It is only light and evidence that can work a change in men's opinions; which light can in no manner proceed from corporal sufferings, or any other outward penalties.

John Locke

9 July 2006: The Invisible Man

If things had gone differently on that first occasion, perhaps I wouldn't have killed all the others. I often wondered about this at the beginning. After all these years I don't even know how many I killed any more and the question has changed: would I be a better person if I had killed only her in a single moment of madness? Today I no longer hate the women I kill — after so many years they're only rag dolls. What I hate are the men full of wisdom, the men who pontificate. Any one of them could have found himself in my place that first time. And it is to these men who live without remorse or honour that I intend to dedicate myself. And to one in particular.

9 July 2006: The Mother

While the left back of Italy's national football team was taking a run-up to deliver the decisive penalty in the 2006 World Cup, Giovanna Sordi got up from the worn sofa in the small apartment where she had lived for fifty years. She had no one to say goodbye to; her husband Amedeo had joined Elisa ten years earlier. From that day on and every day since she had taken flowers to put on their graves. And although she had never received any justice in all those years, she would find the truth now. Slowly she crossed the living room of the small apartment. She passed by the closed door of the room where her dream was born and vanished. She went out onto the balcony, taking no notice of the jubilant cries of the people around and the crowds in the street: she knew exactly what to do. She landed on the pavement twenty metres below at the very moment the whole of Italy exploded into unrestrained joy.

PART I

January 1982

'Pot,' was the first word I heard Angelo Dioguardi say.

I'd only entered the smoke-filled room where they were playing poker because that was where the mobile bar was and I wanted a refill from the bottle of Lagavulin I had my eyes on.

I knew three of the four players by sight, but not the tall young man with long ruffled fair hair, side whiskers and blue eyes, in front of whom almost all of the chips were piled.

'Holy shit, Angelo, that's more than a month's earnings,' grumbled the young lawyer with whom he was battling for the pot. I could see this meant the lawyer earned ten times my own salary.

The fair-haired young man gave a contrite smile, almost apologetic. He was the only one who wasn't smoking, the only one without a whisky in front of him. I glanced at the table as I poured myself the Lagavulin. They were playing a round of Teresina poker. With the cards shown, the lawyer looked to be the winner. There was only one card face down that, if it was the fair-haired guy's, would give him a lead the lawyer couldn't beat.

I shot him a brief glance and he sent me back a friendly smile. I left the room without waiting for the lawyer's decision.

Camilla was waiting for me outside the room. She was the reason I found myself there that evening. Our host was Paola. I'd met her when she came to the local police station to report the presumed theft of her schnauzer, gone missing while it was running about the park. She was very pretty, if a little too refined for my tastes. So I had found her dog for her, which had only become lost, and asked her out for a pizza. Nine times out of ten my rough-edged charm, combined with the badge of rank, worked a treat. She laughed heartily and added, 'I've a very good boyfriend and I'm very faithful. But I might have a close friend I could introduce you to; she likes men like you, a bit surly and macho. Perhaps you'd like to come round tomorrow evening . . .'

She lived in a luxury apartment in Vigna Clara, one of Rome's best districts. She was on the third floor overlooking a quiet little piazza: open, tree-lined, no noise. It was paid for by her parents in Palermo so she could study in Rome. Her friend Camilla wasn't at all bad, except she also was a bit too much of a snob. But during the previous dozen years I'd decided that, given I'd lost the one woman who had counted for something, I'd make do with the sum of the particulars of others. At thirty-two I could manage to think of at least one positive particular in every pretty woman who happened to come within reach. Naturally I'd discovered a long time ago that 'the particulars' of a woman are only discovered during sex, when the gestures, the looks, the words and the sighs manage to be almost truthful.

That evening, however, there was nothing much to be getting up to. Paola's friend was staying the night there, so there was no way to score. Towards midnight I was looking for an excuse to slip away quietly. In that well-heeled circle, a young *commissario* of police like me was sure to be the only one who had to get up at half past six the next morning. I was getting ready to leave when the poker players came back into the salon: three beaten dogs and the fair-haired one with his blue eyes lit up.

'Paola, your boyfriend has the luck of the devil,' said the lawyer as he waved goodbye with the others to the evening's hostess.

The fair-haired guy slumped into the armchair opposite mine. Now that he had finished taking them to the cleaners he had the bottle of Lagavulin in his hand. He poured himself a generous measure and, seeing my glass was empty, filled it without even asking. He raised his glass in a toast. His clothes, his wild hair and whiskers – everything about him made him seem out of place in that house and with those people. In short, more or less like me, except for the fact that I was a master in the art of hypocrisy, a true chameleon of the Secret Service who had learned how to conceal his contempt, while he was just a kid from the outlying suburbs and the one who was genuinely out of place.

'To this magnificent whisky and those who appreciate it!' he said, in the lower-class *romanesco* accent of the outer suburbs.

He offered me a cigarette. He smoked those awful Gitanes without a filter that left tobacco on your tongue and a foul smell everywhere.

'But they taste great,' he said to encourage me. 'And I count them out, no more than ten a day.'

They were cigarettes that no one in Rome's smart set smoked. Marijuana was in, but plain cigarettes smacked of the slums. Of course, it was clear the fair-haired guy didn't belong to the smart set. I thought that if Paola had chosen him and was so faithful to him, then the guy had to have hidden qualities. And the only ones that I could think of were those you demonstrated in bed.

'So you won the pot?' I asked him. He nodded, but showed no interest in the subject.

'Then you really are a lucky sod. There was only a king left with which you could have got a straight. Out of ten possibilities, at least . . .'

He didn't say a word. (Only after a good deal of whisky could I get him to confess that he'd held nothing more than two nines.) 'Professional secret,' he said, making it clear he was letting me in on a very special confidence. By then lawyer was already downstairs and on his way out.

While Paola and Camilla were chatting in the kitchen, Angelo asked what I did for a living.

'*Bravo*, Michele. At least you've got something to get up for every day.'

I shook my head. 'In reality, it's all routine. In a district like this, about the biggest thrill I could get was finding your girlfriend's schnauzer.'

'Oh, it was you who found it, was it? Well, in return . . .' He smiled towards the kitchen.

'Yeah, Camilla's not bad,' I said. 'Pity she's sleeping here tonight.'

He thought about this for a moment. Then I saw him get up and stagger into the bathroom without even closing the door, followed by the sound of retching and moaning. The girls rushed in, as I did too. He was lying on the bathroom floor, looking pale, having thrown up in the basin.

'Shall I call a doctor?' asked Paola in alarm.

'No, no,' he groaned. 'Michele, get the girls out and help me a moment. Meantime, you girls make me a black coffee, could you please?'

So, barred from the bathroom, Paola and Camilla went back to the kitchen and Angelo gave me a big wink.

'Don't worry, it's nothing. But now we have to scare them a little bit more.'

He stuck two fingers down his throat. More retching, and the girls were back in the bathroom.

'I'm going to call a doctor,' said Paola, more concerned than ever.

'No, it's OK, the worst is over. I'll see to him now.' I spoke in the authoritative manner I had when she'd come to report her missing schnauzer. Decisive, calm, reassuring. I knew what I was doing.

Angelo went on a good while longer, with more well-feigned

sounds of retching and groaning. Then I took him on my shoulders to carry him to Paola's double bed.

'Christ, you're heavy,' I said as I tipped him down.

'You have to suffer at least a little in order to get it . . .' He winked at me again and started to moan softly.

The girls came in with the black coffee. Angelo tried it with groans of disgust.

'What shall we do?' The girls were hanging around for instructions, subdued now by my air of calm in the face of his collapse.

'Let him stay the night,' said Angelo, taking Paola's hand. 'If I feel bad again, then at least he'll be here . . .'

I bravely offered to sleep in the lounge with the schnauzer, seeing that Camilla was in the guest room. My gesture was greatly appreciated. Then, later that night, it occurred to Camilla that the dog's snores might be bothering me and so she had me move into her bed.

And that's how I came to know Angelo Dioguardi.

The police station in Vigna Clara was about exciting as a thermal spa. In that residential district of the Roman middle class, a policeman's life ran as quietly as someone in retirement. Well-ordered streets, beautiful homes, greenery everywhere, its inhabitants all formally educated and having achieved economic success by any means, legal or otherwise: tax evasion, bribery and corruption, carefully controlled contracts. All these were means that the Italians, especially in Rome, had discovered after the end of the war as they sought out the good life whatever the cost.

I'd been stationed there for almost two years, thanks to my brother Alberto and his contacts in the Christian Democrats.

'Take it as a convalescence, Mike,' he said when I started there. 'A couple of years to get yourself back together and decide what to do with your troubled life. Time to make some compromises with yourself.'

As if it were possible to cancel out the turbulent thirty-two years of his younger brother. But then Alberto had always been like that. He was an optimist, highly intelligent, forceful – qualities he shared with our father, who left Palermo for Tripoli after World War II.

A Sicilian from the lower middle class, Papa had studied engineering in Rome and became a wealthy businessman in Libya, one of the few who was able to steer through the murky waters of Italian politics, granting it the absolute minimum attention possible and using it only when necessary. And in order to marry the daughter of Libya's biggest Italian landowner, Papa was willing to become the most dedicated of Catholics from conviction and for convenience in order to get into the right circles, and willing to do business with Jews on the one hand, Arabs on the other and Westerners with both hands together.

Alberto was very like my father as regards capability, but he was a better person by far: sensitive, well balanced, generous and even-handed. A model son. In complete contrast, I was the one who, right from the beginning, hated my school run by the Christian Brethren and spent my time with a Diana 50 air rifle, shooting turtle doves from a distance of one hundred metres; and the one who only passed his exams each year because *Commendatore* Balistreri was a really big fish in Libya.

My troubled childhood was divided between serving at Mass as an altar boy with a priest who couldn't keep his hands to himself, and fights with the Arab and Italian boys my age, and it developed into a lonely, turbulent and angry adolescence. As I grew up, I devoured Homer, Nietzsche and early Mussolini. No calculated decisions or compromises: only honour, action, courage. My path was clearly marked: at seventeen I left behind me the first dead in a Cairo shaken by the Six Days War; at eighteen I killed my first lion in Tanzania. At nineteen I was plotting against Gaddafi, who had just taken power. At twenty I claimed the right to decide on the death penalty for those who were traitors.

Then Rome and university. By 1970 I'd even managed to pass a few exams. Over time I made the natural progression from the *Movimento Sociale Italiano* to the ultra-right outside parliament, *Ordine Nuovo*, with its two-headed Fascist axe and SS motto *My Honour is Loyalty*. Three years spent clashing with the Reds – posting up manifestos by night, the days spent attending fiery meetings. Then at the end of 1973, a Christian Democrat minister had *Ordine Nuovo* dissolved and its leaders arrested. An act of madness that let loose dozens of youths, some too young and naive to see the distinction between conflict and the abyss. When many of my friends chose armed conflict, where enemies are actually killed, I paused to reflect. I understood they were moving towards bombing ordinary people, collaborating with common thugs, betraying our ideals, and so I agreed to help the Secret Service block these initiatives. Four years of being a chameleon, undercover for the security forces, still with the semblance of an idea of being on the side of the good people who were preventing massacres of the innocent. Then in 1978 the Red Brigades seized Aldo Moro and right-wing criminality joined forces with left-wing terrorism. Intelligence was ignored, Aldo Moro was assassinated, I protested and my cover was blown. At that point I could have continued and ended up in a block of cement at the bottom of the sea, or else I could renounce changing the world and ask my brother for help.

And so it was my brother, *Ingegnere* Alberto Balistreri, who brought me back from the edge of the precipice. The Minister of the Interior owed him a favour. So I managed to take a philosophy degree, with some help in passing the remaining exams after those taken in the early 1970s. Then they got me into the police and I passed the exam for the rank of *commissario*. And so in 1980 I received my first posting in Vigna Clara, one of Rome's quietest districts.

But at night I wanted to get away from this false Rome and keep my distance from rich middle-class districts or, still worse, the historic centre where the city's chaos and decadence were more in evidence.

I rented a studio flat in Garbatella, a working-class quarter built by Mussolini, where apartments cost very little in those days and true Romans took the cool spring air sitting outside the cheap bistros that served the best food and wine in the city.

In fact, I dedicated myself to the only real passion left to me: women. Any woman, of whatever kind, race, age, so long as she was good-looking and didn't waste my time with the usual runaround. I was voracious; I wasn't looking for friendship, intrigue or protection. They lasted so little time that I didn't take the trouble to learn their names. I only needed to know them in the most thorough way possible, something not too difficult for a young good-looking police officer of some rank. *Hic et nunc* was the way for Michele Balistreri; nothing of sin, confession, regret. I was one of the elect, those the world doesn't understand, those who don't give a damn what the world thinks of them. Nor what God thinks either.

As Alberto used to say to me, and I used to echo, this was only a moment to reflect, a little bit of rest, sailing slowly along a quiet river, carried along by a gentle current. After the turbulent years I'd experienced, this was exactly what I needed: solitude, a cushy day job, eating well, screwing a lot, playing poker, thinking about nothing at all. It was a delicate balance between pleasure and boredom. No emotional ties. Love was a country where it had rained salt and turned into a desert.

But I told myself over and over that I would leave as soon as I could. I'd never become a senile old copper, shut in an office to serve a cowardly and corrupt state. I'd go back to Africa to hunt lions and leopards, far away from a false and sanctimonious Little Italy. Far away from everything I detested. Far away from the battles I had lost.

A few days after our first encounter, Dioguardi agreed without protest to a game of poker with me and two of my friends in the police. This was strange, because we'd only just met and I myself would never have risked putting my money on the table with three strangers who knew each other well. But, as I came to find out, Dioguardi was the opposite of me in many things – and one was being able to trust his neighbour.

We played after supper until two in the morning in the back room of a piano bar near Piazza di Spagna. In less than half an hour I was aware that he was a world-class player. He had technique, imagination and a brass neck. After two hours he'd won a pile of money. Then, in the following hour, he lost more than half of what he'd won.

'You started to lose on purpose,' I said, after the other two had left.

He shook his head, embarrassed.

'I was doing a few experiments, things I could use to improve. I do it when I'm winning comfortably.'

'As in a pre-season friendly against a team of amateurs . . .'

He smiled. He admitted that he played rarely, and only then with wealthy old boys. He won a great deal, was a little ashamed and never boasted of it. I discovered later that he donated all his winnings to charity. His fabulous bluffs in the game were little sins for him, something that – along with his Catholic ethics – was nothing to be proud of.

We went into the crowded bar. A group of young men were singing to the notes of the pianist, led by a beautiful black singer who called out as soon as she saw him.

'Angelo, Angelo, come over here!'

He tried to shy away, but she kept on at him. In the end he went over and the girl pressed his lips to hers. I saw him blush and step back. Then she raised his arm as if declaring him a winner and turned to the crowd.

'This is my friend Angelo, the best unknown vocalist in Rome, who will now sing for us.'

In the field of singing, too, he was in a class of his own. He performed whatever song the crowd asked for and ended with a rendition of *My Way* almost worthy of Sinatra himself. After his singing demonstration he introduced me to the girl vocalist, leaving us alone just long enough for me to get her phone number. By this time he'd gathered what I was.

It was after three when we left the place.

'Michele, if you're up for it, let's go to Ostia.'

'Ostia? It's January. What would we do at the beach?'

'There's a little bakery there. At six they bring out the best crème horns in all Rome and its provinces.'

He wanted to talk. Me too. This was really strange because, over the years, my desire to socialize with the male sex had worn off. We went in his beaten-up old Fiat 500 and half an hour later were parked on the promenade. The stars were out, it was cold, but there was no wind. We opened the windows to smoke. The sea was a millpond; we could smell the sea air and hear the waves lapping a few metres away from us. There was no one at all about.

In contrast to me, Angelo was always willing to talk about himself. He was born poor in a Rome where everyone except his parents was getting rich in more or less legal ways. A lad from Rome's poorest outskirts, he was the son of a bar-room singer and a fortune-teller, two penniless *artistes* who later retired to a country village; two failures according to the social views of the day and both dead from cirrhosis of the liver when Angelo was still in his adolescence. But he said they had both given him a great deal. His vocalist father had given him his singing voice and from his fortune-telling mother came the ability to bluff and think on his feet.

In time he had gained two things: a well-off girlfriend, Paola, who worshipped him and would marry him within a year, and a small job in housing, thanks to her uncle, Cardinal Alessandrini. The Cardinal was just over fifty and oversaw the business of finding lodgings for the thousands of priests and nuns who came to Rome either for periods of study or else a few days of pilgrimage and sightseeing. The Vatican owned hundreds of convents, hostels and apartments and their running had been entrusted to Angelo Dioguardi who, although he'd given up on his education, was a good Catholic and was obviously to be the husband of the Cardinal's niece. Although Angelo was manifestly unsuited to an office job, he applied himself with dedication and energy, exactly the opposite of what I did in my employment. And he was the opposite of me also with women. He knew a great many girls, but never took advantage of this out of his unshakeable loyalty to Paola. In love, he was an idealist in search of the single perfect relationship. Over time this developed into the ideal situation for someone like me, who was always on the prowl: Angelo drew them in and I finished the deal.

'Are you really completely faithful to Paola? I asked. I was expecting him to give a panegyric on love in reply, but Angelo surprised me.

'She's beautiful, well-mannered, intelligent, rich, niece to a Cardinal who's even given me a job, whereas I'm a poverty-stricken nobody who didn't finish school. I can only be thankful to her; I've no right even to desire anyone else.'

We were still there at dawn. We got out to stretch our legs. The bakery was still closed, but you could see the lights on and could smell the baking yeast. I took a cigarette from my second packet. I offered him one, seeing as he'd finished all his.

'No thanks, Michele. A packet of Gitanes every two days, that's me, and no more.'

'You keep too tight a rein on yourself, Angelo. You should let yourself go once in a while.'

He ran a hand through his ruffled fair hair, then gave me a glance and pointed to the sea.

'How about a dip?'

'Are you mad? It's January and dawn.'

'You won't feel the cold once you're in. And it'll give you a perfect appetite.'

That's exactly what he said – a perfect appetite. He switched on the Fiat's headlights and directed them towards the few metres of sand that separated us from the water. A minute later he was in his briefs.

'Come on, let yourself go, Michele,' he said.

Then he took a run up and dived in. I saw him swimming madly in the beam of the headlights. I don't know what took hold of me – certainly something I hadn't felt for many years. A minute later I was in the water. The cold took my breath away, but the more I swam to warm myself up, the more I felt a joy I'd forgotten, brazen, irresistible, that took over my whole body.

And the warm crème horns were the fitting conclusion to such a night.

And so I began to get to know him better. Underneath that affectionate, sunny and angelic face lay a heart left on its own too soon and seeking a safe and permanent harbour. Love and work were that refuge for him. No strange ambitions, no adventures: a more or less regular life. No more than ten Gitanes a day, no more than a couple of whiskies. This was so that he could stay clear-headed when he played poker. Every time we went into one of Rome's piano bars – something we often did in the following months – the same thing happened. The singer knew Angelo and called him on stage. And the female singers always tried to take him home with them, but he was incorruptible. In this he was truly my opposite, or perhaps he was what I could have been. Angelo was unassailable.

As regards our poker, he laid down strict rules for us. The places were limited and fixed, and at the end of the evening the jackpot was divided up according to the number of chips everyone had in front of them. He almost always won and the few times he lost I was sure it was on purpose, like he'd done during our first game. In the beginning we played with my brother Alberto and another engineer, a colleague of his. They tried to persuade Angelo to use their high salaries and stocks and shares to bankrupt a casino but, ever in line with his Catholic morality, Angelo didn't want to know.

We saw each other almost every evening. The standard routine was the four of us for a pizza: myself, Angelo, Paola and my girlfriend of the moment. Then a short stroll among Trastevere's night crowd. We'd stop for a smoke, and drink a last beer in the splendid piazza by the church of Santa Maria. Then there was a choice: either I went off with my girl or, with Paola's blessing, Angelo and I would say goodbye to the girls and go off around Rome in my Duetto or his Fiat 500. (This usually happened when my companion no longer attracted me enough to want to spend the night with her.) We would stay in the car and talk. Unending icy winter nights with the windows down to let out the pall of smoke. Warm spring nights when we squashed the first mosquitoes. Our conversations ranged from chat about sport and politics to deeper existential problems. Despite not finishing school, Angelo was a great debater and could defend his Christian vision of the world divided between good and evil.

We were inseparable on those magical metaphysical nights that filled our lives without any apparent reason whatsoever.

May 1982

Angelo's office was located in the residential complex where Cardinal Alessandrini lived. Two twin low-rise blocks, each three storeys high, surrounded by a park, on Via della Camilluccia, one of Rome's greenest residential areas. Alessandrini lived on the top floor in one of the blocks and had given the other two floors over to Dioguardi for his offices. The first floor was used for administration; the ground floor was open to the public — that is, the young priests and nuns looking for accommodation.

On one of my days off, a Saturday at the beginning of May, I went to meet him there. It was a glorious morning, the skies clear, the sun already warm. In my old Alfa Romeo Duetto I crossed the historic city centre crowded with tourists, stopping every so often to admire a young female visitor. Near the Coliseum I saw a German blonde with huge tits and the words *Über alles* printed on her T-shirt. In Piazza di Spagna American girls in shorts were sitting on the Spanish Steps, and in Piazza del Popolo, where the bars were already full, two gorgeous Japanese girls were taking turns to photograph each other. Eventually I drove up the winding slopes of Monte Mario and came to Via della Camilluccia. A huge green gate barred the entrance to the park where the two low-rise blocks were situated, separated by a huge fountain, a tennis court and a swimming pool. It was a little corner of paradise allowing some privileged people to live a separate life, far above that wonderfully chaotic city crawling with people and traffic.

I drew the car up to the gate. A severe-looking woman in her sixties came out of the gatehouse at the porter's lodge. She looked me up and down sceptically, unable to decide whether I was an encyclopaedia salesman or some lackey of one of the rich people round there. I stared back at her with one of my own surly looks, a gift that came naturally to me.

'Your business?' she asked me brusquely in a Southern accent.

'I'm a friend of Angelo Dioguardi.'

'You'll have to park outside – the inside's only for those who live here.'

She saw my stunned look wandering over the enormous grounds of the park with its few parked vehicles, among them a stupendous Aston Martin, Angelo's clapped-out Fiat 500 and, gleaming in the sunshine, a Harley Davidson Panhead.

'The Count doesn't want non-residents' cars past the gate. And if it was up to him, you know, non-residents wouldn't even be allowed in on foot,' the concierge added with a note of disapproval, whether for the non-residents or the Count I couldn't decide.

Fortunately, parking on that quiet green road was no problem. The residents all had garages and there were no shops or restaurants, only trees, well-tended flower beds, and Filipino au pairs pushing baby strollers carrying the children of the wealthy, who were away having a coffee in Piazza Navona or out on the golf course.

'You have to walk to the far end of the grounds, go around behind the pool and the tennis court, and you'll get to Block B. You can see the balcony from here; you can't miss it,' she explained, as though talking to a small child not altogether there.

As I passed Block A, the one nearer to the gate, I felt I was being watched. I turned to look upwards and caught sight of a reflection on the third-floor balcony. Someone was spying on visitors through a pair of binoculars. I stopped to admire the Aston Martin parked in front of the entrance to the building. The Harley stood beside it. I went around the large fountain and onto the pathways between the tennis court and the swimming pool; tall trees prevented me from making out the Block B I'd seen from the gatehouse.

I came across a lanky and energetic young man. Thick red curls, blue eyes, freckles, probably not more than twenty. He was wearing a priestly cassock.

'You lost?'

'I'm not sure. I'm trying to get to Angelo Dioguardi in Block B.'

'You not priest,' he said, smiling at his witty remark, and went on in his laboured Italian, 'you know, only priests and nuns go Angelo. I Father Paul, assistant Cardinal Alessandrini.'

He accompanied me to Block B's front door.

'Angelo, second floor. Call me if one day you become priest.'

He really was a bit too much of a joker for a first encounter. I recognized it instantly as a way of covering up his insecurity – and Father Paul's insecurity exuded from every pore.

I went up on foot. As I was going past the first floor, a girl with the features of a young goddess came out of a door. She was wearing a long white coat of the kind nurses wear, and I would gladly have fallen ill on the spot. That kind of a uniform tends to disguise the figure, but no kind of dress could have hidden that curvaceous outline.

She stopped dead, her eyes lowered. 'Please, go ahead,' she said, pausing to let me step past. Her voice was soft and childlike, a little dreamy, like her smile. Her arms were full of ring binders.

'Can I help you?' I offered. She kept avoiding my eyes and shook her head, distracted. A ring binder fell to the tiled floor. While I was bending down to pick it up, I caught the scent of toilet soap. 'I'm really sorry,' she said, absurdly over-apologetic.

I couldn't persuade her to give me any ring binders and we went up to the second floor in silence. She ushered me through a small door into a long corridor with several doors leading off it.

'Signor Dioguardi's in the office at the end,' she said, still without looking at me, and quickly disappeared into the first room beside the entrance.

I found Angelo behind a desk, buried under papers, ring binders and folders of every kind. Behind him was a huge photo of the Pope. I felt like laughing at seeing him in what seemed to me such an out of place setting. His complete inability to keep order, when transferred to the workplace, made him look ridiculous.

'I know, Michele, your brother looks just the part for sitting behind a desk, while I only look stupid. And more than that, here I am creating the devil of a mess in a job that demands an ability for planning.'

'Never mind, you seem to have some good-looking helpers,' I said, making a vague gesture out towards the corridor.

'You've already spotted Elisa then,' he replied, bursting into laughter.

'If that's the kind of young goddess you have carrying your bits of paper about . . .'

He explained that Elisa Sordi had been there for two months as a weekend helper; she was still at college and in June would be taking her accountancy exams. She was only eighteen.

'And from whence does this manna from heaven descend on you?'

'Paola's uncle, Cardinal Alessandrini. She was recommended by our illustrious neighbour the Senator, Count Tommaso dei Banchi di Aglieno. The Cardinal and the Count often do favours for each other, even if politically and morally they're far apart: the Cardinal's a Catholic democrat, the Count's an anticlerical monarchist despot.'

'I think they've done you a favour this time, Angelo. Sure, she's a bit young, but you know I don't hang about . . .'

He shook his head with a smile.

'She's not your type, Michele.'

'And why not?'

'She's awkward, incredibly shy, and a very devout Catholic – someone like me, who really believes.'

'Is that what you think of me, Angelo Dioguardi? That I'm only a collector of shags from cheap tarts?' I asked in a tone of disdain that was quite evidently put on.

I expected him to laugh and was surprised to see a desperate grimace on his face. It was the noise of ring binders falling to the floor behind me that made me realise what a disaster it was. Blushing, Angelo rose to help the girl gather them up. I turned round with my most innocent smile. Elisa was standing there with a stunned expression on her face, a look of shock in her eyes. Not having the gift of invisibility at my command, I excused myself and went to the men's toilet, where I remained for a good long while, cursing myself. The face I saw in the mirror was that of a vulgar idiot who had just made a complete fool of himself.

I went back into Angelo's office only when I was sure that Elisa was no longer there. He gave me a sardonic grin that made me furious.

'Imbecile! What's so bloody funny? You could have warned me, couldn't you?'

'I tried to, Micky. Anyway, Elisa certainly knows you now. But if she has a sudden stroke and loses her memory, I'd say you're in with a chance . . .'

We ended up shutting the door to and settling down for a chat over a beer. There was no ashtray, because Angelo didn't smoke in the office, so I used the waste-paper basket. Angelo showed me how his job worked. The Vatican sent him the programme of arrivals and his three regular staff allocated the available housing to the priests and nuns – obviously in separate quarters – while his responsibility was to take care of hostels and convents for any forthcoming conventions. As for emergencies, such as unexpected arrivals, he was always on call, whatever the time of day. That was why he needed extra help on Saturdays and sometimes Sundays too. This extra help came in the shape of that young goddess Elisa Sordi, the girl about to take her exams in accountancy.

'So, on Saturdays here you are alone with her. How do you stop yourself?'

'There's hardly anything to resist. I've already told you, Elisa's a closed door. Go on, admit it: the truth is that my being faithful to Paola upsets you and you'd feel better if I stepped over the line once in a while.'

This wasn't true. I wasn't jealous of the self-control he applied to this renunciation. I'd had to work on self-control a good deal myself and was still alive because I'd learned it at my own cost before anyone had had a chance to kill me. But I really didn't understand self-control applied to sex – it was like sucking mints to hide bad breath. And I wanted my friend to see it as I did: a faithfulness that was self-imposed was like renouncing life itself. And that really was a deadly sin.

At half past one, Elisa knocked and put her head round the door, avoiding my gaze.

'May I go out for something to eat?' she asked.

It seemed an old-fashioned request, like asking for permission to go to the toilet. I went to the window to watch her leave. A young man was waiting for her outside Block B's main door.

'You said she was a little saint . . .' I said to Angelo, confused.

'Shit, Michele, you're even jealous of her! Valerio Bona's an admirer from way back. Anyway, it's no business of ours.'

I looked at her again. The goddess was going off with a boy her own age, a short, skinny guy who wore glasses. It was absolutely ridiculous – such a waste. He even looked like a bum. She'd taken off her white coat. She was dressed simply and modestly in loose-fitting slacks, a sweatshirt tied round her waist serving only to hide her splendid behind.

It would be much more fun with a girl like that.

I intended to do everything I could to cancel out my tactless behaviour. After all, it was only the first time we'd met.

Angelo had to discuss a couple of matters with the Cardinal before we could go down for some lunch.

'Come on up with me, Michele, he'll be happy to meet you. It's always useful to know a policeman,' he said with a grin.

The Monsignor's penthouse was enormous: a spacious lounge, several bedrooms and bathrooms, together with a large balcony over-looking the grounds, from which you could see as far as the entrance on Via della Camilluccia, where the concierge had her lodge. The lounge was full of young African priests and nuns talking in French. It was a kind of de luxe Catholic youth hostel.

'These are the people we have to sort out. They should have left this morning but there's a coup d'état going on in their country and they've closed the airport,' Angelo explained.

The only white face apart from ourselves was Alessandrini, going in and out among the young clergy in his everyday clothes, offering iced lemonade from a large carafe. A short, middle-aged man who radiated great energy, his lively, intelligent black eyes stood out against his cropped grey hair.

He came up to me with a smile and an outstretched hand. 'You must be Michele Balistreri,' he said. Then, turning to Angelo, he added, 'Help yourselves to lemonade. I'll be back in a minute.'

I saw him go to the telephone. The conversation was brief, in perfect English.

'You can tell His Holiness that, with all due humility, I do not agree. There's no violence, it's a bloodless coup. The fact that they're not Catholics is another matter, but we can find a way to dialogue.'

He came back adjusting the spectacles on his hooked nose.

'The current Vatican hierarchy has no love for communists, exactly the same as you.'

I looked at Angelo, who shook his head. No, he definitely wasn't the type to pass on my business to the Cardinal. Either the Cardinal could read in my face what I was thinking or he had made enquiries, seeing as I went around with his niece's future husband. Either way I didn't care.

'I don't think I would agree with the Vatican hierarchy on any topic. Not even on communists.'

The Cardinal ignored my comment and led us to the only corner of the lounge not taken over by noisy young Africans.

'Your Eminence, we have some problems,' Angelo said. 'We can't manage to find places for all of them in our housing and the hotels are full up with tourists. We're looking for about twenty beds.'

This was a different Angelo Dioguardi from the usual one, more awkward and insecure. The Cardinal was too important for him.

Alessandrini laughed. 'My poor Angelo, I see you can't multiply beds like Our Lord did with the fishes! But it's no problem. The priests will stay with me. Naturally, you'll have to accommodate all the sisters. You can never be sure . . .'

'But, Your Eminence, although this is a large apartment, there aren't enough beds. We're talking about twenty priests. Where will you put them all?'

The Cardinal pointed to the terrace. 'I slept out there last night to keep cool. It'll be no problem for them – they're used to it in Africa. I've already sent Paul to get some sleeping bags from San Valente.'

Angelo relaxed and the Cardinal turned to me. 'So, you're a policeman?' I had heard myself so described with a thousand different shades of meaning: often ironic, sometimes even offensive. But in Alessandrini's tone there was only curiosity. At the same time he was letting me know that he knew all about me. In that residential complex, you entered only on foot and after all your details had been checked.

'As a child it was the profession I wanted to follow,' the Cardinal explained. 'But the Lord wished me to serve a different kind of justice.'

I had my own exact opinions about the conflicting relationship between earthly and divine justice, but I judged this wasn't the right moment to speak about Nietzsche and the Gospels. This man, at once both powerful and friendly, was admirable, but I didn't find him likeable. He was a priest and, after years of religious schooling, I knew that a pleasant manner could merely be ash over hot coals. I had learned to be wary even as a young child, from the moment in the fifth year of primary school when a soft hand infiltrated my shorts while I was being told about the goodness of Our Lord.

He read my thoughts. 'Yes, I know, you're very much the lay person and anticlerical or perhaps even against religion. Look, I respect justice on earth, but I also recognize its tragic errors. In this world, justice is often in the wrong hands.'

I was already losing patience. 'If we waited for the next life, we'd be living in tears, tormenting ourselves with our sins. When remorse turns to penitence and absolution, it's only a way of avoiding life.'

Seeing Angelo's look of alarm I stopped, but the Cardinal wasn't the type to be offended by an insignificant non-believer like me.

'Dottor Balistreri, I realize that for you a sin is only what we call crime. And punishment is served out on earth, possibly in prison. But it was the justice of the Enlightenment, not faith, that instigated the guillotine of the revolutionaries, and they didn't only decapitate the guilty.'

'While the Inquisition never made a mistake, is that it?'

'The Inquisition is one of the Church's many embarrassments. And really it was earthly justice.'

And so I discovered that Cardinal Alessandrini had very clear ideas and if necessary would promote them even if they went against the Vatican hierarchy.

I would have preferred to wait in Angelo's office for Elisa to come back, but I realized that after opening my big mouth about easy shags and cheap tarts it was better to allow things to settle. And so I let myself be persuaded to accompany Angelo to the church of San Valente to help Father Paul.

While we were walking back over the grounds towards the exit I glanced up at the second-floor windows. Elisa's office window was the only one wide open. I lit a cigarette and again saw the sun's reflection from Block A's penthouse balcony.

'There's someone up there who likes playing around with binoculars.'

Angelo nodded. 'That'll be Manfredi, Count Tommaso's son. He's a bit strange in the head, but if I were in his place I'd have problems too.'

It seemed impossible to have problems in this branch of paradise. But I'd learned that family wealth doesn't immunize us against the world, especially when we're young.

'What problems does he have, apart from spying on passers-by?'

'Manfredi's problem is his father. The Count's a very powerful politician, leader of the party that wants to bring the monarchy back to Italy. He's got vast economic resources thanks to his family's investments in Africa. Timber, minerals, stock farms.'

I'd also had an important man for a father. I could guess what Manfredi's problems might be. But there was far worse, as I soon learned from Angelo.

'The Count married a very young woman named Ulla from an aristocratic family in the North of Europe. She was only seventeen at the time. She became pregnant straight away. She continued to go riding and the foetus suffered. Manfredi was born with a severe birthmark and a harelip – you can barely look at him. Apart from that he's a healthy kid and highly intelligent, but a difficult character. I feel really sorry for him; I don't know what I'd do in his place.'

The little freak with the binoculars got no sympathy from me.

'There are worse things in life, Angelo. There are people who live quietly with much worse disabilities. Anyway, why can't they operate on him?'

'They've consulted plastic surgeons half the world over and all advise against an operation until the kid's at least physically mature. I hope for his sake that one day . . .'

A blue car entered the grounds and parked next to the Aston Martin. A member of the entourage got out and quickly opened the nearside rear door. The man who then emerged immediately commanded an air of reverential respect. He was about forty-five, dressed in an impeccable blue pinstripe suit despite the heat of the day. Tall, ramrod straight, his black hair was combed back from a wide forehead, his features distinguished by a large aquiline nose, a thin moustache and well-trimmed goatee. He didn't so much as glance at us. He said a word in his bodyguard's ear and slipped into Block A's front door.

'A real friendly neighbour,' I observed.

Angelo smiled. 'The Count doesn't much like human contact, especially with those not on his level.'

The bodyguard came up and, pointing to me, addressed Angelo. 'Is the gentleman with you?'

'Yes, he is,' Angelo replied, somewhat cowed.

'Then please remember to remind your guests that these grounds are private property and smoking is strictly forbidden,' he said sharply, before walking off.

I couldn't believe it. A residential complex where not only was parking forbidden, but smoking too. Where they spied on you from the balcony and knew all your details. I could very well imagine that young Manfredi's life might be difficult. I was careful not to stub my cigarette out on the ground, otherwise I'd probably have been set upon by a pack of Dobermann Pinschers or transferred to some forgotten police station up on a mountaintop.

Angelo explained that the Count occupied the whole of Block A and owned the entire residential complex. The Vatican only rented Block B. As we were going out of the gate, he introduced me to Gina Giansanti, the concierge.

'Next time, have a smoke before you come in, young man,' she said. I still couldn't decide if this was a rebuke or a friendly gesture of solidarity.

At the gate, I turned round and gave a little wave to the binoculars reflected on the balcony. *Ciao ciao, Manfredi.*

The church of San Valente was fifteen minutes from the complex along the Via Aurelia Antica. The Saturday traffic was calm, many shops had closed, and the Roman population was having lunch at home or picnicking in one of the large parks. We drove off onto a small lane and I parked on a patch of unkempt grass between overgrown shrubs and hedges. Everything was tumbledown, left to its own devices. The church was small, very simple, its walls peeling from decades of exposure to the sun. On the opposite side of the grass stood a modest-sized house painted white next to a single small tree that had been recently planted.

A dozen children aged between ten and thirteen were playing football and a blonde girl of about twenty was acting as referee. Another girl was clearing a long table set outside, directly under the tree.

We went around to the house. Disorder ruled everywhere; the place needed a great deal of work. The lanky Father Paul, sweating copiously in his cassock, was loading sleeping bags into an old Volkswagen Beetle.

'Angelo, my friend!' he called out on seeing us. 'Your friend new priest now?'

This time I smiled at him – his desire to reach out was almost painful. We helped him to load up.

'Eat with *noi*?' said Paul finally, in his mixture of English and Italian, as we washed our hands in a simple bathroom with a chipped basin.

We sat down under the tree. The blonde girl brought us plastic cutlery and some lukewarm soup that was certainly nothing special. Then she said she was going to wash the dishes.

'Don't the children help out?' asked Angelo, who from childhood was used to cooking, clearing away and washing his dishes.

'*Difficile*, only at start,' explained Paul. 'You like speak to a *bambino*?'

'Thanks, perhaps next time,' I said. 'I have to be back at the station. I've only got time for a cigarette, assuming we can smoke here?'

Paul burst out laughing. 'I no smoking, but not like Count. Is free to smoke here, if you like kill yourself.'

I opened the second pack of the day and made to light a cigarette. Angelo signalled me not to.

'Long time in Rome?' I asked Paul. I was consciously omitting verbs, as if this would help him understand better.

'Almost one year. *Studio io all'università pontificia* and help out Cardinal Alessandrini. When finish I go Africa, open orphanage like this.'

Then Paul asked me a serious question, which I was able to deduce from the fact that he was now adding verbs.

'How old were you when you had vocation for policeman?' He said it exactly like that, 'vocation'. It was certainly a word that priests knew well.

'I'm still not sure of the vocation, but I became one two years ago.'

I saw him make a quick calculation about my age. He came to the conclusion that he still had some years to go in order to be certain of his own vocation. I imagined that, in the years to come, several of his firmest convictions would be strenuously put to the test.

Sunday, 11 July 1982

I hadn't shut my eyes for almost a fortnight. The World Cup now coming to an end in Spain had affected the life rhythms of every Italian. After an awkward start, Argentina, Brazil and Poland had almost inexplicably fallen to the Italian side. They were evenings of unforgettable joy, followed by poker with Angelo, Alberto and other friends and, for me, often ending up in bed with a girl – always a different one.

On the day of the final against Germany, Rome was in the grip of a creeping sense of triumph that was ready to explode into ecstasy. Shops selling national flags had sold out. Those unable to buy one in time had hung out three coloured towels to simulate the national tricolour. Then even the towels sold out and desperate latecomers were forced to put out painted sheets.

No one no longer doubted that Italy would win the World Cup that evening. Rome woke more peacefully than usual under a clear blue sky: it was as if the whole population wanted to conserve the maximum amount of energy in order to play the final against Germany themselves. Even the usual Sunday exodus to the beaches was largely reduced for fear of getting stuck in traffic coming back and not being in front of the television set at half past eight.

I took the opportunity to stay inside the police station in peace and quiet and sign some papers. Not that there was much to do, but I wanted to be sure I'd have no problems that evening. Angelo called a little before lunch, having just come back from Mass with Paola.

'I have a wonderful evening organized for you, *Commissario* Balistreri.'

'If you organize evenings in the same way as the folders in your office, then I have my doubts. Go on, then, let's hear it.'

'We're all going to Paola's for the final; your brother's coming with his German girlfriend, so we can tease her a bit. We'll eat and have a drink during the match. When it's over, Paola and the others are going to raise Cain out on the streets . . .'

'Sorry, Angelo, what if we lose?'

I already knew the answer. 'It's not going to happen, Michele. That's not in the plan.'

'OK, so we win. What happens then?'

'Then we stay in the flat – you, me, Alberto and a colleague of his – and play a little poker. When the others come back from cele-brating you can go off with one of the girls – they'll all want to carry on partying.'

'OK, Angelo. But I'm not putting the Duetto on the road today, what with all the traffic. You couldn't come and pick me up here at the station in that old wreck of yours, could you? I clock off at five sharp.'

'I don't know if I can. Father Paul called and says there's a bit of problem. I have to drop by the office about five thirty.'

'Shit, on a Sunday? Have you got to find a little bachelor pad for our jumped-up Yankee priest?'

'Don't be blasphemous, Michele. I have to drop in on Cardinal Alessandrini – there've been some unexpected arrivals. I had to call Elisa too – she's working there today.'

Suddenly my hostility to the idea transformed into enthusiasm. I hadn't seen the young goddess again, but remembered her very well.

'Why don't I come with you? That way I can apologize for last time.'

Was I joking or was I being serious? I don't really know myself.

'No, we're not going up to see Elisa – we'd only be in her way. I have to check in with the Cardinal about assigning the housing, that's all.'

'OK, Angelo, I'll go up and say hello to Elisa on my own. Pick me up at five then.'

This promised to be an interesting evening. At Paola's there were always good-looking young women from Rome's bourgeoisie, my ideal target. Euphoria in the case of victory, plus my dark attractiveness, meant one more victory guaranteed.

I went down to the bar opposite the office in the piazza. The roads were totally deserted. Inside, in the cool of the air-conditioning, a crowd with nothing better to do was mouthing off loudly about the coming match. I ordered a sandwich and a beer, listening to the cross-currents of several voices. There was no doubt about the victory – the Germans always lost to us.

'Even in war we've given it to those Nazi Krauts right up the arse!' yelled a long-haired freak with a hammer and sickle tattooed on the back of his dirty hand, who was standing in a group of other long-haired freaks. They were passing around two cigarettes with an unmistakable smell.

I looked at my watch – I still had some time and I had the inclination. I was in civilian clothes, so I took out my ID card. I waited for the joint to get to the tattooed guy and went up to him.

I showed him my ID and took the joint from his fingers. 'You're under arrest for the use of a narcotic substance,' I announced.

He looked at me in shock. 'What shit did you just say, copper?'

'And also for insulting a public official. Would you be so good as to accompany me to the police station this instant?'

I was using the police's bureaucratic language on purpose, knowing how much they hated it. The hairy freak placed a grubby hand on my shoulder. As expected, the owner of the bar went out to call in help from the men on guard outside the police station. There wasn't much time for what I wanted to do.

'Remove your hand immediately or I shall add aggressive behaviour towards a public official to the charges already against you in the proceedings to follow,' I commanded, trying to keep myself from laughing at the guff I was giving out.

The tone and the terminology finally produced what I wanted: he gave me a shove and I fell to the ground like a leaf.

This was the scene that presented itself to my colleagues when they entered. The long-haired freak wouldn't be watching the game that night, not even inside Regina Coeli prison. I would have him slammed in a cell where he would spend a very uncomfortable night.

I gave instructions to the men as soon as I was back in the office. They could watch the match on the set they'd brought in and were very grateful. But I made it clear that in exchange they were not to piss me off – with any interruption, for any reason – after eight o'clock. I repeated myself. For any reason whatsoever.

'What if someone gets up on the opposite roof and wants to jump off?' said one of the men, teasing.

'You can tell him to jump off tomorrow,' I said, in a manner that made it clear I wasn't joking.

By four I'd finished even the most pointless paperwork and started thinking about that goddess Elisa Sordi – entirely alone in her office on a Sunday afternoon in a completely deserted city. I was tempted to not wait for Angelo and go to Via della Camilluccia by myself, but the girl had a lot to do and that first unfortunate meeting with her advised prudence.

My twisted mind hit on an indirect solution. At ten to five I called Angelo's office.

The shy voice I knew very well replied after two rings.

'This is *Commissario* Michele Balistreri. I believe we know each other.'

She remained silent and I went on.

'I'm waiting for Signor Dioguardi, who's about to come and pick me up at the police station. Is he there in the office with you?'

'No, he's not been here at all today. He's dropping in later if that's any use. Should I give him a message, *Signor Commissario*?'

That 'Signor Commissario' softened me and gave me some reassurance. Despite the poor figure I'd cut, she still had some respect for me. Either that or she was afraid of me, which would be even better.

'No thanks. Perhaps I'll drop by with Signor Dioguardi later.'

She said nothing, and I put the phone down without saying goodbye.

I felt a little embarrassed with regard to Angelo over the phone call. As a precaution I called Paola's number. She picked up the phone.

'I'll put him on, Michele. We've just had a siesta and he's coming out to pick you up.'

'OK, see you later,' I said.

'Michele, what's happened?' said Angelo, sounding worried.

'Nothing, Angelo. I just wanted to be sure you wouldn't forget to come and collect me. I called the office thinking you were there, and got Elisa.'

He was silent for a moment, unsure. 'Are you sure it was me you wanted? Anyway, I'll be out of here in five minutes and with you in another five.'

He arrived ten minutes later, just after five o'clock. It was stiflingly hot, so he had lowered the hood of the old Fiat and there was a smell of sweat, beer and Gitanes. We pulled up in Via della Camilluccia a few minutes later; there was hardly anyone on the roads. The street was calm, silent, shaded by its magnificent trees.

'I'm going to have one before going up,' said Angelo. We approached the green gate with our cigarettes lit. The concierge scowled at us, but we stopped outside to smoke.

'What are you doing here, Signora Gina? Today's Sunday,' Angelo asked her.

'Getting my bags ready. I'm off tonight.'

'Without seeing the match?'

'Means nothing to me. I think you're all mad. I'm going to India tonight.'

'India? What are you going to do there?' I asked, surprised.

Gina looked at me with disapproval.

'Young man, I know it'll seem strange to you, but I go there every year to do two weeks' voluntary work. It's Cardinal Alessandrini who organizes the trip for me, so that I can tell him how things are getting on over there.'

'Have you seen Elisa?' Angelo asked her, to stop me saying anything out of place.

'Elisa's been up in the office slaving away since this morning, poor girl. She only went out for lunch – I saw her when she came back with Valerio. She rang on the internal phone half an hour ago and I went up to get the work to take to Cardinal Alessandrini.'

'Well, thanks, Signora Gina,' said Angelo. 'We're going up to the Cardinal to see if everything's OK; that way Elisa can go home.'

'Angelo, I don't want to risk arrest,' I said. 'I'll wait for you here.'

He shot me a warning look.

'Remember, I can see you from the Cardinal's balcony, so no arsing about.'

Although it was some distance away, Block B's balcony was well in sight of the gate, and vice versa. Something of a let-down.

'I won't move from here, I swear,' I promised, with my fingers crossed.

Angelo went off and I was left on my own with Signora Gina. I stood on one side of the gate, having a smoke; she was on the other polishing the gatehouse windows so she could leave them gleaming when she went off. She began to soften a bit.

'I'm sorry about the smoking, but the Count's an overbearing fanatic and his son's even worse.'

Certainly Count Tommaso dei Banchi di Aglieno didn't enjoy the sympathy of the severe concierge. And even less that young idiot with the binoculars.

I looked up towards Block A's balcony. A fleeting reflection, then nothing. Manfredi was acting shy that day.

Angelo came out onto Block B's balcony with Alessandrini. They gestured towards me and disappeared inside. The concierge's internal phone rang. 'The Cardinal's asking for you to go up,' said Gina. 'I'll say goodbye – I have to go to Mass before I leave.'

Damned cleric – as if I was interested in his chitchat. I was trying to decide whether to chance my luck with Elisa, when a blue car rolled up to the gate. The driver rushed to help out Count Tommaso dei Banchi di Aglieno, while Signora Gina opened the wicket gate for him. I found him right in front me, impeccably dressed and without a drop of sweat despite the great heat.

'They tell me you're Dioguardi's friend and a *commissario* of police. Are you here on official business?'

I took it as given that he was having a joke and gave a stupid little laugh. The Count looked at me as if I were an idiot. Without another word he turned and went off to the entrance of his block. I stayed there, watching him go, angry with myself for having felt uneasy – an unpleasant sensation to which I was not at all accustomed.

Then I set off towards Block B, not sure what to do. I risked losing myself again between the tennis court and the swimming pool and again I met Father Paul, just as I had the first time.

'Commissario, the Cardinal's waiting for you.'

This time he was serious – there was nothing of his usual smile. He seemed tense: his blue eyes troubled in his freckled face, his red hair in disarray. He'd even come up with an Italian verb to make himself understood.

'Will you be watching the final tonight, Paul?'

I asked him in order to play for time more than anything else, as I was fighting a little internal battle with myself.

'Yes, in San Valente, with the children. Now late for me.' And off he went without even saying goodbye.

I stopped to look up at the goddess's window. Again it was the only one open and this time there was a flower on the windowsill, which the girl must have put out when the sun was no longer beating down. I still didn't know what to do, so I stayed there a couple of minutes, thinking about her, undecided.

Then I went to the lift and pressed the buttons for floors two and three.

I found Angelo on the Cardinal's landing. We crossed the huge deserted lounge in silence and went into the private study. Cardinal Alessandrini was there, dressed in his red robes, sitting behind a large desk leafing through Elisa's work that Signora Gina had brought him. Seeing him in those vestments and in that room gave a different impression of him. This was not only an energetic and intelligent priest, but also a man who had power and would always want more. Angelo seemed worried; there must be a problem, some work that was unsatisfactory.

'Commissario Balistreri, didn't you want to come up and say hello?' asked the Cardinal, greeting me. His tone was cordial, but you could pick up a slight hint that something was not quite right.

Angelo went out onto the terrace; I saw him smoking while he leafed nervously through some files.

'I didn't want to impose. I know that you and Angelo have some urgent business. Is there a problem?'

Alessandrini pointed to the chair opposite him. 'Nothing that would make you miss the game. May I offer you a lemonade while your friend gets to the bottom of the matter?'

Obviously it was some problem with accommodation that Angelo and Elisa hadn't resolved. That friendly man in red must also have been a very hard man when he wanted to be.

The Cardinal opened a small fridge and filled a glass with iced lemonade.

'You are young, Dottor Balistreri, but with a great deal of experience. I know you've done many things . . .'

This was exactly what he said, confirmation that he had a real and proper dossier on me.

'I've done some stupid things and some things that were right, like everyone.'

'The important thing is to learn from one's mistakes. Even your dear Nietzsche's Übermensch will one day have to stand before God . . .'

Well, I'd committed a grave error twelve years ago. A mortal sin, from which only a priest could absolve me. But I had no desire to talk about it with the Cardinal.

'I see that at least here we can smoke,' I said, pointing to the balcony terrace in order to change the subject.

'Naturally, the Vatican is outside the Count's "jurisdiction", so do join Angelo if you wish,' he joked. He was affable, playful. But he was a little distracted, as if pursuing some thought of his own.

I went outside and, while Angelo was working, smoked a couple of cigarettes one after the other.

Then the telephone rang in the study, and while the Cardinal answered it I asked Angelo how much he still had to do. 'Almost done,' he grumbled. He was serious, full of thought. I cursed Alessandrini and his power over my friend. I didn't like to see him worried by his priestly boss. It stuck in my throat how Angelo was so submissive to the man.

The Cardinal's call was brief, ending with a simple 'We'll meet there at a quarter to seven.'

Angelo went back into the room and handed the papers to the Cardinal.

'Everything's in order, Your Eminence. I'll leave the definitive arrangements on your desk so that tomorrow morning you can confirm everything before the guests arrive. About the other matter, I'll do what I can . . .'

'I'm sure you will. Well now, I suggest we go down. It's ten past six and I have to be at the Vatican. And I believe you have plans for this evening?'

'Won't you be watching the final, Eminence?' I asked.

'I too am flesh and blood, Dottor Balistreri. I shall try to be back for eight thirty.'

We went down in the lift. In passing I gave a last glance at the open window on the second floor. I had to stop thinking about her.

Signora Gina wasn't at the gate, having gone to Mass. The Cardinal said goodbye in a hurry and got into a taxi that was waiting for him by the gate.

We were getting into the old Fiat when we saw the Count coming out of Block A together with a much younger woman and a tall youth with huge rippling muscles below his red T-shirt and who was wearing a full-face motorcycle helmet. As usual the Harley Davidson was parked next to the Aston Martin. The Count placed a hand on the boy's shoulder and opened the gate with his remote control. Then they went out, the Count and Ulla in the James Bond car, the boy on his *Easy Rider* bike.

*　　*　　*

When we got to Paola's there were already a number of people there. Angelo went straight to the kitchen, being one of the cooks, while I offered to lay the large table in front of the TV. Then I helped Paola to welcome the other guests while Angelo was busy cooking. This way I could get a good preview of the female talent coming in. My brother Alberto came along with the elegant German girl who would later become his wife. Every so often I went into the kitchen and found Angelo sweating more than ever over the gas rings and glasses of wine. He was completely taken up with preparing the *penne all'arrabbiata* together with Cristiana, a petite girl with long red hair, large tits and a pair of jeans that perfectly framed her notable backside. From that moment my visits to the kitchen increased, ending with me hanging around there to chat to her.

By eight o'clock, about fifty people were squeezed into every nook and cranny. The heat of that stifling afternoon was still entering the open windows. The neighbouring housing blocks gave off the laughter of groups of friends gathered for the event. I glanced down at the street. Absolutely deserted.

The atmosphere in the house was festive. After several glasses of white wine I ventured into a heated discussion with Cristiana on how different it would be making love as victors or as the defeated.

'You're a likeable idiot, Michele, but a dangerous one. Paola advised me to steer clear of you.'

In reality, Paola was a good friend. She knew very well that that type of advice attracted the girls like flies to honey.

'Be careful – I could arrest you for insulting a public official.'

'And would you have to handcuff me, Signor Commissario?' she laughed.

'Handcuff you first and then question you very thoroughly. If you offered any resistance . . .'

'You'd have to mistreat me a good deal to make me talk, Signor Commissario. Perhaps even use a whip on me.'

I glanced pointedly at her backside.

'It's not always useful as torture – so

She blushed, but laughed. The part of

and the poker was in the bag. Not much

Besides, with all the cigarettes and alcoho

peeped into the kitchen. Sweating like a pi

Angelo was putting the finishing touches to   cent rice salad

in the national colours.

Then the match started. Crouching on the floor between Cristiana's legs, I was drinking, smoking and praying for Paolo Rossi.

The first half finished nil–nil. Strung out with the tension and the intense heat, Italians flooded out onto the streets, balconies and terraces to cool down and find fresh air. When the phone rang, it was Paola who took the call.

'It's my uncle – he wants to speak to you,' she said to Angelo, looking puzzled.

I saw a line deepen on Angelo's forehead as he listened to the Cardinal amid the hubbub.

'I'll come right away,' he mumbled finally, putting the receiver down. His voice was thick with drink.

I met his gaze, concerned. 'Angelo, not more problems with all that housing crap?'

He looked at me vacantly. 'They can't find Elisa.'

'Who can't find Elisa?'

'Her parents. They're really worried. They say that she should have come back home to watch the match with them and she never arrived. They've gone to the Cardinal.'

I could only laugh. 'What a load of bollocks! She'll most certainly be with some friends watching it somewhere else. Typical Italian parents – always worried.'

ook his head. 'Elisa would have told them if she'd changed

y balls went into a twist. 'Holy shit, tonight of all nights! OK,
I'll take you. We'll go in your Fiat, calm down these two old pains
in the arse and get back in time for the second half.'

I was really annoyed at this bother, but it wouldn't take long with
the lack of traffic and I couldn't let him go alone in that state.

We were both drunk. I drove and we were in Via della Camilluccia
within five minutes. I noticed the Aston Martin parked next to the
Harley Davidson. From the illuminated terrace of Block A came the
sounds of a party. The Count had guests for the match.

The Cardinal and Elisa's parents were waiting for us beside the
large fountain. Amedeo and Giovanna Sordi were a little over fifty,
Elisa their only child. The father was a tall, gaunt man, his hair
already white. Elisa had taken her height and bearing from him. The
huge deep eyes, on the other hand, she had taken from her mother.
Those eyes were looking at us worriedly.

'We're so sorry, Dottor Dioguardi, this evening of all evenings.'

It was the mother who spoke, the father keeping to one side. I
noted the respectful use of 'Dottore' to refer to Angelo. The poor
always have too much respect for those in command, which is why
they stay poor.

The Cardinal turned to Angelo. 'Did you see or hear Elisa after
we said goodbye this afternoon?'

Angelo staggered a little, his cheeks flushed. Nevertheless, he
managed to mumble a sensible reply. 'No, I told her that if I hadn't
come past by half past six it meant that the work was all in order
and she could go home.'

'I spoke to her several times on the phone today,' said the mother.
'I also called her in the office just after five. She told me as well that
Dottor Dioguardi was going to the Cardinal and that if there weren't
any problems she'd be home by half past seven. When I saw she

wasn't coming home I didn't worry straight away, thinking there was something unexpected in the office and not wanting to disturb her, so I didn't call.'

The husband looked at her protectively. 'Amedeo wanted to come and get her in the car, but Elisa never wanted to inconvenience him. At eight I began to worry. I rang the office here, but no one answered. Now we don't know what to think . . .'

'I'm a friend of Dioguardi and a police commissario,' I put in, trying not to slur my words. 'Perhaps Elisa simply changed her mind and went to watch the game with some friends.'

Giovanna Sordi stared at me, a little confused by my less than reassuring appearance, but relieved by the fact that I was a policeman.

'But she would have called us, Signor Commissario,' she said respectfully.

Parents fool themselves into thinking they know everything. That thought came to me together with the fact that the second half was about to begin. I assumed an exceptionally professional manner.

'She could have stopped in some place where there's no telephone. We must at least wait until the end of the game,' I said firmly.

I noticed a shade of annoyance on the Cardinal's face, but unlike the two parents he made no objections.

'Let's do that,' said the Cardinal. 'Signor Amedeo, you go back home now while there's no traffic. If Elisa calls or comes home you can let us know. Your wife can stay here with me until the end of the game. Then, if Elisa hasn't called, Dottor Balistreri will tell us what to do.'

I was getting worked up, not about Elisa Sordi but about the Italian side. And I was also drunk. I drove at top speed to Paola's, while Angelo sat beside me with his eyes tight shut.

The second half had just started.

'What's happened?' asked my brother Alberto when we entered the crowded lounge. As usual he was the only one to show concern.

'Nothing serious. One of Angelo's staff hasn't come home. She'll be out with friends watching the match, but her parents are worried.'

Alberto shot me a disapproving glance, similar to Cardinal Alessandrini's, but didn't voice any objections.

I snuggled between Cristiana's legs with my wine and cigarettes. Italy's three goals gave rise to an equal number of roars across the country. Come the third, people left the television to fly down to the streets, or out onto balconies and terraces. The noise of car horns and air horns added to the thunderclap of fireworks.

On the referee's final whistle, tens of thousands were already on the streets. In a few minutes the traffic was jammed solid, folk sitting on car roofs shouting with joy, waving flags, sounding air horns and beating drums. Columns of red, white and green smoke were every-where; the night was painted with the national colours.

Amid this deafening racket the telephone rang. While Angelo went to answer it, I had an uncomfortable feeling in my stomach. Alberto looked at me.

'If she's not back, then get over there right away.'

His tone was calm, but brooked no argument. It was the same tone used by my father when I was little. *You must learn to be more responsible, Mike.*

'The Cardinal says we have to get back there with the office keys.'

Angelo was now less drunk and more worried.

It was no longer possible to go in the car with the uproar unleashed on the streets, but the complex was fairly close by, so we went on foot through the celebrating crowds, pushed and shoved by everyone and pushing and shoving everyone back in turn. It was a ridiculous situation: in the middle of the most unbridled joy, there we were like two drunken branches battered left and right in the wind.

It took us twenty minutes. I was in a state of near delirium about the glorious victory and the probable hook-up with Cristiana. The thought of Elisa just about crept in every once in a while.

Cardinal Alessandrini and Signora Giovanna were waiting for us. She met my look with hope in her eyes and we went straight to Block B. Elisa's window was now closed, the flower still on the windowsill. Alessandrini was very tense, Angelo white as a sheet. The office door had been double-locked, as it should have been. Angelo opened it with a hand trembling from tension and alcohol. I told everyone to stay outside, but the Cardinal objected.

'You're still a member of the public, Eminence. I'm a policeman. You must stay outside.'

But he ignored me and turned to Angelo.

'Stay here with Signora Giovanna, Angelo.'

He went in without even looking at me. I didn't care. I wanted to get away as soon as I could – to play poker, and then take care of Cristiana.

We switched on the lights. Everything was perfectly in order. Folders in storage boxes, windows closed, and no sign of Elisa Sordi. We looked through the papers on the desk in her room to see if there was anything that could indicate any meeting. Nothing. We found her time card in its place in the rack where the staff's cards were kept. She had been the only one in that day. Her departure was properly stamped at half past six.

Angelo locked the office and Alessandrini took me to one side.

'You and Angelo are high as kites,' he said, without any niceties, 'so go back home. I'll take Signora Giovanna home and inform the police.'

I thought this was an excellent idea and only made a feeble protest that the Cardinal didn't even hear. So off we went. As well as our smelling of drink and smoke I'd even let a burp escape my lips.

When we got back my brother had left. No poker. But Cristiana soon returned with Paola. I carried her to the guest room and shut the door.

She stood in the doorway, her cheeks flushed.

'I'm engaged, Michele, to a man who works in Milan. I'll be married within the year.'

I'd heard that story before. Michele Balistreri was every woman's dark little secret, that borderland that girls know, that they fear and dream about without daring to get too close. They soon understood that if they strayed over the line of good behaviour with Michele Balistreri, they could always go back to being cosseted by reassuring guys like Angelo Dioguardi, the ideal boyfriend and companion for life. It was much more enjoyable like this; it was a hoot corrupting their good principles to the point where they not only slipped out of their clothes but also the protective layers built up from years of education and self-control. Along with their panties they handed over that part of themselves they knew existed but were ashamed of, the part that no fiancé had ever seen before and no husband after. They never truly fell in love with me out of an instinct for self-preservation, but when I disappeared they couldn't forgive me. I took away with me the most secret side of their face, even if I was perhaps the only man who had never tried to deceive them.

I undid the cotton belt around her jeans.

'I have no handcuffs, so I'll use this to tie you up.'

She unfastened my leather belt.

'And if I refuse to collaborate with the police, you can use this to smack my bottom.'

Yes, it was going to be a great night. And I forgot all about Elisa Sordi.

Monday, 12 July 1982

Spending the night at Paola's also gave me a huge logistical gain. I was only two strides from the Vigna Clara police station and could therefore sleep in longer. And that morning I needed it. I ignored the alarm completely, having told the station I'd be late. Cristiana was sleeping at my side and from the bedroom next door there was no noise. In the end, what forced me to get up around eleven was hunger.

I didn't even wash. In the general silence, I slipped on jeans and T-shirt and went down to the bar in the piazza. A crowd was discussing the great victory. The pavements were full of folk who should have been at the office, just like me. In the general throng, I put myself right with a tall coffee and a crème patissiere pastry.

'On the house,' declared the barman, obviously a football fan. 'The only ones who pay today are the Krauts.'

I bought the *Corriere dello Sport* and went back to the flat. I wanted to read all the details of the triumph in peace and quiet. I stretched out on the sofa in the lounge with the paper and my cigarettes to enjoy the journalists' hype.

After a while, I heard the voices of Cristiana and Paola in the kitchen and smelled the delightful aroma of coffee. They came in with a steaming cup for me, as well as some toast and jam. They were in slippers and dressing gowns, their eyes swollen with sleep.

'There you are, service for the sultan,' declared Cristiana, offering herself for a kiss, which I gave her distracted and unwillingly.

'Girls, you shouldn't be seen up and about like this. Paola, if Angelo wakes up and sees you in this state . . .'

'Angelo went out at seven thirty. He almost woke me up, damn him.'

I was mildly surprised, but remembered there were those problems to sort out with the priests and nuns. I dived into my second breakfast, then returned to reading the paper. My head felt bad, but my spirits were sky high.

Angelo called a little after noon. Paola handed me the phone.

'The police are here, Michele. They've just arrived from your station.' He sounded scared.

'Who's there?'

'Your deputy, Capuzzo. Elisa's mother made an official report of her disappearance yesterday at midnight in your office, which covers this area. I told Capuzzo I knew you, but I didn't say you were at Paola's. They tried to find you at home, but don't know where you are.'

Good man, Angelo, but this was still a real hassle. 'I'll be right over.'

I phoned the office, pretending to know nothing. They said Capuzzo was looking for me and gave me the number for where he was, which was Dioguardi's office. I called and a secretary answered, who then put me on to Capuzzo.

'What's up, Capù?'

'Dottore, there's this girl gone missing. She works for your friend Dioguardi.'

'Who reported it?'

'The mother. She came to the station at midnight in the middle of that tremendous hell of a racket. She was with a priest. I told him the procedure for an adult is complicated, that we can't make a move until twenty-four hours after her going missing.'

'Exactly. Listen: between ourselves, Capuzzo, this girl's a great bit of skirt who'll be celebrating the victory with someone who's a luckier man than you or me.'

'But the priest was insistent. He must have clout because halfway through the morning came a request from the Flying Squad to go and check out the situation.'

I took some time to make myself presentable. Sure, dressed in jeans and T-shirt I hardly looked professional, but there was no time to go home and change. I made my way on foot through the many knots of idlers discussing Italy's triumph. All the balconies were displaying the national flag. It must have been the first time since Mussolini's era. Perhaps since the day they hanged him upside down in Piazzale Loreto. *A country without honour.* I squashed the thought that had gone with me throughout adolescence; this wasn't the right moment.

The concierge wasn't there; she was probably already flying over India. In her place was a polite girl with features that said she was her daughter. I was smoking when I came to the green gate. I showed her my police ID and entered with the cigarette in my mouth. I was now no longer Angelo Dioguardi's friend on a visit, I was the police. Just let Count Tommaso dei Banchi di Aglieno try to piss me off with his medieval rules and regulations.

The reflection from Block A told me that Manfredi was on the lookout. I was so ill disposed to him I was on the point of gesturing with pouted lips and one eye closed, Mussolini style. I confined myself to waving the cigarette in a sign of greeting. I hoped he would tell his arrogant shit of a father. I knew that all this aggression was justified only by feeling I'd cut a stupid figure on my single brief encounter with the Count. Knowing it only made me angrier.

Capuzzo was waiting for me in Angelo Dioguardi's office. My friend looked as if he'd slept little and badly – dark rings under his blue eyes, which were bloodshot. He was unshaven, his fair hair all over the place.

It was really too much. I took him to one side.

'What the hell's happened to you, Angelo?'

He shook his head.

'We're two turds, Michele, two turds.'

'OK, perhaps I should have taken it seriously last night. But Elisa's only knocking around with a friend.'

'You're a real piece of shit,' he said to me.

This was truly an insult. It had never happened since we'd known each other. I decided to forget about it, knowing that Angelo's sensitive nature was very different from mine.

'So, Capù, who saw the girl last?'

'We don't know, Dottò.'

'What the hell does "we don't know" mean?'

'Her clocking-off card was stamped six thirty, but Signor Dioguardi told us that he went away at six fifteen with you and the Cardinal, and the only ones who live in the other block went away at the same time you did. That young priest, Paul, had already left when you arrived, and the concierge went to Mass at six, before taking the bus to the airport. She was seen in church, but the village where she's staying in India has no telephone and so—'

I stopped the stream of words. Capuzzo had been extremely efficient up to this moment, but this wasn't the point.

'OK. So the girl left a little after we did, two hours before the final, perhaps with the idea of going home to her parents. Then she'll have met someone she knew who took her to watch the match in a beautiful villa at the seaside and she's still there with him recuperating after a long night.'

'No,' said Angelo, giving me a dark look.

'No? And how do you know?'

'I already told you that Elisa's not the kind to—'

I grabbed him by the arm and dragged him to one side. 'Listen, you pillock, you can think that this kid's a bloody saint, but I believe I know women better than you do. Your little goddess has spent Sunday night fucking someone, the lucky bastard. And tonight she'll come back home saying, "Sorry, Daddy, sorry, Mummy . . ." '

Angelo brusquely turned his back on me and went out.

'Then go fuck yourself, Angelo Dioguardi!' I shouted after him.

Capuzzo looked on, appalled.

'The girl's an adult, Capù, and the law's clear. In these cases we can't do a thing unless there's an official report. Yesterday the concierge told us she'd gone up to her after five, just before Angelo and I arrived. Even if she clocked off at six thirty, let's say she disappeared at five. Get a photo of her from the mother; she won't have any difficulty getting a good one. But not in swim suit, or we'll have thousands of sightings from sexually excited fanatics. Anyway, it's enough to see her face not to forget her.'

I carefully stopped myself from saying that I'd heard her on the phone myself around five o'clock, a few minutes before Angelo came to pick me up at the station.

Capuzzo took note. 'Dottò, what should I say to the parents and that priest?'

'Tell them that these are the procedures in this free state with a free Church. And not to be a pain in the arse.'

I went off without even saying goodbye to Capuzzo. I was furious about the fight with Angelo and the cheek of Cardinal Alessandrini.

By the fountain, I met the lean kid with the glasses who I'd seen with Elisa from Angelo's office window. He looked lost.

'Where are you going?' I asked him brusquely.

He gave a half jump from fear and I saw the small gold crucifix swaying around his neck.

'Oh! Who are you?' he asked me in an uncertain voice, adjusting the glasses on his nose.

Of course, the right and proper thing. I showed him my police ID and he became even more nervous.

'OK, where are you going?'

'To see a friend of mine, but I'm not sure if she's there.'

'And who's your friend?'

'She's called Elisa Sordi. She works in the office on the second floor of Block B.'

'Was she with you last night to watch the match?'

He turned pale.

'With me? No, I was at home with my parents.'

'You didn't see Elisa yesterday?'

He thought for a minute.

'Yes, just for a moment straight after lunch. Why are you asking me all these questions?'

'Because since yesterday after work Elisa hasn't been home to her parents.'

'Oh, my God,' he muttered.

'You think that's odd?'

He hesitated again.

'Yes, it's very odd, because—'

'Because she's a very good girl, I know. Is she your girlfriend?'

He stepped back and blushed, running a hand through his smooth fairish hair, and adjusted the glasses again.

'No, no. We're friends, close, but—'

'OK. And what's your name?'

'Valerio. Valerio Bona.'

'All right, Signor Bona. Elisa's not there. Go home. I'm sure you'll see her tomorrow.'

I was angry, but I didn't want to ruin the day. On the way back to Paola's I bought the *Gazzetta dello Sport*. I wanted to read another take on our triumph. When I got back I was covered in sweat from walking in the sun. In the flat the air conditioning was on and Cristiana was waiting for me on the bed wearing only her panties. She was on the phone.

There was little else to discover about her after that night and I wanted to read the paper. But I noticed she was on the phone to her fiancé in Milan.

I pulled off her underwear while she was promising caresses to her fancy man.

Cristiana woke me in the later afternoon.

'There's someone called Capuzzo on the phone.'

What a pain in the arse, having to get back to work.

'Capù, what the hell do you want?'

'Sorry, Dottò. I took the liberty of calling you here—'

'It's all right, Capù. What's up?'

'The girl's not come home.'

I looked at the time. A quarter to six.

'OK, let's circulate word of her disappearance.'

'Already done, Dottò. That priest – the Cardinal – came here at five. He's made some phone calls and Chief Commissario Teodori's turned up.'

'And who the hell's he?'

'Flying Squad, section three,' said Capuzzo in a funereal voice. 'He told me to find you straight away, so I took the liberty . . .'

Section three. The Homicide Squad. This was Cardinal Alessandrini and the power of the Vatican. So much for a free state. The Pope chose the head of government, the cardinals chose who was to investigate the presumed disappearance of an adult girl.

I swallowed a whisky to calm myself and smoked yet another cigarette. Then I took a taxi to Via della Camilluccia. Waiting for me in Elisa's room were Capuzzo, Cardinal Alessandrini and a hugely

ROBERTO COSTANTINI · 58

obese man with his tie loosened and his thin white hair dishevelled, who introduced himself as Chief Commissario Teodori. They were sitting around the girl's desk. I had the impression that Alessandrini recognized the crumpled T-shirt and jeans he'd seen me in twenty-four hours earlier, but he made no comment about it.

'Good day, Balistreri,' said Teodori by way of greeting, without offering his hand or inviting me to sit. His tone certainly wasn't cordial.

Well, I wasn't going to be intimidated by a priest and a fat deskbound bureaucrat. I didn't say hello to anyone, but took a chair and sat down.

'You're already up to date with the problem, Balistreri,' Teodori continued.

Old policemen irritated me in general; they were out of place. It was a profession to follow from age thirty to fifty, then give over. That is, for the unsuccessful, obviously.

Better to starve to death than find yourself at fifty still in the service of this arsehole of a state.

Besides, as my teachers said at secondary school, Michele Balistreri didn't recognize authority either by age or profession. 'Severe problem with ignoring authority, linked to childhood traumas in his relationship with his father' as the psychologist diagnosed years later when he examined me for recruitment into the Secret Service.

'I've already arranged for a notice to be circulated, Teodori,' I declared, omitting the courtesy of a title, as he'd done with me. Then I looked at Cardinal Alessandrini: 'But I see that divine justice considers this insufficient.'

While Teodori's face went up in flames, Alessandrini's opened in a smile.

Real power wears a cloak of cheerfulness.

'Don't take this badly and please excuse me, Dottor Balistreri,' he said, giving me the impression that he was emphasizing the title for

Teodori's benefit. 'The fact is that in these things you have precise rules which you have accordingly observed, but these rules are for normal situations, which I do not believe this to be.'

And obviously between my judgement and his, it was his that counted for more. I didn't refer to this in any way – there was no need. Besides, the presence of Teodori bore ample witness to it.

'On the basis of his knowledge of the family and Signorina Elisa Sordi, the Cardinal considers a voluntary absence of such length implausible,' Teodori explained, as if I were a stupid child and hadn't taken this on board.

I decided not to help extricate Teodori from the difficult situation by telling him what he should do.

He turned to the Cardinal, a little embarrassed.

'Naturally, Eminence,' he went on, 'Dottor Balistreri has followed procedures.'

I noticed the slight trembling of his sweaty hands. The room was stiflingly hot, despite the fact that someone had opened the window after raising the blind. Elisa's flower was still there on the windowsill.

'Now, however, the case is being handed over to the Flying Squad. A purely cautionary measure, naturally. The local station and its officers will continue with investigations, but I have already given instructions that they are to be intensified,' continued Teodori, speaking to the Cardinal.

I looked at Capuzzo, who was staring at the floor. It wasn't true; there was nothing to intensify. Teodori was telling the Cardinal a lie.

The Cardinal read my thoughts.

'In what way will they be intensified, Dottor Teodori?'

I saw the fat man turn pale and look at me uncertainly. But I was damned if I was going to help him out – the semi-retired bureaucrat could sink in his own shit.

'We're going to send out the details to the border police and Interpol,' he said at last.

He was lying, and knew he was lying. Perhaps he could push procedures forward by alerting colleagues on the Italian borders, but being a pain in the arse to Interpol over an adult girl who had disappeared a little over twenty-four hours ago, without any sign of kidnapping or act of violence . . .

Alessandrini decided to take pity on him and rose from his seat.

'Very well, Dottor Teodori. Please thank the head of the Flying Squad for his help so far on our behalf.'

On *our* behalf. On behalf of whom? His and the parents of Elisa? Or the Vatican hierarchy that had called the Minister of the Interior? Perhaps the Pontiff himself?

There was a knock on the door. Father Paul appeared, looking younger and more lost than usual.

'Eminenza, I going San Valente if no more use to you . . .'

Huge improvements: verbs in the present participle. The Yank was making progress.

'Wait for me downstairs, Father Paul,' Alessandrini told him sternly.

I had the feeling that what he had to say wouldn't be pleasant for Father Paul, whose eyes wandered around the room and came to rest on Elisa's desk where they remained for a second. Then he went out, followed by the Cardinal.

'This is a real problem, Balistreri,' said Teodori, sweating like a pig while he filled his pipe, spilling tobacco all over Elisa Sordi's desk. I suddenly realized that the meeting and impromptu search of the evening before had compromised anything that Forensics might want to carry out in the room should it become necessary.

Capuzzo looked at me in alarm. He knew what I thought about detectives who smoked a pipe: low-grade imitators of Maigret. But I didn't say anything. My absence from the office could cause me some difficulties, but fortunately I had Angelo and the faithful Capuzzo to cover for me.

'A real problem? Why is that, Dottor Teodori?'

'Because this isn't any old residential complex.'

He was irritated, as if it were the most natural thing in the world that investigative efforts should vary according to what was being investigated. He had the yellowish eyes of someone who suffered from liver problems and had blotchy skin that also suggested heart troubles. He made me feel sick, him and what he represented.

'Because of Cardinal Alessandrini?' I asked ingenuously.

Teodori swept his heavy sweaty hand over Elisa's desk, disturbing several papers.

'Not only that. In the other block lives someone far more important than the Cardinal: Count Tommaso dei Banchi di Aglieno, a senator and president of the Italian Neo-monarchist party.'

'I met him yesterday afternoon, then I saw him again going out about a quarter past six,' I offered innocently.

'I know, and do you know where he was going? To a meeting with the Minister of the Interior,' said Teodori, shaking his head in a worried manner, bearing witness to the calibre of person a man like the Count might be, who could have a meeting with a powerful Christian Democrat minister on a Sunday afternoon.

'But he was with his wife,' I observed.

'He'll have taken her somewhere else before going to see the Minister. Have you realized who we're dealing with here?'

I had understood, but Teodori felt obliged to inform me in detail. This was a great family with castles, estates and its roots in medieval Italian history. The Count's father's brother had fought on Franco's side with the Fascists and after the war had run off to Africa, where he'd accumulated great wealth and property. Count Tommaso's father had fought with the 10th MTB squadron and, when the association between the House of Savoy and Mussolini was broken off, had remained on the King's side. After the war he presided over the pro-monarchy committee that lost the referendum in 1946, and following this dishonour had shot himself in the head. Count Tommaso was fourteen years old and had assumed the burden of bringing the monarchy back to Italy.

Elisa Sordi, on the other hand, was a beautiful girl from one of Rome's working-class districts who just happened to be in the paradise of a residential complex surrounded by young males and powerful adults.

'Capuzzo, naturally you checked if there were—'

'Everything checked, Dottor Balistreri – everything. Despite the all-night uproar of celebrations, no deaths reported. Only some injuries from fireworks and some youths falling off car roofs – nothing serious.'

'We can do nothing but wait,' said Teodori.

'Yeah, apart from alerting our colleagues on the frontiers and Interpol,' I added sarcastically.

Teodori turned his yellow eyes on me. He wondered if I was more ignorant or arrogant.

'Naturally,' he said at last. 'However, let's hope this beautiful girl is somewhere about sleeping it off with a friend after celebrating all night.'

Clerics and aristocrats. Mussolini had always distrusted both their tribes. He'd flattered them to keep them happy in order to hide the basic distrust he felt. And I felt the same way too. But I wouldn't have allowed myself to be fucked about as he had.

We agreed to get back in touch with Teodori the following morning. Then I tried to find Angelo, but one of his colleagues said he'd already left. I called Paola's apartment. Cristiana replied.

'They've gone out. Paola had tickets for *Aida* at the Caracalla Baths. Can you come and pick me up, Michele?'

I made up an excuse. Having by now got to know all about her,

I didn't want to risk her leaving her fiancé. I wanted to spend the evening drinking and trying to pull in some bar, far away from the luxury life, illustrious people and Elisa Sordi.

Friday, 16 July 1982

For several days there was neither sight nor sound of her. Teodori, whom I spoke to every day on the telephone, maintained that the girl's disappearance could be an 'elopement', possibly even abroad. She had done it secretly, perhaps, because she was lacking the courage to be open about it.

I tried not to think about it, squashing the thought like an annoying insect. I hadn't seen or heard from Angelo and had shut myself away between the office and the studio flat in Garbatella, rotating the casual female company picked up in Trastevere's bars and dives. I was smoking more than usual, drinking more than usual, and screwing more than usual. More than anything else, I didn't want to be alone. As if those things could keep away the gnawing pangs I felt over Elisa Sordi.

Teodori called me on the Friday. A tramp sleeping on the exposed gravel bed of the Tiber, just past Ponte Milvio, had sighted the body of a woman on the riverbank. I shot over there with Capuzzo, as if speed at that moment could have compensated for the time lost when it might have helped in some way.

On the dry gravel bed, exposed by the summer drought, a knot of policemen was grouped around the corpse. The girl was naked, the body attacked by insects was in an advanced state of decomposition, covered with injuries from rats and shrubs along the river, together with obvious knife wounds and cigarette burns. Although heavy blows had devastated the face, I could see it was that of Elisa Sordi. There was no mistaking that incredibly beautiful hair, the figure, the colour of her skin. I had seen other cadavers but this death was new to me; it went way beyond the circle of violence that the violent knew.

Teodori was standing in front of the corpse looking stunned and white as a sheet, his hands trembling, sweating as if he had a fever in his absurd suit and loosened tie. Capuzzo was holding on to his stomach and trying to breathe deeply, his mouth gaping wide. I had to take control of the situation. I sent Capuzzo away before he threw up. A forensic pathologist was bent over the girl's body.

I went up to Teodori. 'We should clear everyone away so that Forensics can—'

'Of course, of course!' he said, shaking himself. He gave some orders and we were left alone with the pathologist.

'Is it Elisa Sordi?' Teodori asked me. It was as if she were a relative and I was there to identify her.

I nodded yes, then walked away to have a cigarette. At the top of the slope, a line of the usual curiosity seekers had formed along the road. They were lazily licking away at ice creams, craning their necks the better to enjoy the spectacle. I called Capuzzo and two officers to move them along. When I finished the cigarette I went back to Teodori, who was talking to the pathologist.

'She's been dead for days. There are several signs of violence to the body beyond the bites inflicted by the rats. I'm afraid it was a long and painful business. Unless she was dead before the blows and the burns – but the autopsy will tell us this.'

Teodori seemed lost in who knew what thoughts.

'And the cause of death?' he asked.

The pathologist shook his head.

'I don't think she drowned. She must have been dead already when they dumped her in the river. Cardiac arrest or suffocation, but we'll see. Anyway, she's been dead for several days, perhaps even since last Sunday.'

I looked with different eyes at that young, devastated body. I thought of that summer, twelve years ago in 1970, while I was escaping over the sea from what I had left in the sea, and from the mistakes I never wanted to call sins, as Christians do. That chain that linked up paralysis: guilt, remorse and repentance. The soul's invisible blood. Wounds that never heal.

I found them sitting on a bench in the police station: parents who would now and forever be in tears. A friend had told them after hearing news of the discovery on the radio. It was the wonderful new world of news in real time with a plethora of private radio stations hunting for the sensation that only bad news could guarantee. No one was taking any notice of the two poor things. Police officers and members of the public walked past them, going about their everyday business. From an open office door you could hear the laughter of those making plans for the weekend.

When they saw me coming, they rose to their feet like two well-disciplined schoolchildren and immediately I realized I couldn't look them in the face. Signor Amedeo put an arm round the shoulders of his Giovanna, who was crying silently. In the summer half-light of that squalid office my eyes went from Amedeo Sordi's grey jacket that was too large for him, to the furrow in his brow now deeper than the lines scored from cheek to mouth in his pale complexion, to the single tear running from Giovanna Sordi's eyes, to the beam of July sunlight that came in through a window and reflected on the glossy photo of her daughter that she was holding in her hands. They spoke not a word and asked me nothing.

The last thing these two parents needed was the condolences of a young policeman frustrated by his own incapacity. In the end I managed a bureaucratic 'I'm sorry for your loss'. Then I shut myself in my office. What was I sorry about? The destruction of a young life, the life crushed out of two parents? That weekend perhaps I wouldn't be dancing and getting drunk in the discotheques along the beach and getting my end away with whoever wanted it. I might even manage a troubled sleep. And so on for several days, a week perhaps. Then I'd start my routine again: office, poker, whisky, women, sleep.

But those two parents would never sleep easily again. Every night they would look in at their only daughter's bedroom, as empty as the rest of their lives. And they'd think of me, blind drunk, saying 'Perhaps Elisa's gone to watch the game with some friends.'

I squashed the thought angrily. What's done is done. Only the future counts.

I downed a bottle of whisky and found myself reflecting drunkenly on the fact that this wasn't the usual childhood melodrama that the infant Mike had fed himself on. I was no longer the 'Michelino' who watched Westerns, the fearless cowboy who killed all the bad guys. I was a man of thirty-two who didn't give a shit about anyone, not even himself. I knew the reasons well enough – they were all very clear.

And now what the fuck was I looking for? Did I want to absolve myself? Did I want to avoid eternal remorse by finding evil? And what was evil?

It changed little; fate was not in agreement with me anyway.

Saturday, 17 July 1982

The investigation was officially handed over to Teodori by the head of the Homicide Squad. At first I wondered why they'd chosen a detective who should have been drawing his pension and was evidently not up to speed. I still didn't know all the subtleties of politics, in particular those of the Christian Democrats.

What I did know was that there were powerful forces around and about Elisa Sordi's death. A luxury residential complex, a cardinal, an aristocratic senator who wanted to bring back the king to rule Italy: spiritual power on the one hand, temporal power on the other. On the other side, two parents from the working class and some girl of theirs from the outskirts. In all probability she'd asked for it, mixing with bad company or some passing brute attracted by her exceptional beauty.

I was assigned as Teodori's deputy in the investigation because I was the district *commissario* and knew the residential complex, its inhabitants and the victim. Moreover, I had been in Via della Camilluccia that day, just before Elisa Sordi went out for her last walk before the World Cup final. I'd even spoken with her that afternoon on the telephone, as the phone records showed. But this was by mistake, of course, as I was looking for Dioguardi. In any case, I was Teodori's ideal stooge.

It was another indication of the superficiality of the Italian police's bureaucracy that no one in the Flying Squad went to check the personal details in my file. If they had, they'd have kept me a thousand miles away from the paradise of Via della Camilluccia and that inquiry.

The reconstruction of the facts was clear. After lunch Elisa was working in the office. Her mother had spoken to her just after six, immediately after my call. Before six thirty the concierge had gone to her office to pick up a file to take up to Cardinal Alessandrini. But no one saw Elisa Sordi when she left at six thirty. By that time, the residential complex was deserted. I had seen Paul go out myself and then all the others afterwards. The priest from the neighbouring parish confirmed having seen the concierge, now in a village in India, in the front row at Mass that evening.

When I went to Teodori's office in the Flying Squad for the first time I immediately noticed his young secretary, Vanessa. She was tall, black hair in a pageboy cut, narrow hips and not much chest, but two superb legs.

Teodori had a small room, a clear sign that he wasn't held in much esteem. The posters on the walls were of Italian seaside resorts in the middle of winter. Pretty depressing. He was slumped behind a desk that was in chaos, pipe tobacco all over the place, no air conditioning and a ceiling fan that made his papers fly about, adding to the general disorder.

'The problem is that we don't know whether the girl was taken away before, during or after the match. The first results of the autopsy indicate that she was already dead on the Sunday, but it's impossible to give a precise time with the body in the condition it's in.' Teodori's tone was funereal.

'We don't know if she was taken away or if she followed someone of her own free will,' I objected.

Teodori gave me a twisted look. 'Balistreri, let's not fly off into fantasy. The brutality lasted for quite a while and is the work of a maniac. One of those animals that takes pleasure in seizing a girl, making her suffer and then . . .'

'OK, but this maniac could also be someone known to the girl.'

'Yes, indeed, one of her friends from the outskirts. In fact where she lives isn't a very nice district,' agreed Teodori approvingly. It was a very ordinary working class area. Certainly a long way from and very different to the splendid Vigna Clara and Via della Camilluccia, but at the same time it was hardly a renowned breeding-ground for maniacs.

I tried to object again. 'The parents say that Elisa didn't mix with anyone, she was always in the office in Via della Camilluccia or at home studying and she didn't ever go out at night. Every so often, on Saturday or Sunday afternoons, she saw that boy, Valerio Bona.'

'We have to know where Bona was on Sunday from six thirty onwards.'

Of course, Bona was a lad from the outskirts, one of the violent working classes. A perfect suspect.

'We really should know the same for the others . . .' I put in.

Teodori gave a start. 'The others? What others?'

'All those who live in Via della Camilluccia, where she worked. You know she was an extraordinarily beautiful girl – she could have turned anybody's head.'

Teodori's eyes turned more yellow than usual. His liver didn't agree with this line of reasoning. 'If you're referring to the Senator, Count Tommaso dei Banchi di Aglieno, you should know that I've already had the entrance and exit register to the Ministry of the Interior checked – just for the record, obviously. The Senator arrived at ten minutes to seven and was with the Minister from seven o'clock until half past. From there he went straight back home where he had guests, and he did not go out again.'

'How do you know he didn't go out again?'

Teodori shot me an explosive look. 'All the general staff of his party were guests at his home, to see the match. Don't you think that's enough?'

'Too many people, plus the excitement of the game . . .' I said, to provoke him more than anything else.

He ignored my comment.

'His son and wife came home about eight and they were there to watch the match and then celebrate on the terrace.'

How Teodori had come to know these details was a mystery.

'But before that? I saw them going out with the Count around twenty past six. What did they do between that time and eight o'clock?'

'I don't know and I see no reason why we should ask them about it.'

Now Teodori was decidedly tetchy, banging the stem of his pipe forcefully on the desk, staring at an indistinct point on the floor, towards which he was directing his thoughts.

'Look, Dottor Teodori, I don't want to be a pain, but a kidnapping by force in the middle of a Roman street, even on a Sunday evening with not many people around, is hardly credible. The girl would have reacted, someone would have heard her screaming . . .'

'Young man, no one would authorize you to question these highly respectable people on a basis of that kind.'

'There's also the proximity,' I added, putting a cigarette in my mouth.

'Please do not smoke. What proximity do you mean?'

I still didn't know if he was really like this or just trying it on.

'The Tiber runs through the whole of Rome. The spot where we found her is one of the closest to Via della Camilluccia.'

'Exactly. The girl leaves office, is attacked, and is taken over there to the river.'

'But how? By car? In broad daylight at six thirty in the evening?

All right, Rome was nearly deserted, but she doesn't scream and no one sees a thing?'

The phone rang and Teodori picked it up.

'No, no, I can't come right away. But tell the pathologist I'll be round later, absolutely . . .'

His whole face was now yellow. He was talking complete shit and we'd already lost a lot of time, which was mainly my fault.

'You were saying, Balistreri?'

He stroked his sparse tufts of white hair with his sweaty hands.

'My reckoning is that the murder occurred in a different manner. Someone she knew gave her a lift and they went down there together in agreement onto the gravel bank. Perhaps Elisa thought they were only going to talk. And only then, among that foliage, the fury of the assassin was revealed. We need to get authorization to question Valerio Bona and all those in Via della Camilluccia.'

Naturally Teodori decided to start with the young kid in glasses.

We tried to find Valerio Bona at his parents'. They told us that, as always at weekends, he first went to Mass and had then gone to Ostia, where he was taking part in a regatta. We could try to speak to him at the sailing club at the end of the race.

It was already lunchtime and Teodori decided that he couldn't possibly go all that way to Ostia with the risk of finding himself jammed in traffic. When I suggested that I go alone he appeared greatly relieved.

'Naturally this would be informal, without a lawyer. He could refuse to speak to us,' I explained.

'We're investigating a murder, not a bag-snatching. If Bona creates any difficulty we can interrupt his weekend and tomorrow morning he can come to us for an official interrogation.'

Our wonderful justice: it was already marked out.

I called Angelo. We hadn't seen each other since the discussion in the Camilluccia complex.

'How about supper?'

'I'm really not in the right mood, Michele.'

It was time to make a move before the rift became unbridgeable. I didn't want to lose this friend because of my stupid pride.

'I was in the wrong, Angelo, and you were in the right.'

The only reply was silence. After a while I heard his voice and it was more friendly.

'It's not your fault. Even if you'd started to look for her straight away . . .'

His generous nature was coming to my assistance. As always.

'We still don't know, Angelo. Perhaps when they called us at the end of the first half Elisa was still alive. Perhaps she still was after the game.'

A sigh. Suffering transmitted by telephone line.

I changed the subject.

'I have to go to Ostia to question Valerio Bona. We want to know where he was when Elisa left the office.'

'Michele, in my view he's a really good kid.'

'Sometimes even really good kids can fuck up.'

Silence. It was his way of showing disapproval. Perhaps even he was thinking that I was only after the weakest link in the chain. We said goodbye.

There was a convenient Metro to Ostia, but I wasn't keen on the idea of mingling with tourists and sunbathers. I hated public transport. Although there was no hurry, I put the siren on my Duetto and got there in half an hour. There was a huge crowd, cars parked everywhere, the beach overflowing with people, the glistening sea full of swimmers and boats.

If she weren't dead, perhaps Elisa would have been there among the Roman citizens who were eating ice creams, getting a suntan and taking a swim. Instead her wounded body was lying in cold storage in the mortuary and two old folk were looking at her empty room in a house in the suburbs.

I found the sailing club easily. The regatta was under way. I sat down at a table under an umbrella on the terrace and relaxed with a coffee and a cigarette. The boats were Flying Dutchmen class, two-man racing dinghies in a regatta. Valerio Bona was in one of them. I deduced from this that Elisa's death hadn't shaken him up too much. Inexplicably, the kid had irritated me ever since the first time I'd seen him. And then that golden crucifix round his neck . . . He was clearly someone inadequate compared with her. Physically insignificant, insecure in character. Thus ran my train of thought while sitting in the sun and smoking, watching those white dots moving along between the buoys on the blue of the sea. I asked the people at a neighbouring table, who were following the regatta through binoculars, if they knew Valerio.

'Of course. He's been coming here to sail since he was a child. He's in second position in number twenty-two.'

They lent me the binoculars. I took a while to find number 22 and get it in focus. And what I saw was a surprise. Valerio Bona, in sailing cap and sunglasses, was at the helm, his crucifix gleaming in the sun. His bearing and every gesture denoted absolute calm and command of the situation. And yet they were at the end of a close-hauling manoeuvre with over twenty knots of wind. I watched his features as they were going about. Only his lips were moving imperceptibly to his partner at the jib. In the stretch before the wind, number 22 gybed continually, forcing the leading boat to do the same, and in the end Bona succeeded in passing it and crossed the finishing line first. Through the binoculars I saw him take off cap and sunglasses. There was no smile on the face of the little swot, only a word of thanks to his fellow crewman.

I kept following him while the crews came back to the marina to moor and lay up the boats. Valerio Bona was receiving compliments from all the contestants, thanking them in a serious and polite manner as he shook their calloused hands. He was confident, relaxed. Then his gaze met mine and he recognized me. I waved a hand to greet him. His face changed rapidly and I saw once again what I had seen on other occasions. He was ill at ease, anxious, insecure. Out of his boat, Valerio was without the shell that protected him from the world about him.

He came towards me, putting on the sunglasses to cover his worried look. It would have been too easy to scare him.

'We've met before, Signor Bona. I'm Commissario Michele Balistreri and I'm investigating the murder of Elisa Sordi.'

I showed him my police ID, but he had already stopped two strides before the table. 'What do you want with me?' he asked hesitantly. I opted for the hard line.

'You must call a lawyer and come to the police station for formal questioning.'

His hands were trembling slightly. While he was standing there staring at me, some yachtsmen came past congratulating him.

'Great stuff, Valerio!' they said, clapping him on the shoulders.

But he was no longer on the waves, he was back on land – a land that he felt was hostile and difficult. Here not even his faith was enough to calm him down and protect him from far worse weather.

'Please sit down. I want to ask some questions. If you don't feel like answering them, we could go to the headquarters of the Homicide Squad back in Rome.'

My peremptory tone helped him decide. He sat down facing the sun, staring at the sea. Most certainly he was wishing he could be out there on a boat.

'When we met on Monday you said that you were a friend of Elisa Sordi. Were you going out with her?'

I deliberately chose a direct and closed question to make things difficult. He shook his head.

'No, we were only very close friends.'

The emphasis on *only* betrayed his disappointment. At the same time I'd seen Elisa Sordi myself. It can't have been easy being only friends with her.

'How long had you known her?'

He pointed to the sea. 'We met exactly here, last summer. She was with a group of friends to see a regatta and a friend of hers introduced me.'

'And you naturally found her of interest?'

I could sense the hostility behind the dark lenses. 'Elisa was a young kid like me, with a simple education and religious. We live in the same area; we're almost neighbours. On Sunday mornings we almost always went to Mass together.'

I'd never had any sympathy for little couples that go to Mass together, especially since adolescence. Did they go there to pray or to be seen together?

'And did you talk only of God and works of charity or did you also do other things, Signor Bona?'

He ignored my irony. 'Elisa was curious about everything; she wanted to know all about boats, about the winds and sails. I took her out for a turn and we talked a great deal. Or rather, I was the one who spoke. She asked the questions and listened.'

I could just see it: he carefree and assured at the helm, she reassured by his shyness on land. Valerio Bona was the only male friend possible for a girl like Elisa Sordi. A faithful little altar boy. But perhaps she hadn't taken into account how in the end a friendship of that kind was impossible for an eighteen-year-old. However shy or awkward he was, he was still a young man with his hormones in turmoil.

'And from then on you saw her often?'

'That summer we used to come to the beach on my moped and go out in the boat almost every day, then we went for a walk and at eight I'd take her back home. Elisa's parents wanted her back for supper. They're kind of old-fashioned . . .'

'So there was nothing between you?'

'I already told you, we were great friends. Is that so trivial?' Now his hostility was stronger than his insecurity. I decided to put him on a more slippery footing.

'A great friendship with a girl almost your age who was so beautiful? And you were content with that, Signor Bona?'

He confined himself to twisting the cap in his hands and skirting round the direct question.

'Elisa wanted to earn some money so as not to weigh on her parents and I helped her.'

'Really? And how did you do that?'

'I work for Count Tommaso dei Banchi di Aglieno. I mentioned her to him and he mentioned her to Cardinal Alessandrini who sent her to Dioguardi.'

Quite a paper trail. 'And what do you do for the Count?'

'I file his papers and correspondence on this new type of computer just out, the PC.'

You could hear from his tone that he had little sympathy for the Count. It was the only thing on which we agreed. I decided this was the moment to change the subject.

'Were you here for a regatta last weekend?'

He nodded to show he was.

'But Elisa Sordi wasn't with you, was she? She had that work that needed finishing.'

He nodded again.

'While waiting I checked the regattas calendar. I saw that you won, but the Sunday regatta was in the morning.'

'Yes, there are three heats: two on Saturday and the third on

Sunday morning. Last Sunday I went to Mass early and alone, because Elisa had to work. Then I came here.'

'What did you do after the regatta?'

'I went straight back to Rome. That evening there was the match – I didn't want to run the risk of getting stuck in the traffic coming back from the beach. I'm a big football fan.'

'Did you go and see Elisa Sordi?' I already knew part of his reply, remembering what Signora Gina had said.

He was hesitant.

'I called her at work from a phone booth about half past one, as soon as I got to Rome. I wanted to have lunch with her, but she wasn't there – she'd already gone out. So I hung around Via della Camilluccia and waited until she came back.'

'You didn't look for her in any of the bars? There surely weren't many open in that area.'

'No,' he replied, quickly. 'I waited for her on the corner, keeping an eye on the green gate. I didn't want to be seen by that crazy guy with the binoculars or by Signora Gina. When I saw Elisa I went up to her.'

'Did you arrange a meeting for later?'

'No, Elisa said she wouldn't finish before six. Then she had to go home to watch the match with her parents. They didn't want her to be late.'

'But you could have waited for her and taken her home on the moped, seeing as you were neighbours.'

It was difficult to decide how much his unease was habitual and how much was due to the question.

'No, Elisa didn't want me to wait for her.' He was now at a point somewhere between scared and aggressive.

'Was she upset? Had you had an argument?'

'I couldn't understand why she didn't want to—'

It was the moment to drive the nail home.

'Perhaps she was meeting someone else, do you think?'

He turned pale. I sensed his eyes were troubled behind the dark glasses, even without seeing them.

'She hadn't arranged to meet anyone else,' he answered stubbornly, his hands worrying the gold crucifix, as if God could help him at that moment.

'And how can you be so sure? Couldn't she have it off with someone without you knowing about it?'

This was too much even for someone like Valerio Bona. 'How can you talk like that about a girl who's just been killed?' he said, standing up.

I stood up as well, towering over him. 'You're right. I meant to say that she could have sex with someone without you knowing about it. Is that better?'

He was both indignant and scared. 'Elisa wasn't that kind of girl—'

'I've heard that one already,' I said brutally, interrupting him. 'Do you know how many times I've heard that about girls who then turn out to be common little tarts?'

I despised myself for using the phrase on that occasion, but managed to come out with it. I wanted to see if Valerio Bona was capable of attacking someone and striking them. He tried to land one on me, but I was too strong for him. I grabbed his wrist with an iron grip.

'Don't be stupid, or I'll arrest you for assaulting a public official.'

A good many people had stopped to look at us. Several yachtsmen came menacingly close. I waved my police ID around.

'Keep your distance and mind your own business,' I ordered.

I was showing the lad up in the only environment in which he felt at ease. I was doing it clinically, because he was hiding something from me. I didn't give a damn about the consequences for him – a pious little neurotic fixated on God, sailing and his computer, who locked himself in the bathroom to masturbate after having had a chat with Elisa Sordi.

I let go of his wrist. 'Now tell me what you did last Sunday.'

Valerio Bona was shaking. 'In the afternoon I went to the park in Villa Pamphili. I had a university exam two days later; I had to revise.'

'And you were there all afternoon?'

'Up until a quarter to eight. The sun was going down, so I took the moped and came home to watch the game with my parents and the relatives we'd invited.'

'You didn't see anyone all afternoon?'

'There weren't many people in the park. I was completely alone with my books under a big tree.'

'And you got home just in time for the start of the match?'

'Just before, but my cousins were already there.'

'And after the match you went out to celebrate on the streets?'

His face grew dark again. 'The others did, not me. I was worried about the exam. I wanted to sleep.'

'You were alone at home? You, the great football fan?'

'Yes. I watched a few commentators on the box, then I went to bed.'

I decided to leave it at that, even if his story was hardly credible.

'You mentioned a crazy guy with binoculars. Who did you mean?'

'The Count's son, he spies on everyone from his terrace.'

'Do you know Manfredi?'

Valerio pulled a face.

'He usually comes down with his helmet on so people can't see his face. But three Saturdays ago I paid Elisa a surprise visit and found him there chatting to her. As soon as I turned up, he found an excuse to leave without even saying hello to me.'

'Did Elisa say what he wanted?'

'She met him outside in the courtyard a few months ago, one

morning when it was raining. He was there with an umbrella and accompanied her from the gate over to Block B. Then he called her on the internal phone about the time she normally went and had a cappuccino in the bar. It was still raining and he offered to take her over again. To my mind he knew her comings and goings, thanks to the binoculars, and liked to keep tabs on her.'

'That's probable. Did you say anything to Elisa?'

'Yes, but she didn't see anything in it. She said he was always very polite and kind and every so often came to the office for a bit of a chat when he was alone. She felt sorry for him.'

'Elisa never said if he tried anything on?'

'She was absolutely certain that he'd never do anything like that, but I'm not so sure. A guy with that face, those muscles and that manner could jump on her at any time.'

Elisa Sordi had to have been a naive, kind-hearted soul or else a cheap little slut.

If I hadn't seen her turn puce with embarrassment at my vulgarity I wouldn't have had any doubts between the two.

'You never saw Manfredi again?'

'Just once, in the courtyard. He was wearing his helmet. I was waiting for Elisa next to the fountain ready to take her home. I was having a cigarette. He came up and told me to go outside the gate if I wanted to smoke. He stayed there beside his Harley Davidson, waiting until I went outside. Then he went off.'

'Did you see him on the terrace last Sunday when you were talking to Elisa?'

'I saw the reflection of his binoculars. He was there spying on us.'

'How did your exam go, Signor Bona?'

He gave a twisted grin.

'Elisa's disappearance made me lose my concentration. I withdrew.'

I nodded over to dinghy number 22.

'But her death hasn't created any problems for you as skipper.'

He looked at me seriously.

'You don't understand. It's only on that boat that I can stop thinking about it.'

'And when you do think about it, what do you think?'

'That that guy Manfredi's dangerous,' he said, immediately regretting his words. 'Well, I think . . . maybe . . . I don't know . . .'

I went away feeling satisfied.

I arrived at Flying Squad HQ after three hours stuck in traffic. Teodori had told me to wait for him and, seeing as Vanessa wasn't there, I went straight into his office.

On the desk stood a framed photograph of an adolescent girl who was pretty enough, if a little too plump. She was wearing a lot of make-up. I knew that Teodori was separated from his wife and that he had an eighteen-year-old daughter named Claudia. A detective who had a daughter the same age as the murdered girl. Had he been clear-headed, he could perhaps have better understood the victim's psychology, but Teodori seemed too fearful of annoying the illustrious guests in Via della Camilluccia. And Claudia Teodori was certainly very different from Elisa Sordi – you only had to look at the photo.

The light on the answerphone signalled two messages. Years working for the Secret Service had taught me that any source was legitimate and every opportunity one to be taken. The first message was from a female voice.

'Good afternoon, Dottor Teodori, this is the Via Alba clinic. We would like you to come to the clinic as soon as you can to see your daughter and talk to the doctors. Goodbye.'

The second message was from a male voice.

'Teodori, it's Coccoluto here. I wanted to say not to worry. I've spoken to the Public Prosecutor and the judge. If we can find out who secretly slipped her the tablets then the severity of the crime changes a great deal.'

I knew that Coccoluto was a colleague who worked in juvenile crime, especially relating to drugs and alcohol. This explained why they'd chosen Teodori for this investigation. He could be black-mailed. His daughter must have got herself into serious trouble. I'd have great difficulty in trying to get him to disturb the tranquillity of the Via della Camilluccia paradise. However, there was one pathway open, even if it was a very narrow one. I left him a message saying I'd call him later in the office.

I parked the Duetto and went up to Signora Gina's gatehouse, now occupied by her young daughter.

Five minutes later I was up in Block B's penthouse. Father Paul, worried and much less his usual sparkling self, came to open the door.

Alessandrini was at the same desk I'd seen him at the previous Sunday. He didn't get up to shake my hand.

'Any news, Dottor Balistreri?'

'Not at the moment. I'm here to ask for a word of advice.'

'Earthly justice isn't my field, Commissario. I wouldn't know how to help you.'

I decided that getting straight to the point was the best way with this man.

'You can help by allowing me to investigate this little corner of paradise as well.'

I caught Paul's glance at the Cardinal. Alessandrini gave me a serious stare.

'And you think you need my permission to do this? It appears to me that you are a firm upholder of the Italian state's freedom from the Vatican's shackles. However, you can ask me everything you think fit, no problems at all.'

'There's also Block A,' I said.

Alessandrini took off his glasses and massaged his temples with a smile.

'I imagine that Chief Commissario Teodori wouldn't approve of this conversation.'

'If you want Elisa Sordi and her parents to get justice you have to help me investigate in whatever direction necessary. The girl worked for the Vatican; you have good reason to ask what—'

The Cardinal interrupted me with a gesture. 'I know very well how to intervene with police authority, as you have seen. But this isn't the point. The body was found by the side of the river. The girl had left the office. Does this make you think that—'

'It's very probable that she knew the killer. The river's too far away to get there on foot. Elisa had to have got into a car or on a motorcycle. It's not easy to kidnap a person without them screaming and without anyone hearing or seeing anything. And in this case no one has seen or heard a thing.'

'Even if this were the case, there are friends in her neighbourhood, school friends – a thousand possibilities,' objected Alessandrini.

'I agree. But then it would have been a meeting totally by chance. Dioguardi told Elisa only the evening before that she'd have to work on Sunday, and until he and I came up to you no one knew what time she'd be able to leave.'

Alessandrini was silent for a moment. 'Very well. I'll see to it that you can question everyone so that you can clear the pitch of even the most minute suspicion. But the Count will not be happy about it and will take his own steps, you'll see.'

'I'm most grateful. Thank you. We need to question everyone who lives or works here.'

Silence. I kept my mouth shut, embarrassed. Alessandrini was perfectly at ease.

'You want to know my movements on Sunday after we left here with you and Angelo? As you'll recall, I took a taxi, which will have been at six twenty. My entrance in the Vatican was recorded as six thirty. I went down to pray in a chapel below the offices, where I stayed for about an hour.'

'You were alone?' I asked. For some reason this powerful man didn't unnerve me. The difficult question came out lightly, easily.

'There are no witnesses who can confirm I was there. I came out of the Vatican towards eight, and the time is recorded. I was here at home about ten past eight. In time to see the match . . . Count Tommaso was parking his car precisely as I was leaving the taxi. We exchanged a wave of greeting – he was in a hurry because he had guests.'

'Was his wife with him?'

The Cardinal thought for a moment. 'No, I don't think so. Before the game started I walked out onto the terrace. Rome was deserted by then. I saw the motorbike arrive, which would have been a quarter past eight.'

'Manfredi was alone?'

'Yes, he was wearing the full-face helmet as usual. He got off very quickly because the game was about to start and went into Block A straight away.'

I wasn't satisfied, but there was little else I could ask. I turned to Father Paul.

'We met downstairs on Sunday towards half past five. I was coming up to see the Cardinal, you were in a hurry – you were off to San Valente.'

A glance at the Cardinal. A small nod of assent. 'Went straight to San Valente. Another volunteer worker waited me, Antonio. He take children with our bus to friendly oratory, until eight.'

'And what did you do in those two hours?'

'I cook. At eight, when Antonio return with children, all ready for us to eat in front of television.'

'And after the match?'

'I and Antonio put children to bed. Then we also sleep.'

'Did you know Elisa Sordi, Father Paul?'

There was a shade of apprehension in those blue eyes that darted to Cardinal Alessandrini for a moment and then turned back to me.

'Of course.'

'Did you ever have the chance to talk to her?'

I noticed Alessandrini's eyes on me, but kept my gaze on Paul. Beneath those freckles something was stirring. I saw him brush a nervous hand through his red curls.

'Every so often Elisa here bring her work. Two, three times.'

'And what did you talk about?'

It appeared to be painful for him to remember.

'About my vocation,' he replied at length, in a whisper.

I had to keep myself from laughing. Valerio Bona went to Mass with her, Father Paul talked about his vocation with her, Manfredi escorted her courteously to the bar. Then someone had taken her under a bridge, slaughtered her, disfigured the body and thrown it in the river. Perhaps after making the sign of the Cross.

'Was Elisa perhaps interested in becoming a nun?' I spat out sarcastically.

To my great surprise, Paul answered seriously.

'Perhaps. She ask many questions on this.'

I turned towards Alessandrini.

'Do you know anything about this, Eminence?'

'I never exchanged more than a few words with the girl when she delivered some documents, and then only on matters of work.'

The Cardinal was deep in thought. It must have been an irritating thought because his affable and serene features had become rigid.

I turned back to Paul. 'Did you ever go to visit her in her office on the second floor?'

Now the flush and embarrassment were clear. 'Not go. She call me Saturday on internal phone.'

'You mean the day before her disappearance?'

'Yes, about five o'clock. Need help bring heavy books to Cardinal. Spoke few minutes, then she go.'

'And what did you speak about?'

'About work she do, she like, comes in Sunday, but OK. She say strange thing: wanted one day me hear confession, her. I say no, me not priest yet.'

'And then she left?'

The young man hesitated. 'I say "ciao ciao" from terrace. She stand by fountain with Signora Gina, they see me and say "ciao".'

There was the motive for the little confession. There was a witness, the concierge, who would be coming back from India and perhaps would remember the exchange of goodbyes.

'Then other thing happened,' added Father Paul, looking pre-occupied.

My instinct told me what, before he could say it. 'She waved goodbye to someone on the terrace of Block A?'

I could read the stunned look on Paul's face and for the first time a mixture of respect and fear in that of Cardinal Alessandrini.

'But you knowing already?' murmured Paul, confused.

'I don't know anything, but now I'm still more convinced that in this little corner of paradise you have there could be a devil hiding.'

Father Paul nodded. 'Boy with binoculars strange being, he—'

Alessandrini decided that it was time to put an end to this conversation.

'This isn't paradise, Commissario Balistreri, but neither is it hell. You won't find any devils in here. However, I will take what action I can, as I promised, so that the Count will be obliged to cooperate with the Italian police. As for Father Paul and myself, I think we have told you everything.'

I had one more question for Paul, but wasn't allowed to ask

him at that moment. *Did you see Elisa Sordi the Sunday on which she died?*

I left as July's unrelenting sun was finally setting on the horizon. I looked up at the second-floor window, the one in the office where Elisa Sordi used to work. The flower in the vase, still there since her death, was now drooping and shrivelled. I caught the usual reflection from Block A's penthouse. From there Manfredi could keep a check on everything and everyone. He could see without being seen, the ideal condition for him. He could see Elisa Sordi's window. And in that moment he could see me. I couldn't resist the temptation. I lit a cigarette and, blowing the smoke out of my nose, gave him a gesture of farewell.

I walked through the magnificent grounds, enjoying my cigarette together with the twittering of the birds. We were in Rome, but it felt like the countryside. I glanced absent-mindedly at the swimming pool. A young woman in a swimsuit was lying on the grass, taking in the sun's last rays. I'd already caught a glimpse of her while she was getting in the car with the Count the previous Sunday. She could have been my age, although her physique was that of a twenty-year-old, lean and slender. I saw her face sideways on, extremely delicate features and tiny crows' feet in the corners of her eyes. She turned to look at me, her eyes a greenish blue.

'Strictly speaking, smoking isn't permitted in the grounds,' she said in a polite and unreproving tone. It was a warning more than anything else. I looked instinctively towards Block A's terrace, but it was hidden by the trees.

I should have said that I lit it on purpose to provoke that overbearing husband of hers and her nosy young son. In that way we could have spoken. Instead, I did exactly what was least in my nature, the diplomatic thing. I mumbled a few words of apology, stubbed the cigarette out on the ground and even picked up the stub and put it in my pocket. I cursed myself; the Count was making me feel an unease that was unknown to me. And yet I'd met men who were just as powerful and dangerous. But in his history and in his manners Count Tommaso dei Banchi di Aglieno had something of which a part of me approved. Or would have approved at one time, in my really bad years: belief in an idea, without compromise, whatever the cost. But there were other things I detested, such as fidelity to a king who had disregarded Fascism and favoured a medieval aristocratic power over the land and the people who worked on it.

Whatever it was, I'd had a bellyful of that unease and wanted to get away from there as soon as possible. I crossed the city in my Duetto with the hood down in the first cool of sunset. Thanks to a special permit I was allowed to enter the historic centre, which was closed to traffic. I parked nonchalantly next to a squad car below the Spanish Steps, showing my ID to the men in uniform. I bought a large cone of pistachio and chocolate ice cream and leaned against the Duetto looking about me, shamelessly eyeing up the most beautiful female tourists. And between the fountain and the steps there were plenty of them, some already looking curiously at the red Spider and the dark suntanned young man not giving a hoot about the cops while peacefully enjoying his ice cream. A platinum blonde signora, suntanned and elegant in high heels, was coming out of Via Condotti with a Gucci shoulder bag and wearing a short Valentino dress. She was about ten years older than I was.

It took me only a moment to see the moped coming and the two kids without helmets. The one behind stretched out his arm to grab hold of the bag and wrench it from her in one swift move. In a moment my pistachio and chocolate cone was plastered over the eyes of the one in front, together with an enormous slap. The moped wobbled off course, hit the edge of the fountain and overturned, taking the two kids with it as it fell.

The patrolmen ran over. I again showed my ID and recovered the lady's Gucci bag, leaving my colleagues to deal with the two little would-be thieves.

'They're juveniles, Dottore. We can take their names, and if they've no previous record shall we let them go?' suggested the elder of the two.

I shot a glance at the two kids. They were Italians from some outlying district. One was wearing an earring, the other had a Che Guevara tattoo on his muscular biceps. 'No, take them to the young offenders' prison. A night inside will be good for them.'

The lady was waiting for me with her shoes in her hand.

'The heel's broken – nothing serious,' she explained with a smile.

She was as tall as I was even without her shoes. Then I noticed the wedding band and diamond ring on her left hand.

'You can't walk about like that – let me take you in my car,' I offered, pointing it out. She smiled.

'It's so long since I've been in a Spider, but I remember it was fun.'

The patrolmen were looking askance at me and I could imagine what they were saying.

'Where do you live?'

'In London, with my husband and two children,' she replied, stretching out her beautiful legs.

'Well, I can hardly take you all the way there. You'll be staying at some place in Rome, won't you?'

She pointed to the Spanish Steps leading up to Santa Trinità dei Monti.

'I'm at the Hotel Hassler up there on a working weekend. But if you're not in a hurry, I'd love a tour. You can feel you're a kid again in this car and I see you can drive through the zones forbidden to common mortals.'

In the open Duetto we slowly crossed the city with the golden cupolas of its churches lit by the setting sun. I drove slowly into the pedestrian zone. It was the only vehicle in the middle of the crowds of Romans and tourists who were off to a Saturday night of revelry. She asked me to take a turn in Piazza Navona, around the fountain of the four rivers, and I obliged her, to the comments of surprised tourists and police patrolling the area.

'This is the car from *The Graduate*, isn't it?' she asked me, while we were driving up towards Santa Trinità dei Monti.

'Yeah, the one Dustin Hoffman has.'

'It suits you. You're as good-looking as he is but somewhat taller, thank God.'

It was dark by the time we got to the hotel.

'Thanks for the bag. And thanks for the forbidden tour,' she said, turning towards me.

This unsettled me, not knowing whether she was teasing or being serious.

'And I'm sorry about your ice cream,' she continued. 'If it weren't impossible to park here in front I'd ask you to come in with me – the ice cream that room service offers is exceptional.'

I put the hood down and left the car directly under a sign that said 'No Parking. Vehicles will be Towed Away', leaving another sign that clearly said, 'Police. On Duty.'

The vanilla ice cream came with strawberries and whipped cream, and champagne was delivered as she was taking a shower. She stepped out of the bathroom in her dressing gown and I opened the bottle.

'You won't believe it, Michele, but this is the first time in seven years of marriage. The idea worries me a little – I don't like taking the initiative.'

'But you don't have to do a single thing – no initiative, no blame.'

She laughed as I slipped the dressing gown off and laid her naked on the bed. She laughed as I tied up her wrists with the dressing-gown belt. She laughed while I placed the little mask on her eyes

and in her ears the plugs kindly provided by the hotel, and distrib-
uted on the most suitable parts of her body the vanilla ice cream,
the whipped cream and the strawberries.

Then I started on the ice cream.

Sunday, 18 July 1982

I didn't go back to see Teodori, nor did I even phone him. After that endless ice cream I'd no wish to — I'd fallen asleep between the hotel's elegant sheets as peacefully as a baby.

I left early in the morning. The elegant lady was going off to Florence where she was to meet her husband coming in from London. I had the impression that she'd perhaps enjoyed things too much and gave her a wrong number so I wouldn't have her on my hands again, then went back to my studio flat in Garbatella where I went back to sleep.

The telephone woke me towards midday. I thought it would be Teodori and replied rudely in a sleepy voice. I'd taken a day off and didn't want anyone being a pain in the arse.

'A nice welcome, Mike! Had a bad night?'

It was my brother Alberto. He was the only one I allowed to use that American distortion of my name. I'd completely forgotten about his invitation to lunch and an afternoon of poker. His German girlfriend was visiting her parents in her native country, and he didn't have one of his usual working weekends. He'd invited Angelo and me to lunch, and then a colleague of his was to join us for the poker.

My exemplary brother was excellent at everything, even cooking. A degree in engineering with the highest marks, a managerial job with a multinational, good contacts in all the political parties with the exception of the extreme Far Right, a beautiful apartment with a terrace, and a girlfriend who would be a perfect mother for the little ones to come. I should have hated him, but venerated him instead. Not only because he'd got me out of trouble, but also because he'd never made a thing of it, and because his manner wasn't my father's utilitarian moderation, which was the acceptable side of arrogance. No, Alberto was a moderate in his soul; he believed that compromise was the source of well-being and happiness for everyone.

Angelo was already there when I arrived; they enjoyed cooking together and complemented each other – Alberto was a sophisticated chef, Angelo a down-to-earth pizza cook. I simply had to set the table, clear the table and put the dishes in the dishwasher.

We ate cold pasta and a Caprese salad, while sipping at white wine. It was extremely hot, but the terrace had a little pergola roof.

'You look tired, Mike. Haven't you slept?'

There was no irony in my brother's question. As usual, he was simply worried about me.

'It's too hot and there's too much noise. Thank goodness this Sunday Rome's at the seaside. Last Sunday a good many gave it up for the final.'

'Just think what effect Italy's win had, Mike. The VAT takings from mid-July were significantly above what was predicted.'

'A country whose citizens actually pay their taxes on the basis of football results isn't exactly a great example of civilization.'

Such a country deserves a police commissario who drives around in his Duetto in the no-traffic zones so he can pick up female tourists.

We talked politics so that we could talk about ourselves without making personal judgements, because we are the way we see the world. And the way I saw it was still quite brutal. On the one hand there were the honest and innocent, usually the impoverished. On the other there were the criminals and cheats, including the many in suit and tie who sat on boards of directors, in Parliament, in public administration and in the Vatican.

In my younger years I dreamed that this system would explode and drag the wheeler-dealers who infested Italy into the mud, shamed and ruined. But the only ruin was mine. I allowed myself to be caught up in the Secret Service as soon as I realized that my neo-fascist friends had become murderers, manipulated by untouchable interests and attacking whole groups of innocent and indefensible people, dishonouring the ideals I believed in. But the Service was linked to those untouchable interests, as I came to understand during the kidnapping of Aldo Moro in 1978. At that point, serving the state in an official capacity became the only way to avoid going permanently out of control.

'I won't ever let myself be caught up in that dirt, Alberto. I think I'll relax for another couple of years and then go back to Africa and hunt lions and take idiot tourists on vacations.'

Alberto shook his head, somewhere between amusement and concern.

'Mike, Italy was a poor country, ruined by the war. Now it's risen up again. These politicians, Catholics and Communists, industrialists and the Church, also did a few things for its good, don't you think?'

'They're the ones who advised Mussolini to go to war and then abandoned him. They were in the big industries and in the Vatican, the same ones who were all suddenly found to be anti-fascists come the end of the war.'

'All stupid conjecture without any historical basis, Mike. It was Mussolini who made the decision to go to war and decreed the racial laws . . . Anti-fascists were persecuted and killed by the Fascists. As was the Libyan resistance by the Italian military.'

Only Alberto could risk making a comment of this kind in front of me and not suffer any consequences.

My history teacher at secondary school in Libya was a skinny guy with a beard who wore a parka, jeans and gym shoes. A young left-wing teacher who had accepted that poverty-stricken posting in Tripoli in order to have a permanent job. He never missed an opportunity to tell us what he thought of our colonialist grandfathers and fathers. One day, an hour before recreation, he was talking about Italo Balbo, Marshal Graziani, and the criminal clique that deported and massacred the Libyan resistance. I knew this to be true, but this guy had no right to talk about it and link our colonialist families with actions like those.

Together with two kids who thought as I did, I went up to him in the courtyard during break.

'My grandfather worked in Libya from 1911. He organized olive-pressing into an industry then, together with other Italian colonists, he built roads where there was only sand, made the water drinkable, and set up the arts and crafts school for young Arabs. Is he a criminal?'

The teacher was having a cigarette, and that also irritated me, given that it was forbidden for the students. He gave us an icy look.

'We'll talk about it next time in class, Balistreri.'

I was beside myself. The advice of my father and my brother Alberto, *Always count up to ten, Mike*, vanished forever. It was as if I'd finally discovered who I was and was fed up with having to hide it.

As I gave the teacher a shove and he fell to the courtyard cobbles, I knew that my life had reached a turning point. I'd read somewhere that very few of our adolescent actions have a determining effect on our adult lives. Well, that was one of the few.

While the teacher was shouting and all our classmates watched us with their mouths open, the three of us grabbed hold of him. I would have preferred to do it on my own, but it would have been impossible. I took his legs and the other two an arm each. We carried him to the goldfish pond like that and chucked him into it, along with our fears and school careers.

I smiled at my brother again. He knew what I was thinking.

'Thank you for always managing to remind me, dear brother. But this decadent and corrupt democracy will hand the country over to the Communist Party or, worse still, into the hands of the Red Brigades.' I was fully convinced of this, while Alberto was very relaxed about it.

'It'll never happen, Michele. You underestimate the Catholics' pragmatism and overestimate Communism. It doesn't make sense any more – it's finished.'

Naturally, as ever, he was right and I was wrong. It was a debate that had been going on all our lives, with variants cropping up according to the circumstances. It was a kind of mantra on our disagreements.

Angelo listened with interest, but in silence, to these discussions of ours, but never offered an opinion. It was one of his ways of getting to know us. While Alberto went to make the coffee, I was left alone with him. We sat there with a last glass of wine and a cigarette watching the slow Sunday traffic crawling alongside the Tiber two hundred metres below.

'Whoever did it knew her,' I said, without looking at him.

'I don't want to discuss it, Michele, not as a friend. As a witness and even as a suspect, yes. But only with Commissario Teodori in an official manner.'

Angelo was sad, and sadness was so out of place in him I was put off from continuing.

'Just one thing, Angelo. Did you see or hear Elisa on the Sunday morning?'

'I've already told you. I was with Paola the whole time before coming to pick you up at five. From Paola's I called Elisa at about two thirty. She reassured me the work would be handed over to the Cardinal by Signora Gina at five o'clock. There was no need for me to call in. I never heard from her after that. Perhaps Teodori hasn't mentioned it, but he's already questioned Paola about my movements and also about yours, Michele.'

So these were the investigations Teodori had been allowed to conduct. Valerio Bona, Angelo Dioguardi, and even Commissario Michele Balistreri. The nobodies, leaving the untouchable ones in peace. Well, it was now time to change gear.

I left Alberto's in the late afternoon and it was evening when I arrived at the Villa Alba clinic. A nice quiet place, green and discreet.

The visiting hour had been over for a while. The reception area was deserted, except for one old nursing sister. I quickly showed her my police ID so that she wouldn't be able to remember my name.

'I'm here for Claudia Teodori,' I said firmly.

'Visiting time is over,' she said, kindly but rigidly.

'I understand and I don't want you to make an exception, only we'd like confirmation of the toxicology examination results and really need them now.'

'But we sent them straight away after the accident, when she was admitted.'

'You sent us a copy that wasn't entirely legible. The Public Prosecutor's office wants me to check the original.'

'And it's so urgent?' asked the sister, perplexed.

'There's a meeting on at the moment – the Prosecutor wants to make a decision on the eventual voluntary nature with regard to the accusation of murder. And the toxicology report is crucial.'

'The voluntary nature? But the girl was driving under the influence of drugs and alcohol. Do you think she hit the tree on purpose so as to kill her friend?'

In the end I obtained a look at the clinical file. When she arrived there with some abrasions, Claudia Teodori was off her face on amphetamines. Driving in that state was equivalent to firing both barrels of a loaded shotgun in the middle of a crowd. So much for the voluntary nature. Unless the girl knew she'd taken them, which was all still to be proven.

Monday, 19 July 1982

I presented myself punctually at eight in the morning at the Homicide Squad offices, ready to put up with Teodori's displeasure. Vanessa shot me a smile while she finished applying black varnish to a long fingernail. It was the first time I'd seen her in a miniskirt.

I gave her an admiring glance. 'You're looking elegant this morning!'

'I've an appointment with my landlord and I'm behind with the rent.' She said it seriously, without looking at me, as she finished off her nails.

Teodori was in his office with a cappuccino and a brioche. His watery eyes were more yellow than usual and his cheeks pale. But he was cheerful, even smarmy. He wanted something.

'Come in, Dottor Balistreri. Do take a seat. Would you like my secretary to order you anything from the bar?'

I declined the offer; his unexpected kindness was suspect.

'There's a lot of positive news,' he began, dunking the brioche in his cappuccino so that some of it spilled onto his desk, 'We have the first results of the autopsy. Death definitely occurred the same Sunday as she disappeared, in the first few hours after the match at the latest. The pathologist doesn't feel able to narrow the time down, but given the state of decomposition, and taking the Tiber's water temperature into account, makes him exclude the death as any more recent.'

He paused for effect. 'The murder took place between six thirty, when Elisa Sordi left Via della Camilluccia, and midnight that Sunday.'

I understood very well why this was good news for Teodori. All the illustrious suspects had an alibi, while Valerio Bona did not. I decided that Teodori's good humour was such that I could risk smoking in his office, and lit a cigarette. He didn't even notice.

'The victim shows multiple lesions, haematomas from heavy blows, cuts from a knife, cigarette burns and some bites. Unfortunately, it was a long and painful process. At least half an hour. She died from suffocation, a cloth or cushion pressed to her face preventing breathing.'

'Were the wounds inflicted before she died?' I asked.

'The haematomas from blows, yes, in particular the one that caused the fracture to the cheekbone and the right orbit. As to the bites, the cuts and the burns, it's difficult to say given the state of the corpse. Besides, some of the cuts and bites could have been caused by branches or by rats. There's one other important point, however: there was no sexual violation.'

I took in the information with some surprise.

'No penetration in any orifice?' I asked, a little incredulous.

I hadn't realized that Vanessa had come in to take away the cappuccino cup. She stood there, a mocking smile on her face, waiting for Teodori's answer. It was the second time something like this had happened to me, but Teodori's secretary was a very different person from Elisa Sordi. She was merely amused by the question's obscene nature and by our embarrassment.

'Would you like anything, Dottore?' she asked me, staring at me as she picked up Teodori's empty cup.

I gave an explicit glance at her long legs in order to make my reply the clearer.

'Not for the moment, thanks, Vanessa. Perhaps something a little later though.'

The young woman went out and Teodori, a little unsettled, continued speaking.

'It's a good job you were with your friend Dioguardi at all times; otherwise I'd be forced to put you down as one of the suspects, given the way you act with women.'

His tone was jocular, but not entirely. And I didn't like that kind of joke, even less coming from someone like Teodori.

'Dottor Teodori, I do not strike, nor cut, nor suffocate. Above all, I like penetrative sex, while it seems our man does anything but.'

Teodori handed over the pathologist's report.

'That may or may not be the case, Balistreri, because there's one final new fact that's important. Read it for yourself.'

Signs of a termination of pregnancy carried out in the previous fifteen days.

No different from the rest, neither more nor less. This was my first thought, transgressive and cruel, accompanied by a small sense of relief, which was shameful. Elisa, like all the rest, was no saint. And in part she was asking for it.

'We must run a check on all her male friendships. At school, in her neighbourhood, that Valerio Bona . . .' said Teodori.

'And in Via della Camilluccia, of course.'

Incredibly, Teodori smiled.

'Certainly, Via della Camilluccia as well, but with great caution. I'll see to that.' He put on a bold and courageous face.

Now I understood all his tiptoeing about. Cardinal Alessandrini must have kept his promise. But the pressure from the Vatican's high spheres was suppressed and it all came down to Teodori's courageous and independent decision. Nevertheless, he didn't want me under his feet with my doubts about those illustrious people.

'Your daughter Claudia, is she feeling better?' I asked him point-blank.

He jumped visibly. His eyes wouldn't meet mine.

'I don't follow. What's my daughter got to do with it?' he asked hesitantly.

'Nothing. I simply wanted to know. Any good news from the medics? Or from Coccoluto or the judge?'

I wanted to make it very clear to him that I wouldn't accept any obstacles tumbling down from on high that he was obliged to submit to because of his family troubles. I didn't give a toss about his concerns.

There was a very long pause, then Teodori looked at me. 'Dottor Balistreri, my daughter's eighteen. She lost her mother six years ago owing to a tumour. I've never been able to keep much of an eye on her, not at school nor outside of it. This year she failed her exams. Ten days ago she also failed her driving test, but in the evening she secretly took my car off to the seaside and went dancing there with a friend. They were dancing and drinking all night and they took some pills. On the way home the car ended up hitting a tree. My daughter was mostly unhurt, but her friend was killed. They're saying that my daughter had the pills with her before going out dancing, but she says that someone secretly put them in her drink in the discotheque. As you know, it makes a big difference.'

He was hoping to attract my sympathy, him and his stupid spoiled daughter, but I'd seen far worse in Africa. Children of three years old wandering the gutters under the open sky, stomachs swollen with hunger, flies clustered around their eyes. I'd never had even a crumb of compassion for the debauched Italian bourgeoisie.

Teodori was forced to accept my presence on the job. The Senator, Count Tommaso dei Banchi di Aglieno, had already been asked to receive us and was expecting us at ten o'clock sharp in his private offices in Via della Camilluccia. Teodori made me promise not to ask any indiscreet questions. As if there were any discreet questions in a murder inquiry.

Going out, Vanessa waved towards me with a promising look and handed me a card. 'In case you need it, Dottor Balistreri.'

It was her telephone number.

The private offices occupied the first and second floors of Block A, underneath the Count's penthouse. We took a squad car and were parked outside the gate in less than ten minutes. It was Teodori's first sign of respect. Signora Gina's daughter opened the wicket gate and said that the Count's personal secretary was expecting us on the first floor. I looked up towards the terrace and saw the reflection there. I immediately lit a cigarette and made the usual mixed sign of greeting and disrespect.

'Who were you waving to?' asked Teodori in alarm.

'The Count's son, Manfredi.'

I saw him give a start. 'Do you know him?'

'We've seen each other a few times, always from a distance.'

Teodori's uncertain look betrayed all his tension. He was being forced to take me there against his will and now things were coming out that he couldn't get a handle on.

The Count's personal secretary was what you would have imagined: an elderly gent with grey hair, impeccably dressed with the monarchist party's badge in his buttonhole. He led us into a drawing room with a few items of antique furniture that were clearly valuable. On the walls hung paintings of great land and sea battles. Heavy curtains blotted out the sunlight. A wealth that was very different from the Roman bourgeoisie; this was aristocratic opulence, dark and serious, and in some ways menacing.

We waited standing, looking at the paintings. Teodori seemed intimidated, as if those painted battles were there to warn him about what was waiting for him. The wait was only brief, however; one of the Count's many fixations was punctuality.

I had already met him, but this time the effect was more striking.

His cold black eyes sat above an imposing hooked nose, below which was drawn the subtle lines of his lips, moustache and a well-groomed goatee. He was half a head taller than I was and towered over someone the size of Teodori. While he was shaking his hand I noticed his restrained repugnance over the head of the investigation's careless appearance.

When it was my turn the grip was stronger than before. He stared briefly into my eyes. 'If you wish to proceed with this case you will have to do so in a dignified manner. At least in this residential complex.'

So the little monster with the binoculars had tipped him off about my excesses. Besides, it was his way of giving us confirmation that at any moment he could have chucked us out and blocked the case. It was not the moment to reply.

A waiter brought coffee and bottled water for the Count, who turned to Teodori.

'I'm somewhat perplexed by the necessity for this visit. I agreed to meet with you because the Minister of the Interior explained to me that there's been pressure from the other side of the Tiber to clear the field of any possible implications in this sad business of the girl.'

He said 'the other side of the Tiber' with a slight grimace of disgust. The Minister of the Interior had asked the Count a favour. Small favours between the powerful. All for the sake of that girl. In those few words and the way he pronounced them lay the Count's vision of the world. A plebeian of no account, a little tart who got herself killed, most certainly by another plebeian like her, and in any case far away from the residential complex of Via della Camilluccia.

'Thank you, and on behalf of the head of the Homicide Squad,' replied Teodori. 'We shall be brief.'

'I can allow you the next half hour, then I have to be off to Parliament for a vote.'

'Then I'll ask you the essentials straight away. Did you know the girl in question, Elisa Sordi?' Teodori began.

'One of my employees, Valerio Bona, gave me her CV. I recommended her to the Cardinal without even knowing her. Usually I have no contact with these people.'

He said it exactly like that, *these people*.

'Not even by sight? She was working here for some time,' I put in.

'I could perhaps have come across her in the courtyard, but honestly, I've never taken any notice. The two residences are quite separate, as you will have observed.'

'We also have to ask you about Sunday the eleventh,' said Teodori, hesitating.

'Please proceed.' The Count knew perfectly well what this was about, but he wanted to make him feel even more embarrassed.

'We're trying to reconstruct the movements of all the people present in the residential complex on that day,' Teodori explained.

'And can I ask what this has to do with a crime that occurred in quite another place by people who have nothing to do with us?'

'You see,' Teodori humbly explained, 'it would be extremely useful to reconstruct the girl's day. If anyone saw her—'

'What time did she arrive on Sunday?' asked the Count, cutting in.

He wasn't rude, but emphasized with every gesture that we were wasting his time without any reason and that he would decide when the conversation was over.

'Her card was punched at eleven. Before that she went to Mass with her parents, then she took public transport to come to the office here.'

'I had already left. I had a meeting of my parliamentary group at the Hotel Camilluccia, five minutes from here. I was there at half past ten and I only came back a little after five, when I met Dottor Balistreri below as he was chatting to the concierge. I then took a shower, dressed, and went out again with my wife and son at about a quarter past six. I believe that you, Dottor Balistreri, were leaving with Cardinal Alessandrini and Signor Dioguardi.'

I nodded in agreement and the Count continued.

'I went to the Minister of the Interior's office for a short meeting arranged some time ago. I think I came back here a little before the start of the game. I had many members of my party to supper. Coming back I crossed paths with Cardinal Alessandrini, who was also coming home. My guests had already arrived. We watched the game and later celebrated quietly on the terrace with a toast.'

Teodori looked at me uneasily. He had no idea how to proceed and if it had been up to him we could have left there and then.

I adopted my gentlest manner. 'Did your wife and son come with you to the Minister of the Interior's office?'

The question signalled a new turn in the conversation. The Count shot me a quick glance and then turned to Teodori.

'I understood that you wanted to know if any one of us had seen the girl here.'

'But also outside,' I said, without allowing Teodori to respond.

This time the Count's eyes met mine and remained there, but I read no embarrassment or fear, rather a brief glimmer of respect.

'Do you think a member of my family could have had a meeting with that girl?'

He was alluding to the insurmountable social distance between the dei Banchi di Aglieno family and someone like Elisa Sordi.

'Not necessarily a meeting – perhaps a chance encounter? Always assuming they weren't with you at the Minister's.'

The Count smiled. 'No, no matter how often the Minister's my guest here, this was a brief meeting to discuss some work. I left my wife Ulla in the centre, near to the Ministry. The shops were open in the area and she wanted to take a walk. She came home alone by taxi.'

'And your son?'

'Manfredi went out on his motorcycle. He went to do a little weight training; he goes to one of the few gymnasiums open on Sunday afternoons. He came home a few minutes after I did, before the game.'

We had reached a critical point. 'We also need to speak to your wife and your son,' I said.

There was a long moment of silence. I had the impression that the Count was weighing up the pros and cons. To prohibit an interview with his family would create embarrassment, with the Minister being leaned on by the Vatican, and this would mean in some way contracting an awkward political debt for him. He decided it wasn't worth the trouble.

'Of course, but I must warn you that my wife Ulla has been very upset by what has happened and my son Manfredi, as perhaps you know, is a boy with some problems and must be treated with a good deal of care.'

'That is all perfectly clear, Signor Conte,' said a thankful Teodori. 'We shall be as brief as we were with you.'

'Then I will escort you upstairs, as they are both at home.'

The penthouse was as large as it was gloomy. Dark parquet floors, heavy curtains, antique furniture. A long hallway led to two drawing rooms in succession. The first was covered in tapestries depicting battles in the Italian colonies and big game trophies from Africa and South America. The second was a museum of eighteenth and nineteenth-century furniture interspersed with modern black leather sofas. I was struck by the total absence of mirrors or any reflective surfaces. The Count sat us down in another room while his personal secretary went to call his wife.

Ulla came immediately, as if she'd been forewarned. She was wearing an elegant tracksuit and her hair, gathered in a short ponytail, made her seem a lot younger than she was, but tiny lines around her mouth and her magnificent blue-green eyes showed that she was over thirty and her life wasn't without stress. She didn't mention our brief encounter beside the pool and we introduced ourselves.

She had little to tell us. On the Sunday morning she had left the apartment early to go to Mass. I caught a tiny grimace of disapproval on the Count's face. She had come back at eleven and noticed Elisa, that beautiful girl she had seen at other times, who was talking to Gina Giansanti before going up to the office.

'Then I didn't leave the house for the rest of the day. I slept a lot because I was tired and knew we had guests for the football match. When my husband returned at about five thirty I gave final instructions to the cook and then went out with him, as I wanted to take a walk. He left me right at the beginning of Via del Corso. It would have been six thirty or a little after.'

'Did you by any chance meet the girl while you were walking in the centre?' asked Teodori.

'No, absolutely not.'

'Did you buy anything?' he asked her.

She looked at me a little surprised, as if she was making an effort to remember.

'No, nothing. I took a taxi in Piazza Venezia to come home and arrived here towards a quarter past eight, a few minutes after my husband.'

'Manfredi was already home?' I asked.

'Manfredi came in immediately afterwards, about eight twenty. When he goes to the gym he stays there at least an hour.'

I understood why Manfredi didn't like the company of strangers and mirrors as soon as I saw him enter the room. Apart from that face, he was a normal kid: he was muscular with powerful but not excessive pectorals and biceps, almost as tall as me, but from the neck up he was a disaster area, a terrible trick of destiny. A harelip and mauvish birthmark as large as an apricot disfigured his face up to the swollen eyelid of his left eye. He had smooth black hair down to his shoulders and kept it over his face to cover the disfigured part. The only visible eye was very striking, having the same sea-green colour as his mother's.

'Ah, the cop who makes the funny faces,' he said. His voice was the slightly guttural one of a young man filled with hormones. He hadn't yet learned his father's art of self-control, but certainly displayed a good amount of aggression.

'Dottor Teodori and Dottor Balistreri have to ask you some questions, Manfredi,' said the Count.

The young guy said nothing, but waited for us. In the air I picked up on something I knew very well: the apparent calmness of someone who's making an effort to contain his anger, an exercise in which I was highly specialized.

I observed this muscular young man with the disfigured face and wondered what thoughts passed through his head every day. It wasn't enough to get rid of mirrors to accept himself – perhaps he had to eliminate the negative reactions of others. Who could tell? A glance too many, a girl's giggle. An opinion was forming inside me. For just a second I wondered if it was an opinion or a prejudice. But I was used to trusting my instincts.

'It would be helpful if you could tell us if you saw Elisa Sordi on Sunday,' said Teodori. I wasn't happy with this opening shot but refrained from making a comment.

'I saw her from the terrace with my binoculars,' replied Manfredi without a moment's hesitation.

'Binoculars?' exclaimed Teodori, taken somewhat by surprise.

'A gift from my father, the Italian Royal Navy model.'

'And on Sunday you saw Elisa Sordi from the terrace through your binoculars?'

'Yes, three times. I saw her arrive about eleven, talk briefly with

Signora Gina and exchange greetings with my mother. Then I saw her leave about one and come back about two.'

'And she was alone?'

'When she went out she was alone. When she came back she was with the young guy who works on the computer for my father.'

'Were they quarrelling?' asked Teodori hopefully.

For a moment Manfredi brushed aside the lock of hair from the left side of his face. I believed it was so he could better observe the idiot in front of him.

'I could see, but I couldn't hear anything. The kid was gesticulating, but I don't know if they were quarrelling.

'How was she dressed?' I asked all of a sudden.

I saw a shadow cross the Count's face, but he couldn't veto that kind of a question.

Manfredi didn't even grace me with a look.

'Blue jeans, white sleeveless blouse and low casual shoes.'

'Was she wearing a bra?'

There was no need to look at the Count to feel his hostility. I saw the embarrassed look Ulla gave her son. Manfredi didn't blink an eye.

'Yes, I remember seeing a strap falling from her blouse.'

As I thought, he was an acute observer.

'May we know what this kind of question has to do with anything?' asked the Count.

'We didn't find the girl's clothes at the crime scene. Every detail is important, including whether she was wearing underwear.'

Manfredi gave me a challenging look.

'Obviously I couldn't say whether she was wearing panties or not.'

There was no trace of irony in his voice; he only wanted to repay me for the provocative gestures I had given from the central courtyard.

'Manfredi!' exclaimed Ulla.

'Manfredi,' repeated the Count, 'this is no time for making jocular remarks.'

'I'm sorry,' he said in a serious tone. 'I only wanted to help the police.'

'Let's go back to Sunday,' said Teodori prudently. 'You didn't see the girl close up?'

'No. Immediately after lunch I shut myself in my room to rest with the air conditioning on. I was drowsy and fell asleep. I only woke up when my father arrived before six, then we went out together about half past.'

'And you went to the gym and obviously didn't see the girl,' Teodori suggested in a humble manner.

'I didn't see her. I came home in time for the match, which I watched in my room.'

'Alone?' asked Teodori.

'I don't like crowded places. The drawing room was full of people.'

'And did you go out after the match to celebrate?' continued Teodori.

'I just said that I don't like crowded places,' the kid replied scornfully.

'Was there anyone in the gym?' I asked. I saw Teodori's look of alarm, but the Count was very calm.

'Only my personal trainer.'

'Did you have a meeting arranged with him?'

'There's no need. We always see each other on Sunday afternoons from six forty-five to seven forty-five, when the gym's deserted.'

'Of course, you don't like crowds,' I said, knowing perfectly well it was a cruel and useless remark.

The kid said nothing. He stared at me with his hard-man attitude, rendered grotesque by his deformed lip and the mauve birthmark on the left side of his face covered by his long hair.

The moment had arrived. I could feel Teodori champing at the bit, wanting to get away. As far as he was concerned, there was nothing more to ask.

I made up my mind and turned to the Count.

'I know that your son has had occasion to speak directly to Elisa Sordi before Sunday the eleventh and I have to ask him if he received any confidential information that might help the inquiry. And given that these things are private among young people, I'd like to speak to Manfredi without his parents present.'

Teodori was pale and looked at me with an air of desperation, as if we were on one of the sinking ships in the pictures on the wall.

'These are routine questions,' I explained humbly. 'But we can't escape them, especially if your son confirms that he spoke to the girl alone at least once in her office.'

The Count looked at Manfredi in surprise. His tone was icy.

'In her office?' he repeated, but it was a question directed at his son.

More than any fear in his tone, it was surprise and disdain that his son, the future Conte dei Banchi di Aglieno, should be gossiping with a little slut from the far-off suburbs. He would have found it more dignified if I'd said that Manfredi had taken her to the banks of the Tiber, hit her, knocked her about, suffocated her and thrown her in the river, rather than wasting time chatting with the worthless girl.

Manfredi looked at his father, then his mother, and got up.

'We'll do it in my room,' he ordered, never losing the hard-man act. Teodori was clearly upset and followed us hesitatingly down the length of the half-shadowed hall.

Manfredi's room was the last one at the end of the hall. It wasn't very large. The ceiling was midnight blue and the walls were completely covered with posters for heavy-metal bands of the 'Black' and 'Thrash' subgenres: Iron Maiden, Judas Priest, Motörhead and

Venom, and album titles like *Killers, Sin after Sin, Overkill* and *Welcome to Hell*. None of the figures had a face showing in those posters – they were masked or with their backs turned or there were no human figures at all. Unexpectedly, there was a photograph of his school class on the wall and I could understand why immediately. Manfredi was half hidden behind the teacher; you could see only his muscular body and the unblemished side of his face. There were no reflective surfaces in the room – the glass in the windows was non-reflective. There was a door to his private bathroom. The light outside entered weakly through the single window covered by a thick curtain.

There were a good many books, a lot for a young kid, and evidently all read. Among works of history, philosophy and art, and collections of prints of ancient Rome, I recognized *Mein Kampf* and Nietzsche, *Beyond Good and Evil*. The last time I had seen those works I was in my own bedroom in Tripoli. On the wall, scrawled in black felt tip in an angry adolescent's hand, was the aphorism I well remembered: *The great epochs of our life come when we gain the courage to rechristen our evil as what is the best in us*.

Manfredi leaned against a wall, as far away from us as possible. Then he turned directly to me.

'So, what else do you want to know?'

'Only if and when you spoke to the girl before Sunday the eleventh,' Teodori said meekly.

'Of course I spoke to her, like all the young people round here. Even the young priest with the red hair spoke to her. Or do you think that I've less right than a priest to chat with a good-looking girl?'

Terrified by his own question, Teodori mumbled something incomprehensible. Now he really was in a painting on the drawing-room wall, standing aboard a sinking ship.

'You had as much right as any one of us,' I said, looking him straight in the eye. 'As for hoping for anything beyond that, well, that's another question.'

I saw his biceps flex and his pectorals swell. I kept a watch on the open palms of his hands. There were many posters of martial arts films and I had no doubt the kid had more than a passing knowledge of the subject.

He told us calmly how he had first come to know Elisa Sordi. He knew what time she came in in the morning. On that particular morning it was raining and through his binoculars he could see she had no umbrella. It was just as Elisa had told Valerio Bona.

'And what did you talk about?'

'She asked me what I was studying. I told her I was doing classical studies at a private institution. A couple of words – she had work to do.'

'Four Saturdays ago you went to see her in her office.'

'She had told me that I was welcome to come and see her.'

He spoke as if this was the most normal thing in the world. As if a monster like that could hold any interest for a young goddess like Elisa Sordi. Perhaps the lad thought that his family status gave him a special right over any plebeian woman admitted into that paradise. A kind of modern *ius primae noctis*.

'Are you saying that Elisa Sordi sought your company?'

I put all the irony and incredulity I could into the question. He looked at me a long time while the only sound in the room was Teodori's laboured breathing. This kid was going to hate me forever, whether he was guilty or not.

'That's how it was. If you don't believe me that's your problem.'

'All right. And what did you talk about?'

He gave a smile that made his disfigured face look even more grotesque.

'About true and false emotions and, fundamentally, we talked about love.'

The little monster was trying to palm me off as if I was a child.

'You talked about love? Would you be more specific, please? It's important. Who was saying what?'

'There was something preying on Elisa's mind; she was sad. I think there were some problems with that boy, the one who followed her around.'

'Did she say so openly?' asked Teodori hopefully.

'Not really. She mentioned the fact that insisting on the impossible in love only brings unhappiness.'

My thoughts went back to the autopsy results. *Signs of a termination of pregnancy carried out in the previous fifteen days*. A relationship that had been going on for some time – she was late in the cycle, a pregnancy test, then abortion. The conversation with Manfredi probably happened when the pregnancy was already discovered, several days before the abortion.

'Did you have sexual relations with Elisa Sordi?' I asked him pointblank, so as to put him on the spot.

It was odd, but he thought about it. 'It occured to me that you might exclude that possibility,' he replied in an ironic tone.

'You could always have raped her,' I said brutally.

'Dottor Balistreri, that's enough! I don't approve of these methods,' exploded Teodori. Then he turned to Manfredi in an attempt to seem impartial.

'You can ignore that comment. But please reply to Dottor Balistreri's question.'

'No,' said Manfredi. 'I'm not obliged to and I'm answering no more questions, seeing as it was not me who killed Elisa Sordi. Whoever it was, was someone more fortunate than me.'

Was this last cryptic admission attributable to his face alone? There was no way of knowing in that moment. We took our leave with many apologies on Teodori's part. The Count and Ulla were nowhere to be seen. The Count's personal secretary accompanied us out with the air of a bouncer getting a tipsy customer off his hands.

★　　　★　　　★

We went back to Homicide HQ in the car, myself at the wheel. Neither of us said a word. Then I saw the tears flowing silently from under Teodori's dark glasses.

'What's the matter?' I asked him. I was used to women's tears, and no longer gave them any thought, but coming from a grown man they got on my nerves.

'I've been in the force for more than thirty years, Balistreri. And now, at the age of sixty, I'm in this embarrassing fix: my hands are tied and someone like you, still wet behind the ears, treats me like a fucking parasite who shits himself at the slightest sign of trouble.'

His words contained both rage and humiliation. In a flash I realized that this was the pain of an ordinary man – humiliated by life, but still a respectable guy.

'Don't worry, I won't say a word to anyone and Coccoluto'll help your daughter out—'

'Oh yes, Coccoluto will help her out, if I look the other way in this inquiry!' he said bitterly.

So a doubt had crept into his mind as well, after seeing Manfredi – his face, those muscles, that room with its violent posters and *Mein Kampf* – and hearing of his sweet little talks with Elisa.

'That's the price your conscience has to pay if you want Coccoluto to invent an imaginary dealer to save your daughter from the charge of culpable homicide—'

'But he really exists, damn it!' he exploded in rage. 'Claudia's told me his name, but I swore not to tell the police because she's out of her mind with fear for this animal. He's in with a dangerous crowd.'

I looked at him in silence. Yellow tears. We only suffer like this for our children. I thought back to my father and what he went through because of me. And what I went through because of him. And Elisa Sordi's parents expecting justice. I was an insensitive shit, but I could sort this problem out. I didn't give a damn about any dangerous drug dealer, having seen far worse. And all of a sudden I felt sorry for this father with his yellow eyes.

I rested a hand on his shoulder.

'Teodori, why don't you assume I'm *not* the police and tell me the name of this dealer?'

After speaking to Teodori I found out more from an ex-colleague in the Secret Service. Claudia Teodori's dealer was a little fish by the name of Marco Fratini. He came from a good family, was the son of professionals, a drop-out from a private religious university, but of good appearance – a cool dude on the disco scene from one of Rome's wealthy districts. Except that one day, after skipping yet another exam, the father hits the roof and cuts him off completely. The good little bourgeois kid isn't studious but he's clever, so he immediately comes up with an alternative source of support. Given his clean appearance and excellent social contacts, he becomes the perfect pusher of amphetamines in the most fashionable discotheques. He then discovers that some of those pills, dissolved in beer on the sly, make the girls easier to bend to his desires.

I could easily have picked him up and beaten the truth out of him. The only real danger was the gang that supplied him with the merchandise. To have them lose an important sales channel purely on account of saving Claudia Teodori could have led to even more serious consequences for the girl. It needed a plan.

'Once you're in the car, don't spend more than a minute, Vanessa. I don't want you running any risks.'

She started to laugh. 'He'll be the only one running any risk. But please explain, Commissario, a minute to do what?'

I told her, running my fingernails from her knee up her thigh: 'As much as you can. Anything to get it over with in a minute.'

She gave me a malicious look. 'Commissario, for years I had a boring boyfriend. Especially in bed. So I learned a couple of speedy tricks. Should I describe them, so you can choose the menu for this piece of shit?'

'I'm not into the theory of these matters. Anyway, please be careful.'

The discotheque *Striscia di Mare* in Ostia was packed with the youth of Rome and its surrounding districts, all of them there to dance on the sand to Olivia Newton John's 'Physical'. I arrived around midnight with three trusted colleagues, chosen from among those with the best build and worst appearance. We made our way through the disorderly sea of motorbikes parked outside the entrance. The bouncer had been notified beforehand and let us jump the queue, to a chorus of muttering and curses.

The dance floor on the sandy beach held an ocean of writhing figures. The guys were stripped to the waist, the girls mainly in shorts and top or bikini top. Many were stunning, but Vanessa naturally stood out, her magnificent legs shooting out from a pair of black leather shorts. She was the only one wearing ankle boots on the sand, and the tightly clinging top advertised her toned and muscular shoulders and arms. Her hands were decked with rings and ended with very long, black-varnished nails. It was a costume I had suggested myself.

Fratini had spotted Vanessa as soon as she came on to the dance floor and followed her with his gaze while she danced alone, drinking beer from a bottle. It was a very promising situation. The extra quantity of pills the guy from Marseilles gave him as a tip for his role as pusher would come in handy for softening up this unbelievably hot girl.

He moved in with his gleaming smile as Vanessa was getting another beer from the bar by the dance floor.

'I'd pay anything for a dance in private,' he said, leaning close to her on the bar. Vanessa looked at him and gave a laugh.

'Maybe, but first let's see how you do it in public.'

They danced for nearly half an hour before he succeeded in dropping two yellow tablets in her beer. I was at the other end of the bar and gave her the sign that everything was going to plan.

In the following minutes, the girl's behaviour became exactly what Fratini was expecting and wanted: uninhibited, wild. When he invited her for a walk outside, she accepted immediately.

They went out into the dark car park, where a cool breeze was coming in from the sea. Fratini was very pleased. No little yellow pills for him – that stuff made you lose control, like that idiot Claudia Teodori who, after they'd fucked, went and crashed her car.

As usual, he'd parked his car a little way off. He opened the rear door to the BMW with its white leather seats.

'Get in,' he ordered.

But Vanessa was laughing giddily.

'Lie yourself down,' she told him with a complicit air, while she pushed him on the seat and crouched down between his knees.

Fratini laughed and tried to undo her shorts, but she brushed her long black fingernails from his knees up to his crotch.

'But I want to explore a bit first, handsome,' she said in a promising tone.

She pulled his jeans and briefs down to his knees and began to caress him. The ten black varnished nails were the end points of unstoppable pleasure.

'Oh, fuck, you're driving me crazy,' groaned Marco Fratini, gasping for breath.

He came in less than half a minute. Immediately afterwards Vanessa herself began to moan, bending over him and throwing up in his lap. Fratini drew back, looking, horrified, at his penis – covered in a mixture of vomit and sperm, which was now spreading all over the BMW's white leather seats. The girl collapsed in a heap, heaving, a kind of froth bubbling from the side of her mouth. A moment later he heard the door open behind his back and two hands of steel grabbed him by the armpits and lifted him from the car. A shove made him trip over his jeans and fall half-naked onto the cobbles of the car park.

Terrified, he found himself in front of me and three accomplices who resembled ex-cons more than they did policemen. Trembling, he tried to hitch up his jeans, but another, more forceful shove was enough to send him back to the ground.

I bent over Vanessa, who gave me a wink.

'The girl's in a very bad way,' I said to my accomplices in a serious manner. 'But no ambulances. If the boss comes to find out, we're fucked. Take her to the car. Her stomach needs a good pump.'

'But then she's going to tell her father,' said one of the three, reciting his part.

'No, I'll talk to her later. She'll keep her mouth shut. If she doesn't, her father'll have her hide and then ours, and then rip the balls off this shit here and feed them to him.'

Lying half-naked on his back on the cobbles, utterly devastated, Fratini began to sob, while one of my guys carried Vanessa to another car and took her away.

'Who are you?' mumbled Fratini, trembling all over.

I gave him a pitying look. 'You only happen to have drugged and raped the only daughter, and underage at that, of one of the Magliana gang's bosses. We were supposed to keep an eye on her, but the little shit gave us the slip and met a weasel like you.'

Marco Fratini saw that he was already dead. He'd always been unlucky; now he'd drugged the underage daughter of a dangerous criminal. Him, a university student from a good family! They'd tear him to pieces.

'But I didn't did do anything bad to her,' he whimpered.

I ripped the jeans brutally from his ankles and pulled out the yellow tablets. His sobs became desperate.

'You're in the deepest shit possible. Even if we do everything we can to keep that inconsiderate little shit's mouth shut, she's used to doing just what the fuck she likes, and if there's a guy that turns her on she comes back to find him.'

'But I'll disappear, I'll leave, I swear it.'

He was on his knees, pulling up his briefs.

'Like fuck we're going to run that risk, eh, guys?' I said to the two giants on either side of me.

'If we beat him to death here in the car park,' one of them proposed, 'they'll think it's only the usual fight outside a club.'

'That way he's out of our way for good,' added the other, totally calm.

'I'm sorry,' I said, shaking the blackjack I'd taken from my pocket, 'we're folk with not much imagination. To be on the safe side, we either put you six feet under or in prison for a good stretch. But *we* can't send you to prison, so that only leaves the grave.'

Fratini had wet himself and was crying and trembling like a leaf.

Then he raised a hand, like a child at school. 'But perhaps *I* could . . .' he mumbled.

In great detail he told us about how he'd drugged Claudia Teodori and the accident that followed. A girl had died. If he confessed to having put amphetamine pills in her glass without her knowing, then they'd give him a good few years in jail. He wouldn't ask for any extenuating circumstances.

I consulted with my two accomplices. We advised him that we also had important friends in the police, that we could check his story, and if he was lying we'd be back to rip his balls off ourselves and then throw the rest to the fishes. When we deposited him in front of the police station in Ostia, he thanked us with tears of gratitude in his eyes.

A short time later, while Fratini was making a full confession about the yellow pills that he'd secretly put in Claudia Teodori's beer, Vanessa and I were alone on a boat moored in Ostia's harbour. It belonged to some wealthy uncle of hers.

The nocturnal sea breeze finally gave some relief from the suffocating heat. We were sitting on the well deck drinking ice-cold beer.

'The most difficult part?' I asked her.

She laughed, now really a little drunk.

'Having to swallow that pill you gave me to throw up. Shit, Michele, it really made me sick.'

'Without my little pill you'd have had to swallow something a lot worse.'

'Do you know how to tie knots? You have to on a boat . . .'

She came up to me with a rope, wrapped it around my wrists, rapidly tied it into a double knot to secure me, and with another tied the rope to the rudder shaft.

'Excellent,' she said, going back to her seat. 'Now you won't fall into the sea, Michelino.'

She took off an ankle boot. Even her toenails were painted black. She stretched out a leg and placed her foot on me exactly where she wanted.

Teodori was less pale, less swollen, and his eyes were a little less yellow. He had shaved and his jacket, tie and shirt were well matched. He was bursting with energy, efficiency and optimism. His office was covered with photos of the Via della Camilluccia victim, the autopsy report and, the biggest surprise of all, the possible alibis of not only Valerio Bona but also the inhabitants of Via della Camilluccia.

'We did a check,' he said, beaming. 'Only Valerio Bona isn't covered for the whole of the afternoon, then, after eight, he's got witnesses to say he was at home, although with all the hullabaloo we can't be sure.'

'Father Paul?'

'The other volunteer, Antonio Orlandi, has confirmed everything.'

'And Manfredi?'

'Same thing. His personal trainer at the Top Top is a Pole called Jan Deniak, who's been living in Rome for some time. He states that Manfredi was with him for at least an hour, from a quarter to seven until eight, doing weight training in the gym.'

The helpful Teodori had even very discreetly verified the Count's movements: first at his party's meeting, then at the Minister of the Interior's. Everything had been confirmed, although there were no witnesses for Signora Ulla's shopping expedition. Then from eight fifteen onwards they were all at home with a bunch of friends. And there was no doubt either about Manfredi. Teodori had even checked Cardinal Alessandrini's times in and times out of the Vatican.

Almost apologetically, he continued, 'We also ascertained that Dioguardi was with his girlfriend all day, then he came to get you at five, and then the two of you were together after leaving Via della Camilluccia.'

So you even checked my alibi!

'And the telephone records for the Sordi house?'

'The girl had nothing arranged for the Sunday, so she didn't tell anyone she was going into the office. She was to spend the day with her parents, going to Mass, and then come home before the match.'

'Did she make any calls from the office on Saturday or Sunday?'

'Only on Saturday, to tell her mother and Valerio Bona that she'd be working the next day. On Sunday no outgoing calls, only those incoming from Angelo Dioguardi and her mother – apart from yours, Dottore, when you were looking for Dioguardi, obviously.'

There was no irony in his 'obviously'. If Teodori were harbouring any doubts about my call, he'd let them go after Fratini's arrest.

When it came time to go Teodori took my hands in his. 'I'm eternally grateful to you, Balistreri. I don't dare ask you how you did it . . .'

I didn't dare tell him for fear of his having a heart attack. The victim of the crime was back after a busy night, right there typing away at her desk, dressed soberly to cover the marks left from the night before.

Friday, 23 July 1982

For three days nothing happened. We had traced all Elisa Sordi's possible friends in her neighbourhood and at school, questioned them, received alibis, checked telephone records. Result: zero point zero. No one regularly met Elisa Sordi except Valerio Bona. No one knew she was at work that day except Valerio Bona, Dioguardi and the inhabitants of the residential complex on Via della Camilluccia.

The last person to see Elisa Sordi alive, just after five o'clock, was the concierge Gina Giansanti, who was in India and couldn't be reached. But the fact had been reported by her directly to me and confirmed by Cardinal Alessandrini, to whom she had delivered Elisa's work.

On the abortion we found nothing. The clinics that practised clandestine abortions were far too many.

On the other hand my informants in the Secret Service made good use of those seventy-two hours. The information on Antonio Orlandi and Gianni, alias Jan Deniak, was interesting. When you dig for information, you find things. Always.

Antonio Orlandi was a physical education teacher in a private middle school. I went to see him at San Valente towards seven in the evening, when he'd just begun his shift, taking advantage of

Father Paul's absence. The kids were having a knockabout game of football, boys against girls, with Orlandi in goal.

It was still hot: you could hear the cicadas and the cool of sunset was still some way off. The grass was overgrown, the white house where the kids lived was flaking, the single tree was pathetic. And yet there was a happy, positive atmosphere. Orlandi joined me under the tree. He was just over thirty with a clean and tidy air about him, though he came across as being perhaps a little too smart.

'Your colleagues have already questioned me several times,' he said, not looking at me. He was watching the kickabout as if it was the World Cup final.

'Children are wonderful, aren't they?' I mentioned casually.

'Sure,' he replied, somewhat quickly. 'All children are angels.'

A reply out of the catechism. 'Which are better, little boys or little girls?'

He looked at me, a little alarmed. 'Aren't you supposed to be asking me about Father Paul's movements on the day of the match?'

'No, my colleagues have already seen to that . . . Father Paul got here before six, you took the kids off on a treasure hunt, and when you came back towards eight Father Paul was here and supper was ready. Then you watched the match, put the kiddies to bed, and about midnight went yourselves. Have I got it right?'

'Yes, that's how it was,' he said, now more at ease.

'How did you come to find a job at the school where you teach, Signor Orlandi?'

Orlandi lit a cigarette and I did the same. He took his time.

'Cardinal Alessandrini brought it to my attention,' he said, finally making his mind up. I knew this already; I was only interested in the difficulty he had in spitting it out.

'Had you taught before?'

'Only in the gym, after graduating in physical education from the College of Higher Education.'

'Did you apply for jobs in state schools?'

'No,' he said.

'Why ever not? Everyone applies for them!'

He said nothing. I was torturing him on purpose.

A little boy and a little girl started to squabble. Orlandi got up to see to them.

'Please stay here and answer my questions,' I ordered. 'Those little kiddies you don't know how to bring up can sort things out for themselves.'

He looked at me, stunned. 'What do you mean? Those children have suffered a great deal—'

I interrupted him as brutally as I could.

'At the age of seventeen you went to a parish on the city outskirts. You were charged with acts of obscenity in a public place in the presence of a twelve-year-old girl. What's a person like you doing in a place like this?'

I saw him stagger. He sat down heavily on the seat, his face in his hands.

'I didn't do a thing,' he murmured.

'Bollocks! The police report says you had your trousers down.'

'It was a public park, I was taking a leak behind a tree, the girl had wandered away from her auntie and she saw me—'

'I don't think so. You were given a six-months suspended sentence. You avoided the charge of soliciting a minor because you were a minor too and because your lawyer was very good. He was paid for by the Vatican Curia.'

'I never touched her, and nothing has ever taken place since,' he said in a low voice, terrified.

'You were given a pardon by Cardinal Alessandrini. Without him you wouldn't be teaching and you wouldn't be here.'

'That's true,' he mumbled, 'but what's this got to do with Father Paul?'

It was a stupid question. Orlandi had been a filthy pervert. He was certainly an idiot. If he was lying about Father Paul's alibi, he had good motives for doing so.

Jan Deniak worked in the evening as a barman in a Trastevere club. I called Angelo to come with me, as we'd seen very little of each other and I was missing his company. He agreed to come, but I could sense that the split between us hadn't completely healed.

We arrived in the open Duetto about ten. Piazza Trilussa was crowded with people who already had a high alcohol intake. You couldn't get anywhere with the car. The kids didn't give a damn about the cars wanting to get through; they continued to down their beers in the middle of the road and didn't even turn round.

'Let's leave it, Michele. We can park along the river and it's only a couple of steps to the club.'

I tooted the horn at the little group that was blocking the way. A girl squealed from the shock and dropped her bottle of beer. The big guy she was with turned round and addressed me.

'Hey, shitface, stuff that horn up your arse, OK?'

I was already out of the car while the little group continued to hurl insults. I turned to the tall guy. 'What did you say?'

Something in my tone or my look warned him off. 'Well, is that any way to behave?' he said hesitantly, while the others kept quiet.

I took the bottle of beer from his hand and tipped it out onto the ground.

'Get out of the way right now,' I ordered.

It was over the top. As with Valerio Bona, I was able to lead him where I wanted. I saw him let fly and ducked, while I let fly back with an uppercut. The blow hit him right in the solar plexus and he bent double, gasping desperately for breath. I was waiting for him to react again; I really wanted to hurt him. I felt a rage inside me, strong and powerful. The guy had nothing to do with it, but

I was careful not to finish him off, so I could continue hitting him. At a certain point, Angelo put a hand on my arm.

'Michele, please, leave off now.'

His look of suffering got to me. He knew where all the anger came from. I went back to the car without even looking round in the general silence and put it in reverse while the guy, still on the ground, was trying to breathe normally. The road along the Tiber was packed with cars, so I parked on a zebra crossing; seeing as I wasn't going to pay any fines, and given I was on duty – not out on a bender like those degenerate young thugs. They were the new prosperous Italy, the Italy of the 1980s: easy money, tanning salons, gymnasia, discotheques, spliffs for the poor, coke for the rich.

The club was impassable, the crowd spilling over outside. Beer, laughter, mopeds passing by, the smell of cannabis. The barman all muscle in the black T-shirt was our Jan Deniak. One of those Poles who, thanks to the Pope, had said goodbye to Communism's crap. A well-built athletic barman. I wanted to observe him a little before I acted.

'Paola and me, we've split up,' said Angelo out of the blue.

So that was why he'd agreed to come with me. Did he want me to feel guilty? No, Angelo Dioguardi was anything but mean-hearted and no, it was only that something unbearable had happened; unbearable, that is, for a sensitive guy like my good friend, not for a cynic like me. What really was unbearable was our superficial behaviour on that wretched night, so unbearable as to split Angelo and Paola's relationship apart.

'And the job?' I asked, imagining the reply.

'I've given notice to the Cardinal to find someone to take my place. I don't feel I can carry on there.'

'Bullshit, Angelo. You're not responsible for what happened.'

I said it in a rage; if there was any superficiality it was all mine.

I was the policeman, not him. He shook his head, but said nothing. I could hardly recognize him. I tried to make him laugh.

'You could always make money from singing. With your voice any Trastevere piano bar would find themselves full.'

'No, I'm going to make money with poker. Gambling's my real talent. And with the proceeds I'm going to make charitable donations, if I'm a success.'

'So you're going to become a professional player?'

I had no doubt about his exceptional ability, but it was a tough world. For a good guy like him it didn't look too promising.

'They won't eat me alive, Michele. I can look after myself, you'll see.'

'Shame. I was counting on your presence in the piano bars in order to pull. Now you're a free man we can really get down to it.'

Again, I was trying to make a joke, but he didn't laugh.

It must have been very difficult for Angelo Dioguardi to live with a sense of guilt. He was a Catholic who believed in the Last Judgement, while I was a cynic who didn't believe in anything any more.

Jan Deniak wasn't happy to see my police ID. No one was ever happy to see it, whether they were guilty or innocent, so imagine a young foreigner in his place of work. He told the other barman he'd be away for five minutes and led me out via the fire door to a deserted back yard behind the bar. It was filthy, full of overflowing sacks of rubbish. You could hear the laughter and the mopeds outside, but we were alone.

'I've got five minutes,' he announced, pumping up his powerful muscles.

I gave a scornful laugh. 'Oh yes? Would you answer that way to the police in your wonderful communist country?'

He gave me a surly look. 'I know my rights. I can turn right round and go back to the bar whenever I like.'

'And I can ask you to come down to the police station and hold you there for twenty-four hours. Have you learned the word "homicide" since coming to Italy?'

'What are you on about?' he said, cutting me off. He was a cheeky bastard. I had to soften him up a bit before we got to the point.

'Anabolic steroids and other gear to juice the muscles.'

There was a moment of hesitation. 'I don't know what you're talking about.'

It was satisfying still having friends in the Secret Service. The lives of others were as wide open as a steamed mussel: ministers, entrepreneurs, ordinary citizens, and every so often someone suspected of a crime. Jan Deniak just happened to be unlucky, because no one should have been interested in him. But he was the personal trainer to a famous surgeon for whom he also did special sexual favours, and in exchange he received illegal drugs which he then sold on at exorbitant prices to wealthy clients in the gym. Unfortunately for him the famous surgeon happened to be the brother of a minister who was under surveillance by my ex-colleagues.

'All right, so let's talk about Sunday, July the eleventh. Do you remember that day?'

'Of course – you won the World Cup.' He was relieved by the change of topic. Poor deluded fool.

'And you did weight training with Manfredi that evening from seven to eight, half an hour before the start of the match. There couldn't have been a many people in the gym.'

'Only Manfredi and me. I already said this down the station.'

'A load of bollocks. You must only tell me the truth now.'

Pumping his muscles, he gave me a contemptuous look.

'Because you're the tough guy, is that it?'

He hadn't noticed the rubber truncheon slipping out of my left sleeve. The blow to his right elbow paralysed his arm and the pain travelled right up to his brain. I gave him a second blow to the kneecap before he could mouth a word.

A wonderful instrument of work, the rubber truncheon – it leaves no visible mark.

Jan fell to his knees, swearing. 'Bastard policeman, I'll kick your head in.'

I gave him a slap on his forehead with my open hand so that he rolled over in the middle of the rubbish. While he was trying to get up again, moaning with pain, I showed him the first photograph.

'You must be really good at giving blow jobs, Jan – the surgeon looks very pleased.'

He opened his eyes wide, incredulous, his mouth gaping to take in breath. He cursed. I gave him a kick in the balls, but not too hard.

'Look, your Polish friend in the Vatican doesn't approve of swearing. And nor do I.'

I waited while he tried to get up. After several attempts, he leaned heavily against the backyard wall so that he wouldn't fall over. I showed him other photographs, in which his little friend was handing him boxes of pharmaceuticals. His eyes fluctuated between the photos and mine.

To be sure of leaving nothing to chance, I added, 'The friends of mine who took these photos get really mad if anyone lodges a complaint. And if they get really mad they don't make a report – they do away with the people and that's an end to it.'

'What do you want from me?' he asked, now with a good deal of humility.

'I told you before. The truth. Manfredi was there in the gym with you between seven and eight, is that right?'

His hesitation was enough to give me the reply I wanted, but not enough to resolve the question for Teodori, the Prosecutor and the Chief of Police. Jan Deniak was between a rock and a hard place, two opposing threats that were paralysing. I had to help him decide.

'You're in deep trouble, Jan. You won't go to prison for giving blow jobs to the surgeon, but you will for trafficking in anabolic steroids.'

He looked at me. 'We were there, Manfredi and me, I swear to it. A tough session on a very hot day.'

The phrase was left dangling in the air. I took a little while to understand. He was sharper than he looked.

'But the gym has air conditioning?' I asked.

Jan even managed to laugh. 'Sure. It's a top-notch gym. What do you think? No one could train in this heat.'

It was enough. Jan Deniak preferred being charged with giving false evidence to any possible trouble with Manfredi and the Count. I had a full house with aces.

Saturday, 24 July 1982

Despite it being Saturday, the electricity company supplied us with the records of the gym's consumption by the end of the morning. Between seven and eight there was no noticeable consumption. The air conditioning had been shut off for the whole of Sunday afternoon, after the last clients had left at lunchtime.

Jan Deniak was brought into police HQ for questioning and his lawyer advised him to tell the truth.

'I must have mistaken the day,' said Jan. 'Manfredi probably came at that time the day after – I had them confused.'

'But his personal timetable is filled in between seven and eight on Sunday,' countered Teodori, still unsure as to how to proceed and at best hopeful there was another explanation.

'I don't fill that in – the client does it.'

One question still remained to be asked, but neither Teodori nor the Public Prosecutor wanted to address it. So I did.

'So let's say you were confused about the days, Signor Deniak. Could we know if anyone contributed to that confusion?'

He gave me a hateful look. I stared at him with half a smile and a finger in my mouth. I wanted to give him a good reminder of the photo with the surgeon before replying.

Jan capitulated. 'Two or three days after, Manfredi reminded me that during the training we did together on Sunday afternoon I'd promised to let him try the new machine for the dorsal muscles. I told him that it hadn't been Sunday but Monday, but he insisted on it. In the end, he convinced me I must have been mistaken.'

The rest of the afternoon was long and extremely busy. Teodori and the Public Prosecutor spoke on the telephone to the Chief of Police, who called them to a meeting in his office. Teodori ordered me to go home and I had the feeling that he wanted to take the credit for it all, but I didn't give a damn. I had a threesome in mind with Vanessa and Cristiana, on which my imagination had been playing for some time.

Teodori kept me abreast of things on the phone. At the Ministry of Justice and the Flying Squad they must have regretted having involved him as well as me now that he was inflexible, freed as he was from his personal problems. The order for Manfredi dei Banchi di Aglieno's arrest was signed just as the fiery red sun was bowing out to the citizens of Rome.

Teodori called me back a little after Manfredi's arrival in police HQ.

'The young man's acting tough, Balistreri, insisting he was in the gym and that they didn't have the air conditioning on.'

'Bollocks. It was him. We all know it – me, you, the Chief of Police and the Minister. And even that shit of a father of his, the King's big buddy. Now he'll have something else to occupy him instead of bringing a cowardly monarchy back to Italy.'

I was over the moon, but feeling wicked. I only wanted to slam that little monster in the cells and get my friendship with Angelo Dioguardi back on the rails. I wasn't thinking of Elisa Sordi, or her parents. Only of Michele Balistreri . . .

'The Count's here at the Flying Squad, Balistreri, together with his wife Ulla and the best criminal lawyers in Italy.'

'Are you worried, Dottor Teodori?'

I heard a little laugh under his breath. His voice softened.

'The charge against Claudia's been dropped. And Manfredi is going behind bars this very evening, you have my word.'

I wasn't invited to the gathering, nor was I invited to Manfredi's questioning. I couldn't have cared less – it was Saturday night, the case was over, and I was satisfied. There was nothing else I could do. I couldn't give the girl back to her parents and I couldn't give life back to her.

What's done is done.

I wanted a good dinner out, and whisky and cigarettes in the company of Vanessa and Cristiana. They were made for each other – the first a sadist, the second a masochist. There was no reason to argue over me, so long as they made me a gift of one of their secrets.

Sunday, 25 July 1982

The phone was drilling into my brain. I felt the weight of Vanessa's head on my thigh, and caught the damp smell of sex from Cristiana where my cheek was resting. My eyelids were heavy roller blinds shut down on my studio flat's stale smoke, my tongue was stuck fast to my teeth, palate and gums. It had been one of those magical nights when my wildest fantasies had finally come true.

I didn't want to answer; I only wanted to sleep. But the ringing wouldn't stop. One eye managed to open. The digital clock said seven twenty.

'Oh, fuck off, will you?' I groaned and shut the eye again.

Several minutes passed. The phone continued to ring. It was like drops of water eroding my brain, going ever deeper, up to the point where I began to wonder what was reality and what was dream.

Cristiana stared at me while I listened to Teodori's funereal tones.

'Come down to Via della Camilluccia right away.'

'Sod it, now what's up?' I asked, suddenly awake.

'Manfredi's mother Ulla threw herself from the terrace at dawn.'

The rain was tipping down over Rome. A summer storm. I heard the drops beating hard on the Duetto's hood while I was parking in front of that violated paradise. I'd never liked rain. In Africa the sun was always out, while in Italy it rained even in summer. I couldn't bear the sense of sadness that rain gave me. It was as if something were coming between life and me and slowing it down.

There were screens all around Block A. Behind them were Teodori, the forensic guys, the forensic pathologist and Cardinal Alessandrini in a jumper and dark trousers. Parked in a corner were the Count's Aston Martin and Manfredi's Harley Davidson. Ulla's body was covered by a sheet from which a stream of blood was mingling with the rain. I felt a desperate need to smoke, but it was neither the time nor the place.

Teodori was shattered. He put a hand on my shoulder and pointed to the sheet.

'I'm having the body taken away.'

I gently lifted a corner of the sheet. Ulla was fully dressed, perhaps after a sleepless night had eaten away at her soul; her delicate features had been mangled by the drop onto the pavement.

'Any witnesses?' I asked Teodori without much hope.

Teodori pointed to Gina Giansanti's young daughter, who was collapsed in a chair under the roof of the lodge.

'She starts work at six o'clock prompt. From the lodge window she saw the Countess come out onto the terrace, climb onto the balustrade, make the sign of the Cross and throw herself off. It was five past six.'

'So she waited until there was a witness,' I muttered.

'I don't follow, Balistreri. Why should she want a witness?'

'To be certain that no one could accuse that bastard of a husband of having thrown her off.'

Teodori looked at me, terrified.

'That's enough accusations, Balistreri. Manfredi's in prison and rightly so. But this is a broken family now, including Count Tommaso.'

However, I still wasn't convinced. Something had come out in the talk with Ulla – some detail, a fear. Now I was certain something was missing. All of a sudden I felt a little twitch of anxiety.

You did what you could. And that monster's guilty.

We were interrupted by the Chief of Police and the Minister of the Interior's undersecretary. They came up to Teodori and Cardinal Alessandrini, deliberately ignoring me.

'We're really in the shit . . . Oh, I'm sorry, Cardinal!' groaned the undersecretary, looking at the sheet. Typical example of Christian Democrat piety, I thought.

I was in time to hear the Chief of Police whisper under his breath to Teodori. 'You're certain about the arrest last night? It is OK? I mean, a hundred per cent certain?'

I caught Teodori's worried look and nodded to say yes.

'I'm certain it was this young man who killed Elisa Sordi,' Teodori replied without hesitation.

Cardinal Alessandrini turned round to stare at me. There was no need to speak. He didn't agree with that certainty. We were ordinary mortals, therefore fallible.

I felt a sudden chill. It was the ridiculous cold dawn at the end of July, the rain sticking my shirt to my skin, or else it was the fear of having got it all wrong. Irritated, I went over to the young concierge.

I had her repeat in detail what she had seen. Between her tears, she confirmed everything, with no space for the slightest doubt. The Countess was alone on the terrace; she climbed onto the balustrade of her own accord, then made the sign of the Cross and leaped into the air.

'Your mother's back from India today, is that right?'

'She got into London from Bombay yesterday and she landed in Rome an hour ago. She called me to say she was taking a taxi. I didn't have the courage to say anything – she'll be here soon.'

'She doesn't know about Elisa Sordi's death?'

'I don't think so, she was in an out-of-the-way village without even a telephone.'

At that moment Block A's main door opened. Count Tommaso dei Banchi di Aglieno was dressed as usual in his impeccable manner, his proud face set in a fixed, inexpressive mask.

The Christian Democrat undersecretary came forward. 'Excellency, may I extend to you my most heartfelt condolences and those of the Minister of the Interior.'

The single icy glance from the Count gave him a start and had him take two steps back, sending him straight into the approaching Chief of Police. The rain was coming down more strongly now. It would take a lot of rain to wash away Ulla dei Banchi di Aglieno's blood from that pavement. Rivulets of water, mud and blood were coursing over the ground. When the Count went over to the sheet and lifted it a clap of thunder exploded overhead, making us all jump. All except him. He put the sheet back with icy calm and his gaze fell on the undersecretary and the Chief of Police, who had lowered their eyes.

'Please thank the Minister on my behalf,' he said, then turned on his heel and went back inside.

Ulla's body was loaded onto the ambulance and carried off to the mortuary. I was the first one to see the taxi arriving at the green gate; the young concierge rushed to open it and the Cardinal turned to follow her.

'No,' I said rudely, barring his way.

He looked at me. 'No? And why not?'

'Signora Gina is a witness and must be questioned by the police before anyone tells her about what's happened.'

'I thought you had already solved the case, Dottor Balistreri,' said Alessandrini icily.

I ignored his comment. 'We're not in the Vatican State here. I

ROBERTO COSTANTINI · 142

expressly forbid you to speak to Gina Giansanti before we do.' I was beside myself, numb with cold and fear.

Alessandrini turned round and saw the two women embracing, mother and daughter holding tightly on to one another. The young woman was speaking between sobs, while tough old Signora Gina listened to her. I moved towards her, but was too late. Gina Giansanti ran up to us and went to kiss the Cardinal's ring, tears streaming from her eyes.

'Eminence, help me. I can't believe it . . . First Elisa, and now Countess Ulla . . .'

I saw Teodori approach a little uncertainly; he'd not yet met Gina Giansanti. The Cardinal grasped both the woman's hands without saying a word. She stared at him, begging him for comfort. I put myself between them.

'Signora Gina, we need to speak with you straight away.'

The concierge looked at me, bewildered.

'But what do you want with me?'

Teodori introduced himself in a manner that was certainly more reassuring than mine. We went into the little house beside the entrance gate where Gina Giansanti lived. Her daughter put coffee on the stove and we sat around the kitchen table. I could distinctly smell wax and detergent, the girl having polished everything for her mother's arrival.

'Signora Gina,' began Teodori, 'you know that before this morning's tragedy, precisely on the day you left for India, another terribly unfortunate event occurred?'

Signora Gina lifted her eyes red with tears. 'My daughter's just told me about Elisa Sordi.'

I had the impression that her look went beyond the window behind me towards an indistinct point in the open square. Teodori shook his head in annoyance, watching the daughter pour out the coffee. 'What have you said to your mother, young lady?'

The girl was trembling. 'Only that Elisa Sordi had been killed and Countess Ulla committed suicide.'

'And you're saying that it was Manfredi who killed Elisa?' asked Gina Giansanti suddenly. The harsh mask of her face had become fossilized in pain.

Teodori looked at her in amazement.

'How did you know that?' he asked her.

'Because that boy's a monster, and his father's worse than he is. The poor Countess, on the other hand, was an angel, like Elisa.'

I decided to get the point, before the blanket of impressions and emotions veiled Gina Giansanti's recollections like a mist.

'Do you remember the Sunday afternoon of the final? I came here with Angelo Dioguardi towards half past five; you'd already packed your bags to leave.'

'I remember very well. I'd gone up to Elisa a bit before and she'd given me the work to take to the Cardinal. Then you arrived with Dioguardi. He went up to see the Cardinal while you finished a cigarette. When Dioguardi called you she'd already joined them.'

'When Dioguardi, the Cardinal and I went out about ten past six you weren't there any more.'

'No. I went to Mass and I bought some holy pictures from the priest to give out as gifts in India. I chatted a while with some of the parishioners and then came back here about half past seven to fasten up my bags. I'd booked a taxi to the airport for eight.'

'All right, Signora Gina, we've already been able to check all this. Both your parish priest and the parishioners remember you, the taxi driver too,' said Teodori.

'And why did you have to check up on my movements?' she asked resentfully.

'Because Elisa Sordi was killed away from the premises here precisely during those hours, after having punched her card at six thirty,' Teodori explained patiently. 'And in these cases we're obliged to check accurately on everyone.'

It was Gina Giansanti's look that gave me the first sign of alarm. The second came from inside my body, from a hidden corner of my brain where I'd wanted to bury all my doubts. My eyes travelled beyond the kitchen window towards the pavement stained with Ulla's blood. The blood was there; we couldn't go back. The invisible blood came from wounds in the soul.

Gina Giansanti's words came from a great distance away, like the first breath of wind that precedes a storm.

'No, you're wrong. Elisa Sordi left while I was getting in the taxi to the airport, at eight that evening.'

The cup of coffee slipped from Teodori's fingers and dropped onto the tiles and shattered, along with our certainties.

We had her repeat her story three times. The taxi to the airport, as the radio taxi company confirmed, had been booked for eight sharp. Gina Giansanti was keeping her eye on the green gate from the kitchen window. At five to eight she saw Elisa Sordi coming from Block B, crossing the grounds in a hurry and then leaving through the wicket gate on Via della Camilluccia. She didn't see if anyone was waiting for her. She only noted that she was moving in a hurry, and assumed she was late for the game. Five minutes later her taxi arrived – a fact we'd already checked. Signora Gina checked in at Fiumicino at eight fifty-two and got on the last flight to London, from where she would take the flight to Bombay at six the following morning.

There were no doubts of any kind. At five to eight Elisa Sordi left from Via della Camilluccia, just before Manfredi got in. It was ruled out that the long business of her death could have taken place in a few minutes in the middle of Via della Camilluccia still in the light of day.

We'd had it: me, Teodori, the Chief of Police, the Minister. Ulla killed herself through our blundering. Through my blundering, because of my certainties. The Count would destroy us; he'd annihilate the lot of us.

'Where's your car, Balistreri?' Teodori asked me. We got into the Duetto in the deafening rain.

Teodori took out his pipe and lit it. He seemed calm, absorbed in his thoughts, whatever they were.

'I'll tell the Chief of Police you didn't agree with me,' I told him, knowing it wouldn't be enough. He was the boss; there was no way I could save him. They would send him into retirement with a dishonourable discharge.

He looked at me with his yellow eyes and smiled. He was a humble bureaucrat, not very intelligent and with big troubles. But I had solved the most important problem in his life for him. And he was a good man.

'You can't save me, Balistreri. Hierarchies are all-important. I demanded Manfredi's arrest, you weren't even there.'

'But I was the one—'

He interrupted me with a gesture. 'I took all the credit for the investigation. I said I had the idea of consulting the records of the gym's electricity consumption, and I was the one who explained everything to the Public Prosecutor, the Chief of Police and the undersecretary. I never mentioned your name; I took all the credit that was yours. So you don't come into it – you haven't done a thing.'

I stared at him in amazement. Now I understood. 'You weren't a hundred per cent sure and so you kept me out of it.'

He avoided my eyes. 'That was my mistake. I had some doubts and I shouldn't have arrested Manfredi. The Countess would be still alive.'

'You had some doubts . . .' I muttered, bewildered.

'I have a daughter, Balistreri; I know things you couldn't know. Elisa Sordi would never have gone down to the Tiber with Manfredi of her own free will. With another man, yes, but not with him.'

I looked at him, appalled. It was a very simple explanation. And true. 'But you can't assume responsibility for my mistakes, Dottor Teodori.'

He now looked at me more firmly. 'I'll say it was all my idea, that it was you who were against it. I'm old and have hepatitis that's turned into cirrhosis. In exchange, you can do me another favour, the biggest one I can ask of you.'

'Claudia?'

'Exactly. My daughter. I'll be dead before too long; you must be a guardian and a friend to Claudia. I think that you'll know how to protect her until she's more certain of herself. And you can do it far better if you remain a policeman.'

'You trust me to do all that?'

He forced himself to smile. 'Not entirely. You have to swear to me that you'll never touch her. Look, you would be an excellent guardian and a very poor boyfriend.'

I was at a point in my life where I was fully convinced of what my father had said and that was that I'd never amount to anything good because I had no talent and no will, nor the application to make up for it. And I didn't really care at all – whatever happened to me from that day on was indifferent to me. It was for this reason I accepted Teodori's offer, not to save my own backside but because I was worn out. All I wanted was to say yes, and then float away and fall asleep forever.

INTERMEZZO

2005

Antonio Pasquali came from Tesano, a small town halfway up the mountains in Abruzzo, a photo of which hung behind his desk at a respectful distance from the rigorously symmetrical ones of the Pope and the President of the Republic. It was a sober but important office, worthy of one of the highest-ranking officers of the Italian police. Not the highest ranking of all, but the most influential in the circles that count.

As a boy he had shown a marked talent for acting and for politics, two spheres with many points in common in contemporary society. The young Pasquali divided his time between drama school and the local branch of the Christian Democrat party. His academic progress suffered a little as a result, but he made up for it with a lively intelligence and the help of his father, who had been mayor of Tesano for almost eight years. His teachers looked favourably and with understanding at the bespectacled boy, who was serious, but sharp and witty when he needed to be. With his personal gifts and those of his family, it was clear to everyone that Antonio Pasquali would make a career for himself.

When secondary school was over he spent several months in London studying acting, then his father brought him back to harsh reality. He took a degree in political science in Rome and passed the exam for entry into the police. After completing two years of the course for the rank of commissario, his father spoke to the Minister of the Interior, who was also from Abruzzo and a fellow party member, who was able to confirm that the young Pasquali was a hard worker, decidedly on the ball, and aware of how to handle interpersonal relations.

And so in 1980, the Minister brought him to Rome as his assistant on secondment from the police and there Pasquali built up the network of political contacts that would support him for his whole career. He had friends everywhere, from neo-fascists to the extreme Left, but he remained strictly a man of the centre, a man for all seasons, ready to dialogue with everyone.

At the beginning of the 1990s the Public Prosecutor's office in Milan sprang into action with the *'Mani pulite'* trials that led to the disappearance of the Christian Democrats and the Socialist Party, decapitating that part of Italy's ruling class. One evening in 1993 his father and his friend the Minister were sitting in the drawing room of the family home in Tesano in front of an open fire, with a good glass of the local aperitif. The two older men were discussing the by now obvious necessity of repositioning themselves politically. The Christian Democrats were splitting into two – one half centre left, the other centre right – under the new first-past-the-post electoral system. Young Antonio, who was by now moving up the ranks of the Flying Squad, came up with a solution for his two benefactors.

'I think you should split up, one into each half.'

The two looked at him a little in amazement, then agreed that this was the most prudent thing to do as they waited for developments that would clarify who would win in the new bipolar system. Everyone was well aware that the local electoral system of political favours, which had developed in the post-war period and had ruled for forty-five years, was now at risk of falling apart under the attack of the 'Communist' magistrates in Milan and the new power of the media, and they had to find a place in both of the new alliances.

They discussed briefly who should go with whom, but the personal and political histories of the Minister and Pasquali's father were identical. But here too the young Antonio found the solution. Turning to the one higher up the ladder, the Minister, who was also the elder of the two, he took a hundred-lira coin and asked him, 'Excellency, the choice is yours. Heads or tails?'

Then his father asked him, 'And what about you, Antonio? The police need political contacts as well.'

Antonio was evasive. He said that in any future scenario it wouldn't be appropriate for a policeman to have any direct membership of a party; it would be more useful to have a simple sympathetic leaning. Nevertheless, he would think about it. What he did not say was that in reality he was waiting for the imminent birth – according to whatever more authoritative voices were saying – of a new very strong political party with limitless funds that would absorb sizable groups of Christian Democrats and Socialists and sweep the field. Antonio Pasquali wanted to keep his hands free: his youthful gifts as an actor would be appreciated in the new television world of politics.

In 2000 he was transferred from the Flying Squad to the Anti-Mafia section, where he conducted several brilliant operations that led to the arrest of historic Mafia fugitives whose places had in the meantime been filled by other Mafiosi. He took good care to see that no politician, present or past, of whatever persuasion, came to be involved. He was honestly convinced that in this way he was serving his country's true interests.

By the end of 2002, all the non-EU criminals in Italy became 'politically relevant'. Urged by the people and several political parties, the government decided to create a Special Foreign Section to support the Flying Squad in the regional capitals. The name of Pasquali as super coordinator *inter pares* among the regional police chiefs was suggested to the Minister of the Interior in office by both the majority alliance and members of the opposition. He was a candidate with support on both sides: a capable and well-balanced man, an excellent policeman who was attentive to the political world's demands.

The Rome Chief of Police, Andrea Floris, was a man who had been recommended by the Left and knew of Balistreri's neo-fascist past, but he also knew that Michele Balistreri was better qualified for the post, having successfully directed Homicide for the previous three years, and that he was Pasquali's age. He asked to speak to the Minister of the Interior, but was passed to the relevant undersecretary who in turn shifted him on to his first assistant, a young man not yet thirty with a degree from a prestigious university, who maintained that, given his distant past as far-Right activist working with the Secret Service, Balistreri's candidature would cause incomprehension precisely among the centre Left where the Chief of Police had his political support. Floris countered by saying these were events that went back thirty years and which Balistreri had redeemed himself for by serving and risking his life for the state, as well as keeping his distance from all political factions. But this was insufficient for the young man; indeed, keeping his distance from politics actually made him 'suspicious'. Balistreri still used terms like *fatherland, honour, loyalty*. This was baggage from the past, an obsolete language, and was indicative of an older generation, the young man concluded. Used to Rome's political theatrics by now, the Chief of Police gave in: the politicians didn't want anyone like Balistreri for the position – a man who didn't speak to them, didn't go to their dinners on terraces or in the most exclusive clubs, a man who never spoke to journalists, a kind of maverick already in decline.

But Floris managed to secure one condition in return for supporting Pasquali's nomination: as head of the Special Section in Rome, which was the most important of all, he wanted Michele Balistreri. Pasquali had no liking at all for this particular policeman who paid so little attention to under-the-table relations with the political world, but he agreed to it in order to ingratiate himself with Floris, whom he needed. At the same time, this meant he could take the opportunity to see that Balistreri did not move to the Flying Squad's fourth section dealing with crimes involving property, where the most politically sensitive investigations into fraud, corruption and false accounting were under way. So he entrusted Rome's Special Section to him in the hope that there he would go up in flames, after which he could replace him with a more trustworthy person. But Balistreri did everything so damned well for two and a half years.

That is, until the case of the letter R.

23–24 July 2005

Samantha Rossi stole a glance at the clock on the kitchen wall. It was half past eight in the evening. The last of the daylight was coming in from the open window on the ground floor, along with the sounds of a few cars setting off for the sea or the countryside. It had been a long hot day, the end of an interminable week of work. She turned off the gas and poured out the soup, then added some Parmesan cheese. Only a little, because Assunta, the ninety-year-old woman she was looking after, had been forbidden cheese by her cardiologist. She placed it in front of her on the chipped Formica table and slowly fed her, a spoonful at a time.

Usually, at exactly ten minutes to ten, Samantha would pick up her rucksack and, having kissed Assunta, would run to the other side of the piazza to take the bus to the Termini station and then the Metro to Ostia. At eleven she would be at home with her parents in their house by the sea.

From eight onwards the Bierkeller was a madhouse. It was where Romanians from the nearby travellers' camps, together with those who lived in the poorest housing on Rome's east side, gathered. After spending a whole day under a blazing hot sun placing one brick on top of another, or at a crossroads cleaning the windscreens of the Roman motorist, they were thirsty. Very thirsty.

Amid that hubbub, in the Bierkeller's most dimly lit corner by the toilets, the man with long straight black hair, Lazio supporters' cap and large sunglasses had been sitting by himself for over an hour. He had drunk little, only half a glass of beer. However, in a white sports bag he had two unopened bottles of excellent whisky that he wouldn't touch. And in the pocket of his jeans were several plastic sachets of cocaine he would never snort.

He lifted his beer glass and winked at three eighteen-year-olds from his own country who were coming out of the toilets. They all had razor-cut heads and were wearing sleeveless white vests and jeans. Only the tattoos on their swelling biceps and necks differed: little swastikas, eagles, two-headed Fascist axes, gladiators, crossed swords. They were perfect for what he had in mind.

Balistreri was having supper at his brother Alberto's house with his deputy Corvu, his friend Dioguardi and one of Alberto's colleagues. It was a light supper of Parma ham, melon and chilled white wine, in view of the poker game to come. Balistreri had cut his smoking down to the strict limits dictated by his unhealthy heart and had almost completely cut out spirits. Playing poker was a substitute pleasure for the many others he had slowly abandoned over the years and was one of the few sources of excitement left to him.

With supper over, Samantha helped Assunta move from the kitchen to the only other room that served as tiny sitting room and bedroom. At twenty to ten she got up to get ready to leave. She conscientiously checked the many tablets that Assunta had to take at different times to keep her heart under control. The timetable Samantha had worked out for her was very precise. She had photocopied it and sellotaped it to the wall in the bedroom, the kitchen and the bathroom. She lost time in giving her some last-minute advice.

'Signora Assunta, did the concierge get you your anticoagulant?'

The old lady smiled absent-mindedly. 'I forgot to ask her, Samantha, but don't worry about it . . .'

At five to ten she raced out of the door.

At ten to ten, he took them out of the Bierkeller. The three young lads were drunk and high, but not too much – just as he wanted. Not clear-headed, but still strong and ready for action. The lonely piazza with its gardens was deserted. They saw her running up in great strides like an athlete and then shoot past, leaving all four with their mouths open.

'Wow, what a piece of ass!' exclaimed the gladiator in Romanian.

Dioguardi was winning, as he had regularly for more than twenty years. His greying fair locks and blue eyes surrounded by wrinkles did nothing to change the air of eternal child who always won apologetically and lost every so often so that his friends weren't always humiliated. Alberto played in his regular scientific manner and lost with the same regularity.

'He's bluffing,' Balistreri said to his brother, who had just passed on Dioguardi's most recent raise.

'I don't think so,' Corvu put in. 'He's got a sixty per cent probability of winning the hand. I think Alberto was right to fold.'

As usual, Dioguardi said nothing. He smoked and drank much more than he'd ever done in his youth, but his bluffs and non-bluffs remained a professional secret.

Samantha noticed them out of the corner of her eye as she went past. She could smell them: drink and sweat. She could feel the eyes undressing her, then the arms that grabbed and held her.

While she was being dragged away, struggling and kicking, she could see the bus two hundred yards away beginning its turn around the piazza. One of the men immediately put his arm round her neck and pushed a dirty rag in her mouth to stop her from calling out. With her eyes staring wide, Samantha saw the bus set off and its tail lights disappearing as many hands pushed her into the brushwood and bushes of the little gardens.

'Mamma!' she wailed. 'Papa!'

An old man taking his dog for a walk at midnight found the girl's body in the vicinity of a rubbish tip not far from the site of the attack. The proximity of the Casilino 900 travellers' camp and other squatter camps of the Roma people meant that the Special Section was called in and Balistreri was immediately contacted on his mobile. He ended the poker game with his friends and, together with Corvu, rushed over to the scene. When he arrived, the forensic pathologist was already there. But it didn't need an expert to see that the girl had suffered multiple rapes and had then been strangled.

In less than twenty-four hours, both the press and a large part of the population were convinced that the perpetrators came from the Casilino camp. The centre-Right opposition had for some time initiated a campaign of zero tolerance against the gypsies 'protected' by the centre-Left administration that had ruled Rome for years. The murder of a young Italian student detonated a request for the immediate dismantling of all the travellers' camps and the forced repatriation of all Roma people.

Gangs of ultra-Right youths attacked a squatter camp with studded clubs and knives, wounding several people, including a woman who tried to protect her husband against them. Romanian flags were burned outside the Romanian Embassy in Rome and the city's walls were daubed with abusive graffiti. A Romanian foot-baller in a first-division Italian team refused to train in protest against the insulting whistles he was bombarded with by his own fans. The Romanian government and press protested in turn and the Italian media were very happy to raise the level of tension. The two Prime Ministers met in Brussels and promised reciprocal collaboration in isolating the few delinquents who were damaging both the Romanian community's good name and relations between the two states, which were now strained.

The mayor and his centre-Left party discussed the problem without finding a solution. Now, with their backs forced to the wall by the opposition, the media and public opinion, they called for a meeting with Chief of Police Floris and Antonio Pasquali in order to settle the issue quickly.

Since the first day, the investigation had obviously been directed towards the travellers' camps. Balistreri was alone in refusing to follow that path to the exclusion of others. His reason was a detail that had been kept strictly secret, known only to the top ranks of the investigating team and absolutely unknown to the press and public opinion. On Samantha's back the letter R, five centimetres high and the same length across, had been carved using a sharp blade. And to Balistreri, the carving of a letter on the victim pointed to a level of premeditation that didn't square with the blind herd instinct of a group of gypsies, even if they were drunk and high as kites.

Pasquali immediately grasped this as an excellent opportunity to damage Balistreri's very solid reputation. At the end of the morning, during a press conference with his colleague sitting beside him, he launched on an impromptu theatrical scene using his great talent for dialectical debate. 'The head of the Special Foreign Section holds that there may be paths to follow other than the one of the non-EU immigrants.' In front of the obvious bewilderment of the journalists, he handed him the microphone. Balistreri's face went dark. 'I can't say anything more,' he said, cutting things short and infuriating the journalists, particularly those in the media agitating the most for the removal of the travellers' camps and putting the blame on the Roma. The headlines in the next day's papers were of the kind that read: *Head of Special Section says 'It wasn't the Roma'*.

All through Saturday night and Sunday morning, there were spot searches in all of Rome's travellers' camps. During a blitz by the Carabinieri in a squatter camp not far from Casilino 900, a bracelet with the initials S. R. was discovered hidden under a mattress in a caravan where three young Roma males were living, having arrived in Italy ten days earlier from the countryside around the Black Sea. They had neither jobs nor a residence permit. The DNA evidence was incontrovertible. The three were blind drunk when they were picked up.

After two hours of questioning, they confessed to everything. That evening they were in a bar where they'd drunk a great deal with a fellow countryman, who had also given them coke to snort. They'd left the beer joint about ten and he'd gone up to Samantha to rob her, but she'd resisted so they'd dragged her over to the rubbish tip. There they'd raped her, in the middle of the plastic bags, refuse, syringes and dog shit. Taking turns, one held her by the neck, one held her arms and the other raped her. In the end, she'd fainted. Each accused the other of strangling her, then they said it had been this mythical fourth man they knew nothing about. But the traces of organic matter on Samantha's body were all from the three of them; there was nothing to indicate the presence of a fourth man. When they emerged from the Carabinieri station a thousand people were waiting, baying for blood. The forces of law and order were only just able to stop them and several officers would willingly have torn the boys to pieces with their own hands.

The media attacked the Romanian community and the police, paying particular attention to the Special Section and its head, Michele Balistreri, the former Fascist agitator and, according to many, soon to be former policeman. And yet Pasquali didn't remove him. He also knew that the three Roma lads could neither read nor write and were therefore incapable of carving a letter on the murdered girl's body. His instinct and his caution told him to wait. He had learned among the Christian Democrats that you always had to have a scapegoat and an escape route ready and waiting.

PART 2

Thursday, 29 December 2005

Morning

He was woken by the sound of someone cursing. Balistreri turned over in bed and looked towards the window. Dawn was breaking. He glanced at the alarm clock: five forty. He put his head underneath the pillow, but couldn't get back to sleep. Things started turning over in his mind.

This part of Rome was a mixture of heaven and hell. For three years he'd had to live in the historic centre, which he hated; it may have looked magical at night, but during the day it was smelly and chaotic. He lived in a building near the Ministry of the Interior reserved for its employees and executives, in a small apartment on the second floor over a small street in the middle of the traffic noise, waves of tourists and shopping frenzy. Almost every evening he shut himself away, alone in his little bolt-hole with a CD or a good book, ever more rarely with a woman, and closed the windows on the world outside. He slept little and badly, hearing every noise – great and small – of the damned city. He couldn't take sleeping pills because they counteracted his antidepressants.

There was the curse again, more loudly this time. Resigned to the fact, he got up, opened the window and looked down onto the street. Two non-EU types were unloading goods from a white van into the clothes shop below. The owner, an elderly Jewish man, was in discussion with an enormous guy who had got out of an SUV as large as he was. It was obvious that the SUV was blocked by the white van. The SUV owner swore a third time, gave the elderly man a push and screamed at him in a strong Roman accent.

'Get those bloody gypsies out of the fucking way!'

The two young guys stopped unloading and moved towards the SUV. Balistreri saw the man with the mouth on him reach a hand underneath his black leather jacket.

'I think you better not,' he said to the man. He was near enough to make himself heard without raising his voice. The four men looked up at him.

'And who the fuck are you? Get back to bed, you piece of shit,' the man with the mouth shouted to him.

'I think I better not,' said Balistreri. 'If you take that pistol out and cause any trouble, you won't get very far in any direction. And I happen to have a pistol as well.' He waved jauntily at the big thug with the excellent facsimile of a Magnum 44 presented to him years ago when he was on a course with the FBI.

The man with the mouth on him took shelter below the main entrance, out of shot. The elderly Jewish man stood in the middle of the road and looked uncertainly at Balistreri.

'Signor Fadlun, have the van go once around the block so that this gentleman can drive through.'

'The road is now free, sir; you can drive off, no worries,' Balistreri said to the hidden thug.

The huge brute looked up uncertainly from his hiding place. 'The pistol's only a copy,' said Balistreri reassuringly.

The thug got his courage back. 'OK, get down here and I'll break your neck, you bastard.'

Balistreri smiled patiently, wondering if he had become too reasonable over the years or too soft.

'Calm down,' said the shop owner to the man as sweetly as he could. 'This gentleman's a policeman; he certainly wouldn't fire at you.'

The white van had gone round the block and was now behind the SUV.

'But I can always shoot the tyres of your lovely big vehicle if you don't piss off within five seconds,' Balistreri warned him, this time shaking his unloaded Beretta.

The SUV departed instantly. Balistreri shut the window and went off to make himself some coffee.

After a few minutes, he heard the doorbell ring. It was Signor Fadlun. He was standing on the threshold with a packet in his hand that smelled sublime.

'My wife has just taken this baklava out of the oven. I know you like it very much.' Signor Fadlun was full of contrition. Balistreri had told him, he didn't know how many times, that he should unload after six a.m. like all good Christians did.

'Please thank your wife, Signor Fadlun.'

'Again, I'm sorry,' said Fadlun, now smiling a little. They had known each other well for three years. 'It's business – what can you do? Over the Christmas period you have to have plenty to sell.'

Balistreri looked at the old man's wrist on which you could still clearly see the number that identified him as a Holocaust survivor. He thought with a shudder what the Balistreri of thirty years ago would have thought of this old man. He thanked him kindly and said not a word about him opening his shop before hours.

The last two weeks of the year had been impossible. As usual, the centre of Rome had been full of people hunting for Christmas presents and had turned into a pit of hell that was impossible to live in.

Balistreri took his gastro-protection pill, ate a wholewheat crispbread while looking regretfully at the packet of baklava made by Fadlun's wife, then drank his decaf coffee, smoked his first cigarette of the day and checked that there weren't more than five in the packet. His coffee was like his life: insipid. Like a good Sicilian, his father used to say that decaf was like coitus interruptus or a cigarette you didn't inhale. But Balistreri had wiped out the Sicilian half on his father's side, the part he detested and had forgotten about, in favour of the half he loved.

He took a shower and dressed. His trousers flapped loosely about him. He had lost more weight and was greying even more at the temples. He swallowed his antidepressant with the last sip of coffee.

Once I wasn't frightened of death. Now I'm reduced to putting it off for as long as possible.

It wasn't yet seven when he left the flat. He arrived at the office in five minutes. The guard at the entrance obsequiously rushed to open the lift door for him. It was a gesture that Balistreri had no liking for, but they were habits dictated by other high-ups. And his fall from popularity advised against any criticism of the system. In any case, it was a system he'd worked in for twenty-five years. He'd been an integral part of it for too long.

He went up to the third floor that housed the Special Section's offices. His own was in the corner, a large room with a sixteenth-century frieze three and a half metres high in the centre of the ceiling and a view of the Coliseum and Roman Forum.

All the other offices were empty except for the cubicle belonging to Margherita, the new switchboard operator and secretary, who greeted him with a smile. She wore no make-up and had the appearance of a good clean girl.

She could be my daughter. If I tried it on with her, she'd laugh in my face . . .

Over the years, he'd gradually eased up on his womanising. He no longer had the ability to inflict wounds as thoughtlessly as he did with no feelings of guilt. Slowly the number of areas he had forbidden himself had spread into almost all female categories: those who were married or engaged, and singles at an age when they still entertained hopes of marriage. As a result of these self-imposed moral limits, and his physical and mental decline, the field was reduced to the occasional one-night stand.

He had a good half hour before the arrival of his two deputies, Corvu and Piccolo. He started in on his routine, the same as he did every day. He put the stub of an extinguished cigarette in his mouth, switched on his computer and checked his e-mails. As he did every morning, he read only the two most important ones. The first was from Graziano Corvu, his 'update on investigations'. It was a summary of all investigations begun in the past two years that hadn't been solved, with the latest findings highlighted in red. There were only four cases: three recent ones plus the case of Samantha Rossi, the case of the letter R.

There was only one new case: a young Senegalese had been stabbed to death outside the Bella Blu nightclub behind the Via Veneto on the night of 23/24 December. Papa Camarà was a bodybuilding instructor at the Sport Center gym. In the evening he also worked as a bouncer at the Bella Blu. There had been an argument at the club entrance between Camarà and an unidentified motorcyclist just before the stabbing, which took place about two thirty in the early hours of the morning. The Bella Blu's manager was a lawyer, a certain Francesco Ajello, who had called the police.

He made a note on a Post-it, stuck on one side of his desk and lit his second cigarette. He turned to Giulia Piccolo's e-mail: new cases. The Special Foreign Section dealt not only with serious crimes, but also any offence or relevant aspects of any investigation involving foreigners – affray with grievous bodily harm, rape, missing persons. Over the holidays Piccolo's e-mails had been quite short. Towards Christmas nothing very serious happened: women's bags were snatched as they were out shopping, shop tills were robbed and merchandise stolen by bored young boys on holiday who turned to shoplifting in the shopping centres. Then there were the tramps found frozen to death and fights between relatives of different ethnic groups rashly gathered together for the holidays, and obviously road traffic accidents increased tenfold because of the number of Italians on the roads and the abundant drinking. It was all commonplace and you could live with it. Nothing that warranted his attention.

But that day there was something new. The morning before a Romanian prostitute had reported that her friend had been missing since the night of 24 December. Another Post-it.

Beyond the blinds, which Balistreri kept lowered, Rome was lazily beginning to wake up. He left only the table lamp lit and put a Leonard Cohen CD on at low volume. The psychiatrist whose patient he was had told him to give up on Cohen, Lennon and De André and let them stew in his memories a while. He went to stretch out on the worn and split leather sofa, which was almost a symbol of his status and state of mind, and dozed off. He dreamed of lighting up a cigarette.

His two deputy commissari entered his office together at seven thirty sharp. What they had in common was punctuality and absolute dedication to the job, but apart from this they couldn't have been more different.

Graziano Corvu came from an impoverished family in a small village in the Sardinian interior. He'd studied like mad and gained a first class honours degree in maths at Cagliari. When he was already working for the police he'd taken an evening course for an M.A. in Economics. The youngest of five sons, he possessed the innate skill of pleasing everyone and had friends everywhere for whom he had done favours. Corvu was the ablest analyst in the Rome police. His Achilles heel was women. In this field, the indefatigable little Corvu was a mixture of awkwardness and bad luck, despite the advice and encouragement of an old hand such as Balistreri.

Giulia Piccolo, on the other hand, had grown up in a small coastal city near Palermo, from which she had upped and left as soon as she was eighteen, followed by gossip about her ambiguous sexuality. Big and strong, one metre eighty of well-honed muscle below the features of an angular – but good-looking – face, she had graduated in physical education in Rome and had a black belt in karate. There was no talk of men in her life, which – according to Balistreri – was a bad sign. She was perhaps too impulsive in character, but her evident courage and uncompromising nature were the very qualities the head of the Special Section knew to be the ones that over the years he himself had lost.

'Good morning, Dottore.' It had taken everything to persuade Corvu not to address him as Assistant Deputy Chief of Police, which was Balistreri's actual rank. Corvu had agreed to call him 'Dottore' only after Balistreri had brought to the attention of his colleague's analytic qualities the fact that two of the three words of his rank were diminutives.

'You look tired, Dottore,' observed Corvu.

They're worried. They've heard rumours in the corridors that have me down for early retirement.

'Any form?' Balistreri asked Corvu, in order to change the subject.

'Both Camarà and Ajello have clean records – immaculate, in fact,' replied Corvu, not knowing which of the two he was referring to.

'Have you checked with Interpol?'

'Yes. Nothing there.'

'Civil court?'

'Checked.'

'And SISDE?' It was a rather impertinent question. Corvu didn't have sufficient authority to access the Secret Service computer records department.

'Checked. Nothing came up there.' Corvu looked away. Balistreri preferred not to ask how he'd managed it.

'Doesn't it seem strange to you that the manager of a nightclub with cage dancers and bouncers, who are most certainly paid cash in hand, doesn't even have a tiny bit of form? I don't mean a conviction, but being reported for stealing apples, that sort of thing . . .'

'When you're dealing with a lot of cash, there's always something,' added Piccolo, piling it on.

Corvu's face grew dark. 'Sorry, Dottore, I should have thought. I'll check with the Revenue Agency.'

'You can tell me tomorrow. For now, tell me about the dead man.'

'Papa Camarà worked at the Bella Blu from the beginning of September. He started at ten in the evening and left at six when the club closed. He stopped any "unsuitable" types from coming in, so Ajello said. There was an argument outside the club.'

'And what do we know of this argument?'

'A witness, an American tourist who turned up about two o'clock, saw Camarà arguing with a motorcyclist who then sped off. Camarà was found dying on the pavement outside the club at two thirty. Stabbed in the stomach with a knife.'

'Any description of the motorcyclist?'

'The American guy was drunk. But he did say the rider was wearing a full-face helmet.'

'OK, find out more from him. And about the victim, Ajello and the takings – everything.'

He turned to Piccolo, picked up the other Post-it and passed it to her. On it was written '28!?' with an exclamation and a question mark.

'You're right, Dottore. The girl waited four days. For a variety of reasons, so she said. I've got the statement she gave at the Torre Spaccata police station yesterday. She's called Ramona Iordanescu and had known the missing girl, a certain Nadia, for only a month. She didn't even know her surname, only that like her she came from a Moldovan village near Iaşi. She hadn't heard from Nadia since late afternoon on December the twenty-fourth.'

With a gesture Balistreri held Corvu back from the torrent of clarification he was about to request.

'Could you summarize?' he asked Piccolo politely. He was always very careful not to tread on her susceptibilities. He used the formal third-person 'lei' with her and the informal 'tu' with Corvu, out of a form of respect for her, and she showed no signs of taking offence.

'Ramona Iordanescu, born April the 4th, 1986, in Iaşi, Romania.'

'You said Moldavia,' interrupted Balistreri.

'No, Moldova, Dottore, not Moldavia. It's a region of Romania,' Corvu explained.

'She's been resident since December the first, 2005 in a flat in Via Tiburtina owned by a certain Marius Hagi, who's also the owner of the billiards bar next door and employer of a distant cousin of hers, Mircea Lacatus. She met Nadia X on the coach journey from Moldova to Rome at the end of November. They liked each other and decided to share the room rented by her cousin Mircea's employer. Once they arrived in Italy they were forced into prostitution by Mircea and his cousin Greg under the threat of serious physical violence. Usual "place of work" was Via di Torricola, a long road out into the countryside between the Via Appia and the Via Casilina. On December the 24th Ramona arrived at the customary patch with Nadia about six. She got into a client's car towards six thirty and didn't see Nadia when she came back, either there or in the room in Via Tiburtina when she got in at daybreak on the 25th. Nadia was to have gone with her to spend the New Year in Romania. Ramona says that she didn't make a formal report before, thinking that her friend had managed to give their pimps the slip, but she did hand in a photo of herself with Nadia.'

Piccolo handed them the photo. It showed two young girls hugging each other in St Peter's Square. Someone had drawn a heart around them in red biro. They didn't look any more than twenty. One was taller than the other and dark, the other small, slim and blonde. Someone had marked an R underneath the brunette and an N under the little blonde.

'And so yesterday she decided to report her missing?' asked Corvu.

Piccolo read directly from the statement: 'Iordanescu came in today, December the 28th 2005, at 5 a.m. to make a formal declaration because in one hour she was taking the coach to Iași.'

She looked up at Balistreri indignantly. 'It seems no one ever dreamed of stopping her.'

Balistreri showed no sign of annoyance.

Who do you think is going to give a damn about a Romanian prostitute, without a residence permit, who disappears?

Now the car horns were hooting outside the window, you could hear them even through the double glazing. It was raining hard and Balistreri was happy.

Rain cushions life, like an antidepressant.

He looked at the time.

'It's ten past eight,' he said to Piccolo.

'I asked about the change of shift. It's at nine o'clock.' Piccolo was already on her feet.

'Take Nano with you and use the siren. Rome's a disaster area in the rain.'

Inspector Antonio Coppola was a fifty-year-old from Naples noted for three things: his low stature, from which came his affectionate nickname 'Nano' or 'The Dwarf', then there was his way with women and, finally, the barely concealed racism of a Southerner who has been discriminated against himself. When he was younger, he'd been married twice to women much better looking than he was. Both of them had kicked him out for his blatant infidelity. He said he suffered from a compensatory illness. In a nutshell, this womanizing was his way of compensating for the sense of inferiority over his height. Then he married Lucia, a Neapolitan girl, his first love at secondary school, who was tall and beautiful. And so Ciro was born, now a very tall sixteen-year-old and captain of his basketball team. Nowadays Coppola confined himself to coming on to beautiful women, without then going on to taste the fruit.

Nevertheless, Balistreri was resigned to the need to keep him well away from any women under investigation who were too attractive. He didn't want to be either the cause or a witness to any romantic crises.

Coppola took the driving seat and set the siren going, while Piccolo put him in the picture with regard to Ramona Iordanescu's statement. He drove through the chaotic traffic as if he were the only driver on the Monza circuit.

After a while they got out of the centre and the beautiful ancient buildings gave way to the shabby tower blocks of Rome's eastern outskirts, the result of the 1960s' property speculation boom.

They arrived at the Torre Spaccata police station at a quarter to nine. The entrance was the rusty gate to a six-storey block with hundreds of windows and not a single balcony. They rang the entryphone. 'Police station,' replied a young Sicilian voice.

The duty officer, Giuseppe Marchese, was not much older than twenty with very short dark hair and watchful eyes. He was in civilian clothes and immediately addressed his male colleague.

'What can I do for you?' he asked, completely ignoring Piccolo.

'Inspector Coppola.' Nano showed his police ID. A knowing pause. The officer became nervous, an effect the Special Section always produced. Then Coppola pointed to the woman beside him. 'I'm here with Deputy Commissario Piccolo.'

'I'll . . . I'll . . . call my superior immediately,' mumbled Marchese, reaching out a hand towards the telephone.

'No,' said Coppola, brusquely stopping him. 'It's you we want to talk to. Is there an office where we can do this discreetly?'

'To tell you the truth,' said Marchese in a feeble attempt to escape, looking at the clock on the wall, 'my shift's over in five minutes.'

'Excellent. So no one will disturb us. Where shall we go?' Coppola persisted even more pressingly, feeling a touch of anger. Marchese was still a kid – he couldn't have seen more than his local village and this police station in one of the ugliest parts of a treacherous city. But on the other hand, if they'd let Ramona leave, it was his fault too.

Marchese led them to a little room to one side, while other officers attached to the station greeted each other in the changeover. Some looked at them inquisitively, but Coppola shut the door in their faces. There was a table and two chairs in the room. Coppola offered the larger chair to Piccolo, who took it into a corner and sat down. Coppola leaned heavily on the desk.

'Sit down,' he said to Marchese. The poor kid sat on the edge of the seat with Piccolo behind him.

'Ramona Iordanescu. You took her statement, right?' began Nano. Marchese shot to his feet. 'Inspector . . .' he tried to say.

Coppola placed a hand on his shoulder and sat the kid down again. He was visibly uncomfortable. Piccolo had learned to recognize fear instantly. Even for an emotional young man, his reaction seemed too extreme. Of course he was dealing with the Special Section and Nano's tough-guy attitude, but no one was accusing him of anything. She got up and stood in front of Marchese with perfect timing, while Coppola moved out of the young policeman's field of vision.

Piccolo squatted on her heels in front of Marchese so that their eyes were at the same level.

'Giuseppe,' she began in a very calm voice, 'you've done nothing serious – you can't have with your rank.' He looked at her as if she were Our Lady of Sciacca come to save him from the pit of hell. Piccolo gave him time to calm down, then in a low voice addressed him in Sicilian dialect. 'There's only one thing I want you to tell me right now. Who told you to let her leave for Romania?'

The kid's eyes shot towards the door, outside which raised voices could be heard. Piccolo glanced at Nano, who went and stood in front of it. Someone knocked. Coppola opened the door, went out into the corridor and shut the door behind him. The voices increased in volume. She had a minute, perhaps less.

'We're not on home ground here – you better tell the truth or you'll be fucked,' Piccolo continued in Sicilian.

'It's always us poor folk who get fucked,' he moaned, then whispered a name.

In the corridor, all hell was breaking loose. Piccolo opened the door wide. A fifty-year-old in the uniform of a deputy commissario and a good thirty centimetres taller than Coppola was screaming in his face: 'I'm reporting you to the disciplinary body! We're not in Chicago here. Just who the hell do you think . . .' Then he saw Piccolo and his face set in a stunned expression as he wondered who the bitch with the muscles was.

As though reading his thoughts, Piccolo showed him her ID card. The man looked at her, but straight away reacquired his aggressive stance. 'Whatever, you can't just come in here and subject one of my men to an interrogation.'

He stared at her contemptuously and showed her his ID in turn: Deputy Commissario Remo Colajacono. He was tall and well built, his thick grey hair combed straight back with brilliantine and hung over his collar; he had a boxer's nose and close-set, dangerous-looking black eyes.

'We can talk about it in your office, if you wouldn't mind, not out here in the middle of the corridor,' said Piccolo politely.

The man turned rudely on his heel and showed her the way to an office in a corner, sitting down in his armchair below the crucifix and photo of the President of the Republic. Without inviting her to sit down, he pointed to Coppola and said, 'The Inspector stays outside.' Coppola went out and closed the door.

'All right, let's talk about Ramona Iordanescu,' Piccolo began.

'Oh yes, she made a statement yesterday morning,' he said, rather too quickly.

Piccolo restrained a smile. Violent men were often too quick like that.

'No, about the time before. Did you speak to her?'

Colajacono was uncomfortable because Piccolo didn't correspond to any of the pigeonholes into which he was used to categorizing women: mothers, sisters, whores and murder victims. He was tall, but she was taller. He had quite a high rank, but so did she and in a more important section. In order to give himself time, he lit a cigar.

'Does smoking bother you?'

'No,' said Piccolo. She got up as if she were at home and went to open the window.

Colajacono decided on the path he thought he could best control. 'I spoke to her for a few minutes that time. She came in mid-morning on the twenty-fifth of December. Officer Marchese told me there was a young Romanian girl who wanted to speak to the Commissario and so, as to spare him any aggro on Christmas Day, I spoke to her instead. She told me that her friend Nadia was missing. I asked her if her friend had a mobile and she said no, they couldn't afford one. I asked her if her friend was happy working the streets and she said no, that she wasn't happy either, no one could be happy. They were all prostitutes, but no one was happy.'

Piccolo said nothing, but her look became darker.

'I told her to let us know if her friend continued to be missing,' Colajacono ended, looking relaxed.

Piccolo raised an eyebrow. 'Really? You were that vague?'

Colajacono gave her a piercing look with his cold black eyes. 'Who can remember? What's clear is that the slut found some idiot Italian who kept her on the game a while and then she did a bunk.'

'You think anyone can easily do a bunk from Via di Torricola?'

'You tell me, seeing as you know everything,' answered Colajacono with irony, blowing smoke in her face.

You can't lay a finger on him, Giulia. Not here, not now.

Piccolo got up.

'We'll start looking for Ramona,' she said. Then, looking him straight in the eye with an angelic expression, she murmured, 'Let's hope nothing happens to her in the meantime.'

She found Marchese in the corridor, having finished his shift. They went out accompanied by Coppola. Despite it being almost half past nine, the traffic was very heavy. They crossed the road in the rain at a zebra crossing in between the cars and mopeds that brushed past them without stopping. The bar was full of people, almost all of them employees late for work but calmly stopping for breakfast. There were also some non-EU types in overalls.

'These Romanians, drinking beer at this time of day . . .' said Coppola, barely hiding his contempt.

Nano had now assumed a fatherly role and Marchese was more relaxed outside the police station.

Piccolo left them in the bar to have a coffee. She went and sat in the car and switched on the heater. It was still raining hard and the street was blocked with cars moving at a crawl to get over some subsidence filled with twenty-five centimetres of water. Get rid of the potholes and the Roma gypsy camps. That's what the opposition was urging the mayor to do. Potholes and Roma gypsies.

You could fill the potholes with Roma bodies. Many would agree with that.
She called Balistreri. She told him everything.
'All right, Piccolo. Bring Marchese here and I'll deal with Colajacono.'
Piccolo smiled. Balistreri wanted to keep her away from trouble.

'Corvu, I need to have a meeting with Linda Nardi after lunch. Max security.'

This was Balistreri's way of saying 'in secret'. Corvu went off, truly shocked. Linda Nardi was a journalist, a type that Balistreri usually avoided like the plague. Moreover, she wrote for a paper that often attacked the forces of law and order and which Balistreri had cancelled from his press cuttings. When there had been the Samantha Rossi case five months earlier, Linda Nardi had been particularly persistent in pointing out the Special Section's mistakes. Then, strangely, she hadn't joined in the subsequent press campaign that had called for Balistreri's head.

The Assistant Deputy Chief of Police lit his third cigarette of the day. Linda Nardi, he thought. How old could she be? She had to be about thirty-five, even if there were days and moments when she seemed to be ten years younger or ten years older. A good-looking woman or a good-looking girl, whichever way you looked at it. A baby face that was too serious, the eyes switching from intensity to detachment. A woman who was as polite and open as she was firm in her opinions and uncompromising in making them known. Balistreri knew that they considered her indispensable at the newspaper for the interest her articles aroused in their readers, but also dangerous in the past for the trouble the same articles had caused within political circles, the extremist fringe of the Church and with several foreign countries.

According to rumours circulating in the corridors, many men – including police and journalists – had tried it on with her, but without success. She was cultivated and courteous, but on that level a total zero, which was sometimes humiliating for the suitor. Balistreri's predecessor in Homicide, Colicchia, was a fanatical Don Giovanni and having a beautiful woman about without having sex with her disturbed his sense of equilibrium, partly because of his innate presumption and partly because he thought all women were of easy virtue. So Colicchia had sent Linda Nardi a bouquet of red roses and a card inviting her to dinner wherever she chose. She had politely declined, but when Colicchia had continued to persist, adding a veiled threat about cutting her off from privileged channels of communication, she had accepted and chosen Il Convento. Colicchia, who was notoriously tight-fisted, nearly had a heart attack: this was a restaurant with only eight tables where the food was heavenly but you paid outrageously for it, certainly well beyond the budget of an honest policeman. But by then his reputation was at stake. He had taken her there and rattled off the usual selection of crimes he more or less romanticized and with which he usually impressed his prey, only to discover that Linda Nardi was as insatiable at the table as she was chaste away from it. She ordered multiple dishes and the most expensive wines, which she barely touched. Then she began to ask Colicchia to tell her his bloodiest tales. In the end, when they were the only customers left, she began to tell him in all seriousness about her research into certain crimes committed in America by women against men. Tales of horrifying mutilation. In the end Colicchia who, like almost all of the Flying Squad, suffered from gastritis and had been forced to drink all the wine she'd ordered and barely tasted, had to run to the bathroom and throw up the contents of his stomach, returning to the table as white as a sheet. So ended the night out.

As usual, Balistreri decided not to use an official car. It was still raining, Rome was awash.

It was a little after nine thirty, the time when the city was opening its shutters: shop owners finally raising the roller blinds, hordes of tardy employees still down in the bars, as well as those who'd already punched their cards and the lackeys and office boys from the world of politics. Around the Ministry of the Interior there was a mishmash of buses, taxis, official cars and private vehicles with permits to enter the historic centre to reach their place of work, which was practically half of Rome. They were all sounding their horns like crazy, as if the cacophony would help move the traffic jam along.

He walked as far as the Via Cavour Metro. The carriage was dirty and almost empty. He saw two non-EU types leap the turnstile laughing and run down the stairs while the ticket collector shouted after them, then turned to a colleague and added, 'Fucking black bastards . . .'

Leaving the underground, his BlackBerry regained its reception and showed two messages from Corvu: the first with details and news about the Romanians that he was going to find, the second with an address and a time: *L. N. – Sant'Agnese in Agone, 3 p.m.*

He took a bus the rest of the way. At least the traffic was moving here, unlike in the narrow alleys of the centre. But the stench of refuse was evident, the rubbish collectors having been on strike since the day after Christmas. A private company had cleared the centre so that the tourists wouldn't see an eyesore, but in the suburbs, the contents of the bins were spilling out onto the pavements and into the middle of the streets.

When he got off the bus Balistreri saw two tramps picking up wrappers from all the special Christmas cakes, hoping there might be something left inside. He passed by them, noticing the smell of piss and alcohol. One of the two addressed him without ceremony.

'Gi' us a smoke, boss, will yer?'

Balistreri handed him a cigarette. So much the better – one less for him to smoke.

The billiards bar was part of a derelict block whose main entrance was next door. The bar door was glass and coming off its hinges and although it was only morning the blue sign was lit up, except the neon letter B had gone. Behind the bar was a slim, smart young man with perfect features and a ponytail. Two Filipinos were playing the slot machines.

Balistreri ordered a coffee. The barman made it immediately and served it with a chocolate. As in every bar in Rome, *Out of Order* was written on the toilet door – except that here, instead of a piece of cardboard, they had written on the door itself, thus making it permanent. Next to the toilet door was another one that remained closed. Above it was written *Billiards Room*.

A young thickset guy came in with a shaven head and three-day stubble, wearing a long black leather coat.

'Do you want a beer, Greg?' the barman asked politely. He had an East European accent. Greg nodded. He leaned on the bar and lit a cigarette right underneath the sign that said *No Smoking*. At which point the two Filipinos at the slot machines also lit up. 'There's no smoking here – put them out,' ordered Greg.

The Filipinos stubbed their cigarettes out on the floor and started playing again. 'Pick up the ends and throw them out – you're not at home here,' he barked.

The younger of the two Filipinos turned round in a temper, but the other stopped him. They picked up the cigarette ends and went away.

'Don't let these shitty slitty-eyes in here any more, Rudi,' Greg told the barman. He took up his beer, gave a burp and went off into the billiards room, closing the door behind him.

'Where are you from?' Balistreri asked the barman.

'Albania, sir,' replied the barman.

Balistreri showed him his police ID, but not the one for the Special Section.

'I'd like to speak to the Lacatus cousins.'

'There's only Greg.'

'His cousin's not here?'

'Mircea went off this morning.'

'I was expecting to meet him here,' said Balistreri, feigning surprise. 'When did he leave?'

'Actually he was here with Signor Hagi. Half an hour ago he took the car and left. And Signor Hagi went off to Marius Travel, his travel agency.'

'What's Mircea's car?'

The kid thought a moment. 'I don't know, but I have to pay his car tax, so I've got a note of the registration here.'

Balistreri sent the details to Piccolo on his BlackBerry with an order to stop the car and come to the bar as soon as possible. He then changed the subject.

'Do you know Ramona and Nadia?'

The kid from Albania looked at the door to the billiards room and began to tremble.

The first difference between the gophers and the real villains: the first lot look upset, the second don't give a shit.

'Don't worry about Greg and Mircea. If I have a mind to I'll put them away and when they come out you'll be a long way away from this bar.'

'With your criminal system they'll be out before I even get to the bus stop,' objected the barman.

He's pretty on the ball.

'If you tell me the truth – everything – then I'll help you.'

'And then where will I be able to hide?' whined Rudi, holding his temples in his hands.

From behind the door came Greg's voice.

'Hey, arsehole, another beer!'

Balistreri went to the door and quietly turned the key. He then went to the bar door and turned the sign to *Closed*. There came another shout from Greg behind the iron door.

'Hey, shift yourself with the beer, will you? Or do you want your head kicked in again?'

The Albanian looked agitated. 'I want a lawyer,' he said in fit of rebellion.

Balistreri shook his head. 'Wouldn't do you any good – you're not accused of anything.'

He took him outside the bar to the pavement, where the threats couldn't be heard. It was certain that Greg would have called an associate or two on his mobile to come and get him out. He sent a text message to Piccolo asking her to get to him with a team.

'What's your name?'

'Rudi.' The kid was more relaxed now. He took a packet of cigarettes out of his pocket and a slim blue lighter. 'You know, we can't smoke in the bar. You want one?'

'Thanks, I've got my own, but I don't want one now.'

Rudi lit his cigarette, his hands shaking. 'Greg and Mircea brought them back here at daybreak.'

'Did Hagi exploit them as well?' asked Balistreri.

'No. Signor Hagi's not like those two, he pays me and gives me food and lodging. He doesn't live here, but he comes in to keep an eye on things in the morning.'

'Where do the girls live?'

'They have a room in the flat on the first floor. Greg and Mircea have one room, I'm in another, and the two of them are in the third. They used to go out at five when it began to get dark and only went out later when they had work from a private client, but in that case Mircea would take them.'

'Do you know where he took them?'

'No. I once asked Ramona and she said she couldn't tell me.'

'Do you remember the last time Mircea took them out?'

'That's not difficult. It was the 23rd of December. He only took Nadia. Ramona went out at five as usual. He picked her up at eight thirty. Then Ramona came back early that night – she wasn't feeling well. It was midnight. I'd already shut the bar. A bit later Mircea arrived with Greg, but no Nadia. They stayed down here to play billiards. I went up to the flat and I found Ramona being sick. So I came back down and then brought her up a jug of hot lemonade, without telling Mircea and Greg that she was back. We had a toast at midnight with the hot lemonade because we wouldn't be able to on the twenty-fourth.'

At that moment, two young men in leather jackets and jeans got off a motocross bike and approached them.

'Hey, you faggot, what you doing outside? Pulling old men during working hours?' said the taller one in a strong East European accent. He was huge, hairy, with tattoos on his neck and shoulders.

'I think they'll kick your head in again, queer boy,' said the second one, a small guy with yellow teeth. 'You locked Greg inside so you could pimp yourself to this old guy?'

Balistreri assumed an embarrassed air. 'Sorry, sorry, it's my fault. I asked Rudi—'

The larger of the two bikers addressed him. 'Fuck off, Granddad, and go and find someone else to suck your cock.' He spat on the ground. 'You Italians, all poofters and whores.'

Two unmarked cars drew up in silence. Piccolo and four detectives stepped out. They looked like villains themselves. Balistreri gave them a signal and they entered the bar. The two Romanians went in as well, followed by Rudi and Balistreri, who locked the door behind them.

'What the fuck you think you're doing, you old poof . . .' said the large guy, but he couldn't finish. Piccolo showed her ID and the four plainclothes men showed they were all clearly armed.

'Hands in the air,' ordered Piccolo. They searched them. They were both carrying flick knives. Very good.

Piccolo read them their rights and declared them under arrest. They handcuffed them, Rudi first.

Then they pulled out Greg, who was beside himself. He had a plastic sachet of coke in his pocket. Seeing he was about to jump on the policeman who was searching him, Piccolo delivered a single blow to the solar plexus that made him fall to his knees gasping for breath. A perfect blow, in that it leaves no marks. While Greg was groping about, they handcuffed him. Balistreri shot Piccolo a warning look.

She's just like I was. I'll have to teach her to be a bit careful.

Piccolo had already called for more cars from the local police stations. They sent all of them off to headquarters except Rudi. Balistreri turned to him.

'Who's in Ramona and Nadia's room now?'

'No one. I've got the keys – I do the cleaning.'

Balistreri shot another look at Piccolo. She was pushing the boundary.

'Perhaps the door's open,' suggested Piccolo. 'Is it, Rudi?'

The young guy was sharp.

'Well, now I think about it, it is.'

'All right, Dottoressa, up you go with this young man and take a look. Then join me later.'

'I'll call Corvu as well to notify the Prosecutor about the custody orders,' she suggested.

Balistreri nodded. 'All right. And remember the refuse collectors are on strike.'

Giulia found the young Albanian instantly likeable. He was polite, helpless and also, she was surprised to find, very handsome.

When they left the bar to slip into the entrance next door, she kept the handcuffs on and gave him a vicious push.

Just in case one of those shits happens to be looking.

They entered using Rudi's keys. The flat had three rooms with two single rusty iron-frame beds in each, a kitchen, a bathroom and no living room. The furnishings were basic, mostly junk. In the first room, which belonged to Mircea and Greg, there was a television and a DVD player. The one in the middle was for Rudi and any occasional guests. The last room at the end belonged to Ramona and Nadia, an illegal extension common over half of Rome: a lumber room knocked into a balcony and finished off with aluminium and plastic sheeting. Two ramshackle beds, an old chest of drawers, no wardrobe. Patches of damp showed through the walls. The bathroom had no windows, no toilet seat, and only the most basic in the way of basin, bidet and shower. There was a smell of cigarette ends and ammonia everywhere.

They went into the girls' room. Rudi was now agitated again.

'Signora, thank you for the handcuffs and the push down on the street.'

'Please don't call me "Signora".'

'Dottoressa?' he asked hesitantly.

Damn that Balistreri!

'I'm a Deputy Commissario,' Piccolo told him.

Both the beds had been made. On one the sheets were clean, but not on the other.

'Which one is Nadia's?'

He pointed to the one with clean sheets.

'Mircea told me to change them.'

'When did he tell you?'

'On the 25th about six in the evening after Ramona went to work. I was down in the bar. He told me to go up and make everything tidy.'

'In what sense tidy?'

Rudi ruffled his hair. He was obviously uncomfortable in that room.

'I don't know – it was in a mess with stuff all over the floor. Some of it was Nadia's clothes, I'm sure. I put some of them back where they went, but there were also Ramona's, who's usually tidy. They were scattered on the floor. Nadia used to leave things lying about and I'd put them away, but it was never such a mess as that. Then I changed the sheets on Nadia's bed and made the other one . . .'

'Have you been back in this room since then?' she asked.

Rudi was now trembling.

'I can't talk any more in here right now . . .'

'No worries – we can go now.'

They went down to the bar. Piccolo stepped into the billiards room. Two billiard tables, a table football, two card tables, two more slot machines, a phone on the wall. Three plastic sacks tied with black thread had been thrown in a corner.

The refuse collectors are on strike.

'What are those sacks?'

'Mircea told me to throw the ones that smelled out on the pavement and keep the others in here until they came to collect again with the truck. There were only two, I thought . . .'

Piccolo had the plainclothes men open the three sacks. The first two were full of beer cans and bottles, cigarette ends, newspapers, magazines and waste paper. In the third was a red raincoat, two T-shirts, two polyester miniskirts, a pair of jeans, a pair of worn trainers, a blue jumper and several pairs of stockings, bras and panties. The underwear was of two types: for a prostitute and a normal adolescent, all inferior quality bought by Nadia in some clothes shop back home.

Piccolo saw Rudi burst into silent tears, crying with the dignity of the destitute. She placed a hand on his shoulder.

The kid pointed to one of the open sacks from which spilled some Romanian language magazines. From the cover photos they seemed to be the typical weeklies full of celebrity gossip.

'That's Nadia's stuff too,' he said.

Piccolo bent down, picked up two or three magazines and started to leaf through them. A card fell out of one that looked like a ticket.

She retrieved it. *Roma – Iaşi. Stazione Tiburtina. 29 December 2005. 6 a.m. Seat 12.*

She stepped outside thinking about that empty seat on the coach back home.

It had stopped raining, the sun had come out and the pavements were gleaming. There was less traffic and so Balistreri took a taxi back to the centre.

He looked out of the window at the passing suburbs: pedestrians, streets ruined by potholes, now filled with rainwater, rubbish every-where. The taxi driver was in full flow against the mayor.

'Look at them potholes, Dottò. I have to change me tyres every two months. You think they had potholes under Mussolini? No way. Meantime, them dirty politicos just do their own thing! And we're the ones that have to drive round San Basilio, Tor Bella Monaca, Tor de' Cenci and Quartuccio at night . . . I'd like to see that Communist prick of a mayor live in one of them places with the blacks and Romanians . . .'

As they approached the centre, the refuse grew less and the street life began to change. They went past the Coliseum and the Roman Forum, now bursting again with happy tourists.

Here Rome's at its most beautiful – the ochre-coloured buildings, the marbles, the pathways along the Tiber.

He arrived back in the office in time for lunch and asked the new switchboard girl if she wouldn't mind going down and getting him something from the bar on the street. Five minutes later Margherita came back with a bottle of beer and a *pizza bianca* piled high with Parma ham and buffalo mozzarella.

'Margherita, you're a mind-reader, you know just what I like.'

The girl blushed and left in a hurry.

That's all that's left to you, Balistreri. Double entendres.

Balistreri was eating heartily as he read Piccolo's e-mail about what she'd discovered. At that moment Corvu came in, a satisfied smile on his serious face.

'OK, Corvu?' He didn't invite him to sit down, knowing that he was more relaxed if he could move about as he talked.

Corvu looked at the notepad in his hand.

'Something new on Ajello, the lawyer who's manager of the nightclub where the Senegalese man was killed. The Bella Blu belongs to a company called ENT and we've got something new from the Revenue Agency,' he added, again looking satisfied.

'OK, later. Right now I want to know about this Marchese. Where've you put him?'

Corvu's face grew dark as his carefully planned debrief went pear-shaped.

'He's in my office, but you told me not to question him—'

'Officially,' said Balistreri, finishing the sentence for him, 'but don't tell me you just sat there staring each other in the face.'

'We talked about our two islands.'

Balistreri went quiet and Corvu continued, a little uneasily. 'He said the Sardinian sea seems more beautiful in appearance because it's more transparent, but the really beautiful sea is Sicily's, which has more soul—'

'All right, so he didn't say anything about Ramona?' cut in Balistreri, getting impatient.

'I'm getting there.' Corvu was searching carefully for the right words.

'Marchese was saying that it's the same with girls. Sardinian women seem more willing, but in essence Sicilian women—'

'In essence? Look, would you mind telling me just what the hell you two were talking about? And what's this got to do with Ramona?' Corvu went red in the face, plainly embarrassed.

At that moment, Piccolo entered. 'Dottore, we've brought them all here, including Mircea.'

'Tell Mastroianni and Nano to be ready. You two, plus those two, makes four, and there's four Romanians . . .'

'Five,' said Corvu, correcting him. 'Marius Hagi's coming in this afternoon with his lawyer.'

'I'll question Marius Hagi when you've finished with those four.'

'There's also the Albanian kid.' Corvu was now really insistent.

Piccolo intervened immediately. 'We have to protect Rudi. I brought him with us. Right now he's locked in my room.'

'You did right. Let's leave him in peace. Now . . .' Balistreri looked with regret at the empty bottle of beer. 'Corvu was telling me about what we've learned from Marchese.'

Still muddled and embarrassed, the deputy commissario began again.

'I'm sorry, Dottore. As I was saying, Marchese said that Ramona was different from Sicilian women, who . . . who are . . .' he stammered again, looking desperately at Piccolo, his face burning.

Before Balistreri went completely ballistic, Piccolo finished what Corvu was trying to say: 'Saints on the outside and sluts on the inside! Sicilian men are so full of shit.' Then she remembered her boss's origins and looked out of the window.

Balistreri broke the silence, pretending he hadn't heard the last part.

'So according to him, Ramona Iordanescu is a saint.'

Corvu latched onto the investigative turn in the conversation.

'Yes, a saint. She had the courage to go back a second time for her friend after Colajacono told her that if he ever saw her again he'd have her on his office desk and then throw her in prison.'

Balistreri saw the muscles in Piccolo's face grow tense.

Trouble ahead. Have to keep her under control.

Afternoon

He was happy to go on foot to Piazza Navona even though it was full of people, as it always was towards New Year.

He walked past the stalls, the acrobats, portraitists and charity collectors to the church of Sant'Agnese in Agone. Linda Nardi was already there. She had extraordinary eyes, wore no make-up and dressed like a fifty-year-old. Balistreri had noticed a vertical line that sometimes appeared in the middle of her brow and ran to the bridge of her nose. One day, during an interview, he had stared at her breasts. They were well shaped, not huge but promising, so he certainly wouldn't have embarrassed her. And yet that furrow had appeared straight away. This frown was as inexplicable as the woman herself, who was far too detached in a way that was so different from all the other women he'd known. In a world where the gentler sex could obtain a great deal by seduction, she could have put her good looks to use in so many ways. But Linda Nardi wasn't trying to seduce anyone.

'Dottoressa Nardi, thank you for agreeing to meet me.'

'No problem. I'm just a little surprised. You're not in the habit of asking to meet journalists.'

'No, not really,' he agreed.

'Then we better go inside. I don't think you want to broadcast our meeting.'

The silence in the church was in direct contrast to the noise in the piazza. There were a good many tourists wandering silently through the aisles, and several Italian families with children pulling at their parents to make them leave. Mass was about to start.

Linda pointed to the seats with hassocks. They sat down in a quiet place. She looked about her calmly, as if they were actually there to visit the church.

'Do you know the story of St Agnes, Dottor Balistreri?'

'Why don't you tell me?' He wasn't particularly interested, but neither was he ready to ask her what he wanted without some kind of preamble.

'The Roman Prefect's son took a fancy to this Christian girl, Agnes, but the feeling wasn't shared and the pain of rejection made him seriously ill. So what do you think the Prefect did?'

Balistreri tried to make a joke. 'Fell in love with her himself?'

She shook her head. 'Knowing Agnes had taken a vow of chastity, he ordered her to be cloistered with the Vestal Virgins of Rome's protective pagan deity.'

'But she wouldn't go?'

'Exactly. Agnes refused and the Prefect locked her up in a brothel. Am I boring you, Dottor Balistreri?'

He had no liking for the story, nor for the way she was telling it. In some ways she was making him feel almost a distant accomplice of that Prefect.

'Agnes also refused to go with the clients?' he asked, knowing that was not how it went.

'Women can refuse to do almost anything, but they can't defend themselves against men's physical violence. Agnes was lucky. Everyone knew the reason why she was there, and for a long time no client dared touch her, until a blind man fell in love with her, who tradition has it was made that way by an angel. Agnes wanted to intercede with the Lord to get his sight back and was accused of witchcraft,' continued Linda.

'And this was her real mistake, don't you think? A vain attempt to challenge authority, an act of pride. Did she want to cure a blind man who loved her or show off the power of her God to the people?'

Linda looked at him for a long time in silence, but without hostility. It seemed as if she was also trying to get to know him better through his reactions to the story. Then she went on.

'Perhaps Agnes didn't want to heal the blind man as much as to bring to light the weakness of the powerful and the strength of the persecuted. Anyway, she was stripped naked and killed: with a sword stroke to slit the throat, like they did to lambs.'

She told the whole story without any emphasis, as if it were that of Snow White. Only her eyes were dark, as if the blackness of a storm had condensed inside them.

'I'm investigating the possible disappearance of a young Romanian prostitute,' Balistreri announced without ceremony, and also to change the subject.

Linda Nardi looked at him, confused.

'I'm sorry, I don't follow. It was you who said that in the world of non-EU foreigners here the line between perpetrator and victim was never clear.'

The words escaped my lips during a heated press conference after dozens of stupid questions from you journalists.

'Dottoressa, that's not the case. You're taking a statement based on statistical evidence for a racist comment. Anyway, in this case we're dealing with a very young Romanian girl and—'

'Your boss Pasquali certainly wouldn't approve of the head of the Special Section wasting his time over such trifles,' she cut in.

'For that very reason I need you to do something for me. But I can't offer you anything in return.'

She considered the proposal with attention.

'I won't do anything illegal.'

'I'll be committing a small legal infraction – you won't run any risk at all.'

'And you trust me?' There was no irony in her voice, only perplexity.

I'm doing something stupid. But it's the only way. Only you can put the wind up Pasquali.

'I'm forced by circumstances. But I'm not telling you anything about the investigation, not before—'

'I didn't ask you anything. I also want to speak to you about something else. But not here, right now. If you're free, we can do it one evening over dinner.'

From Linda Nardi's lips it was different from how any other woman would have said it. There was no shade or play of meaning. A working dinner. He remembered poor Colicchia.

She read his thoughts, knowing that he and Colicchia had been great friends.

'It'll be on me.'

Balistreri looked straight at her.

'I'm not promising you anything.'

'You've already said so, Dottor Balistreri. Would you now like to tell me what help you want?'

As he told her, she listened in silence right till the end. Then she shook her head as if to say no, but instead said, 'Very well.'

Inspector Marcello Scordo was a young man in his thirties from Calabria whose film-star looks had earned him the nickname Mastroianni, after the famous actor. He was closely attached to a woman from his native region and faithful to her – despite the fact that many beautiful female colleagues had come on to him, sometimes quite openly – so in many ways the nickname was ironic.

'Giorgi and Adrian have a normal resident permit and are employed by the travel agency Marius Travel,' began Mastroianni. 'They say that Marius Hagi is an excellent boss, good natured, honest.'

'If it was up to them, they'd make him Pope,' said Nano, sarcastically.

'Giorgi and Adrian know nothing about the girls. On the 24th they went directly from the travel agency together with Hagi, Mircea and Greg, taking the Metro straight to Casilino 900, where they arrived at six in the evening. They were together the whole time and by ten o'clock they were in St Peter's Square. They weren't the ones who picked up Nadia.'

Nano shook his head, incredulous. 'Pieces of shit like that in St Peter's Square!'

Balistreri turned to Corvu. 'And what about Mircea and Greg?'

'Greg and Mircea Lacatus come from Galati's poorest suburbs in Moldova near the Black Sea, like Marius Hagi. He brought them here at the end of 2002. They've got clean records in Italy, but we're checking in Romania. They also turn out to be employees of Marius Travel.'

'What do they say about the girls?'

'They maintain that Nadia and Ramona were prostitutes of their own free will. They declined positions as waitresses in order to make a pile and get quickly back to Romania. Mircea and Greg found them free lodging at Hagi's place. In short, two guardian angels for the girls.'

Balistreri turned directly to Piccolo. 'Rudi told us that on the evening of the 23rd Nadia didn't go to work in Via di Torricola because she went out with Mircea.'

Piccolo nodded. 'Mircea says he took her to out to a restaurant and nothing more. After supper they had an argument because she didn't want to have sex, so he left her where she was and went back home with Greg, who was in the area. Rudi confirms that they were both there at midnight and did not go out again.'

'Corvu, get a printout of the records from the phone company,' ordered Balistreri. 'Find some charge or other and we'll hold them for forty-eight hours. As for Rudi—'

Piccolo raised her hand. 'Rudi should be in a safe place before they get out.'

Balistreri smiled. 'All right, you can see to that. Mastroianni, you go off to Via di Torricola now – the prostitutes'll be starting shortly. Pass yourself off as a client—'

'Beg pardon, Dottore,' interrupted Corvu, 'but Mastroianni's hardly a credible client. Much better . . .' and with a little embarrassment he pointed to Nano.

Coppola exploded in fury. 'Listen, Corvu, if there's anyone here who looks like he's gagging for it, needs to go with prostitutes—'

Balistreri patiently cut them short. Over the years he had learned the art of mediation that he had detested as a young man.

'Corvu's got a point – Mastroianni's not right. You go, Coppola, because I need Corvu elsewhere,' he said, to avoid any further argument. 'Corvu, can you rustle up your Romanian contacts for an informal word with Ramona in Iaşi tomorrow morning? I think there's time to get on the last flight to Bucharest.'

While the others were exiting, Corvu was diligently taking down the note. He raised his head and looked at Balistreri. 'Mastroianni's going to question Ramona, right?'

Balistreri stood up. 'I thought you'd made that decision. Did you want to tell me something about the killing of the Bella Blu bouncer?'

In his hand Corvu held two printouts. Balistreri stared at them in disgust.

'Listen, Corvu, we'll do it this way. Just fill me in on the conclusions to your analysis. If I have any doubts, then we'll look at the sheets of paper.'

Corvu got to his feet. 'Would you mind if I walk about while I talk?'

Balistreri imagined Corvu out at dinner with a girl, with a stack of papers in front of him full of figures, diagrams and formulae. She asks him a question whose answer isn't on the sheets of paper. He gets up and starts walking about.

'Corvu, if you walk about I can't concentrate and I lose the thread. It's better if you sit down.'

Resigned to the fact, Corvu perched on the edge of a chair and glanced sidelong at his notes.

'Well, the Bella Blu's part of a chain of nightclubs, gaming rooms and amusement arcades that belong to a company named ENT. Ajello's been the sole director since the end of 2004, when he took over ten per cent of the stock from the heirs of a previous partner and director, a certain Sandro Corona, who died in an accident at the end of October 2004. The remaining ninety per cent of the company, since it was constituted in the middle of 2002, is in the hands of a trust.'

'Which means that we need a judge and a valid motive to get to know who's behind it,' observed Balistreri.

'However,' the deputy continued, 'Ajello has an immaculate record. And ENT makes a fearsome profit, five million euros, half a million of which goes to Ajello.'

'And we have nothing against this ENT?' asked Balistreri.

Corvu consulted his notes. 'Yes, proceedings on a charge from the finance police in September 2004. In one of the arcades they found some games that weren't linked up to the telematic network for tax, so were illegal. At the time the director was Corona, not Ajello.'

'All right, Corvu, we'll carry on later. Signor Hagi should be here by now.'

Balistreri had known Hagi's lawyer, Avvocato Massimo Morandi, for over thirty years. They had first met in 1971 when they were students at Rome's Sapienza University, both of them active on opposite political fronts. Morandi, already a recognized student leader on the far left, had spoken last at a meeting. A group of right-wing students had created a disturbance in the hall with sticks and clubs and in the end Morandi and Balistreri had found themselves exchanging insults in the same Carabinieri police cell. Now Morandi was a left-wing senator who defended managing directors for very large fees when they were accused of false accounting and also, very occasionally, non-EU residents such as Marius Hagi who were able to pay through the nose for his services.

When Balistreri and Piccolo entered the room for the informal questioning they had no idea whether to expect a kind of senior underworld boss or someone like Greg. Hagi was neither the one nor the other. He was extremely thin, almost ascetic, with short black hair, hollow cheeks scored with deep furrows, and black eyes set below thick eyebrows and with dark bags underneath. He was dressed in an almost nondescript fashion, and was resting against the chair with his bony hands placed loosely and calmly on the table. He didn't seem worried, as if the matter was nothing to do with him. He had a weary air, a sharp cough and the rough voice of long-term smoker.

'So, Dottor Balistreri,' began Morandi. 'What is the charge against my client?'

'Nothing, officially. We're asking for his help,' replied Piccolo.

'But, Dottoressa, there's no reason to ask for it,' said Morandi, speaking as if to the most stupid assistant in his practice, without even deigning to look at her.

'Not about three persons, who were armed, and one of whom was in possession of cocaine – among his employees?' continued Piccolo.

'The cocaine was not in Signor Hagi's possession and he knew nothing about it. As for the two with knives, they weren't even in the bar.'

'Nevertheless we should like some voluntary information from your client about certain details,' Piccolo insisted.

'Let's hear what this is about, then I'll suggest what my client should do.'

'We should like to know how an honest businessman comes to have two prostitutes as guests in his house and gives employment to people who go around armed with knives and with cocaine in their pockets,' said Piccolo.

Morandi didn't even look at her. He gave a little laugh and addressed Balistreri. 'Do you really think I'd let my client reply to questions of this kind without any corresponding charge? I want to know now, right now, what this is about. We're in the Special Section here, not the local police station.'

'That's right,' replied Balistreri, 'the fact is that one of the two young Romanian girls in Signor Hagi's flat in Via Tiburtina disappeared on December the 24th and the second young girl reported the fact only yesterday, the 28th, then left straight away for Romania. We have reason to be concerned about the fate of the missing girl and the possible involvement of your employees.'

Hagi turned his deep black burning eyes on him.

'Do you suppose all Italians are honest? There are many prejudices against Romanians, although the majority are normal inoffensive people. Among those I help, giving them a home or work or a gift, there are extremely honest people and also some young men who are difficult. It would be easy to wash one's hands of them, but then what help would it be if I abandoned precisely those who had most need?'

'So you know about their illegal activities,' insisted Piccolo. Hagi didn't look at her either.

'If by illegal activities you refer to the fact that Nadia and Ramona sell their bodies on the street, yes, I do know, as do the Italian police, which see them there every night. Except that I don't earn a single euro from it, whereas your police . . .'

Morandi shifted about a little uneasily.

'They're all employed by your travel agency, aren't they?' continued Piccolo.

'Yes. And they work hard at least twelve hours a day. I often send Greg and Mircea to Poland and Romania to find new hotels and restaurants to do business with. Giorgi and Adrian look after the office in Rome.'

'While carrying a knife?' put in Piccolo, interrupting him.

Hagi gave her a mocking look. 'They live in the Casilino 900 camp. If you lived there, the muscles you have wouldn't be enough to let you sleep in peace.'

'Are you telling us they're good guys?' asked Balistreri. Hagi had another fit of coughing and gave half a smile.

'You're asking me if Greg and Mircea are good people. No, they're the worst kind of people, very difficult. But their parents helped me get out of Ceausescu's Romania when I was young. In 2002 they told me that Greg and Mircea had moved on from contraband goods to drugs. They asked me to take them to Italy and find work for them. I did this willingly, because those guys saved my life. I set down clear rules for Greg and Mircea: they had to work seriously for the agency, not use weapons of any kind, nor engage in illegal activities.'

'Apart from dealing cocaine and living off immoral earnings,' said Piccolo. Balistreri shot her a warning glance.

'If they so much as push a single gram of cocaine I'll send them away, they know that. They have it for personal use, as do many Italians, including the police and politicians.'

Balistreri caught a trace of deep embarrassment on Morandi's face.

'All right,' said Balistreri. 'Now let's talk about Ramona Iordanescu and Nadia. Do you know her surname?'

'No. She was a guest and paid no rent, therefore I wasn't obliged to report her presence.'

You're almost as good as a lawyer yourself, Marius Hagi. This country's brought you up well.

'The girls were there almost a month and you never saw them?'

'I can understand that it may seem strange, but I don't live there and our daily routines were completely different.'

'But you knew that Nadia had gone missing and Ramona was about to leave?'

'Greg told me that Nadia was perhaps missing on the evening of the 25th and I learned that Ramona had left today from Mircea.'

'And what did you make of this?'

'About what?' Hagi seemed genuinely surprised by the question.

'Nadia went missing five days ago. What do you think has happened to her?' insisted Piccolo.

'I haven't the faintest idea.'

'All right,' said Piccolo, pressing on, 'let's go back to the 24th. We're interested in what happened from six o'clock onwards.'

Morandi raised a hand and said something in his client's ear. Hagi shook his head calmly and replied.

'At six o'clock I went out together with the other four from Marius Travel and we took the underground as far as Via Togliatti. They went to Casilino 900 and I continued on foot to my house to pick up the presents for the children. I stowed them in the car and joined the others in Casilino 900. We celebrated Christmas there with sparkling wine and cake and the children opened their presents. At half past nine I went back home while the others went to St Peter's.'

'And why didn't you go there?' asked Balistreri politely.

'Because I was very tired. My health isn't what it was and I have to go to bed early.' After a long pause, he added, 'And because if God existed he'd live nearer Casilino 900 than in St Peter's.'

Pasquali's secretary Antonella was a typically Mediterranean beauty of forty. She had had a relationship with Balistreri several years earlier, but it had been nothing more than a physical affair. He had subsequently lost interest and the sex had grown less until it disappeared altogether. However, in its place a friendship was born in which Antonella was able to lavish her maternal instinct on this man who had so little enthusiasm for life.

She ushered him into the small meeting room, the more luxurious one that was furnished as if it were a stylish domestic interior: an Ultrasuede sofa and armchairs, a low table in precious marble, a nineteenth-century drinks cabinet in a corner and a balcony with an angel supported by sculptures of the fine arts. Pasquali said this was his guardian angel.

'Pasquali's with the Chief of Police; they'll be here soon. In the meantime, how about a coffee?'

Balistreri knew he couldn't smoke and that coffee would make him want a cigarette, so he declined.

On the one hand, the Chief of Police means problems, but on the other there are advantages.

On the marble table was a telephone and magazines. He glanced at the cover of a magazine with a photo of Casilino 900 and a headline that read *Europe's Gift to Italy*.

The scent of quality aftershave announced Pasquali's presence as he showed in the Chief of Police. Pasquali's dark-grey suit from a high-class tailor was impeccable, as was the cut of his grey hair and his super-lightweight rimless titanium spectacles. Compared to him the Chief of Police looked like a peasant recently come up from the country, and Balistreri simply a tramp that had been given a quick wash and brush-up.

Pasquali's greeting was cold and formal, whereas the Chief of Police shook Balistreri's hand and gave him a fleeting smile. Floris belonged to those Leftists Balistreri had fought when he feared them. Nowadays, when he found them as inoffensive and confused as a ninety-year-old in the middle of traffic, he looked at people like Floris with more objectivity. Floris was no genius, but he was a good man.

Over the years he had had to learn to live with people who were incapable as well as those like Pasquali, who were capable of anything.

The inevitable compromises, as my Papa used to say. The ones that make a child into a man.

Pasquali offered the Chief of Police a seat in one of the two large armchairs, while he took the other. It was obvious that the sofa went to Balistreri.

'So,' began Pasquali, turning to Balistreri, 'the Chief of Police is present at our meeting for two reasons: one for an urgent contingency, the other more fundamental.'

The fundamental one concerns my backside that you would like to kick right out of here. All you need to do is convince the Chief of Police.

'I say we start with the urgent one,' suggested the Chief of Police tactically.

Although it was obvious that the balance of power was in Pasquali's favour, there were appearances to save: rank, age, hospitality. All things in which Pasquali was a master. He made a polite affable gesture towards the Chief of Police.

'The Chief of Police has received a telephone call from the Deputy Prefect of the Head of Police . . .' Here Pasquali paused to try to read any sign of guilt, fear or at least embarrassment on Balistreri's face. He was a master of the pause, of silences and the unexpected question. A supreme actor.

'It would seem,' put in the Chief of Police in a subdued manner, 'that one of your deputies, together with a colleague . . .' He hesitated, searching for the most suitable words.

'Has created a disturbance in a police station,' said Pasquali, finishing the sentence.

Balistreri raised an eyebrow and frowned, as if he were trying to remember something. He turned directly to the Chief of Police.

'I'm sorry, but did the Prefect use the word "disturbance"?'

'No, no,' said Floris immediately. 'They're complaining about the alleged offensive and intimidatory behaviour towards Deputy Commissario Colajacono followed by the seizure of a policeman in the station.'

'Did they use the word "seizure"?' asked Balistreri, with an even more bewildered air.

'I think that's enough of linguistic niceties,' said Pasquali, cutting him short. 'We are here to ask *you* the questions and receive an explanation. And when I say "we", I mean the two of us plus the Prefect.' His voice was soft and calm, as he was used to giving orders without ever raising his voice.

Balistreri stood up. He knew that his attitude would irritate not only Pasquali but also the good nature of the Chief of Police. It was essential, however, that some time should elapse. He went to the drinks cabinet and chose a still unopened bottle of Delamain cognac and twisted the cap. He turned to the two men. 'Excuse me, but I need a drink of something.'

Balistreri sat down with his 1971 cognac. He needed another forty minutes. He spent thirty of them relating the history of Nadia and Ramona.

'And where are Marchese and the Albanian to be found?' asked the Chief of Police with a look of concern.

What a good man you are.

'No need to worry,' Balistreri reassured him. 'They're both safe in our offices.'

'Have you arrested the policeman?' asked Pasquali.

'Certainly not. He's with us of his own free will.'

'But you have questioned him?' insisted Pasquali, failing to hide his irritation.

'He only had a couple of chats with Corvu, one of my deputies. Sardinian women against Sicilian women . . .'

He turned to Pasquali with a submissive air. 'I meant to tell you during this meeting, certainly not hide it from you. Also because I want to proceed with the arrest of Deputy Commissario Colajacono.'

Pasquali was truly a cold-blooded beast. Balistreri watched him while he paused to reflect, weighing up the pros and cons – the political implications, of course, not the ones regarding the investigation. Now Pasquali was forced to give his opinion directly in front of the Chief of Police.

'First the Chief of Police and I will have a word with the Prefect. In the meantime, you will refrain from action of any kind.'

There was no hint of menace in his voice, but without question it was an order that clearly re-established who was in command among the three men in the room.

The telephone on the table rang. Pasquali made an irritated gesture and replied, 'Antonella, during meetings like this I don't want . . .'

He was suddenly quiet. 'Put her through to my office,' he said at last, regardless of any slight to the Chief of Police. Not only was he interrupting the meeting, he also didn't want to be overheard. For someone like Pasquali, this action was almost inconceivable.

Balistreri decided this was the right moment for a visit to the angel. He could allow himself his fourth cigarette of the day. He nodded to the Chief of Police. He knew that Floris always had half a smoked cigar in his pocket.

'I'll come with you,' he said to Balistreri with a smile.

Up on the fourth floor the sound of the traffic was a little muted. The streets were all lit up and full of people coming and going in and out of the shops. It was cold but no longer raining. The balcony was dirty; in the humidity, the dust on the balustrade had turned into a spongy coating.

'Your relations with Dottor Pasquali are a little strained,' said Floris all of a sudden.

'I'll try to do better,' said Balistreri obediently. His fate depended on the Chief of Police. Pasquali couldn't decide to demote him alone.

'You know,' Floris went on, puffing on his Tuscan cigar, 'it's a real shame. Until the Samantha Rossi case, the two of you saw eye to eye. Since then . . .'

'Since then you've had to back me up. Why have you done that?'

The Chief of Police took his time to think about it. 'For two reasons,' he concluded. 'The first is because I happen to think you're one of our best men. Although since Samantha Rossi, that's not been enough. The second reason . . .' He then hesitated.

Floris was one of the few people up to speed on the case. Balistreri drew a letter 'R' on the dusty balustrade.

'It seems easy enough, but you have to know how to write.'

'Exactly. And we've arrested three illiterates who have no idea how to write,' Floris finished.

Pasquali reappeared in the room. He started tapping his fingers on the arm of the chair, which for someone like him was a sign of deep agitation.

'We have a problem,' he began, addressing the two of them. 'That was Linda Nardi, the journalist. My secretary told her that I wasn't available to speak to her and she told her to give me a message, immediately.'

'What message?' asked the Chief of Police.

Pasquali fixed his eyes calmly on those of Balistreri. 'It was: "The Torre Spaccata police station".'

The Chief of Police started visibly, while Pasquali kept his gaze fixed on Balistreri.

Yes, you know I'm capable of it. But you can't do a bloody thing. Not now.

Balistreri looked both interested and at the same time concerned. He had to be very careful not to overdo either his indifference or his concern.

If the Chief of Police had the slightest inkling of what Pasquali suspected, he was in trouble.

'And what did you say to her?' asked the Chief of Police in a decidedly worried tone.

'She told me that her informant . . .' Pasquali's mouth twisted as he pronounced the word . . . 'brought to her attention a certain bust-up in the Torre Spaccata police station this morning.'

Pasquali paused, expecting Balistreri to say something. But it was the Chief of Police who intervened. 'But that's absurd. No one involved had any interest in—'

'Excuse me,' said Balistreri, interrupting him, 'there were a good many officers in the police station and also some members of the public who were there to report things. Unfortunately, Colajacono made such a scene in the corridor before Dottoressa Piccolo could ask him to speak in a more private place.'

'The fool.' Pasquali let the words slip out from between gritted teeth. He must have been very annoyed, as the word was the most vulgar that Balistreri had ever heard him utter.

'There's more,' Pasquali continued. 'Nardi sent one of her reporters to the station and a policeman told her that the fight occurred between the Special Section and Deputy Commissario Colajacono over a report made by the friend of a missing Romanian woman.'

'What does the blessed woman want?' asked the Chief of Police, already picturing the headline to a front-page article: *Disappearances: police opinion divided*.

And so they might have got away with it. But Linda Nardi wasn't the kind of person to stop there. Unlike her colleagues, she wasn't after any scoop, but something far more dangerous: the truth. He would have to warn the mayor and ask him to call the newspaper's managing director, or better still the owner.

Now, with a touch of sadism, Pasquali landed the Chief of Police with what Linda Nardi had said on the telephone. 'She wants to have a look at Ramona's missing person report in the original.'

Balistreri had difficulty holding back a smile. The bit about 'in the original' was Linda Nardi's touch. An extra slap in the face. Treat the dishonest as dishonest.

'But how can we . . .?' complained the Chief of Police.

'If we refuse, she'll only ask us to do it in tomorrow's article,' said Pasquali calmly.

The Chief of Police poured himself a generous shot of Delamain.

He sank into an armchair and relit his cigar without asking Pasquali's permission. Balistreri could read his thoughts. *The article comes out, the entire press demands an explanation. We refuse on the grounds that an investigation is under way. But who can assure us that the person who spoke to Nardi didn't also tell her that Colajacono had sent Ramona packing the first time and discouraged her from coming back? This would mean serious trouble for everyone, starting with the Chief of Police.*

Pasquali had already arrived at the same conclusion during the telephone conversation. 'I told her that I wasn't aware of any fight, but that an investigation is under way about the way the report was taken and that I can give it to her not tonight but tomorrow.'

'And she agreed?' asked the Chief of Police anxiously, already mentally praising the superior negotiating skills that Pasquali always showed.

'She asked me a question before she agreed. She wanted to know if this time was also needed for questioning Colajacono and the policeman who wrote down the report.' Pasquali looked at Balistreri. 'Naturally I said yes.'

I know, you'll make me pay dearly for this. But this evening we're doing it my way. And you can take it as you like, along with that guardian angel on your balcony.

Evening

Before he went out, he allowed himself a few moments' reflection. Panting a little with the effort, he climbed the last flight of stairs that led to the roof of the old building. He had the key to the unused terrace where washtubs once stood, and hung the washing out to dry. As the building was at the top of a slope it was as if you were on a tenth floor. It was dark and the noise of the traffic was only a distant hum. To his right he could see the floodlit Quirinale with the Italian flag fluttering on it, while in front of him stood the white marble of the National Monument and Mussolini's balcony in Piazza Venezia; to his left was the Coliseum and the Roman Forum with the headlights of the traffic queues.

This was the centre of the new political power that had replaced the traditional parties after the 'Tangentopoli' scandals of bribery and corruption in the nineties. New only in a manner of speaking, of course. The only new things were the problems: a country that was too well nourished and therefore lazy, too old and therefore weary. A country that needed its young immigrants but was so damnably scared of them, and with no culture of integration and an economic model to help it. In addition, St Peter's majestic cupola reminded the city and the whole world that behind those walls was an immense power enclosed in less than half a square kilometre.

I thought I could change the world, at least a little. But the world wasn't in the least bit interested and instead it changed me.

He had witnessed the decline of the West as it turned into reality at the same rate as the decline of his own body and spirit. The mistakes he made as a reckless and thoughtless youth had gradually turned into sins. In the cloud of remorse, his dreams had finally dissipated.

Slowly, inexorably, he had become what he had thought it was impossible for him to become: a bureaucratic old civil servant like his old boss, Teodori.

If I were offered the chance to be a child and start over again, I'd refuse. The effort would be unbearable.

When he came down he found Corvu and Piccolo waiting outside his office. They had been worried about him for some time.

'Marchese maintains it was Colajacono who suggested that he and another policeman, Cotugno, swap shifts with him on the night of the 24th as a favour to them, even though he was dog tired,' declared Piccolo with some irony.

'And who was on duty in their place between nine on the night of the 24th and the morning of the 25th?' asked Balistreri.

'Colajacono and his right-hand man, Inspector Tatò,' declared Piccolo joyfully.

Corvu was impatient. 'It's half past eight, Dottore. We have to go if we want to catch Colajacono at the police station.'

'You can see to Colajacono, Corvu. His boss has already been told, thanks to the Chief of Police.'

I don't want Piccolo getting into any trouble.

'And if he won't cooperate?' asked Corvu, ever attentive to the rules.

'Either he comes voluntarily or you can arrest him for twenty-four hours. No interrogation tonight, nothing until tomorrow morning. But he's to have no contact with the outside world – he can sleep here comfortably in our guest room.'

He turned to Piccolo. 'You can talk to this Tatò, Piccolo, but outside the police station. And one last thing—'

'I won't lay a finger on him, Dottore, rest assured,' said Piccolo, crossing her fingers behind her back.

'Dottore, today's Thursday,' Corvu reminded him, consulting his notes just as he was leaving.

Thursday. Supper with Alberto. Poker.

He grabbed his mobile to postpone.

His brother picked up on the first ring. 'Michele, don't distract me, I'm finishing off preparing the pig's cheek. Tonight I'm making you a *carbonara* that will be divine.'

Colajacono showed no surprise at seeing Corvu arrive. His massive form filled the whole threshold to his office door. Smoothing his hair, he said, 'Can I help you?'

Corvu introduced himself respectfully. He was tiny compared with Colajacono. A twig next to an oak.

'This is a polite invitation to the Special Section for an informal meeting, not for questioning, and we'll put you up for the night.'

'Oh, in your grand central hotel? That would be a pleasure, but I've another engagement for tonight.'

The steel hidden in Corvu's tough Sardinian soul came to the fore.

'If you don't come tonight, tomorrow I shall be forced to come back with a warrant and everyone here will know about it.'

Colajacono spat a metre from Corvu's feet.

'OK, I'll come and sleep in your grand hotel. Is the room service any good?' he said in lofty disdain.

They went out along the corridor where several policemen were standing. Colajacono turned to them with a smile, his small eyes gleaming with irony.

'Lads, I'm just taking a stroll down to the offices of the smart police down in the centre. I'll be back tomorrow.'

EUR, south of Rome towards the coast, was a suburban area planned under Fascism to house the 1942 Universal Exhibition in Rome, but it was never held for the obvious reason of the conflict worldwide. The work was completed in the post-war period, keeping to the original architectonic criteria inspired by Ancient Rome on the basis of monuments, rationalism and Classicism.

In the evening the district is almost deserted. The bars and restaurants that work frenetically until early afternoon for its thousands of workers are already closed by dinner time. On the whole, the atmosphere is almost weightless, in contrast to the hubbub, chaos and heat of the historic centre.

The villa where his brother had moved with his German wife and two adolescent sons stood at the end of a narrow road under the watchful presence of a patrol car, necessary because an important politician lived there. For Balistreri that car's eternal presence, even when the politician had no official engagements, was one of the signs of what the country had become.

Alberto opened the door wearing a chef's apron. He was the elder brother, but had looked after himself better than Michele. More physical activity, no smoking, little drinking, a happy marriage with two fine boys, a career as a well-paid executive: the ideal outcome after an engineering degree and a Master's in the United States. He lived on future plans, positive thoughts.

They clasped each other around the shoulders, then went into the kitchen. The house was hot, a halogen lamp lit the lounge and the background music was the old Pink Floyd album *Meddle*. It wasn't Leonard Cohen or De André, but one of his favourites, nevertheless.

'You've lost more weight, Mike.'

Balistreri was aware that his clothes were now too big for him, but he didn't want his brother to worry. Not any more – he'd done it for long enough.

'I know, it's odd. Perhaps I skip a meal now and then, but I do eat. Anyway, tonight I'll make up for it. What are you making besides the *carbonara*?'

Alberto pointed to his nose. It was his chef's obsession: you could tell good things by their aroma.

'Lamb, Roman style,' said Michele enthusiastically. 'And I can smell strudel.'

'But we'll wait for Angelo and Graziano to eat that,' said Alberto, opening a bottle of white Frascati to go with the *carbonara*. 'The strudel's too hot now, but in an hour or so the pastry'll all suck up the apple juice and be ready to serve. Would you bring in the red wine for the lamb?'

Balistreri saw the bottle of Brunello di Montalcino that had been opened two hours earlier and decanted into a wooden Piedmontese loving cup. His brother really did love him: in order to serve him his favourite wine he was breaking a rule he adhered to rigidly, dishes and wine from the same region.

The table was laid for two. He wandered around the room. So many photos, a peaceful life framed in silver. Alberto, his elegant wife, two boys with sunny faces. In the only wooden frame was a black and white shot taken along the Tripoli seafront. Alberto and Michele as children dressed in English-style shorts and long socks. Beside them stood their mother Italia and their father, *Ingegnere* Salvatore Balistreri, the captain of industry.

She was looking at the sky, he at the ground. Honour and strength. An obviously unequal duel.

Alberto brought him back from his thoughts.

'OK, Mike, it's ready. Angelo and Graziano will be here soon.'

The *carbonara* was delicious. The pig's cheek was crispy – you could just taste the egg – and the spaghetti were cooked *al dente*. The chilled Frascati was a perfect accompaniment.

'I wanted to ask your opinion about the slot-machine market,' said Michele.

'For investigative reasons?' Alberto felt more stimulated if his help was going towards a good cause.

The oven timer was ringing. 'I'll go and get the lamb and we'll talk about it,' he said, taking away the white wine glasses.

While they were taking a sip of water to clear the palate, Alberto picked up the thread.

'After an investigation into illegal video-poker games in 2004, the government decided to regulate a situation that was about to explode. Also because, with the difficult economic climate caused by the national debt, an avalanche of money coming in to the state is always attractive.'

'What kind of sums are we talking about?'

'Fifteen thousand million euros a year turnover for the legal sites, the others . . .' said Alberto, beaming seraphically.

'And you're sure about all those zeros?'

'Absolutely sure. About three quarters of the money goes back to the players in winnings. Let's say that the system keeps almost four thousand million euros and hands one thousand five hundred million over to the State. Before 2004 this last amount stayed in circulation. Think what hidden fortunes could have amounted over ten years of uncontrolled video-poker. And despite all this, there are still two thousand five hundred million floating around each year today. Plus the illegal part . . .'

'And that is?'

'The games still not linked to an official payment tool – the telematic network for collecting tax on them. No one can do anything about it. So much so that even if the financial police arrive, sanctions are purely administrative.'

Balistreri pulled a face and sweetened his taste buds with the last piece of lamb and a sip of Brunello.

At exactly ten thirty the entryphone rang. It was Corvu, who had been home to spruce himself up. Out of consideration to Alberto he was wearing a matching jacket and trousers, where during the day he went around in jeans and jumper. His hair was still wet from a shower, but he would never have arrived late. He had brought along a bottle of homemade alcoholic cordial made from Sardinian bilberries. They put it in the fridge and Corvu sat down at the table with them.

'Have you eaten, Graziano?' Alberto asked him. He addressed him by his first name, which Balistreri couldn't bring himself to do, even in private. It was his involuntary way of maintaining a correct distance.

'I have, but when you cook, Alberto . . .' said Corvu, shooting a languid glance at the remainder of the lamb. Afterwards, while nibbling at the lamb, he turned to Balistreri. 'Everything's in order. Colajacono's lodged in our offices for the night.'

Their Thursday evening poker sessions had been going on for three years. Corvu had taken the place of Colicchia, Balistreri's predecessor in Homicide, who had retired and gone to live outside Rome.

'Alberto was telling me how the bar owners make money out of their slot machines,' Balistreri said to Corvu.

'But where does ENT stand in the value chain?' Corvu asked Alberto, displaying his knowledge of the technical terms picked up on his evening Master's course in economics.

'Corvu, what the hell is a value chain? Would you mind telling me?' said Balistreri irritably.

The entryphone rang again and Balistreri went to open the door for Angelo. With growing irritation he heard Alberto explain the famous chain to Corvu and Corvu reply, 'Oh yes, I see. That explains it all.'

Piccolo took advantage of the wait to call home. Rudi replied at the first ring.

'Dottoressa Piccolo's residence.'

'Rudi, I told you to answer the phone only after two consecutive calls of three rings each. And not like an English butler either. I don't want anyone to know you're there.'

'I'm sorry, Dottoressa. You have a very beautiful apartment. I'm very grateful for your hospitality.'

'That's all right, Rudi. The fridge is full, so help yourself.'

'No, I'll cook something and wait till you come home. I'm really good in the kitchen.'

A little surprised, she ended the conversation because Tatò was coming out of the police station. He was a fat forty-year-old with thinning hair and watery eyes. She followed his car for two kilometres. The Capannelle racecourse was lit up and the car park very crowded. Tatò parked on the pavement and Piccolo was forced to do the same.

The racecourse was almost full, and she had a job staying behind him as far as the bar in the home straight grandstand. Once inside, Tatò sat down at a table with three middle-aged guys, clearly gambling men like himself. She saw him take out a wad of hundred-euro banknotes and speak animatedly. They were deciding where to place the bets.

She caught the words '. . . the jockey swears he'll go slow . . .' and Tatò saying 'If he fouls up, he knows I'll have him inside, no problem.'

Glasses of whisky arrived while one of the men went off to the tote windows. Piccolo sat down nonchalantly in the vacated seat,

"Ey,' said one of Tatò's companions. 'Somethin' wrong with your eyes? That seat's taken.'

Piccolo ignored him. She looked at Tatò. 'I need to speak to you.'

There was no need to produce her ID card. He had had a good look at her that morning in the police station.

He looked around him. He had no wish for a scene in this, his other place of work. 'I'm off duty, Dottoressa.'

'So I can see. Unless this here's your real work.'

Tatò turned to the other two. 'It's all right, boys, I'll see you later.'

They got up without a word, but the look they gave Piccolo clearly expressed what they would have liked to do to her.

Why don't you try it? You'd be in for a nice surprise.

'Can I get you anything to drink, Dottoressa?' Tatò had decided to take the path of politeness.

'No, thanks. I *am* on duty.'

'So go ahead. How can I—'

Piccolo got straight down to business. 'Let's talk about the evening of December the 24th when you and Colajacono were in the station standing in for Marchese and Cutugno. Why did you do that?'

'The two lads had an awful shift to do during the festive season, nine at night to nine in the morning every day. They asked if they could at least spend Christmas Eve with relatives. As you know, everyone in the South has some relatives in Rome – we're home to the whole world here.'

That's the first lie you're telling me.

'Actually Cutugno and Marchese say that it was Colajacono's idea. The lads didn't ask for anything.'

Tatò looked slightly uncomfortable. 'Well, perhaps it was. I don't exactly know how it was. They were jumping for joy that morning, that's all I know.'

'And Colajacono suggested that you and he stand in for them?'

He thought for a moment. This time he decided to tell the truth as a lie would have been a waste of time. 'He suggested it to me on the morning of the 24th. Colajacono's like that. He believes that bosses should sacrifice themselves and set an example. Besides, neither of us is married.'

'And neither of you went to midnight Mass, I suppose?'

'I went to Mass at six o'clock in the local parish church – it's next to the police station.'

'And after Mass?'

'Colajacono was waiting for me outside the church. It was almost seven. We took a drive round the district. It was all quiet. Everyone was going home for Christmas Eve dinner. We stopped to eat something in the little restaurant opposite the station; it was the only one open. We were back in the office again just before nine.'

That was a lot of things to check. Mass and the meal in the restaurant were easy, the drive around more difficult. For details of this kind you needed the patience of Corvu.

The roar of the crowd announced the start of the race. The group at a gallop was at the other end of the circuit. Piccolo saw that Tatò was following the course of events with some trepidation, little drops of sweat forming on his forehead. The horses were approaching their stand and the crowd was on its feet, Tatò waiting for the final furlong with the eyes of a man possessed. In the final thirty metres number 6 went ahead and won by a clear length. Tatò relaxed, visibly satisfied.

Piccolo brought him back to the present. 'Let's get back to the 24th after Mass. Did you drive past Casilino 900?'

Now that he had won, Tatò was more relaxed. 'There was no need. Everything was quiet. They were setting up for a party themselves. You know, it seems that even these gyppos celebrate Christmas and they do it with all the money they pinch from us Italians,' he concluded scornfully.

Piccolo clenched her fists but remembered Balistreri's advice. 'So you have no idea where Colajacono was between six and seven while you were at Mass,' she said calmly.

Tatò nodded thoughtfully. A crowd of people was moving towards the tote windows to place their bets.

'From nine o'clock onwards you did not once leave the police station?' Piccolo asked.

'That's right, we didn't leave until the morning after.'

'Neither of you went out?'

'No, neither of us.'

'How can you be so certain? You were together for the whole twelve hours?'

Tatò let out a guffaw. 'Well, not exactly. I don't know about you, but when I go to the loo it's usually on my own.'

Concentrate on the objective here. Don't let yourself be distracted by anger. Do as the boss told you.

She counted to ten, then started calmly again. 'Apart from calls of nature, you were always together. Therefore you would be ready to swear that Colajacono was with you from seven o'clock until nine, and in the twelve hours from nine that night until nine the following morning he never left the station.'

'Absolutely,' replied Tatò. 'Can I get back to the horses now, Dottoressa?'

Balistreri opened the door and was confronted by the beaming smile of the man who for more than twenty years had been his best friend – his only friend in fact, given that Alberto was his brother and Corvu a kind of stepson; a friend who was barely showing the signs of age, as if his very simplicity was protecting him from growing any older.

But Angelo Dioguardi had become a lot stronger over the years. Breaking off his engagement with Paola and resigning from his employment with her uncle the Cardinal in 1982 had opened up a new path for him. Paradoxically, while Balistreri's life was slowly in decline, Angelo's had gone in the opposite direction.

They had never stopped their endless nights of conversation about things great and small, but their roles in life had become reversed. Now it was Angelo who, not often but every once in a while, went after women in search of the ideal he never found, while on the same front Balistreri had retreated: endless repetition, the sense of guilt and the lack of stimulating women had all played a part. And while Balistreri had become ever more involved in the mechanisms of networking and in the bureaucracy he had so hated, Angelo Dioguardi had become one of the ten strongest professional poker players in the world. He continued to donate a good part of his winnings to charity, but he now oversaw their use directly.

While Alberto and Corvu were talking about balances of payments and that damned value chain, the two friends went into the living room. Angelo lit his thirtieth cigarette of the day and poured out a double whisky, Balistreri lit his fifth and took a glass of water. Whisky was too much for his stomach.

'I have a question for you, Angelo. I'd like some information about illegal gambling dens. I know you haven't been to any in years, but at the beginning of your career—'

Angelo frowned in amazement. 'They've not thrown you into Vice . . .?'

'Don't be a prick. I just need some information about those circles.'

'Michele, times have changed. Today they have Texas Hold 'Em tournaments in several private clubs, with very high stakes, but now it's all legal, taxes paid and all.'

'How much is staked?'

'Depends on the jackpot. I think it's quite high in the middle-range tournaments. What exactly do you want to know?'

'I'm investigating a company that runs a nightclub and poker tables, slot machines and gaming rooms. It's controlled by some trust abroad. I have my ideas, but I wanted to hear what you might have to say.'

Angelo thought for a moment. 'There could be a link, Michele. Criminality and money-laundering. They're only small sums – for laundering large sums you need other channels . . .'

'Such as?'

'Michele, remember that I know these things from the circles I mix with – it's not that I've ever been involved. My poker winnings are more than enough to pay for my vices.'

'All right, I know you're a born saint. Now tell me something useful.'

'Real money-laundering's done through property and obviously not in Italy, but the places where you can buy a skyscraper for cash in a week – the Caribbean, Dubai, Macao . . .'

'And where does the money come from?'

'The large amounts from the proceeds of criminal operations: drugs, armaments, prostitution. And not only Italian criminals, of course. Even here we're losing ground to the Russians and Chinese. The Russians fly in with suitcases loaded with cash and over a weekend buy a couple of apartment blocks.'

'But even the Italians . . .'

'Sure. But the Italian underworld prefers to invest the money back in Italy, at least in part. Real estate, chains of retail outlets, hotels, service industries, nightclubs. It helps to create jobs, therefore approval, therefore votes to influence politicians.'

'And the money from kickbacks – all the scams between politics and business?' Balistreri asked.

Angelo smiled. 'Which no longer exist since the "Tangentopoli" trials, right? Look, anyone with his finger in the public purse is much more careful now. They prefer to sweeten a contract with a beautiful penthouse bought in cash for the children or renovating a house in the country or, if it's small potatoes, with a whore. They're people with a good deal of imagination, on all levels.'

'And my slot machine and nightclub company, where does that fit in?'

'Right in the middle. It invests the illegal money that's been laundered abroad back in Italy.'

Angelo lit another cigarette. Balistreri watched him with envy. 'How many do you smoke?'

Angelo shook his head. 'The number varies according to my mood. Between one and two packets a day. Now you're not going to lecture me, Michele. I can take it from others, but not from you—'

'I'm no longer the reprobate here, remember? And women?'

He smiled. 'It's a moment of great freedom, of transition. I like to take time to consider. I like to offer continuity, but after a while they get bored with all my chat . . .'

'Of course, you're a real drag with your fixation about love. After all these years you still can't be satisfied with a simple healthy fuck?'

'Well, I think you've reached rock bottom there as well.'

'I'm fed up with feeling guilty for others' illusions. The price is too high for the value you get.'

Angelo thought for a moment, looking perplexed by the affirmation and sorry for his friend.

'Michele, if you're going to confuse value with price . . .'

'Compare, Angelo. Not confuse.'

'I wanted to say that there are values that have no price.'

He said it with the humility of an uneducated lad from the working-class slums in the face of an educated middle-class friend. For Balistreri that 'I wanted to say', which Angelo sometimes used, almost to excuse himself when he wasn't in agreement, was the starting point for their great friendship and kept it alive.

Alberto called them to order. The card table was ready. Things went as they nearly always went. Angelo won, almost without wanting to. In all this time, they still hadn't understood when he was bluffing and when he had a good hand. In the end he won and the winnings went to a foundation that ran several shelters for the poor and homeless.

As Angelo drove him back home in his car, Balistreri felt drained from that interminable day.

'I'm claiming the right to the last one,' he said, pointing to the packet of cigarettes.

'Then I'll keep you company,' replied Angelo, lighting up his fortieth of the day.

They ended up talking until four in the morning.

Friday, 30 December 2005

Morning

Mastroianni's flight from Bucharest landed in Iaşi at eight in the morning local time. The airport was small but modern and functional, like many things built in Eastern Europe after the end of Communism. A thin, lanky young man in jacket, tie and jeans was waiting for him at the Arrivals exit.

'I'm Florean Catu, Deputy Inspector of Police,' he said.

'Marcello Scordo. So you speak Italian? I'm not very good with Romanian . . .'

Catu was happy to show off his linguistic ability. 'My aunt lives in Florence; I visit her every summer.'

They drove off in Catu's Golf. There were few people about. It was very cold, but the sky was clear. The city's architecture varied according to the successive periods of Romanian history: a few ancient buildings, the small low terraces from the interwar years, stark monumental buildings from the Communist period and last of all the post-1989 era, which was the most modern but less solid, at least in appearance.

'We're carrying out inquiries in the country villages near Iaşi to discover Nadia's surname. If anyone was expecting her for New Year perhaps they've reported her missing, but I doubt it,' said Catu, driving between the few vans and bicycles.

'If she has any relatives, wouldn't they be worried about not hearing from her?'

'You'd hope so, but here we only start to worry after several months, not after several hours as in Italy. We're picking Ramona up in the University area, but we can't force her to reply to any of your questions.'

'I'd like to do this in a different way, Florean, and speak to her alone, precisely because it's an informal thing and if there is an eventual crime it wouldn't involve the Romanian police.'

Catu appeared to be weighing up the pros and cons. On the one hand, it was annoying that an Italian policeman should come onto their patch to question a Romanian citizen without a local police presence. On the other hand, there was the advantage of the leaving all the responsibility to the Italians, including Ramona's probable lack of cooperation.

'All right, but you'll have to question her outside the police station. There's a bar in December XIV Square that makes the city's best espresso. It's also the most expensive.'

Balistreri had slept only a couple of hours, and in that brief time there had been nothing but dreams full of unanswered questions. Tiring dreams. He had his breakfast of decaf and wholewheat crisp bread, then walked to the office in the cold drizzling rain.

At seven thirty Corvu arrived punctually at his office together with Piccolo, who looked a little too subdued for her normal self.

'Did you find a safe place for Rudi?' Balistreri asked her straight away.

He caught her off balance. She flushed and looked at Corvu for help. He came to intervene like a wise old uncle.

'The witness is receiving the best protection, Dottore. Piccolo's putting him up at her place. There'll be no risk there.'

Balistreri felt a twinge of anxiety. 'Oh, really? What a good idea. Well done! A homosexual linked to a criminal gang sleeping at the home of our deputy commissario – a deputy commissario who also happens to be female.'

You've become an old pain in the neck. And she's not your daughter.

'Precisely,' continued Corvu. 'And seeing as we're dealing with a male homosexual, we decided that Piccolo's apartment would be more suitable than mine.' Before Balistreri could reply, he changed the subject. 'Dottore, Nano's outside to report on the prostitutes he's questioned.'

They brought Coppola in.

'Well,' Nano began in embarrassment, 'I'm sorry to say I found out very little.'

'Well, let's hear it,' encouraged Balistreri.

'I chatted to the two pairs of girls who were there on the night of the 24th and who stood just before and just past the spot where Ramona and Nadia usually stood. I asked for information about charges, services offered, et cetera. You know, a little chatting up to break the ice.'

'OK, Coppola,' said Balistreri, 'spare us the rates for services. Did you get any information?'

'When I told them I was the police they were a bit touchy, but I sweetened them up by saying I'd send them any young colleagues in need of a bit.' He shot a quick glance at Corvu.

'Coppola . . .' said Balistreri, losing patience, but Nano went on quickly.

'I learned two things. First, for safety, the girls watch out for each other. They take the clients' number plates. Second, there was little trade on the evening of the 24th. You know, Dottore, going with prostitutes at Christmas is a mortal sin . . .'

'Listen, Coppola, if you've got anything useful to say, say it. If not, we've got other things to do,' Balistreri warned him.

'They didn't see Nadia go off with anyone and they haven't seen anyone acting strange. But there is one thing, and that's a car one girl told me about. It had a broken headlamp so from a distance it looked like a motorbike.'

'And would she recognize the model?' asked Corvu, showing interest.

'She didn't see it herself – it was her cousin. That evening she didn't have her usual companion and a cousin had come to keep her company.'

'Good. If you can bring her in I'll question her and see if we can reconstruct the model with CAD-based vehicle recognition,' said Corvu. 'Did the girls on the other side of the street see anything?' His analytical brain wanted every detail.

Coppola shook his head. 'They don't remember seeing it.'

Balistreri looked worried.

He persuaded Nadia to get in. He switched off the headlights. Bad sign.

The area was full of young people on foot or on bicycles. While Mastroianni rang the entryphone for Ramona a pair of female students gave him an inviting wink, which he returned with an in-offensive smile.

Ramona Iordanescu was good-looking – tall and dark, with a country girl's healthy face on a great body, as he'd already noted from the photo with Nadia. But she came down without make-up in baggy tracksuit bottoms, a shapeless pullover and a black imitation leather jacket. She spoke decent Italian: without articles, but with the verbs more or less correct.

She was a little taken aback to see this handsome young Italian with the innocent puppy look. And she was very happy about the invitation to the bar in the centre. 'Bar very expensive. German student took me there once – he must have been son of Herr Volkswagen,' she warned him.

The traffic had eased and the taxi took them to December XIV Square in ten minutes. The bar was on the ground floor of an ochre-coloured eighteenth-century building; it was a beautiful, well-heated place, with wood panelling and circular wrought iron tables.

'What would you like, Ramona?'

'Cappuccino. Very good here.' She hesitated.

'Would you like a croissant?' Mastroianni added. Those he'd seen looked to have come straight from the oven.

She gave him a nod. 'What's your name?'

'Marcello.'

'Oh, like Italian actor. Did you know you look like him?' She flashed him a smile as she bit into a croissant.

Mastroianni let it pass – he was used to it. 'You had to go twice to report Nadia missing, I gather.'

'It was three times. First time was dawn on December 25th. It was seven in morning. Police station seemed closed. I rang entry-phone and that man opened for me.'

'Deputy Commissario Colajacono?'

'Yes,' she nodded, attacking a second croissant, 'but I know only face, not name.'

'You already knew him by sight?' asked Mastroianni, astonished.

Outside the large window, grandmothers were pushing prams with newborn babies wrapped up against the cold. A few brave cyclists chanced the freezing roads. In the bar someone put a romantic Romanian song on the jukebox.

Ramona was lost in thought. Probably she was wondering why she couldn't meet someone like Mastroianni, marry him, have loads of kids, a job as shop assistant and a little house on the Iaşi outskirts.

'That man has wicked eyes. Eyes that say you don't exist.' She wiped away a tear and added, 'For him I nothing more than piece of dog meat.'

Mastroianni was deeply embarrassed. 'I'm sorry, Ramona. Not all Italians are like that.'

She smiled at him. 'Can you ask more cappuccinos and croissant?'

Mastroianni ordered them and she went on with her story.

'I met him in nightclub, the Cristal, maybe ten days ago. Mircea bought me trousers and top all black leather. He told me wait for him in bar and left me mobile. At midnight it rang and Mircea told me come out. Outside was big policeman, Colajacono.'

She paused, bit into another croissant and made up her mind. She spoke very quickly, all in one breath, becoming agitated. 'He asked me if I know how to use whip and I say yes, even if not true. To get him excited I said I happy to whip him. He looked me with those evil eyes and gripped my arm with huge hand. He asked me if he looked type to be whipped by Romanian bitch and I said it was mistake and was sorry.'

Mastroianni stroked her hand while another tear rolled down her cheek.

'Then big policeman showed me studio flat on first floor beside nightclub. Big bed in middle, big mirror on ceiling. There are whips, handcuffs and plastic dicks. He give me house keys and said I leave them in house after. Then he explained what I to do. Go back to Cristal and sit at bar. Wait for gentleman, a little old, very well dressed. I had to say straight away that I like to be slave owner.'

'And Colajacono went off?'

'Yes. He goes off. Then elegant gentleman comes and I do my job in apartment. He was real pig, liked me whipping him.'

'You never saw the man again?'

'No, never.'

He had to get to the point. 'And when you went to the police station in the early hours of the 25th to report Nadia missing you found yourself in front of Colajacono.'

'Yes, I rang and he opened door. I was surprised and frightened. He asked what I want and then he made great big laugh. Said me not to piss him off.'

'But was he embarrassed or surprised? He must have had a shock seeing you there, now you knew he was a policeman.'

She seemed to think about it a moment. 'He not care at all. For him I was nothing.'

'You went back to your room?'

'Yes, to see if Nadia come back. She no there, but not gone off with anyone. She left clothes there.'

'Are you sure they were there?'

'Yes.' Ramona smiled at a thought that touched her. 'All over floor and on bed of Nadia, as usual. She very untidy, you know. Rudi tidy up and Nadia give him little presents.'

'You went back to the police station later. Weren't you afraid of Colajacono?'

'Yes, but it was almost eleven, Nadia not come back and I worried.'

'But why were you so worried, Ramona?'

'We never got in car with customer unless the other there.'

'I don't follow,' said Mastroianni.

'We always in two standing by fire we have. We never get in car unless other takes number plate so customer sees, and so he afraid do bad things.'

'Very clever. But what do you do if a customer comes while one of you is working and the other's alone?'

'We make him wait. Our jobs last only few minutes.' She gave a little knowing laugh.

'And you went off with a customer and when you came back Nadia wasn't there?'

'Yes, it was six thirty, there was few customers because at Christmas Italian men no go to women on street. I went with client, she wrote number. When I come back, Nadia no longer there.'

'You were only away a few minutes?'

'Well, a little longer. I tried but this client not get pecker upright,' she said, sniggering like the young girl she really was.

'All right, now tell me about when you went back to the police station.'

'It was almost eleven, I couldn't do nothing. I looked in police station and saw that there were people. I have to be brave. I rang bell, young policeman opened.'

'The one called Marchese?'

'I don't know what he called. Young man take me to Colajacono in his office, then go away. He says I am whore, Nadia whore. He say put me in prison if I come back. Coming out, I saw sheet with times and Colajacono no come to work until nine.'

She was a brave girl and smart too. Colajacono was really unlucky. Another girl wouldn't have dared return, but Ramona was different. She then seemed to read his thoughts.

'Not because I am brave,' she said. 'Nadia love me like my mother . . .' She burst into tears.

'Was Nadia upset the day before? Had anything happened to her?'

Ramona appeared to think about it. 'No upset, no, instead more happy. She not talk much, but that day she happy.'

'And why was she happy?'

'I not know. That night she come back very late. I had been ill. I asked her what she had done and she said that perhaps fortune had smiled on her.'

'Can you tell me about Nadia's clothes?' asked Mastroianni, as the bar began to fill up.

'Afternoon of 25th I went to work and clothes still there on bed. When I came back morning of 26th everything was tidy, clothes there no more, and bed of Nadia had clean sheets.' She was speaking in a very low voice. There must have been something more than the memory of the clothes and the bed.

'And then you decided to report her missing and leave?'

She shook her head. 'No. I went to work as usual evening of 26th. Then when I came back on 27th that thing happened. Mircea said that if Nadia had left me something I must give it him immediately. But Nadia not left me a letter, card, nothing. I say but they not believe me. They say they beat me to death. I was crying, no understanding what they looking for. Then . . .' She stopped, staring at the next table where a young man was sitting by himself, reading a newspaper and smoking.

She got up with a start. 'That's enough now,' she said sharply. 'You pay and we go.'

Mastroianni paid and they went out into December XIV Square. It was extremely cold, a freezing wind was blowing in from the Urals and the pavement was icy. The shops still had their lights on although it was now half past nine. They walked in silence to the taxi rank. When they found one that was free, she told him, 'I take bus.'

'Why?' objected Mastroianni. 'We still have to—'

She shook her head. ''Bye, Marcello,' she said quietly, adding 'be careful' as she jumped on a bus that had just stopped.

When Mastroianni turned back towards the taxi stand he saw the young man who had been in the bar at the table next to theirs. The newspaper was sticking out of his pocket. It was an Italian newspaper.

A beep on the computer signalled Mastroianni's e-mail with his report from Romania, which was an hour ahead because of the different time zones.

Balistreri read it out pensively. 'Nadia's clothes left untidy and then they disappeared. That follows.' Then he looked at Piccolo.

'But it's Ramona's clothes that I don't get. You told me that Rudi had said . . .' He thoughts became confused and he let it drop.

There was Colajacono to question. He decided to take Piccolo along. With him she was under control and a little provocation would be helpful.

Colajacono was waiting for them where they'd questioned Marius Hagi. He was rested and shaved, his thick grey hair combed back and brilliantined. He watched them in silence, a sly look in his small closely set eyes.

His lawyer was sitting beside him and immediately put out his hands. 'My client is here to make a voluntary statement. If this takes a turn into something I don't like, we'll stop immediately. Or you may proceed formally to custody.'

Just like Morandi for Hagi. Besides, he knows we don't have the authority.

'Well then, let's hear what the Deputy Commissario has to tell us voluntarily,' said Balistreri with courtesy.

'With regard to what?' Colajacono asked provocatively.

'Ramona Iordanescu,' said Piccolo sharply.

Colajacono didn't even look at her, continuing to address Balistreri. 'About her two visits to the police station?'

'Three visits,' said Piccolo.

Colajacono's boxer's nose flared dangerously, while his thin mouth stretched into a sneer. He turned slowly towards Piccolo.

'That's right, that bloody Romanian slut. She came three times, as if we had fuck all else to do.'

'Tell us about the first time,' Piccolo asked him calmly, conscious that Balistreri was keeping his eye on her.

'She came at dawn on Christmas Day. It was still dark; there was just Tatò and myself. I opened the door and I found this whore rabbiting on. She was saying that this other whore hadn't come back. You can imagine what a huge problem that was. I didn't even let her in the station, having much more important things to see to.'

'At that time on Christmas Day?' The irony in Piccolo's voice was plain.

'Listen, love, in my station we deal with scum like her every day. We've got Casilino 900 with six hundred and fifty inhabitants as well as other camps, then the common criminals. They're animals. If me and my men didn't watch them they'd be attacking all the women in the neighbourhood, the elderly and kids. Besides the good-looking ones like yourself, of course,' he ended with a snort.

'You should have taken her statement,' said Piccolo icily.

Colajacono shot her a scornful look. 'You sit here in your beautiful office in the centre of Rome and tell us what to do! Street cleaners in paradise, that's all you are.' He spat on the floor. His lawyer whispered something in his ear.

'Tell us what you felt when you opened the station doors and found Iordanescu there,' continued Piccolo.

He looked at her in annoyance. 'What did I feel? Am I a child? What the fuck should I have felt?'

'I don't know,' replied Piccolo impassively. 'Surprise, fear—'

'Fear?' Colajacono burst out, and his lawyer placed a hand on his arm. 'Me, frightened of some gyppo whore?'

Balistreri stuck a half-smoked cigarette in his mouth. It was the signal agreed with Piccolo. It was time to hand over.

'You weren't surprised to see the young Iordanescu woman at the station?' asked Balistreri suddenly.

Colajacono looked at him and for the first time hesitated. In the end he decided that it was wise to have an escape route ready.

'Well, a little, yes, at that time . . .'

'And the young Iordanescu woman wasn't surprised to see you there?' he went on.

The lawyer decided to interrupt. 'Dottore, this conversation has taken a cryptic turn that I don't like at all. If you'd like to put a clear question to my client . . .'

'The question is crystal clear, Avvocato. But to repeat it: given that Deputy Commissario Colajacono wasn't surprised to see Iordanescu, having already met her, we were wondering if Iordanescu was at least surprised to see him there in uniform, having met him a few days earlier in plain clothes outside a nightclub.'

The lawyer shot straight up and addressed Colajacono. 'Do not say a word.' Then he turned to Balistreri. 'The voluntary statement is now over. If you wish to continue, you know what you must do.'

Colajacono raised his huge form up and, standing a few inches taller than Balistreri, placed himself in front of him, staring at him with open disdain.

'Well then, are you arresting me or am I free to go?' His breath smelled of garlic and whisky.

Balistreri lit his cigarette. The interview was over. What disturbed him more than Colajacono was the clearly visible Italian newspaper mentioned in Mastroianni's report. It was a symbolic language he knew, even if he could hardly believe it.

As a youth, Nano had been a warehouseman at the NATO base in Naples and had learned a little American English. So for him to be given the job of asking a few questions of the witness who had observed the fight outside the Bella Blu between the bouncer Camarà and the motorcyclist was a gratifying recognition of his linguistic ability. Thus he switched from Romanian prostitutes to a young American professional who worked for a multinational, a category that in Coppola's mind consisted only of superior beings.

Mid morning, the bar in Piazza di Spagna was full of the citizens of Rome who were both wealthy and idle. The north wind had cleared the sky, which was now an intense blue, and you could look down below on Piazza del Popolo, filled with tourists. They sat outside under the veranda next to a gas heater that made the temperature acceptable.

Fred Cabot was in his thirties, a young man with a likeable manner. Nano immediately reassured him of the fact that he could speak his language.

'I speak American,' he declared.

Cabot ordered a juice and Nano a cappuccino and a currant pastry with cream.

'Rome is wonderful. I come from Houston, a very modern city. One of your churches is older than all our buildings put together. *Chiese molto vecchie, sì?*'

Coppola realized that, what with the Texas drawl and his own lack of knowledge, he could only understand half of what Cabot was saying. He kept things simple.

'First time in Rome?'

'Yeah, first time.'

He decided to get to the point in order to avoid excessive linguistic stress. He pulled out a sheet of paper on which he'd written out the questions with the aid of a dictionary. In the meantime an elegant waiter had served them.

'Please tell me about the night of December the 23rd.'

'Well, you know, it was late. I'd been in various nightclubs and, frankly, I was drunk, *ubriaco, sì*? I wanted one last drink and some music.'

'And some girls?' added Nano, giving him a wink.

The American laughed. 'Yeah, but a drink first.'

'What time you arrive Bella Blu?'

'I think it was two o'clock, maybe a little later. This black guy was on the door and he had to check me for security. He was just starting when this motorcycle stopped in the middle of the road and the rider yelled – *gridato* – and drove away, *andato.*'

'What he say? What language?'

'I don't really know. It was certainly Italian or Spanish, *gridato* this bad word: *testa . . . casso*?'

'*Testa di cazzo?*' suggested Nano. 'Dickhead.'

'Yeah, certainly something rude, *parola brutta*. The black guy was angry, *arrabbiato, urlato vafanculo*,' explained Cabot, proudly showing off his own linguistic progress.

'Where motorcycle come?'

'Well, I'm not sure, *non sicuro*, but my impression is that it was just around the corner. *Sentito* engine starting, and it came out of the darkness, *da buio.*'

'You see the person?' asked Nano hopefully.

Cabot thought about it. 'The guy wore a helmet. You know, it's queer . . .'

Not having understood a word, Nano held up a hand in desperation to stop him. He pulled out a pocket dictionary and with a melancholy air looked up 'whore'. With surprise he found it meant 'prostitute'. A prostitute in a helmet, that is, a crash helmet. And then he seemed to recall that 'queer' meant a faggot. This was a real tangle – a prostitute in a crash helmet on a bike with a faggot.

'Two people,' he said, holding up two fingers for the number. 'But how you know she is prostitute and he is gay?'

Cabot looked at him as if he'd just swallowed the cup as well as the cappuccino. Then he burst out laughing.

'No, no,' he said, trying to contain himself while Nano stared at him, offended. '"Wore" means "to wear", *avere casco*. And "queer" means "strange", *strano.*'

Coppola asked for confirmation. 'One person, no prostitute, no gay?'

The American realized that Nano was offended and chose careful, simple words. 'One person with helmet.'

'OK,' said Coppola, relieved. 'So this person say to black "Dickhead" and black say him "Fuck off" and motorcycle go away.'

Cabot nodded confirmation, choking back his laughter.

'And you remember motorcycle?' asked Coppola, again hopeful.

'It was a great bike, handy and speedy.'

Coppola shook his head sadly. His American needed refreshing. He'd understood that the bike was large, but for the rest he needed a dictionary. With some relief he said goodbye to Fred Cabot, who was leaving for the United States the following day, yet with the clear feeling of his having missed something important.

Giulia Piccolo was unsettled. The decision to bring Rudi home had been made on the spur of the moment. Now, in the cold light of day, the positive side to it was still there but the problems had also become clear. The most troubling of these wasn't what other people might think, but why she had made the decision. She felt lonely, that was true. Indeed, she was lonely, and had been for a long time, ever since the moment Francesca had left. And Rudi was excellent company – sensitive, witty, gay and very handsome.

Where does a good-looking Albanian homosexual fit into the mess your life's in? Serious wounds can't be healed by the dying. Neither one of us is what we'd like to be and together we're even less where we'd like to be.

She arrived at the restaurant around ten. She'd telephoned the manager to make sure that he'd be there at that unusual time with the waiter who'd served Mircea and Nadia. She was greeted by a well-dressed man in his forties in a jacket and tie, whose shoes were in need of a good clean. The waiter, on the other hand, was nearer seventy than sixty, and below his slightly greasy white jacket the flies of his black trousers were open.

'I'm Carpi, Signorina. I was waiting for you.'

No one here was likely to call a policewoman 'Dottoressa'.

The restaurant was quite large with two dining areas, one set aside for smokers. From the menu in English, French and Japanese, you could tell it was a typical tourist restaurant in the historic centre, one that was a little showy judging from the photos of actors and actresses who had certainly never set foot in the place.

Carpi pointed to the waiter. 'Tommaso here served them. He recognized the couple from the photos you sent.'

Piccolo turned to the leering seventy-year-old. 'Did you recognize him or her?'

'I remembered the girl very well – she was pretty. You see me now with only half my hair left, but I still have an eye for the young ladies, I have—'

'All right,' said Piccolo, cutting him off. 'Now tell me all you can remember from the moment they came in, starting with the time.'

'Well, the exact time I'm not sure. But they had booked ahead; I remember this because he kicked up a fuss straight away. He said he'd booked a smoking table. Luckily we're never full, so I was able to accommodate them. He looked the touchy sort, ready to start a fight.'

'And where did they sit?'

Tommaso led them to the smoking area. 'He complained here as well. I offered him a table in the middle and he said he wanted to have his back to the wall. Like someone in the Mafia, you know? Besides, these Romanians, they—'

'So then what did you do?' Piccolo was losing patience.

'Well, I changed tables with a reserved one and gave him the one he wanted, then I took down the order. She spoke in Romanian and he translated. He ordered *penne all'arrabbiata*, she didn't order a first course.'

'How come you can remember an order from a week ago?'

'Because he complained about that as well.'

'About what exactly?'

'He said the *penne* weren't spicy enough, there was no flavour to them. He also said something rude about where the chef could stick his red pepper—'

'Tommaso, please,' put in Carpi.

'Altogether a real fusspot. I was trembling when he ordered the wine. I had him try it twice before I poured it out.'

'Did they talk much between themselves?'

'When I went past they were either silent or he was talking. She seemed not to talk at all.'

'Did anything in particular happen?'

'Well, yes. To begin with, he was taking it really easy – they were here for more than two hours. You know, couples usually only stay here a short time; they eat and then go off to—'

'Tommaso!' said Carpi, rebuking him.

'But the guy went on sipping away at the wine until he'd finished the bottle, while the girl drank only water. Then he ordered dessert, then coffee, some bitters, then a whisky. And then in the end he raised his hand to her. These people really don't know how to treat a lady. An Italian would never dream of—'

'He actually beat her?' asked Piccolo, interrupting him.

'Not exactly. I was in the other room, but I heard him raising his voice in that ugly lingo with all its "u"s and then the sharp sound of a slap. So I went in and she was holding her face in her hands and everyone at the other tables was looking at them. And the man turned to them and said, "Mind your own bloody business." Then he left two fifty-euro notes on the table, got his leather jacket from the cloakroom and left.'

'And the girl?'

'She stayed there a while, as if she didn't know what to do.'

'What did the bill come to?' Piccolo asked.

Tommaso looked at Carpi. 'Well, that I don't recall.'

'More or less,' Piccolo insisted, 'given that the girl ate little and drank water . . .'

'It'll have been seventy euros,' interjected Carpi.

'And you, Tommaso, took the change to the girl?'

She saw the waiter wring his hands before deciding the risk was low. 'Yes, though I don't remember how much it was, but she left a good tip.'

'All right.' Piccolo turned to Carpi. 'Would you have a look through the receipts for that evening?'

Useless question, Piccolo. Imagine them giving an official receipt to foreigners.

After a moment, Carpi came back with a fine receipt for eighty euros.

'Tommaso, what time would it have been when the Romanian left?' Piccolo asked.

'About eleven thirty.'

Piccolo held the receipt out to Carpi, pointing out the date and time: *23 December, 22:15.*

'Could you find something more believable?'

The manager turned red in the face. He swore underneath his breath and went back to the till.

Then she asked the waiter, 'Did you see her to the door?'

'I saw her leave. She had a raincoat that was too long for her – it touched the ground.'

Ramona had lent it to her. Nadia didn't own a coat.

'And did you see which way she went?'

'No, she stopped just outside. She looked around, as if thinking about where to go. Then she nodded to someone and turned left towards Piazza del Popolo.'

Corvu was worried about Balistreri. After the Samantha Rossi business and the different opinions over the travellers' camps, now there was also Colajacono. The possible indictment of a deputy commissario of police, one who was extremely popular with his colleagues and among the local population, was going to be a thorny issue.

He had checked and everything was confirmed. On 24 December the four Romanian employees had left Marius Travel and arrived at Casilino 900 a little after six. But Hagi had stopped by his home to pick up presents for the children. Same for Colajacono. In both men's alibis, if there was any point in speaking of an alibi, there was a gap of an hour – enough time to pick Nadia up from Via di Torricola.

Corvu was dissatisfied though. Investigative work was undertaken with one per cent intuition and ninety-nine per cent sheer bloody analytic drudgery. You could only develop an intuition on the basis of analysis, and the facts were so damned few.

At ten o'clock he was told that the Ukrainian prostitute who had seen the vehicle had arrived. Corvu had permission to use Balistreri's office instead of his little glass cubicle when he had to make an impression on anyone brought in for questioning.

The girl was slender, petite, with a lively little face that was both kind and make-up free under straight black hair with purple streaks. She looked even younger than her twenty years.

'What's your name?' Corvu felt a little embarrassed. He had been expecting a slut and she was more like a schoolgirl.

'Natalya. And yours?'

Suddenly taken aback by the confidential manner, Corvu blushed and stammered 'Graziano', keeping his unattractive surname to himself.

He offered her the armchair in front of the desk and sat down in the one next to it. He didn't want to make her feel ill at ease by taking Balistreri's swivel chair.

'How long have you been in Italy, Natalya?'

'Only two months.'

'So how come you speak such good Italian?'

She smiled. A beautifully open smile. 'I've had an Italian boyfriend for three years. I came to Italy to see him.'

'And he makes you prostitute yourself?' asked Corvu, feeling uncomfortable as he did so.

She burst out laughing. She had clear green eyes and beautiful small white teeth. 'But I'm not a prostitute,' she protested, still laughing.

Corvu didn't like surprises. He blushed violently. 'So what were you doing at night on a street like that?'

'Graziano, I only went there that day and it wasn't night. I was there about two hours, then I went to work.'

Embarrassed by the casual use of his Christian name, Corvu looked for a diversion. 'And what work is that?'

'I'm a waitress in a snack bar. Breakfast, lunch and supper.'

'But what were you doing in Via di Torricola on December the 24th?'

'It was Christmas. I went to keep my cousin company for two hours. She was on her own until eight. Unfortunately, she does prostitute herself . . .'

'Weren't you frightened when she got in a car with a client and left you there on your own? Anything could have happened to you!'

'It only happened once for ten minutes. Luckily no one stopped. Anyway, we'd agreed that I'd play for time and would wait until she came back.'

Natalya was surprised by Corvu's obvious discomfort and concern.

'And in those ten minutes when you were alone a car came past with a missing headlight.' Corvu shuddered at the thought. Fate had spared Natalya and chosen Nadia.

'Yes. When I saw it coming up I was frightened. I thought it was going to stop for me but instead it slowed down, passed close by, then accelerated.'

'Do you remember the make of car?'

Natalya shook her head. 'No, it was dark. But I think I know the make. You see, my brother in the Ukraine sells used cars, and I don't know if I've seen it there or here in Italy . . .'

Now was the moment to show her what he could do. 'Natalya,

I have a computer programme with the bodywork of all makes of car: bonnets, doors, roofs, everything. Now we can sit down here, I'll show you them and you can pick out the ones most like it.'

She found this a great deal of fun. Without their realizing it, two whole hours went by. When the Gianicolo gun fired its noonday salute, they looked at each other like two schoolkids found smoking in the toilets.

'Oh my God, it's late. I have to go to work,' she said, looking sorry she had to go.

'But we're not even halfway through,' protested Corvu.

'OK. Look, Graziano, today I'm on till five, then I'm going to the hairdresser and I'll be free after that because it's the restaurant's evening closure. I can come back then and we can finish off the work. All right?'

'All right,' said Corvu immediately. Then, as she was leaving the room, he was struck by his usual misgivings. 'So long as your boyfriend doesn't get mad, Natalya.'

Have you gone crazy, Graziano? What the hell are you saying? Who do you think you are, Brad Pitt?

He blushed at his own audacity and then, closing the door sharply behind Natalya, barricaded himself in Balistreri's office.

While he caught his breath he heard her cheerful voice from the corridor.

'I don't have a boyfriend any more. See you later, Graziano.'

Corvu was overcome with embarrassment.

After the meeting with his team and the interview with Colajacono, Balistreri was even more out of sorts. He wanted a smoke, but was already one cigarette over his ration. He wanted a coffee, but his stomach was protesting against the idea.

In the meantime, Margherita announced that Pasquali expected him at one thirty sharp. And it certainly wasn't to offer him lunch.

Pasquali was an ascetic who didn't eat and did nothing but work. He needed a break. Margherita was busy with piles of paper and her computer.

'Can you help out with an investigation?'

She stared at him, clearly surprised, but made no objection.

'Of course, Dottore. I'm all yours.' She said it without looking at him.

Years earlier that 'I'm all yours' would have carried other meanings and consequences. These days the use of 'Dottore' irritated him a bit, but it was better that way. Only power could confer a certain charm on a human wreck of nearly sixty who needed to keep himself in check.

Having pondered these thoughts, he wondered if by chance he'd forgotten to take his antidepressants. This could have been a direct consequence of the depression. The sufferer can become self-destructive. The psychiatrist had mentioned this after Balistreri's last visit, while he was writing out a hefty cheque.

They went into his office and Balistreri closed the door. The wood was thin, so he could hear Nano's comment clearly.

'What's this turning into, a knocking shop? First you go off on the borrow of an Albanian queer, then Graziano gets friendly with some Ukrainian pro, and now the boss's screwing around with Margherita.'

Balistreri opened the door while Piccolo was already making a threatening move towards the inspector. He shot her a look and she went back to her seat. He called out to Coppola, who came over shiftily, his eyes lowered.

'Have you nothing to do, Coppola?'

'I'm meeting the girlfriend of that Senegalese guy at the Bella Blu in the gym where Camarà worked during the day.'

'All right, off you go. But regarding the observation you just made . . .'

Nano turned pale. 'Dottore, I'm really sorry.'

Balistreri calmed him down. 'Just curious, Coppola. I wanted to know about Corvu . . .'

Nano told him. 'I told you Corvu went with prostitutes, didn't I?' he rounded off triumphantly.

Balistreri already knew from Corvu's report that Natalya wasn't on the game. His look made Coppola take a step backwards. 'Please don't take advantage of my forgiving nature, Coppola,' he warned him.

He shut the door again and turned to Margherita.

'Margherita, I've a problem that perhaps a good-looking young woman like you can help resolve.'

Startled, she went bright red. The double entendre had been made on purpose, just to see her reaction.

Old games I no longer have any use for.

'It's to do with work, Margherita,' he explained, trying to reassure her. 'You have to imagine that you're a prostitute who works as a couple with a friend and is waiting for customers in a dark street.'

'As a couple? You mean they . . .' she asked him, still more disconcerted.

This conversation's becoming embarrassing; the girl's too awkward.

'When one of you gets into a customer's car the other one has to be there to make a note of the number plate,' he explained patiently.

Margherita calmed down. 'Ah, I get it. OK, Dottore, what do I have to do?'

'You and your friend are on a dark street at some distance from any housing. Only pairs of other prostitutes are around, the nearest about fifty metres away. One gets in with a customer and the other takes down the number.'

'Right. And then?'

'A car stops, your friend gets in. You get the number, they go off towards the little roads out in the fields. You're alone, you see the glow of the other girls' fires down the street. Two minutes go by. A car comes up with only one headlamp lit – the other one's broken. It pulls up and stops. What do you do?'

She looked at him a little uncertainly. 'I take my time. I start chatting while waiting for my friend to come back.'

'He's in a hurry, tells you to get in,' Balistreri insisted.

'I continue to play for time,' she repeated, not knowing what to say.

Not happy, Balistreri got up and pulled down the blinds. The room was now dark, lit only by the red pilot lights of the television and the telephone that glowed like tiny fires.

'Close your eyes, Margherita. Try to live out the scene if you want to be of help.'

She looked at him bewildered, then her innate docility and the desire to help overcame her fears. She closed her eyes and sank back into the armchair.

'Now think about it, Margherita. He's insistent. What's going to happen?'

She collapsed further into the chair. 'He gets out, drags me in.'

'No, if he gets out you'd scream and the others could see you and get suspicious. You get in of your own free will.'

In the dark Balistreri could hear the young woman's laboured breathing.

'He knows my name . . .' she whispered.

Balistreri nodded. 'Yes. He addresses you by name and invites you to get in. You go up to get a better look. The car's interior light comes on. Can you see him now, Margherita?'

Her breathing was heavier now, her voice stifled. 'Yes, I recognize him.'

'He smiles at you, beckons you to get in. You do get in. Why?'

'He's someone I trust,' she whispered, lying almost flat in the chair.

At this point Margherita wanted to open her eyes, but the desire to help Balistreri forced her to resist.

'I was waiting for him,' she added, as a tear welled up in the corner of her eye.

Balistreri's voice seemed to come to her from far away. 'He's promised you the world, hasn't he? And you know what he'll give you instead, don't you?'

Suddenly Margherita saw the face of her Latin teacher at school who'd invited her to take a ride. She let out a scream.

Five seconds later the door sprang open. Giulia Piccolo was there – five foot eleven of muscle ready for action. Corvu held her by the arm and was literally dragged into the room.

'Come in and close the door,' Balistreri commanded, calmly switching on the light.

Piccolo's face was grim, but Margherita had already calmed down. Balistreri put his hands on her shoulders. 'You were excellent, Margherita.'

While Piccolo couldn't see what was happening, Corvu was petrified by doubt. They had heard the scream, seen the blinds pulled down, Margherita in that state and now that ambiguous phrase.

Balistreri could read their doubts. Was it possible he'd fallen so low?

He brought them back to reality. 'Nadia recognized him and was waiting for him. It was all arranged.'

Afternoon

The gym was on the ground floor of an office block near Via Veneto. When Coppola arrived at the entrance to the Sport Center at one o'clock, several people could be seen through the windows working out on the equipment, weights and cycle machines. Others were dancing to deafening music around a large swimming pool.

Professionals, well-heeled women and some high-class villains, for sure.

Carmen was waiting for him. Like Camarà, she was of African descent. She wasn't good-looking, but had a trainer's well-developed body.

'I'm from Miami,' she said, introducing herself in decent Italian.

Coppola felt a sense of relief. His American English couldn't have withstood another test. She led him into a tiny cubicle that must have been her office. On the wall was a photo of her and a large-muscled black man standing in front of the gym.

'You were very good friends?' asked Coppola.

'We'd been together for three months,' she replied simply. 'Papa was a hoot, a real honey.'

'Was there anyone who could have held a grudge against him? A slight disagreement, some argument?'

Carmen shook her head. 'No, it was that terrible man with the motorbike, I'm certain of it. With no cause at all to—'

'We know that they'd had words just before. We have a witness, an American from Texas,' Nano added to give it more credibility.

'You don't say,' she added scornfully. 'A lying Texan, just like our President.'

'The witness states that they exchanged pretty heavy insults,' Coppola went on.

'That's not right. It was the motorcyclist who shouted "dickhead" to him and Papa told him to fuck off.'

'I'm sorry, how do you know this?'

'Because he called me immediately afterwards and told me about it. You see, we were in touch a lot that evening because Papa wasn't well – he'd caught a urinary infection because of me . . .'

Coppola had checked the phone records. There was a call Camarà made to Carmen's mobile at two fourteen, just after the altercation with the motorcyclist and just before he was found dead. A call that lasted two and a half minutes.

'What did he say exactly?'

'He called to reassure me how he was. He often had to pee, but he didn't have a temperature. I asked him if it was a quiet evening and he told me about this guy on a bike who had shouted out an insult for no reason, a strange guy—'

'There was no previous argument?'

'Papa said no.'

Nano went away with the renewed conviction that urinary infections were common among people of African descent. He was too distracted to notice the man watching him from the opposite pavement.

A little before one thirty Balistreri went up on foot to see Pasquali. He realized he was short of breath and decided he ought to cut out even his last few pathetic cigarettes.

'He's waiting for you in his office,' said Antonella. 'If you like, seeing as you're five minutes early, I can make you a decaf.'

From lover to sister, concerned about me and my dodgy ticker.

He beamed a grateful smile and accepted the offer.

When Balistreri entered, Pasquali was sitting at his imposing eighteenth-century desk. The little glasses on the end of his nose gave him the air of a calm intellectual, which suited him very well. He could have been a harmless retired teacher. Instead he was the Ministry of the Interior's most influential official.

'Take a seat,' he ordered without any opening courtesies. 'I have to be with the Undersecretary in ten minutes so I'll be brief. We don't like this business at all.'

He put an emphasis on the 'we' without making it clear who else he meant. The Chief of Police, Prefect, Minister of the Interior, his father . . . But the mention of the Undersecretary was not by chance. Balistreri said nothing.

Pasquali continued in his calm, subdued manner. 'It's out of the question for you to bring any kind of a charge against Deputy Commissario Colajacono. You have nothing against him. He sent away a Romanian prostitute who didn't know where another Romanian prostitute was. I mean, how can this be a crime? It's not even an oversight. It's nothing at all. Colajacono's highly respected by his colleagues and the local population.'

'And I imagine he's respected by the inhabitants of Casilino 900, or somewhat more than respected.'

'By pure coincidence you and Colajacono share the same opinion of Casilino 900.'

Balistreri shook his head. 'We don't share the same opinion at all. For Colajacono, dismantling it means the use of arrest, followed by a good hiding and forced expatriation.'

'And your view?'

'My concern is for the security of the citizen, not politics. It's a disgrace having these camps right in the middle of Rome; they're a time bomb waiting to go off. They should be transferred outside the city as soon as possible, to more dignified surroundings.'

'We need a political consensus for it, but we'll get one.'

'Politicians today are only concerned about the electoral implications of any question. On the left, as usual, they have no idea what to do. And on the other side they know only too well: procrastinate and let trouble brew, so in the meantime we have an increase in kidnapping, rape, and car theft by drunks who run people over. And perhaps with this tactic next year we can say goodbye to this mayor and one from the other side can take over.'

'This is simply fantasy politics, Michele. The truth is that this is a complex problem. We need time and a wide consensus in order to do as you suggest. We have to find where we can transfer them in agreement with the local mayors, and we need to construct new camps in accordance with European regulations. And the Roma also have to be willing. A forced transference would be frowned on by the Vatican and by the city corporation's current centre–left coalition.'

Of course, let's be patient until someone gets killed.

'Look,' continued Pasquali, attempting to placate him. 'Perhaps Colajacono's methods are sometimes heavy-handed. And you know that, as a policeman and as a Catholic, I don't agree with them. But you've nothing to charge him with.'

'He knew the Iordanescu girl and didn't tell us.'

'He denies this. And it's the word of a highly esteemed Deputy Commissario against that of a prostitute.'

'There's something else much more serious,' Balistreri went on. 'Ramona says that Colajacono wasn't at all surprised to find her outside the police station.'

'Precisely, Michele. Because he'd never seen her before.'

'Look, imagine for a moment that the Iordanescu girl's telling the truth and that they were already acquainted. Only for a moment. So what would you deduce from the fact that Colajacono wasn't surprised to see her there at daybreak on Christmas Day?'

Pasquali remained impassive and silent, only a slight frown betraying his concern. Then he pushed the thought away, as if it were a warning of bad weather at the weekend that he didn't want to believe.

'He didn't know her, Balistreri. End of story. Let's not open any doors that only lead to a brick wall.'

The switch to his surname signalled the end of the discussion. Taking his time, Pasquali smoothed his grey hair. 'There's another thing,' he said. 'There's the problem of Linda Nardi. We promised her the Iordanescu girl's statement today.'

'We can let her have it. There's nothing compromising in it.'

'I know. In fact, I authorize you to give it to her. But yesterday she asked me something else on the telephone in exchange for keeping quiet about the fight in the Torre Spaccata police station.'

And you didn't want to mention this in front of the Chief of Police. It must be a serious problem for you, then.

Pasquali looked out of the window towards the cupola on his beloved St Peter's as if searching for divine inspiration. 'She wants to know what we're hiding on Samantha Rossi.'

So now you're starting to worry about the R carved on the poor girl's back.

'All right, I'll see to it, Pasquali. I'll try to see her this evening.'

'I'm sure this Nardi woman will be happy to see you again – it's been so long since you last saw each other,' he concluded icily.

Corvu arrived immediately after lunch at ENT's head office situated in a handsome apartment in the city centre. Parquet floors, expensive carpets, photos of casinos, old pinball machines and period jukeboxes, a beautiful and elegant secretary.

Avvocato Francesco Ajello, the lawyer who was ENT's director and manager of the Bella Blu nightclub, was very different from what he had supposed. He looked nothing like the owner of a gambling den or even a gambler.

Instead, he was tall and well-dressed, hands manicured, hair recently cut, his face fresh from a beautician, his body trim from the gym, a wonderful tan from a sunlamp.

Behind him hung his degree certificate in law. On his modern desk were photos of a refined-looking blonde and a muscular adolescent. He was clearly a successful man with an aura of utmost respectability.

'We're sorry about our young employee,' he began contritely. 'To be killed like that over a pathetic argument. Of course, it's an everyday occurrence in the world we live in today.' He shot an apprehensive look at his son's photo.

'Of course, Avvocato. An unexpected occurrence, but unfortunately part of our modern world,' said Corvu.

They were interrupted by the arrival of the beautiful secretary. She had urgent papers to process, which Ajello signed quickly with his designer fountain pen. Then he turned to Corvu with an obliging air.

'So, what can I do for you?' he asked, taking a quick glance at the showy Rolex on his wrist.

'Well, I'd like to ask you some questions about Bella Blu and ENT. If you don't mind, that is.'

Ajello raised an eyebrow to show his slight surprise and a polite difference of opinion. 'I thought you would want to ask me about the night the young man was killed. I don't see where ENT comes into it.'

'The young man could have made enemies in his workplace, you know, either in the gym or in your place. I don't know . . . a customer mistreated at the entrance, or someone who lost a lot on the slot machines in the club, or—'

'Are you telling me this could have been something premeditated? The American tourist spoke of an argument with a motorcyclist.'

'At the moment we can't discount any hypothesis. If you could help me by clarifying what it is you do . . .'

'All right. ENT's a company formed in 2002 by a group of partners from various nightclubs, amusement arcades and gaming rooms. I own ten per cent, which I took over at the end of 2004 from the widow of the previous director, Sandro Corona, who had died a couple of months before.'

'Corona was the director when there was that trouble with the finance police?'

Ajello shrugged his shoulders. 'A trivial business, a fine for tax evasion. Slot machines had just been made legal. During a surprise check they found some that weren't officially linked up to the payment tool.'

'Which means you played on them without paying the tax,' Corvu clarified.

Ajello pulled a little face of disgust, as if mentioning tax evasion was the equivalent of uttering a vulgarity. 'Shall we say revenue that wasn't in the books?'

'Who are the partners holding the other ninety per cent?'

'I don't know them and I don't think they want to be known, otherwise they wouldn't use a trust company. I'm only in touch with their administrator.'

Sure, and without just cause no judge would force a trust company to reveal the names of its partners. And there's no link between ENT and Camarà's killing.

'All right. Now let's talk about the night Camarà was murdered. You were at the Bella Blu, were you?'

'Yes, there was a private function in one of the club's rooms. I arrived at the club about one thirty. I let the guests in at the back and took them to the room they'd booked.'

'You came from another club?'

'Yes, we have a nightclub in Perugia where there was another private party. I knew the person for whom they were holding the party. I blew out the candles on the cake at midnight and slipped away.'

'And in an hour and a half you were already in Rome?'

'I travel in the company plane. I couldn't do without it given the number of clubs in different cities I have to visit in an evening.'

'And later?'

'Later, about two thirty, I heard shouts. I rushed outside and found the American. And Camarà in a pool of blood. Then I called the police.'

Corvu had nothing more to ask him. He nodded to one of the photos on the desk. 'A fine young lad, that – my compliments.'

Ajello smiled at the photo with evident pride. 'Yes, it was actually

Fabio who introduced me to Camarà, who was his bodybuilding trainer at the gym.'

While he was on his way out, passing the secretary, Corvu saw a light on the phone come on. It was Ajello's private line.

The south wind had veered to the south-west and huge black clouds were filling the sky. It was still afternoon, but the shops had already switched on their lights. Balistreri went by bus to Casilino 900. Marius Hagi was waiting for him at the camp entrance. He was alone, as had been agreed with his lawyer Morandi.

Hagi was wearing a grey flannel shirt, corduroy trousers and a black woollen pullover. Despite the cold and damp he wore neither overcoat nor hat. His cough was more pronounced than ever.

Balistreri held out his hand.

'Good afternoon,' said Hagi without taking the offered hand. His attitude wasn't hostile but neither was it friendly.

'Thank you for coming, Signor Hagi – you know you're under no obligation. I wanted to have a little informal chat and take a tour of the camp with you.'

Casilino 900 had existed for more than thirty years and housed about seven hundred people, mostly women and children: Romanians, Macedonians, Bosnians, Kosovars, Montenegrins. They went in by the main gate, beside which a police car was parked. Between the containers and makeshift huts, the camp's unmetalled roads were full of muddy puddles and strewn with rubbish and organic refuse.

The panorama offered nothing more than mounds of waste, washing lines and skeletons of cars. There were no connections to water or gas supply. Some of the huts were linked by homemade cable connections hooked up to an electricity supply of dubious provenance. In others you could see the lights of flickering candles in the middle of all kinds of inflammable materials. Public hygiene was served by Portaloos and the overall smell was a combination of waste and urine. While they were walking among the huts, Hagi and Balistreri were surrounded by children, adults, and stalls – selling things more or less fished out of wheelie bins around Rome, or else lifted from someone's bag. The children were playing with a ball, chasing after each other between the puddles, smiling and shouting.

Beyond the confines of the camp you could see the dump where the remains of Samantha Rossi's tortured body had been found. Behind the dump at the time had been a small unofficial squatters' camp, since cleared, where the three Romanians had been discovered with Samantha's bracelet.

Hagi caught the direction of Balistreri's gaze and his train of thoughts.

'You'll release them after a few years for good conduct. In my day in Romania they would have been impaled.'

Balistreri wanted to tell him that there could be more of such animals among those Hagi was protecting, but he was there to talk about Nadia, not Samantha Rossi.

'We try to be a civilized country, Signor Hagi.' He said it without much conviction, a conditioned reflex of the institution he represented.

'Look, Balistreri, the severity of justice is a measure of civilization. You're not civilized, only cowardly. Your tolerance is based only on the need for care workers, prostitutes and people to pick your fields of tomatoes. If they weren't of any use to you, you'd take any immigrants who stepped out of line and nail them to crosses along the road like they did in Ancient Rome.'

While Hagi led him through the huts, Balistreri noticed that dozens of eyes were watching them. Word must have got around that he was a policeman. Hagi felt his unease.

'You're safe here, don't worry.'

'Because I'm with you?'

'No, because no one's stupid enough to lay hands on a policeman inside the camp.'

At that moment an old Roma woman came up with two steaming tin mugs, which she offered to Hagi and Balistreri. They thanked her and sipped the tea. Hagi was smoking all the time, lighting a fresh cigarette from the stub of the last, despite the fact that he was wracked by coughing. His ascetic face was very pale, but his black eyes were dark coals below his thick eyebrows. The dark rings under his eyes accentuated his Mephistophelian look.

They stopped near a caravan a little better maintained than the rest. Someone had written the number 27 on it in felt tip.

'Let's go in,' suggested Hagi. 'This is where Adrian and Giorgi live.'

Behind the caravan there was a lightweight motocross bike chained to a bench. Inside it was bare, but not dirty as one might have expected from the outside. They sat down on the only chairs beside a small painted table that was now covered in rust.

'Your good little boys will be released tomorrow, Signor Hagi.'

'If you'll bear with me, I'd like to tell you something.'

Balistreri lit his fourth cigarette of the day. 'Be happy to hear it.'

Hagi began to tell his story, interspersed with bouts of harsh coughing.

'I'm forty-six years of age. I was born in Galati near the Black Sea. My brother Marcel and I were already orphans by the time I was twelve and he was sixteen. We moved to Costanta on the Black Sea where we both found work in the port as stevedores. We slept in a shed there. We were, as you would say, good little boys.'

'With a difficult childhood behind you . . .'

'Now comes the worst part. My brother was a great goalkeeper,' Hagi went on. 'At the beginning of 1978 he was invited to play for a first-division team in Bucharest. They gave him a small salary that allowed him to take me along and he sent me for maths lessons with the team's accountant. One morning in May 1978, in the final of the national championship, Marcel saved a penalty in the last minute and his team won the cup against the team that was managed by Ceausescu's son.'

Hagi paused, struck by yet another bout of heavy coughing, then he continued.

'Two bastards from the secret police came to the room we lived in and broke his fingers one by one. Then Marcel did something crazy. He went to the police and reported them. A few days later, when I came in, the room was turned upside down, blood all over the place. They'd cut off his hands and Marcel was lying there, having bled to death.'

Hagi stopped a moment to light another cigarette, then went on with his story.

'I was saved by pure chance, but they did look for me and wanted to do away with me. I was nineteen and had nothing to lose. My friends knew someone in Krakow and I went there. I was lucky. I met Alina. She was only sixteen and an orphan, living with her uncle, a priest who'd worked with Wojtila and ran an orphanage. When the Pope invited him to Rome six months later, Alina and I married and left with him. We arrived in April 1979 and Alina found work immediately thanks to her uncle.'

'And you became a businessman, exploiting the fact of your knowledge of Eastern Europe.'

'I knew very little about anything, but immediately discovered that Italians like Eastern European girls a lot. They would set off for Warsaw, Belgrade and Budapest with suitcases full of nylons, jeans and beauty products. I used my contacts with friends in Poland and started to organize these pleasure trips. There was nothing illegal – I simply put the two parties together to their mutual satisfaction. Then I opened bars and restaurants in the area where all the Poles live. I became a wealthy immigrant and respected member of the community.'

'Italy is very hospitable. You've been happy in our country?'

Hagi thought for a moment, as if the question were a difficult one.

'Italy's made me a rich man, Balistreri. But it's because of Italy that I lost the thing most precious to me. When Alina died in 1983, she was only twenty.'

Balistreri had read all about it in the dossier. A moped accident. They happened every day. It was one of the most common causes of death for a young person in Rome. But why did Hagi blame Italy for his wife's death?

'Cardinal Lato, who helped you to come here, made a statement. He maintained that Alina was running away from you when she had the accident.'

Something gleamed behind Hagi dark eyes. 'Alina was like a daughter to him. He was driven mad with grief.'

'In his statement, Cardinal Lato said that you beat her.'

Again that slight shudder like the shock wave of a distant earthquake. Then Hagi replied coldly. 'The statement was withdrawn of his own free will after a month, when Monsignor Lato calmed down and reason prevailed over grief. And now enough about that – it's all beside the point.'

'All right. What happened to you after the death of your wife?'

'I went on with my business activities for six years, but with no enthusiasm for them. Then in 1989, when Romania was freed from that swine Ceausescu, I sold everything I had in Italy and went back there, where I used my savings to purchase real estate that's now worth ten times more than I paid. I've got bars, restaurants, estate agencies and travel agencies in Bucharest and go there twice a year.'

'You sold up everything in Italy?'

'I have only a little house where I live, some apartments, the Bar Biliardo and the travel agency Marius Travel. All of which I use to give a home and work to my fellow countrymen. I help many young people settle into the community as well as the Roma gypsies that you keep herded together in travellers' camps and whom your police treat like animals.'

'Do you know a Deputy Commissario Colajacono?' Balistreri asked.

Hagi grimaced and suffered a bout of coughing. He immediately lit another cigarette.

'I know who he is. Everyone in here's acquainted with him, some of them to their own cost.'

'You've never seen him yourself?'

'Yes, once here in the camp. They were carrying out a search and found a working moped in the middle of the scrap heaps of cars, and he wanted to know who'd stolen it. It was the moped Adrian had before the motorbike outside – he bought it for cash from a scrap dealer.'

'What happened?'

'I told Adrian to go and explain that it was his. He and Giorgi went out, while I watched and listened from this window here. Colajacono and another guy brought them into the caravan, and I hid in the cupboard. Colajacono wanted to see the registration document, which Adrian didn't have, of course. Then the other policeman said it was stolen, and that they would take it away and arrest him.'

'Can you remember this policeman?'

'Yes, he was short, fat and balding . . . He asked Adrian to hand over the keys to the moped and Adrian said "Like fuck I will . . ." and the guy whacked him on the shoulder with a rubber truncheon. They beat both of them. Then they took the keys and confiscated the moped without making a report or anything. He found it again in pieces outside the camp. That's how I know about Colajacono.'

'Colajacono's the man who took the Iordanescu girl's missing person statement about Nadia.'

It seemed as if Hagi had completely lost interest in the conversation. He said nothing.

'Yesterday I asked you if you had any opinion about Nadia's disappearance. You think that Mircea—'

A light flashed in Marius Hagi's eyes. 'My employees know that I would be highly offended if they did anything serious behind my back.'

You happen to be a benefactor of the destitute, but it's not wise to rub you up the wrong way.

'I'd like to ask you one last thing about your wife Alina.'

Hagi stared at him in silence. He said nothing. In the end he got up. The conversation was over.

Coppola went by tram. He was early for his appointment with Sandro Corona's widow. He used the time to look in the elegant district's shop windows and lingered in front of a shoe shop. There were several extremely smart pairs with significantly raised heels that were well disguised. He looked at the price labels and turned pale. And yet the shop was full of people trying items on and making purchases. The most he could have afforded were the heels alone.

The glass reflected a passing face. He had a fleeting feeling of unease. He continued his stroll, stopping in front of other windows. Nothing came to mind. It was only just before he arrived at the front door of Signora Corona's apartment block that he placed the face. It was the young lad who had been sitting in a corner of the tram.

He sent Balistreri a text message, informing him that someone was tailing him, adding a question mark out of discretion.

The concierge of the apartments where Corona's widow lived was a particularly suspicious type. Coppola's appearance made the man even more aggressively so and Coppola was forced to show his card. At that point he decided to take advantage of his official role and ask for some information.

'Did the lady live here with her husband?'

'No, she bought it six months ago. The husband was already dead.'

'Does she live by herself?'

The concierge looked at him askance. 'I mind my own business. Anyway, she lives by herself.'

Ornella Corona was a package – a de luxe model, just like the costly apartment she'd bought. She was much younger than he'd imagined. Her late husband was nearly sixty. She could have been forty but looked thirty-five at most. Her hands and feet were well taken care of, she was long and lean, her muscles toned, her legs sheathed in clinging black leggings. Her eyes were bored and distant. The photos on the wall showed her, much younger, on a catwalk – modelling clothes by Valentino, Yves Saint Laurent, Dior. It couldn't have been easy for a man like Corona to provide for a woman of that taste.

She showed Coppola into a living room full of expensive furniture. 'Would you like anything to drink? A liqueur? Fruit juice?'

Nano went for the fruit juice. He was uncomfortable. He couldn't take his eyes off her and was certain she was well aware of it. Luckily she sat down, sipping a grapefruit juice. 'What can I do for you, Inspector?'

'A young man's been killed at the Bella Blu, a nightclub run by ENT.'

'I know all about that. I saw poor Camarà at the Sport Center – they've got excellent facilities for spinning.'

Coppola looked at her in surprise. 'So you knew Signor Camarà?'

'I didn't know him – I'd seen him and knew who he was. Then a few days ago I read that he'd been stabbed during an argument outside the Bella Blu.'

'But you knew he worked there?'

Ornella Corona had a way of crossing her legs that was distracting, to say the least. She was wearing a flashy wristwatch, its black face a winking feminine eye with long eyelashes.

'He wasn't working when my husband was there, then at the end of 2004 I sold my shares in ENT and since then I haven't had anything to do with the Bella Blu.'

'You sold them to Avvocato Ajello?'

She pulled a slight face. 'Yes, to him. Besides, who else could I have sold them to?'

'And you bought this apartment with the proceeds?' said Coppola, the words slipping out.

For the first time it looked as if she was paying attention to Nano. She thought about it, then made up her mind. 'I suppose it's pointless asking you how you know I've only recently bought this apartment. But I can ask you what this has to do with Camarà's death.'

'To be honest, I don't think it has anything to do with it, and forgive me for mentioning it. So you would also rule out the possibility that your husband knew Camarà?'

'I would rule it out in the most absolute terms,' she said in irritation. Then she went back to being more cordial. 'And can't you tell me why these questions about me and my husband? Perhaps I'd feel more comfortable and could be of more help if I knew.'

I can't think straight for this woman. Come on, Coppola, buck up and don't make a mess of it.

'Look, we're simply going into the background of Signor Camarà's place of work, where the crime took place.'

'But I read that there was an argument with one of the clientele . . .'

'There was an argument, certainly. And it could have been with a previous employee at the Bella Blu – who knows? Do you remember if your husband ever spoke to you of anyone particularly violent there?'

'Well, there was the barman, Pierre. I believe he's been in prison,' she admitted readily. She got to her feet to pour herself some more grapefruit juice and Coppola found himself with his eyes less than a couple of feet from her exquisite posterior. He went red in the face and caught her swift glance in the mirror. He blushed even more. Caught out like an adolescent reading *Playboy* in the bathroom. She sat down again.

'I think my husband would have left ENT anyway, even if he hadn't had that accident.'

'He would have left ENT anyway, even if he hadn't had that accident,' Nano repeated, still swooning over the mystical vision he'd received.

She went on. 'He was earning little compared with the trouble he was getting, including that from the partners.'

'Do you know them?' Nano asked in a gleam of recovered lucidity.

'No. Perhaps I did happen to hear one of them on the telephone. There was a call to our home number. The man said my husband's mobile was off, so would I contact him and tell him to get to Monte Carlo that same evening. He didn't say please or thank you, only to pass the message on. I objected that it was already five o'clock in the afternoon and he said that was why they had a private aeroplane. Then he put the phone down.'

'Was he Italian?'

'Yes, he was Italian. A man used to giving orders.'

'Was your husband angry?'

'More than angry about having to go to Monte Carlo. It seemed to me he couldn't understand why they'd called the home number. It had never happened before and from then on he began to complain about the job, saying there was too much pressure from them.'

'In September 2004 your husband was hit by a truck while he was on a zebra crossing.'

This time she didn't ask what this had to do with anything. 'The traffic police said that the driver possibly wasn't even aware at the time of having knocked him down. Anyway, there was a very long and interminable investigation.'

She sighed in a melodramatic fashion, crossing her legs in the opposite direction, and leaned forward towards Coppola to pick up a cigarette case from the table. The extremely low neckline of her T-shirt delivered the coup de grâce to Nano. He realized how little self-control he had.

He took his leave in a hurry. As soon as he was out of the building he contacted Balistreri. He gave a meticulous account of the facts, at the same time omitting any description of Ornella Corona.

'Coppola, the investigation into Corona's death is odd. I've only had a glance at the date it opened and closed. It took twice as long as normal. Any idea why?' asked Balistreri.

'I couldn't get any more information, Dottore. I'll go to the traffic department and ask.'

'What's Signora Corona like?' Coppola wondered if he'd somehow given himself away.

'Nothing out of the ordinary – a widow,' he said hesitantly. He thought he heard a little laugh.

'Are you sure?' asked Balistreri, admiring a photo of her in the folder they'd delivered to him.

'Of course, Dottore. Nothing special.'

'Are you sure? Quite sure? Shall I come and check?'

Silence. Then Nano gave in. 'She'd make you go weak at the knees, Dottore.'

Balistreri laughed. 'One last thing, Coppola, from a purely investigative point of view: top or bottom?'

This came from one of Nano's vulgar remarks for men only about a very beautiful woman under investigation. Balistreri had redeemed the remark from its vulgar meaning, using it to refer to the character of the woman under investigation and thus giving it true investigative weight.

Nano relaxed. He was very pleased that a noted expert, albeit an aging one like Balistreri, had faith in his judgement in this field.

'Bottom, Dottore, one hundred per cent. A woman who'd let you do anything you wanted while she filed her nails, and then, when you'd finished, she'd start to paint them. She even has a watch that winks at you.'

Seeing that Balistreri was in his office and he couldn't borrow it, Corvu had polished and tidied up his little glass cubicle before Natalya arrived. While he was cleaning the wall with a cloth, Margherita came up to him. They had become friends from day one, which wasn't difficult with Corvu. She stepped into the little office and leaned against the door.

'Graziano, look,' she began, embarrassed. 'I wanted to tell you something.'

Without stopping his cleaning, he gave her an encouraging smile.

'I'm all ears, Margie. Whatever I can do to help . . .'

'It's not about me, it's about you.' She was even more embarrassed.

Corvu carried on regardless, now dusting his computer keyboard. 'About me? You're worried about me?'

'No, no,' she said quickly, remembering how touchy Corvu was on the subject. 'I'm not worried. But I wanted to speak to you about the girl who's about to pay you a visit.'

Surprised, Corvu stopped dead. 'About Natalya? Why?'

'Well, I don't really know how to say this. To us . . . that is, to me . . . I've seen . . . no, it seemed . . .'

'Look, Margie, there's no need to worry.'

'But she's a . . . that is, she . . . I mean, she works as a . . .'

Corvu explained the misunderstanding and Margherita began to laugh. Then her manner changed. In an instant she was beaming, full of enthusiasm, as if Corvu had just announced he was about to be married.

'That's wonderful, wonderful. She likes you a lot, Graziano.'

Corvu blushed violently and began to stammer in embarrassment. 'What d'you mean? How d'you know?'

'I'm a woman. I saw how she greeted you. And she told you she no longer had a boyfriend. When a girl says that to a man it means that she likes him.'

Corvu went red as a pepper and brooded in silence.

'However, you have to know what to do.'

'Margie, for goodness' sake, you're getting me all agitated,' said Corvu, dropping into his Sardinian accent, which only happened when he was stressed.

'I've got a brilliant idea,' Margherita exclaimed, and ran off. She came straight back with a framed photo of a good-looking blonde girl who looked like Natalya. 'This is my sister. I keep it on my desk.'

'So? What's her photo got to do with it?' Corvu was getting more and more disturbed.

'We'll put this here,' she said, placing it on a corner of Corvu's desk and looking approvingly at the effect.

'Are you crazy?' he burst out, grabbing the frame and looking anxiously at his watch. Natalya could arrive at any moment.

Margherita grasped the frame and pulled it from one side, Corvu from the other. Balistreri came in at the same moment. 'What's going on here?'

Corvu's face was burning. 'Nothing, Dottore. Margherita was—'

She interrupted him. Quickly she explained the situation to Balistreri, who listened with growing interest.

'Corvu, I order you to put that frame on your desk,' Balistreri commanded at last.

For the first time since they had known one another, Corvu protested, his accent ever more pronounced. 'But you can't, Dottore. This is something private—'

'All right,' said Balistreri. 'Then there's no questioning of Natalya. When you saw her before, you got nowhere. You may be able to use a computer, but you know nothing about female psychology. I'll have her questioned tomorrow by a real expert in the field.'

Corvu turned pale. 'Who?' he asked, full of anxiety.

'What time does Mastroianni get in tomorrow?' Balistreri asked Margherita maliciously.

At that moment, Natalya knocked on the glass. Corvu was white as a sheet.

Balistreri gave her a friendly greeting and ushered her in while Margherita held onto the frame in her hand. Natalya was prettier than ever. She had blonde highlights in her hair and was wearing the make-up of a young girl.

'Please sit down,' said Balistreri. 'We've almost finished. Dottor Corvu tells me you've been a great help.'

'It's good to help the police when they're so kind.' Natalya shot a smile at Corvu, who went from white to red.

'Excuse me, Dottor Corvu,' said Margherita, placing the frame in clear view on the desk. 'I replaced the broken glass on it. I won't disturb you any more.' Turning to Natalya, she explained, 'That's Dottor Corvu's fiancée, who died a year ago.'

To avoid Corvu going into a faint, Balistreri quickly distracted Natalya's attention. 'Now, young lady, could you tell me everything about when you saw the car with the single headlamp.'

The young lady was a little surprised by this recent succession of events. She stared at the photo of Margherita's sister and Corvu almost collapsed on the chair.

At last she spoke. 'As I was saying to Graziano, I was alone at that moment, my cousin was working. It had already been dark for quite a while, and I thought it was a motorbike. When it came up to me it slowed down as if to stop and I realized it was a car, then it accelerated away and was around the bend in seconds . . .'

You didn't tell me, Corvu, that it slowed down so much. And you didn't wonder why?

'I suppose you didn't get a good look at the driver.'

'No, but he was wearing a beret and dark glasses,' Natalya replied readily.

Balistreri looked at Corvu. His face was so mortified that Balistreri could only think of saying goodbye and leaving the room to save him from embarrassment.

If I hadn't popped in here by chance I'd never have known. Look what a bloody disastrous effect a young girl can have on this chump here! Beret and dark glasses in a car in the dark.

Evening

Balistreri had almost an hour to spare. It was enough to get him to Trastevere on foot. He felt the need to walk, and all the better through the steady drizzle with which the year 2005 was taking leave of Rome and its inhabitants.

He went down Via Nazionale. The shops were about to close and customers were leaving, while restaurants were opening and filling up. Money was shifting from clothes to food.

While he was crossing the Tiber – from the dark city centre lowering its rolling shutters, over to Trastevere lit up by its restaurants – his mood darkened, as it did every time he put the river between himself and the capital's temporal power and came closer to the Vatican's spiritual one.

The one whose judgement no one escapes.

The doubt had been growing slowly inside him since 1982, inexorably and against his will. It was the revenge of the Catholic education that he had rejected as an adolescent.

He suddenly found himself in front of her. Linda Nardi's profound and distant beauty was as usual equalled by her total lack of interest. The contrast was as irresistible as it was permanent.

It's as if she were a nun from an enclosed order temporarily visiting the outside world.

Balistreri had purposely booked a table in a pizzeria crowded with young students and families. A lot of people, nothing classy. She showed no signs of dissatisfaction.

They ordered a pizza. He allowed himself a beer and she told him she didn't drink. Balistreri now understood that those costly wines had only been ordered to teach that loudmouth Colicchia a lesson.

For a while they talked of nothing much – Christmas, purchases, presents. It was perfunctory conversation that interested neither of them, but he wanted to maintain a certain distance before speaking of other things. And, very politely, she allowed him to do so.

Then Balistreri began to tell her about developments in Nadia's case, only the barest details. But she seemed even less interested.

It was very hot in the pizzeria. At one point Linda took off the long jacket she was wearing over her grey trousers. Her breasts were hardly noticeable under her blouse, but Balistreri was unable to resist the habitual glance he gave them under those circumstances. And then it appeared: the vertical line that divided her forehead.

They were quiet for a long time, until the arrival of the *tiramisù*. Only in front of the pudding did Linda relax again, taste it, and give the waiter a satisfied smile, asking him to pass on her compliments to the chef. After a while the chef came out in person. He was a young Egyptian man.

'You are very kind, Madam,' he said humbly.

'And you're an excellent chef.' She got up and put her arms around him.

Balistreri watched with some surprise.

Unselfish kindness, tenderness towards the weakest. A distant memory.

Stunned and frightened by the thought, he fought it off almost angrily.

He waited for her to sit down. 'There's another matter you want to speak to me about, is that right?'

'Only if you're willing to – you're under no obligation.' The politeness was almost irritating.

'Look, let me thank you for the phone call to Pasquali. You really helped me. I gave you the information on Colajacono and the Iordanescu girl's report, and I can guarantee you'll be the first—'

'I'm not here to speak of any future crimes.' She said it simply, with no aggression.

You're not interested in the next crime. You want to speak about the one before. But I don't.

'All right. But don't expect anything important you can write about.'

'I only want you to tell me why you're not convinced.'

The question took him by surprise. The feeling of not being in control of the situation was fascinating and at the same time unpleasant.

'What are you talking about?' he asked sharply.

'Those three Roma boys and the fourth man they spoke about.'

'What makes you think I'm not convinced?'

'Because you can't stop thinking about it and it shows. Regret isn't a positive quality in the character, but sometimes it's the only way to the truth.'

He didn't want to engage in a conversation of this kind, even less with a woman who appeared to be able to read his mind.

'Dottoressa Nardi, there's been no injustice in that case, except for what happened to Samantha Rossi. Whoever's in prison is guilty, without any doubt.'

'But perhaps not all the guilty are in prison.'

'The matter's closed, it's over.' He felt the doubt echoing in his own voice.

'And the fourth man?' she asked.

Don't get yourself involved in this business, Balistreri. This woman has things in her head you don't fully understand. Things that could cause you a great deal of harm.

'I'll get the bill,' said Balistreri ill-temperedly.

She appeared to be thinking a moment, then said softly, 'And if he carves up another girl?'

She wasn't expressing a challenge or an accusation, only a concern, and even appeared apologetic about making him feel embarrassed by the question.

Balistreri visibly lost it. He was a little frightened at himself, hearing his own voice before having thought what he was going to say.

'I'll find the person who passed this information on to you and, believe me, I'll do everything to destroy them.'

'Then the best of luck, Dottor Balistreri.' There was no challenge or trace of arrogance in her voice.

As if I'd made her a promise, not a threat.

Linda Nardi got up, left money for the bill and made her way out.

An analytical appraisal of the risks and advantages should have put her off, but Giulia Piccolo wasn't Graziano Corvu. They had nothing to hand to ask for a search warrant of Mircea and Greg's flat before they were released.

Rudi wasn't at all happy about accompanying her. But he was necessary for various reasons. First, he lived in the flat, and if they surprised them there she was simply accompanying him and nothing more. Second, he knew the building well. Third, Rudi was scared of the place, therefore he was hiding something.

She let him smoke as they drove there in the car. 'Don't worry, we're going there to pick up your things and take them to my place. Ten minutes and we'll be away.'

'What if someone comes in?'

'Mircea, Greg and the other two are being held until tomorrow. Don't worry.'

'Why don't you call a couple of uniformed guys . . .' he suggested.

She suddenly realized that Rudi was afraid for her safety as well, because she was a woman among a bunch of beasts.

'I have my pistol,' she smiled reassuringly, showing the holster.

The policeman they had put on guard on the street confirmed that plenty of people had come and gone in the building, but no Marius Hagi. Piccolo had wanted to put him on the landing outside, but Balistreri had said no.

It was already late and only a few windows were still lit. They went in using Rudi's keys. The flat was completely dark, no light coming in from the outside.

'Didn't we leave some of the blinds up yesterday?' recalled Rudi fearfully.

Piccolo took the pistol from its holster and signalled to him to stand still close to the door of the first room. She moved silently along the hall with the pistol in her hand. When she came to the third door into Ramona and Nadia's room she quickly switched on the light. It was all upside down: mattresses ripped open, drawers pulled out – even the radiator had been wrenched from the wall.

Slowly she turned to Rudi's room. She stopped on the threshold and suddenly switched on the light. The mess was even greater – all of Rudi's things had been scattered about the room. She heard the boy's fearful breathing coming from behind her. 'Stay here in the hall,' she whispered to him. The doors of the wardrobe were closed. She went into the room and approached it, pistol in hand. As she put out her hand to open it she heard a cry from Rudi, then a muffled thump and the door slammed. She rushed back into the hall and almost fell over him. She had a moment of doubt, then bent down. Rudi was groaning, his hands cupping a bloody nose.

She rushed to the window and called to the policeman. 'Someone's coming out – stop him!'

Then she ran down the staircase. The policeman looked at her, incredulous. 'No one's come out at all, Dottoressa.'

Piccolo went back in followed by the policeman. 'The cellars,' she shouted, pointing to the staircase that went down to them. 'You stay here to watch the main door.'

'But Dottoressa . . .' he objected. She was already on her way down the stairs.

You're crazy, going into an apartment block full of sleeping families with a pistol in your hand. And what if the guy also had a pistol? Would you blaze away in there like a 'Gunfight at the OK Corral'?

The cellar was a real labyrinth. She switched on the light and followed the passages all the way round. Nine floors, four apartments per floor, thirty-six storerooms. Thirty-six locked metal doors. He could be behind any one of them. The light, on a timer, went out, and she couldn't find the switch. In the dark she felt the sweat trickling down her neck. She performed a breathing exercise her karate teacher had taught her. Her anger was stronger than her fear. The bastard was in here, a few metres away.

She waited in absolute silence. Several minutes went by. The policeman called to her from the top of the stairs. She made no reply. Soon after a gust of cold air travelled along the passage. Piccolo held the pistol in her two hands and released the safety catch. In the dark and total silence she heard the rustling of footsteps. They were coming towards her, rather than moving away. She aimed the pistol in that direction.

'Stop where you are and put your hands up,' she called out, her voice wavering slightly.

'Dottoressa, it's me.' The policeman found the switch and put the lights on. He stood stock still at the sight of Piccolo pointing the pistol directly at him.

Another moment and I'd have fired at him. You're crazy. Now stay calm.

They went up to the ground floor, the policeman in shock. Piccolo called Balistreri. 'Are you eating?'

'No, I'm on foot on my way home from Trastevere. What's up?'

She told him everything briefly, including the fact that she had been about to shoot a fellow policeman. Balistreri listened to her without interrupting.

It's about time this dear girl grew up.

'Piccolo, the person driving the car was wearing a beret and dark glasses.' It was a stark message to make her desist from her useless stupidity.

She said nothing, then she angrily ended the call and switched her mobile off. Rudi was coming down the staircase holding his nose, his face and pullover covered in blood.

She put an arm around his shoulders and took him to the car while the uniformed man stayed on guard.

'You'll have to wait for me a while, Rudi. Stay in the car and stop the bleeding with these.' She handed him a pack of tissues.

'Be careful, Dottoressa, and don't worry about me.' She gave him a quick hug and got out of the car. She opened the boot, took out a canvas bag and went back into the building.

'You can go outside again now,' she said to the policeman. 'Check on anyone who comes out. Call straight away for a colleague to help you.'

Without another word she went back down into the cellars. From the bag she took out a jemmy and a pair of steel cutters. A couple of minutes per door.

Half an hour later, Balistreri arrived. He was out of breath and panting a little, while she was almost halfway through her task, perspiring heavily, her make-up mingling with the sweat and tears trickling down her face. He looked at the disaster area but made no comment.

'I have still twenty to go,' she said in a rage.

'There's no point,' he said gently. 'He's not here in the cellars.'

'Then according to you where the sodding hell is he?' she hissed.

Balistreri nodded up above. 'In order to have cellar space you have to have an apartment.'

She looked at him, nonplussed. Then she let the cutters fall and collapsed on the floor, bitter tears of frustration coursing down her cheeks. Breaking open the doors of thirty-six storerooms was one thing, but searching thirty-six apartments without a warrant was something else entirely.

'However,' said Balistreri with a smile as he picked up the cutters, 'a robbery is more believable if we open them all.'

He gave her a little pat on the head and immediately regretted it as being too affectionate.

You'd be a real disaster as a father.

Piccolo then went back to breaking open the storeroom doors. When she had them all open, Balistreri told the policeman to go home and make no report until his commissario had spoken to Balistreri.

He asked Piccolo for a lift back to the office. Rudi was asleep in the passenger seat, so Piccolo fastened his seatbelt and Balistreri got in the back.

'I know this district's commissario – he's a good man. I'll sort things out,' he said to calm her down.

They spoke no more until they arrived. Before he slipped into the main door, she quickly mumbled, 'Thanks.'

He imagined no one would be up on the third floor, it was almost midnight and he was exhausted, but as soon as he entered the corridor he heard giggles.

Then came Corvu's voice, his Sardinian accent at its most pronounced. 'But we'll find it, we'll find it.'

Balistreri peered round the corner. Corvu and Natalya were in his little cubide in front of two empty pizza boxes. They were sitting in front of the computer with their heads together and cans of beer in their hands.

When he tapped on the glass Corvu leaped up and the can fell into his lap, spilling beer over a crucial spot.

'We were, we were . . .' he stuttered, trying awkwardly to wipe away the foaming beer.

Natalya began to laugh, then she took out some tissues. 'Can you do it, Graziano?'

'Yes, better let Graziano clean himself off, unless we want to see him have an attack of something,' said Balistreri sarcastically.

When Corvu had regained his self-control, they went into Balistreri's office and sat down at the computer. There were several images of a car. Corvu started to explain.

'We began with reconstructing the rear that Natalya saw for a few seconds while the vehicle was driving away. We're almost certain it was white or grey, a light colour anyway.'

Balistreri stopped himself from asking why they'd accomplished so little in all this time. He was so happy for Corvu he didn't even want to admit it, even to himself.

First of all, he's not your son. Second, he'll never manage it.

All of a sudden he felt very tired.

'I'm shutting the computer down and we can all go beddy-byes,' said Balistreri.

Natalya pointed happily at the screensaver, where a young Balistreri was posed with a group of equally young fellow officers in front of his first police station.

'Oh, that's amazing!' she exclaimed.

Corvu's face immediately clouded over. Balistreri, who had no knowledge of his young deputy's jealous side, was embarrassed himself. Of course, in that photo he was young, perhaps handsome, but 'amazing' was pushing it a bit. Then Natalya moved closer to the screen and pointed her slender finger at the police car that could be seen.

'I'm positive that's it. I recognize it clearly from behind, with those long tail lights . . .'

Balistreri and Corvu looked at each other in astonishment, staring at the old model on the screen that was no longer in production: an Alfa Romeo Giulia GT.

Saturday, 31 December 2005

Morning

The search for the light-coloured Alfa Romeo Giulia GT 1300 with a broken headlamp began straight away, but the night of the 30th passed without any result.

Corvu had slept in Balistreri's office. Balistreri had given him permission to use it – hoping that Natalya would stay with Corvu – and had himself then gone home to sleep.

When Balistreri came back at seven, he found his deputy asleep on the worn sofa. Naturally, he was alone.

He went down to the bar and ordered a cappuccino-to-go in a glass and bought a still-warm doughnut. He went back up and put the hot cappuccino under the nose of Corvu, who woke instantly and dragged himself up in embarrassment.

'Dottore, I'm sorry, I couldn't manage it.' Balistreri put the cappuccino and doughnut down for him.

'There was an e-mail from Mastroianni in Romania,' said Corvu, biting into the doughnut. 'In 2002, before Hagi brought them to Italy, Mircea and Greg were acquitted of a charge of double homicide on the grounds of insufficient evidence and thanks to the best defence lawyer in the whole of Romania. Anyway, Mastroianni's on his way home now.'

'However,' he went on, a dab of crème and sugar on the end of his nose, 'I have gone through all the vehicle databases. Fortunately, there are only a few left in circulation. In the whole of Rome only fifty-two came up, a good twelve of which are in the name of non-EU nationals. As you know, it's a very old model but fast, and those people like that.'

'Have you got the owners' names and addresses?'

'Yes. Of course the records are possibly not up to date – there could have been changes of ownership still to be registered or not recorded at all. As you know, with vehicles that age they tend to save on the paperwork.'

'All right, check on them all by phone. But divide up the twelve foreign ones between you and Piccolo, Coppola and Mastroianni. And work in pairs, not alone. You need to do it before the fireworks go off for New Year.'

When he was alone, Balistreri turned on the radio and lit his first cigarette of the day. He took another gastro-protector pill so he could drink at the New Year party at Angelo Dioguardi's flat.

The mail with the press cuttings came in, and contained Linda Nardi's article. A front-page headline: *Samantha Rossi: Is the case closed?* The question mark was in colour. Below the headline was the girl's photograph, the one every Italian had known for months. A gleaming smile in front of a sailboat.

Reluctantly, he forced himself to read the article. No hint at all about the carved initial or the fourth man. The main point was all in the question that concluded the piece.

Are we looking at the chaotic fury of someone who lost control or the premeditated barbarity of someone in full control of themselves?

The question caught him off guard – which happened only rarely, yet always with this woman.

Fury or premeditation? Linda Nardi's question brought back a particular unease, something whose roots were sunk in well-hidden depths.

Piccolo came in punctually at seven thirty. Balistreri could sense a new disquiet in her that left him feeling anything but easy. He was hoping she would have calmed down with regard to the previous night, but that wasn't the case. On top of her anger there was a determination that was too personal, and experience had taught him that in that state you could a lot of damage.

'How's Rudi?' he asked her.

She gave a little smile. 'He's sleeping on my couch.'

He forced himself to find the right words. 'Piccolo, I don't want to intrude, but Rudi could . . . could . . .'

'He had an HIV test last week – he's fine. And if it'll make you any happier, you should know that we're not having sex,' she said, looking him in the eye.

Balistreri faltered. He was saved by his mobile ringing. 'Alberto, up already? You're not working today, are you?'

'No, we're off to the Maldives after lunch, the whole family. I wanted to wish you a Happy New Year.'

'You're taking the boys diving?'

'This year, yes. Have you read the papers yet?'

So that's what was worrying you . . .?

'I read them. I spoke to Linda Nardi yesterday. I thought she'd write something of the kind.'

'Linda Nardi thinks you're right to have doubts.'

'Alberto, I never expressed any doubt after the arrest of the three Roma. I did before we found them, and I was wrong.'

They both knew he didn't believe what he was saying.

'So why are you on antidepressants? Samantha Rossi died quickly, whether you were right or wrong. And yet you're positive you didn't get justice for her.'

'You're a believer, Alberto. You should understand that better than me.'

It was a gratuitous wicked comment dictated by frustration. But his brother pretended to take no notice.

'There's no antidepressant against regret, Mike. You can only repent, make a confession if you believe, and atone for it if you can.'

'I tried for many years, but it's not enough.'

'Mike, not even the truth can close certain wounds. Not on this earth.'

At lunchtime Balistreri called Angelo on his mobile. They were to see the New Year in at his little penthouse on the Janiculum. From up there you could see the whole of Rome and enjoy the midnight fireworks.

'Have you arranged poker as well after the champagne?'

'No poker. Your brother Alberto's away and Corvu says he can't.'

'Then it's women,' said Balistreri, cheering up.

'Well, let's hope so. Anyway, there should be plenty going spare here tonight.'

'Excellent, Angelo. Shall we celebrate with a couple of goers and dance in front of the TV at midnight?'

'Perhaps an old-style night of recreational sex would do you good.'

'I think a little recreational sex would also do you good once in your life. Perhaps you might discover that there's an alternative to the ideal woman, something more simple and realistic.'

'When you were a cynical womanizer you were amusing. But a cynical ascetic's only pitiful.'

They went on in this manner for a while, then said goodbye.

Balistreri then called Coppola. 'Any news, Coppola?'

'Indeed, Dottore. Some interesting news.'

'You've found out what colour of underwear the lady wears?'

'No, but I've understood why the investigation took so long. There was a life insurance policy on Sandro Corona.'

'Payable to the lady with the nice behind?' said Balistreri provocatively.

'Exactly, Dottore. The lady found herself with three million euros thanks to that policy.'

'Thanks to an unknown lorry driver, you mean.'

'Perhaps she persuaded him in some way. You know, a prick-teaser and a lorry driver?'

'Where are you now, Coppola?'

'Out with Piccolo – we've got eight names on the list. The others have been dealt out to Corvu and Mastroianni, who landed in Fiumicino just now.'

'OK, get busy. And keep an eye on Piccolo so she doesn't do anything stupid.'

Afternoon

The office was much quieter than usual. It seemed that 2005 had no wish to end. Balistreri settled down to the inevitable wait. He was in pain because he couldn't smoke. He looked at the drawn blinds outside which the rain was pelting down on and thought of the stalemate he was in: no brainwave from which to launch a fresh initiative, only the hope that the dragnet would come up with a bigger fish.

The hours passed slowly. Margherita popped in every now and again to see if he wanted a sandwich, a beer or a coffee.

He politely declined. His mind, on the other hand, was full of memories he was trying to resist. They were bouncing off the walls of his brain and coming right back.

Summer 1967. Summer 1970. Summer 1982. Summer 2005.

Every so often he heard a phone ring somewhere and a voice answer it. Then even those sounds diminished – everyone was leaving.

At six o'clock Margherita stopped by to offer her best wishes. He watched her as she left and wondered who would be taking her out that evening.

Certainly not you, Balistreri, but perhaps someone her own age.

The thought reminded him of Ramona's story that Mastroianni had told him: the client who couldn't get it up. The bastard had been lucky – he had gained extra time. As for Nadia, she'd got into the car with someone without making a scene because she knew him. She was waiting for him. And he'd met with that good luck.

The room was far too hot, the radiators boiling. Balistreri opened a window to let in some fresh air. The first sounds of fireworks were mingling with the sound of thunder. In the distance, beyond the Coliseum towards St Peter's, a bolt of lightning lit the sky. The year 2005 was now ready to come to an end.

Evening

The last shops were lowering their shutters and everyone was rushing home to get ready for the big evening. Piccolo and Coppola were soaked to the skin, cold and tired. Coppola also felt shivery, and had a temperature coming on. The red tail lights of cars painted intermittent blotches on the wet asphalt. Inside the car they were looking down their crumpled, wet list.

'Finished,' said Nano. 'And, pardon my French, but it's been fuck all help.' Nano wasn't usually crude in front of women, but the many hours he and Piccolo had spent questioning people mystified by their interest in an old wreck, while all around them the New Year fireworks were starting to go off, had worn his nerves to a frazzle. He wanted to get home to Lucia and Ciro and help them prepare the grand supper. Instead, eight people questioned and eight lots of wasted time. And all in the rain.

'All right, Coppola, let's go home. We've seen seven vehicles, head-lights intact, although they could have put another one in later. Owners who can remember very well where they were on the evening of the 24th and say they have alibis. Then there's the Egyptian who no longer has his because he sold it to an East European with no name and without registering the change of owner. But he's sure the headlights were working.'

'Exactly. A complete waste of time. In four hours it'll be New Year and I'm off home. And you'd do well to go home yourself: take an aspirin and have a ball.'

'I'll drop you at yours, then go on with the car from the pool.'

When they got to his flat, Nano invited her in. 'The wife'll make you a steaming hot mug of milk – your eyes show you've got a temperature.'

She shook her head. 'There's something I have to do, but thanks anyway. Give my best to Lucia and Ciro.'

Coppola looked at her suspiciously. 'Are you sure?'

'Don't worry, I'm going home. Happy New Year.'

At half past eight she drew up outside the Torre Spaccata police station. There was hardly anyone still about – everyone was at home getting dressed up for the evening. Piccolo let her phone ring the agreed number of times, then hung up and called again straight away.

'Hello?' said Rudi.

'What are you up to?'

'I'm cooking. You said you didn't want to go out tonight and that I couldn't—'

'Did you go out shopping? I expressly told you not to—'

'Only to the supermarket downstairs. And I put on one of your berets and pulled it right down over my eyes.'

Piccolo felt her forehead. It was burning.

'Listen, Rudi, you're not to go out. I'll be late. I'm not sure when I'll be back. You cook for yourself and eat.'

'No, I'll wait for you. I've also bought some sparkling wine. With my own money,' he clarified.

She could picture him: all hot and sweaty over the hobs. She wanted to be there, right now, in the warmth and in the company of this extremely good-looking gay chef.

'All right, but I could be late. Promise me you won't go out.'

'Not until next year,' he said.

Piccolo grinned. 'If you do, I'll arrest you.'

'OK. But remember it's the traditional lentils tonight.'

Both her head and her throat were sore. She fished around in her pockets and found a sweet. She settled herself on the seat to keep an eye on the entrance to the police station. She wanted to switch the heater on, but couldn't leave the motor running – the exhaust would be seen in the freezing air.

They came out shortly afterwards, both out of uniform, Colajacono towering over Tatò. They got into a private car and Tatò took the wheel.

She followed them at a distance. They went down a long boulevard with high rises, then turned off to an unlit area. The roads became ever more desolate until they came to one with no houses or street lamps, open countryside to the right. The road went up and down following the curves of the hills. Piccolo switched off her headlights and followed Tatò's tail lights at a distance of fifty metres. Every so often on the right, dirt roads wound steeply up the hill. The countryside beyond the city stood out under the lights of fireworks and flashes of lightning, although a couple of kilometres away on the left the illuminated outlines of the outlying high-rises were visible.

At a certain point the red lights slowed down, then shifted over to the right and went out. It was a lay-by at the top of a slope, totally deserted in the freezing rain.

Piccolo stopped immediately. She couldn't stay there in the middle of the road. Ten or so metres back she'd seen a metalled road on the left, so she reversed to it and put herself out of sight. A flash of lightning lit up Tatò's car parked in the lay-by.

Will I see them if they get out in this dark and this rain? Keep calm — they can't see you.

Piccolo felt for the pistol in its holster. In the silence she could hear only the constant beating of the rain and the intermittent noise of the fireworks. She was stretched out almost flat so as not to be seen. Feeling herself begin to shiver, she was tempted to switch on the heater, but resisted. She zipped up her jacket and tried to breathe through her nose. Every so often she cleaned the condensation off the window with her sleeve. The lightning allowed her to keep a check on the other car. Two glowing red ends told her that Tatò and Colajacono were having a cigarette in the car. The time passed — ten o'clock, eleven — and she was growing steadily colder.

They're waiting for someone or something. But who or what? Should I tell Balistreri I'm following two policemen without any reason after what I got up to last night? First we'll see what happens, and then I'll tell him.

She decided to call Rudi again, but there was no signal. She saw the glow of a cigarette as someone got out of the car and a flash of lightning illuminated Colajacono's grotesque figure taking a piss in the rain with the cigarette in his mouth.

Her headache was worse, her throat burning. What she needed was to lie down, warm and peaceful, and have some of Rudi's lentils. In the distance, she saw a motorbike headlight coming towards her.

Who rides around on a motorbike in this weather half an hour before New Year?

The headlight turned off about half a kilometre before them down a dirt road. Then the latest flash of lightning lit up the scene. It wasn't a motorbike. It was a Giulia GT struggling up the slope with only one headlight. Tatò's car began to follow it at a distance.

*　　*　　*

Half an hour before the end of 2005, Angelo Dioguardi's penthouse was overflowing, fifteen people in seventy square metres. A cold north wind was blowing. Balistreri and his host were on the terrace protected by the glass surround.

'Graziano phoned. He was really looking forward to the poker. He'll join us around two with a friend, so there'll be four of us.'

'Shame. If he doesn't get it on with Natalya tonight, she'll lose interest.'

'Graziano takes his time.'

'That's your bad influence, Angelo. The ideal woman is a childish illusion.'

It was one of those cutting remarks that Balistreri had made on many occasions, but this time Angelo took issue.

'I still have that illusion, Michele. You don't even have that left.'

Balistreri looked at him in surprise. It wasn't in Angelo's character to criticize. In fact what he read in Dioguardi's eyes wasn't an accusation, it was his sorrow for a friend who, while still alive, was already dead on the inside.

You make certain decisions in a moment and they stay with you for the rest of your life. She was twelve years old on the beach at Palermo when she dived into the waves to save a little boy. She was fifteen when she flattened the best looking guy in the school with a karate blow for copping an uninvited feel. She was seventeen when she first went to bed with a girl. Now she'd brought a male homosexual home and, with the onset of a fever, was about to face corrupt policemen and potential killers.

She drew the pistol from its holster and placed it on the seat next to her. She switched the engine on and turned to follow Tatò's car, which she only managed to see when the tail lights came on as he braked. With her own lights off and at that distance they couldn't have seen her. The important thing was not to lose them.

They turned off where the Giulia GT turned. It was a dirt path now, all mud and puddles, that wound up around the dark hillside. Piccolo's car slid about and went off the path, but fortunately it was a front-wheel drive.

Every so often she touched the metal of the pistol for good luck, breathing heavily because of her temperature and the tension. They passed along several curves, then a crossroads. Now the potholes were enormous and she had to keep further back so as not to make a noise, her eyes trained on the intermittent tail lights – there was no other light source. Then all of a sudden Tatò and Colajacono stopped the car. She did the same and switched off the engine. The tail lights she'd been following completely disappeared and the darkness became total. There was only the wind whistling in the night and the distant sound of fireworks. It was biting cold and the damp entered the bones, but at least it was no longer raining. She looked at her watch face, the only weak light in all that surrounding blackness: five minutes to midnight.

A torch came on and moved away from Tatò's vehicle. Piccolo got out of the car. It would have been better to turn it round in the right direction to go back down the hill, but there was no time. She grabbed the pistol and began to follow the torchlight. She slipped on the mud and fell down, banging a knee.

She got to her feet again and pressed on. She was dog-tired, her legs felt like lead and her head was on fire, but she couldn't lose them. One last slope, and a curve gave on to a grassy patch where the Giulia GT was parked near an abandoned farmhouse, inside which she could make out the flickering light of an oil lamp and hear male voices. It was impossible to tell the language, but they were probably foreigners.

The torch had been switched off. Piccolo had no idea where Colajacono and Tatò were. Gripping the pistol in her hand, she hid herself behind the last tree before the open space in which the farmhouse stood. She tried breathing only through her nose and inside her jacket to hide her breath as it condensed in the freezing air. The explosions suddenly multiplied as the fireworks all went off. She huddled behind the tree.

Her head was bursting, her legs about to give way. She had to make a decision – she couldn't stay there forever. She held the pistol in her two hands and ran behind the farmhouse. As she paused for breath a hand was pressed over her mouth and an arm grasped her from behind. Without thinking she let go a karate blow and heard the cartilage of a nasal septum breaking and a curse in Roman dialect. She pointed her pistol at the forehead of Tatò, who was on his knees and groaning as he held onto his bleeding nose.

In a moment the farmhouse door opened and two men stepped out in the lamplight, one armed with a knife and one with a club. Piccolo moved behind Tatò and pointed the pistol.

'Put down the knife and the club,' she ordered.

'Who the fuck are you, bitch?' the one armed with a club shouted in a strong East European accent.

'Police,' Piccolo yelled back, while her eyes searched for Colajacono.

The two men looked at each other, then with an understanding nod started to walk towards Piccolo.

'Stop or I'll shoot!' she warned.

Twenty metres. They hesitated a moment, then carried on walking forward. Piccolo calculated the time. If they got to within five metres they'd jump on her together. She only had a few seconds.

She fired a single shot in the air. She couldn't spare any more than that. The two men hesitated again.

'On the ground, now!' Colajacono's voice exploded like a cannon shot, making them jump.

The two Roma gypsies turned round and saw the giant standing with his legs apart and the pistol in both hands, his arms tensed.

They looked at each other and began to run towards the path. Piccolo heard a shot fired and saw the Roma with the club fall over, holding his leg. The other stopped dead in his tracks. He no longer had any doubts: Colajacono would fire if he tried to escape.

In that moment Piccolo realized that the not-too-distant sounds she heard weren't fireworks going off but the blades of a helicopter that was coming down above them. A spotlight illuminated the scene from above while a voice from a loudspeaker warned the escaping man to stop and put his hands up. They heard the sirens of squad cars as they screeched up the hill and other headlights came on lower down.

Colajacono approached Tatò. 'Come on, you'll have a new nose now,' he said and then, turning to Piccolo, added, 'and you can thank this big stupid bitch here.'

Piccolo saw the slap coming. Under normal circumstances she'd have parried it with one arm while striking with the other. But the fever, the tension and the cold had made her sluggish. The slap sent her reeling into the mud.

Sunday, 1 January 2006

Night, 31 December–1 January

The phone call reached Balistreri just after the midnight toast. He listened in silence, then called Corvu and ordered him to drop Natalya and meet him straight away with a car from the pool.

At one o'clock they were on top of the rise. Floodlights powered by photoelectric cells lit up the scene. As they drove up they met the ambulance taking away the shepherd wounded by Colajacono; the other was in handcuffs guarded by two policemen. A paramedic was getting to grips with Tatò's nose.

He saw Piccolo sitting alone in a police car wrapped in a blanket.

'Corvu, while I talk with Piccolo, check out the farmhouse. On your own. Have you got your equipment?'

'Of course, Dottore.' He went off to get his bag with all the gear necessary to analyse the scene without contaminating it.

Balistreri slipped into the back seat of the car, sitting next to Piccolo. He saw she was trembling, but didn't ask her anything. She told him everything freely, except for the slap she received from Colajacono. She'd have time to think about that by herself.

'I'm sorry,' she concluded. 'I was afraid that they'd get away and I didn't know if Colajacono was on their side or ours.'

This was going to be the worst part to explain to Pasquali. Even worse than Tatò's nose.

'All right. Now I'll get someone to take you home,' said Balistreri softly.

'Let's look for Nadia first,' she replied, determined.

'We'll look for her. You're going home right now. I'm getting someone to take you.' It was an order that brooked no discussion and several minutes later Piccolo was in a car finally taking her home to Rudi's lentils.

Balistreri turned to Colajacono.

'I'm sorry about Tatò's nose. Anyway, there'll be time to talk about that and how you came to be here.'

Colajacono looked down on him with undisguised contempt. 'Whenever you like, Dottore. Then you can explain why you had us followed by that madwoman.'

Balistreri didn't bat an eyelid. 'In the meantime, why don't you tell me what you two were doing here.'

'The farmhouse is occupied by one of the Roma – that one,' he said, pointing to the young shepherd in handcuffs. 'The flock of sheep's his, and the car. We had an anonymous tip-off after putting out word that we were looking for a Giulia GT with a broken head-lamp.'

'Anonymous? So you trust all anonymous tip-offs?'

'I've already explained to you, Dottor Balistreri. We're not in your elegant offices in the centre – there's no messing about with us.'

Balistreri kept himself calm. 'And who's the other one?'

'Another shepherd. He also lives in an abandoned farmhouse, but on the other side of the hill, a kilometre away. This evening they took advantage of New Year when many folk are out and about.

They entered a nearby villa and took away the television, stereo, a video camera and some silver. It's all in the boot of the Giulia GT. This one's called Vasile Geoana. He's one of those Roma.'

He went up to the shepherd. He was thin and bony with a long beard, wearing a leather jacket over a T-shirt and jeans. He smelled strongly of sheep and alcohol.

'Do you speak Italian?'

With a hard, sly look he nodded that he could.

'Is that your car?'

'Yeah, mine.' His voice was rough, his accent guttural.

'Who did you buy it from?'

'Egyptian who makes pizza. Two hundred euros.'

'With a broken headlight?'

'What means "headlight"?'

'Front light, lamp.'

He shook his head. 'No, broken after. I lend it sound, broken after.'

Corvu came out of the farmhouse. He went up to Balistreri and showed him two long blonde hairs in a plastic bag. Balistreri let the shepherd see them.

'Where's the girl?' Colajacono asked him brusquely.

Vasile took a sharp intake of breath and stared at a point on the ground.

'What girl?'

'This girl,' persisted Colajacono, pointing to the bag with the hairs.

'I bring whores. Sometimes.'

Colajacono placed his enormous hand around the shepherd's hand-cuffed wrist. He howled in pain.

'The girl that you picked up in your car on Via di Torricola. Where is she?' asked Colajacono while he squeezed the man's wrist. Vasile screamed out in pain, his face contorted.

A gust of icy wind swept across the field. Tears were streaming down the shepherd's face.

Balistreri turned towards Colajacono. 'Leave him alone,' he ordered.

Colajacono didn't even turn to look at him. His face was twisted in a grimace of cruel satisfaction.

'I not know,' whined the shepherd. 'I not know where she go . . .' He was now on his knees, his face turning blue.

'Leave him alone or I'll place you under arrest,' Balistreri warned Colajacono.

This time Colajacono turned round, openly mocking him.

'Oh, really? You think these animals who screw Italians over should be treated with kid gloves, do you?'

He spat on the ground and ended scornfully, 'But then I was forgetting, you're the street cleaners in paradise.'

Giving the shepherd's knee such a powerful kick that he fell face down in the mud crying, Colajacono turned to Balistreri with a defiant air.

'I'll leave him to you, Balistreri. See what you can do with all your nice ways of protecting civil liberties, your DNA and your long words in English . . .'

Balistreri managed to keep himself under control – there were enough problems already.

Or perhaps I know that you're partly right.

The ground was a mixture of water and mud. Going over it by the light of photoelectric cells would be difficult, but it had to be done. It was one thirty and dawn was five hours away. Balistreri gave instructions to Corvu to call for the dogs and make a start.

Finally he succeeded in lighting his first cigarette of the year. He looked over at the city, lit up by the last fireworks. He wanted to be sitting in the warm with Angelo, playing a game of poker. Or else with Linda Nardi.

He drove the thought of her away angrily and set off through the freezing rain.

Morning

By dawn on the morning of 1 January they had found nothing. The wind had died down and the sky was a dense iron grey. Nevertheless, its light would help the search. The area was half deserted; the police were all out on the hill. As soon as Forensics had completed their examination, Balistreri went into the farmhouse with Corvu and the shepherd.

There was one empty whisky bottle and another half full next to a broken armchair. It was a real dump, smelling of alcohol, sheep and faeces. A stained mattress was lying in a corner on the floor. There was also a television set and remote control, certainly stolen, and a satellite dish next to them.

'Now tell me about the girl,' said Balistreri to the shepherd, who was still moaning about his painful wrist.

'What the fuck should I know?'

'In Sardinia we feed people like you to the pigs,' said Corvu.

Balistreri looked at him in surprise.

Hagi would have them impaled; Colajacono would break every bone in their bodies, one by one; even the shy Corvu would feed them to the pigs. What is it that's not right?

They had examined the car. Besides the stolen goods there were more blonde hairs, a beret, and a pair of glasses with dark lenses.

'Listen, Vasile,' said Balistreri patiently. 'This girl was seen getting into your car. You were wearing the beret and the dark glasses we found in the car.'

'Not my stuff. Girl was here, waiting me.'

'She was here, waiting for you. When?'

'When I come back from house of friend. The one you shoot.'

'Why did you go to his house?'

'Afternoon I leave sheep with him, has sheep pen and dog. Then we drink something and we talk. I come back always at seven.'

'You always come back at seven precisely?'

'TV, *L'eredità* programme start then. I always watch.'

Marvellous. The wonders of social integration.

'And the girl was already here by seven. What day was this?'

'December 24th. He said present for me.'

Balistreri decided to ignore the 'he' for the time being and concentrate on the gift part.

'Why the present?'

'For car,' Vasile replied quickly.

Balistreri pointed to some rags in a corner, underneath which was a bucket with a rope attached to the handle.

'Is there a well here?'

'Yeah, near my friend's house, but well no good no more, water no good.'

They exchanged looks. Corvu was already out of the door.

'All right, Vasile,' said Balistreri, continuing, 'a present for the car. Explain.'

'I lend him car, he give me one hundred euros and fuck with whore.'

'And what does he do with your car?'

'He take bed, my car has luggage rack.'

Of course, a blind. A fast car, not registered to the real owner, ideal for a robbery. And Vasile was well aware of it. He wasn't running much of a risk because he rarely went out, only in the evenings for some burglary. And the car wasn't registered in his name. It was a good deal: one hundred euros and a whore for lending out a car.

'Where did you hand over the car to him?'

'No, I leave here open with keys inside. He say he come and pick up and then bring back in evening. With whore.'

'I don't follow, Vasile. You don't know this man?'

'No, he call my cell, offer deal, I say yes.'

'When did he call?'

'Day before – 23rd.'

'He was Italian?'

'Spoke Italian, accent Italian.'

'Then?'

'Then evening of 23rd I come back and find hundred euros here, as he promise. Then morning of 24th before I go out with sheep, I leave car with keys in and when I come back at seven car is here, blonde whore is here. As him promise. She have two bottles whisky because he break lamp on car. We fuck, she make me drink much, I no remember when she go, I drink bottle and half whisky, too much . . .' He pointed to the bottles on the floor.

'And he?'

'He nothing, no see, no more hear. Disappear.'

Balistreri had a mournful thought and heard footsteps approaching. He recognized Corvu's gait. He stood up, but he already knew.

'Come on,' he said to the shepherd and they set off along the path behind Corvu. The three of them walked Indian file in silence through the mud. It had started to rain again. Somewhere sheep were bleating. When he came within sight of the well surrounded by police, Balistreri stopped. He met Colajacono's stare. 'Keep close to this piece of shit here,' he told Corvu, pointing to Vasile. 'No one lays a finger on him.'

Nadia's body was in the water fifteen metres below. It was Corvu who went down the ladder. They hauled the body up on a wire. The girl was naked, her legs broken perhaps from having hit the bottom of the well. To judge from the state of the body it was likely that Nadia had been there for some days, perhaps since 24 December. The marks of cuts and cigarette burns were still visible on her arms and thighs. The letter E, three centimetres high, had been clearly carved in the middle of her forehead.

At seven on the first morning of 2006, while they were returning to the centre, Rome was deserted under a leaden sky and drizzle.

Balistreri called Pasquali on the car's speakerphone. 'The girl's dead,' he declared. Silence. Pasquali was waiting for the rest. 'We have a suspect,' he added.

'How long has she been dead?' Pasquali's voice was a whisper. First of all, of course, he was concerned about possible comments on their efficiency.

'From the state of the body, for several days. She was probably killed the same evening she was taken away.'

'Thank goodness,' said Pasquali, letting the words slip out, relieved.

'It was a Roma shepherd here without a residence permit.'

'Lord, more problems for the mayor,' Pasquali muttered. As a good Catholic, he limited himself to invoking the name of the Lord where other policemen would turn to a curse.

'There's something else,' added Balistreri.

He could imagine Pasquali lying on his comfortable bed below the crucifix, whispering into his mobile so as not to wake his wife, deeply content about this news that would even further upset the city's centre-Left administration.

Pasquali was silent. He could smell the bad news coming. The really bad news.

'She had the letter E carved on the centre of her forehead,' Balistreri ended. Silence.

Perhaps now Pasquali was getting up and going silently into his well-appointed bathroom. The letter E inescapably reopened a door that he had closed shut with a double lock.

He's congratulating himself now on having resisted the temptation to get rid of me. Congratulating himself on his prudence.

'Michele, I'll inform the Chief of Police, and you inform the Public Prosecutor. Only what we've spoken about. As regards the journalists, we'll do a short press release in the early afternoon. We'll meet in my office in an hour.'

At nine o'clock Rome was dull in colour and deserted, the roads soaked in rain and strewn with the remnants of the New Year's Eve festivities. Despite the fact that it was a holiday and the office was half empty, Pasquali was wearing an iron-grey suit with a blue polka dot tie, impeccable as usual and having already been to Mass.

Floris, the Chief of Police, was less formal in the sports jacket he had been wearing to take his dog out in the early morning, despite the fact that it was 1 January and pouring with rain. Balistreri was still in the jumper he'd put on to go to Angelo's. He was unshaven and his shoes were covered in mud.

They sat down in Pasquali's little lounge. Balistreri recounted the events without omissions. It wouldn't have helped to hide anything, as Colajacono would have ensured they knew everything anyway.

'How is Inspector Tatò now?' asked Floris when he'd finished speaking.

'They're operating this morning. It's nothing serious.'

'Dottoressa Piccolo attacked him.' Pasquali wanted to be one point up for what was to come.

Balistreri shook his head. 'She didn't attack him. She was in a dangerous situation, she felt her shoulders grabbed and reacted out of instinct. Tatò acted in an imprudent manner and was struck.'

'So according to you Tatò was imprudent. What about Piccolo then? Throwing herself into a situation like that without informing anyone.'

'There was no telephone reception, Pasquali. She couldn't inform anyone.'

'She wasn't using her head. Let's say it was the fever, but I'd like to know why she was following Colajacono and Tatò.'

'Because she had her doubts about them, as I mentioned to you yesterday.'

Pasquali shook his head. 'But instead we now know that these doubts were foolish. If we've found the vehicle, the girl and the guilty party it is thanks to Colajacono and Tatò who, as true professionals, sounded the alarm in Headquarters by radio before going up the hill.'

'How did they know where to look for the car?' asked the Chief with good reason.

Balistreri pulled a face. 'An anonymous phone call came in about half past eight last night. Some guy had seen the Giulia GT with a broken headlight coming down the hill a little earlier. It was Vasile and his mate going off to commit a burglary. End of story. If we believe it.'

'We certainly do believe it,' said Pasquali, cutting him short, 'and anyway, Dottoressa Piccolo should remain at home to recover from her fever, and to rest. And I say this for her own good: she should keep away from this case.'

Balistreri said nothing. Pasquali showed slight signs of nervousness, twiddling his glasses in his hands. The fact of having kept quiet to the Chief about Linda Nardi's request was putting him in an embarrassing position. Still more, the fact that Balistreri might know about it.

'Let's talk about the letter E,' said Floris. 'And about the R, naturally.'

Pasquali felt for the knot in his tie. He must have already weighed up the pros and cons – the political ones as usual, not those concerned with the investigation.

'We should reopen the Samantha Rossi investigation, which was never officially closed anyway,' he said, as if it were the truth. 'But the press must be kept out. No official link between the two cases.'

'The E on Nadia will get out – it was too visible. Those who pulled her out will have seen it, at least, and those in Forensics,' objected Balistreri.

'Even if it does get out, no worries. But no one knows about the R in the Rossi case. And who says they're linked?' replied Pasquali.

'We have the same modus operandi,' remarked Balistreri. 'The guilty Roma handed up on a plate and another figure who disappears.'

'A plot against the Roma?' said Pasquali sarcastically. 'They're surely not important enough to unleash a series of murders.'

'Apart from the Roma, we perhaps have a serial killer who carves initials in his victims. First an R, then an E. He could even be writing a word,' said the Chief, expressing his bewilderment.

'There are important differences between the two crimes,' said Pasquali.

Balistreri preferred to let this theory take its course without any rebuttals from him.

'Differences precisely in the modus operandi,' Pasquali went on. 'Samantha was attacked and raped by persons unknown to her. Nadia gets into the car of a person she knows and goes of her own free will to have sex with the Roma shepherd. So long as the autopsy reveals there was no violence there.'

'There's another important difference,' Balistreri added. 'Samantha Rossi was an Italian student and Nadia a Romanian prostitute.'

'Exactly,' said Pasquali approvingly, 'they could be two unrelated cases and the letters purely a coincidence. Or else the three Roma boys in the first case knew this Vasile and they told him how they'd murdered a girl and carved a letter on her before we arrested them. And then he imitates what they did.'

Balistreri shook his head. 'Vasile's only been in Italy since last September and the three Roma boys were in prison by August.'

'When you interrogate Vasile more thoroughly you can gather whether he's invented it all,' said Pasquali firmly. 'This story of the vehicle he lent out sounds like fiction. He picked Nadia up for sex and instead of paying her threw her down the well. The end.'

'If it weren't for the E carved on her forehead,' Balistreri pointed out.

Pasquali got up. 'We'll do a short press release in the early afternoon without mentioning the mark. A simple case, little to write about. A Romanian prostitute, a Roma shepherd. We have everything – let's close the case there. Officially. But unofficially we continue with the Samantha Rossi case.'

It was an intelligent solution. It could even stand up if the letters were kept secret.

And if the murderer had finished writing.

Corvu had called her and told her about Nadia. Piccolo had told Rudi. He had cried for a long time in silence, while preparing compresses for her.

She was lying in her tracksuit stretched out on the sofa, the thermometer showing a temperature of over 39°. It was hot in the living room of her two-room flat. Rudi maintained this would make her worse and had opened a window to let in fresh air.

He took the rubbing-alcohol compresses and placed them on her forehead, wrists and ankles.

'I'll squeeze you some more fresh orange juice,' he told her. Since Piccolo had come back in a dreadful state and he had taken care of her, they had become even more friendly.

'You've already made me two.'

'You have to drink. Liquids and vitamins.'

'I haven't tasted your New Year lentils,' she said weakly.

'Nor the boiled sausage that goes with them. But tonight you'll feel better and then . . .'

'I've messed up for two nights running, one after the other, doing really crazy things.'

'Well, all things come in threes. Today you're not going out, so you can do crazy things at home, if you want.'

She recognized a slight hint and was surprised to feel a certain pleasure.

The dim grey mid-morning light filtered in from outside. Piccolo didn't want the lights on – they hurt her eyes. Rudi was sitting on the floor at the foot of the sofa. He hadn't tied his hair into a pony-tail and she saw him as even more handsome: slim, angelic and kind, but still frightened.

'If there's anything you know, you should tell me, Rudi. Help us find the one who did this to Nadia.'

He shook his head. He was trembling. In the semi-darkness of the flat they heard the first muffled sounds of people waking after the carousing of seeing in the New Year: sounds of chairs being moved in the flat above, voices, the television being switched on. While the world was waking to the New Year, Piccolo felt sleep finally overcoming her.

But Rudi had begun to talk, his voice sounding distant, as if it came from one of the neighbouring flats. 'Mircea and Greg were in Ramona's room. They were insulting her, slapping her about. I was in bed, scared out of my wits. I could hear they wanted something off her, but couldn't understand what. Then Mircea came to get me.'

Piccolo felt the throbbing in her head easing off and the waves of tiredness disappear. She liked the smell of the rubbing alcohol, the same as she liked the faint sounds coming from the other flats and the morning's grey light.

'Ramona was crying, the room was again turned upside down.

Greg said that if she didn't help them they'd take it out on me, but she begged them to leave me alone and promised she'd do anything she could. But she didn't have what they wanted. So Mircea went to get the broom . . .'

Piccolo felt him take her hand. Half asleep, she heard him still talking, now closer. He went on for a long time, lying next to her. Then she began to feel his light breath on the end of her nose, his lips brushing against hers. She became aware that it was her very own hand that was guiding Rudi's under the elastic of her tracksuit bottoms, then lower down inside her underwear. Then everything became mixed up in her sleep.

The last man who had tried to touch her had been the guy at school. Awkward, rough, hurried. The exact opposite of Rudi.

The violence of that time, all the violence of all the men in the world, faded in that moment and she melted under those delicately exploring fingers. The pleasure came from a distant past, at first cocooned, then ever more intense and unstoppable.

She woke many hours later. The fever had gone.

Balistreri knew the Samantha Rossi file off by heart – every name, every photograph, every list of times. But he wanted to read it again now that he'd seen the E on Nadia's forehead. He opened the window. *Wonderful. Fresh air, silence, rain.*

First, the autopsy. Multiple blows to the body and sexual violence. Then strangulation. Then the incisions. He lingered over the description of the actions that had been the cause of death. Prolonged pressure at the base of the neck by both hands. Clear signs of the thumbs. Strong hands with a firm and deadly intent.

He moved on to the confession made by the three Roma youths. They had come to the bar early and only had money for beer. Inside the club, coming out of the toilets, they had met a fourth man. He spoke Italian, was rolling in money, but had no friends and wanted to celebrate. He'd given them a hundred-euro note so they could drink to his health. Then he disappeared and they drank like fish for an hour. At a certain point they saw him again. He led them into the toilets to sniff some coke. They lost sight of each other and then at a quarter to ten he was at the entrance to the bar calling out to them. 'Let's get some women,' he said.

They thought he meant to pay for some whores as well and followed after him. As soon as they were outside, the fourth man offered everyone more cocaine. Then they saw a girl running towards them. The piazza was empty, no one at the bus stop. He was the one who got hold of her first; they helped him drag her into some gardens while the bus went past. It was he who delivered a sharp blow to the face and knocked her out. They helped him drag her as far as the rubbish tip. He had whisky for everyone in his rucksack. Then the girl came round and they got stuck in. None of the Roma could say exactly what they or the fourth man had done. One of the three said that he'd confined himself to watching and smoking. When the girl fainted he was no longer there. They went back to their caravan. They didn't remember taking the bracelet either, never mind having carved the R on the girl's back. They'd undergone a handwriting test, for what it was worth. All three could neither read nor write.

Balistreri moved on to the part that interested him more: the iden-tikit of the fourth man. Unfortunately, the three Roma youths had only supplied vague details. Indistinct features, long straight hair over forehead and cheeks, beret, large glasses. About his height they were even more confused: one saying medium, another very tall.

He looked at the picture. It could have been anyone. The hair was probably a wig, the glasses too large. Like the beret and dark glasses of the driver in Via di Torricola.

He went back to the last part of the description. After having struck Samantha the first blow, the fourth man had moved aside, stepping into dark shadows until he disappeared altogether.

Vasile the shepherd had said the same thing about the man to whom he'd lent the Giulia GT. The man who'd sent Nadia to him with two bottles of whisky. Two very similar men. Or else they were one and the same.

The thoughts clashed with one another in the mix of facts. It was useless trying to find the end of the thread to untie all the knots – the tangle seemed too complicated.

While he waited, Balistreri drank water and listened to music, shut in the silence of his office in the early morning of 2006. He was waiting for inspiration.

A thought began to take shape slowly in his head, unfocused and hazy: the Invisible Man.

He walked by just before lunch. He saw Linda Nardi coming out of the newspaper offices. She looked rested, as if she'd gone to bed very early, giving a miss to New Year festivities. Perhaps after reading a good book and sipping away at a herbal tea while everyone else was popping champagne corks.

'I was just going to have a coffee at the bar opposite,' Balistreri lied shamelessly.

She showed no awareness of the evident lie, nor was she angry after the stormy supper. Instead she seemed happy to see him, as if nothing had occurred. But there was the same extreme politeness again, the borderland that separated them.

'I heard about it on the radio a little while ago,' she said simply.

'The newspapers published the details of the vehicle we were looking for and Colajacono received an anonymous call about the Giulia GT.'

Linda Nardi looked at him in silence, but asked him nothing.

'I'm happy to give you some answers – that was the pact, in exchange for the favour of calling Pasquali.'

She surprised him with a different question from the one he was expecting.

'Who is Marius Hagi?'

Balistreri was thoughtful for a moment, lost in a memory that this woman kept alive each time she managed to catch him off guard. Then he told her about Hagi, Greg, Mircea and his dinner out with Nadia.

She listened to the whole story without comment. At the end she posed another unexpected question.

'When did Hagi's wife, Alina, die?'

'In 1983,' he replied on an impulse. He had no idea from what line of reasoning the questions came, but in some way he liked talking to her. It was like walking on a very thin sheet of ice towards the gates of paradise.

Linda Nardi traced the line of a drop of coffee with her finger on the steel counter. He watched her as if she were a fairy that had stepped out of a children's book.

Afternoon

Corvu must have had time to rest; he was dressed in a more sporty mode than usual, a loud dark-green shirt hanging out of his jeans and a scoop of gel on his short black hair.

When Nano saw him he started to whistle the theme from *Love Story* and Corvu gave him a blazing look. They were sitting around the table in Balistreri's office.

Mastroianni was recounting in minute detail all the particulars of his talk with Ramona.

'What did she say to you about the bachelor pad where she took the distinguished-looking customer?' Balistreri asked.

'In what sense, Dottore?' asked Mastroianni.

He's handsome but not quick off the mark. He's still not got it. Or else I'm the one who's seen too many of them.

'The bedroom, Mastroianni. Where was it? How was it set up?'

'She told me there were pornographic objects, plastic dildos, whips, handcuffs, a large mirror on the ceiling . . .'

No, you couldn't trust him. Unless I'm the one who's too much of an expert in these things. A mirror on the ceiling, a video camera.

Ignoring Balistreri's silence, Mastroianni went on. 'Then I went from Iaşi to Galati to check on the information about Mircea and Greg. They have a serious previous record. Double homicide with intent.'

'And who did they want to kill?' Corvu asked.

'Two retired ministry officials. A couple of friends who were ex-colleagues. They'd bought a small farm outside Galati with the lump sum and their pension. They'd gone to the market one day and sold thirty lambs, getting paid in cash. While they were going back to the farm our two suspects attacked them with the intent to rob them. The two retirees put up a fight and the other two simply cut their throats. A witness saw them coming out of the farmyard just after the crime. They were arrested, but two days later an important Romanian barrister took it upon himself to defend them. He obtained their release from detention and the return of their passports. After that, the charges against them were completely dropped.'

'It's pointless asking who was paying for the barrister, I take it,' said Corvu.

'As a matter of fact, we don't know,' concluded Mastroianni.

'But all of this takes us a long way from the problems we're facing today,' said Corvu, 'First an R, now an E. And what if this has only just begun?'

'Let's not mix chalk and cheese,' put in Coppola. 'Samantha Rossi was a respectable girl, an Italian student; the other was an East European trollop, who should have stayed at home.'

'Aren't you ashamed of what you've just said?' exploded Corvu, stammering with emotion.

Balistreri decided it was time to end the meeting.

Evening

He kept imagining conversations in which they spoke different and incomprehensible languages, but where she understood everything and he nothing.

A different level of understanding. A level that I recognize and that scares me. That of total trust.

In order to not think about Linda Nardi, he made a decision.

'Margherita, today is New Year's Day and I don't want to eat dinner alone.'

She was nonplussed for a moment, then her inborn trust and the desire to please prevailed.

'Thank you, Dottore. It would be an honour. I'd be happy to have dinner with you.'

He took her to a well-known and crowded little restaurant near Piazza Fontana di Trevi. Margherita kept on calling him 'Dottore'. She certainly had no fears about her old boss coming on to her after dinner.

At one time I'd have had her in my Duetto as soon as we came out of the restaurant, or perhaps already on the way there and saving on the money for dinner.

Margherita was staring at two old Japanese tourists like they were ancient statues, as they threw coins into the fountain for good luck. 'They're so sweet, hand in hand like teenagers.'

'Yeah, wishing for another hundred years together,' said Balistreri sarcastically.

'You don't believe in love, Dottore?' She blushed after saying it, as if she'd gone too far.

'In what sense?' he asked, a little astonished but mainly amused.

'You don't believe that a woman could change your life.' She said it almost in a tone of contrition.

Balistreri was about to say something, but was interrupted by a hand on his shoulder.

'Michele.' It was Dioguardi with his usual open smile.

'Angelo, what are you doing here?'

'I started the New Year with a high-stakes online poker tournament. And I came here to celebrate my first win of 2006.'

On his own. As I would be were it not for this little angel, Margherita.

'Sit down with us and have a coffee,' Balistreri offered immediately, happy to have him there.

Angelo sat next to him facing Margherita. He always looked like a great big kid with his hair awry, his light beard unshaven, his large blue eyes.

Margherita was fascinated by him. He reined himself in, not wanting to be intrusive, but she bombarded him with questions about his career as professional poker player. Then Balistreri made things worse by mentioning the charity works Angelo financed with the winnings. Angelo said nothing. He was looking at Margherita while Balistreri was telling her about the early days of their friendship, their evenings together, the women, and how Angelo's life changed completely from undistinguished employee to world poker champion while the young extrovert Balistreri was growing old and grey in an office. Then he told her of their first meeting in Paola's apartment, when Angelo threw up his very soul in order to procure a fuck for him.

Margherita laughed. 'So you were the bait, Angelo! Shame on you.'

'He was engaged,' Balistreri clarified. 'And unlike me he's always believed in love.'

Angelo started at the words, as if they were slanderous accusation.

'And did you ever find love?' Margherita asked him.

Balistreri listened to them absent-mindedly, as if he were sitting at another table. They liked each other, those two – it wasn't difficult to see. He made the decision instinctively and felt relieved, almost light-headed. He feigned a call from the office and shot out into the night. He knew where he wanted to go.

By now he was on the hunt for murderers, not love.

It wasn't far away. He was happy to walk in the cold evening to the pavement outside the open nightclub entrance. It was here that Papa Camarà had died, his stomach slit open by a knife. He recognized the corner from where the motorbike had emerged. Fifteen metres. The rider had waited with his engine just turning over before the insulting the Senegalese. And then, perhaps, he came back to kill him. A murderer who was very stupid. Why insult him precisely at the moment when there was a witness?

It was early; there were still few customers at the tables. The waiters were chatting quietly among themselves. He ordered something to drink, then called the barman over to his table. Pierre wasn't frightened off by his police ID card – he was a laid-back guy with a pleasant manner, and he showed no surprise when Balistreri told him he was there about Camarà.

'Did you have any reason to speak to him that night?'

'No, your colleagues already asked me. I bumped into him a couple of times when he was going to the toilet and coming up the stairs again in a hurry. Ajello – the manager, you know – wants the main entrance covered at all times.'

'Is there another entrance?'

'Yes, in the alleyway behind. But it's always locked; the manager's the only one with the keys. He uses it to let in the guests who go straight into the private lounges. There's two of them, one large and one small.'

'And that night?'

'There was a party in the larger one after one o'clock. Friends of the manager's son – the boy himself was there as well. The manager came over specially from Perugia to welcome the guests and let them in by the rear entrance.'

'Whose was the party?'

'A young girl from Roman society was celebrating her eighteenth birthday. She's a friend of Fabio, Ajello's son.'

'I understand you had a different manager before.'

'Yes, Corona. Poor sod. Snuffed out like that. But maybe it was a release.'

'How come?'

'Well, you're not married, are you? Corona was a married man . . . and how.'

'Pain of a wife?' suggested Balistreri.

'The devil of a pain.' Pierre agreed. 'All the messes that Corona found himself in were caused by her. In the end she made him lose everything.'

'You mean this place?'

'Not only this place. Corona was director of the company that runs this and other nightclubs. She always wanted him to make more money, no matter how he did it.'

'And he did what a good director shouldn't do . . .' suggested Balistreri.

Pierre nodded in the affirmative, with a sad look. He was really upset about Corona.

'He was in trouble with the finance police. Some business over slot machines that weren't registered for tax. The problem was that the money ended up in Signora Corona's account, not in that of the partners,' Pierre explained.

Balistreri saw him stiffen. A well-dressed and distinguished-looking forty-year-old was approaching the table.

Pierre made the introductions. 'Avvocato Ajello, our manager. Dottor Balistreri, police.'

The tall athletic man held out a hand fresh from the manicurist. A gold Rolex, diamond cufflinks, a Marinella tie, made-to-measure monogrammed shirt, clearly expensive shoes.

Ajello addressed Balistreri. 'If you're not in a hurry, why don't we have a drink in the private lounge?' He wanted to be rid of Pierre.

They went down a long corridor at the end of which was a toilet and a security door and before them two private lounges. They entered the smaller one. Leather armchairs and sofa, drinks cabinet, DVD player and video projector.

'Very comfortable,' commented Balistreri. 'Just a little water for me, however.'

Ajello pointed to an armchair and served him.

'This room is reserved for our more important guests. You know, faces too well known to mingle with the general public in the main room.'

'People in the film world?'

'No, footballers mostly, television actresses, some politicians with unofficial company,' Ajello explained with ill-concealed scorn for those who in his eyes were only half civilized. 'People who don't blink at spending five thousand euros on champagne before the evening's halfway through.'

'And the night Camarà died there was someone in here?'

'No, at that time only the large room was occupied. A party for one of my son's female friends.'

On the glass coffee table stood a huge ashtray and a large wooden box. Ajello opened it.

'Cuban cigars. Real ones,' he announced, pointing to them. 'I don't smoke them myself, but they tell me they're very good. Do help yourself.'

Balistreri shot a glance at the box's contents. There were five compartments and five cigars, each cigar attached by a silver thread to a small pocket lighter with a stylized dancer in blue, the night-club's logo. A courtesy gift for the customers.

'I'll stay with my cigarettes, thanks. And now perhaps you'd like to tell me something, Avvocato?'

Again that condescending smile.

'To be frank, Dottor Balistreri, I found the curiosity of your officer a little out of place. It was like being interrogated by the finance police. Thousands of questions about ENT, its partners, the previous managing director . . . Nothing serious, but a little strange for a murder that has nothing to do with—'

'Avvocato Ajello, I don't think you've taken into consideration the fact that Camarà's killing could have something to do with the Bella Blu, or its business associates, or the previous manager or yourself . . .'

'We have no enemies, Dottore. We operate in a difficult field and are extremely careful to do everything by the book.'

'But the finance police found unregistered slot machines here.'

Ajello made a gesture of irritation with his hand as if brushing away a fly. 'An oversight by Sandro Corona, the previous manager. He left several slot machines unregistered as in the heyday when there were no regulations. Nothing serious, Dottor Balistreri. Don't tell me you're one of those narrow-minded purists who thinks that those who don't pay their taxes down to the last euro should be in jail? Corona was only one of the poor unlucky ones who avoided paying a few pennyworth of tax.'

'Meaning that tax evasion today is only in millions of euros, Avvocato?'

Ajello maintained his composure. He stared at Balistreri as any young lawyer who was cultivated, rich and had good contacts would stare at an ill-dressed, greying civil servant.

'Corona didn't understand life, Dottor Balistreri. And in order to live life well, it's necessary to understand it.'

'Or else perhaps he did understand it, but someone close to him was pressurizing him too much,' Balistreri threw in deliberately.

Ajello now looked at him with decidedly more attention, silent and on guard.

'Do you know Signora Ornella Corona well, Avvocato?'

Ajello weighed up the question. 'I knew her well when I took up the ENT shares she inherited from her husband.'

'So you knew her before, less well . . .' said Balistreri, interpreting his words.

Ajello shifted uneasily. He chose to gain time by getting up and going to the drinks cabinet.

While he poured out a whisky, Ajello spoke with his back to Balistreri. 'We used to go to the same gym.'

Well done. All doors now open. We went to the same gym and we didn't so much as say hello to each other. Or else we went to the same gym and frequently fucked in the toilets.

They said goodbye with feigned politeness. Outside the Bella Blu he called a taxi, noticing a grey saloon car parked on the corner. Two men were calmly smoking cigarettes inside, totally uninterested in him.

They know that their presence is enough to let me get the message, because I know the house style.

He was at Piccolo's before midnight. Rudi came to open the door wearing a tracksuit twice his size bearing the initials G. P.

'The Dottoressa's resting on the sofa, Dottore.' Balistreri tried to suppress his annoyance at the protective tone.

Rudi seemed different. He looked ridiculous in Piccolo's tracksuit, but seemed more at ease, no longer afraid. Balistreri tried to show his indifference.

Piccolo also seemed to be calmer. The latest events must have tried her sorely. Instead she was only sad for Nadia. Otherwise she seemed rather pleased with herself, like a schoolgirl who had just received top marks.

'Rudi insisted I rest on the sofa all day, even though I could go out. The fever's passed.'

'In Albania you only go out after a whole day without a temperature,' pronounced Rudi, like a wise old aunt.

'Yes, but in Albania you're a bunch of do-nothings, while I have things to do in the office,' insisted Piccolo.

'A little rest is what you needed,' said Balistreri, interrupting them. 'And keeping still for a while gives you better time to reflect.'

'Rudi, you know the flat by now. Offer the Dottore something to drink. Still water, I believe.'

'How do you like it here, Rudi?' asked Balistreri.

'Very well, Dottore. But I also have to get back to work, and not at the Bar Biliardo.'

'Because of Marius Hagi?'

'No, I already told you, Hagi has never done anything wrong to me. But Mircea and Greg—'

'Beat him up savagely, the bastards,' Piccolo put in.

Balistreri shot her a questioning look.

'The morning before Ramona left. They wanted something from her, but she knew nothing about it. In order to make her talk they took it out on Rudi.'

Rudi served the glass of water and sat on the sofa beside Piccolo. He was smoking nervously and was grateful for the fact that she didn't go into details and that Balistreri didn't ask.

'They said that Nadia had stolen something precious from somewhere. They were sure she'd given it to one of us because they hadn't found it in the flat,' Rudi explained.

Balistreri nodded. 'Look, Rudi, you've already told us that – unlike Nadia – Ramona was very tidy. But when you went up to tidy her things everything was upside down.'

'Yes, it was Mircea and Greg. They were looking for something.'

'And they didn't tell you what it was?'

'No. I think they didn't even know themselves, but they were sure that Nadia had stolen something valuable.'

'All right. Now listen, Rudi, you often used to tidy up Nadia's things, right?'

Rudi gave a sad smile. 'Yes, the little one was really untidy. I used to put everything away and she called me her little brother.'

'And she gave you presents . . .'

'No, Nadia had no money for presents. But she treated me very well, like Ramona.'

'A little present, perhaps something she'd lifted from some-where . . .'

Rudi seemed to remember something. 'But Mircea said it was something valuable . . .' he murmured.

'Valuable perhaps for reasons other than its economic value, Rudi. Valuable because of its meaning.'

Rudi went pale as he put his hand into a pocket.

The lighter passed in front of Piccolo's eyes as Rudi handed it to Balistreri.

'Sweet Jesus!' exclaimed the head of the Special Section, holding Rudi's hand still while the stylized dancer winked from the little cigarette lighter.

Monday, 2 January 2006

Morning

'That's incredible,' said Corvu, stammering in excitement.

'Isn't it?' Balistreri agreed, lighting his first cigarette of the day and opening the window on the cold morning of the first working day of the new year. 'Well, it seems incredible, but I don't believe in coincidences of this kind. Rudi had completely forgotten about the lighter, as it wasn't worth anything. Nadia gave it to him on the 24th. He thought she'd found it lying around and given it to him as a present for the favours he did for her.'

'But we can't rule out a coincidence,' Corvu objected. 'Nadia could have been given it by one of her clients who went to the Bella Blu.'

'It doesn't explain the frenzied way Mircea and Greg were looking for it, and someone was still searching for it in the Via Tiburtina flat when they were surprised there by Piccolo and Rudi.'

'Dottor Balistreri's right. Nadia must have picked it up at the Bella Blu herself,' said Piccolo. 'Except that these freebies are only found in the private lounges, not the club itself. They're handed out to important customers, attached to Cuban cigars. Therefore Nadia was in Bella Blu's private lounge on the night of the 23rd.'

'It could have happened before the 23rd,' objected Corvu, who didn't want to leave anything to doubt.

But Piccolo had all the answers. 'In that case, Mircea and Greg would have acted earlier to find it. No, Nadia comes out of the restaurant alone towards half past eleven and later she's in the Bella Blu's private lounge and there she pockets the lighter which she gives to Rudi.'

'Perhaps Mircea was waiting for her outside the restaurant and they went to the Bella Blu together,' Corvu suggested.

'No,' objected Piccolo. 'Rudi told me that that night Mircea came back with Greg just after Ramona, who was feeling ill. This was about midnight, therefore he came out of the restaurant and went straight home.'

'So someone else picked Nadia up and . . .' put in Corvu.

'They were sitting at the table for two and a half hours. Mircea kept on ordering drinks. That's a bit odd for an uncontrollable guy who's in a hurry to get into bed with the girl in front of him,' Piccolo responded. 'Then he hits her because, he says, Nadia won't have sex with him. He gets pissed off and leaves. Does this seem credible?'

'So you think Mircea wanted the waiter to remember he was there and then left all on his own? Why should he want to while away the hours until a certain specific time?'

Balistreri had let his two deputies continue back and forth while a dark cloud was forming in his mind. 'In order to deliver the girl to someone else,' he said.

The two of them looked at him in surprise, having almost forgotten about him in the heat of the discussion.

'In order to deliver her to someone who took her to the Bella

Blu,' concluded Corvu, using the logic he so prized. 'But how come they knew about the disappearance of a lighter? It's almost impossible . . .'

'It's perfectly possible,' explained Piccolo. 'I went to the Bella Blu early this morning and met the woman who does the cleaning. The private lounge is run like a hotel mini-bar and has to be filled up. She checks it every morning and puts down what needs to be replaced. And she clearly remembers that on the morning of the 24th a cigar and its lighter had gone – it's written down on the stock sheet for refilling.'

'Who does the stock sheet go to?' asked Balistreri.

'To Pierre the barman – that's his job. But anyone can get hold of it.'

Silence. Each of the three was considering the consequences of this line of reasoning and coming up with the inevitable conclusions.

Someone had noticed the sheet of paper. Someone who knew that the private lounge was occupied the night before and had made a check and knew that the girl could have taken it. So they mentioned this to Mircea and Greg, but without telling them what to look for because they couldn't know the whole story. And they couldn't know about the Bella Blu.

It was Piccolo who did the summing up. 'Someone who didn't want to run the risk of any link being found between Nadia and the Bella Blu.'

And Corvu finished it off. 'Someone who knew that Nadia was already dead.'

Balistreri's thoughts wandered darkly further back and further forward in time.

A depressing scene, Roma and Casilino 900. A prostitute used to film a sexual encounter. The world of nightclubs, slot machines, illegal gains. And that grey saloon parked outside the Bella Blu. A picture I know very well. But where does Samantha come into this, and the letters carved on the girls?

All of a sudden he had a definite feeling of grave danger. Something had begun a great distance away and was slowly, but inexorably, coming closer.

Linda Nardi was about to do something that her editor would perhaps not have encouraged and of which Balistreri almost certainly wouldn't have approved.

She went out on foot and crossed the centre flooded with sunlight. She came to Piazza Fontana di Trevi, which as usual just after midday was packed with tourists. Even this piazza was daubed with graffiti and hung with political posters. Next to the historic fountain, a small publicity truck was parked showing a smiling face and the words *Augusto De Rossi, Deputy Mayor* next to an image of Casilino 900 and the words *Only integration can put a stop to the violence*.

When she arrived at the restaurant, she took a good look around her. Nadia had left the place before midnight on 23 December. According to what Balistreri had told her, the waiter had said she'd wrapped herself up in a raincoat that was far too big for her and then waited outside for a bit. Didn't she know where to go? It was possible, but the large sign of the Piazzale Flaminio Metro was visible a few metres to the right. Instead, after a while she'd gone over towards Piazza del Popolo, where there were taxis, but no Metro. Could she have taken a taxi?

She stepped inside. An elderly waiter came up to her and she showed him her press card. 'Are you Tommaso?'

She noticed the waiter's gaze falling on her bosom and tried to hold in her anger.

'Yeah, but look, the police have already been here.'

'I need you to make another effort of memory,' she said, passing him a fifty-euro note, which he rapidly tucked away.

'What do you want to know?'

'I want you to tell me exactly what the girl did after the Romanian guy left.'

'How should I know? There were other people about. I was the only one still waiting on the tables . . .'

'You liked the girl, didn't you?' Linda's tone was kindly, almost knowing, and tuned to the same wavelength as the waiter.

'Well, after that piece of shit had gone I thought she'd be off as well, but she went into the ladies. When I saw her again she'd already taken the raincoat from the cloakroom and put it on.'

'Did she have a handbag?'

'No, a little rucksack.'

'And you can't think of anything else?'

Tommaso looked at her with half a smile. 'You know, I think she'd changed. Her clothes, I mean. In the ladies.'

'She changed her clothes? How could you tell if she was wrapped in a raincoat?'

'Well, I'm not sure. I only had an impression . . .'

'Do you remember what she was wearing when she came in?'

'Yeah, sure I do. It was jeans, all torn.'

'All right. And on top?'

Tommaso thought for a moment, then his face lit up. 'That's why I said she'd changed! When she came in she was wearing a big baggy jumper with a roll neck.'

'And then?'

'Well, there was no roll neck poking up out of the raincoat, nor any jeans.' Then, satisfied, the waiter added, 'And before she went out she put on a pair of gloves, which seemed odd to me because it wasn't at all cold that night.'

She changed into a low-neck top and a miniskirt to go to a nightclub, dressed for pleasure.

Linda Nardi felt better as she left the restaurant, even though she was bitter as well. Her eyes looked over towards Piazza del Popolo, as Nadia had done that night going towards whoever was waiting for her.

Going out to meet her fate.

Margherita appeared at the door a little breathlessly. 'Hello, I'm sorry but I have to take the afternoon off. May I?'

Balistreri could see the girl was uneasy. 'No problem, but would you slip down to the bar and get us two coffees, please? Mine's a decaf.'

'No coffee for me,' said Corvu. 'I'll have a fresh grapefruit juice.'

Balistreri gave him a disgusted look. 'Grapefruit? Before lunch? You'll feel a real hole in your stomach.'

'I've given up coffee,' he declared firmly.

'All right, Margherita, a coffee and a fresh disgusting grapefruit juice. Can you send Coppola and Mastroianni in and ask them what they want from the bar as well?'

Coppola and Mastroianni listened closely to the latest.

'We should talk to Ramona again,' said Mastroianni.

'And Ornella Corona,' added Coppola.

'Mastroianni, make arrangements to get the Iordanescu girl back to Rome – we'll pay the fare. As for Signora Corona, I'll see to her.'

'I don't see why I—' said Nano, trying to raise an objection.

'Because you have to talk to the American tourist again – Fred Cabot.'

Coppola didn't like the idea of another conversation with the American and the linguistic humiliation that went with it.

'Cabot's gone back to America,' he objected again.

'We've got all his contact details. Talk to him on the phone.'

Cursing silently, Coppola nodded unhappily.

'And there's another thing I want to know from Carmen, the Senegalese's girlfriend. What kind of urinary infection had he caught?'

They all looked at him in amazement.

'Oh, Dottò, there's no way I'm asking personal questions like that!'

'Very well, you can go and question those shepherds in prison,' Balistreri suggested with a mean look.

Coppola's eyes were wide open. 'All right, Dottore. I'll get in touch with Cabot and go and talk to Carmen.'

'Good,' continued Balistreri. 'Corvu and Piccolo will question the two shepherds, along with the Public Prosecutor.'

Corvu raised a hand. 'We have authorization from the judge to get the names of ENT's partners from the trust administrator now that there's a direct link with the crime.'

Afternoon

Corvu was in a very good mood. It worried Balistreri to see him so unusually happy and full of self-confidence, as if his deputy's reliability depended on a feeling of insecurity, and this lightness of being after falling in love was a forerunner to his taking his job lightly.

They were early for the appointment, which was for two o'clock, so they mingled with the people swarming towards St Peter's Square, bought two slices of pizza and made their way towards the great dome, which stood out in a sky that was finally blue after so much rain. Young Roma women with their children were chasing after the tourists. The citizens of Rome recognized them instantly and steered well clear to avoid any trouble.

The main office of the ENT trust was a small apartment on the third floor. There was a nameplate on the door and a pale secretary led them into a sober office.

A gentleman of a certain age, who introduced himself as Davide Trevi, was waiting for them. On his visiting card was written *Sole Administrator* and there was a landline and e-mail address, but no mobile number.

'Naturally, gentlemen, we are willing to cooperate. If you'd like to explain what you need, then within a few days—'

Corvu shook his head. 'We need something very simple – just one thing. But we need it now.'

'But, Dottore, as you can well imagine we too have our procedures—'

'Signor Trevi,' Corvu explained, 'one of the nightclubs run by ENT is linked to a murder, perhaps two. We need to know the names of its partners.'

'I understand, but you are aware that we have the right to see any official request before supplying the documents requested. With all due speed, of course, but not the speed you require.'

Balistreri stood up and went to collect his raincoat from the hallstand.

This shit is well used to all kinds of problems and to resisting them, procrastinating. We won't get anything in the normal way.

'You say that you need some time, Signor Trevi. Very well, please take it. However, these two murders could be linked to a previous one and the sequence could well be followed by another.'

Alarmed, Corvu shot him a glance of strong disapproval.

'Dottor Balistreri means to say that not being able to exclude with certainty the risk of a recurrence, it would be advisable to—'

'I mean to say,' said Balistreri, interrupting Corvu sharply and staring into Trevi's eyes, 'that if by any misfortune there is another victim and we ascertain any link whatsoever with ENT, then we will carry out a check on how you have used the intervening time you're asking for with particularly close attention.'

Like Pasquali, Trevi was evidently a man who was used to weighing up the pros and cons. Unlocking a drawer, he took out a grey file with *ENT* written on the spine and drew out a sheet of the trust's headed white notepaper.

'This is our authorization to act as agent,' he explained. 'There's only one shareholder who's entrusted us with ninety per cent of the ENT shares. The authorization's renewed automatically every year in the absence of a written order countermanding it.'

'And who is this shareholder?' asked Corvu impatiently.

Although still somewhat shaken, Trevi allowed himself a little smile. 'ENT (Middle East), a company registered in the Dubai Free Zone, United Arab Emirates.'

Balistreri and Corvu looked at each other, stunned. 'But there must be a name on the authorization,' Corvu objected.

'Of course – the ENT (Middle East) administrator, a certain Nabil Belhrouz, a Lebanese. Here are his details and his address in the Emirates.'

'It's a post office box,' Corvu protested.

'That's how they do it over there, but there is the company's sponsor, Free Zone Media City. We have the address for that.'

'And how often do you have contact with Mr Belhrouz?'

'I've never seen him or spoken to him,' Trevi declared serenely. And as they stared at him, stupefied, he added, 'Look, this is quite normal. Trusts are employed by anyone who doesn't want to be known. No client comes here to us. Mr Belhrouz's signature was gathered by means of an Italian notary who has a corresponding number in Dubai.'

They had a photocopy made and went to the door. While they passed by the secretary's desk, Balistreri saw the pilot light of Trevi's external phone come on.

Linda Nardi was walking in the cold air of the early afternoon, lost in her thoughts. The lives of these women meant nothing to anyone. She knew this little scenario very well. The politicians never gave a damn about any Italian deaths, let alone a little Romanian prostitute. And the police cared even less.

And Balistreri, an ex-Fascist now working for justice? Can you put any trust in him?

Graffiti was beginning to appear on the walls saying *Romanian murderers, Roma go home, Let's burn the travellers' camps*. No distinction between the Roma and the Romanians. Rather, the fact that the victim was Romanian and the presumed murderer a Roma gypsy only served to link them in people's opinion. And the political party posters had already leaped into the argument, milder in tone but the same in substance. The opposition laid all the blame on the city council and promised they would dismantle the camps as soon as they were in power. The mayor's party underlined what had already been done and what would soon be done. Faces and names of senators, MPs, city assessors – all had something to promise. The electoral implication of these circumstances was a juicy bone for some, a bitter pill for others. No doubt there were those among the politicians who were hoping cynically for another Samantha Rossi.

At the newspaper offices Linda had discovered that there would be a decisive city council meeting the following day. For the first time, perhaps, there was a majority prepared to vote to move the travellers' camps outside Rome immediately. For the mayor and the council there was now no other choice if they wanted to avoid an electoral massacre.

She was now about to do something that both her editor and Balistreri would not only have disapproved of, but forcefully deplored. She was prepared, having brought along something to use as a weapon, but it was still a dangerous business. This was a part of her she knew well, ever since she used to ask her mother questions that she couldn't answer.

Linda demands the truth, even when it could do a great deal of harm.

The Marius Travel office was closed for lunch. Behind the glass door she could see two young men, who had to be Mircea and Greg, eating a sandwich and drinking a beer. Two ordinary employees. No one would have thought they were exploitative pimps or perhaps worse.

When she knocked the taller of the two glanced at her, sizing her up. She gave the smile she hadn't given for a good many years but remembered perfectly well – the smile that men interpret as freely as they wish.

Mircea opened the door, locking it behind him as he let her in. They looked at her with mocking smiles of condescension.

'The agency's still closed,' said Greg, 'but if there's anything we can do for you . . .'

Linda showed her press card. 'I'd like to speak to Mircea.'

They stiffened a little, but then Mircea sniggered and signalled to her to take a seat in front of the desk at the back of the room. Linda was aware that there they couldn't be seen from outside, but there was nothing else she could do. Mircea sat opposite her and Greg at her side, blocking any escape route. She saw that the key was no longer in the lock.

'So what d'you want to speak to me about, lady journalist?'

'About supper with Nadia on December the 23rd,' Linda said calmly. For many reasons, she had no fear of them. Yes, they were two dangerous young men, but she had no more fear, ever.

'And what do I get in return?' Mircea asked, looking at her breasts provocatively, without worrying about the vertical crease on her forehead.

'If you have any information useful for my piece I'll make you a present.'

'What kind of a present, lady? Some cash?'

After a huge effort, she managed to give that smile again.

'All right then,' said Mircea. 'It's very simple. Me and Nadia went there on the Metro, about nine. We ate, argued, I left there and called Greg, who was nearby in an amusement arcade. We took the Metro and were at the Bar Biliardo by midnight. You can ask the Albanian barman and the other girl Ramona, who were there.'

'What were you arguing about?'

He looked at her in a provocative manner. 'Nadia had said she was tired and that I'd promised her a night off. So she didn't want to have sex. And I don't waste my time with women who don't want to have sex.'

'And so you wouldn't even have taken her out to dinner.' Her tone was still polite, understanding, as if a child had told her why it was eating chocolate in secret. In reality, what Mircea was saying was only what men in general thought.

'Yeah, I don't waste time and money like that.'

'Then you took her straight to Piazza del Popolo at eleven thirty.' She said it softly, as if stating the obvious, knowing she was stepping dangerously close to the mark.

A slight hesitation, a fleeting glance at Greg. The chair squeaked. *So that's the truth. You were just the delivery man.*

'I don't follow,' Mircea said at last.

'All right, let's change the subject. Do you know a nightclub called Bella Blu?'

His features relaxed and he looked relieved. 'Never heard of it,' said Mircea straight away.

'OK, tell me about the Cristal place. You know the club, don't you?'

'Of course,' Mircea replied, more relaxed. 'Me and Greg go there once in a while.'

'Some beautiful pieces of ass there, like you,' said Greg, feeling obliged to emphasize the point with a wink.

'You took Ramona there,' Linda said to Mircea. She could feel the danger clearly as she got close to the crucial area, but she had to press on. She tried not to look at the door and confined herself to taking out her mobile phone with its send message ready and pressing it as she transferred it from her bag to her pocket.

'Could have, I don't remember.' Mircea was now looking menacingly at her, and Greg was almost on top of her.

'You had to introduce her to a policeman, Colajacono, and he had to introduce her to someone else,' Linda concluded.

Greg was already on his feet. Linda saw him go to the glass door and draw down the blind.

'Does Marius Hagi know about this business of the Cristal and the Bella Blu?' she asked, looking Mircea straight in the eye.

He lost control and grasped her hand savagely. 'Now take my cock out and suck it, slut!'

She went on looking him straight in the eye. 'You wouldn't like that at all.'

Mircea read something in that look, something that made him loosen his grip.

Before he could make a grab at her again, she'd taken the canister from her bag and aimed the stinging spray right in his face. As Mircea staggered back screaming, they heard a violent knocking on the glass door.

'Who the fuck's knocking like that? Fucking . . .' swore Greg, pulling back the blind.

He instantly recognized the mountain of muscle with the pistol in her hand and jumped back a step. He still remembered the blow she had landed on his solar plexus. He pulled out the key, quietly opened the door and let Linda Nardi go over to Giulia Piccolo's side.

While they were returning on foot to the office after the visit to the trust administrator, Corvu called Media City in the Arab Emirates on his mobile. He obtained Belhrouz's number and then rang him. He spoke surprisingly good Italian and said he could meet them in Dubai the following day with no trouble.

Soon after, Corvu's mobile rang. He lowered his voice as he answered. 'Yes, of course, but I can't take you to the funfair tonight. See you later. 'Bye.'

'Your little niece?' asked Balistreri sarcastically. Corvu blushed violently and said nothing.

Balistreri suddenly stopped in front of a shop window to tie his shoelace. 'You've a good memory for faces, haven't you, Corvu?'

'It's one of my specialities. I'm a walking archive of names and faces.'

'Then take a look.'

Corvu was appalled to find himself staring into a window full of women's risqué underwear. It was a shop for sexy lingerie. 'I don't understand, Dottore . . .'

'Don't look inside, look at the reflection,' said Balistreri, turning to the other shoe. 'On the opposite pavement, next to the lamp post.'

Corvu stiffened. 'The guy with the newspaper?'

'Yes.'

'He was outside the pizza place when we bought two slices.'

Balistreri nodded and set off at a brisk pace.

'Nano had the feeling he was being followed before he visited Ornella Corona,' Corvu recalled.

And I saw a grey saloon outside the Bella Blu. And other little things . . .

'All right, let's leave it there. You go back to the office.'

'You're not coming?'

'I'll meet up with you later. I have to explain our trip to Pasquali. But first I have to make the acquaintance of a beautiful lady.'

Bottom, one hundred per cent. A woman who'd let you do anything you wanted while she filed her nails and then, when you'd finished, she'd start to paint them.

A first glance at Ornella Corona was enough to confirm to Balistreri that Nano was infallible in that field.

Her deep black hair, smooth and shiny, was gathered in a pony-tail that fell to her hips. Her distant and bored eyes regarded him without curiosity. The wristwatch with the eye and eyelashes winked from the slender wrist.

'So you're the famous Michele Balistreri, the supercop we hear so much about.'

She said it with no irony, but slightly puzzled, as if she thought he'd look different.

'Would you like to see some proof of identity, Signora?'

'No, it's just that you don't fit my idea of a coldly analytical detective, you know, like those in English detective novels.'

'You were expecting someone with a pipe and moustache?'

Instead you get someone who looks like a retired punch-drunk boxer.

Ornella Corona smiled and Balistreri could easily imagine how many men she had knocked out with a smile like that. It wasn't a real smile, more like 'I'll let you play a while with me if you like, but when I get bored, you stop.'

She moved like a former model when she brought him something to drink and when she bent down to sit on the large sofa, folding her long legs sheathed in leggings beneath her. She wore no bra under the baggy cotton shirt.

'You can smoke if you like, Dottor Balistreri.'

'You don't smoke yourself?'

'No, it's a vice I don't have. But I'm very tolerant about the vices of others.'

All right. Let's play. Just for a while.

'I interrupted your manicure.'

Ornella Corona didn't even look at her hands. 'It's a habit,' she said. 'Every couple of weeks I change the colour, but I only paint some of the nails. I choose which ones on the spur of the moment, according to my mood at the time.'

Balistreri smelled the heavy odour of the dark purple varnish on the middle and index fingers and the thumb of her left hand. And resisted the temptation to go any further.

'I'm left-handed,' she pointed out, 'I use my left hand for a lot of things.'

'I bet you do.'

'Yes, I use these three fingers for creative things. A brush to paint with, a pen to write a poem . . .'

Balistreri tore his gaze away. He wondered what he would have done at one time with a woman like Ornella Corona and her three purple fingers. Various hypothetical activities came to mind, none of which attracted him at that moment.

I've become a sinner in thought and omission. How sick . . .

She was going on in the same tone. 'That man of yours who came to pay a visit, the little one . . .'

'Inspector Coppola.'

'Yes. He asked an awful lot of impertinent questions.'

Damned maniac, Nano . . .

'My apologies for him. When he sees a beautiful woman, Inspector Coppola sometimes—'

She started to laugh. 'I used the wrong term. I meant to say "not pertinent".'

Balistreri looked her in the face. 'I'll put one to you that he didn't ask.'

She tucked herself up a little more and looked him directly in the eye. 'Not pertinent or impertinent?'

'Pertinent, Signora, because the situation has changed a little. We have reason to believe that the Bella Blu wasn't the scene of the crime through accident. And therefore any questions regarding the Bella Blu are all pertinent.'

'But I haven't been there in ages,' she protested, suddenly serious, concerned.

'That is, from the time you sold your ENT shares to Avvocato Ajello?'

'No, even before that, when my husband was still alive. The Bella Blu's a tiresome place.'

Ornella Corona got up. With her graceful walk she went up to the drinks trolley and poured out a grapefruit juice with her back turned. The leggings fitted her like a glove.

You have to turn round. I want to see your face, not your behind, when I put the question to you.

When she turned round she was ready. 'And what would your question be, Dottor Balistreri?' She sat down again, but this time leaning forward towards Balistreri. The baggy shirt now offered a clear view of the panorama that must have tormented the dreams of Sandro Corona and many another man.

'Did you already know Ajello before your husband died?'

'Yes,' she replied immediately. Then, after a short pause, with a malicious gleam in her eye, she clarified: 'Fabio Ajello, the lawyer's son.'

Seeing his momentary bewilderment, she came to his aid. 'You know, I often met up with Fabio. We went to spinning sessions at the Sport Center.'

Balistreri nodded thoughtfully. 'You met Fabio Ajello through his father, I imagine.'

'No, the opposite. It was Fabio who introduced me to Avvocato Ajello once when he came to lunch at the Sports Center.'

'But how old is Fabio?' Balistreri asked, and regretted it immediately.

Now she's laughing at me. An old fool who's thinking the unthinkable. And she's amusing herself by having me think it.

'Nineteen, I think. He finished secondary school a year late and is still trying to decide which university course he should take. He's come of age, anyway,' she finished, staring at him with the most innocent look in the world.

There remained one last possibility.

'Have you been going to the Sport Center for long?'

'Five years.'

'And Fabio Ajello?'

A slight hesitation. To lie or not. She decided on the not.

The gym has books of registers.

'He's a member of the Center's water polo team – he's been one since he was a boy, I think.'

'How did you come into contact? He was a little boy, you were a young married woman.'

'I knew his mother, Signora Ajello, and Fabio through her. Then Fabio grew up and gave me swimming lessons. Then one day he introduced me to his father.'

'The father who some years later took up your husband's ENT shares.'

She remained silent. That was her way. Evasiveness instead of a lie – only a few privileged people can allow themselves to do this in a relationship where the powers are unequal. Balistreri imagined the good soul of Sandro Corona in this woman's grip and felt sorry for him.

'Ajello's always been in the business. Was it him by any chance who put your husband in touch with ENT?'

He cursed himself straight away. His best card, the only ace left in the pack, thrown down far too soon. And all for his male chauvinist solidarity with a dead man he never knew.

Morally done in by this siren. Perhaps physically as well.

Ornella Corona was no longer smiling. She was considering her options. One was obvious. She could say 'It's none of your business, Dottor Balistreri. What's all this got to do with Camarà?'

Naturally she was too clever to make a mistake like that. So she chose her usual tactic, evasiveness. 'I haven't the slightest idea.'

She wasn't confirming that she knew Ajello before 2002, nor that she had introduced her husband to him. She hadn't confirmed that it was Ajello who had introduced Sandro Corona to ENT. And even less had she confirmed that that it was Ajello who had suggested the life insurance policy with which she had bought the very nice apartment.

Her answer neither denied nor confirmed anything. He could now ask other more detailed questions, go deeper, dig further, get her into a corner. She knew this very well as she shamelessly showed off her splendid bosom. And he was looking at it, thinking of Linda Nardi and the vertical crease that scored her forehead each time he let his gaze fall in that direction.

She got up uncertainly. 'My head's spinning, Dottore. I'm going to lie down in my bedroom. We can carry on talking in there.'

He followed her, already having an idea of what he would find there. A large circular bed, an enormous mirror in front of it. Once upon a time he would have handcuffed her in front of the mirror, taken her leggings down to her knees and thrashed her with his belt until he drew blood. Which was what she wanted.

He stopped on the threshold.

I'm stopping on the threshold of a conscience I detest . . .

'I'll let you rest, Signora. Please don't bother to see me out.'

Ornella Corona was only a fork in a road that started from very far away. And only when he was outside once again and saw the posters with the face of the Deputy Mayor, Augusto De Rossi, preaching the words *Only integration can put a stop to the violence* did he feel certain of it. The man with the newspaper leaning against a traffic light was watching him, smoking calmly.

'They're all in there questioning the shepherd. The Public Prosecutor's there and the lawyer,' Margherita informed him.

She was a little embarrassed but happy, which touched Balistreri. There was a flower in half a glass of water on her desk.

'All right. And Mastroianni's made arrangements for Ramona?'

'He's come to an agreement with the Romanian police and the Iordanescu girl. She'll be back in Italy on the plane arriving late in the evening the day after tomorrow.'

'Any news from Nano?'

'Inspector Coppola's also in there for the questioning. He's still not managed to trace the American tourist.'

'And what about Carmen, Camarà's girlfriend? Has he seen her?'

'Yes,' Margherita replied. 'He's sent you an e-mail with a summary.'

'Well, you have access to my e-mail. What does he say?'

Margherita was as red as a pepper. 'I think I'd rather you read it yourself, Dottore.'

When he was alone, he lit a cigarette and opened Nano's e-mail. *Subject: Camarà's urinary infection. After a lot of insisting I received a copy of the certificate from the doctor they went to. Symptoms: itching, a burning feeling, swelling, urgent and frequent micturation. Diagnosis: acute prostate inflammation. Therapy: systemic and local antibiotics. P.S. A friend of mine who specializes in men's diseases says this often happens to those who practise unprotected anal intercourse. Black people's poor hygiene makes the inflammation more likely.* Naturally, the last racist supposition came from Coppola, not the specialist. But the picture in Balistreri's mind was filling up.

Camarà's prostate inflammation and Nadia's small theft had upset the murderer's plans.

He called in Corvu and Piccolo from where they were questioning Vasile. 'Let Coppola and Mastroianni carry on with the Prosecutor; we'll come back to it together.'

He read out Coppola's e-mail on Carmen and Camarà.

'I don't see what this has to do with it, Dottore. We already have the lighter to link Nadia to the Bella Blu,' said Corvu, confused.

'Precisely, but the lighter doesn't link Nadia to Camarà. Why was he killed?'

When it came to intuition, Piccolo was always the first to get there. 'Because he saw Nadia that night . . .'

'I don't think so,' Corvu objected. 'Nadia would have entered the private lounge directly from the back alley.'

'Exactly,' agreed Balistreri. 'The meeting between Nadia and

Camarà occurred when he went to pay an urgent visit to the lavatory, just as Nadia was coming in from the back alley. The doors are all along that corridor. Unfortunately for Camarà, Nadia's not alone. Someone else sees him and in that moment his fate's sealed.'

'But why? It doesn't stand up,' Corvu protested. 'You don't commit a murder for things like that.'

Again it was Giulia Piccolo who came forward, her voice heavy with rage. 'Unless the bastard knew he was going to murder Nadia the following day. And that's why they wanted the lighter back.'

Keep your cool now, girl. With prejudices and a hot head you only make grave errors.

There was another point that needed immediate clarification. The most dangerous connection. All three went into the interrogation room. After greeting the Public Prosecutor and the appointed defence lawyer, Balistreri noted the plaster cast on the wrist Colajacono had crushed. He asked the Prosecutor for permission to ask a question and turned to Vasile.

'When they brought the Giulia GT back to you, was there any difference apart from the broken headlight?' he asked him.

'No, nothing,' murmured the shepherd.

'Was there any new smell in the car?' He noticed Corvu's amazement and then saw him blench. Then came the shepherd's subdued voice.

'Smell of cigarettes – yes, much more than usual, very much. I smoke only when other man offer.'

'But no stubs, right? Because smoke doesn't reveal any DNA but stubs do.'

He heard Corvu swearing in Sardinian. Balistreri then addressed the Prosecutor and the lawyer. 'Do carry on. Please excuse us.'

His deputies followed him into his office again.

'Dottore, I'm sorry, my mistake.' Corvu's voice was a whisper. 'I'm mortified. I don't know how it could have happened.'

Balistreri knew very well what had happened. *The Natalya effect.*

He felt for Corvu's embarrassment, but couldn't avoid the fact that there was worse for him. 'One of the three Roma boys said that the Invisible Man was smoking while they were raping Samantha Rossi.'

Corvu and Piccolo staggered. 'It's not possible!' they exclaimed in unison.

The three folders were still on his desk: Samantha Rossi, Nadia X, Marius Hagi.

We're only at the start of the game. These are only the first three cards on the table. The decisive ones are yet to be revealed.

Evening

He had decided not to annoy Pasquali or cause him any concern, otherwise he might create a fuss about the Dubai trip. So nothing about suspicions of being followed and nothing on any links between the murders of Samantha and Nadia. The Bella Blu lighter was enough to justify the short visit.

Antonella greeted him with a decaf and made a slight fuss over him, as a sister would over her unruly brother.

'You look tired, Michele. You should rest if you can.'

She ushered him into the less well-appointed meeting room. So there was no Chief of Police, Floris. Pasquali came in after a minute, more impeccably dressed than usual. His hair was fresh from the barber and he wore a new made-to-measure suit. He shot a slightly disapproving glance at the sleeve of Balistreri's jacket. If he knew that breaking into the cellars of an apartment block under investigation had caused the tear his disapproval would have been more evident.

'I know that you and Corvu are leaving tonight for Dubai,' he began without preamble. Of course, all requests of this nature passed across his desk, even if Balistreri had his own independent budget.

He illustrated the link between Nadia, Bella Blu and ENT, including the outcome of the visit to the trust's administrator. He had to credit Pasquali's excellent capacity for listening and asking few but pertinent questions.

'Where does ENT fit in with Nadia and Camarà?' he asked at last.

Now you're worried. Is it about the R and the E or ENT? Or both things together?

'Camarà was killed there – at the moment we know nothing else. But Nadia was in the private lounge the night before they kidnapped her. We can't exclude the possibility that she might have been with one of the ENT business partners. If we didn't investigate we might be overlooking an important lead.'

'There's no need for subtle threats. Isn't there a less costly method of finding out the names of these business partners?'

'It would appear not. Corona's dead, Ajello says he's never met them and his only contact is with Trevi, who deals only with the Lebanese lawyer Belhrouz. Signora Corona once spoke with one of them on the telephone, but she didn't know who it was . . .'

Pasquali stared fixedly at him. 'Do you think there's a serious link between the murder of Nadia and that of Camarà?'

It's no use, he's too sharp.

Balistreri knew how slippery the ground was, but under those inquisitive eyes he had to make a reply. Pasquali would catch on to any possible lies.

'Perhaps Camarà unwittingly saw whoever had it in mind to kill Nadia.'

Pasquali fiddled with his glasses while he weighed up his reply. 'And after a few hours, this whoever-it-is dresses up as a motor-cyclist, feigns an argument and kills him.'

'No, it can't have been exactly like that,' said Balistreri.

'I don't follow,' objected Pasquali.

'Let's say that this character, let's even call him the murderer, already intended to kill Nadia out of some sadistic sexual compulsion. But at that moment he hasn't yet killed anyone. Does it seem logical to you to improvise something so complicated as this in order to protect himself against a crime he hasn't yet committed? And what crime? Killing a Romanian prostitute? He could have given up on her and killed another one just the same three days later. Unless . . .'

You're an idiot, Balistreri. Pasquali's managed to get you to reveal your innermost thoughts. And now you can see something in his eyes you don't understand.

He immediately backtracked. 'Naturally, there are more plausible explanations. This character wanted to kill Nadia specifically, her alone. Perhaps he was a disappointed lover. You know, an obsessive-compulsive . . .'

Pasquali looked at him closely from behind his spectacles.

OK, we both know this is bullshit. I'm asking for a truce. Let me have it and let me check things out in Dubai. Pretend you believe me and let's post-pone the Samantha Rossi problem.

Pasquali stole a glance at his expensive Piaget. It meant the truce was granted.

'One last thing,' he said, stopping Balistreri before he could leave. 'Linda Nardi.'

Since Balistreri was a boy he had learned to his own cost how to sniff out real danger, so he said nothing.

Pasquali wasn't even looking at him, he was staring at the computer screen. 'A most intelligent woman. And very dangerous for us and for you. Be very careful, Balistreri, and keep as far away from her as you can.'

Angelo offered to take him to the airport for the night flight to Dubai. He was both cheerful and thoughtful at the same time.

'Michele, you're not upset about Margherita, are you?'

'No problem, Angelo. I've already had her in every single position.'

He saw him turn pale, his knuckles tight on the steering wheel. Then they burst out laughing together.

'You shit! You piece of shit, Michele. Margherita would never let you have it.'

'If I'd wanted to, she'd have let me. But I've no longer got any interest in cradle-snatching the inexperienced.'

'While Linda Nardi, on the other hand . . .'

Balistreri looked at him, amazed and a little disconcerted. 'How the hell do you know . . .'

'A snippet from Graziano. Don't get mad.'

'I'll wing him back to his mountain goats in Sardinia. Corvu's in love and has lost his senses. The usual equation.'

'He thinks a lot of you, as if you were his father. He wants to see you happy, like we all do. And he says that Linda Nardi is just your type . . .'

Balistreri interrupted him with a threatening gesture. 'You can stop all this bullshit. The Nardi woman's an arrogant and presumptuous shit − lesbian or frigid, I don't know, and I don't want to know. I wouldn't touch her, not even—'

For some strange reason Dioguardi burst out laughing.

'What the fuck are you laughing at, Angelo? Are you simple?'

'Nothing. It's just that I've never heard you talk so unkindly about a beautiful woman in all the time I've known you.'

Tuesday, 3 January 2006

Morning

During the night flight to Dubai Balistreri couldn't sleep a wink, the seats were so small and uncomfortable. Business class on expenses was only for politicians and top executives, not for those who went about trying to find those who committed murder. Beside him, Corvu was making use of the small screen on the back of the seat in front for endless poker challenges.

He fell asleep exhausted during the last hour of the flight when they were already over the Arabian Peninsula, music from the headphones still penetrating his ears.

The Ottoman odalisque had her face half-covered, but her body was draped in transparent veils. When his eyes fell on her breasts a vertical line furrowed her brow. He murmured words of apology, but couldn't manage to shift his gaze and realized with horror that his hands, which were no longer linked to the control of his brain, were loosening the knots and progressively revealing the girl's nakedness. She let him do as he wished, silent and unmoving. Her eyes stared at him from the opening in her veil. It's your choice, they were saying.

He awoke bathed in sweat when the undercarriage hit the runway. Corvu was already prepared: map of Dubai, address in Media City, Nabil Belhrouz's telephone number, passport, landing card, sunglasses, baseball cap, Lacoste shirt and light cotton trousers.

Balistreri looked at him, astounded. 'Corvu, I think you forgot the butterfly net.'

'Dottore, I think you should take the woollen jacket off. It's only eight in the morning, but it's already twenty-five degrees.'

The airport was a super-modern building, full of noisy shops. Courteous officials in long white robes helped them quickly through the formalities.

Huge hoardings advertised new residential centres in the middle of the sea in the shape of palms. Outside the terminal they were met by a clear sky and a late spring temperature, together with a horde of drivers with placards waiting for business executives. To their surprise they saw one that read *Mr Balistreri – Mr Corvu*.

'It must be part of the travel package with the hotel, but our travel bureau didn't say anything,' said Corvu.

The driver in his dark blue suit was a young Pakistani who continually called them 'sir'. He led them through a forest of big-engined cars and SUVs to a limousine. Inside it was air-conditioned, with a bar and television screen.

Corvu was about to pass the address to the driver, but he anticipated them. 'Media City, yes?'

Balistreri immediately asked him to turn up the temperature inside, which was freezing owing to the air conditioning. The traffic was already very heavy. The driver explained that Dubai had exploded from the demographic and residential point of view and it would take some time to reach the centre. The limousine moved slowly between Porsches, Ferraris and Lamborghinis rolling along brand new roads. The number of cranes and skyscrapers under construction was incredible. They crossed the bridge over the Creek that divided the two halves of the city and came into the more modern side.

Gleaming skyscrapers soared in bold forms of glass and marble. Corvu took up his role of guide with enthusiasm.

'It's the emirate nearby, Abu Dhabi, that has the petroleum. But the smart place is Dubai – skyscrapers, seven-star hotels like the Vela, shopping centres out of sci-fi, a ski slope perfectly covered in snow right next to the beach. And drink, nightclubs, girls . . .'

They took the wide Sheikh Zayed Road that led to the new built-up areas and hotels along the sands of Jumeirah Beach. They arrived in Media City at ten o'clock and it was decidedly hot. Balistreri insisted on keeping his jacket and tie on and was sweating copiously as he thought longingly of Rome's rain and cold.

The driver deposited them right in front of the main door to the building that housed the offices of ENT Middle East. They comprised only two elegant rooms plus a meeting room on the third floor. A Filipino secretary greeted them and accompanied them to the meeting room, which had a beautiful window with a view of the green sea furrowed by motorboats and catamarans.

Nabil Belhrouz was a handsome man with gleaming black hair and sunburnt complexion, thirty-five at the most.

'I can speak a little Italian, if you like.'

Balistreri accepted the offer, relieved not to need Corvu as interpreter.

'Perhaps you're surprised at my age,' said Belhrouz after having offered them a cup of American coffee, 'but here in Dubai it's all like that – a world of huge opportunity where there's room for the young.'

Balistreri liked him – an active younger man who operated with energy in a complex world. Corvu, on the other hand, was a little in competition with him and kept to himself.

'Now, Avvocato Belhrouz, you know that we're here because one of the ENT nightclubs in Rome, the Bella Blu, was the scene of a crime before Christmas,' Corvu began.

'Yes, I read your e-mail and will give you all the information I have, even if I haven't really understood the connection with the crime.'

Corvu decided to ignore the implicit request. 'We know that ninety per cent of ENT's shares are held by an Italian trust that receives its orders from ENT (Middle East). We need to trace the ENT (Middle East) shareholders.'

'Of course,' Belhrouz agreed. 'Naturally, you gentlemen being Italian, you'll understand certain questions. Anonymity is totally protected here.'

Balistreri and Corvu exchanged a worried glance.

'I mean,' Belhrouz explained, 'that if you are expecting to find the first and second names of persons residing physically in Europe, then you won't ever find them here in Dubai. And this is the case with ENT (Middle East).'

He handed a sheet to each of them. It was a type of simplified shareholders' register, certified in the Media City Free Zone for the Dubai Chamber of Commerce. On it was the single shareholder of ENT (Middle East): ENT (Seychelles) with its headquarters in the Seychelles.

Corvu gave Balistreri a troubled look. 'I should have known,' he muttered.

'So we have made a completely wasted journey,' said Balistreri in Arabic. Surprised by the language, Belhrouz thought for a moment, then replied in Italian.

'Not entirely, Dottore. Yours is a difficult quest and this is a difficult world, almost impenetrable for various reasons – nearly always for tax, but also for less legal motives. As far as I know, absolutely legal in the case of ENT. I'd like to help you, however . . .'

He was a likeable young man, clearly well recompensed to act as front man and ignore any seamy traffic underneath. But you could see that he was worried. He wasn't a citizen of the Emirates and a murder investigation wasn't a joke. Italy had an embassy in Dubai and even a polite protest over a far from satisfactory cooperation could cause him problems. The sheikhs wanted to live in a clean and ordered civilized country. A young Lebanese lawyer would have been expelled even if he wasn't really guilty of anything.

'There are no night-time flights to Italy so I imagine you'll be leaving early tomorrow morning. Which hotel are you staying in?' Belhrouz asked.

'The Hilton Jumeirah.'

'Excellent. You have all the day free. So please enjoy the sunshine and I'll pick you up at seven. I'm taking you out to dinner. We can talk in a less formal way.'

It was clear that he didn't want to talk inside the office. They had no choice but to accept. Before leaving, Balistreri said, 'Thanks, too, for the car you sent to pick us up from the airport.'

Belhrouz looked at them bewildered. 'I didn't send anyone – you didn't ask me to.'

Balistreri had an annoying thought. 'Then it was our own travel bureau. We'll see you this evening.'

Afternoon

They had arranged to meet the day before, after the brief explanations outside Marius Travel.

'I could have managed with the old pepper spray,' Linda said, 'but thanks all the same for the help. I imagine you'll have to say something to Dottor Balistreri.'

Piccolo smiled. 'I was following you after I heard about your visit to the restaurant. But it was my idea. Balistreri wouldn't have approved. It's better we keep this to ourselves.'

They agreed to meet the following day in the bar, where they were now quietly taking tea like two old ladies.

'I have a proposal for you, Giulia.'

Piccolo looked at her. Linda Nardi was beautiful, intelligent, sensitive. But it was also clear she had no sexual interest in her whatsoever.

She listened to the proposal in silence, while her blood ran hot and she felt ripples of excitement.

An older sister. More sensible than I am, but prepared to do anything, like me.

'Aren't you afraid?' Piccolo asked, for the sake of hearing her say what she wanted to hear her say.

And Linda said it, with her peaceful look. 'My only fear is that this business will continue.'

The well-organized Corvu had brought two pairs of swimming shorts along, one for himself and one for Balistreri. They spent the day on the hotel beach until five o'clock. Every so often Corvu phoned Natalya and told her what he was seeing. He took pictures with his mobile phone and sent them to his beloved. He took a tour in a parachute attached to a motorboat. He went on the ski slope. He swam for over an hour. Balistreri refused to follow him in any kind of activity and fell asleep on the beach.

He had a confused dream in which Linda Nardi spoke to him in a language he didn't know.

Evening

When Belhrouz came by to pick them up in his Audi A8 it was dark, but there was a light breeze and the temperature was mild and pleasant.

The restaurant was on a rotunda in the middle of the sea. They sat outside by the water illuminated by the lights from the skyscrapers.

The average age of the diners was about thirty and the standard of girls was stratospheric, as were the prices that caught Balistreri's eye in the menu and the tiger prawns he ordered.

During the meal Belhrouz talked about his family, who were of Palestinian origin: his grandparents driven out by the Israelis, and his parents who miraculously escaped the Lebanese Christian army in 1982 in Shatila. All the while the young lawyer was drinking white wine and following the magnificent toing and froing of the girls.

At the end of dinner, with a scotch on the rocks and a good cigar, Belhrouz said: 'Dubai is one huge game of chance and the bank is the state of the world economy. You see, here it's the same as in your Gospels – the loaves and fishes get multiplied every day. Real estate, finance, tourism, everything.'

'Because no one asks where the money comes from,' observed Corvu.

'Exactly. The Russians, Chinese, Iraqis, Iranians, Saudis – all come with suitcases full of cash to buy a skyscraper. No one asks where the money comes from. Industrial activity or contraband weapons? Supermarkets or traffic in organs? No difference, the money is always good.'

'But if the economy slows down and the recycling comes under pressure from governments who want to tax everything . . .' said Corvu.

Belhrouz pointed to the magnificent silhouette of the world's most elegant hotel.

'Those suites costing a minimum of four thousand dollars a night are booked up for the next two years. But they can become void in two days. And I'll go back to East Beirut,' he concluded with a sad smile.

Balistreri decided it was the right time to pick up from where they had left off that morning. 'And what would we find by going to the Seychelles?'

Belhrouz smiled. 'More beautiful beaches. Another nominee. And so on.'

'And at the end of all these circles?'

Knocking back his fourth whisky, the young lawyer was looking avariciously at the Russian waitress' behind.

'In the end, Dottor Balistreri, you would find yourselves at the point where you started in Italy. The truth lies there.'

'But how can we—'

'Listen to me,' Belhrouz said in a low voice. 'You seem to be a serious man. I only need your word on two things.'

'I'm listening.'

'You must never mention my name.'

'Agreed. And the second thing?'

'My sister's studying at an Italian university in Aquila. Once, when I was staying with her, she answered my mobile by mistake and it was one of ENT's partners. I might need a favour sometime.'

'You have my word.'

Belhrouz drained his fifth whisky and paid the bill. He was clearly tipsy. He handed them a visiting card. 'I don't want to talk here and I have to pass by the office to pick up some papers for you. We'll see each other at my house in an hour. Give the taxi driver the card with my private address on it.'

They went with him to the exit. His Audi was brought to him and a little shakily he said goodbye in the hoarse voice of the happy drunk. 'See you later, my Italian friends!'

Balistreri's gaze followed the car as it left in the direction of Sheikh Zayed Road. A huge SUV set off behind it as soon as it was out of the car park.

He took out his mobile, called the hotel and spoke to the porter.

'I wanted to know if the journeys to and from the airport were included in the booking our travel bureau made.'

He heard the Filipino checking his computer. 'No, sir, this service was not included.'

He shut his mobile and ran towards the taxi rank. Corvu followed him in surprise.

'What's going on, Dottore?'

'Get a move on and no questions.'

Balistreri immediately gave fifty dollars to the Pakistani driver and pointed to the Audi A8 and the SUV two hundred metres ahead.

At that hour there was less traffic and the taxi's acoustic warning signal for excess speed was going crazy. The driver looked at him in the rear mirror. 'We go prison, sir.'

Balistreri showed him a hundred-dollar note and the driver accelerated. He saw the rear lights of the large SUV and the Audi entering the series of bends before the flyover.

'Have you got Belhrouz's mobile number?' Balistreri barked at Corvu.

'Yes.'

'Then call him immediately and hand him to me.'

Belhrouz answered on the second ring, his voice thick with drink.

'My Italian friend,' he said happily.

'There's an SUV on your tail. Slow down and try to stop.'

'What do you mean?' laughed Belhrouz.

Balistreri saw the SUV accelerate and swerve alongside the Audi.

He distinctly heard Belhrouz's exclamation of surprise – 'What the hell?' – and the metallic clash of the two vehicles as the Audi was rammed. It careered to the right, hit the guardrail, overturned and skidded back over to the far side of the lane where it hit the other guardrail and reared up over it. Then it fell the twenty metres below it.

The secret mobile rang three and a half minutes after Belhrouz's Audi A8 crashed along the Sheikh Zayed Road and burst into flames.

Pasquali had just arrived home and was greeting his wife. When he heard that mobile ringing he knew he had to leave even her company. Only one person had that number: a person who Pasquali both respected and feared, and by whom he was trusted.

Lord, I did it for the good of the country, perhaps for power, but not for money . . .

He went into his study and answered the caller without saying a word.

It was the voice he knew well. 'It was necessary to intervene seriously.'

Pasquali gave a deep sigh and said nothing. This really was quite unforeseen. But protesting was as dangerous as it was useless.

'We want no problems here when your man returns. Please see to it,' the voice finished.

The call was over. Pasquali had not said a word. Before leaving the room he gave a fleeting glance at the crucifix and bowed his head.

As foreseen, Colajacono left the police station at nine. Piccolo had let the news that Giorgi and Adrian had spoken about him filter down to him by means that were untraceable to her. They saw him enter Casilino 900 without any difficulty; he was in uniform and well known.

After a few minutes, they followed him in. They were dressed like two gypsies and no one asked them anything. The camp was lit feebly by oil lamps in the huts; few adults were still about given the cold. The smell of rubbish and excrement was very strong.

They went in further, following Colajacono at an appropriate distance.

'Stick with him – I'll be behind you,' said Piccolo. 'If Colajacono sees me we've had it.'

Linda went on, trying not to lose sight either of Colajacono or her way in the maze of huts and piles of refuse.

I knew what fear was many years ago. And since then I've wiped it out.

Colajacono entered a caravan. 'That one belongs to Adrian and Giorgi,' Giulia told her.

Linda positioned herself under a half-open window.

'I'll tear you to bits with my own hands!' Colajacono's voice sounded furious.

Linda crouched down, knowing she had to be patient as she calmly prepared the small portable infrared video camera.

She clearly heard the sound of the first slap, then the second. The two Romanians protested feebly.

'Now tell me the truth or I'll grind your fucking balls into a pulp!'

This was the moment; she breathed in and rose to her feet, ready to film. The scene was perfect: two youths on the floor and a uniformed policeman pointing a pistol at them. She filmed for a few seconds, then Colajacono saw her. Before he rushed outside, she threw the camera to Piccolo who hid herself behind a nearby shack.

Colajacono came out swearing, the pistol still in his hand. 'You ugly little slut, I'll break your neck.'

His backhand swipe caught Linda on the cheek, sending her to the ground.

The violent are so predictable. Get it well filmed, Giulia.

'You gypsy piece of shit, hand me that video camera,' said Colajacono menacingly.

'I'm an Italian journalist,' she said, picking herself up and wiping the blood trickling from a split lip. He stepped back, confused, then stared in amazement at the press card. He knew the name. He thought for a moment, then made up his mind, his piggish eyes reflecting pure hate.

'Then it is my duty to search you for it,' he said, prodding her with the pistol barrel into the caravan where Adrian and Giorgi looked on, bewildered.

Piccolo continued to film, torn between her satisfaction over the plan that was working and the desire to intervene. But Linda had been insistent: 'Only when I give you the signal.' She moved closer to the caravan.

'OK, my clever journalist, where've you put the camera? Is it perhaps between your lovely pair of tits?'

Piccolo heard the guffaws of the three men. Now Adrian and Giorgi were getting some fun. She managed to see Linda shaking her head. It was a sign addressed to her.

No, not yet, wait.

'Well, all right, I'll have to search you – you'll like that. Then I'll also make a nice film of you giving a blow job to these two good lads here, so if you feel the need to create any problems for me I'll post it on the internet.'

Piccolo kept filming, shaking with rage as Colajacono lifted off Linda's coat, jumper and blouse. He stopped at her bra.

'Right, lads,' Colajacono said to the two Romanians. 'Let's see if she's hiding it between her tits or her legs.'

'No, wait.' Linda Nardi said. 'I'll tell you where it is.'

This was the signal. Piccolo quickly hid the video camera under the caravan, took out her pistol and in an instant pulled the door open.

'Hands up, all of you,' she said, pointing the pistol with savage pleasure.

Don't shoot them, Giulia, don't shoot. We can fuck them over better alive.

Incredulous, Colajacono hesitated a moment, glancing regretfully at the pistol he'd laid on the table. The look on Piccolo's face dissuaded him – it was clear she needed no excuse to shoot him. Slowly he began to understand the shit into which he was sinking.

'Now lie down on the floor,' she ordered, while Linda got dressed again and left with all due speed.

Piccolo let several minutes pass, giving her friend time to get out of the camp with the video camera. In the meantime, she listened in amusement as Colajacono swore and gave out obscene threats.

'You're finished, Colajacono. The whole scene's been filmed, including the attempted rape of a journalist.'

'You're a stinking whore, you filthy dyke. You think we don't know what cunt-lickers like you get up to with each other?'

Piccolo laughed. 'I shouldn't bother provoking me. I won't lay a finger on a piece of shit like you. I'll let your cellmates see to that. D'you know what they do to police who end up inside? You'll spend a few years sucking cock and taking it up the arse. Now get up.'

Colajacono rose up, trembling with rage.

'The video camera's outside the camp, already on its way to the newspaper. You have till tomorrow midnight to tell us who was with Nadia in Bella Blu's private lounge on the night of December the 23rd. If you tell us we'll check it out, and if it's true the story will end there. Otherwise you'll see yourself on TV and the internet.'

Colajacono looked at her, bewildered. 'Who Nadia was with at the Bella Blu? How in God's name should I know that?'

'Ask your mate Mircea – he knows for sure. He took her out to dinner and handed her over to someone who took her to the Bella Blu and then killed her.'

'You're a fool, as usual. It was that shepherd, Vasile.'

Piccolo shook her head. 'Give us that name – the right one. If not, you'll be watching yourself on YouTube.'

She left him, incredulous, to meditate on the disaster.

Wednesday, 4 January 2006

Morning

Thanks to the three-hour time difference, the return flight had them back in Rome before lunchtime.

The night before in Dubai, Balistreri had decided not to go after the SUV. The taxi driver was already terrified, even if he had fortunately not understood their connection with what had happened. A chase along the roads of Dubai was ruled out – a shooting could have followed and a huge diplomatic incident. He had ordered Corvu to write a report saying only that Belhrouz had had a fatal accident after getting drunk at dinner. No hint of the meeting at his house, the hit-and-run SUV or of the driver who came to pick them up at the airport.

It wasn't only Belhrouz's accident that was troubling him. He was also worried by the driver who knew about their arrival and intended destination. We always know where you are, who you're with and what you're talking about. Certainly their conversation with Belhrouz either at the ENT offices or at dinner had been heard. And it had decreed the young lawyer's fate.

A warning – a card dealt – from someone who feels untouchable. They knew he would recognize the style, because he had

practised it for years. The threat was real, concrete. Whoever entered
the circle was at risk. It was essential not to involve others in the
game. It was now necessary to choose between his life or finding
out the truth.

*Once I wouldn't even have given it a thought. But today I don't want any
more regrets, any more sins to atone for.*

Piccolo met him at Leonardo da Vinci airport with Nadia's file.
She had that euphoric air that Balistreri associated with big trouble.
As they drove towards the centre of Rome, there was none of the
usual congestion. The schools were closed, offices operated with
fewer staff, the well-heeled were skiing in the Alps, and others were
touring the Roman hills.

Balistreri gave Piccolo the censured version of the Dubai events.
Then she gave him her summary of events.

'The first thing the autopsy says indicates that she died quickly,
the same night of December the 24th. Sexual intercourse with no
marks of violence. Then strangulation. The other shepherd confirms
Vasile's version of events. And now that he knows we're dealing
with a murder I don't think he'd lie. Vasile didn't pick up Nadia on
Via di Torricola.'

'So,' concluded Corvu, 'someone else picked Nadia up, took her
to Vasile, who was drunk, they had sex and he strangled her.'

'There's one problem with that,' said Piccolo.

'Vasile's left wrist,' said Balistreri.

Piccolo looked at him in surprise. Corvu was the first to react.
'It was sprained, we know, but that was done by Colajacono during
capture.'

Balistreri shook his head. 'No, when Colajacono grabbed his wrist,
Vasile squealed immediately like a stuck pig. Now, however strong
Colajacono is, Vasile had to have injured it before . . .'

'Then he sprained his wrist in the act of strangling Nadia,' Corvu
replied.

'That's what I was hoping too,' looking at Piccolo with a questioning air.

'Unfortunately, that's not the case,' Piccolo said. 'The doctor who saw him said it was a sprain that was at least ten days old – you can tell by what's left of the swelling. Vasile maintains that he injured himself playing football in a field with some friends, and the other shepherd confirms it. He says that during the recent burglaries he had to drive and carry the heavy objects because—'

'That's not possible,' Corvu burst out. 'That means that Vasile didn't kill her. Whoever picked the girl up killed her too.'

'That's more or less it, yes,' Balistreri agreed.

Corvu was sceptical. 'But, Dottore, so this hypothetical killer goes to great lengths to get himself the Giulia GT which has nothing to do with him, he picks up Nadia without being seen, he takes her as a present to the shepherd so he can have sex with her, he waits there until the shepherd's finished taking his pleasure, and then strangles her?'

'Yes, more or less. Before strangling her, he waited until Vasile had drunk a good deal of whisky and fallen asleep,' Balistreri confirmed. 'Does it remind you of anything?'

Piccolo and Corvu stared at him incredulously.

'I know who it was,' said Piccolo at length.

'Me too,' Corvu exclaimed.

'Not me, and you two will come out with different names,' Balistreri concluded.

Our preconceptions, our certainties. Disaster's taught me to be wary of them.

Pasquali was less impeccable than usual. It was in the details. One shirt cuff protruded more than the other from his jacket sleeve. His parting was a little crooked, as if he'd dressed in a hurry after a night of clandestine sex, which in his case could almost certainly be ruled out.

He listened in silence to Balistreri's summary, which omitted to mention the tailing, the driver at the airport, Belhrouz's promise of help and the SUV.

'So now you want to go to the Seychelles, Balistreri?' There was no irony in his voice, only a sour and troubled note.

Balistreri shook his head. 'That path's closed – we'll never discover the real partners in ENT.'

'Assuming that it may have some bearing on the crimes against Nadia and Camarà,' Pasquali pointed out.

Balistreri refrained from spelling out that they were dealing with three crimes. Talking about Samantha Rossi to Pasquali only meant creating more problems.

He changed the subject. 'Pasquali, I know that this evening there's an important council meeting and that you'll be seeing the mayor, the Chief of Police and the Prefect beforehand. Could you please explain to them that—'

Pasquali nodded and pulled a face, as if he'd just bitten his tongue.

'The time frame of politics isn't the same as that of the police. To move Casilino 900 and the other camps you need a bipartisan agreement that's not there at the moment. And the Vatican's opposed to it. Would you prefer us to take the Roma out to the middle of the Mediterranean and drop them into it?'

'Pasquali, it's gone OK this time because the victims were a Romanian prostitute and a Senegalese bouncer. If it had been two Italian girls, perhaps from good families . . .'

Pasquali brushed the image away with a brusque gesture, as if to exorcize it.

'In order to avoid that,' he said, 'we need men like Colajacono too. And in any case, no one here would be lynching a Roma.'

Balistreri shook his head, disconsolate. He knew that Pasquali didn't believe what he was saying but was forced to. Indeed, another crime linked to the Roma would play into the hands of one of his new political supporters.

'Pasquali, with all due respect, I wouldn't be too sure. Someone has an interest in stoking the fire of intolerance. And racism in Italy does exist. Take a tour of the schools or the tiers of certain stadiums.'

'Nevertheless,' said Pasquali, cutting him short, 'the outcome of this evening's meeting is truly in the balance. It only needs one vote more or less on one side or another.'

'Listen, Vasile did not kill Camarà. He wasn't at the Bella Blu on the night of December the 23rd, he was with his three accomplices emptying the villas whose proprietors had left for the Christmas holidays.'

'And you believe people like that?'

'No one is going to lie for someone like Vasile and run the risk of being charged as an accomplice to murder.'

'But he killed Nadia.'

Balistreri told him about the sprained wrist.

'It makes little difference,' said Pasquali. 'It's all part of the same circle: Roma, Romanians, Casilino 900. It's there you have to look, among those people.'

Balistreri felt the disquiet start to circulate in his veins. Pasquali was insisting on the absurd. And when an intelligent person does that, it means that he has a hidden agenda.

Afternoon

The telephone call from Avvocato Morandi came out of the blue. Hagi wanted to have an informal talk with him. They settled on the Bar Biliardo immediately after lunch.

On the bus to Via Tiburtina Balistreri realized that it was less than a week since his first visit. And yet the look of the district had changed. The Christmas decorations had been put away, and out had come the political posters. He saw them from the window as they drove past. Attacks on the council, the mayor's laboured and heartfelt defence. Everyone blaming each other, everyone saying that the integration model was the wrong one, no one coming up with a solution. They were even prepared to speculate about more deaths.

The strategy of tension was the product of lofty minds. This was a tactic of mediocre ones, a real mixture of the incapable, the profiteers and the common criminal.

He looked around him in the bus. Only the old and non-EU immigrants. No suspicious tail. He concluded that they knew who he was going to see and that the trail had no interest for them. It was ENT that was the sensitive issue, certainly not the Bar Biliardo with Hagi and his acolytes.

There was a new man at the bar. Hagi was waiting for him with Morandi in the billiards room, which was closed to the public. He was coughing more than usual, but there was a happy gleam in his eyes. He made no mention of Rudi's disappearance but offered him a coffee, and they sat down by a billiards table.

'Do you play?'

'As a boy in the oratory we played with our hands – playing with cues was forbidden.'

'In my country, back in Galati, we thought playing with the hands was only for queers.'

Hagi was in no hurry and Balistreri didn't want to put pressure on him. Besides, the ENT trail having come to a dead end, they had to wait for the autopsy results and Ramona Iordanescu's return to Italy.

It was Hagi who broached the subject. 'I'm worried about Mircea. You think he may have had a role in Nadia's end. Can I ask you on what basis you make this judgement?'

And I can ask you your motives in asking me. Is it part of your mission as protector of those two delinquents?

'First I want to ask you something. If you seem sincere, I'll answer your question.'

'Fire away, Balistreri,' said Morandi, his hand smoothing his gold Rolex. 'I will decide whether my client will reply or not.'

Balistreri turned to Hagi. 'Mircea and Greg were accused of two murders in Romania the year before you brought them to Italy. Two retired employees of the Interior Ministry.'

Hagi's ambiguous aura, always teetering between the messianic and the Mephistophelian, became slightly accentuated, and he remained silent.

'They were released from prison thanks to the best barrister in Romania and then acquitted. I was wondering who paid this lawyer.'

Hagi didn't wait for Morandi's go-ahead. 'Obviously it was me. As I've already told you, I owe my life to their parents. And when they asked my help for their sons it was my duty to intervene. It was a debt of honour. I had to pay.'

'Even if it meant helping two murderers?'

'There was no proof against them. Only a witness who said he'd seen them near the farm and then retracted his statement. They would have been absolved anyway, perhaps after ten years in jail. In Romania we don't have any protectors of civil liberties, as you call them.'

As he was shaken by a cough, Hagi's eye peered into the soul of the Special Section's boss.

Balistreri remembered the last encounter with Linda Nardi and the Romanian's forbidden subject, so he asked: 'Would your wife Alina have approved, had she been alive?'

Marius Hagi assumed a slightly harder expression. 'I've already told you not to touch on this subject, Balistreri.'

'It's you who asked to see me. And now we're no longer dealing with an investigation into a person's disappearance, Signor Hagi. There's at least one murder involved.'

The man held back one of his mocking laughs. 'And what has the death of my wife in 1983 to do with that of Nadia in 2006?'

There was something in Hagi's feverish eyes that was difficult to decipher. It certainly wasn't fear. It seemed more of a mocking threat. Balistreri rose to leave.

'You didn't answer my question,' Hagi reminded him.

'And you didn't answer mine.'

'Then I'll hold onto my curiosity. Goodbye, Balistreri.' He spoke through his coughing, as he lit another cigarette.

'I'll show you out, Balistreri,' Morandi offered.

And it was there on the pavement outside the Bar Biliardo among the harmless housewives with bags of shopping, that Balistreri had confirmation of what he suspected.

Morandi was smiling, almost friendly, as he shook his hand. 'It's as cold as anything here in Rome, Balistreri. It would have been better if you'd stayed in Dubai and taken a long vacation.'

Piccolo was waiting for him not far from the Bar Biliardo. It was cold and already almost dark, but she was standing there with her leather jacket open. She gave off an air that was half euphoria and half embarrassment, which was what Balistreri feared most.

'I hope you've managed to avoid any more visits down to cellars.'

'I did better than that and worse, Dottore. If we can step into a bar I'll tell you over a nice hot cup of tea.'

When they were sitting down she pulled out a notebook. 'Some doubts came to mind and I wanted to make some checks.'

'About what?' Balistreri asked, with a tinge of apprehension.

'About Colajacono and Tatò.'

Balistreri felt relieved. The important thing was to keep his deputies well away from any risk, and after Morandi's warning he was sure that those risks were serious. But they were to do with the investigations into ENT, not in the wretched world of prostitutes, pimps, travellers, shepherds and violent, racist policemen. No one tailed them there; they could do what they wanted.

'All right, let's hear it.'

'So, let's start with that fateful December the 24th. Before they finished their shift at nine on the morning of the 24th, Colajacono told his men Marchese and Cutugno that as a reward they could skip that evening's shift. They accepted – a little surprised, but happy. Colajacono notified his right-hand man, Tatò, that they'd be standing in together for the two young policemen. Are we agreed up to now?'

'I have a few questions already and I need to smoke, but you can't in here, so I'll content myself with listening.'

'Right. But why does he want to stand in for them himself? In order to set an example, he says – to show the young policemen that real bosses make sacrifices for them. True? Let's say it is – it fits in with Colajacono's personality. But why dump this on Tatò, his most faithful deputy, as well? Because the two of them are bachelors, he says, so no one would have any hard feelings. And we can go along with this as well. What do you say, Dottore?'

Balistreri had already moved ahead, spurred on by the desire to go outside and smoke. 'Fine, Piccolo. Let's try another hypothesis. Colajacono has his own reasons for being on duty there that night and also a reason why he wants Tatò there with him. However, we'd have to show that the reasons he's given aren't the truth, or find some proof about the real reason.'

'When I questioned Tatò he was at first worried, then relaxed, and then worried again at the end of the meeting.'

'So you think he lied about something at the beginning and at the end of the questioning?'

'At the start we were talking about Colajacono's idea of their standing in for the night shift. I checked the civic registry office records. Actually Colajacono lives alone in Rome – his parents are already dead and his closest relatives live outside the city. Tatò's from the South, his parents don't live in Rome, but he has a younger sister in the city who lives by herself. She works on the checkout in a supermarket.'

'But we don't know if they usually spend Christmas together—'

'Oh yes,' replied Piccolo triumphantly, 'we do know that now. Since Tatò came to Rome they've spent every Christmas Eve together. I sent Mastroianni to the supermarket where she works. She was really upset when her brother told her that he couldn't come over. They almost had a row.'

Balistreri looked at her, astounded. 'I need to smoke – let's go outside.'

With regard to his ration, he was owed two cigarettes because of the flight – and he really needed one.

Outside it was almost dark; the lights of shop windows and vehicles were on. The Roman suburb was swarming with people coming and going in the supermarkets, shops and bars. There were a large number of immigrants in the area, hence the graffiti were against the travellers' camps. That evening the city council would come to some decision with a only very narrow margin, according to the opinions he kept hearing.

The train of his thoughts was full of heavy consequences that Balistreri had no wish to discuss in that moment. He limited himself to asking a question. 'Why did he choose Tatò?'

'Because the alibi's false and only Tatò could play ball with him about it,' said Piccolo immediately.

'What alibi are you talking about?'

'Well, the one that Tatò's giving Colajacono . . .'

'And this would be the alibi for what?'

Piccolo looked at him in surprise. 'What do you think? For Nadia's kidnapping and murder.'

'No, that doesn't hold up. You said yourself that Tatò was relaxed while telling you about this part and therefore, according to your interpretation, he wasn't lying.'

Piccolo showed her irritation. 'Not necessarily so. Suppose Colajacono was in the Giulia GT on Via di Torricola at six thirty in a beret and dark glasses.'

'That's precisely why it doesn't hold up.'

Piccolo finally saw the point. 'Shit, the Mass.'

'Please don't blaspheme,' said Balistreri, reproving her.

'He would have said that Colajacono was at Mass too between six and seven to give him a full alibi,' Piccolo muttered disconsolately.

Then she became angry, more with herself than anyone else. 'So you believe all those bastards' bullshit,' she said, almost shouting.

Balistreri waited for her to calm down. The girl had to learn to control herself.

When he saw she was less upset he said, 'No, I think both of them are lying. But we still don't know exactly what about. And therefore we don't know why.'

Piccolo seemed embarrassed, as if she still had something important to say. She walked on in gloomy silence.

They suddenly found themselves outside the Torre Spaccata police station. 'Have you brought me here on purpose?' Balistreri asked in surprise.

Now Piccolo avoided looking him in the face. 'I've done something else, Dottor Balistreri.'

Balistreri was seriously worried, but the reality was worse than anything he could have imagined.

He listened with growing horror to the account of the exploits of Linda Nardi and Giulia Piccolo at the Marius Travel agency and then at Casilino 900 while a veiled anger rose up from his stomach to his head against Piccolo, who always wanted to do things her way. But what could he do? Slap her? He risked getting two back. Send her packing from the Special Section? He'd lose a formidable member of the team. And then Giulia was just like the young Mike Balistreri. Could he repudiate himself? So the person he took issue with was the brains, Linda Nardi, the true perpetrator. Damnable still waters, polite and kind. Polite and kind, like hell! That one was made of tempered steel. In the end he realized with a certain shame that he was angry not with the two women but with Colajacono, for what he had dared to do to Linda Nardi.

That pig had no right to come anywhere near her.

He sent Piccolo back to the office and went into the police station. Colajacono's door was open. The deputy commissario was sitting with his feet up on the table; in his mouth a large cigar that had gone out. He made no move to get up or offer Balistreri a seat when he appeared in the doorway.

Colajacono pointed at the table full of piles of paper. 'Look at this, Balistreri. Exactly a hundred reports to examine. Stupid little matters for someone like you. Bag snatches, little thefts, some breaking and entering, stolen cars. And in ninety per cent of the cases the perpetrators are your friends the Roma gyppos.'

Balistreri said nothing. Colajacono sat up in the chair. 'All right, I'm all ears. But this is my patch here and I'm not having anyone question me. So watch that you don't start to piss me off.'

He's very sure of himself. He must have found a way of resolving the problem with Linda Nardi and Piccolo.

Balistreri stood right in front of him. 'Someone on the morning of December the 24th was scared. A small object from a nightclub had disappeared. Nadia had stolen it. So this someone asked you the favour of staying in the station and slowing down the investigation into Nadia's disappearance. They invented a little story for you, such as the girl had been with a politician for a little blackmail, seeing as you had already helped out in similar matters. But in reality they wanted time to get this object back.'

Colajacono shrugged, unmoved. 'I don't know what you're talking about, Balistreri. If you have any proof, well and good, otherwise it's all hot air, as with all you bureaucrats.'

'Your attitude towards Ramona Iordanescu held up the start of an investigation for several days. I have proof of that.'

'We would have found Nadia already dead anyway. The autopsy report says she was killed before nine on the evening of the 24th, so it changes nothing.'

'Perhaps it would have been easier to catch the murderer,' said Balistreri provocatively.

But Colajacono didn't bat an eyelid. 'Vasile's the murderer. We've caught him and he's in prison. And it's thanks to my informants, certainly not yours.'

He's being sincere; they've made an idiot out of him and caught him in a trap. He really believes it was the shepherd.

Images of Colajacono stripping Linda Nardi were torturing him. It had taken him many years and much remorse to manage his anger and become a good policeman, sensible and prudent. But the thought was too much for him.

With a sadistic pleasure, looking him straight in the face, he said, 'Vasile did not strangle Nadia.'

Colajacono was taken aback for a minute by the tone of conviction. Then he pulled himself together. 'Yet more conjecture from an intellectual policeman, Balistreri. Listen to me: go back to your office in the city centre and thank God that I can't give you a good hiding.'

He stripped Linda, this prick of a racist, this animal in policeman's uniform.

Anger prevailed completely over prudence. The words slipped from him without control, as they had so many years ago.

'Vasile's left wrist was sprained several days before. That was why he screamed out so much as soon as you grabbed him. We have the medical report. There's not the slightest possibility that he strangled Nadia.'

Madness, Balistreri, sheer madness. They should expel you from the force.

He saw Colajacono turn pale and suddenly get to his feet. 'Just what the fuck are you saying?' he hissed, closing in.

Balistreri went to the door. He was sure he could flatten him, but he hadn't gone that far back. A fight there would have marked the end of his investigation. He preferred a verbal uppercut.

'They had you there with Tatò, you stupid prick, to leave you without an alibi while they murdered Nadia.'

The effect was a lot worse than a physical uppercut. As he made his way towards the main entrance, he gave Colajacono a last look. He was as white as a sheet, leaning against the wall, staring into space. He had understood he was sitting at a card table where the stakes were too high for him.

When he returned to the office at the end of the afternoon, Margherita told him that Corvu wanted to speak to him urgently.

'Have him come into my office.' He pointed at the flower in the glass on the girl's desk. He winked at her and she blushed.

Corvu had the agitated manner of a high-school student on the day before final exams began.

'Dottore, I'm sure I'm being followed.'

Balistreri cursed under his breath and felt anxiety as well as anger growing inside him for the members of his team who were too enterprising.

'You weren't at your desk today?'

Corvu looked at the floor. Balistreri had an ugly presentiment. He could have expected if from Piccolo, but not from Corvu.

'First I analysed all the data we have on Nadia's discovery. I spoke to Forensics and asked for any early details. There are traces on the body of organic fluids that point to one DNA alone, which is that of Vasile, without any doubt.'

Faced with Balistreri's silence, he decided to continue.

'Then I compared the alibis of all the possible suspects between six and nine on the 24th.' He held out a chart.

Balistreri cast an eye over it. He saw 'Full alibi' written beside the names of Greg, Mircea, Adrian and Giorgi and 'Incomplete or uncertain alibi' written next to those of Hagi, Colajacono, Tatò and Ajello. The last name caused him a brief shiver.

'How do you know what Ajello did in the early evening of the 24th?' he asked, attempting to hide his anxiety.

'I called ENT and the secretary said that Ajello was coming back from Monte Carlo this evening. So I said that we urgently needed to check the books of Bella Blu in order to get confirmation of the date that Camarà was taken on. She got in touch with Ajello, who said it was OK.'

'And you went over to ENT?'

Corvu was looking at the toes of his shoes. 'With Mastroianni,' he whispered.

Balistreri gripped the arms of his chair until his knuckles were white and clamped his lips so tight he crushed the unlit cigarette he had stuck in his mouth.

Damn Corvu! And damn Mastroianni with his big-time Italian hotshot looks!

When he felt he had regained control over himself and was ready for the worst, he asked, 'Tell me exactly what happened.'

Corvu spoke to his shoes.

'We went there by bus. When we got to ENT I introduced Mastroianni to Ajello's secretary as an expert in accountancy. She had laid out the Bella Blu's books in a meeting room, then offered us some tea, and Mastroianni left the room with her a couple of times on the pretext of making some photocopies. Then he asked her to help him decipher some abbreviations, keeping her talking. She was distracted and flattered. It was then I went out with the excuse of going to the toilet.'

'The appointments diary.'

Corvu nodded. 'Ajello had a last appointment in his office at six thirty on the 24th. Then the diary was empty until seven, when it said "Grand Hotel: Cocktails".'

Balistreri groaned softly. Then he waited in silence, resigned.

'I called the Grand Hotel and asked for the management with the excuse that I was from the finance police and I was checking the invoices of a catering firm. I asked if there was a reception there in the early evening of the 24th. They told me that every 24th of December there were aperitifs for the season's greetings at seven for the members of a charity group that raised funds for a humanitarian organization. It'll be easy to check if Ajello was there and if he donated a cheque.'

'Like fuck!' shouted Balistreri in fury, jumping to his feet.

Corvu quickly stepped back and shielded his face with his arms as if he feared a slap.

'Corvu, you will not venture to take even the most minimal of initiatives with ENT, Bella Blu or Ajello. If you step a millimetre out of line I'll send you back to the mountains of your delightful island to count the goats. Have you understood that quite clearly?'

'Yes, Dottore, I've understood,' stammered Corvu, mortified.

'Now tell me about being followed,' Balistreri ordered him.

'It happened on the bus, coming back. I noticed him because he was the only one to get on with us. I didn't notice him as we were going there, but it was the same one as the other day.'

Evening

There wasn't a minute to lose. The actions of Piccolo and Corvu and his own words to Colajacono had set a time bomb ticking. He called Coppola and Mastroianni in.

'I want you to follow Colajacono and not let him out of your sight. Take it in turns and don't let yourselves be seen. Now get a move on.'

'I wanted to say that I haven't yet traced Fred Cabot, but I spoke to Carmen again and a strange thing came to light . . .' Nano ventured.

'I don't give a shit, Coppola. One of you must be outside the police station before Colajacono leaves — it's almost eight.'

Mastroianni lifted a finger like a schoolboy. 'Coppola will have to do the first shift as I have to go to the airport at midnight to take Ramona Iordanescu to the barracks to stay the night. Reasons of security, and all that.'

'But I've got my son's basketball match — it's the final tonight,' Nano protested.

Balistreri looked at him askance. 'Coppola, there will be other finals. Stick to Colajacono and don't ever let go of him for any reason. I'm giving you an important job — it's a serious responsibility.'

Nano reacted in the way Balistreri expected. 'Dottore, you're right. Ciro's a champion anyway and there'll be time for other finals. I won't let go of that bastard Colajacono even if we descend into hell.'

Left to himself, Balistreri tried to reflect. The Bella Blu had been chosen simply as a meeting place to introduce Nadia to someone. Then a real disaster happens. By pure coincidence, Camarà has a prostate inflammation and urgently needs to pee. He goes down to the toilet, and going past the private lounge he sees Nadia with someone. The person who's organized Nadia's death for the following day feels they're in danger. And so he does away with Camarà, feigning an argument with a motorcyclist.

But that's not enough. Worse happens. On the morning of the 24th, the housemaid notes that there's a missing lighter in the private lounge that need replacing. They call whoever was with Nadia in the lounge, but he doesn't know anything about it. A link between Bella Blu, ENT and the future crime is absolutely unacceptable. They think they'll find the lighter on Nadia when they kill her, but they don't. They panic and tell those two delinquents Mircea and Greg that Ramona must have it, but in order to protect the Bella Blu they don't say what they're looking for, otherwise Rudi would have given it to them without any problem rather than get beaten up.

What troubled him most was the sense of inescapability. Up until 23 December nothing had happened that would compromise the Bella Blu, ENT or its partners. Why couldn't they put a hold on everything? Not kill Camarà, not kill Nadia, change the target and the date. But no, it was as if there were no other choice. Despite all the risks the plan had to go ahead, so Camarà dies, Nadia dies, and they beat up Ramona and Rudi in order to find the lighter. They continue to search for it in Nadia and Ramona's room and happen to be surprised by Piccolo and Rudi.

He came to a stop, exhausted. He saw the powerful image of Colajacono suddenly trembling and pale as a ghost. He had to do something to stop what he himself had set going. He called Linda Nardi on the phone.

Both the police and the Carabinieri use the Beretta 92, 9mm Parabellum, not available commercially because it was a military calibre. The 92FS was the latest weapon, possessed by the majority of police officers with less than fifteen years' service. Balistreri had the 92SB, a model that was a little older but still in use.

He took the weapon reluctantly from his office safe. He cleaned it, loaded it, put the safety catch on and slipped it into the holster, which he fastened under his left armpit. He had been familiar with pistols since he was a boy and they weren't associated with happy memories. He hadn't touched a weapon with the intention of having to use it for many years. But now old phantoms, his dangerous ex-colleagues, were reappearing on the horizon.

He made his way through the centre on foot, while a few customers were leaving the shops that were about to close and people shivering with cold were beginning to slip into restaurants. There was a pleasant drizzle again and when he got to the Pantheon his hair was wet and plastered to his forehead.

She was already there. She was wearing an unfashionable raincoat and below it a jumper and baggy trousers. The contrast between her childlike eyes and the mature woman's outfit was greater than usual. And yet Linda Nardi was thirty-six, neither a child nor a mature woman.

He came straight to the point, not being able to abide any more madness.

'So you've decided to get yourself killed, Dottoressa Nardi?'

She thought for a moment, as if it was a serious question. 'In a little while no one will remember Nadia any more, nor Samantha, nor the many other poor things, and their families who will mourn them forever. I asked you before in Sant'Agnese. Is this business boring you?'

He stared at her. A beautiful woman, polite and kind, but incorruptible in her principles and therefore dangerous. In her eyes was the steady calmness of those who are right.

The eyes of someone I loved, the values that I lost.

The thought took him back forty years. Something collapsed inside him, something that came from very far away like the distant shock of an explosion at the bottom of the ocean when it finally reaches the shore.

The words came out uncontrollably. 'You're crazy.'

They both knew what that 'crazy' meant. The word that had slipped out was an impossible bridge over the raging torrent between them.

What do you think you're doing, Balistreri? You're an old man. Don't make yourself any more ridiculous to others than you already are to yourself.

She gave him a smile, a little smile, the first real smile since they had known each other.

'Finding out the truth is part of my life, of what I am. I never knew my father. And I still don't know why. And I was a horrible aggressive child. I used to hit my schoolmates, male and female.'

Balistreri stared at her in amazement. 'I don't believe you.'

'Well, I can show you photographs. I was an early developer, physically and psychologically. I was already fully developed at age eleven. I went to a private middle school, the Charlemagne. The upper school was there as well, with the older boys. I was missing a father and I looked for one in them – at least that's what the psychologist said when all the trouble began.'

'What kind of trouble?'

She shook her head, lost in one of those unwelcome memories you can never get rid of and of which Balistreri was a great expert.

'There was a problem and I had to leave the school. Fortunately, love heals any illness. It was my mother's love. She helped me get better, always there beside me until I was able to go back to school, which I did with excellent results, because it seems that, without deserving it, I am intelligent.'

'And it's precisely because you're intelligent that you should understand that looking for a murderer isn't the job of a journalist, but that of the police.'

She nodded. 'Colajacono has to give me that name before midnight. I promise that I will give it to you immediately. Is that all right?'

He paused, having no wish to ask her, but he had to do it. 'I need another favour.'

This time again she listened to him without any interruption. She placed no conditions on doing what he asked. They left each other soon after in the Pantheon's deserted piazza. He had wanted to hug her in the rain, but instead let her go off with a brief goodbye.

While he was walking home in the rain he was struck by a feeling of disquiet. Halfway there, he decided to stop in a bar that was still open near the Termini main railway station. It was full of non-EU citizens. The Asians were crowded round the slot machines, the East Europeans were drinking shots of spirits and the Africans were trying to sell counterfeit designer bags to the few passers-by shivering with cold. All of them were smoking, not caring in the slightest about the prohibition.

Balistreri took advantage of this to light the last of his daily cigarette ration. The surrounding square was lit by the headlights of the few cars in circulation. It was a little after midnight.

He called Coppola. 'All's well, Dottore; Colajacono's still in the station. He went out with Tatò to eat at the little restaurant opposite and then they came back. Rest assured I won't lose him.'

'Thanks, Coppola. That's great.'

'And, Dottore,' Coppola added, 'I wanted to say that my son won the final and scored thirty-two points.'

'How do you know that he's really yours, Coppola?' Laughter. Goodbyes.

Then he called Mastroianni.

'All's well, Dottore. Ramona's here with me, we're coming into the city from the airport.'

'Mastroianni, I want to talk to her straight away. Come and meet me. I'm in a bar on the Via Marsala side of the Termini station.'

★　　★　　★

He had of course imagined a different and more private setting for questioning Ramona Iordanescu, but there was no time to lose. An official interrogation in the barracks or in the office was impossible without the Public Prosecutor present, so they found themselves sitting at a little table in the bar filled with people, smoke and muffled voices.

The photo with Nadia taken in front of St Peter's hadn't done justice to the girl's statuesque figure. The harsh features of her face were immediately belied by her adolescent's manners. She was making eyes at Mastroianni, which was no surprise, and had him bring her two crème horns.

'I really love them,' she said, trying to justify herself, wiping a streak of the filling from the side of her mouth.

'You can have as many as you like,' Mastroianni said to her.

'All right,' Balistreri cut in, 'but meanwhile let's have a little chat.'

Ramona nodded, her mouth full of crème and flaky pastry.

'You don't need to worry about this. Tomorrow we'll have a meeting with you and Deputy Commissario Colajacono. Immediately after Mastroianni will take you to the airport and you can go back home.'

He read the fear in the young girl's eyes. 'He'll go straight to prison on the charge of being an accessory to Nadia's murder and won't come out again for many years,' he said to ease her.

Mastroianni and Ramona both jumped. 'Accessory to murder?' whispered Mastroianni.

Balistreri ignored him and turned directly to Ramona.

'Tell me about the apartment near the Cristal. Did it have a false ceiling or a real one?'

'I don't understand,' said Ramona, confused. Mastroianni, who was looking after her like his little sister, explained the question.

'I don't know. How can you tell?'

'By the lights. Where the ceiling wasn't covered by the mirror was there a chandelier or spot lamps?'

'Spot maps?'

Another explanation from Mastroianni.

'Oh yes, yes, pink spot lamps.'

For filming from above. Real pros.

'All right, then what happened?'

'I did as Colajacono said. When well-dressed man arrive to Cristal he comes over to me after little while, and offers me drink. After I take him to flat, he wants to be as slave. I did my job, he very happy, and give me hundred-euro tip, then go away.'

'Would you recognize this man if you saw him again?'

'Every centimetre of him,' she said, and began laughing like a child while Mastroianni blushed.

Balistreri took out his BlackBerry and looked for the e-mail Mastroianni had sent from Iaşi. He frowned as he read part of it.

'Ramona, you said that Colajacono wanted to convince you that Nadia was safe with the man she got into the car with. Is that exactly what he said?'

He felt Mastroianni was about to interrupt and gave him a sign to keep quiet.

'Yes, I'm sure, he said exactly like that.'

'And you told him that she had got into a car?'

Balistreri clearly noticed the sound of Mastroianni's cup tapping against the saucer and shot him a warning glance.

Ramona appeared to be making an effort to remember. 'Well, I said that Nadia and I worked as couple, that we not get in car ever if other not there. Then I told him I was away with limp dick client and on return I found Nadia gone. And that I waited and also asked other girls—'

'Did you tell him what the other girls said to you?'

'No, he said straight away not to piss him off.'

Mastroianni emitted something between a groan and a wheeze. Exasperated by a long day with distracted and insubordinate underlings, Balistreri lost control and snarled in his ear, 'If you can't hold it in, go to the loo and change your nappy.'

Mastroianni got up, staggering a little, and went off to the toilet.

'What's happening?' Ramona asked, disconcerted.

'Nothing. He has to go to the toilet. So you hadn't told him about the car . . .'

This is what happens when you delegate questioning of this kind to the most inexperienced and you sit down comfortably in your office to read it via e-mail. You're a fool, Balistreri. And this simpleton of a Mastroianni thinks that women tell him everything without him even having to ask the right questions.

Then he remembered what Corvu had got up to, to say nothing of Piccolo. In the end, the only one who hadn't messed up was Coppola. Immediately he felt a note of apprehension. He picked up his mobile to call Coppola, but at that moment a cry of joy rose up from the Romanian group, followed by rounds of toasts.

Balistreri looked up at the television screen that was on, convinced he would see the replay of some goal. Instead, there was the face of a newscaster. He managed to hear the closing words.

'. . . and so, with only one vote between them, the city council has postponed moving Casilino 900 and the other camps, committing itself however to seeking a path forwards shared by all the parties concerned. The council has received the Vatican's approval . . .'

He moved a little closer to follow the comments of interviewees. The mayor was torn between conflicting emotions. He declared he was surprised but in the end happy about De Rossi's unexpected choice of voting against the move. A brief interview with De Rossi followed.

'Deputy mayor,' asked the journalist, 'a large part of the electorate, including the part you represent, is certainly not in agreement with this postponement.'

'Apart from his own electors, each one of us has to answer to his own feelings of morality and his own conscience,' De Rossi said pompously, staring at the television camera.

Now even more furious, Balistreri turned away and found Ramona opposite him looking at the screen in astonishment.

'But that –' she stammered, pointing to De Rossi – 'that's my dirty pig from Cristal.'

Balistreri was already dialling Coppola's number. Nano answered immediately – you could hear his car engine.

'Where are you?' shouted Balistreri, now beside himself. The whole bar turned to look at him.

'Take it easy, Dottore. Everything's OK. I'm following those two bastards in the car.'

Balistreri took a huge breath, trying to control himself. 'All right, Coppola, everything's fine. Can you tell me where you are?'

Nano's voice was little more than a whisper. 'Colajacono and Tatò are taking the road to the shepherd's old farmhouse, where we found Nadia. You're very faint, there's no signal . . .'

The line went dead. The sharp pain in his chest was so strong that it left him without breath for several seconds. He leaned against a table so as not to fall over, his sight dim and his hands trembling.

What an inglorious death, Balistreri. A heart attack, perhaps even shitting your pants, in a grubby dive.

But that was not his destiny. Mastroianni was back, white as a sheet. 'Give me your keys – I need a car with a siren. You can call a taxi, take Ramona to the barracks, and don't either of you move from there.'

Thirty seconds later he was driving at breakneck speed through the pouring rain towards the city's eastern outskirts.

He was there in twelve minutes, at ten to one, consumed with anxiety. He parked in the same place as Piccolo did on the night of San Silvestro, halfway up the slope, where the potholed road became a boggy unmetalled lane. Coppola's car was now parked up there, and a little ahead, in the same place as a few nights earlier, was Colajacono and Tatò's car. He tried calling Corvu's number. There was no signal. He swore – Piccolo had already told him about that. The nightmare was repeating itself in all its particulars.

A good thing Coppola always has his pistol.

He remembered what Coppola had said on the subject: 'Dottò, it makes me feel taller. My son thinks I'm important when I come home and take my holster off from under my jacket.'

He had no torch. He took off his anorak, jacket and holster and began to run up the slope in his shirtsleeves with the pistol in his right hand and his mobile in his left to give himself a little light. He felt the mud slipping under the soles of his shoes, the drizzle bathing his forehead and the leaves on the low trees scratching his face.

He realized he was afraid and this made him all the more so. He was afraid for Coppola and for himself. He was afraid of dying too soon, before he had atoned for all his misdeeds.

He was about to start up the slope towards the clearing when he heard Coppola's voice at the top.

'Hands up.'

There was total silence for a few seconds, then all hell broke loose, with pistol shots and shouting. He looked towards the clearing that was dimly lit by an oil lamp. Tatò's body was lying on its back by the door. The shots were coming from inside the farmhouse and behind it and from an oak tree twenty metres ahead on the left. That had to be where Nano was. He made it up there in time to see Colajacono, terrified and in handcuffs, taking refuge behind the trunk of the huge tree.

Mircea was giving orders in Romanian – he heard him calling out to Greg, Adrian and Giorgi. He managed to understand what he was saying – 'There's only one.' He was tempted to call out to Coppola, but that would have been doubly damaging, revealing that he was there, and also his whereabouts.

A burst of fire issued from inside. He immediately recognized it as covering fire. Then he saw the outline of Adrian, who set off behind the old farmhouse firing like crazy.

Balistreri came out into the open taking advantage of surprise, but his hand was moving in slow motion, a last resistance before squeezing a trigger after so many years. Coppola came out from behind the tree taking two quick side steps and, holding the Beretta in two hands, opened fire as they had taught him in training school. Adrian fell with his arms open while Coppola quickly took shelter again.

Giorgi came running and shooting at Nano from the other side of the building while Mircea gave him covering fire from inside.

Balistreri felt his own hand stiffen on the trigger while Coppola shouted at him to take cover. He stood rooted to the spot in a daze, watching Coppola come out into the open. He fired a single shot that struck Giorgi in the head.

'Dottore, get behind the tree!' Coppola shouted at him. Balistreri shook his head and started to run. He had almost got there when Mircea's bullet hit him in his left side, making him twist in a half pirouette on himself. As he limped forward, he saw Greg coming towards him under Mircea's covering fire.

Who would ever have said that you'd die like this, petrified with fear?

Coppola went down on one knee and rolled towards the oak tree, firing like crazy. Greg fell face up in the mud, hit in the heart.

When you tell this to your son, he won't believe you. You'll never ever have to wear false heels again.

Nano quickly got up to get back to safety. The projectile hit him between the shoulders. He fell forwards and began to crawl towards the oak tree.

Taken by surprise, Balistreri swung to where he thought the shot had come from. As he hesitated, another bullet from Mircea in the farmhouse hit him below the right knee. The tree was only two metres away, but he would never get there with his leg broken and his side split open. In that moment, he met Colajacono's staring eyes.

'Help him,' he ordered, pointing to Coppola lying on his back on the ground. Despite being handcuffed, Colajacono dragged Coppola behind the tree as if he weighed no more than a child. Then he came out into the open again and with more effort dragged Balistreri behind the tree as well. Oddly, the shooting had stopped.

Nano's wide-open eyes were staring at him and a stream of blood was coming from his mouth. 'You're a big man, Coppola. Ciro'll be proud of you,' Balistreri told him. Nano nodded in agreement, then closed his eyes.

Balistreri was losing a lot of blood. He knew he was going to faint at any moment. He tried not to lose consciousness and control the savage hatred that had got hold of him.

Now I'm going to kill these vile animals, this scum we need to sweep out of Italy. Colajacono's right.

Suddenly, he was not afraid. His mind was clear, conscious that he had only one possibility.

'Haul me up and hold me by the waist, without blocking my arms,' he said to Colajacono, who nodded in a daze.

The deputy commissario held him up while Balistreri leaned all his weight on his left foot. Despite the handcuffs, Colajacono's huge biceps managed to keep him balanced.

He steadied himself. He knew he had only one shot. With Mircea hidden and himself in the condition he was in, he would have no more than one chance. He saw the flickering light in the farmhouse and Mircea's shadow falling across the wall in the shelter of the corner next to the window. He weighed the rock, calculating the distance: seven or eight metres.

He needed a loud thud. Strength in the right hand, accuracy with the left. As a boy in Africa he had won shooting matches firing from his left hand because with his right there was no question, it wasn't even any fun.

There was a target that Mamma gave you as a present when you were seven. The bear's head appeared only for a moment at the little window. And in that moment you went pow! You only know how to shoot and punch, Michelino. Like your father says.

The pain was getting worse, the bleeding wouldn't stop, he felt his head spinning and he knew he had no more time. He gripped the Beretta in his left hand. He gave himself a little push and let fly, as he did when he was a boy to get the crows out of the eucalyptus. The rock described a perfect arc and hit the farmhouse wall exactly where Mircea's head was. He jumped forward from the shock. The bullet entered his eye. Balistreri saw Mircea's shadow totter and fall.

Colajacono could no longer hold him. Balistreri collapsed on the ground and in the last moments before losing consciousness he thought he saw a shadow come out of the woods and slowly approach him. His eyelids refused to open. From the slit that remained open he could only see Colajacono's boots in the sloppy mud. He wasn't sure if it was real or a dream. The deputy commissario's voice came to him from a thousand kilometres away.

'Holy fuck! Now take these fucking handcuffs off.'

The other voice was an even less distinct whisper. 'Don't worry, policeman, it's coming now.'

'What the fuck's coming?' Colajacono hissed savagely.

The whisper became confused as he lost consciousness. 'Your death.'

Balistreri fainted before he could hear the shot being fired.

INTERMEZZO

Thursday, 5 January 2006

The morning papers came out too early to mention anything about the killings – they could only report the news of the city council's decision not to move Casilino 900 and a short article by Linda Nardi entitled 'If a policeman dies . . .' A curious coincidence, but in the general chaos no one asked her about the piece.

But the unhappy coincidence of the postponement of moving the travellers' camp and the shootings in which three brave policemen – Colajacono, Tatò and Coppola – met their deaths, and the head of the Special Section, Michele Balistreri, was gravely wounded put the mayor and his supporting majority well in the shade. It also created more embarrassment for the Church, which had defended non-EU immigrants and their rights to the last. Accusing voices were raised even in parliament and the Senate, which, usually silent, were now explicitly clear about the Vatican's interference. While the Church had hoped for tolerance by conviction rather than convenience, several political groups were cynically riding on events for their own electoral ends. Someone openly hazarded the hypothesis of reviewing the Concordat between the Vatican and the Italian state.

Appearing on his balcony in St Peter's Square for the Angelus, the Pope deprecated the violence and hoped for mutual understanding.

When he said that he would pray for the dead and that intolerance had already been the cause of serious violence in the past, a salvo of disapproving whistles rose up from a part of the crowd below, composed principally of Italian citizens. Italian television channels cut the shots from the news, but CNN and the internet broadcast them to the whole world.

Linda Nardi was able to see all the footage, including that censored by Italian television. Later she heard that, after operations on his spleen and tibia, Balistreri was out of danger. At that point she bought a vast quantity of food from the supermarket and shut herself in her apartment. Then she called her editor-in-chief to tell him that she would now be writing from home.

At dawn she went down to the news stand below to pick up the papers and then returned to her living room. She read all she could – picking things out, cutting out, underlining and cataloguing. She made a sizeable synthesis of everything on her computer and saved the file in a folder that already existed, *Michele Balistreri*.

She named the file 'For When You're Well'.

Tuesday, 10 January 2006

Unable to move in hospital, Balistreri had time to reflect. The seriousness of his condition gave him six days to prepare himself properly for the first questioning.

He had asked a nurse to get him a copy of the 5 January edition of Linda Nardi's newspaper. He had seen the title of the short article 'If a policeman dies' and made his decision. He didn't want to endanger the life of anyone else after those of Belhrouz and Coppola, Colajacono and Tatò, least of all that of Linda Nardi. And that 'least of all' worried him. A woman he really didn't know had wormed her way into his thoughts against his will.

He had spent years becoming a rational adult, aware of duties, risks and wrongdoings. This was the definitive moment to bury Mike Balistreri, the adventurer who knew no fear or compromise, who was arrogant and cared only for himself. He had several deaths on his conscience other from the latest. And there was no way at all he could wipe them from it. He could only try to move on, limiting the damage and asking pardon for his errors.

Truth had a price and in this case it was too high. He made a silent agreement with the Invisible Man.

The manhunt is off. I'll hold onto my dead and my remorse and look for you no longer. But you have to stop.

The questions put by the Public Prosecutor and Pasquali were too easy. The dynamics of events had already been reconstructed and were clear. Colajacono and Tatò had their informants and had gone there to find something. They had been surprised by the four Romanians, the Lacatus cousins plus Adrian and Giorgi, the ones who had kidnapped Nadia and taken her to Vasile, who had later strangled her with the help of the other shepherd. Colajacono and Tatò had been handcuffed and killed in cold blood. The heroic and unfortunate Coppola had followed Colajacono on Balistreri's orders and Balistreri himself had raced over there when Coppola had contacted him by phone. They merely asked him formal questions, so as to have confirmation of this reconstruction.

Neither of them asked him if he had seen anyone else besides the four Romanians. Besides, there appeared to be no other traces and the shots to the bodies of Coppola, Tatò and Colajacono and the ones that had nearly killed Balistreri had all been fired from the six pistols found beside the four Romanians. The Public Prosecutor and Pasquali complimented him on the final shot at Mircea, no one asking him how he had managed to save his own skin alone under those conditions.

Because the Invisible Man didn't want to finish me off. He wanted me like that, permanently defeated.

Linda pored over all the old newspapers she had had brought, the oldest from 1970. She knew that up to the summer of that year Balistreri had been living in Libya, but had found nothing on that period. Then in autumn 1970 he appears at Rome University.

A young Balistreri, looking very full of himself, with groups of other equally proud young men full of conviction. Rallies about honour, loyalty, courage, the fatherland. Then the two-edged axe with the fasces, SS slogans, the Roman salute, black shirts, the wounded, police wagons, tear gas and stones inside the university and among the bridges over the Tiber. But he was never directly linked to political crimes, atrocities, acts of terrorism.

The Christian Democrat government disbanded *Ordine nuovo* at the end of 1973 and arrested its leaders, but from 1974 there was no trace of Michele Balistreri. Linda Nardi found nothing more, neither in the newspapers nor among the official records of the Ministry of the Interior. There was no home address or bank account. Nothing.

Until June 1978, that is – one month after Aldo Moro's death. At this point Michele Balistreri reappears. He finishes university and graduates in philosophy, joins the police, passes the exam for the rank of commissario, and from 1980 he's in Vigna Clara, twiddling his thumbs in Rome's quietest district.

In certain matters she found it easy to link the present man to that young man, but in others it was impossible. Honour, loyalty and courage were still there, but only as old memories blurred under the thick glue of reality. It was easy to imagine the Balistreri of 1970 with a pistol in his hand, but the Balistreri of today must really have been forced to shoot at those Romanians on the hill.

She wondered if it would still be possible to lead that man back to his old nature in order to drag the evil out of hell and annihilate it.

His brother Alberto, together with Mastroianni, Piccolo, Corvu and Angelo Dioguardi, had organized things so that he was never alone during visiting hours. In the middle of February they were able to twist the ward sister's arm enough to allow for afternoon poker sessions in Balistreri's room, but despite Mastroianni's seductive powers, she was not giving in on smoking. They played with the window open to the cold outside to allow Balistreri a few drags. No one mentioned the crimes that had been committed, ENT or work. It was only poker and an afternoon cigarette.

Balistreri hadn't heard from her, but it was as if Linda Nardi's occasional articles were always addressed to him. Their fresh composure and irrelevance were a message. Empty articles, waiting for them to be able to talk. And on this imagined promise Balistreri built his hopes. *Take time to heal, Michele. I'll be waiting for you.*

When the doctors decided that it was time for him to go home and continue with his physiotherapy beyond the hospital, Balistreri felt almost lost. He had become used to the place where only muffled echoes came in from the outside world, along with the good things brought him by his brother and friends.

The thought of going back to the apartment near his office filled him with anxiety, as did any direct contact with the city. The hospital walls constituted the ultimate alibi for his giving in. Inside them, he could do nothing. Once outside, it would be his choice alone whether or not to engage with the world and its friction.

Only one thing attracted him in the idea of leaving hospital, and that was being able to see Linda Nardi again. His mind refused to obey: the more he told himself not to think about it, the more he came back to it. What worried him were the conversations he imagined between them and the apparent absence of physical desire. He felt very clearly that he had grown old.

On the morning of 15 March, the date set for his leaving, he opened the windows on a radiant day, one of those special ones that in Rome give a foretaste of spring. He was sitting in his armchair signing the papers for his discharge, when the nurse came in and said he had an out-of-hours visit.

Linda Nardi had grown much more beautiful.

That's because I'm seeing her for the first time with other eyes — those of a soldier coming back from war, defeated but alive.

She stood still for a moment, then held out her arms. He rose up tottering, then, leaning on his crutches, allowed himself to be embraced. It was a silent embrace, perfectly still, that emerged from somewhere far away.

Spring 2006

From that day on, after the crutches, Linda became his third support. They didn't talk about it, or make a conscious decision. It simply happened. She set him up in the guest room of her small top-floor apartment. In the morning she took him to his physiotherapy sessions and in the afternoon, taking advantage of the Roman spring, she insisted on his taking long strolls through the streets of the historic centre and Trastevere, even though they were crawling with young people and tourists, in order to get him used to walking again.

When he was tired they went back home and sat on her flowery terrace with its view of St Peter's dome, and there they enjoyed the supper she made for them. They never spoke of the night Michele Balistreri almost died, nor of the crimes that had been committed. He never mentioned them and she avoided them completely.

Linda met his friends and his brother's family, and so began a humdrum middle-class home life that Balistreri always imagined he would detest. Several couples came to visit them: Alberto and his wife on Saturdays, Angelo and Margherita almost every evening. Corvu and Piccolo often came by after work. They even resumed their weekly ritual of poker, and on those evenings Linda usually went out with Margherita.

They could have been an ordinary couple, except for the lack of sex. At midnight they went their separate ways, each going to their own room to sleep.

Am I in love with her? Then why do I feel there's an insurmountable barrier?

Days passed and one evening at the end of May, arriving home, they set two chairs together on the little terrace facing St Peter's.

In those ten weeks of living together, many things had become dear. Now all that he wanted was silence and Linda, the same as he had thirty-six years before on that beach on the other side of the Mediterranean.

He saw his arm going around Linda's shoulders. She turned slowly towards him, her face a few centimetres from his; there was no furrow in her brow, her eyes were clear and calm.

It's your decision, Michele.

He remembered the silent pact he had made with the Invisible Man on that distant night.

The manhunt is off. But you have to stop.

Suddenly he felt he was only an old policeman who was protecting something inestimably precious, something that should never suffer even the slightest harm, something he had to protect from everyone, beginning with Michele Balistreri, his sins and his remorse.

Because you can't harm the fairies in a nursery tale . . .

The moment passed as the thought came to him. Linda laid her head on his shoulder and fell asleep.

The following evening they were there again, not saying a word, enjoying the warm sunset that marked the beginning of the long Roman summer. Balistreri had fixed on the following day for his return to work.

'Michele, I have to ask you something very personal.' Linda's tone was odd; direct questions were not a part of their everyday life.

'Now that has me worried, Linda,' Balistreri joked.

But she was serious, clearly unhappy about asking the question. 'I'd like to know if, when you were involved in politics, you caused anyone's death.'

Balistreri was struck by her use of those circumlocutions.

When you were involved in politics . . . you caused anyone's death . . .

And yet she knew for certain that, up until November 1973, Michele Balistreri had been a Fascist agitator and a leader of Ordine Nuovo, which was later dissolved by government decree on a charge of being a new incarnation of the old Fascist Party. And, being a good journalist, she certainly wondered why he hadn't been arrested and put on trial along with the movement's other leaders.

'Would it change anything between us, Linda?'

She thought for a while. 'I need to know who you are today, Michele, and in order to know that I have to know something about back then.'

Balistreri didn't ask why. He trusted her and her good intentions in asking him.

'I never killed an innocent person nor ordered any to be killed. In the group of youths I was among, though, there were several who thought that bullets and bombs were the only means with which to fight.'

'And you?'

'After Ordine Nuovo was disbanded I tried to lead the group back to a political movement, but they only had armed struggle in mind and I lost.'

'Where were you between 1974 and 1978?'

She said it in an affectionate tone, but that question opened up an insurmountable gap.

I was still in with that group of youths, one of the leaders. But I'd signed a contract to spy on them.

'I can't tell you, Linda. And it's for your own good that I can't.'

She took one of his hands in hers. 'I know you didn't kill any innocent people. But when you found yourself next to those who did want to kill them, did you let them do it? Or did you stop them?'

My former friends, the guys with whom I started out, those I betrayed because they betrayed themselves and thought that combat was putting a bomb in a litter bin in a crowded square.

'I did what I could, Linda – everything I could to combat what I thought was unjust and dishonourable.'

'And you'd do the same again today?'

Linda Nardi had left him taken aback by a question several times before.

'Today I'd only kill someone if I were forced to do so. As happened five months ago on that blasted hill.'

She nodded in agreement, but her eyes said no. She opened her hands and Balistreri's hand was free, light as a feather, and on its own.

PART 3

Sunday, 9 July 2006

Morning

He had been back at work for a little over a month. It was a peaceful time. After his return to the office, no one mentioned the shooting or the crimes that had been committed. By now they were in hands of the Public Prosecutor's office and the killers were in prison. Vasile's accomplices, Hagi's four employees who had traded Nadia for a vehicle to use for a robbery, were dead. Camarà's killer was an unknown motorcyclist, who had almost certainly killed him following a disagreement about entrance to the Bella Blu. There was no connection between the two cases. And even less between ENT and the Secret Service.

Balistreri was living with Linda and also without her. With love, but no sex. He did things he had never done, such as fixing a leaking pipe, watching a detective film on television, and trying to play golf. He spent a whole Sunday in Linda's garage, getting oil and grease all over himself, trying to repair her old moped.

The peace we spoke about thirty-six years ago. A couple, a house, friends, work, children to bring up. A peace I never deserved.

In the summer drowsiness, a passion was reborn for the national football team. The previous few days had passed by in a growing collective ecstasy. The triumphal march in the FIFA World Cup in Germany towards the final against France was as unexpected and all-consuming as it had been twenty-four years before. There were Italian flags on all the balconies and every evening the centre was blocked by the crazy traffic of rejoicing cars. In offices, churches and hospitals and on the streets, the talk was of nothing else. Only 'national' dishes were being served in bars and restaurants: tomato, mozzarella and green salad, or else watermelon, cantaloupe and kiwi fruit. In short, it was the rediscovery of the old national tricolour in a country nagged at by the secessionist pull of Lombardy. In the heat-haze of a scorching July, all true Italians were participating directly in the national team's adventures on German soil.

Even politics and the great disagreement with non-EU residents had been put on the back burner in the newspapers, on television and in conversation. Indeed, many foreigners – some from conviction, others out of pure opportunism – had become Italian supporters, making a great deal of money selling counterfeit national team shirts on every street corner. People hugged each other in the celebrations after the matches. No one could give a damn about killings any more.

In the middle of the morning, Balistreri and Dioguardi were talking on the phone.

'While the match is on and the city centre's empty, let's take Linda and Margherita for a good long stroll,' Balistreri suggested.

'Margherita really wants to watch the final – everyone's going to Alberto's house. Your brother's even persuaded Linda and they're saying we're antisocial.'

'Then let's the two of us go and they can join us later. Italy's only going to lose and the centre will still be deserted.'

'We're going to win, Michele. And Margherita and Linda will be out celebrating with the rest of them.'

'Linda wouldn't ever go out celebrating on the streets, Angelo.'

'But Italy'll win and it'll take Linda three hours to get home from Alberto's.'

They were both highly conscious of a feeling of déjà vu and studiously avoided it as they talked. They had never again spoken of that night in 1982, but football had sunk inexorably to the bottom of their list of passions. Together they came jointly to the only possible solution: a stroll through the deserted city centre, and after the match a further stroll if Italy lost or a strategic retreat to Linda's little terrace in the case of victory. Just the two of them.

For Giovanna Sordi, it had been a Sunday morning the same as all the others for the past twenty-four years. The half past eight tram to Verano cemetery, Sunday being the day she changed the flowers: tulips for Elisa's romantic heart, red carnations for Amedeo's socialist one. A brief moment of concentrated silence without tears and then 'Grant them eternal rest, O Lord' recited in a whisper: twenty-four times for Elisa, ten for Amedeo. Then the tram again to the old home on the outskirts from which she had never moved. Midday Mass at the local parish church, and then confession, with no sins to declare except the only, the habitual one, the one that the old priest no longer listened to and for which he granted absolution without penance.

Lord, at least tell me who did it.

Evening

Strolling through the centre of Rome, they had the sensation of being on the moon. Even innocent tourists who had never seen a football match in their lives came to be drawn into the squares where the final was being shown on enormous screens. Down the deserted streets, the total silence was broken by collective roars. It was impossible to ignore the match's progress completely, the result in the balance, the beginning of extra time. Along with the sounds, Michele Balistreri and Angelo Dioguardi were accompanied by an emotion that had nothing to do with the match. They walked along without saying a word, and the more they walked the more the memory wormed its way in gradually, subtly, inexorably. It grew very slowly, soft as a heavy fall of snow on a winter's evening. For almost two hours they wandered about without exchanging a single word, surrounded by the historic centre's overwhelming, incomparable and silent beauty.

When the match reached the final gruesome lottery of the penalty shoot-out, they found themselves standing pale and exhausted outside the front door of Linda Nardi's apartment block. In the silence of millions of people holding their breath, they lit a cigarette that went back twenty-four years. Balistreri and Dioguardi hurried up the staircase while the crazy crowds rushed down onto the streets. They took refuge on Linda's little terrace while the joy around them spread out irresistibly together with the explosions and colours of the fireworks.

During an uproar like this, a monster cut her to pieces while we couldn't give a damn.

Balistreri heard a whistling sound close by and turned to see the fireworks display. A line of white was running directly up on high; at any moment it would explode in a thousand colours. Instead, it reached a point in the sky, couldn't manage to go any higher and went out.

Monday, 10 July 2006

Afternoon

It had been a tiring night of celebrations followed by a day of endless chatter and newspaper headlines, with T-shirts of the world champions on sale even outside cemeteries and hospitals. Hardly anyone was working and whoever tried to was looked upon as an idiot. To distract himself from the inane office chatter, Balistreri allowed Linda to persuade him to take a late afternoon walk.

After half an hour, his bad leg and his age demanded a rest and a good coffee. They sat down at a bar in Piazza Navona.

At the next table sat a couple with their two adolescent children. Balistreri heard the mother reading out from a guidebook. 'Piazza Navona came into being in the first century AD, but as a stadium rather than a square . . .'

The son was grumbling with half a chocolate pastry stuffed in his mouth. 'And did Roma play there?'

The mother carried on unperturbed with the history of the fountain, the rivalry between Bernini and Borromini, and the raised hand on the Rio della Plata statue that blocks the view of Sant'Agnese.

'Well, it is a bunch of crap,' opined the girl, wiping a blob of crème with the back of her hand.

At a certain point the two teenagers got up without a word and went off to look at the shop windows full of designer knitwear, iPods and the latest mobile phones. The mother put the guidebook down and looked at her husband buried behind the *Corriere dello Sport* that described the great Italian triumph in every detail. 'Bloody hell, aren't you going to do anything? They're your kids . . .' He interrupted her by lowering the newspaper a little. 'You bring the kids up, I bring home the money.'

Their two coffees arrived together with two little glasses of water. By now there were very few bars that kept up this tradition. Balistreri liked it. It reminded him of the *mabrouka* who performed the same ritual for his father when he was in his study. Papa thanked her with a little nod of the head without taking his eyes off his papers, took a sip of water and then started on the coffee.

He glanced at the next table, where the sporting father had spread the paper out on the table and was continuing to read. His eye fell on a headline buried among the interviews with the national heroes. It was hidden away in a corner so as not to disturb the population's joy: *A Tragedy of Two World Cups*.

He got up and went over to the table and the father absorbed in his reading. 'Excuse me,' he said.

The man raised a pair of hostile eyes, imagining it would be some nuisance of a non-EU street seller, but when he saw a typical Italian face, he softened a little.

'Yes?' he replied, irritated nevertheless.

'It doesn't matter, thanks,' said Balistreri, having just noticed a newspaper stand open at the other end of the piazza.

Followed by Linda's wondering look, he asked for the *Corriere dello Sport*.

The vendor laughed. 'My dear Signore, all the newspapers were already sold out by ten o'clock.'

'Even the current affairs ones?'

'Even the current affairs ones only talk about the national team. All sold out.'

Balistreri went back to the avid reader at the next table.

'Look, I need your paper. I'll give you ten euros for it.'

The man shook his head. 'This newspaper is above any price and will be hanging up in my front room for the next fifty years. You're Italian, aren't you? You should have thought about it before.'

'All right. Look, I just wanted to read that little piece that interests me there, and then I'll give it back to you.'

The other man was now curious. 'What is it you want to read?'

Balistreri pointed it out to him. The man looked at it with a frown. 'What the hell's that got to do with a glorious day like today?'

The look on Balistreri's face made him change his attitude.

'Keep the page, I'm not interested in it,' he said in order to get rid of him.

Sitting with Linda in the joyful piazza overflowing with crowds of people, Balistreri read the article.

A TRAGEDY OF TWO WORLD CUPS. Giovanna Sordi committed suicide yesterday evening by throwing herself off the balcony at her home. Just like her daughter Elisa, who was brutally murdered twenty-four years ago on the day of Italy's World Cup victory in Spain, the elderly lady died as the national team were lifting up the cup. A chilling coincidence, or had the latest national victory awakened unbearably painful memories in her? The Elisa Sordi case, which at the time filled the front pages for weeks, has remained unsolved all these years and no one has ever been formally charged with the murder. Unfortunately, this great joy for many of us coincides with this huge personal tragedy.

An extremely sensitive sub-editor, a piece that escaped the chief editor's notice.

A pang in the stomach, different from all the others he had felt for years. It didn't even seem to come from the usual point at the bottom of the oesophagus, but somewhere deeper, distant and clear.

He lit a cigarette and thought about Elisa Sordi's parents again: humble origins, a worker in early retirement and a waitress. He remembered the couple's persistence – for him, petulance – during the World Cup final, the desperation and restraint they showed after Elisa was found, and Signor Amedeo's coming down to Homicide every morning to ask if there was any news. He would sit himself down in a corner to read *l'Unità*, and remain there in silence for hours, no one taking any notice of him. He had kept it up for two whole years until someone, perhaps his own lawyer, had gently let him know that it was pointless and was annoying them.

Giovanna Sordi had waited twenty-four years for someone to tell her who had taken Elisa from her and why. And when, after twenty-four years, World Champion Italy had replied no, she really couldn't know who'd done it, she had decided to end it all.

On an impulse, he tried calling Angelo. Linda was watching him, the vertical groove clearly furrowing her brow. Angelo replied happily at the first ring.

'Michele! Got over the fireworks yet?'

He read the article to him. A long silence followed. Finally Angelo Dioguardi hung up without saying a word.

Tuesday, 11 July 2006

Morning

He had waited too long to make the visit. It was Giovanna Sordi's suicide that spurred him on to make it.

You can at least ask to be forgiven.

Linda offered to drive him in the car. They took far less time to get from Rome to the outskirts of Naples than from there to the city centre. Balistreri took advantage of the delay to read the newspapers, avoiding the stream of articles on the World Cup triumph. Several newspapers remarked on the great participation of the majority of immigrants in celebrating Italy's victory, as if that made them worthy of living there. Such was football's power.

Linda drove calmly through the hellish traffic while Balistreri hurled curses at the cars hooting at them to get moving again after stopping for a red light. The city was even more strewn with flags than Rome and hordes of people were spilling out everywhere. They had told Lucia Coppola they would arrive in the morning, but it was almost one o'clock before they got there.

The apartment was small, but you could see the whole of the bay from its balcony. 'It belongs to my parents,' Lucia explained as she welcomed them in. 'They're on holiday in Capri.'

She was a good-looking woman, unbelievably more so than Nano, and much taller. Inside, there were photographs of Coppola everywhere: photos with Lucia at secondary school, on their wedding day, on holiday, and with the wonderfully handsome Ciro getting taller at every stage. Lucia was calm and relaxed, as if Nano would be home from work at the end of the day. She showed them a photo she had taken when they'd celebrated Giulia Piccolo's entry into the section. On the steps outside the offices, Balistreri was standing in the middle with Piccolo, Corvu and Mastroianni, while Nano was knowingly perched a step higher.

The table was laid for four in the shady part of the balcony. The wonderful smell of pasta sauce and fresh basil drew Balistreri into the kitchen.

'Ciro's out training; he'll be back any minute,' Lucia told him.

While she and Linda watched over the cooking pasta, the bell rang and Balistreri went to the door. He had prepared something to say, but the lanky teenager held out his hand and, looking him seriously in the eye, said, 'Papa found fault with everyone, but never with you.'

At the table they talked about Italy's victory and the incredible fireworks display that had lit up the bay like daylight. Then Ciro told them about his successful trial with Napoli Basket. He would be starting with the team the following year.

'And school?' asked Balistreri, remembering Coppola's fixation about his son finishing secondary school and going on to study law.

Ciro's eyes sought his mother's. 'Not very well,' said Lucia lightly. 'It's been a difficult year, but he'll make up for it.'

After coffee, Lucia and Linda started to clear the things away and Balistreri went along to Ciro's room. It was full of posters of star players and singers. Above the bed was an extraordinary photo of Nano in basketball strip completing a three-point shot at the hoop.

'He wasn't a bad player,' said Ciro. 'When he was young, he got to a decent level as point guard.'

They sat down on the edge of the bed, one already an old man, the other still a boy. Without saying a word, they stared for a while at the photo that said so much. Then Ciro spoke. 'Mamma says you were absolutely not to blame.'

Balistreri had no idea what to say.

The boy went on, smiling at him. 'You were wounded going to help Papa.'

Coming to Naples, he'd sworn to himself that he wouldn't tell this lad what violence could mean. But that photo changed things. He told him that his father had emerged from cover to save his life, rolling over on the ground just like in the films and had scored a bull's-eye on the man who was about to kill him. He told him that they'd only succeeded in stopping him by hitting him in the back. Ciro's eyes glowed with pride.

You'll never ever have to wear false heels again.

When they came to say goodbye, Ciro brought him a small flat packet. 'Papa kept an appointments diary at work – they returned it together with his things. I want you to have it.'

Looking at this gentle boy who would no longer have a father to applaud him scoring three-pointers or a praise a good result at school, he felt a cold rage rising inside him, the rage he'd tried to put behind him and forget after that January night on the hillside of Vasile the shepherd.

In twenty-four years' time, will Lucia and Ciro still be without justice, just like Giovanna Sordi?

Evening

When they arrived back at Linda's flat, Balistreri opened Inspector Coppola's diary while he drank a little white wine on the terrace facing the sunset. As usual, Linda drank water and seemed lost in distant thoughts.

Nano was a stickler for detail, under each day noting down the time as well as the event. It was a 2006 diary, just begun, and yet in three days there was a good deal set down in it. The last note was for eight in the evening on 4 January, made immediately after he'd been sent to keep an eye on Colajacono.

Tell B. about Carmen. Call Cabot again. I spoke to Carmen again and something new came up.

These were Nano's last words as he came out of Balistreri's office on that wretched evening.

At the back of the diary were phones numbers, clearly listed. He immediately found the one he wanted. He was still angry at the thought of Ciro and Lucia alone in that apartment, otherwise he wouldn't have been so rash as to use his personal mobile.

A foreign voice answered at the first ring. 'Carmen here.'

'Good evening. It's Balistreri from the police, boss of Inspector Coppola, who in January—'

'I know who you are,' said the woman, interrupting him. 'The papers spoke a lot about you a few months ago. I'm sorry about Coppola.'

'Thank you. Look, I could do with your help. Coppola came to see you the day he died.'

'He did, poor man. I remember he told me his son had a basket-ball match that evening.'

'Right. Unfortunately he didn't have time to report on what you talked about and I was wondering if—'

'Look, I'm happy to help you, but it's been a long time. Anyway, nothing new came out over and above the first time we spoke.'

He was conscious that Linda was listening there in silence.

'Please bear with me and try to remember. I'd asked him to go over with you the phone call your boyfriend made to you that night, before the . . . before he was . . .'

'Before that bastard on the motorbike killed him,' she said, helping him find the words.

'I wanted to be sure about the times.'

'I've told you a thousand times, he called me at two forty-five. It shows up on my mobile records and Papa's. He called to reassure me about how he was. He said he had to urinate a lot, but he didn't seem to have a temperature. I asked him if it was a quiet night. He said it was, then he told me about this fool who went past on a motorbike and insulted him for no reason.'

'And you asked him if he'd had any other problems with this guy?'

'I asked him, but he said nothing else had happened that night.'

'Then what did he say to you?'

'Nothing. I can't recall anything else.'

'The call lasted two and a half minutes. Did he describe the motorcyclist to you?'

A moment of confusion. 'No, Coppola also asked me that the last time, but Papa only said that it looked odd, and he was wearing a full-face helmet.'

'Why odd? He couldn't have seen him if he was wearing a full-face helmet.'

'No, it wasn't the rider who was odd, it was the bike.'

'Odd? How do you mean?'

'He only said it was odd. Nothing else. And that the man was wearing a full-face helmet.'

Balistreri said goodbye to Carmen and started to think. He quickly found the summary of Coppola's questioning of Fred Cabot on his BlackBerry. Rereading it, he realized now that it was highly condensed. Coppola was probably having difficulties with the language and had summarized a good bit. Cabot had spoken of a motorcyclist with a helmet and a large bike, easy to handle and fast.

He noted the number of adjectives used – three was a lot. Either Coppola was exaggerating or Cabot was a motorcycle enthusiast. He wondered what the English words were. Was the bike 'big' or 'large'? Was it 'handy' or 'easy to handle'? 'Speedy' or 'fast'? He turned to the diary's last page. There were two numbers for Cabot, a landline and a mobile. He recognized the prefix as San Francisco. Nine hours' difference. Eight in the evening in Rome, morning in San Francisco.

Cabot answered in a sleepy voice, but he had a sharp mind and it took little time for him to grasp who was on the phone. And because the newspapers in California had spoken about Balistreri and the deaths of 4 January.

'I'm sorry about your guy. He was a good man.'

'Thanks, Mr Cabot. I just need to clarify something with you. In your conversation with Coppola you described the rider and the motorcycle, but Coppola translated it into Italian. Could you tell me what you originally said?'

A little embarrassed, Cabot explained Coppola's misunderstanding about a prostitute and a gay.

Balistreri couldn't help smiling quietly.

'Why did you say queer?' he asked.

'I was thinking of the bike, not the rider. You see, I love motorbikes – I have a collection of them.'

An expert in bikes, so the description was based on something real, not a simple impression.

'You said the bike was big, easy to handle and speedy.'

'It was easy and speedy, but certainly not big. I probably said "great".'

Great – that meant beautiful, not Coppola's translation of 'big'. And queer was 'odd'.

The truth hit him a second before Cabot's voice announced it from the other side of the world.

'You see, it was a motocross bike. Odd to see one in the middle of a city.'

An evening breeze was blowing across the little terrace. Everything was as it had been on the other evenings during the previous months. But then everything changed.

'Linda, you asked me one day about when Alina Hagi died . . .' The question came out without thinking, by an association of ideas.

Linda was motionless, as if she were making up her mind. Her eyes were fixed on St Peter's dome, which was starting to light up. The vertical crease was there in the middle of her forehead.

Balistreri remembered her two questions at the end of their first dinner. *And the fourth man? And if he carves up another girl?*

He couldn't bear the silence any longer. His voice became urgent.

'Who told you about the carved letters?'

'No one told me, Michele.'

'I don't believe you any more.'

She stroked his hand. 'Find out who killed Nadia and Samantha and you'll also find who killed Coppola.'

Angrily, he took his hand away. 'You don't want to help me. But I'll find out who it was and throw him in jail.'

She took the phrase in, as if it were confirmation of what she'd known for some time. Then she made a decision. She got up, went inside, and took a thick folder full of newspaper cuttings from a drawer.

Balistreri went over a little uncertainly. She held the folder out to him without saying a word. On it was written 'For When You're Well'.

Now he was well, he could do what he wanted. But without her – that was the message.

'I'm not well, Linda.'

She shook her head as he left. 'It's an illness only you can cure.'

Going back on foot to his own flat, he thought about her embrace in the hospital, about the past months together, about the evening when he thought of kissing her and she had fallen asleep with her head on his shoulder, about the moped grease between his fingers.

There are no dreams without waking up. There's no freedom without truth.

Antonio Pasquali had given himself a few days off in the cool of Tesano, his family's hometown. His private mobile vibrated briefly. He was chatting to his wife, so gave her a smile to excuse himself and went outside into the open. He felt brief shiver of fear on hearing the voice again.

'Your friend's made two strange phone calls. Perhaps there are problems again.'

They had tricked him, dragging him into something so base that he couldn't even have dreamed of it. He had believed he was serving his country better by helping them make sure an ex-Communist mayor lost the election, because he was convinced that the Communists couldn't ever change and with them in power Italy would be poorer and less free. But he had never imagined finding himself involved in anything like this and wouldn't tolerate any more deaths among his policemen, least of all Balistreri.

He gathered all the courage he could muster.

'No drastic solutions this time,' he whispered.

'I beg your pardon?' The voice appeared to be mocking and warning him at the same time.

He didn't dare say anything more. It wouldn't have helped. He had to make a rapid decision, a different one that would satisfy Balistreri, putting him out of danger.

'Keep an eye on him,' said the voice, 'and the woman too. Don't ever forget that article.'

Wednesday, 12 July 2006

Morning

Corvu's affair with Natalya had rejuvenated him. Everything about him was different, from the cut of his hair to the clothes he wore. Even the way he played poker was a little more daring, less analytical.

'Alberto says that tomorrow's poker is off. Angelo can't make it.'

'All right,' said Balistreri.

He hadn't slept a wink, thinking of Linda and that voice on the hill that had announced Colajacono's death. And a motocross bike.

'But Alberto's expecting you anyway for dinner around eight thirty.'

'All right.'

It was the second 'all right' that aroused Corvu's suspicions.

'Is anything the matter, Dottore?'

Balistreri lit a cigarette, the first of the five he continued to allow himself.

'Sit down, Corvu.'

That 'sit down' left no room for doubt. Playtime was over.

Balistreri pointed to the blackboard. It was an old habit. Sometimes, when an investigation had hit the rocks, he asked Corvu to set his analytical gifts in motion and write up all the important details on this board, where they stayed until the investigation was over.

'You can start writing,' Balistreri said.

Corvu remained rooted to the chair.

'What do you want me to write, Dottore?'

'Whatever you want. Details, questions, doubts,' said Balistreri encouragingly.

Corvu found the courage to look him in the eye. 'Up there? After Dubai you told me that—'

'We'll keep the office locked.'

Corvu went hesitatingly up to the board. 'Let's do it like this,' said Balistreri to encourage him. 'Let's put down an exhaustive list of questions, along with any doubts. You do one, I'll do another, until we can't think of any more. We'll write the answers next to them as soon as we know them.'

'What does the letter R mean? And E? Does it come after?' began Balistreri.

As he wrote this down, Corvu found renewed confidence and energy. They went on with growing enthusiasm for two hours. The blackboard was very large and Corvu's writing was minute. By the end they were exhausted.

What does the letter R mean? And E? Does it come after?

Why did Colajacono want to stand in for Marchese and Cutugno? Because he knew that Ramona might come in about Nadia.

And how did he know that? Mircea told him.

Why was Colajacono already dog-tired on the morning of 24 December?

Why did Ramona offer her services to deputy mayor Augusto De Rossi? In order to blackmail him and make him change his vote.

Who blackmailed him? Mircea and Colajacono.

On behalf of whom and why?

Is there an Invisible Man in the Samantha Rossi case? Who is he? There is, but we don't know who he is.

Is he the same person who phoned Vasile for the Giulia GT?

When was the Giulia GT's headlamp broken?

Where was Hagi between six and seven on the evening of 24 December when Nadia was taken away? And then after nine?

Same question for Colajacono and Ajello.

Where was Hagi the night Coppola and all the others died?

Same question for Ajello.

Were Mircea and Greg guilty of murder in Romania? And who were the two victims?

How did Alina Hagi die in January 1983?

Why did Colajacono want Tatò with him even though he knew he should have been with his sister?

Why did the Giulia GT slow down when the driver saw Natalya?

What was the relationship between Ornella Corona and Ajello and his son before her husband died?

Who suggested life insurance for her husband?

How did Sandro Corona really die?

Why did Camarà die? Because he'd seen Nadia with someone in the private lounge on 23 December.

Who owns ENT?

They decided not to write down the reply to the last question, nor to the question about the instigators of the Augusto De Rossi blackmail. The Secret Service would anyway have been an inadequate reply. The question was who was behind it.

'For goodness sake,' said Corvu, looking at the blackboard. 'With all the things we don't know, it's a miracle we've got any guilty parties in prison.'

'Always assuming they're the true culprits,' said Balistreri, correcting him. 'I've got two more questions to add, but I'd prefer you not to write them down.'

'Why's that?'

'Let's just say I'm superstitious. The first is this: where was Adrian's bike on the evening of December the 24th while he was at Casilino 900?'

Corvu looked at him wonderingly. Then he checked the statements made during questioning. 'What does that mean?'

'Well, it means there are at least two things we don't know, which I'd like you to deal with. Where was that bike on December the 23rd when Camarà was killed? And where was it on December the 24th when Nadia was kidnapped and killed?'

'I still don't get it. What's Adrian's bike got to do with the one outside the Bella Blu? Adrian's is a motocross bike.'

Balistreri told him about his calls with Carmen and Cabot. Corvu frowned. A second connection between Nadia and the Bella Blu. Bella Blu meant ENT. And ENT meant big trouble, as Balistreri himself had spelled out to him.

'And the second question, Dottore?' he asked, now visibly worried.

'There are too many invisible men in this business. And the easiest to find is the one with the bike.'

'Right. What do you want me to do?'

'Organize the workload to get answers to these questions. Except the ones about ENT and Alina Hagi – I'll take care of those. And send Margherita in.'

Corvu looked away, embarrassed. 'Yesterday when you were in Naples she asked me if she could take the rest of the week off.'

'Just like that, all of a sudden?'

'Yes, it must have been a snap decision. Perhaps she and Angelo have gone off somewhere – who knows . . .?'

Afternoon

The death toll was never-ending. No one gave a damn about it, except the victims' parents. Everyone said that mopeds had been Rome's salvation, otherwise traffic would have ground to a halt twenty years earlier. The centre could have been pedestrianized, but the shop owners were against it. The numerous public administration offices could have been moved out to the suburbs, but the public employees were against it. They could at least have maintained better roads and done away with the traditional cobblestones on which the mopeds bounced about like skittles, but the administration for the city's historic fabric was against it. And so the death toll went on.

Alina Hagi had been only one of the countless victims. In Rome, recording the details of a road traffic accident in which a twenty-year-old girl lost her life on a moped was a purely routine matter. The record of her accident was perhaps more detailed than many others because of the statement made by her uncle, Monsignor Lato, but there wasn't even a photo of the girl. It had taken place on a rainy night in January 1983, after ten o'clock. Many witnesses saw her take the curve around the Coliseum at top speed, hit one of the holes between the cobblestones, swerve off the road and crash into a plane tree. She was not wearing a crash helmet, which was still not obligatory at that time. No one had cut across her, and nothing else had occurred.

He read Monsignor Lato's statement, which he later retracted. He said that a few days earlier Alina's arms had been covered in bruises. One of Alina's friends had told him after the girl's funeral. However, there was no direct link with the accident and after a month Monsignor Lato had retracted the statement.

It was mainly Linda Nardi's question that troubled him. *When did Alina die?*

The one-way roundabout suggested that Alina was coming from home and going off somewhere in the dark after ten on a rainy January night, riding a moped at an idiotic speed. And Alina Hagi was an exceptional young woman, very polite, religious and with her head firmly screwed on.

He called Angelo many times during the day, but his mobile was always switched off.

He called Corvu to tell him to get hold of Monsignor Lato. Corvu told him that all the inquiries to be followed had been organized and set in motion and that Piccolo was enthusiastic to start the hunt again. It was this enthusiasm that worried Balistreri. The last thing he needed was a mountain of female muscle ready for anything in order to avenge wrongs against women.

The desire to call Linda came over him in waves, but he resisted. Not out of pride – there was no trial of strength between them, but that point beyond which he hadn't wanted to go now had a precise reason. Secrets are a barrier against complicity.

He spent hour after hour sitting at his desk. He read all the statements again on his computer, then the list of questions on the blackboard. He knew that the solution was there in the replies to those questions. He read the first one again.

What does the letter R mean? And E? And what comes next?
When did Alina die?

Linda's question bounced backwards and forwards in his head.
When? Why 'when' and not 'how'?

Corvu called him towards nine o'clock while he was walking home, alone, without Linda for the first time in so many months.

'Monsignor Lato went back to Poland ten years ago. But he's alive and well and I dug up his phone number.'

'Excellent. You're still very efficient.' Corvu didn't catch the wry comment.

'I also thought it worthwhile bothering a friend of mine in the Vatican. That's how I found out where Alina Hagi worked. I've sent you an e-mail.'

'Good, I see you're in tip-top shape. I'll read it straight away.'

'One last thing, Dottore. Natalya and I are going out for a pizza, if you and Linda would like to . . .'

'No, thanks. Not tonight.'

He ended the conversation with Corvu. Now the desire to call Linda was irresistible.

I'll read the e-mail and then call her.

Corvu's e-mail was very short. It began with the Monsignor's phone number in Poland and continued: The parish where Alina Hagi worked in 1982 was that of San Valente on the old Via Aurelia.

I did it, memory says. I couldn't have done it, says pride. In the end, it's memory that has to give in.

Linda Nardi was looking beyond St Peter's towards the river that now divided them.

She had tried with all her might to convince herself that he could understand or at least accept it.

But that wasn't the case. She knew that very well now, from that evening on the little terrace. She spoke to her mother. She made the necessary phone call.

Thursday, 13 July 2006

Morning

For years he had avoided that stretch of the Via Appia Antica that climbed up as it passed by the well-maintained low-rise housing lost among the greenery of the trees. It was an unconscious avoidance, as if his memory's immune system had driven his consciousness away from the place.

Because remorse has a face, a name, a habitation.

He knew that the man who supervised the activities of the voluntary association whose headquarters were in San Valente parish was his old acquaintance, Father Paul.

While he was parking, looking past the sunlight filtering through the trees, he noticed that very little remained of what he remembered. The squat church had been repainted, the greenery was thicker and better tended, and at the end of the lawn the large house had at least doubled in size. Walking over the small carpet of grass he became aware that something had grown, as if the place itself had passed from infancy to adulthood.

Father Paul had been notified of his arrival. He came across the lawn to meet him. His red hair was tinged with grey, his blue eyes were more cautious, less open to the world. His handshake was firmer than he remembered, and it was obvious that the man in front of him was a lot stronger than the uncertain talkative young man he'd known before. It was the first time he'd seen him without his priest's cassock.

Paul welcomed him in a cordial manner and led him to the back of the house. The tree where they had chatted the first time had grown. There were three chairs, a table set with glasses and mineral water, the latest BlackBerry and a packet of cigarettes.

'I never imagined you'd still be here after all this time,' Balistreri observed after they had taken a seat.

'Do you mean Rome or right here at San Valente?'

'Well, both, I suppose. I remember you as a young man with a great desire to travel.'

Paul smiled, but no longer in the manner of a young American kid; now he smiled like a adult who was sure of himself and his place in the world. And his Italian was perfect.

'You're right, Dottor Balistreri. When I look back I'm a little surprised myself. Every year I thought to move on, and every year they asked me to stay. And little by little, with the passage of time, San Valente's become the world that I wanted to visit. You know, the orphans and the voluntary workers come from all over the world. So I never needed to travel.'

The chorus of birds in the trees mingled with the joyful sounds of the children in the house.

'How many are there?' asked Balistreri, pointing to the huge house.

'We doubled in size ten years ago. At the moment we have thirty children ranging from ten to fourteen and two voluntary workers who take turns on the night shift. But we have dozens of houses like this spread over several continents.'

'And you run the whole lot?'

'No, not at all. I'm in charge of selecting and training the volunteers, and the direct running of San Valente here.'

Paul took a cigarette from the packet and offered one to Balistreri. 'You smoke, if I remember correctly.'

Balistreri looked at Father Paul, the typical Californian health maniac, lighting a cigarette and inhaling with the relaxed and confident manner of someone who had achieved what he wanted to achieve. And he couldn't resist having a smoke with him, even if it was already his fourth of the day and his stomach was burning a little.

'And His Eminence?'

'Cardinal Alessandrini?' Paul smiled. 'He's the real creator of this miracle. Without his determination not even the Vatican would have been able to take these children out of the hell they were living in. Now the project has worldwide importance.'

'Is he still in Rome?'

Paul pointed to St Peter's, visible in the distance. 'Cardinal Alessandrini's never been one of those who aspires to the limelight. He's always been happy to make the decisions rather than make appearances. Today he's one of the new Pontiff's closest advisors, but he still lives in the Via della Camilluccia place where we met.'

Paul enthusiastically set out the details of Cardinal Alessandrini's project: the number of children saved from terrible circumstances, the number of dictators bending under the influence and determination of this little man of steel to allow the exit of exploited and abused children who were victims of corrupt and immoral regimes, and the huge influence he had with the Pontiff.

When his BlackBerry rang he answered briefly and then turned to Balistreri. 'If you don't mind, Dottore, I thought to give you a surprise. I told Valerio you were coming and—'

'Valerio?' asked Balistreri in amazement. 'Valerio Bona?'

'Yes, of course. Perhaps you don't remember, but he also sometimes lent a hand here in the parish.'

'I remember him very well. But I didn't think he was still about in these parts . . .'

'Valerio graduated in IT, worked a few years for IBM and then came back to us.'

'To you? I don't understand . . .'

'Dottor Balistreri, the organization set up by Cardinal Alessandrini has grown and today its running is as complex as that of an international concern. We have thousands of orphans, hundreds of volunteers, dozens of employees, more than twenty houses abroad. Valerio Bona runs our computer system.'

Balistreri couldn't hold in his incredulity. 'But I seem to remember there was some bad blood between the two of you . . .'

Paul brushed away his embarrassment. 'I know, at the time Valerio and I weren't what you might call friends. But we were young and time sometimes produces miracles.'

Valerio Bona arrived with his uncertain gait. He seemed a little hunched and there was no hair on his shaven head. He came up and offered his hand without looking Balistreri in the eye. The golden crucifix round his neck was the same one he had worn twenty-four years before.

The shy and touchy kid had aged more than Paul. Time hadn't been kind to him. His eternally worried look was hidden behind very thick lenses.

'Well,' said Balistreri, 'this really is a surprise. And do you live here as well, Valerio?'

'No, I work in the association's offices in a house near here, where I also have a small flat.'

'Are you married?'

'No, I'm not married. I live by myself.' He said it quite calmly, but Balistreri caught a hint of regret.

Valerio told him about his IT degree, the money he earned at IBM and the feeling he had of falling into a void, until he met

Cardinal Alessandrini who suggested the job. In that way he could put his science in the service of his faith.

'He didn't accept right away,' said Paul. 'I don't think he wanted to work with me.'

Valerio gave half a smile. 'That may be so, but then I met you and—'

'And you found that I'd become much more likable!' Dottor Balistreri, I imagine you're here to discuss what happened on Sunday to Elisa's mother.'

The sound of the name gave rise to an immediate unease. He preferred to distance himself from the subject immediately.

'No, I'm not here about Signora Sordi's suicide.'

'No?' Paul and Valerio exclaimed together.

'No. I'm here about a question from that other time. But it has nothing to do with Elisa Sordi.'

Valerio listened gloomily, Paul with curiosity.

'At that time there was a Polish girl among those who worked at San Valente,' Balistreri said.

'There were a good many Polish girls around,' said Paul, interrupting, 'ever since Wojtila's election—'

'Her name was Alina. Alina Hagi.'

For a moment in the still July air they heard only the chorus of birds and the children's cries. Paul lit a cigarette and Valerio poured some water.

'You don't remember her?' Balistreri asked.

'We could hardly forget her,' said Paul, staring at the huge white house. 'Alina Hagi, the indefatigable blonde – you met her yourself.'

A dozen children aged between ten and thirteen were playing football and a blonde girl of about twenty was acting as referee.

He tried to draw on his photographic memory, keeping out the emotional one. 'The girl who refereed the football and served at the table?'

'Yes, she had an incredible energy. She'd been working with children for several years and the voluntary workers all came to her too to ask for help or advice.'

'Did you ever meet the husband?'

Valerio shook his head. 'Never saw him, but I knew she was married.'

'I met him,' said Paul, 'but I only saw him a few times at the beginning. I think he was Polish as well.'

'Romanian,' said Balistreri, correcting him. 'Marius Hagi.'

There was a long silence. Balistreri was aware that something in the air had changed.

'Do you know what happened to her?' Balistreri asked after some time.

He met Paul's eyes and caught a look of disapproval bordering on harshness – a strength that hadn't existed twenty-four years before.

'I see you haven't lost the habit of asking questions to which you already know the answers,' Paul said.

'Was Alina still working here when she had the accident?' asked Balistreri, ignoring the comment.

'Yes,' Paul replied. 'After Alina's death, Cardinal Alessandrini held a special Mass for her in the Vatican with all the children and volunteers.'

'And were you here at the time, Valerio?'

'No, I was working for Count Tommaso dei Banchi di Aglieno while I was attending university. After that the Count didn't want me any more, because of what I said about Manfredi, I think, and the fact that I was too close to the Catholic world.'

He didn't say 'after Elisa's death', as if that name couldn't be mentioned. It was Balistreri who came out with it. 'Did Alina know Elisa Sordi?'

'I'd rule that out absolutely,' Valerio answered straight away. 'Elisa never came to the church here and Alina never went to Via della Camilluccia.'

As these names and people slowly emerged again from the past, Balistreri had the feeling that he couldn't ignore them, although the people involved at the time were different and the connection between Elisa's death and the present remained only an unfocused vision.

'Does the Count still live there?' he asked.

'He's never moved from his penthouse. As you can see, we've all stayed rooted in our places,' Paul replied.

'Manfredi as well?'

Paul considered the question. 'No, Manfredi's been the only one who really got away. After Ulla's suicide, the Count sent him off to Kenya where they have huge family estates. I know that he graduated in medicine in South Africa.'

'Does he ever come to Italy?'

'He comes to see his father every so often, but no more than once or twice a year. Cardinal Alessandrini tells me that among the native Kenyans he's a kind of god because he treats them gratis and with great efficiency and helps them in every way. As you see, everyone can change . . .' he said with a cruel irony of which Balistreri wouldn't have believed him capable.

The perfect guilty party that I wanted to nail has turned into a medical man who's a benefactor to the destitute.

'Was Alina particularly close to anyone?' Balistreri asked.

Paul and Valerio consulted each other by looks. It was Valerio who spoke. 'There was a small group of youngsters who were attached to each other. Alina was the one they looked up to.'

'Did one of the girls hint at any problems Alina had with her husband?' he continued.

Paul shot Balistreri a penetrating look. 'We've already said we didn't even know this husband.'

Valerio's voice was dull. 'This was a world of good Catholic youngsters, Dottore. Not like . . .'

Not like Balistreri and Dioguardi.

He decided it was time to take his leave. They said goodbye, but without any warmth.

Afternoon

Waiting in the office were Corvu, Piccolo and Mastroianni. They had ordered sandwiches, water and beer for a working lunch round Balistreri's table. It was the first time they had done this since Coppola's death and everyone disguised their grief in a different way for the loss of a colleague and the way in which it had come about.

'The first answers to the questions are starting to come in,' Corvu announced with satisfaction as he went up to the blackboard.

'But we have other questions to add,' said Balistreri. He told them what he had discovered about Alina Hagi.

Corvu scratched his head sullenly. 'I'm not sure I follow. Are we saying there's a connection between this case and the Elisa Sordi one?'

'No, that's got nothing to do with it,' Balistreri replied. 'We're saying that Alina Hagi's death twenty-three years ago, even though it was certainly an accident, could be concealing something. And this something could be linked to what we're facing today.'

'All right, I'll tell you what we've discovered,' Corvu proposed hesitantly. 'In reality, it occurred six months ago, immediately after the events of 4 January. Then you got better and things took a certain turn . . .' Corvu was now truly embarrassed.

'Look, Corvu, it's OK. What you mean to say is I was no longer interested in the case, all right? So now you can tell us what this is all about.'

'It's about Colajacono.'

Piccolo's head suddenly shot up. 'I knew it!'

Balistreri stopped them all with a gesture. 'Listen to me very carefully,' he said. 'We've already had one death in the squad. Whatever we say, and I mean *whatever*, stays inside this room. I – and only I – will decide if and how it is to be acted on. I don't want any personal initiatives, in particular about Colajacono and ENT.'

There was a moment of silence. Then, as if the words had been addressed to her alone, Piccolo said, 'All right, I understand.'

'Now let's hear it, Corvu.'

'After the events of January the 4th, the newspapers published Colajacono's photo. And Pierre, the Bella Blu barman, called me and told me he'd met this guy. I told him I'd call him back, but then you . . . anyway, I only did it this afternoon.'

Balistreri swore to himself and Piccolo started to say something, then bit her tongue.

Corvu continued. 'I went to meet him. And now we have the answer to the fourth question on the list. Why was Colajacono already dog-tired on the morning of December the 24th? Because he'd spent almost the entire night before at the Bella Blu. Pierre's certain of it.'

Piccolo couldn't contain herself. 'The night of December the 23rd, when Nadia went there and they killed Camarà. That bastard, he did it—'

'That's enough, Piccolo!' Balistreri exploded. 'I won't tell you again. Until we have proof to the contrary, Colajacono and Tatò were two policemen brutally murdered and decorated for bravery who discovered Nadia's killer. You broke the nose of one and the other you blackmailed with Linda Nardi.'

'But I'm sure that—'

'Your intuition's not enough here – we need serious proof, which we don't have. And which we won't ever have if, instead of looking for the truth, we look for confirmation of a truth that happens to suit us.'

Piccolo lost it. 'And what truth would suit you? Do you want it all to end with those four illiterate Roma in prison and those four animals you killed on the hill? And what about Colajacono, who was waiting for Ramona – or have you forgotten? And what they did to Rudi for the Bella Blu lighter? And blackmailing the deputy mayor, De Rossi? Or do you believe in the fairytale that Colajacono and Mircea didn't know each other?'

Silence fell on the room. Only the sound of the new air conditioning could be heard. After a while Balistreri rose up, dragging his bad leg, and went to the door of the office. He opened it and Giulia Piccolo went out.

Balistreri then went back to his seat and addressed Corvu and Mastroianni. 'Piccolo's out. You are not to share a single detail with her.'

The silence of his team members was clearly one of disagreement, but he decided to ignore it completely.

'Let's move on. What else have you discovered?'

Corvu was overcome by the whirl of events, so it was Mastroianni who carried on. 'I checked the alibis for December the 24th and January the 4th. Those for the night when Samantha Rossi was killed are too far in the past.'

'All right. Results?'

'We already know about Hagi on December the 24th. He has no alibi from six to seven, when he says he went home to pick up presents for the kids in Casilino 900. Nadia was presumably kidnapped around that time. And he doesn't have one beyond nine thirty, when the others went off to St Peter's and he says he went home. And Nadia was presumably killed around that time. We don't know where Colajacono was between six and seven when Tatò went to Mass. After that, there's Tatò's word, which – if we believe it – gives Colajacono an alibi; if not, then he doesn't have one.'

'And Ajello?'

'He went to the charity benefit, but nobody knows exactly what time he arrived there. The drinks finished at eight o'clock with donors handing over their cheques, his among them. Afterwards he went home and celebrated Christmas with his family. His wife and son stand as alibis. But we haven't checked.'

'And the night of the 4th and 5th of January?'

'Hagi says he was at home in bed. He was ill and asleep at that time. No alibi. We know where Colajacono was. We're not certain about Ajello.'

'Why?'

'At nine o'clock he was certainly at the opening of a new ENT gaming room in Florence. But we checked and his private plane landed at Urbe airport around eleven. He picked his car up there and went off, presumably home, because there's no sight of him at the Bella Blu that night or in any of ENT's other nightclubs. We'll have to question him directly.'

'Let's leave Ajello and ENT for the moment. And Adrian's bike?'

Corvu came in. 'We asked a whole lot of people who knew Adrian at Casilino 900. That night he came on the Metro with the others, without his bike. And he didn't have it when they went off to St Peter's. Therefore we could deduce that it was used by Camarà's murderer on December the 23rd and the day after for going up the hill to the shepherd, Vasile.'

'All right, you've done a good job. Now concentrate on Hagi and his past.'

Corvu was evidently in a black mood over Piccolo's exclusion from the investigation.

'I wanted to speak to you, Dottore, if I may . . .'

Balistreri's head was aching, along with his leg. And he was missing Linda.

'Cut the tone, Corvu. What do you want?'

'I wanted to tell you about Margherita.'

'Not now,' he replied sharply, and sent him away.

★ ★ ★

Alberto was setting the table in the garden. Faced with an excellent plate of cold pasta and a white wine, Balistreri managed to relax a little.

'So even you have the Italian flag on the villa gate . . . Aren't you ashamed of yourself?'

'If you had teenage children, Mike, you'd understand. And once upon a time, between the two of us, you were the football fan.'

'But I came to my senses, while you've lost yours.'

'Anyway, you can't deny there's been some positive effect. Look how the mood's calmed down now that we've seen non-EUs waving our flag and celebrating.'

'You think it's a symptom of progress, Alberto? Once upon a time we wanted to deport them for raping our women and murdering our policemen and now, after a game of football, we suddenly discover they're well integrated?'

'That's how we are, we Italians. And the Roma problem's a complex problem. It won't be resolved by any edicts, but with agreement, patience and hard work.'

'I think I'm hearing Pasquali. Alberto, everyone knows what has to be done – shift the Roma from those filthy camps in the middle of the city.'

'All right, Mike. We'll see what the next mayor does, whoever that is.'

'I'll tell you what he'll do. He'll take them out of Casilino 900 and we'll see his photos in the papers as he closes the gates. And he'll shift them elsewhere. All things that could be done right away. Except that the politicians of this country are split into the incapable and the cynical. They don't give a damn about any deaths, unless they can use them to win an election.'

'Mike, there are many honest politicians who are trying to do something, even if it's true that some think only of their personal careers or votes. And yet votes are useful, fortunately.'

'Fortunately? You think it's very fortunate having a democracy where no one thinks about resolving issues but only about the stealing and getting of votes?'

Alberto's mood darkened a little. The words took him back to the worst times with his brother, when he himself was forced to resort to unpleasant compromises in order to get him out of trouble.

He hadn't heard him say anything of this kind for years. It seemed he had become more prudent, or perhaps nothing mattered to him any more. It must have been Giovanna Sordi's suicide that brought all that aggression out.

'Mike, do you remember the senator, Count Tommaso dei Banchi di Aglieno? Would we be better off with him in the government?'

Balistreri sank into silence. The Count was part of the memories that had slowly distanced him from life.

He had no wish to answer that question. He couldn't. He would have had to think about too many uncomfortable things again: his father, his mother, the crimes that had never been solved, and those last terrible hours in Tripoli that had left a mark on his life. Alberto understood him straight away and didn't press the point. He served up the king prawns and changed the subject.

'Heard anything from Angelo, Mike?'

'I've been trying to get him on his mobile for days, but no luck. I believe he's gone off with Margherita to some desert island.'

'Yes. When he called me to cancel the poker he told me that he was going out of Rome. They'll have left.'

'I hope that Margherita's a help to him,' said Balistreri, thinking of Giovanna Sordi and the remorse they both felt.

'And you and Linda?' asked Alberto. 'Will we see you this weekend?'

Balistreri shook his head, but gave no explanation. Alberto asked for none. After all these years he felt the disastrous shadow that was coming back over his brother's spirit. He promised to pray for him again, and pray seriously.

Friday, 14 July 2006

Morning

Monsignor Lato had been notified in advance about the phone call. He had a warm voice and spoke Italian with traces of a Roman accent.

'I read about your mishaps, Dottor Balistreri. I hope you're now fully healed.'

'Thank you, I'm well. I'm sorry to disturb you, and for something so painful for you that happened many years ago.'

There was a short pause at the other end of the line. 'I read in the papers that the men who shot at you were employees of Signor Marius Hagi.'

That was exactly how he said it: 'of Signor Marius Hagi'.

'They were,' confirmed Balistreri. 'But you'll also have read that it's been proved that Hagi had nothing to do not only with that night's events, but also all the illegal activities of those employees.'

'Yes, and I'm not surprised.' He heard a touch of irony in Monsignor Lato's voice.

'You've known Hagi for almost thirty years,' Balistreri said.

'Since 1978. From the day on which I saw him for the first time with Alina.'

'Alina was your niece?'

'The only child of my sister, who died the year before together with her husband in an aeroplane accident. I took her with me to Krakow, helped her continue her studies and taught her how to work with orphans. Alina was sixteen but had the maturity of an adult. Unfortunately, she also had a single-mindedness that was unusually strong . . .'

'Do you mean with Marius Hagi?'

The bitterness was now apparent in the Cardinal's voice. 'You see, Alina had a very strict Catholic upbringing and a genuine vocation to help others. And she got it into her head that young Marius was one of life's victims that she'd saved from perdition.'

'Did you try to disabuse her of this?'

'Unfortunately I didn't understand the danger immediately. At first, it was only friendship between them, then Alina involved Marius in her work, and he really did seem a poor devil. Then my transfer to Rome came in the wake of Karol Wojtila's election as Pope John Paul II and Alina came to me with Marius to tell me they were getting married. He was an uncommunicative boy, but quick-witted and too much so. I read in his eyes that the violence he had suffered had left its mark. But I could not block the marriage; I only made the condition that they follow me to Rome. I wanted to keep an eye on the situation. Contrary to what I expected, Hagi accepted this with great enthusiasm. It was I who officiated at the marriage ceremony.'

'And in Rome . . .'

'In Rome everything went well at first. Through Cardinal Alessandrini I found a job for Alina in the San Valente orphanage. She adored the work even if it paid very little, as the orphanage had no serious funding at the time. After a short time Marius started in business – travel agencies, bars, restaurants. It was incredible for a Romanian immigrant with no education and so young. Whatever

Marius touched became gold. They bought a house opposite the Coliseum and had hundreds of friends . . .'

'Alina was happy?'

'Yes, and very proud of Marius. And the orphanage was a focal point for everyone. It lasted almost three years. Then, I don't know exactly when, things changed. I used to see Alina and Marius every Sunday for the Angelus in St Peter's Square. One Sunday she arrived on her own, and from then on Marius never came with her. At first Alina said he was out and about on business, and after that she didn't say anything. I saw she was beginning to lose her looks; she was less calm, less sunny and looked tired. I tried to speak to her, but I could see she didn't want to share her feelings. This went on for months; I didn't see Marius again until the Christmas of 1982, when there was a huge party in the parish. Marius came with enormous presents, amazing ones, for all the children. I was looking at Alina hoping to see the old pride with which she regarded Marius, but found only pain. I decided to tackle him and asked if everything was all right.'

'And he said?'

'He told me that both he and Alina had to abide by the oaths of fidelity they had sworn on the day they were married in church. I gathered that Alina was his prisoner. And that there was something the matter which was making her suffer deeply.'

'After Alina's death you lodged a complaint against Marius Hagi.'

Monsignor Lato allowed himself to sigh. 'It wasn't a real complaint as such, more of a statement. The circumstances of the accident left no doubts – there were many witnesses. But it was clear that Alina was running away. She died for escaping from Marius Hagi.'

'Did you have any proof?'

'Indirectly. Alina had made close friends with several of the young women who worked at the orphanage. She was inseparable from one in particular. When I met her at Alina's funeral she was in a state. I offered her a coffee after the ceremony and she told me that a few days before she had caught Alina in the orphanage bathroom, where she was applying some ointment to her badly bruised arms. She asked her who had done it and Alina refused to tell her.'

'But this friend thought it was Hagi?'

'Who else? If it had been anyone else Alina would have told her.'

'The statement was withdrawn soon after.'

Now Monsignor Lato's voice was full of bitterness. 'I couldn't ask the other girl to testify – she would have found herself in who knows what trouble. And to what end? Alina was dead.'

'There's one more thing I'd like to ask you, Monsignor, and that is the name of this girl, your niece's friend.'

'I don't think I ever knew it, but I couldn't remember it anyway, it was so many years ago.'

'You have to help me, Monsignor. This tiny thread from the past is important. I have to know what took place between Alina and her husband.'

'In order to do what, Dottor Balistreri?'

Just like Alessandrini. The final judgement is reserved for God.

'My business is earthly justice, Monsignor, not divine. If you don't know her name, at least describe her, then I can ask someone who was around at the time. I'll find her one way or another.'

Monsignor Lato gave a little laugh. 'I can do more than that. One day Alina and her friend asked me to take a photo of them . . .'

Balistreri held his breath.

'I have a copy on my bedside table. I imagine you'd like to see it.'

'Monsignor, I really don't know how to thank you. You perhaps don't know what a scanner is . . .'

'Even things divine use technology, Dottore. You'll have an e-mail with the photo in a few minutes.'

He spent those few minutes thinking about Linda Nardi.

You sent me to Alina Hagi. And what am I to expect now?

He had the reply straight away. A beep announced Monsignor Lato's e-mail. The photo was sharp. Two smiling girls were looking at the lens: Alina Hagi and Samantha Rossi.

They met in Pasquali's office in the middle of the morning. Ever since he was a child Pasquali had learned – from his father and his Christian Democrat friends – to put off, water down and soften, with a smile on his lips and rage in his heart; and all with the consummate artistry of someone who could have been an actor.

He adjusted his spectacles and studied the photo that Balistreri was showing him. 'Yes, a remarkable likeness,' he commented.

He added nothing more, waiting to hear what Balistreri had to say. The head of the Special Section was holding out a photo that had appeared in the papers the year before at the time of Samantha's murder. It was of her mother, Anna, rigid with grief, as she was following the funeral procession.

'Yes,' said Pasquali. 'It could be Samantha's mother as a young woman. It would be a remarkable coincidence.'

'You find it a remarkable coincidence? The possibility that back in 1982 the wife of Marius Hagi, a man involved in two murders in 2005, could be the friend of the mother of one of those two victims, Samantha Rossi, seems only a coincidence to you?'

Pasquali assumed his most patient manner. 'Remember that Hagi's still not officially involved in any murder, let alone that of Samantha Rossi, with which he had absolutely no involvement at all.'

'Unless he's the Invisible Man,' said Balistreri, trying to provoke a reaction.

Pasquali would not allow himself to be troubled even by this. 'The Invisible Man, as you call him, is so invisible that he's only been described by guilty parties attempting to shed themselves of part of the burden.'

If I told you about the voice that announced Colajacono's death, would you say I was delirious?

'All right, but I'm going to speak to Samantha Rossi's parents.'

'Fine, that's something to check,' Pasquali said in approval.

'And I want to question the three Roma in jail for Samantha Rossi's murder.'

Pasquali's lips twisted a little. 'The Public Prosecutor's Office will want to know why.'

'Because of the link with Nadia, it's a new lead.'

'Link?' Pasquali didn't want to take the R and E into consideration. 'There is no link at all, nothing of the kind.'

'There's another question,' said Balistreri, annoyed.

Pasquali stiffened, having a sixth sense for serious problems. Balistreri told him about the motocross bike seen at the Bella Blu and the one belonging to Adrian.

Pasquali listened in silence. 'So?' he asked coldly when Balistreri had finished.

'So it could be the same bike.'

'Or it could be one of the hundreds of motocross bikes circulating in Rome.'

'I don't often see any motocross bikes myself in the centre of Rome down among the Via Veneto nightclubs.'

'But you do sometimes see one, Balistreri. And as a good policemen you know that's sufficient.'

As usual, the change to his surname was a clear message: that was enough. But it wasn't.

'Colajacono was at the Bella Blu on December the 23rd, the night Nadia went there and Camarà met his death.'

Long moments of silence passed in which the things unsaid weighed as heavily as those said openly.

'I also have something to say to you,' said Pasquali at last.

Balistreri waited expectantly. He had a presentiment.

'I know that you have been very close to Linda Nardi these past months. I suppose you saw this little article that came out on the morning of January the 5th.'

Balistreri looked implacably at the photocopy: *If a policeman dies . . .*

'Yes, I read it months later, during my convalescence.'

There's no need to tell him everything.

'And what do you think of it?'

'A remarkable coincidence,' suggested Balistreri maliciously.

From the look directed towards the stone angel on the balcony, Balistreri realized that irony was not Pasquali's strong point, nor was patience.

'If you read this piece in the light of what has happened, doesn't it seem to you more of a warning than a hypothesis?' said Pasquali, shifting his gaze to Balistreri.

'In that case it would be a warning that went totally unheeded.'

'Who was it meant for according to you?' Pasquali asked, staring directly at him.

He was aware of the danger, but no longer disposed to be cautious. It was as if his brush with death on the hill, Nano's death and Giovanna Sordi's suicide were dragging him back to his true nature, the one that the weight of remorse and time had crushed.

'Let's say, as a hypothesis, that the article was meant for whoever ordered the ambush on Colajacono and Tatò, except that it came outside the time limit,' Balistreri replied.

Pasquali looked like a corpse. 'Ambush? But if all the reconstructions say that Colajacono and Tatò decided to go to Vasile's farmhouse to find more proof and by chance bumped into the four Romanians that were there to make them disappear?'

'And if, on the other hand, Colajacono and Tatò were two accomplices who had become inconvenient? They could have drawn them to the place by means of one of their informants and had them killed by the four Romanians,' Balistreri continued.

Pasquali gave him an icy look. 'Did you dictate the article to the Nardi woman?'

Balistreri feared what could happen to Linda if Pasquali thought it was her idea.

'I suggested the article, yes.'

Not a muscle moved in Pasquali's face. He was waiting for an explanation.

'I didn't explain the reasons for my suspicions. She agreed to publish it in exchange for a future exclusive.'

Pasquali picked up the telephone and spoke to Antonella. 'Could you make me one of my herbal teas, the one for an acid stomach, please?'

'I suppose you'd prefer something else,' he said to Balistreri, pointing to the bar.

'I cut out all alcohol before dinner during convalescence. If Antonella could bring me some tea . . .'

Pasquali called Antonella and told her about the tea.

It was as if his confession had calmed their souls. Showing the weaknesses of their respective stomachs created a reciprocal act of trust, no matter how minimal. Two policemen who suffered from gastritis and fear.

'Colajacono first became involved because he was useful, then he was turned into a scapegoat. But Coppola's unexpected intervention and then mine on that hill turned him into a hero,' Balistreri explained.

'I can accept the first part,' Pasquali conceded. 'Colajacono became involved because of someone. This someone wanted to be certain there was a friend inside the police station to meet Ramona if she went to report Nadia missing.'

'Pasquali, I tell you what's seriously troubling me: that day I stopped by the station and confronted Colajacono. He was calm about everything, even when I accused him of having stood in for Marchese and Cutugno in order to be able to delay Ramona's report. No reaction – he was imperturbable. But then I said something to him . . .'

The tisane and tea arrived. Pasquali gestured to him to stop. 'Let me have a bit of this herbal tea before you tell me what you said to him. In fact, hang on a minute and I'll tell you myself.'

He drank, then took off his glasses and massaged his temples. 'Only a madman like you, Michele . . .' he murmured. 'You told him about Vasile's wrist.'

You're a damned bastard, but you've got a great brain.

'When I told him about the sprained wrist I saw Colajacono tremble with fear. He suddenly realized they were framing him. He had no alibi for the hour between six and seven, the hour in which they kidnapped Nadia, probably because someone had sent him off somewhere else. He had only Tatò, who they suggested to him as company for the night precisely because he couldn't give a credible alibi. And he certainly didn't know that Nadia would end up dead. He'd have thought it was another blackmailing of a politician, as they'd done to the deputy mayor, De Rossi.'

'You mean they ambushed him on purpose?' Pasquali was shocked.

'Yes. First they tell him that Nadia has to perform a little service for a politician, then they tell him there was an accident because of that shepherd who got drunk and killed her. They give him the information to find Vasile, so he cuts a good figure. He's happy. But he suddenly discovers that it wasn't the shepherd. He knows very well who it was, but he also knows that he's open to being framed himself. He'd already been forced to show himself with Ramona at the Cristal for the blackmail on Augusto De Rossi. Now we also know that they'd deliberately called him to the Bella Blu on December the 23rd when Nadia was there. You can imagine how Colajacono must have felt. They'd pulled the rug out from under his feet.'

Pasquali frowned. 'And you've surmised that he turned on those who were giving the orders and they decided to silence him. Linda Nardi's article was supposed to have helped avoid all this, but there was no time. You, however, could have done without telling Colajacono about Vasile's wrist.'

Three policemen, among them Coppola, are dead because of this, because I wanted to punish Colajacono for having stripped Linda.

'They'd said to Colajacono that he only had to stop the police searching for her for those two or three days when Nadia would be used for blackmailing a politician. I discover his game and he calls somebody. They arrange to meet him at the farmhouse to calm him and Tatò down. But he goes there before the appointed time to look for proof that would put the blame on someone else.'

'Could you explain yourself better?' Pasquali was looking pale and that pallor worried Balistreri.

'Along the dirt road that leads to Vasile's farmhouse Forensics found no other tracks apart from those of the Giulia GT and the cars driven by Colajacono and Piccolo.'

'So I read. Another reason for ruling out the Invisible Man. How would he have got away from there? Did he have wings?'

'He could have come down on foot, in spite of the dark and the cold. But there was also a hill to climb to get to the Giulia GT. I agree it's too complicated.'

'Therefore no Invisible Man – a mere invention of Vasile.'

'So who killed Nadia, given Vasile's sprained wrist?'

'The other shepherd, his accomplice in the burglaries,' Pasquali replied immediately.

'Could be, but then Colajacono wouldn't have been scared. Things went wrong and he knew it. He went to search for the tracks of the motocross bike with Tatò, but they were lying in wait to kill them.'

Pasquali paused to reflect. 'Forensics would have found the bike's tracks,' he murmured, confused.

'Not if the bike went up off the main path. A motocross bike comes in handy for that.'

'So your theory would be that the Invisible Man goes up the hill on the morning of December the 24th on the motocross bike, takes the Giulia GT and leaves the bike, then comes back around seven in the evening with Nadia in the Giulia, kills her and then departs on the bike.'

Balistreri said nothing. There was an anomaly in that reconstruction but this wasn't the moment to mention it.

Pasquali wanted a conclusion. 'And where does all this take us?'

You know very well where it takes us. To that wonderful example of integration, the enlightened entrepreneur and benefactor of the destitute, Signor Marius Hagi.

Balistreri waited silently. It wasn't up to him to make the connection. If someone is resistant to logic it means that he has another agenda.

Pasquali was a man of great experience and great intelligence. He knew when the game was up and it was necessary to bow out without incurring catastrophic losses.

'I'll find a way of persuading the Public Prosecutor to let you speak to the three Roma who attacked Samantha Rossi. You go ahead and see her parents and clarify the link with Alina Hagi. But don't mention the letters R and E to anyone, least of all Linda Nardi.'

'I'll keep my distance from her.' And as he said it, he was well aware that he had no choice but to keep the promise.

He was glad that Samantha Rossi's parents had moved house. His visit to San Valente had already reopened uncomfortable memories. Going back to see the house where Samantha was born and grew up wasn't top of his life's wish list.

They received him in the early summer evening, after working hours. It was a modern house: new, white and clinical, like a hospital for anaesthetizing grief.

Anna Rossi was a good-looking woman in her forties. Samantha resembled her mother in her features, while she'd taken her height and bearing from her father. They welcomed Balistreri with cold politeness; after all, he believed the Roma boys to be innocent, and had made the great blunder.

Balistreri knew he had to keep the visit as short as he could, his presence giving rise to more grief.

He wanted to be clear straight away.

'I'm not here about your daughter, at least not directly.'

While they were looking at him bewildered, he placed on the table the photo sent him by Monsignor Lato.

Anna Rossi's sad look was lost in a memory that for a moment softened the bitter twist to her mouth.

'Alina,' she said in a flash.

Her husband looked at her perplexed. 'Alina who?'

She gave him an affectionate look. 'She was my best friend at the beginning of the 1980s. I've spoken about her sometimes – she was the one who died on her moped a year before we met.'

'And you saw Alina Hagi regularly at that time, Signora Rossi?' Balistreri asked.

Anna Rossi plunged into her memories.

'She was an extraordinary person, a real force of nature. She looked like a fragile little girl with blonde hair, but she was a bundle of positive energy. Alina was capable of organizing anything and of helping anyone, from the orphans to us voluntary workers when we were having a crisis.'

'How did you meet her?'

'I came to San Valente through my boyfriend, who was studying law and gave a hand in the parish with the paperwork in getting the orphans expatriated. He introduced me to Cardinal Alessandrini and he in turn introduced me to Father Paul. This was 1981, and Alina was my teacher on the training course. We became inseparable immediately, even though she was there almost full-time and I only came when I was free from the university.'

'Did you know her husband as well?'

'A little. He came to pick her up in the evenings to take her home. He was a very serious young man, not very communicative, but he had his wits about him and was full of determination. Then I gradually saw less of him, until Alina's funeral.' A shadow crossed Anna Rossi's face.

'On that occasion you spoke to Alina's uncle, a priest. Do you remember?'

'Yes, I remember it well. I was in pieces with grief and he was consoling me. I unbuttoned a little and told him about something that had happened a few days earlier.'

'The bruises on Alina's arms?'

'Ugly bruises on both her arms. She said she'd fallen, but it wasn't possible. I asked her if her husband had done it, and she strongly denied it.'

'Alina saw eye to eye with her husband?'

'Certainly, at the beginning. Later, in my opinion, the relationship fell apart. I'm not entirely sure, but she gradually talked less about it, unwillingly.'

'Had you been in touch the night she died?' Balistreri asked.

'Yes, she phoned me. She asked if she could come and sleep at my place. She'd never ever done this before and I didn't ask her why. Then, as soon as she left home, the accident . . .'

'Was there another man perhaps?' Balistreri suggested.

Anna Rossi laughed for the first time. 'Alina Hagi was a kind of saint, Dottor Balistreri, a very devout Catholic. She'd have died rather than betray her husband.'

'You've had no more contact with Marius Hagi?'

'None. After Alina's death it took me a long time to forget. It was as if I'd lost a sister. And then Samantha . . .'

Her husband put an arm around her shoulders. He tried distracting her. 'I didn't know you had anything serious going on then?'

'With Francesco? He was only a boyfriend, and turned out to be on the make. It was Alina who helped me see the reality; it was thanks to Alina I found the strength to leave him. We were a really good group of volunteers, you know? We were real believers. Francesco, on the other hand, was using the voluntary service as a political lever for his career, nothing more.'

On an impulse, Anna Rossi got up, crossed the living room and rummaged about in a large drawer full of photo albums. 'Here we are,' she exclaimed happily. 'The group photo in 1982.'

She handed it over to Balistreri. There was the San Valente church in the background, a smiling group of young men and women. He recognized Father Paul, Valerio, Alina Hagi and Anna Rossi, and next to Anna Rossi, an arm around her as her husband's now was, impeccable in jacket and tie, was the future lawyer Francesco Ajello, now manager of the Bella Blu nightclub and director of ENT.

Balistreri decided to keep his questions to the minimum.

'How did this boyfriend of yours become involved with the group of volunteers?'

'This boy here introduced him – they were friends.'

Her finger pointed to the skinny figure of Valerio Bona.

Many remarkable coincidences, as Pasquali would have said.

It was a Friday summer evening. Pasquali had probably already left to spend the weekend in the cool of his hometown and there was no need to get him on the phone. He immediately ruled out the idea of contacting Corvu. Ajello's appearance on the scene put ENT at the centre of the case again, and Ajello was ENT. And ENT meant very serious trouble. He had already lost Coppola and Corvu had witnessed Belhrouz's demise in Dubai.

He knew that the struggle between caution and the truth was one between what he had become and what he had been, which was unhappy in either case, albeit in very different ways. Now he had to find a synthesis that left the living still living and gave justice to the dead.

He had made a note of Father Paul and Valerio Bona's mobile numbers after their meeting. He called Paul first, having an idea where he might be.

'Dottor Balistreri! Keeping up again after so many years of silence. Would you like to meet up?'

He could hear the cries of children in the background along with the clattering of plates. They were starting supper at San Valente.

'Could I drop by now?'

'You can do more than that, if you like. We're about to sit down and eat. I'll get a place laid for you.'

Paul greeted him in front of the large illuminated house. Several children were serving up the dishes prepared by the cook in the kitchen. They were waiting for him to start. Paul pointed out an empty place between a little Asian boy and a small African girl who must have been between eleven and twelve years old.

They were serving up an excellent spaghetti with tomato sauce. The two children were joking among themselves and stealing sly glances at Balistreri. After a while, the little Asian boy plucked up courage.

'My name's Luk. What's your name?'

'Mine's Michele. I'm a friend of Paul. You speak good Italian.'

'I've been here three years, thanks to Paul. He and the Cardinal saved me.'

'And where do you come from, Luk?'

The boy replied hurriedly, as if to push away dark memories. 'From Cambodia.'

The small African girl also found her courage and tugged at Balistreri's sleeve. She was a beautiful child, with enormous eyes. 'My name's Bina. I'm from Rwanda and I'm older than Luk.'

She said older, not bigger. The two of them started taking turns to talk to him, speaking only of their lives in San Valente, as if the first part of their lives had been entirely put to one side. Balistreri noticed that every so often Paul was watching him. For half an hour he managed to forget all about rapes, murders, Hagi, Ajello and ENT. It was as if he'd been transported into another dimension in which the miseries of everyday life had been wiped out by the innocence and happiness of these orphans. The chaotic passion of 1982 had become transformed into an efficient organization that dispensed only that happiness. He could readily understand how Paul was justly proud of it.

When the fruit had been served, Paul signalled to him to join him outside. They sat down under the usual tree in the flickering light of a lamp. A girl of about thirteen brought over a tray with two coffees. Everything at San Valente had changed; everything had grown, like Father Paul.

'Coffee and a cigarette?' Paul proposed, confirming the changes.

It wasn't decaf and it was excellent. Balistreri accepted the cigarette from Paul, his sixth of the day, after years of keeping to his limit.

'I went to visit Anna Rossi, Alina Hagi's friend.'

Paul nodded. 'I read about her daughter's tragedy a year ago. Cardinal Alessandrini called to comfort her.'

'And do you remember anything about Anna Rossi's boyfriend?'

A slight, barely perceptible shadow crossed Father Paul's face. 'Francesco Ajello. He worked with Valerio for the Count. He never came here; he worked in the office. He was studying law and helped to get the orphans out of their country of origin.'

'Did the Count introduce him to you?'

'I think so. Valerio knew him – he introduced him to the Count, who had a word with Cardinal Alessandrini about him. The same as with Elisa Sordi.'

'Did you find him likeable?'

Father Paul lit another cigarette and Balistreri accepted his seventh without giving it a second thought.

'You tend to forget, Dottor Balistreri, I'm first and foremost a priest.'

'But you were a young man then, with likes and dislikes, as any young person. Don't you remember?'

Paul shook his head.

'What I said to you about Manfredi was poisoned by anger. I've had occasion to regret those words very deeply.'

'And you can't tell me anything about Francesco Ajello?'

'It would only be the personal opinion of the confused young man I then was.'

Balistreri decided not to press him further. They were forecasting a night and weekend of high temperatures. There wasn't a breath of wind in the dark of San Valente's garden. The children had gone to bed, the lights and the cries extinguished. Around the lamp fluttered a lazy moth.

He took his leave of Father Paul and that unbearable peace with the feeling of having entered the darkest of labyrinths.

Saturday, 15 July 2006

Morning

Valerio Bona had always loved the sea at Ostia, Rome's holiday beach. His parents had taken him there every summer since he was little. It was there he had met Elisa Sordi in 1981, when she was seventeen and he was an eighteen-year-old, a school leaver who had just enrolled in the Faculty of Information Technology. They had taken many walks by the sea in the endless summer when he had shoulder-length hair. Then came autumn. Elisa had picked up her studies again for the final year of accountancy and he was starting his first year at university. And things had changed. For him the friendship had turned into love, but not for her.

Balistreri called him at eight on Saturday morning. Valerio was preparing his dinghy for a solo outing, just himself and the sea. It was a moment of peace, when memory mingled with the lapping of the waves on the hull and the whistle of the wind. But Balistreri wanted to see him straight away and Valerio felt obliged to wait for him.

The weekend traffic was very heavy. Balistreri preferred to take the Metro line. He stepped out onto the sea front surrounded by bathers off to the beaches. Valerio was waiting for him on his moped. 'I've got a helmet for you as well. Let's go to the harbour – we can talk in the boat.'

Ever since the summer of 1970 Balistreri had avoided going out in boats as much as possible. He realized, however, that this would be the best place to talk to Valerio Bona. Valerio hoisted mainsail and jib and chose a close-reach course that allowed a little coolness and a seat in the shade of the sails. In ten minutes they were out on the open sea and the sounds from the crowded beach had become faint.

The cockpit was plastered with photos of Valerio at different ages at the helm of various boats. The two odd ones were one of Pope John Paul II and one of Italy's 2006 World Cup-winning team.

Valerio was relaxed at the helm. The gold crucifix round his neck gleamed on his sunburnt skin. He was completely at ease in the boat, as if he were inside a shell in which he was able to control the situation. The insecure, awkward kid had once more been left on the quayside.

Balistreri tried to relax, but the peace was broken by his worst memory. 'This'll do here,' he said, lighting a cigarette every five minutes. The iron rules he had set himself were starting to crumble.

'When you came to San Valente the other day, Paul and I were sure it was about Elisa's mother's suicide,' Valerio said, looking at the sea. 'Instead it was about Alina Hagi. We were flabbergasted.'

Valerio Bona was incapable of forgetting. Inventing a new life is a justifiable defence after a great tragedy and he had tried: his degree, IBM and a career. But something had pushed him back on his tracks, something that was stopping him from going too far away.

While Paul was only a kid back then and in time had matured into an adult, in 1982 Valerio Bona was already an adult who could only grow old.

'Do you both think I don't care about Elisa Sordi and her mother?' Balistreri asked.

Valerio gave a start. Balistreri's direct approach wasn't one he shared and he had never liked it.

'No, no,' he murmured. 'We were just surprised. But you're here about Alina Hagi, I imagine.'

'And about her friend Anna Rossi and her boyfriend at the time.'

A long silence.

'We're going to come about – mind the boom,' Valerio announced at last.

After the manoeuvre, Balistreri found himself with the sun in his eyes.

'It was you who introduced Francesco Ajello to the Count, is that right?' he asked, shading his eyes from the sun.

'Yes, I introduced him to the Count, who offered him a position as intern with the law firm that looked after his properties, the same one where I looked after the first PCs.'

'Where had you met him?'

'Right here in Ostia, during a series of regattas for two-man crews in 420s. He came from a wealthy family, had the best-looking boat and was looking for a good helmsman. The sailing club put us in touch and we tried several outings. It worked a treat and we won eight of the ten regattas and the title in the summer of 1981.'

'Why did you introduce him to the Count?'

'Francesco was very smart and was studying for a law degree. He knew that the law firm that took care of the Count's business was looking for an intern and he wanted the experience.'

'And after several months the Count introduced him to Cardinal Alessandrini?'

'Yes, the Cardinal wanted a legal assistant to work for free on the orphanage's paperwork. The Count introduced him to Francesco, who was more than happy to lend a hand.'

'Most generous of him.'

'Well, several people, like Paul, said that he was just a social climber who poked his nose in everywhere. The fact is, he was very smart.'

'And he had a girlfriend, Anna Rossi.'

Valerio thought for a moment. 'Francesco was pretty casual with women. Yes, Anna Rossi was his steady girlfriend, but perhaps not the only one. He was a bit, how should I say . . .'

'Someone who tried it on with everyone?'

'With all those he took a fancy to,' said Valerio, lost in thought.

'And was Elisa Sordi one of these?'

Valerio gave a start, and for a second lost control of the boat, the sails losing wind and beginning to flap. Suddenly the sun went from Balistreri's eyes and the face of an old man appeared in front of him: the lines across Valerio Bona's hollow face were now deep furrows.

Valerio took control of the boat and himself once more. 'Elisa was off limits. And I don't think Francesco was top of the list of the people she liked.'

Returning to Rome on the Metro, mingling with the bathers, Balistreri fell asleep. The sun, the wind, the sea and too many cigarettes had taken their toll. In his dreams, surrounded by the festive cries of families, he met Linda Nardi. He looked at her breasts, the vertical crease appeared in the middle of her brow, and in the place of Linda Nardi's face came the very sweet and childlike one of Elisa Sordi.

Afternoon

He was astonished that Count Tommaso dei Banchi di Aglieno had agreed to see him straight away. Either he never bore a grudge or he was simply curious. The second was the more likely hypothesis. On his part, Balistreri would happily have avoided the meeting, but it was indispensable. He remembered the incompatible feelings of respect and repulsion the Count gave rise to in him. Moreover, the man was the living memory of his most egregious investigative failure.

When it became clear that the investigation had become a shameful shambles, the Count had taken his leave of him, along with his boss Teodori, with the same icy contempt he had shown for them from the first. It was a contempt mixed with the commiseration that superior beings absent-mindedly display to imbeciles. The humiliation that accompanied that contempt had haunted him for years.

The residential complex on Via della Camilluccia was more elegant that he remembered. The trees had grown taller; the pair of three-storey blocks had recently been repainted.

The great green gate through which Elisa Sordi had exited for the last time a little before the 1982 World Cup final was covered in ivy, as was the porter's lodge and gatehouse next to it.

Naturally Signora Gina was no longer there, but a young man in uniform from beyond the EU. And this complex was in the same city as Casilino 900 and the area where Nadia's body had been found at the bottom of a well.

Before approaching the gate he smoked a cigarette, knowing it was totally forbidden inside.

'The Count is waiting for you, Dottor Balistreri. You can park beyond the fountain,' the young concierge told him courteously as he opened the great gate.

Democracy has reached here as well. The Count really must have grown older.

The sun illuminated the twin penthouses: the Count's and the Cardinal's. He crossed the grounds, circling the fountain, and parked his old Fiat in a shady corner beside the Aston Martin, which was definitely a later model than the one he remembered. Behind the swimming pool and tennis courts Block B had all its blinds lowered, and Balistreri quickly took his eyes away from Elisa Sordi's window.

He took the small lift in Block A's atrium and pressed the button for the penthouse. On the landing the gloomy prints of Ancient Rome had been replaced by fine photographs: bright-green highlands, a lake that looked as broad as a sea, a river that was almost white in colour.

The Count's personal secretary, a young man in jeans and Lacoste shirt, welcomed him. The residence that he remembered as always being in the dark, with its curtains drawn and the blinds pulled halfway down, was now completely open to the sun. The heavy curtains had gone.

They crossed the two reception rooms. There was no trace of the black leather sofas and the disturbing tapestries – these had been replaced by modern furniture and mirrors.

The young man ushered him into a small air-conditioned sitting room, containing two light and comfortable armchairs, where the blinds were raised.

'The Count will be with you in a moment. May I offer you anything to drink?'

Balistreri asked for a coffee and sat down. It was another transgression against his gastric rules, but he was no longer able to get by on decaffeinated coffee. The French windows gave onto the large terrace, and he peeped out. He saw a large open parasol and a work table with a PC on it.

'Dottor Balistreri.'

He hadn't heard him come in. Count Tommaso dei Banchi di Aglieno was as straight as a ramrod. His smooth hair, beautifully combed straight back, was only slightly thinner and sparser with a few grey streaks that broke up the black. A short, well-trimmed grey beard had replaced the goatee. His double-breasted blue suit was impeccable. The changes were all to do with the surroundings, not the man himself.

'*Signor Conte* . . .' Balistreri held out his hand, which the other man shook with the strong grip he remembered well.

'We'll be undisturbed here, and cooler. Do sit down.'

The Count showed not the least touch of surprise, annoyance or hostility. In front of him sat the man who, twenty-four years before, had unjustly accused his son of causing his wife's suicide. But nothing in his calm manner gave rise to any suspicion that he was still brooding on the past. By now he was probably bored with it and this visit had simply stimulated his curiosity.

'Thank you for seeing me at short notice.'

'I'm not as frantically busy now as I was back then, Dottor Balistreri. Moreover, I hope the circumstances will be less unpleasant.'

'I won't take up too much of your time, in any case.'

'Please, don't be concerned. I'm now a retired landowner. Very busy with many things but still in retirement. And perhaps I may also have something to ask of you. You know, your adventures of recent months have interested me a great deal, even if they haven't come as a total surprise.'

Balistreri decided not to pick up on the implication.

'A war was about to break out between Romania and Italy.' The Count was amused by the thought.

'But, as you see, a well-placed penalty kick has been enough to settle things back into place.'

The Count nodded. 'I agree. We live in a more or less superficial world. The country's values lie buried under the rubbish the refuse collectors leave in the middle of the street when they go on strike.'

Things change around us, but not inside us.

'I know you left politics many years ago.'

The Count gave an ironic smile. He commanded the same respect, but not the fear he did before, as if he really was the retired landowner that he said he was.

'After the business of 1982, I gave up trying to bring back the monarchy to this country where no one would dream of being king. I was destined to failure, my dear Balistreri.'

'I don't think you're afraid of a fight, Signor Count.'

'It was an unequal one. The Christians were already Democrat, the Communists have become so, and with the benevolent neglect of the Vatican everyone is democratically becoming wealthy. Too many enemies for an old aristocratic idealist.'

Balistreri began to feel uneasy. It was annoying to share even a part of this man's ideas. Finding them in some way similar to his mother's was unacceptable and revolting. It was on these occasions that Alberto, always the respectful one, was the rebel.

Don't trust the Catholics, my sons. It's a religion founded on resentment, bad conscience and repentance. Don't trust the morality of the weak that distances you from life's joys.

The Count was perfectly calm and at ease. He was talking to him as if they were old friends.

'Nevertheless, you are not here to discuss politics with me, Dottor Balistreri. I imagine that the suicide of that girl's mother reopened a tragic wound.'

Here he was after twenty-four years, a few days after Giovanna Sordi's suicide. Father Paul, Valerio Bona and now the Count – how could they think he wanted talk about anything else?

'Right now I'm here for other reasons, fortunately or unfortunately.'

The Count politely raised an eyebrow. 'Reasons to do with your recent adventures?'

'To tell you the truth, at this point I don't know. Perhaps, but I'm not sure.'

The man smiled. 'I see that time has allowed the wisdom of doubt to creep in. It's one of the few advantages of growing old.'

'I have to reconstruct several links from the past that partly concern you.'

'Before you do that, Dottor Balistreri, I'd like to understand how I can help you.'

'I'm a policeman, Signor Count. I'm conducting a very confidential investigation.'

'But you know that I am a most confidential person. And I could help you better knowing what we are speaking about.'

Balistreri decided that, leaving aside ENT and the incised letters, he could risk it.

'I'm on the trail of an elusive phantom,' he began.

'Good,' the Count said. 'An interesting question would be the ideal thing to put some life into a Saturday afternoon in summer. And to encourage you – ' he pressed the button on a remote control, 'this is the only room with a smoke extractor.'

The Count watched him, enjoying his astonishment. A little hesitantly, Balistreri lit a cigarette, nervously awaiting a reaction.

The Count listened in silence to the summary of Nadia's kidnap and murder, carefully pruned of any links with ENT and Colajacono's possible involvement.

'It was Alina, the deceased wife of Marius Hagi, who took me back to the church of San Valente,' Balistreri explained.

The Count kept his peace, his deep black eyes impenetrable.

'Yes, I remember Alina Hagi. Cardinal Alessandrini introduced me to her one day together with her husband Marius. Two singular young people, both blessed with great energy.'

Balistreri knew very well how useless it was to put direct questions to this man. He remained silent while he enjoyed his cigarette.

'I'll check the records for you with my accountants. I think I gave Marius Hagi some work to do, as I did with everyone, perhaps too generously.'

Balistreri shifted uncomfortably in his armchair. Moving on to Anna Rossi and Francesco Ajello would be very complicated without revealing more of his cards.

'Do you happen to know if Alina Hagi was particularly close to any of the voluntary workers?'

The Count gave him another ironic smile. 'I never saw Hagi's wife again. As you know, unlike Ulla I kept strictly away from San Valente and Catholic circles. However, I imagine you've already questioned Father Paul and Valerio Bona on the matter.'

'Yes, I've spoken to them. And we came up with a very close friend of Alina whose boyfriend was another one of your employees.'

'And what would all this have to do with the death of this Nadia and with Marius Hagi?'

Balistreri took the only possible line. 'You see, we're not convinced that Alina Hagi's death was completely accidental. A few days before she died, her friend saw that her arms were covered in bruises. We don't know if this was Hagi's work, but if we find evidence of violence in Marius Hagi's past it would reinforce the hypothesis that he was a party to the crime this Christmas.'

It was a logical explanation. It wasn't entirely without fault, but it stood up. The Count mulled it over in silence, as if he were weighing up a distant memory. After a while, he came to a decision.

'Dottor Balistreri, if you're not in a hurry I'd like to show you something before we continue this conversation. Now that the sun is starting to set we can go outside.'

The French windows that gave onto the terrace surrounded by tall plants were wide open and the sun's setting rays fell on the parquet flooring. On going outside, Balistreri saw the parasol, the work table with the PC and the powerful shoulders.

A tomb on which I put a lid that was too light to last over time.

Hearing the sound of footsteps, Manfredi turned round. Balistreri turned into a pillar of salt. The disfigured youth was an adult with a normal face and calm demeanour. There was no angioma, no harelip, no swollen eyelid. His black hair had no need to hide anything. The plastic surgery had worked a miracle in aesthetics; the rest must have been worked by the medicine of the mind. Now Ulla's angelic face could be clearly seen beside the aquiline nose and features of the

Count. The slender lines of the scars could just about be seen, but the surgeons had done an incredible job. His powerful muscular structure was the same as it was then, now covered with a suntan that must have been natural. The ugly duckling had become a normal man, handsome even in the contrast between his father's marked features and his mother's delicateness.

Manfredi rose to come and meet them. He had grown a little in height and was taller that Balistreri by half a head. He held out his hand and Balistreri shook it in silence.

'I'm glad to see you, Dottor Balistreri.' His voice was quiet, soft and deep. And, like the voice of a good doctor with his patients, it was soothing. His eyes were bright and shining. His manner was unruffled, as if he were greeting an old acquaintance, not one of the pack of hounds that had been out to hunt him down.

Balistreri decided to be sincere. 'I'm glad to see what I see.'

'Let's do this,' the Count proposed. 'While the two of you exchange a few words, I'll go and do a little research in my records.'

They sat down at the table. Balistreri stole a glance at the computer screen. *Paris: Tenth Conference on the Pathology of Infection. Presentation by Professor Manfredi dei Banchi di Aglieno, Nairobi University.*

'I'm presenting our latest research,' Manfredi explained. 'The Paris Conference starts on Monday, then I have another in Frankfurt on the following Monday. After which I go back to Africa.'

'I'm told you've been living in Kenya for many years.'

'Since August 1982. The family has a large farm and estates on the border with Uganda. I graduated in South Africa and now I practise medicine in Nairobi. Look.'

He turned to a new screen that showed Manfredi in a white lab coat surrounded by hundreds of applauding local Kenyans and wealthy bourgeoisie. He was something between a wizard and a saint. He was standing in front of a new white extension closed off with a ribbon: *Nairobi Hospital: Opening of the new Unit for Infectious Diseases. 25 December, 2005.* That was only a few months ago.

'With my father's financial help, we've built a new unit for the care of infectious diseases. Unfortunately, diseases in Africa multiply like the trees and mosquitoes there. It's a kind of natural extermination programme we're gradually trying to reduce. But as soon as a conference crops up in Europe I stop off in Rome to stay a while with my father.'

The more he observed him, the more Balistreri wondered how it had been possible. Could a fully-grown human being experience a trauma that would turn him into another human being? Because that was what Manfredi was – an entirely different person.

Manfredi recounted everything with great composure. After Ulla's death, his father had decided to send him away from Rome to the family's extensive estate in Kenya. Subsequently he had put him in a luxury clinic and entrusted him to the care of the best psychiatrists and plastic surgeons in South Africa. Then followed his medical studies in Cape Town, graduation and research into the most serious diseases among the local populations in the desert and highland villages. There was no hint of any new attachments in the story. No wife or children, only his father.

'I'm amazed,' Balistreri murmured. 'I can't hide the fact that—'

'I know,' Manfredi said, interrupting him in his calm voice. 'It's a miracle. And perhaps if all that happened hadn't happened I'd still be shut in the semi-darkness of my room here with my posters, music and disfigured face . . .'

'The price was too high, however,' said Balistreri.

Manfredi let the statement pass by, along with flight of the swallows over the terrace lost in the greenery and last shadows of the dying sun.

'Nevertheless, Ulla was very unhappy. She made a mistake

marrying my father, and being a practising Catholic she didn't know how to escape from it.'

'Your mother was the victim of many people's shallowness, starting with my own. I don't know how you could ever forgive me.'

Manfredi's blue eyes wandered over beyond the trees towards the twin block. The windows of the second floor were all closed. Balistreri tried not to look while he lit another cigarette.

'In fact, I haven't forgiven it.' His voice had only a trace of the old arrogance. 'What have you been doing all these years, Dottor Balistreri?'

'Taking sleeping pills.'

'And now you have another reason to seek the truth?'

'Giovanna Sordi.'

'Precisely. You owe it to her more than to me.'

At that moment the Count came back with two freshly printed pages. He handed him the first. It was an invoice made out to Marius Hagi.

'He worked for me only once, in the spring of 1982. It was about organizing a visit to Auschwitz for my wife. Ulla had begun to study the persecution of the Jews. She was interested in understanding the role the Catholic Church played in either stopping it or supporting Nazism. At that time it wasn't a tourist destination and Hagi had contacts in the place for a trip of that kind.'

'And your wife went?'

'Yes, in May. Anyway, we never used Signor Hagi again. I suppose we had no reason to.'

Balistreri glanced at the other sheet.

'Here's the other person you wanted to ask me about,' the Count explained.

'I didn't mention anyone,' Balistreri protested.

'There was no need to,' said the Count simply.

He handed him an account sheet for Francesco Ajello. It was a decidedly longer summary than the one on Hagi, with the description and date of every piece of work – all items regarding the Count's property. Every so often a payment was mentioned. The work began in January 1982 and broke off in November 1985, after nearly four years. The Count anticipated his question.

'Ajello graduated and set up a practice for himself.'

'And since then?' asked Balistreri.

'Since then nothing on a professional level. Every year I get a Christmas card from him.'

'But in the years before, did he come here to work?'

'No, never. This is my home. And as you know, I'm something of a private man. Ajello worked at the law firm that looked after my affairs.'

'Did you ever meet his girlfriend, Alina Hagi's friend?'

'No,' said the Count. 'I never knew much about Ajello.'

'I saw Alina Hagi's friend once.' They both turned towards Manfredi.

'You knew Alina Hagi?' Balistreri asked in surprise.

'Not really, but I met her here and she introduced herself. She was very kind, I think she was moved by my looks.'

'And what was Alina Hagi doing in your house?' asked Balistreri.

'Ulla had called her over. She wanted some advice before going on the famous trip to Auschwitz. She was with this other girl – her closest friend, I presume.'

'Do you recall her name?'

Manfredi shook his head. 'No, she never told me. But I remember she was the opposite of Alina Hagi. One was small and blonde, the other tall and dark.'

It was incredible. The one tenuous thread he had followed without much conviction was now unravelling into thousands of others all linked to a past that he had buried in the depths of his consciousness. And those threads, shaped like a spider's web, were dragging him backwards in time towards a memory that over the years he'd succeeded in blotting out.

The people in the present – Hagi, Ajello, Samantha Rossi's mother – were now getting mixed up with those of the past. He wondered where the line of demarcation was, if there was such a line. He left the residential complex on Via della Camilluccia, as he had left it many years before, with the feeling that the truth was at the same time both very near and very far away.

Returning home he passed through the centre, full of people crowding into bars, restaurants and theatres. It was a splendid Saturday evening in summer; everyone was out to have fun. He looked over at St Peter's dome, in the direction where Linda Nardi lived. He picked up his mobile then put it down for a while. Then he dialled Angelo Dioguardi's number. There was no answer.

Before going to sleep, he took up an old habit he'd broken off for many years. Straight whisky and a cigarette.

Sunday, 16 July 2006

Morning

He slept little and badly, no more than two hours. It was the heat, the sounds of festive nights, the mosquitoes buzzing around and the annoying thoughts he couldn't manage to eject from his mind. His stomach was burning from the spirits he'd drunk. His head hurt from the amount he'd smoked.

He got up at dawn feeling terrible. From Signora Fadlun's oven came the smell of baking cakes. On Saturdays Jewish people rested, but on Sundays they worked. He took a cold shower and gulped down a coffee with no sugar. He immediately smoked a cigarette, then got himself ready for the office.

His need for action increased at the same rate as he was physically and mentally tired, which was doubly dangerous.

At seven in the morning Rome was silent, full of sunshine and absolutely deserted after a Saturday night of the high life. Few bars had raised their rolling shutters at that hour. He bought a paper and drank another coffee, sitting down at a table to smoke a second cigarette. It would either be extremely easy to speak to Cardinal Alessandrini or impossible. Corvu would have found a way.

His deputy arrived at the office at seven thirty. He had told him a thousand times that on Sundays he could take it a little easier, but Corvu never listened. And with him came Giulia Piccolo, who immediately retreated into her little cubicle.

Corvu's manner was more resolute than usual. 'Dottore, I've thought at lot about this and I have to say that I'm not absolutely in agreement,' he said, nodding to Piccolo in her cubicle.

'Absolutely'. A word that this shy and respectful young man rarely used.

'I've thought about it too,' Balistreri replied, taking him by surprise. 'Call her in. I hope she's got the message.'

Corvu gave him a look, smiled and quickly went out.

Piccolo came in with her eyes lowered. 'Dottore, I'm sorry. Please accept my apologies.'

'All right, Piccolo. Now I'm going to tell you of a case that you know about only in part.'

They drew closer with enthusiasm and listened attentively. They knew that the Elisa Sordi case was still considered Homicide's worst botch job and that their boss was indirectly involved in the humiliation of its remaining unsolved. Piccolo was also told about how Belhrouz came to die. The only thing Balistreri kept to himself was the question over Colajacono's death. He needed to break his feeling of isolation, but not to that extent.

Corvu immediately called his trusted friend in the Vatican. After a few minutes, Balistreri was speaking to Cardinal Alessandrini's personal assistant.

'Via official channels, it would be impossible, as you well know, Dottore. But the Cardinal will see you informally before the Angelus at half past ten this morning in the Pontifical Lateran University. After that he leaves with His Holiness for Castelgandolfo.'

'Right, you two, try to start filling in some answers on this damned blackboard. And find Ornella Corona. I want to speak to her before I see Ajello.'

'With your permission, I'd like to take Natalya out to lunch on the Janiculum. She's leaving tomorrow to visit her family in the Ukraine.' Corvu looked guilty.

Balistreri tried to be encouraging. 'Why don't you go with her to the Ukraine? Then you'll be able to see a bit more of the world beyond that Sardinia of yours.'

Corvu looked at him in shock. 'But the investigation . . . You've just told us that—'

'Just ask Natalya if she'll have you,' Piccolo butted in. 'If she does, I'll give Dottor Balistreri a hand.'

He left them in heated discussion on the matter. At nine thirty he began to make his way unhurriedly on foot to St Peter's Square. The citizens of Rome were still asleep, but dozens of groups of tourists on foot or in coaches were converging on the Vatican for the Papal Blessing.

He arrived early. The personal assistant ushered him into a large university hall filled with young priests of every race and colour, exactly as he had met Alessandrini the first time in his penthouse. He made out the Cardinal's minute figure on the dais handing out diplomas.

As opposed to the Count, Cardinal Alessandrini had never made him feel uneasy but rather irritated more than anything else. In 1982 he had been a newly appointed cardinal; now he occupied one of the Vatican's highest positions. Alessandrini had to be around eighty, almost the same age as the new Pope. His hair was white, but his face beamed with the same intelligence and energy. Alessandrini saw him and, without worrying about protocol, gave him a small sign of welcome.

At ten thirty the hall emptied rapidly and the Cardinal beckoned him to come forward. 'They're running off to get the best seats for the Papal audience,' he explained as, full of curiosity, Balistreri's eyes followed the festive swarm of young priests.

The Cardinal had his usual air of a thinking man who preferred action, greeting him as if they had seen each other every day over the past twenty-four years.

'I'm happy to see you in good health. I read that they thought your last hour had come.'

'I'm well, Your Eminence. I've been lucky.'

Alessandrini smiled. He hadn't forgotten his verbal duels with the younger Balistreri, when he had tried to persuade him that only divine justice had the blessing of infallibility.

They sat behind the professorial chair. 'I've thought a great deal about Elisa Sordi over the years,' the Cardinal said, 'and even more this week after her mother's action.'

'I've thought about it myself, Eminence, and I haven't found a solution to the crime nor an excuse for my sins back then.'

A shadow passed across the Cardinal's face. 'God forgives all sins if the repentance is sincere.'

'But there are sins for which there's no redemption, isn't that so?'

'No, there's forgiveness and possible expiation for every sin. If you confessed and were really penitent, then any priest would absolve you.'

Balistreri decided to change the subject.

'In any case, I must thank you for seeing me, Eminence. The agreement between Italy and the Vatican doesn't permit me to bother you. Besides, I'm embarrassed to tell you, but—'

'But you aren't here about Elisa Sordi. Oh, don't bother about the formalities, I should be happy to help you. Paul has informed me about your visits to San Valente.'

'Father Paul has become what you hoped for – a well-balanced and effective adult.'

'Paul was already an extraordinary soul all those years ago, but very confused. We have helped him to channel his positive energies and I'm pleased you have noticed this.'

'Valerio Bona, on the other hand . . .'

'Each individual has his own way of behaving. Valerio has his demons, as have we all. He's more troubled because he's more fragile.'

The Cardinal paused. He seemed to be reflecting on something. 'Alina Hagi. This is the name that's taken you back to San Valente, isn't it?'

'Yes, Marius Hagi's wife.'

'Marius Hagi. Isn't he connected to the men who shot at you?'

'I see you're well informed, Eminence. Hagi was the employer of the men who shot me, but he hasn't become implicated in their activities in any way.'

'And isn't the death of that young Romanian girl, Nadia, connected with this?'

'Yes, Your Eminence, it is. We should like to know if Signor Hagi was a mild-mannered, hard-working young man or a violent one. It would help us a great deal.'

The Cardinal paused again. 'Are there links to Elisa Sordi's death?' he asked finally.

That unexpected question shook Balistreri. He couldn't understand the reasoning behind it. And yet the Cardinal wasn't the type to make inconclusive deductions.

'There's no evident link among these crimes. But there are people in common with them, and not only Hagi. Father Paul will also have told you about Anna Rossi and Francesco Ajello: two people who were connected with the church of San Valente and the residential complex in Via della Camilluccia.'

'They are two very different and distinct places, Dottor Balistreri.'

The atmosphere had changed imperceptibly, as if the Cardinal were troubled by a sudden thought.

'Distinct but connected, Your Eminence. And at least three people involved in these current events had something to do with San Valente, directly or indirectly.'

'How do Anna Rossi and Francesco Ajello fit into your present inquiries?'

Balistreri stared straight into his eyes. The Cardinal knew the official response. They were dealing with a confidential investigation. Not even a close confidant of the Pope could have been allowed to know.

Balistreri, however, decided to tell almost all the truth. 'Francesco Ajello runs a nightclub where Nadia spent the evening before she was killed.'

'And Anna Rossi, Samantha's mother? Are the two cases of Nadia and Samantha linked?'

He couldn't tell him this. It would put the lives of his squad at risk. He had already had to mourn the loss of one. No matter how much of a saint he had before him, for Balistreri the Cardinal was still a mortal man with a man's weaknesses and secrets.

'I can't tell you, Eminence.'

He felt that the Cardinal was more worried than offended. His eyes wandered over to the balcony where the Pope would make an appearance in little more than an hour. The young priests' exit had brought a silence that was more in keeping with the surroundings. Balistreri realized he was asking a lot, too much perhaps.

The Cardinal pulled up the sleeves of his red vestment, as if it were a young man's shirt.

'You have your work cut out, Balistreri. I shall try to be less of hindrance to you this time.'

'Do you think you hindered the investigation back then, Eminence?' Balistreri asked, surprised.

Again, the Cardinal was filled with distant thoughts. He wasn't the kind to wear sackcloth and ashes without a reason.

'Perhaps,' he said, but he didn't seem willing to explain.

'We had two different opinions. Yours turned out to be the correct one,' Balistreri admitted.

'Yes, I'm still convinced it was. However, you wish to know from me if Hagi was a mild or a violent man. All right then, I honestly don't know. I saw him with Alina on no more than two or three occasions.'

'You will have had your own personal opinion, nevertheless.'

Alessandrini looked at him with a smile. 'I see you haven't changed that much. I think in the past we've already discussed the danger of personal opinions in these kinds of things.'

Balistreri nodded. 'That's right, but I'm convinced that there's always a reason behind certain feelings. And the feeling I have about Marius Hagi—'

The Cardinal stopped him with a gesture. 'I told you that I would help you this time, and I'll tell you one thing about Marius Hagi. The man I knew as Alina's husband was an absolutist – you could read it in his eyes. For him there was only good and evil. He could take on four men single-handed, but he wasn't the kind to take pleasure in strangling a defenceless young girl. He would have seen that as too cowardly.'

'But Alina? And Anna Rossi?'

'Hagi adored Alina like the Virgin Mary. Anna Rossi I saw very few times, and then again a year ago at her daughter's funeral.'

'That leaves Francesco Ajello.'

There was a slight pause, the usual slight irritation that Ajello's name evoked in many people.

'Francesco was a highly promising and motivated young man; he saw to some paperwork for me very ably. Then he broke off with his girlfriend and kept away from the parish. But Paul will certainly be able to tell you something else about him. Today he's taking the orphans to the seaside, but you'll find him at San Valente tomorrow.'

It was half past eleven. He could have said that the Pope was waiting for him, but he didn't.

'If I have to make confession one day, would you give me absolution, Eminence?' Balistreri asked as he rose to say goodbye.

Alessandrini put a hand on his shoulder. 'Yes, but only if you are sincerely penitent.'

'Ornella Corona's at the seaside at her home in Ostia. She's expecting you after dinner,' Corvu announced at lunchtime.

'All right, I'll take the opportunity to work here in the office for a bit today while there are fewer people around.'

'And Angelo called from London. He sends his greetings.'

'From London?' asked Balistreri in amazement.

'Dottore, you live a cloistered life. Today's the Texas Hold 'Em World Final, live on TV from four o'clock if you want to see it. Angelo's among the finalists.'

'Is Margherita with him?' he asked.

Corvu pointed to the open letter on her desk. 'That's from Margherita. She's asking to extend her holiday for a week and to be transferred.'

Surprised, Balistreri glanced at the girl's tiny desk. There was nothing on it apart from a glass with a wilted flower inside. It seemed a bad omen to him.

'All right, Corvu, off you go to lunch with Natalya.'

'Shall I come back afterwards?'

'Look, Corvu, it's Sunday, your girlfriend's off tomorrow morning. Didn't they teach you anything at university about—'

'All right, Dottore, thanks. But if you need—'

'And tell her you're going with her to the Ukraine tomorrow. Do I make myself clear?' he ordered menacingly.

Corvu was about to protest but his boss's grim look pushed him to disappear.

Afternoon

For a while Balistreri did nothing but smoke and drink beer, looking out of the office window at the flow of overheated tourists walking below. He realized that he was now nearly at the rate of a packet a day and his stomach was beginning to burn from the cigarettes, too much coffee and beer. He shelved the thought as irrelevant. Then he realized he'd forgotten to take his antidepressants. Despite feeling tired he wasn't depressed, rather the opposite. So many things had happened all in one week, starting with Italy's victory. Linda had left him. Or perhaps it was he who had left her. He thought about it continually and was no longer sure. Something in him was changing. His buried memories were rising up again, together with that anger he had managed to quell by himself.

In that week, so many years before, he and his friend had continued to chat a great deal, almost always in the car parked on the pavement, and they had tacitly avoided going back to that terrible night. But from that July in 1982, Angelo Dioguardi had reacted by throwing off his previous existence and, with a great effort, had tried to live a little for himself and a lot more for others. Balistreri, on the other hand, had slowly started to disintegrate in his remorse.

I've gone to sleep, leading a life that's not mine in a world I have no liking for.

But now Giovanna Sordi had taken him back to that night. Angelo had disappeared and had finally called from London, sending his good wishes but no invitation to call back.

He went down to buy a slice of pizza and a beer, followed by a coffee and a cigarette. He then went back up, closed the blinds and switched on the air conditioning. He looked at the blackboard. By now he had plenty of answers. Not all, but most. And now there were other questions and old acquaintances from 1982.

He switched on the television and found the right channel. The poker final still hadn't started. He stretched out on the sofa; the quiet, the beer and the semi-darkness had their effect.

Pasquali's private mobile rang immediately after lunch while he was playing a hand of *tressette* with his old hometown friends under the shady porch of his country house in Tesano.

He excused himself and went some distance away to reply. As usual, he said nothing, but simply pressed to receive the call.

It was the icy voice he knew very well. 'Serious risks have come up. Let's start with the removal.'

'Couldn't we—'

'No.'

He attempted a feeble protest. 'But my view—'

'I'll send you a more detailed message.'

The call was broken off. Pasquali returned to the card game with his legs feeling like lead. With his head in a daze he wasted a magnificent hand and lost the game.

Balistreri awoke with a start in the middle of the afternoon, sweaty and dazed. Angelo Dioguardi was staring at him from the television screen as he pulled a large number of chips towards him in a gesture that Balistreri knew from experience.

He followed the game without trouble. He knew Angelo's tactics by heart. Twenty minutes from the end there were only two players left, his friend clearly in the lead. At this point he only had to declare himself out all the time, until he had the hand for the freezeout, the elimination of the last opponent.

The game was coming to an end and Angelo Dioguardi had the Texas Hold 'Em world title in his hands. All he had to do was be cautious and wait for the right hand to close.

On the table were the four community cards face up: the three, six and nine of clubs and the nine of diamonds. The hole cam that allowed viewers to see the players' two private cards showed two clubs for the opponent, who therefore already had a flush before the river, the fifth card. Dioguardi had the four of spades and the jack of diamonds, and no possibility of winning that hand, no matter what the river card was.

His opponent made his call, high enough to dissuade Angelo from attempting a bet on the last card in case he only had a two pair or three of a kind. It was a common situation. Balistreri was expecting to hear him call 'check', or pass.

Then he saw Angelo Dioguardi turn and stare out at him from the screen. He immediately knew two things with absolute certainty: Angelo was turning to look at him personally and he would do the same thing that Balistreri had seen him do on the first night they met, which was to call and see his opponent.

He was looking out at him, Michele Balistreri. It was the last thing left to Angelo Dioguardi to pass on his thoughts.

All in, for everything.

It was obvious to everyone present and to the viewers that Dioguardi had gone mad, pointlessly putting back on the table a world title that was already his. The dealer dealt the fifth card, the nine of hearts. Dioguardi's opponent turned pale, thinking long and hard, twisting his hands. He could risk everything in order to gain an unlikely victory, or else he could keep the chips he had in front of him and try another hand. 'Fold,' he said, shaking his head.

Angelo's face wore the same disinterested and absent expression as it had on the first night on which Balistreri had seen him bluff at the card table in Paola's apartment. His opponent looked at him one last time, then shook his head and put his cards down.

Angelo didn't even smile as he took the pot. The freezeout came in the next hand. Dioguardi was world champion.

★   ★   ★

When Balistreri came out of the office, the sun was beginning to set but the blanket of heat had made the asphalt burning-hot all day and he was sweating copiously as he walked home. The sound of his mobile shook him out of his thoughts.

'Corvu, you haven't gone back to the office, have you?'

Corvu wasn't the type to get excited easily, and yet he could hear him breathing with difficulty. 'I'm running there now to get a car. Where are you, Dottore?'

He understood immediately that something serious had happened. 'On my way home. I'll wait for you on the pavement outside,' he replied, without asking any questions.

Corvu arrived five minutes later.

'We're going over to Aquila. They found the body of a girl there this afternoon.'

'Another prostitute?'

'No, a foreign student at the university. The last time her friends saw her was on Sunday night during the World Cup celebrations, but they hadn't reported her missing because the day after she was going to Rome and flying home.'

'I've got that, Corvu. But I don't understand what it has to do with us.'

'It's Selina Belhrouz, sister of the lawyer in Dubai.'

Balistreri turned to stone.

It was me. I broke the pact. The truce is over.

Corvu drove flat out along the motorway and they arrived at the destination in an hour. The body had been found down the well of an abandoned farmhouse near Tesano, Antonio Pasquali's home-town. Balistreri refused to dwell on the fact, but he found Pasquali at the scene. He was there for the weekend and had been attracted by the number of police vehicles passing by his villa.

He was dressed differently this time, wearing a jacket and an open shirt, and he looked very shaken. 'What are you two doing here?' he asked Balistreri.

'If you don't mind, I'll tell you afterwards in private. Right now I'd like to see what's happened.'

'Then hurry up. Forensics have finished their examinations and they'll be taking the body away shortly.'

But Balistreri was already on his way to the well, near which the girl's body had been placed on a stretcher and covered with a sheet. He introduced himself to the local commissario.

Incredibly the area was an exact copy where Vasile the shepherd lived. A clearing, a little wood, a tumbledown farmhouse and a well. And only a few kilometres from the country retreat of Dottor Antonio Pasquali. There was nothing to see apart from the body under the sheet. Forensics would have seen to the rest. As the smell of decomposition was overpowering, everyone was wearing masks. Balistreri and Corvu followed suit.

The paramedics were waiting to load the body onto the ambulance. Aquila's regional pathologist was finishing off his notes.

'Has she been dead for long?' Balistreri asked him.

'I'll know better after the autopsy. At least three or four days, in any case.'

'And the cause?'

'There are clear signs of strangulation at the base of the neck, besides the bruising, cuts, cigarette burns and various fractures.'

Just like Samantha, like Nadia, like . . .

In his anger, he dismissed the thought of the last name. But he couldn't drive away the feeling of dismay. It was there, fixed, immovable in a corner of his mind. He turned to the commissario. 'I'd like to see the body before they take it away.'

'Please, be my guest. It's not a pleasant sight, but I imagine you're more used to it than I am.'

Struggling for breath, the paramedics lowered the sheet as far as the feet. The body was in a poor state of preservation, but the signs round the base of the neck were very clear. She must have been an active girl, a little dark complexioned like her brother.

'Can you turn her over?' he asked the paramedics, who unwillingly performed the task.

At the base of her spine Selina had a tattoo, one of those half-hidden ones that rose above the panty line. They were popular among young girls. This one depicted a sun surrounded by its rays and a five-centimetre V had been scored at its centre.

Evening

The Pasquali family villa was as sober-looking as its owner. His wife served them supper and left them by themselves.

Corvu was clearly uncomfortable. 'If you'd like me to leave you . . .'

Pasquali put him at ease. 'That's not necessary. Let's try to gather something from this awful mess.'

His usually smooth and relaxed face was marked with deep lines. Pasquali waited until the end of the meal, then offered a stiff drink. He lit up a cigarillo and led them out onto the patio. 'It's cooler outside. It'll help us think.'

Balistreri realized he could no longer skirt around the issue. He told him what they'd seen in Dubai: the SUV, the death of Belhrouz, who happened to be the brother of the girl found in the well. As usual, Pasquali showed he was an excellent listener. He also decided not to enquire why this had never been mentioned to him before.

'You don't know if it was an accident or murder, then?' he asked finally.

'We weren't sure,' Balistreri replied, 'until this afternoon.'

'This too could be a coincidence,' Pasquali offered, more to bolster his courage than anything else.

'Like the fact that they chucked her down a well behind your house?' replied Balistreri in irritation.

Pasquali let out a kind of resigned groan.

'And there's more,' added Balistreri.

The account that followed of the events and people that had collected around San Valente made Pasquali markedly nervous. 'You went bothering Cardinal Alessandrini?' he murmured, incredulous. 'And he actually saw you?'

'He's a very friendly person.'

'Friendly's not the most exact term to describe one of the Vatican's five most powerful men. And to ask him what, if I might know?'

'ENT's mixed up in something serious,' said Balistreri, cutting him off.

'Even I have gathered that,' replied Pasquali, ever more tense. 'But that doesn't mean to say it's mixed up with these murders. And what's Cardinal Alessandrini got to do with it? To say nothing of Count dei Banchi di Aglieno . . .'

'Do you know the Count?'

'By reputation, everyone does. Besides, we play golf at the same club.'

'May I say something?' cut in Corvu, timidly. His manner showed he was worried.

'What is it?' Balistreri asked him, struck by the look of concern.

'It's just that there was an anonymous call and I—'

'What are you saying, Corvu?' Balistreri's manner changed distinctly.

'Yes,' Pasquali explained. 'The local commissario's office received an anonymous call today about five o'clock. It was about the terrible smell coming from the well. It must have been someone passing by who didn't want to get involved.'

Corvu looked at Balistreri, trying to read his thoughts. 'I'm sorry, Dottore. I'd completely forgotten—'

'I'm not sure I follow. Does this change anything?' Pasquali objected.

Balistreri suppressed an evil thought. 'It's the second anonymous call after the one made to Colajacono. And now we have the third letter, a V. Another coincidence?'

'All right. Next week you can go and speak to the three Roma youths who killed Samantha Rossi. But not a word to the press about the letters.'

I should tell you how Colajacono died on the hill. But I can't, not yet.

They said goodbye about eleven and were back on the motorway, Balistreri overcome with tiredness, his stomach burning. He smoked in silence in the dark, his eyes fixed on the tail lights of the car in front.

They managed to distract themselves by chatting about Angelo Dioguardi and his great win. Having his number, Corvu decided to call him at his London hotel, using the hands-free set.

They heard the typical English ringtones, then the hotel desk, which put them through to Angelo's room.

'Graziano.' There was noise from a television in the background.

'Angelo, you were great. I'm in the car and Dottor Balistreri's here with me.'

Silence. Then Angelo said, 'Ciao, Michele.'

Those two words and the way in which they were spoken were enough for Balistreri to feel in that moment – for the first time since he'd known him – that there was an unbridgeable distance between them.

'Well done, Angelo. We must talk about that bluff sometime.' It was his way of telling him that he'd understood the message.

'Yeah, sometime, perhaps, Michele.' Angelo's tone didn't encourage further conversation.

They said goodbye to each other like that, with a sense of empti-
ness that left Corvu astonished and embarrassed.

Inevitably, he and Balistreri began to speak once more about the
afternoon's events.

'I don't like anonymous calls, Corvu, and this one less than ever.
I wonder if—'

Balistreri suddenly stopped himself short. 'Did you tell Ornella
Corona that I wasn't coming this evening?'

'It wasn't necessary. She said she'd be home anyway after dinner.'

'Call her on the hands-free.'

'Dottore, it's almost midnight. She'll be asleep.'

'Call her, right now.'

Corvu knew this was the tone that meant no more discussion.
He punched the number. The message said the mobile was switched
off.

'Call the landline,' Balistreri insisted.

'I don't have her home number in Ostia.' Now Corvu was more
agitated than he was.

'Never mind,' said Balistreri. 'Switch the siren on and get there
as fast as you can.'

Ornella Corona had heard that voice on the phone, just like Selina Belhrouz.

They didn't exchange a word for the rest of the journey. It took
less than an hour. Corvu only switched off the siren once they entered
Ostia. Along the seafront there were crowds around the ice cream
parlours that were still open. They entered the calm, silent residential area. Ornella Corona's two-storey villa was completely dark,
surrounded by a small garden.

They rang the bell on the gate. No reply. They rang again. Nothing.

'I'll climb over,' said Balistreri.

'But, Dottore—'

'You stay here.'

Corvu stiffened. 'Let's call a local patrol. Let's not risk—'

But Balistreri was already at the top of the gate. He didn't have his pistol, but he knew there'd be no use for it. If the Invisible Man had paid a visit, he'd already have left.

He landed in the dark garden. The only light was coming from the back of the house. He rang again at the front door. Nothing. He decided to go round the back to find a way in. As soon as he turned the corner, he saw a parked Golf, its doors closed but with a single light glowing on the dashboard. It was Ornella's car.

He stopped to inspect it. Beside him was a small lamppost. He pressed a switch and a white light illuminated the scene.

He knew where to look. The light was the one that indicated the boot was open.

Ornella was inside the boot, her eyes wide open and filled with fear. She was dressed, but her leggings were pulled down around her thighs. The letter I carved on her began at her navel and went right down to her pubis.

Thursday, 20 July 2006

Morning

Balistreri passed the ensuing nights between the television set and his front-room window, his cigarettes and whisky consumption now out of control, accompanied by insomnia and unpleasant conjectures about the past, present and future. The everyday normality to which Linda Nardi had accustomed him for a few months now seemed like a last moment of quiet in his life, a last failed attempt to forget who Michele Balistreri really was and to round off his existence living with his dark memories. He brushed her angrily from his thoughts, but she always came back.

The summer's dawn found him worn out after his thinking, smoking and drinking. His eyes were red, his beard unshaven, his clothes even more dishevelled. All caused by Linda and his other obsession, the Invisible Man.

A serial killer who carves letters on his victims, or a plot by my ex-colleagues in the Secret Service? Who am I chasing after? Two shadowy figures, one on top of the other, which then split into two, like two phantoms. Or was there only one?

From a good, sensible policeman, albeit one that was a little depressed, he was turning into someone disturbed; halfway between an alcoholic and a homeless vagrant. Corvu and Piccolo defended him strenuously against the cruel comments going round the Flying Squad offices. The Special Section had never been accepted by the other divisions and now its much talked-about boss, who was unpopular with both suspicious politicians and jealous colleagues, was on his knees.

Pasquali was also defending him strenuously, as was Floris, the Chief of Police. There had been three days of hellish media frenzy. Fortunately not a single journalist had a spark of illumination to link the discovery of Selina Belhrouz's body with Pasquali's house in the country. But Balistreri, who knew Pasquali well, was aware that he was eaten up by the possibility.

Information about the letters carved on the victims didn't reach the media. Even its 'Deep Throats' were keeping quiet on account of reprisals threatened by Floris and Pasquali.

In this way, no one saw any link between the two crimes. Selina Belhrouz's murder was likened to Nadia's because of the way in which the body was found, although no one questioned the guilt of Vasile, shut away in prison. The most strident criticisms were about Ornella Corona's death. A beautiful Italian woman killed like that in her seaside home, probably by an ordinary thief – surprised in the garden – who had also tried unsuccessfully to rape her. Moreover, some witnesses had seen and heard a man, probably a Romanian, speaking in an East European language into his mobile, wandering around outside the villa after suppertime.

The first reports from Forensics and the pathologist on the two cases were clear enough. In both cases there were no fingerprints, nor traces of any organic nature. This already spoke volumes about the theory of the thief surprised by Ornella Corona. Whoever went into a house wearing surgical gloves and a balaclava so as not to let a hair fall had something far worse than a robbery in mind. There was no sign of sexual violence at all in either case, but there were significant differences.

Selina Belhrouz had been taken off to an isolated place and stripped, bound and tortured. But she hadn't been raped. The bag with her personal effects and mobile had disappeared. It didn't really look like a robbery. There were fractures, bruises, cigarette burns. An act of sadism or an interrogation? She had already fainted by the time she was strangled.

After coming back from the beach, Ornella Corona had had consensual sexual relations shortly before being killed. She had gone out into the garden, perhaps drawn there by some noise, and there she'd been attacked and strangled. The winking wristwatch had disappeared, but as a robbery it was a poor effort. The leggings had probably been pulled down immediately after death in order to carve the letter 'I'. The car was open because it was parked in the villa garden. It was clear the murderer knew there was little time. The pathologist had calculated the time of death as between eleven and midnight.

Once again, the campaign against Casilino 900 and the other camps exploded, this time more violently than ever, and the city council was again in a fix. The opposition had launched a vicious attack and the Catholic Church alone was trying to defend the Roma from generic and total condemnation. In the outlying suburbs patrols of young Italians began throwing Romanians out of bars, then chasing after and assaulting them. When the police tried to arrest one such juvenile for making mincemeat of his grandfather's Romanian carer, after having accused her of theft, they found themselves facing the entire neighbourhood opposing the arrest and praising the boy for having taken the law into his own hands. The police were drawn up in force to protect Casilino 900 and the other camps, but the idea of leaving it up to the crowd was beginning to circulate among them. In July's torrid heat the peace created by football was swept away by the latest murders, and by now it needed little for the situation to become explosive, to the joy of those who were expecting that very thing.

Balistreri hadn't seen Linda Nardi at the press conferences. She hadn't even published an article on the matter, until that morning.

Sitting in Pasquali's office at eight o'clock were Floris, Balistreri and Pasquali.

'This is worse than a tsunami,' moaned Floris gloomily, looking at the newspaper.

The headline was clear: *Four points along the same line?* The four murders of Samantha Rossi, Nadia, Selina Belhrouz and Ornella Corona were given out according to the police's official version. Linda Nardi made no comment about that; it was a dry and faithful description of what had been reported from official sources.

But there was a final question: *If there was a common element among these four crimes and the investigators were aware of it, have they the right to remain silent about it so as not to compromise inquiries or should they tell us how things really are?*

Pasquali was his usual cool self. 'Linda Nardi is posing a question for us. We can either ignore her or reply. I say we should analyse the pros and cons.'

'If the analysis you want to make is investigative and not political, then I'd bring in Corvu and Piccolo.'

Pasquali looked at the Chief of Police. 'I'd say we make an investigative analysis to use as the basis for a political decision.'

Corvu and Piccolo were brought in. Corvu was a little intimidated by the Chief of Police's presence, Piccolo not at all.

'Balistreri,' said Floris, 'would you guide us through this minefield?'

'Linda Nardi's asking if there's a common thread to these four cases and whether we have the right to keep it to ourselves. I'd like to clear the field of any doubt about one point. In the past, as Dottor Pasquali knows, I have used Linda Nardi as a channel for investigative ends, but I have never mentioned the letters in the first two crimes, nor have I seen her since July the 11th.'

'All right,' said Pasquali. 'There are no doubts about Dottor Balistreri's discretion. Let's continue.'

'We have four letters,' continued Balistreri, 'probably carved by the same instrument: a scalpel or a sharp knife. An "R", an "E", a "V" and an "I". And they come in this order, assuming that the order makes sense and the letters themselves do. This is the one sure common thread along the four murders. And it can no longer be a coincidence.' He addressed the last point to Pasquale.

'The letters may not be over,' Piccolo added, just to lift everyone's morale.

Balistreri saw the Chief of Police quickly make an automatic superstitious gesture, touching the wood of his chair.

'Agreed,' Pasquali cut in. 'So I propose we shelve the letters, for a moment only, and ask ourselves if there are any other common elements among the four cases.'

Corvu raised his hand to speak. 'Actually, there are five cases. There's Camarà as well, and that's leaving aside the deaths on the hillside. If we want to analyse the deaths of the four women, we have to remember that Nadia's death is linked to Camarà's.'

'And the last two murders could be connected more closely to Camarà's death than to those of Nadia and Samantha,' said Balistreri.

'Necessity killings,' observed Pasquali.

'Exactly. The first two crimes were preceded by a sexual attack and concern two females chosen at random, although we'll have to come back to this. But if we hypothesize a connection, the last two victims are not random at all but two women linked in some way to the investigation into Nadia's death, and the motive could be the same as that in Camarà's case: doing away with an inconvenient witness. And all of this disguised as part of a sequence. The letters could simply be a cover-up.'

'Then what you're saying,' interpreted Pasquali, 'is that we're not dealing with a sadistic serial killer who attacks, kills and carves letters into his victims, but with premeditated murder that evidently gives rise to more on the part of one or more other murderers?'

It's as if the Invisible Man had two different selves and two different masks. But the hand that does the killing is only one.

Corvu was aware of the impasse and obviously put forward his own analytic approach.

'If you'll permit me, I'd like to pick up on Dottor Pasquali's question about any other similarities among the four cases. It's here that – ' Corvu looked at Balistreri as if to ask his permission, 'the Invisible Man comes into play.'

The Chief of Police stared vacantly at him. 'What Invisible Man?' he asked looking first at Corvu, then Balistreri, then Pasquali.

'In the case of Samantha,' Corvu went on, 'the three Roma boys say there was a fourth man – who later disappeared – who got them drunk, gave them drugs, and was the first to attack the girl. In the case of Nadia, according to Vasile, there was a man who telephoned, and in exchange for the loan of the Giulia GT brought him Nadia and two bottles of whisky.'

'But there's nothing of the kind in the other two cases,' Floris protested.

'*Signor questore,*' Corvu replied obsequiously to the Chief of Police, 'there was an anonymous phone call that led us to Selina Belhrouz's body in the well, and a suspicious individual who was speaking on his mobile in Romanian near Ornella Corona's villa. Furthermore, there's a motorcyclist involved in Camarà's case.'

And there's the phantom that announced Colajacono's death and killed him in cold blood.

'Help me to understand here,' said Pasquali. 'Let's suppose – for a moment only – that the murders are all by the same hand and that the perpetrator is this Invisible Man, as you call him. You're saying that the choice of the first two victims was random or in some way different from the last two, which came about by necessity. But while I can understand that Camarà was killed because he'd seen someone at Bella Blu he shouldn't have seen, I don't understand where Selina Belhrouz and Ornella Corona come in. What had they seen?'

'They'd heard a certain voice on the telephone,' said Balistreri, suddenly deciding to come out with it.

While they all looked at him dumbfounded, Pasquali shifted uncomfortably in his seat and favoured him with a long stare. In the general silence, Balistreri felt as if he were undergoing an X-ray.

It's the fear I see in your eyes that worries me more than anything else.

At last Pasquali gave a sigh. 'I hope you know what you're saying. And I'm letting you know that if you have any more hidden cards you'd better show them now, as I don't think there's much time left. Tell us about this voice,' he said in a tone that betrayed no menace, only concern and great foreboding.

'One day Ornella Corona received a phone call at home. The person at the other end said that her husband's mobile was off and asked her to find him and tell him he had to go to Monte Carlo that evening. When she protested that it was already five o'clock in the afternoon, the man told her in no uncertain terms that this was why they maintained a private aeroplane. Then he hung up.'

Then came a long silence. The dark shadow of ENT was again falling across the murders. And no one dared think what it could mean.

'This ENT . . .' Floris began feebly.

'I beg your pardon, *Signor questore*,' said Pasquali, interrupting him. 'I'd like Balistreri to finish his explanation with regard to Selina Belhrouz as well.'

'In Dubai, just before the accident in which Selina Belhrouz's brother lost his life, he told us that during one of her visits to Italy, his sister accidentally answered a call on his mobile. According to him, this was a problem because it was a voice Selina wasn't supposed to hear.'

Pasquali had turned very pale. He made a single note in his diary. 'All right,' he said, taking charge of the meeting again, 'let's leave ENT for now. We have two women chosen at random and killed, then Camarà and two other women eliminated because they were inconvenient witnesses, and the letters are only a red herring to put us off. Is this the picture?' he concluded, turning to Balistreri.

'No,' said Piccolo, without asking permission to speak. Everyone turned to her. 'We can argue about Samantha, but Nadia wasn't chosen at random. They twisted the arms of Colajacono and Tatò and got them involved and they went ahead with Nadia even after Camarà saw them, at the cost of killing him and getting the Bella Blu and ENT involved. They could easily have dropped her and chosen another victim. But no, they wanted Nadia. For some reason, she had to be the victim.'

'I really don't follow,' Floris protested. 'A poor young Romanian girl who turns to prostitution – why go after her . . .?'

'It's possible that she had discovered something she shouldn't have . . .' Corvu suggested.

'But that's absurd,' said Pasquali. 'They would have shot her and thrown her down a well. End of story. Instead of this pantomime with the trip to the Bella Blu, the motocross bike, the Giulia GT, Vasile.'

Balistreri knew that Pasquali was perfectly correct. But so too was Piccolo: Nadia wasn't chosen at random, but for a particular reason – which, at that moment, he couldn't fathom.

'And where does the question of Elisa Sordi come into all this?' asked the Chief of Police, ever more confused and preoccupied. 'Pasquali's told me that you've been to question Count Tommaso dei Banchi di Aglieno and Cardinal Alessandrini.'

'A simple friendly chat, not an interrogation. And neither of them was upset. They thought I was there to reopen the Elisa Sordi case after her mother's recent suicide, but I was actually there for another matter. Everything starts with Alina Hagi, who at that time was often around San Valente. Her best friend was Samantha Rossi's mother, who was then going out with Avvocato Ajello, who today is director of ENT and linked in some way to Ornella Corona.'

'But this is worse than science fiction! These coincidences are unbelievable.' The Chief of Police was appalled.

Balistreri shook his head. 'Exactly, unbelievable. *If* they were coincidences.'

It was Pasquali, as ever, who drew the conclusion.

'Let's go back to the beginning, to Linda Nardi's question about the investigators having something to link the four murders. Yes, we do. Do we have reasons for not revealing it? Yes, we do. If we said there was a serial killer about who carves letters of the alphabet on his victims, it would set off a general panic. Can we still keep this a secret among ourselves indefinitely? I would say no. Certainly, a fifth murder with another letter would be totally unacceptable.'

'Then what do you propose, Dottor Pasquali?' asked the Chief of Police.

Balistreri met Pasquali's look and saw that he had made a decision. The business of the voice heard by Ornella Corona and Selina Belhrouz had had its effect.

'Balistreri, you now have forty-eight hours to arrest the murderer. Once the perpetrator's in prison we could tell the press a part of the truth and they'll forgive us the untruthful part.'

Pasquali's voice was cool, calm and decisive. There was no room for any doubt or objection.

Floris stared at him incredulously. 'I'm sorry, Dottor Pasquali, but who would this perpetrator be that you're speaking about?'

Pasquali wasn't in the mood to mince his words. 'He wields an influence over the whole Romanian community. He never has an alibi. He speaks both Romanian and Italian. He could have used Adrian's bike to go up the hill to Vasile. Samantha's mother was his wife's friend in 1982. Nadia lived in the apartment he owned. The four tearaways who killed three policemen, and almost killed Balistreri, were his henchmen.'

'But we have no proof . . .' the Chief of Police tried to say.

Pasquali looked at Balistreri. 'You'll find the proof, Michele. Tomorrow morning you can see Vasile and the three Roma boys who murdered Samantha. By Friday I want you to have nailed Marius Hagi on a charge of multiple murder.'

Balistreri left the meeting with the uncomfortable feeling of having revealed too many things to Pasquali, and with regret for not having told him about the most dangerous.

'I imagine you have a very good reason for calling me.' The voice was calm, but hardly encouraging.

'We have to meet,' Pasquali whispered.

'I don't think so,' came the frosty reply.

'You've gone too far, and – what's more – on my own doorstep!' Pasquale was trying to keep a check on the tremble of rage in his voice.

'A merely fortuitous coincidence.'

'We have to stop this here, right now,' Pasquali muttered in desperation.

'On this we're in agreement. I'll see to it. Keep yourself prepared for tomorrow.'

Pasquali ended the call. He turned to the crucifix and began to pray. 'Our Father, which art in Heaven . . .'

He felt Christ's gaze on his head. It had been a dreadful mistake, and now the game was out of his hands. Or perhaps it had never been in them.

'. . . and lead us not into temptation, but deliver us from evil. Amen.'

Balistreri was aware that speaking with with ENT's director was a final act of defiance towards whomever had warned and advised him in every possible way to keep his distance; an act of defiance that could only end in yet more serious difficulties.

But it was as if Giovanna Sordi's suicide had unleashed those instincts in him that time and regret had slowly put to sleep. His antidepressants were no longer any use, nor his gastro-protector pills, nor cutting down on smoking and drinking, and it was no longer any use going to bed early with the solitary company of a good book. And it was no longer any use putting off the uncertain encounter with God, no use waiting for or fearing His judgement. The only thing that was any use was what he had sought ever since he was a boy, no matter what trouble it cost, and that was the truth. Without any compromises, with whatever force necessary, even at the cost of his destruction.

Avvocato Ajello appeared relaxed. Balistreri caught up with him mid-morning, along with Corvu, at the golf club where he had just finished a round with his son Fabio. The four of them sat down at a table in the shade.

'It's far too hot,' Ajello complained, wiping away his perspiration with a perfumed face towel while his son was finishing off a soft drink. 'It's only ten thirty and already boiling hot.'

'You're not at work today, Avvocato?' Corvu asked.

Ajello brushed away the idea with an irritated gesture. 'I work at night, as you know. But I was at home yesterday, so this morning Fabio and I were on the first tee by seven.'

Balistreri was stealing glances at the son, who appeared totally disinterested in the conversation and was fiddling with a brand new BlackBerry.

'To what do we owe this visit? Have you found the man on the bike?' asked Ajello, lighting a cigarette.

'Can you talk about this in front of your son?' Balistreri asked.

'No problem. Fabio's an adult and we have no secrets.'

'All right. Let's talk about Ornella Corona.'

Ajello shook his head in consternation, while Fabio stopped playing with the new device and looked at Balistreri for the first time with all the scorn his adolescent eyes could show for an adult who was so far from his ideals of success: a nobody of a civil servant, unshaven and badly dressed.

'We live in a ridiculous country,' said Ajello. 'We allow young tearaways to go about raping and killing—'

'I'd like to know when you last saw Signora Corona,' Balistreri said flatly, annoyed by the usual bullshit.

Ajello stopped smiling and examined the fresh manicure of his long sunburned hands as if he had found a small defect.

'And what would be the relevance of this question to your investigation?' he asked, with an air of irony.

'That of determining as far as possible Signora Corona's movements on the night she was murdered. We know for certain that she was sunbathing at the beach resort until sunset. She left alone and we presume she came directly home. We found a plate with the remains of a salad and a used glass with traces of wine. Then, towards midnight, before she was murdered—'

Ajello held up a hand to stop him there. 'Fabio,' he said to his son, 'could you pop into the Pro Shop and see if the new bags are in?'

The fair-haired mountain of muscle got up. Above him Balistreri was aware of a look that was somewhere between menacing and scornful.

'Please, do carry on,' said Ajello, all politeness.

'Before she was killed, she had consensual sexual relations,' Balistreri concluded.

'And you want to know if she had them with me? I still don't see the relevance—'

'If you were there, you could have seen or heard something.'

'Or I could have killed her.'

'Depends on your alibi.'

'At that time I'll have been in my car on my way to the Bella Blu. I got there about midnight, I think.'

'Then I'm afraid that's not a proper alibi, unless you went there straight from home, although as you know a spouse's testimony counts for little.'

'I wasn't going there from my house,' Ajello said calmly. 'I was coming from Ostia, as I'd been with Ornella Corona.'

Corvu and Balistreri exchanged glances. 'Naturally,' Ajello added, 'Ornella was alive when I left her, around eleven thirty.'

'And did you see anyone about the villa when you left?' Corvu asked.

'Absolutely not,' Ajello replied immediately.

'Please think carefully,' Balistreri insisted.

A small shadow appeared to cross the lawyer's impeccable features. 'I saw no one. But the car hood was down and I did hear a voice – someone speaking loudly into a mobile phone. In Romanian, I think.'

'Would you recognize the voice of Marius Hagi?' Balistreri interjected nonchalantly.

There was a lengthy pause. Ajello took his time, lighting a cigarette. He gave Balistreri a sideways look.

'I know that name,' he muttered, 'but I can't manage to place it . . .'

'He's the husband of Alina Hagi, Anna Rossi's best friend,' said Corvu.

Balistreri thought that Ajello could have been a very able poker player, but not a world class champion like Angelo Dioguardi.

Something inevitably showed on his face. Fear? Anger? Guilt? It was difficult to say.

'Anna Rossi,' he continued with a smile, recovering his composure. 'My God, how many years have passed since then? Alina Hagi I certainly remember, but this husband of hers, Mario . . .'

'Marius,' Corvu pointed out, wanting to unnerve him.

'Marius Hagi. Yes, I must have met him once or twice. But I don't recall, I haven't seen him since then. After graduating, I didn't mix with the San Valente parish crowd. I was working for—'

'Count Tommaso dei Banchi di Aglieno,' said Corvu, anticipating him.

'How did you know?' asked Ajello, bewildered.

'The Count told us himself. We went to ask him about this Marius Hagi and your name popped up.'

Ajello acknowledged the coincidence, but had in any case already decided to play ignorant about it.

'And Valerio Bona also spoke about you,' Corvu added.

'Valerio Bona! My expert helmsman.'

'Valerio Bona was working at San Valente with Father Paul for Cardinal Alessandrini.'

Ajello absorbed the information in silence. He seemed neither surprised nor disturbed.

Balistreri decided it was time to get to the point. 'There was a major crime at that time, do you remember?'

Ajello met his gaze. 'Elisa Sordi, poor little thing,' he said hurriedly.

Balistreri was struck by his manner. 'Did you know her?'

Ajello shook his head. 'Only by sight. I never went to Via della Camilluccia. But Valerio introduced me to her once and we went for a coffee together . . .'

Balistreri saw that Fabio was coming back. He looked directly at Ajello. 'Do you remember where you were on the day Elisa Sordi died?'

Ajello again gave him his ironical look. 'Another pertinent question, Dottor Balistreri? Well, if it had been any other day I wouldn't remember, but it was the World Cup final in Spain. You would have seen it yourself, wouldn't you?'

It was difficult to say if there was any irony in the question.

'Anyway, I'd been alone in the boat all afternoon, and at seven thirty I was in the sailing club with friends to watch the game. And later, naturally, I was out around the Coliseum celebrating.'

Ajello looked at him in amusement. 'You'll have celebrated yourself that evening, Balistreri, or maybe not?'

This time the message was very much clearer.

Afternoon

It was lunchtime. Summer storms always break out when the temperature is higher. Thunder and lightning accompanied them back to the office, while hundreds of tourists in T-shirts and shorts sought refuge in the bars and Metro stations.

It began to rain heavily as Corvu parked the car. It was the first downpour since the beginning of July. Balistreri decided to take advantage of it for a restorative walk through the city centre's now deserted streets. He sent Corvu up to the office and set off towards the Tiber in the pouring rain.

R.E.V.I. Was it a red herring or the key to something? Only the first letters of their names could directly link Samantha, Nadia, Selina and Ornella. But the Invisible Man wants us to find another link. He wants to enjoy our fear.

He felt the drops of rain trickling down his back through his open shirt collar. Absorbed in his thoughts, he suddenly found himself on the riverbank. On the other side lived Linda Nardi.

When did Alina die?

It was a ridiculous question. Linda Nardi could easily have found out when Marius Hagi's wife had died, but what did it matter?

He and Angelo Dioguardi had spent the evening of 11 July 1982 watching Italy's World Cup victory. That same day Elisa Sordi was killed, after having been tortured by beatings, cuts and cigarette burns.

Balistreri's mind had resisted the similarities from the moment that San Valente came back onto the scene. But similarities there were: a young girl beaten and tortured, albeit not raped, then suffocated and thrown in the Tiber, but with no mark of a letter on her.

Was there one? Are you sure, Balistreri? Do you remember how distracted you were?

He leaned on the balustrade. The river's grey surface was running slowly by, stippled by the rain. Elisa's body had been in the water for days. The effect of the water and the rats had been catastrophic. He remembered the autopsy photos with a grimace. Bruises, burns, bite marks, but nothing scoring the skin.

Bite marks? The pathologist had noted a semicircular scar on what remained of the left breast. Possible cause: bite, cut, scratch. A cut.

He was soaking wet, alone, disturbed, exhausted. His eyes were burning and he was dropping with fatigue. He looked over towards St Peter's and Linda Nardi's place and then, with an ugly premonition, turned his back on the Tiber.

When he returned to the office, without having eaten, it was already three.

Corvu and Piccolo made no comment about the state he was in. His clothes were drenched, his stubble was thick, his shoes caked in mud. If they didn't know him, the policemen guarding the entrance would have rudely sent him packing, taking him for a tramp.

'Important news,' Piccolo declared.

'Two items,' Corvu pointed out.

'Mastroianni's gone back to Romania. With the help of a friend, I got permission for him to see the secret archives opened up after

Ceausescu's death. The two murders that Mircea and Greg were accused of were those two retired employees of the Ministry of the Interior. They were Secret Police with wonderful CVs. Among others, they had seen to the elimination of Marius Hagi's brother.'

A man who never forgives. Alina must have found out as well.

'Excellent information,' said Balistreri. 'Not directly linked to our present enquiry, but—'

'The second piece of information has a direct bearing,' Piccolo cut in. She was radiant. So she had nailed Colajacono, or at least the memory of him.

'After today's meeting with Pasquali I asked Rudi if he could think of anything strange that Hagi did or said on the morning of December the 29th, when I went to the Torre Spaccata police station and spoke to Colajacono. Rudi remembered that Hagi was ending a phone call when he came into the billiards room to bring him a coffee. He only heard the final phrase, but I think it's enough.'

Piccolo paused.

Balistreri couldn't wait. 'All right, Piccolo, what did Hagi say?'

'He said, "Don't worry about them, they're only the street sweepers of paradise".'

He shut himself in his office, thinking of Marius Hagi. What was he doing on what would be his last day of freedom? The following day, Pasquali would have him arrested at the cost of fabricating further proof beyond the evidence that was emerging everywhere. On an empty stomach, he drank two beers and a double whisky and smoked four cigarettes.

He turned the air conditioning up to maximum and closed the blinds against the sweltering afternoon. Finally, he switched on the reading lamp and took it over to the sofa along with three folders. The first contained all the interrogations of the three Roma youths who had brutally attacked Samantha and killed her. The second contained those of Vasile, Nadia's presumed rapist and murderer. It took over two hours to read through them all.

Then he took a magnifying glass and opened the third folder, containing Elisa Sordi's autopsy report. After twenty-four years, he still remembered it. The photograph was number 43. Semicircular scab of recent scarring to left breast, broken sharply by the loss of a part of the breast. Possible causes: bite from the superior dental arch of a human being, cut or gouge from branches or piece of metal in the river.

Truly an amateur investigation: a real collection of doubts, superficialities and absurdities. A textbook example of what errors not to make.

There was no need for the magnifying glass to discount the idea that the cut or gouge mark was accidental. The line of the curve cut into what remained of the breast was continuous and regular, a quarter circle. Superior dental arch? It could match the central and lateral incisors and the canines. He used the magnifying glass to see it better. It was no line of an ellipse, it was definitely a circle. A piece of the letter O. Certainly, no pathologist would have sworn it was a cut. The letter O cut into the flesh.

But now we know many things we didn't in 1982. Four young women murdered: R.E.V.I. And perhaps an O. Perhaps the same hand for all of them – the Invisible Man's.

He worked until the evening, fighting off sleep and hunger. He called in Corvu and Piccolo. They read Elisa Sordi's file together three times. It was a job he should have done all those years ago. All the details, all the alibis. But now there were new names to add: Hagi, Ajello. And new facts.

Finally Corvu noted down on a sheet of paper: *Check alibis of the following people for all the crimes.*

Pasquali and Floris would have been appalled to see some of the names, and would have ruled them out. But Balistreri had no intention of asking their permission.

Evening

At the end of the day, Corvu offered to take him home in his car.

'You're tired, Dottore, and it's late. It'll be a tough day tomorrow what with questioning the Roma boys and arresting Hagi.'

'Take it easy, Corvu. I still need to walk on my own for a while.'

Rather than head towards home he set off again towards the banks of the Tiber, which were crowded with excitable and noisy young people. He had no idea where he was going, not consciously. It was suffocating in the heat and humidity as he walked wearily, smoking one cigarette after another.

It was his thoughts that spurred his steps on over the bridge, where he should not have gone, and as far as the street where Linda Nardi lived. It was fate that decided it for him. A few seconds more or less would have changed everything. But destiny led him to turn the corner at the precise moment when Linda Nardi was opening the front door to the apartment block, accompanied by Angelo Dioguardi whose arm was draped around her shoulders.

He decided to try sleeping in his office with its air conditioning on, when he came back at midnight. There were few policemen about and no one on his floor. The flower in the glass still on Margherita's desk was now completely dead and he knew with certainty that that flower had always been destined to wither.

Taking off his jacket and shoes he made himself comfortable, switching off all the lights and turning the air conditioning on full. He poured out a whisky and lit a cigarette. Then he went into the bathroom and threw all his medicines into the toilet bowl. First the gastro-protectors, then the antidepressants.

He felt easier now that he had a few answers. Angelo and Linda: two adult children, insensitive as only children can be and clever at hiding themselves as only adults can be. And traitors, like those other two thirty-six years ago.

Friday, 21 July 2006

Morning

The private mobile rang at seven, while Pasquali was getting ready to go to Mass and then to the office. That morning he had been less punctilious than usual. He had cut his chin and his parting was crooked.

The usual voice spoke. 'Everything is set up, we'll end it this morning.'

He tried to sound confident. 'I've arranged a meeting for him at ten o'clock, so he'll give us no trouble.'

'Excellent. You must see to it yourself with no outside help.'

'The subject must be armed. And react in a certain way when arrested.'

Pasquali had never thought of having to shoot at anyone, not even a multiple murderer. But if he shot at an armed multiple murderer it would be more than justified. He dared not look at the crucifix as he formulated the thought.

'Obviously. You'll become a national hero, a star.' There was a mixture of irony and contempt in the voice.

'This thing has gone beyond everything we agreed; we must talk later.' It was only a small act of rebellion, the maximum his fear would allow him to say.

'Of course. Our friend will be in suite 27. Be careful not to get your shoes dirty.'

A last impudent gesture to his compromised respectability. He did not dare take Communion that day.

They arrived punctually at ten. He had chosen Piccolo to come with him so as to have her under control, given she was always over the top. They had brought the three Roma boys to Regina Coeli, the prison nearest to Trastevere.

They left pistols and mobiles at the entrance and were accompanied to a room where the three Roma were waiting for them with an interpreter and a lawyer. They were aged between eighteen and twenty-one, but seemed much older than Balistreri remembered them.

Piccolo started at the beginning. When had they arrived in Italy? What were their casual jobs? Thefts. How had they met? The boys replied in monosyllables. They weren't particularly interested. When they came to the evening of the murder, Piccolo's questions became more detailed. Which of them had been approached by the fourth man? His description? Medium height, black hair, long and straight, metal-rimmed glasses. Where was he while they were drinking his whisky? In the bar, maybe. Maybe outside. Did he invite them to go outside? Yes. And the cocaine? Yes, it was his. Now, Samantha. Who suggested the idea? He did. Who hit her first? He did. Then they'd dragged her to the rubbish dump. He had more cocaine and more whisky. The story became much more confused. Who had raped her first? Who had been last? And where was he all that time? There, somewhere around. They could hear him coughing as he smoked.

'Stop,' said Balistreri. Piccolo nodded, having picked it up herself. He asked each of the boys again in turn: 'Where was he while you were raping the girl?' One of the three was a little more specific. 'He was somewhere near. We couldn't see him, but heard him coughing as he smoked.'

'You never mentioned the cough,' Piccolo observed, checking their statements.

The lad shrugged his shoulders and replied directly in Italian. 'Does it fucking matter?'

They showed them a recent photo of Hagi. They looked at it with bad grace. 'No,' said the first. 'Don't know,' said the second. 'Could be, maybe,' said the third.

Then they showed a photograph of Hagi recreated by computer graphics with long hair and glasses. 'Yes, that's him,' they all said.

'Which one of you was the last to speak to him?'

No one could remember. The man disappeared at a certain point, as if vanishing into thin air. They all confirmed the same story. Samantha was alive, she was moaning, when they left. This time Balistreri had no doubts: they were telling the truth. It was the Invisible Man who had finished her off.

Every time a mobile phone disappeared that was connected in any way with a crime, the phone company was informed and told to take note and notify immediately the eventual reactivation of the SIM card. The news came to Corvu in the office at exactly ten o'clock, at the precise moment when Balistreri and Piccolo were entering Regina Coeli. Selina Belhrouz's SIM card had been reactivated and the phone company was very precise in its information. The microchip had been pinned down to the very narrow area of Rome that took in Casilino 900.

Not being able to communicate with Balistreri, and wanting to follow procedure, Corvu informed Pasquali.

'We'll go there immediately with two men. No sirens – we don't want to give a warning to anyone,' Pasquali decided on the spot.

'But Dottor Pasquali,' Corvu protested, 'I can go over there with a few more policemen. It could be dangerous; you shouldn't—'

'The arrest will be carried out by us. You will confine yourself to placing a car at each exit, discreetly. We'll meet downstairs in five minutes,' said Pasquali, cutting him short.

Corvu put on his bulletproof vest and his holster containing his Beretta. He got hold of two plainclothes men. It was the standard format for a simple arrest. But there was no saying this was a standard arrest. He tried the mobiles phones of Balistreri and Piccolo again. No answer. He left both of them a text message: *Call me soonest*.

Pasquali did three things at great speed. He put on his bulletproof vest, readied his Beretta and turned to the crucifix.

'Lord, forgive me for what I am about to do.'

Corvu and Pasquali sat behind the two plainclothes men in the car.

'Good,' said Pasquali. 'The telephone company's circled an area containing a total of six broken-down mobile homes. We'll go in quietly, as if it were a normal patrol. They're used to seeing the police these days. After we've gone in, no one must leave without being searched and having their ID checked.'

Corvu objected. 'Dottor Pasquali, I think it would be better to search in groups—'

'No. We'd only find the mobile in a rubbish bin and never know who to link it to. I want to apprehend someone with that mobile in their hands.'

'It could be dangerous,' Corvu protested.

'That's precisely why we are here. And I want to be extremely clear on one point. We have already lost three able policemen and Dottor Balistreri only survived by a miracle. If you see so much as the sign of a pistol, fire immediately. Don't wait for anyone else to fire first.'

The two plainclothes men were clearly intimidated by Pasquali's authority. They looked at Corvu.

'Dottore,' said Corvu, chancing it, 'procedure insists that before firing—'

Pasquali gave him a withering look. 'Dottor Corvu, I will not allow another criminal to shoot at a policeman. I will take full responsibility. Rest assured that there'll be no shortage of political support should you shoot an armed Roma in order to avoid being shot yourself.'

His face strained, Corvu inclined his head. 'All right, how are we to proceed?'

'We'll start with the caravan nearest the entrance to the camp. One of you will knock. If they open up, we go in, check IDs and continue to search until the Belhrouz woman's phone turns up.'

'And if no one opens the door?'

'We go in and search anyway.'

Corvu went rigid. Balistreri would have been furious.

Vasile affirmed that the man who had phoned on 23 December spoke excellent Italian. 'With a foreign accent?' asked Piccolo.

'I don't know, it sounded like Italian to me.'

'And what else do you remember about the call?'

He repeated the details of his statement.

'Can you remember what kind of voice he had?'

'Rough. He coughed a lot.'

Balistreri and Piccolo exchanged glances. Perhaps this wouldn't be enough for the Prosecutor's office. All they had was circumstantial evidence. Many people have a cough. Many people have friends with motocross bikes. The deaths in Romania weren't attributable to him. His wife Alina was running away from him when she had her accident on the moped, but so what? And he didn't have any alibi? Neither did millions of people.

Piccolo tightened her lips in rage. 'But we know it was him.'

Balistreri got up, troubled. Something wasn't right. He'd never liked coincidences, and here there really were a great many – too many.

I must tell Pasquali how Colajacono died. And as soon as I can.

They entered the camp under a blazing sun that had dried the mud left from the previous day's storm. There were a good many people about, mainly women, old men, and children playing at jumping off a heap of old mattresses. The rubbish gave off a dreadful smell in the sun and mingled with the smell of urine from the chemical toilets. Groups of children swarmed happily around the policemen. Corvu shivered – this was sheer folly. Their holsters were open below their jackets and visible to the expert eye. He saw Pasquali sweating in his impeccable grey pinstripe and looking about him a little disoriented.

He made a last attempt to call Balistreri. Nothing. They were still in Regina Coeli.

They knocked on caravan 28. A toothless old woman holding a child in her arms opened the door; she could as well have been the mother as the grandmother.

They went in. The heat was suffocating inside the caravan, as was the stench. Tea was boiling on the small enamel stove. There was no one besides the old woman and the child.

'You carry out the search, Corvu. I don't see any danger here. I'm going on to number 27,' ordered Pasquali.

'But Dottore . . .' Corvu protested. Pasquali was already out the door.

Corvu imagined that he wanted to make the arrest because he wanted to be seen to play the leading role. He made a sign to the two plainclothes men to go with Pasquali.

'Do you have a mobile in here?' he asked the old woman as he looked around. It was a stupid question, but he had to ask it.

The woman didn't understand Italian. The child began to cry while the pungent smell of its faeces spread through the caravan along with the stink of rubbish.

Corvu had a feeling he was going to vomit and went to a window to get some air. From where he was he saw one of the policemen knocking at the door of caravan 27. Pasquali and the other policeman were a yard behind him. A moment later the door opened. It was another old woman. Three small children ran out between the legs of Pasquali and the two policemen.

Corvu saw with surprise that there was a motocross bike parked behind the caravan. And he didn't notice the old man in a beret and dark glasses coming up behind the men and Pasquali. Then he heard the sound of a cough.

He swore in Sardinian and, turning sharply round, bumped into the old woman, knocking her to the ground along with the child, whose faeces spattered over the floor. He lost a few seconds apologizing and helping her get up again, then he burst outside with the Beretta in his hand, shouting, ready to shoot.

Pasquali turned but did not raise the pistol in his hand quickly enough. He only managed to see Marius Hagi's malicious grin below the dark glasses as he squeezed the trigger. He had no time to ask God to forgive his sins before the bullet passed through his head. Hagi threw the pistol far away and raised his arms above his head in the sign of surrender. The plainclothes men pointed their weapons at him, trembling with fear and rage.

'Stop, stop!' shouted Corvu to the plainclothes men as he ran towards them, keeping his Beretta aimed at Hagi. The latter looked at him calmly with a mocking smile.

'Call an ambulance and block all the exits,' Corvu shouted desperately.

'No accomplices – it's only me for the lot of you,' Hagi said, completely unruffled.

Corvu didn't dare look at Pasquali's body lying on its back on the ground. He ordered the other policeman to handcuff Hagi, who offered no resistance. A huge crowd had gathered about them and many patrolmen were running towards them, weapons in hand.

Hagi watched the scene in amusement. He smiled at Corvu. 'Where's your boss, our wonderful street cleaner of paradise?'

Afternoon

Balistreri refused to participate in the press conference arranged for the early afternoon. He watched it on the television in his office along with Corvu, Piccolo and Mastroianni. First the Minister of the Interior spoke a few words of praise for the police and Dottor Antonio Pasquali's heroic sacrifice to rid the Italian people of this source of evil. He promised that within a few days the government would take drastic measures to control all non-EU immigrants, using a decree with the force of law so as to avoid bureaucratic delays in Parliament's red tape.

To a question from a French journalist about possible protests from the UN, the Vatican and humanitarian organizations, he replied with scant diplomacy: 'We do not expect protests from anyone and they will not be welcome.'

He then handed over to the Chief of Police for a reconstruction of events. Floris was visibly shaken, but maintained his composure. He gave a succinct precis of the deaths of the four young women, which were linked by the four incisions in their bodies. He spoke about the Invisible Man and, by way of illustration, the mountain of indirect evidence that converged on Marius Hagi on whom, incidentally, Selina Belhrouz's mobile had been discovered. He recalled that four Romanians linked to Hagi had been killed in an exchange of fire in which three heroic policemen had lost their lives and the head of the Special Section, Michele Balistreri, had been gravely wounded.

He ended by saying that he was certain that Marius Hagi's arrest had delivered the city from a nightmare and added that, together with the Minister of the Interior, he had summoned the Mayor of Rome for urgent talks. He used the precise word 'summoned', as if calling for a servant.

Then all hell broke loose, the journalists unleashing a barrage of questions at the tops of their voices, but there were no further statements.

Corvu was overcome. Television's merciless footage had shown his face drained of colour as Pasquali's body was taken away from Casilino 900 and Hagi was loaded into the police van that would take him to prison. Balistreri had tried everything to get him to go home, but without success. He had explained in every way that he was not at fault, that it was only Pasquali's rashness and desire to play a leading role that had led to this outcome.

'Listen, Corvu, there's no way you can be present at Hagi's questioning. You're in a state of shock. You've made your statement, now take three days off and go and see Natalya in the Ukraine, would you?'

Corvu shook his head. 'No, Dottore, thanks all the same,' he said, in his most pig-headed manner.

But Balistreri had made up his mind. 'I've already had the flight booked for you – you're leaving this evening. Piccolo's been in touch with Natalya, who's expecting you. My brother Alberto's coming to pick you up at home in two hours' time to take you to the airport.'

I have to protect you right now, Graziano, because it's not finished here. Or rather, it's only just begun.

Corvu raised his head. His normally serious and unruffled look was shaken. 'Thank you, Dottore,' he whispered, getting up. Then in a last effort to perform his duty, he added, 'I've checked the list of the alibis that you asked for and given it to Mastroianni. Perhaps it doesn't matter now . . .'

Piccolo and Mastroianni gave him a hug, then Balistreri put an arm around his shoulders and accompanied him to the exit. He could feel him trembling.

They were out on the pavement when Balistreri asked Corvu, 'How much time did Pasquali have from the moment he saw Hagi to the moment he tried to fire?'

'Less than a second.'

Less than a second. He already had the pistol in his hand.

In the middle of a baking hot summer afternoon, Balistreri went to Regina Coeli for the second time that day. Imagining what was in store for him, he avoided taking Piccolo.

Avvocato Morandi was waiting for him outside the interrogation room, his eyes lowered. 'I'm sorry to hear about Pasquali.'

Balistreri stared at him.

You're only feeling sorry for your own reputation, you son of a bitch.

'What happened was totally unexpected,' Morandi went on, 'but it confirms what I told you last time.'

'It was better if I'd stayed in Dubai?'

'You now have the perpetrator. My client will confess to everything, keeping nothing back.'

'Really? Will he tell me why he staged an argument in order to disembowel poor Camarà?'

Balistreri saw him turn pale under his artificial suntan.

'Be satisfied with the evident truth,' Morandi said icily.

Balistreri resisted the temptation to lay his hands on him or else they would have relieved him of the investigation; this time he wanted to get to the truth. He congratulated himself on his self-control. He turned his back and went into the room, Morandi following.

The Public Prosecutor was already there. He muttered a few words to the lawyer and then turned to Balistreri.

'Avvocato Morandi has already told me that his client will declare himself guilty of all the murders, including that of Camarà. He will give a full confession and every detail.'

Hagi was brought in wearing handcuffs. His black eyes rested calmly on those of Balistreri. He had grown thinner since he had last seen him seven months earlier and was coughing much more. But his eyes now burned even fiercer above the huge dark bags beneath. The resemblance to a demon was now complete.

After the usual preliminaries, the Public Prosecutor let Balistreri lead the questioning.

'Let's start from the beginning, Signor Hagi.'

'That's fine. Let's start with Samantha Rossi.'

Balistreri shook his head. It was time to make the direction clear. 'No, Signor Hagi. The beginning was in 1982.'

Hagi nodded with a smile. 'Elisa Sordi?' It was as if it were the most obvious thing in the world.

The words surprised everyone: the Public Prosecutor, Morandi, the prison officers. Only Balistreri remained unruffled.

I'm offering you your own show, the one you want, in order to take a step towards the truth.

'And you did such a lot back then, didn't you, Dottor Balistreri?' His contempt was now evident.

'I must ask you to limit yourself strictly to answering the questions, Signor Hagi, without making any comments,' said the Prosecutor, his face pale.

'One moment,' put in Morandi, a little disturbed. 'I must first confer with my client. I don't understand where Elisa Sordi comes in.'

'It's not necessary, Avvocato,' said Hagi placidly, to calm him. 'You only have to see that these gentlemen don't distort what I say. I want everything to be extremely clear and in here there are some notable bunglers. They were already that way in 1982.'

'When did you come to know Elisa Sordi?' Balistreri asked, ignoring the contemptuous remark.

'I don't remember exactly – a little before the summer of 1982. I went to the residential complex on Via della Camilluccia and there I came across one of the young men that Alina had introduced me to and Elisa was with this young man.'

'What was his name?'

Hagi shrugged his shoulders. 'I don't remember. He was a non-entity, while the girl was an extremely tasty morsel.'

He wants to provoke you. Keep cool.

'Why did you go to Via della Camilluccia?' asked Balistreri.

'Through Alina I had received some work. I had to organize a trip to Auschwitz for a good lady.'

'And do you remember her name?'

'She was a foreigner from Northern Europe. Her husband was an Italian nobleman with a very long surname.'

'All right. We'll come back to this later. So you came to know Elisa Sordi there. And then?'

'What would you like to know?'

Balistreri saw the Prosecutor and Morandi shifting uncomfortably on their seats, exchanging bewildered glances.

'What took place afterwards?'

Hagi stared at him brazenly. 'Have you not understood that what was around her left breast was an "O"? Not then, you were too young. But have you finally understood now?'

Morandi almost fell from his chair. The Public Prosecutor turned white and suddenly jumped to his feet.

'The first letter you made?' asked Balistreri impassively, as if they were exchanging pleasantries.

'I took the body out to the middle of the river in a small boat with a good ballast of rocks, thinking that the rats too would find her to their taste.'

Balistreri gestured to the Prosecutor and prison officers to calm down. Hagi's game was clear: he wanted to drag everyone down to his own level.

'And why did you hide such a work of art with so much care?' Balistreri asked.

'I couldn't be sure I hadn't left traces of organic material or finger-prints on the girl. So I let the river see to it.'

Balistreri came to the most complicated point. 'Alina found out everything, didn't she?'

Hagi had a fit of coughing. Balistreri saw some blood on his hand-kerchief. Then Hagi was himself again.

'I've already told you I have no intention of talking about my wife. And anyway, I would never have done anything untoward to her.'

'Allow me to doubt that, Signor Hagi. I know what an end you put to those two scoundrels who killed your brother in Romania.'

Hagi raised his shoulders. 'I couldn't care less about your doubts, Balistreri.'

'How many women have you killed in the twenty-four years between Elisa and Samantha?'

'None,' said Hagi immediately. 'And I have obviously have no reason to lie to you. It was Alina's death that changed my life.'

'Then why did you kill Samantha a year ago?'

'Because a year ago I became ill. Lung cancer.'

The Public Prosecutor looked at Balistreri, who gave him a placatory sign and continued.

'We can verify this later. And so you found out you were ill and for this reason alone you picked up on your old bad habits? Well, I don't believe you.'

Hagi wiped away a trickle of blood that was dripping from his mouth. 'If you want any more answers, then take off these cuffs. I want to smoke.'

The Prosecutor looked over at Balistreri, who nodded consent. A prison officer removed them. Balistreri offered Hagi a cigarette and lit it for him with the Bella Blu lighter. Then Hagi took up his story again.

'Alina knew the truth – she was too intelligent. I beat her because she was going to report me, and for a while she calmed down. Then Anna Rossi began to interfere. Seeing the bruises, she suggested that Alina leave me and go and stay with her. That wretched evening I tried to make her stay, but Alina ran away on the moped to that whore.'

There was another fit of coughing, more blood on the handker-chief. By now his face was contorted with rage and hatred.

'I don't forget a friend, but neither do I forget anyone who does me wrong. It was a real pleasure to have her daughter killed by those three Roma. But the greater pleasure is the thought of when you'll explain to Anna Rossi that her daughter died because of her.'

Balistreri was extremely thankful that he hadn't brought Giulia Piccolo with him. No one could have managed to hold her back from tearing Hagi apart, limb from limb. Hatred filled the room as if it were a layer of poison gas. Morandi held his head between his hands, incredulous, while the Public Prosecutor was no longer even taking notes, his face parchment white. The prison officers appeared ready to jump on Hagi and take him apart right there in the room.

'And why did you kill Nadia? How did she come into it?'

'Nadia was Alina's exact twin. I wanted to avenge myself symbol-ically on my wife as well. It was she who ruined my life, flitting off and dying like that.'

A well-rehearsed reply, far-fetched. This is a point on which you don't wish to reply.

'Your wife ruined your life because she'd discovered you were a murderer, and she died escaping from your home. Whose fault was that, Signor Hagi?'

'A wife doesn't betray her husband, she remains with him come what may. It was the atmosphere in San Valente parish that turned her against me, her uncle the Cardinal and that joke of a Catholic religion of yours . . .'

'Couldn't you switch your target? The risk with Nadia was enormous after Camarà had seen you together in the private lounge and she'd taken the lighter away, the one I just lit your cigarette with.'

Hagi hesitated, hearing this point. 'She was the spitting image. It would have been difficult to find another like her. As to that nigger, it was child's play to slit him open on the pavement.'

'And with Selina Belhrouz and Ornella Corona? What had your vendetta to do with them?'

Hagi coughed for a long time, spitting blood into his handkerchief.

'You didn't like the letters "V" and "I"?'

He doesn't want to answer certain things. Let's try another route.

'We have five letters, Signor Hagi, starting from 1982, in the order "O", "R", "E", "V", "I". Do you want to give us an explanation?'

'I don't think I do,' Hagi said, as if it was a matter of a simple game, 'but I can give you a hand. You have to take my wife Alina into account, killed as you say because of my evil deeds.'

'And what letter would that be?'

'Very simply her initial, "A".'

'So therefore: "O", "A", "R", "E", "V", "I". All right, what does it mean?'

Hagi stared at him with the eyes of Lucifer. 'I see that nothing that I say surprises you, Balistreri. Well, I'll have to give you something new to think about.'

Balistreri understood beforehand what Hagi was about to say. In that brief moment he was certain he was facing not a simple serial killer but a merciless plot, and that they had no idea where it began and where it would end.

'Wait for the next letter, Balistreri.'

Fiorella Romani, twenty-three, granddaughter of Gina Giansanti, the former concierge at Via della Camilluccia, newly graduated and recently employed by a bank, had left her home in the suburbs at seven thirty that morning, the same as every day, to take the Metro to the office. Except that she never got there. At six that evening, seeing that she wasn't home, her mother Franca called her mobile repeatedly, but it was switched off. After calling all her friends, she decided to report her missing.

'Too many hours have gone by,' observed Mastroianni at the start of the meeting later in Balistreri's office. 'It's likely that Hagi kidnapped her at seven thirty, as soon as she left home, and killed her straight away, burying her in some woods or dumping her into the river or down a well. Then he went to Casilino 900 to kill Pasquali.'

Balistreri listened in silence, smoking and leafing through Mastroianni's report on the search of Hagi's house. They had found the Invisible Man's disguises — wigs, glasses, berets.

'There's also this work that Corvu did, Dottore,' Mastroianni said. It was the check on the alibis he'd asked for.

In order to avoid any trouble they hadn't directly questioned the Count, or his son, let alone Cardinal Alessandrini, on the murders of the previous year. Corvu had confined himself to checking minutely the official record.

In the Nairobi newspapers were photographs of the opening of the new hospital wing, which had taken place on 25 December in the presence of Manfredi, Count Tommaso, Manfredi's colleagues and the local authorities. Corvu had even checked that the only direct flight from Europe that could have taken Manfredi to Nairobi in the early morning left Zurich at midnight and that the last flight from Rome to Zurich on the evening of 24 December left at six, before Nadia was kidnapped. There was no sign of Manfredi in Rome either on the passenger lists or in passport control. So while Nadia was being killed, Manfredi was in Nairobi. On the other hand, for the murders of Samantha, Selina and Ornella, neither the Count nor Manfredi had a secure alibi.

Corvu had also noted Cardinal Alessandrini's movements in the Vatican for official events during the whole of the afternoon and all the evening of 24 December, but it wasn't possible to check if he had been temporarily absent. On the day of Samantha Rossi's death he was in Madrid, but it wasn't known when he had come back. And on the evening of Ornella Corona's death he was at home alone.

Ajello, Paul and Valerio had been questioned. They had seemed more worried and surprised than angered. Paul and Valerio were together in San Valente on the evening of 24 December for the orphans' Christmas Eve supper; from at least eight o'clock onwards their movements could be traced. Ajello was certainly at the opening of an ENT nightclub in Milan the night on which Samantha was killed, and there were many witnesses. There was a ridiculous coincidence in that, for different reasons, all three found themselves in Ostia on the night of Ornella Corona's death. Ajello had had sex with her, Paul had taken the orphans to the seaside and had slept over there with them, Valerio had been out on a boat on his own and no one knew at what time he'd returned. As for the case of Elisa Sordi, there was no one who could confirm Ajello's alibi after so many years had elapsed.

One result was clear: Hagi alone never had an alibi. And he was the one charged with having committed all the crimes.

Balistreri felt exhausted. Around him he saw looks on his colleagues' faces that fluctuated between commiseration, contempt and derision.

Before the day was over, he received a phone call from the Chief of Police.

'Balistreri, this is a disaster, starting with the victims and their loved ones and ending up now with the media blowing it all up and then the political consequences.'

'*Signor questore*, we're facing something that is highly complex and planned down to the last detail.'

'So you don't think Marius Hagi could have set up all this business entirely on his own?'

'I really don't know. We could simply be at the start.'

'The start?' Floris blustered in exasperation. 'After five young women have been brutally murdered, the first being twenty-four years ago, then Camarà, Colajacono, Tatò, Coppola, Pasquali – you were nearly killed yourself – and now Fiorella Romani! What do you mean, we could simply be at the start? The start of World War III?'

There was no way that Balistreri could reassure him with certainty. The fact that Pasquali already had his pistol in his hand while the plainclothes man knocked at the caravan door was a real concern.

He was too cautious a person to go to Casilino 900 and end the case himself with a pistol in his hand. Unless he was very frightened.

'I have to speak to Hagi again,' said Balistreri.

'And what do you hope to get from that monster?'

'He has a plan. If we want to try and save Fiorella Romani we have to go along with him.'

'Go along with him? What does that mean?' Floris asked in irritation.

'Either Fiorella Romani is already dead or she will be soon. If Hagi's hidden her away somewhere and we don't find her, she'll die of starvation. If, on the other hand . . .'

'On the other hand?'

'If, on the other hand, he wants us to find her, it means Hagi's playing with us.'

'What are you talking about?' the Chief of Police asked, exasperated.

'It's too complicated a business,' Balistreri concluded.

Floris sighed, exhausted. He was a well-balanced man, compassionate and respected, who was now without any points of reference, chained to a chair placed on quicksand.

Evening

It was already dark when Balistreri returned for the third time to Regina Coeli. The image of Angelo with Linda was continually tormenting him. He brushed it aside angrily and tried to concentrate on Hagi and Fiorella Romani. But that former image took him back to his worst nightmares, back to Africa in the summer of 1970.

Corvu called him from Kiev, wanting to know how things were going. Balistreri told him that Hagi had confessed to everything, including the killing of Elisa and the letter 'O'. Then he told him about Fiorella Romani's disappearance.

'Then I'm coming back tomorrow, Dottore. Natalya's happy I'm here, but I can't stay any longer.'

'Very well, Corvu. Tonight I'm going to ask the Chief of Police for your urgent transfer to the beautiful mountains of Sardinia, where you can count the number of goats. That should calm you down.' And he closed his mobile phone.

He entered the room along with the Public Prosecutor and Morandi, who felt it his duty to mutter some more words that Balistreri ignored completely.

Hagi appeared rested after the few hours' pause. The special guards who were watching him said that he had eaten a little and had also slept. The medical reports following his first questioning confirmed the presence of a tumour in the lungs that was at an advanced stage. The doctors were sure he had little time to live.

'You're tired, Balistreri. The bags under your eyes are getting more swollen and darker. If you carry on like this you'll die of a heart attack before I die of cancer,' said Hagi cheerfully.

'You needn't worry about me. I'd like to talk about Fiorella Romani. Is she alive?'

Hagi appeared to consider the question thoroughly. 'I think so. Naturally it depends on her powers of resistance.'

The Public Prosecutor could contain himself no longer. 'You should be thankful that in this civilized country, which has given you a place to live for so long, no one can torture you like Ceausescu's hired killers did to your brother. If it were up to me, I wouldn't hesitate to imitate them in order to find out where you've hidden the girl.'

Hagi looked at the Prosecutor pityingly. 'You wouldn't have it in you to harm a hair on my head, not even if we were on a lawless desert island. You're just spineless people, as you were in the last years of the Roman Empire. In time, the people you call barbarian will come to rape your women, steal your houses and take over your country, while you watch impotently.'

Even Morandi felt moved to intervene. 'Signor Hagi, I beg you to save Fiorella Romani's life. The court will take it into consideration.'

Hagi laughed. 'I'll die well before I see any judge. But I'm willing to save Fiorella Romani's life on certain conditions.'

Balistreri bent towards Hagi. 'What do you want in exchange?'

'Only the truth, Balistreri. It would be simple if you weren't so incompetent.'

The Prosecutor and Morandi looked at him, disconcerted.

But Balistreri was ready for him; he knew what truth he meant.

The one I haven't found. The one I gave up finding all these years. The one I thought to atone for by giving up on life.

'This means speaking to Fiorella Romani's grandmother and

reopening the investigation on Elisa Sordi, and Fiorella in the mean-time could be dead,' said Balistreri, while the Prosecutor and Morandi looked at him astounded, as if he were talking in Chinese.

'We'll do our best to keep her alive a little longer. But I'm advising you to be quicker this time, Balistreri. Fiorella won't live for another twenty-four years.'

The Prosecutor cut in. 'I don't follow. You said before that it was you who killed Elisa Sordi, Signor Hagi. What truth are we talking about?'

Hagi looked at them all with scorn and hatred.

'I never said that I killed her, only that I threw her body in the Tiber. You're a bunch of incompetents like Balistreri, this street cleaner in his paradise. I want the truth – only that can save Fiorella Romani.'

The Chief of Police and the Public Prosecutor agreed that the investigation be reopened immediately and that the now 84-year-old Gina Giansanti be contacted. Her daughter Franca, Fiorella's mother, told them that Gina was ill and had been living in Puglia for over twenty years in a residential quarter on the outskirts of Lecce, her birthplace. A military aeroplane was made available for Balistreri and Fiorella's mother on the following morning.

It was almost midnight when Balistreri left Regina Coeli. He had smoked at least thirty cigarettes and drunk a dozen coffees. He was physically and psychologically in pieces. Resisting Marius Hagi without reacting had been extremely tough. His nerves were in shreds, his thoughts uncontrollable and savage.

He'll be kissing her on the little terrace, where I hesitated. Then he'll take her to bed . . .

He took the walk home from Regina Coeli through Trastevere, where the chaos was greater because it was Friday night. There were cars everywhere tooting horns, music at top volume, ice creams, kids with bottles of beer walking in and out of the traffic. And yet he didn't hear a thing – he was walking down a tunnel that had only one possible exit.

And if he carves up another girl? This had been Linda Nardi's question the first time they had gone out to supper on 30 December 2005. It was time to know where that idea had come from.

Don't confuse the investigation with your anger. Stop here, Michele, while you still have time.

But his footsteps led him towards her flat on their own. When he got to the main door it was a little after midnight. He looked up and saw a faint light in the windows. He still had the key she'd given him. Breathing heavily, he walked up the staircase.

Linda Nardi's door was the only one on that floor. The lock was gleaming, evidently new. He rang the bell. He heard steps coming to the door. He was tempted to run away, but remained nailed to the spot in front of that door like a man condemned to death in front of the firing squad.

'Who is it?' came Linda's voice.

'It's me.'

There was a brief silence, then Linda opened the door but left it on the chain.

Her face wasn't surprised, but sad. 'What do you want, Michele?'

'We have to speak. Right now.'

He saw the vertical line furrowing her brow. She could have said no, never. Or else, not now, we can speak tomorrow. But that would not have been Linda Nardi.

She can leave you outside her life, but not outside her door.

When she took off the chain and opened the door, Angelo Dioguardi was standing in the middle of the small living room that was softly lit by a table lamp. His hair was more ruffled than usual, his eyes tired, the lines deep on his face.

'He has to leave,' Balistreri said to Linda.

Angelo didn't wait for her reply and stepped towards him as he went towards the door. As they brushed past one another, Balistreri felt him hesitate a moment and halt as if he had something to say, a last attempt to clarify things. But it was only an exchange of silences and then Angelo went out, pulling the door behind him.

Linda stared at him, arms folded. She wasn't angry. 'I'm listening, Michele.'

She was so beautiful. He had never seen her so attractive. Her blouse was buttoned almost to the neck and held those breasts he'd imagined so often, but only now wanted to fondle and kiss. Her trousers as usual were baggy, but were more intriguing precisely because of that, and he wanted to put his hands inside them, where perhaps a few minutes earlier Angelo's hands had been.

The desire he had repressed during the months they had spent together suddenly erupted with a violent force, making him almost reel. He felt his knees buckle. He should have taken her in his arms instead. He should have told her that he did not understand her, but trusted her. He should have promised her that he would do everything for her, anything at all, even without understanding. He should have. But he didn't want to, not any more. Linda Nardi was now only flesh and blood, a woman he desired, a woman who had sent him packing and thrown herself into the arms of his best friend.

Surprised, he heard his own harsh voice. 'Who told you about the letter carved on Samantha Rossi?'

There was a sad look in her eyes. Linda was sorry for him and this he found intolerable.

'You told me yourself, Michele, by your reaction that night in the restaurant.'

The desire added to the frustration and the frustration added to the anger, which was flowing into his veins like heroin entering the circulation.

'Bullshit! You knew, all right, someone told you.'

'I had my doubts, but your reaction that night made me certain,' she said calmly.

'I don't believe you. And besides . . .' He stopped a moment before he could finish the sentence that would have cut any tie between them forever. The uncontrolled anger had returned, that of the young Mike Balistreri when things didn't go the way he wanted – the anger he'd tried to bury at the bottom of the Mediterranean in the summer of 1970.

She tried to stop him. 'Angelo really doesn't come into this.'

'Really? If someone's a liar in one thing they can be in everything. Did you play the nurse here with me to be sure I'd get better and continue the hunt for the Invisible Man? Did you want the scoop when I found him?' He heard his voice getting louder and more threatening.

'Michele, get out of your prison cage now or you'll never get out of it.'

'I should have fucked you like an ordinary whore. So much for all your shit about Saint Agnes.'

She was looking at him now with a different light in her eyes. It was regret and goodbye.

'Yes, Michele, you should have. Perhaps then you'd finally have understood this business.'

The words themselves, the calmness with which they were pronounced, her eyes shining in the semi-darkness. He found himself as he was thirty-six years ago, at that precise point where there was no repentance from remorse.

His slap sent Linda reeling against the wall. He held her wrists together with one arm while the other grabbed her hair, forcing her to look at him. He kissed her violently, trying to put his tongue in her mouth. She didn't cry out or offer any resistance. She was lifeless, defenceless.

It was that passivity that was the last straw, that absence of any attempt to defend herself. He ripped off her blouse and bra and flung her on the sofa. Linda confined herself to covering her breasts, crossing her arms while he took off her trainers and trousers. Then he leapt on top of her, breathing heavily from desire and fury.

'Have you already had sex tonight?'

She turned her face away so as not to look him in the eyes and he tore off her briefs. He had to stand up to unfasten his trousers. He was ready. But in that moment when their bodies separated in the dim light and total silence broken only by his own heavy breathing, Balistreri saw the slim figure of a semi-naked woman with her clothes torn, her breasts shielded by her arms, her pubis exposed. It could have been Elisa, Samantha, Nadia, Ornella, Alina or Saint Agnes. It could have been another woman, one never forgotten since that last night of August 1970.

And as Linda had predicted, he saw the first glimmer of truth. It was only a sensation, not a real and proper idea. Incredulous, horrified, he took a step back, staggering. He crashed into the table lamp, which fell and broke, and left the flat in utter darkness. He took advantage of it to escape into the night.

Saturday, 22 July 2006

Morning

Balistreri arrived at the airport after yet another sleepless night, his beard unshaven, his clothes dirty and creased. He smelled of drink and tobacco. He wasn't sure if his excitement, wedded to his fatigue, was the result of his stopping taking the antidepressants or simply caused by the rapid chain of events.

I don't care. I'm going to get to the bottom of this, wherever that may be.

The last time he saw Franca Giansanti was twenty-four years ago on that wretched dawn when Ulla launched herself into the air and the concierge had come back from India with her part of the truth. She was somewhat bewildered to find him in a state of total disintegration, but acted as if nothing were amiss.

During the flight to Lecce, Franca spoke in tears about her daughter Fiorella. She was thirteen when Franca's husband had died from a tumour. Cardinal Alessandrini found a place for her in a boarding school, where they encouraged her studies. Then Fiorella went to Milan, where she graduated from the Catholic University, and recently she had begun working for a bank in Rome.

Balistreri's thoughts wandered from Linda Nardi to Fiorella

Romani – locked up without food and water in an isolated farm-house where they would find her starved to death.

When they landed, a car with two policemen was waiting for them. They passed through Lecce's splendid Baroque centre, which was already hot in the morning sun. On the bypass they encountered the Saturday summer traffic and Balistreri ordered them to switch on the siren.

'My mother suffers from heart trouble. We haven't told her what's happened to Fiorella.'

He well remembered Gina, the touchy old concierge, devoutly religious and of few words. It would not have been easy to tell her. 'We may have to, Signora Franca, in order to get her to help us.'

They stopped outside a row of terraced houses in a quiet street in Lecce's outskirts. Franca rang the bell and Signora Gina came to answer the door. Her severe, tight-lipped face was now wrinkled with age. The dark shadows under her eyes, her trembling and her swollen ankles were signs that she wasn't well.

The house was full of crucifixes and photographs of Padre Pio, the Pope and Cardinal Alessandrini, as well as many shots of her daughter and granddaughter Fiorella: recollections of a life that was about to be shattered.

'I'm not surprised you want to see me, after Elisa's mother's suicide,' said Gina Giansanti. 'Have you come to arrest me?'

'I'm here to talk about Elisa Sordi, but not to arrest you, although I suspect that twenty-four years ago you perhaps forgot to tell us about something.'

'You've waited all this time to be suspicious?' replied Signora Gina with her customary harshness.

Franca intervened. 'Mamma, did you hear on TV about that Romanian that killed the top policeman and all those women?'

'Of course. The TV said that animal also confessed to having killed Elisa Sordi.'

'No, Mamma. He said that he'd killed them all except Elisa.'

The lines on Signora Gina's face became more drawn. 'Where does that gypsy come into it?'

'He was there at the time,' Balistreri replied. 'He was working for Count Tommaso dei Banchi di Aglieno.'

'Oh, the Count . . .' Gina mumbled with the same age-old tone of resentment, 'Only a man like him could have given work to an animal like that.'

'It wasn't the Count's fault – he didn't know what kind of a man Hagi was. But please try to remember now, is there something you didn't tell us at the time?'

'No,' Gina Giansanti replied decisively. 'There's absolutely nothing I didn't tell you.'

Balistreri looked at Franca Giansanti. The woman was biting her lips.

'Mamma, this is very important. I want you to swear on the head of Fiorella that you're hiding nothing from Dottor Balistreri.'

Gina Giansanti reacted against her daughter. 'How do you dare to ask me to swear to something over Fiorella!' she hissed with all the contempt and authority of the Southern mother.

'Because if you lie Fiorella will die,' Franca replied.

Balistreri saw the pale shadow of death transfigure Signora Gina. There was no limit to the pain that Marius Hagi was able to inflict on his victims even from inside prison, using Balistreri as his blunt instrument.

'I don't understand, Franca . . .' she stammered. All of a sudden she was an old woman, trembling with a heart condition.

Franca burst into tears. 'That man's kidnapped Fiorella and hidden her somewhere, Mamma. And he's said that he'll let her die if you don't tell us the truth.'

Gina Giansanti wavered. 'Oh, my God, oh, my Lord, have mercy upon me.' She clasped her daughter and wept in silence.

Balistreri saw the tears of these two small women embracing each other, their bodies distorted with pain, the bony hands of one clutching the other's shoulders tightly. He remembered them embracing like that on a rainy morning outside the Via della Camilluccia gate, while Cardinal Alessandrini was shaking Gina Giansanti's hand.

He clearly remembered the sound of Commissario Teodori's cup as it shattered on the floor tiles, the end of Michele Balistreri's mad dreams of omnipotence, and the beginning of his slow goodbye to life.

Elisa Sordi left while I was getting in the taxi to the airport at eight.

He cursed himself for having believed her, for having given up thinking and reacting, then and for the next twenty-four years, and for not having the courage to follow his instincts and his convictions, for not remembering Christ's words to the Jews, when he said that faith comes before morality for God's children, and also Cardinal Alessandrini's words about divine and earthly justice.

How many times since then must Gina Giansanti have remembered that untruth before cursing herself for telling it? What was the huge debt she had paid with that lie that she could no longer maintain today?

Balistreri knew he had little time. 'Signora Gina, I understand. But you must tell me when you really saw Elisa Sordi for the last time.'

Gina Giansanti lifted up her sorrowful face to him. 'Elisa called me on the internal phone just before five, before you and Angelo Dioguardi came. I went up to collect the work from her to take to Cardinal Alessandrini. She was glad to be finished. That was the last time I saw her, poor child.'

Franca Giansanti looked at her old mother astounded. There was no time for Balistreri to ask any more questions.

'I have to leave immediately,' he said.

The old lady embraced him, and for a moment rested her face on his chest. 'I beg you, Dottore, please save my granddaughter.'

In the car, Balistreri looked at the marks of Gina Giansanti's tears on his jacket: damp rivulets that ran from his collar to his heart, along with all the ugly memories.

Twenty-four years earlier, in a residential complex that seemed like paradise, a group of people above suspicion had deceived the inexpert and distracted investigators with lies and cover-ups.

Balistreri thought of poor Teodori again and the inglorious end to his career, and of all the deaths caused by that shameless lie. The truth that everyone was looking for had been buried for twenty-four years under that untruth.

Everyone together, investigators and those under investigation, had contributed to leaving a horrendous crime unpunished and had put in motion an infernal mechanism whose victims they still hadn't finished counting.

Afternoon

He spent the return journey rereading the Elisa Sordi file. Gina Giansanti's false testimony had turned the case upside down, raising suspicions again against Manfredi and all the other possible guilty parties associated with the Via della Camilluccia residential complex. By saying that she had seen Elisa leave the office at eight o'clock, Gina Giansanti had given an alibi to everyone. With the World Cup final beginning at eight thirty and the following celebrations, everyone had a friend ready to swear they were somewhere.

Now they were coming back to the point of departure, to the time card that Elisa had stamped regularly at six thirty. Between six thirty and eight o'clock, no one had a solid alibi: certainly not the three young men Valerio, Manfredi and Paul. The Count had gone to see the Minister of the Interior, and it would be necessary to reconstruct the details of that visit. Cardinal Alessandrini had gone to the Vatican, which would be difficult to check up on. And there were other people to add: Hagi, Colajacono, Ajello – and who knew where they had been on 11 July 1982 after such a long time?

The aeroplane landed in Rome early on Saturday afternoon. Balistreri crossed the blazing city by taxi; it was empty of its inhabitants, the streets full only of tourists. Graffiti against non-EU immigrants was again everywhere. He saw that the little Pakistanis, usually eager to offer to clean windscreens at the traffic lights, now only approached very cautiously. Passing by the Termini central train station he noticed that the Africans' counterfeit goods stalls had completely disappeared. And you couldn't see a single Romanian about, not even if you were willing to pay cash. They had vanished into thin air.

When he arrived at the office, Piccolo and Mastroianni were waiting for him but said nothing about his appalling appearance. The air conditioning was on and the blinds were half closed. Balistreri immediately noticed the changes on the blackboard, the latest answers added in capital letters.

What does the letter R mean? And E? Does it come after? OR BEFORE? AFTER THE 'V' AND THE 'I' OR BEFORE THE 'O' AND THE 'A'.

Why did Colajacono want to stand in for Marchese and Cutugno? Because he knew that Ramona might come in about Nadia.

And how did he know that? Mircea told him.

Why was Colajacono already dog-tired on the morning of 24 December? BECAUSE HE'D BEEN AT THE BELLA BLU ON THE NIGHT OF THE 23RD.

Why did Ramona offer her services to deputy mayor Augusto De Rossi? In order to blackmail him and make him change his vote.

Who blackmailed him? Mircea and Colajacono. AND HAGI.

On behalf of whom and why? THE SAME PEOPLE IN DUBAI.

Is there an Invisible Man in the Samantha Rossi case? Who is he? There is, AND IT'S MARIUS HAGI.

Is he the same person who phoned Vasile for the Giulia GT? YES.

When was the Giulia GT's headlamp broken? DOESN'T MATTER.

Where was Hagi between six and seven on the evening of 24 December when Nadia was taken away? And then after nine? FIRST COLLECTING NADIA, THEN KILLING HER.

Same question for Colajacono and Ajello. WE DON'T KNOW, BUT IT DOESN'T MATTER.

Where was Hagi the night Coppola and all the others died? WE STILL DON'T KNOW.

Same question for Ajello. WE DON'T KNOW, BUT IT DOESN'T MATTER.

Were Mircea and Greg guilty of murder in Romania? And who were the two victims? THE MEN WHO KILLED HAGI'S BROTHER.

How did Alina Hagi die in January 1983? SHE WAS RUNNING AWAY FROM MARIUS HAGI.

Why did Colajacono want Tatò with him even though he knew he should have been with his sister? HE WAS ADVISED TO, IT WAS A TRAP SO THAT HE'D HAVE NO ALIBI.

Why did the Giulia GT slow down when the driver saw Natalya? HAGI TOOK HER FOR NADIA.

What was the relationship between Ornella Corona and Ajello and his son before her husband died? SHE ALREADY KNEW THEM.

Who suggested life insurance for her husband? AJELLO.

How did Sandro Corona really die? IN AN ACCIDENT PERHAPS LIKE THE ONE IN DUBAI.

Why did Camarà die? Because he'd seen Nadia with someone in the private lounge on 23 December.

Who owns ENT? SAME PEOPLE IN DUBAI WHO WERE BLACKMAILING DE ROSSI.

WHERE WAS HAGI WHEN ORNELLA CORONA DIED? HE WAS THERE TO KILL HER.

WHERE WAS AJELLO WHEN ORNELLA CORONA DIED? HE WAS THERE JUST BEFORE.

WHAT DO THE LETTERS 'R', 'E', 'V', 'I', 'O' AND 'A' MEAN? WHAT WILL THE NEXT LETTER BE?

WHAT'S THE CONNECTION BETWEEN HAGI, BELLA BLU, DUBAI, DE ROSSI, ETC?

IS FIORELLA ALIVE? WHERE IS SHE?

The writing in capitals was Piccolo's, but Balistreri recognized Corvu's style. 'Where did he call from?' he asked Piccolo brusquely.

'He's come back and shut himself up at home. He says that if you don't want him in the office, he'll take some leave and spend it in Rome.'

Balistreri decided to ignore the implied tone of disapproval in Piccolo's voice. This series of calamities had forged an indissoluble bond of solidarity between these deputies who were otherwise so different.

'Tell him to come here immediately. The most important questions are missing.'

Piccolo smiled and immediately sent a text message that Balistreri guessed had already been written. Then he went up to the blackboard and added his latest questions.

WHY NADIA ESPECIALLY?

WHOSE WAS THE VOICE THAT SELINA AND ORNELLA HEARD ON THE TELEPHONE?

DID HAGI DO EVERYTHING BY HIMSELF?

★   ★   ★

Corvu arrived in a quarter of an hour, his eyes lowered.

'What did Natalya say?' Balistreri asked him.

'That I had to come back here, finish off this business, and then come back to the Ukraine. If you don't pack me off to count goats, that is.'

'You'd be a pain in the arse even to them, Corvu.'

He told him about the new details linked to his visit to Gina Giansanti while Corvu stared at the latest questions on the blackboard.

'So it's certain that there's a link with Elisa Sordi?' Piccolo asked.

'Yes, it all starts there, from Alina Hagi and the church of San Valente. And Hagi wants to know the truth. Why?'

'To get his revenge on someone who injured him. We've seen how cruel and vengeful he is. He waited years to get even with his brother's killers.'

'Hagi played a role in Elisa's death,' Balistreri explained, 'and Alina came to know about it from Ulla, I think. That's where the crisis between them started, followed by her running off on her moped, and her death.'

'And in his sick mind Hagi blames everything on Elisa's murderer,' observed Piccolo, 'as if he'd killed Alina.'

'Precisely,' continued Balistreri. 'But if he knew for definite who it was he would have taken revenge immediately – he's not lacking in means and imagination. Marius Hagi knew, however, that Gina Giansanti had lied, and to take revenge chose her granddaughter Fiorella as the latest victim. But did he know back in 1982 or has he only recently come to know?'

'But how could he have known?' asked Mastroianni.

Balistreri reflected on Mastroianni's question. The answer was obvious.

Hagi knew that Elisa was already dead at eight o'clock that evening.

Corvu made a few calculations. 'Now we know that Elisa did

indeed leave at six thirty, as her time card shows. And no one has an absolutely certain alibi. In the space of an hour and a half someone she knew could have led her away with some excuse to a secluded place, attacked her, tortured her and killed her. Then tied weights around her and thrown her in the Tiber and come back in time for the match.'

Balistreri listened, thinking deeply.

Corvu went on. 'Then there are the letters.' They could almost hear his analytical mind at work. 'I've thought about it over the last few hours. Hagi was determined to let us know that we have to consider the letter "A" as well, the initial of his wife Alina, whom he wants to include among the victims. And that there's still a letter missing. Now, if we accept for a moment that this isn't a red herring—'

'Only for a moment,' said Piccolo, not entirely convinced.

'That's fine, Corvu. We'll accept it for a moment. Let's say there's a message in those letters. What would it be?' Balistreri asked.

'What would you think was the most ordinary meaning a series of letters could have?' Corvu asked in return.

Mastroianni laughed. 'The name of the killer, as in a good crime novel!'

Balistreri saw that Corvu wasn't laughing.

Piccolo voiced an objection. 'I don't follow, Graziano. We already know who the killer is: it's Hagi.'

'Except in the case of Elisa Sordi. He knows the details of the case perfectly, but says it wasn't him. And I don't see why he should lie; one extra murder isn't going to change anything. Besides, the man is dying.'

'That's all right, Corvu. Carry on,' Balistreri conceded.

'Hagi says that the last letter's missing, the one that will be carved on Fiorella Romani. I think it'll be an "L".'

Balistreri looked at him thoughtfully.

Too simple. Or too complex.

'And what would those letters mean then?' Mastroianni asked, looking puzzled. 'One moment,' Balistreri put in. 'Why on earth would Hagi go to all this trouble?'

'To suggest a solution for us. Because he knows who the perpetrator is and wants us to find the proof so we can nail him before he succumbs to his cancer.'

'But Corvu, if he knew who it was already, he'd have killed them,' Mastroianni objected.

Piccolo the psychologist intervened. 'Unless Hagi prefers to think of them locked in a cell for the rest of their lives – a worse revenge than a pistol shot. Hagi's suffered all his life for Alina's death. An eye for an eye.'

Balistreri came to a decision. 'Notify the Prosecutor and the judge. Today's Saturday so he'll be out on his boat at Ostia. Go and pick him up – we'll see if you're right. But before that I want you to fix up another meeting with Cardinal Alessandrini.'

Halfway through the afternoon he spoke to Floris, the Chief of Police, in order to bring him up to date on his intentions.

'Cardinal Alessandrini will refuse to be questioned, Balistreri, and the treaty between Italy and the Vatican is clear: we can't force him.'

'Leave it to me, *Signor questore*. It'll be an informal chat. I don't think he'll refuse.'

'Is there a link though?'

'Yes, there is. It all starts in 1982. According to Hagi, whoever killed Elisa was also the cause of his troubles with Alina. Of course, he could be wanting to frame an innocent person, but it's a risk we have to take.'

'Those letters start with Elisa Sordi in 1982 – it's too early,' Floris objected.

'*Signor questore*, the absolute priority is not to find Elisa Sordi's killer – we've waited too many years for that. We have to save Fiorella

Romani if she's alive. Elisa Sordi's the key to making Hagi tell us where Fiorella is.'

'Dottor Pasquali's funeral's on Monday afternoon, that's in forty-eight hours, and the worry of both the government and the city council is that if we don't solve this case then the press will crucify us. That doesn't concern me, Balistreri, but I am anxious to save that young girl's life.'

Linda was looking at the dome of St Peter's in the mid-afternoon light. There were so many things she could have spoken to him about, but in the end none of them would have changed the reality. He wasn't the one she needed. He had been, at one time. But not any more.

Now she needed someone who could play for everything, putting it all into one hand. And that man was someone else.

At five o'clock on that boiling hot afternoon, Balistreri arrived in St Peter's Square, which was full of priests, nuns and tourists. The assistant had notified him that Cardinal Alessandrini would be waiting for him in his private study. This time Corvu's contacts wouldn't have been enough to part the Vatican's gates for him again, but the kidnapping of Fiorella Romani had thrown them wide open.

He followed the assistant along the silence of the wide marble corridors, with their huge religious frescos. He found Alessandrini in grey slacks, the sleeves of his white shirt rolled up, sitting at his desk buried under a mountain of paperwork. This time he greeted him without a smile and came to the point straight away.

'Dottor Balistreri, I'm afraid you were right about Hagi. He seemed to me the type with a moral code that didn't entertain the deaths of young women. Evidently I was wrong.'

Balistreri made no comment. He had no more time or patience

for useless digressions. He had chosen a route towards the truth, impassable but necessary.

'I'm here for two reasons, Your Eminence, one professional and one private although closely connected. I'd like to begin with the private one.'

Alessandrini was always swift to catch on. 'Why exactly do you want to confess to me, Dottor Balistreri?'

'No one better than you can judge if my penitence is enough. Besides, there's a second private reason, which I'd prefer to talk about during the confession.'

Alessandrini put on his Cardinal's cassock, which was on a clothes hanger nearby. 'We can go into a private chapel – there'll be no one there at this time.'

Balistreri followed Alessandrini down a short corridor. The chapel was very small, semi-dark and cool, smelling of incense. There were a few simple hassocks, an altar, a confessional. Alessandrini entered and closed the door. Balistreri knelt down at a grille through which he could only see the Cardinal's face in outline.

'I'm listening. Please go ahead.' In the confessional's semi-darkness the Cardinal's voice seemed different, nearer and yet further away.

'I haven't made confession for over forty years, since the priests wanted me to serve as an altar boy when I was in middle school.'

'Don't worry; the Lord has no deadlines.'

'In forty years of sinning, I've committed a great many. But some are worse than others.'

'You don't have to tell me all of them. The ones that trouble you the most will do – the ones whose weight has brought you here today.'

Balistreri began to speak of what he had never spoken, except thousands of times to himself.

'I lived in Tripoli, Libya, as a child. I had a friend, a very great friend. And there was a girl I loved.'

For the first time he told someone else the story that had influenced his whole life and, in doing so, moved slowly towards a different and deeper level of understanding. His guilt was serious, but even more serious was the way he had chosen to atone for it: a progressive renunciation of life, a self-inflicted penalty, like millions of paternosters and Hail Marys.

Alessandrini listened to the whole story in absolute silence, making no comment.

'Now you know everything, would you grant me absolution, Eminence?'

He knew the reply, even before he heard it. 'Do you repent, my son?'

A strict Catholic education. An overbearing, obsessive father. An adolescent incapable of being what that father wanted and who, in order to run away from his lack of success, invented a directly opposing model of behaviour, following the heroes of his childhood films. Honour, courage, loyalty.

'Eminence, my continual repentance and the need for salvation and forgiveness haven't done anything for me, except to die a living death.'

The Cardinal's voice was a whisper. 'My son, if you want God's forgiveness you must allow God to be your judge; you cannot be the judge of religion.'

Fundamentally, that was what he wanted to hear; it was where his adolescent rebellion had started. And he was coming back to it, to the one really great disagreement with his brother Alberto that had continued through the years. The only thing they had seriously quarrelled about, the thing that with time he had forgotten about.

Nietzsche. Mamma. It's not loving thy neighbour so much as the impotence of loving thy neighbour that stops today's Christians from putting us on the pyre.

Balistreri rose from the hassock.

'Eminence, if there's a penance I can pay, I'll pay it here on this earth, whatever its nature. But it'll be neither you nor God who decides.'

Alessandrini sighed and came out of the confessional. They were standing facing each other. Now they were two adversaries and, finally, equally armed.

'There's one more thing, Your Eminence. The professional reason.'

There was a pause, then Alessandrini gave another sigh.

'Did you want to speak about Elisa Sordi, Dottor Balistreri?'

'I do, Your Eminence. About an evening in July 1982 when I wanted to watch a football match in peace.'

'You were a young man, Balistreri. You wouldn't make those mistakes again today.'

'It wasn't those mistakes I was thinking about, but others. All through the years I've always said that the killer was impossible to find among the crowd celebrating the victory, and so I tried to silence my conscience. I slowly buried Elisa Sordi in a very small dark corner of my memory.'

'And now that's no longer the case?'

'Eminence, as you know, before his arrest Marius Hagi kidnapped Fiorella Romani. This morning I went to Lecce and spoke to Signora Gina.'

The silence lasted a very long time. Balistreri realized that he was finally succeeding in controlling the anger he felt towards Alessandrini and turning it into positive energy. There was no doubt the Cardinal had performed good works for a great many people and little evil for a few. Whatever reason he had in 1982 for asking Gina Giansanti to lie, it was unacceptable and had caused many other deaths. No earthly justice would absolve him, and no God either. But now the thought was useless. What was needed was the truth. The truth that Hagi was demanding in order to free Fiorella Romani.

The Cardinal went to kneel at one of the benches. Balistreri let him pray undisturbed. He was a little light-headed from the smell of incense, on edge with tension and lack of sleep, shattered by Angelo and Linda's betrayal and by disgust for what he had done to her himself the night before. But it was precisely that madness he had pulled himself back from that had brought him back to life, to seek the truth, whatever it was.

After several minutes Alessandrini signalled him to come over. Balistreri knelt beside him.

'Gina Giansanti is not to blame. It was I who asked her to say she'd seen Elisa Sordi leave at eight o'clock that evening. I knew how to reach her in India and I told her what to say. She had no wish to save Manfredi, but I swore to her that he hadn't killed Elisa Sordi. I said the same to Ulla, poor soul. Unfortunately, Gina came back to Rome too late to save the unfortunate woman.'

'I already know all this, Eminence, but I was wondering why.'

Alessandrini was plainly suffering. 'In order to save an innocent man, Balistreri. I assumed the right to correct the mistakes that earthly justice was about to make. Manfredi was innocent. I knew this and know it to this day with absolute certainty.'

'Then you should have said so to the police. Here we're on earth in a secular and sovereign state. You should have given us the proof you had, not try to distort the truth.'

'I couldn't. I was bound by the secrecy of the confessional. What I had learned couldn't be made known.'

'It was a case of murder committed in Italy, not the Vatican. I could have you arrested, Your Eminence.'

They both knew he could not, not even if Alessandrini had confessed to having done away with Elisa and all the other women himself. But the prelate had a more valid reason to speak out than Balistreri's useless threats, and that was the life of Fiorella Romani.

'From six forty-five to seven forty-five on that day Manfredi wasn't in the gym, nor was he murdering Elisa Sordi. But I couldn't tell you and I decided to save him from those unjust accusations by means of Gina Giansanti's lie.'

'Eminence, you have to tell me the reasons for your certainty. You have done a lot for Fiorella Romani. If you want to save her, I have to know the truth, the real truth.'

Alessandrini had also lived with his spectres for twenty-four years. And now, as both a Christian and a man, he would have to live with a good many more if Fiorella died as well. He made the only possible decision.

'Ulla was very religious, but this came up against the Count's principles. Unknown to him, she came to me to confess almost every day.'

'Even after Elisa's death?'

Alessandrini nodded. 'The afternoon of the final, before the game started, something terrible happened while the Count was out at his party's conference. After lunch, Ulla had gone to her room to sleep. She was very upset, so took a tablet and fell into a deep sleep. About five o'clock she was woken by loud noises coming from Manfredi's room. Behind the door she heard lacerating cries, like those of an animal in its last throes. She entered without knocking. Manfredi was covered in blood, coming from superficial cuts. The Count came home at that moment and sent Ulla away, but she stayed to listen in at the door.'

'And what did she hear?'

Alessandrini ignored the question. 'After twenty minutes, the Count called out for her. He'd given Manfredi a powerful sedative and had seen to the cuts, which were only slight. He ordered Ulla not to tell a soul what had happened, otherwise there'd be a permanent stain on Manfredi's future. Then they went out together, he to see the Minister and Ulla to do some shopping, and Manfredi left on his motorbike. The Count had ordered him to go to the gym as usual.'

Balistreri was trying to put his thoughts in some order as they started to crowd in on him. 'When did Ulla mention these things to you?'

'That same evening, before the final. While the Count was changing before he went to see the Minister, Ulla managed to persuade Manfredi not to go to the gym and come with her to the Vatican instead so that he could speak to me. Ulla telephoned to ask me while you, Balistreri, were in my home and Angelo Dioguardi was on the terrace looking over Elisa's work.'

Balistreri remembered the call and shortly afterwards the Cardinal hurrying to leave. 'Ulla and Manfredi came to see you in the Vatican?'

'Yes, they came to see me without the Count's knowledge. He'd forbidden Ulla to involve Manfredi in anything that had to do with the Catholic Church. They arrived a little after half past six on Manfredi's motorbike. I was waiting for them in a taxi outside a side entrance and we went to my private study.'

'Fine. What did you talk about?'

'Manfredi made confession for the first time in his life. He was shattered, poor young man.'

'Shattered by what, Eminence?'

'It was a confession, Dottor Balistreri. As with your own a little while ago, I can never reveal the contents to anyone. But I am also concerned for Fiorella Romani's life, so I will swear to you by the Virgin Mary that Manfredi was with me between six thirty and seven thirty and therefore could not have killed Elisa Sordi.'

'This is ridiculous! Why didn't Ulla tell the truth in order to prove his innocence?' Balistreri objected.

'You don't know Count Tommaso dei Banchi di Aglieno very well. Ulla was afraid to tell him that she'd taken Manfredi to confession. To do so would have destroyed the marriage and the relationship between the Count and Manfredi as well. When I spoke to her she begged me to keep quiet, so binding me forever to the secrecy of the confessional. And then I asked Gina Giansanti to lie.'

Balistreri realized that there was some sense to the explanation, but there were other consequences to the lie that Alessandrini could not pretend to ignore.

'There are other people who have benefited from Gina Giansanti's lie, Your Eminence.'

'I know. And that's why I spoke of pride, because I decided that saving an innocent man was more important than punishing the guilty. In reality, I thought that the police would find the real culprit – someone in the middle of the crowd out there.'

'And you don't think it could have been someone much closer inside, someone to whom Gina Giansanti gave a cast iron alibi?'

'No,' Alessandrini replied sharply, 'I don't think so at all. Valerio Bona wouldn't have done anything like that. And Paul is out of the question – he was at San Valente and never moved from there.'

'It seems to me you could also be mistaken, Eminence.'

'I could have made a mistake about Hagi, but not about Valerio Bona and Paul.'

Balistreri decided to say nothing about Valerio Bona's forthcoming interrogation.

'There's also the Count,' he said instead.

'Of course,' said Alessandrini, getting up. 'And there's also myself, Dottor Balistreri. Now, however, I must see to the living.'

The conversation was at an end. The Cardinal rose, made the sign of the Cross and left.

Balistreri went back to the office by bus, winding past sun-baked tourists in shorts and Romans out for a walk at that hour to avoid the worst of the heat.

When he arrived, Valerio Bona was waiting for him in the interrogation room. Balistreri wanted to see him under pressure. He was the former boyfriend, the one without an alibi. And the letters carved on the girls formed an anagram of his name.

He was accompanied by a young female lawyer who went sailing with him. The Public Prosecutor had assumed responsibility for the Elisa Sordi investigation on the grounds that it was linked to the principal enquiry. Balistreri sat in front of Valerio, with Piccolo and Corvu at either side.

'May we know the grounds for this arrest?' the lawyer asked the Prosecutor.

'We have reopened the investigation into Elisa Sordi's death on the grounds that new evidence has emerged. Dottor Balistreri will question your client, then we'll decide whether to hold him.'

Valerio looked at him aghast. 'You've decided to reopen the investigation! The other day—'

'New evidence has emerged in the last few hours, some of which affects you directly. We have to reconstruct the events of the afternoon of 11 July 1982.'

'But why? What's the point?' protested the lawyer. 'Marius Hagi has made a confession.'

Balistreri remembered Valerio Bona very well, including his insecurity and apprehension. He showed little resistance to pressure.

'Hagi didn't kill Elisa Sordi,' Balistreri declared sharply.

He saw Valerio turn pale and start fiddling with the gold crucifix round his neck.

'There's one fundamental new piece of evidence,' Balistreri went on. 'Elisa Sordi could have been killed at any time from six thirty onwards. That's the time she left the office, not at eight o'clock.'

What he read in Valerio Bona's face in those few seconds was the incredulous, dazed look of someone called to account after twenty-four years. But there was something more than fear. There was also a touch of relief. And this mixture surprised Balistreri.

The lawyer cut in. 'I imagine that for the moment you have no intention of telling us on what this new conviction is based.'

'Correct,' Balistreri replied sharply. 'Now, Signor Bona, let's start at the end. Where were you after six thirty?'

'You already know; I told you at the time. I saw Elisa straight after lunch, near the gate on Via della Camilluccia. Then I went to Villa Pamphili on the moped. I sat down under a tree to study for my exam. Towards eight fifteen I went home to see the game with my parents and relatives. And then I went to bed. My parents' friends testified to that effect back then.'

'I'm well aware of it. You had gone out with friends to celebrate all Italy's other victories, but after the most important one you decide to go to bed.'

'As I told you, I was concerned about the exam, I wanted to get some sleep.'

'And because of this exam, which you never took, you didn't go out to celebrate Italy's win. I don't believe you, having seen the pictures on your boat of the 2006 champions. I think you were upset, Signor Bona, about what had happened that afternoon.'

Valerio Bona was already shaking. 'No. I didn't speak to her again that day, I swear to God.'

Balistreri had noted all of the emotions that were crossing Valerio's face: pain, shame and remorse.

He shook his head. 'I don't believe you. And, leaving God aside, there are other reasons why I can't believe you. Serious ones.'

The lawyer lost her patience and turned to the Prosecutor. 'I think we need greater clarity here.'

The Prosecutor made a sign of agreement to Balistreri, who then continued.

'We think that there's an outside accomplice in the series of crimes attributed to Marius Hagi in the past year. You knew him as far back as 1982. And you have no alibi for these crimes. Indeed, we know for certain that on the day Ornella Corona was killed you were in Ostia on your boat.'

Valerio Bona's eyes were filled with horror. 'You're joking . . .' he stammered.

'I'm not joking at all. And this time, I won't be superficial or distracted. I'm considering the matter very thoroughly and I would advise you to do the same, Signor Bona. I want the truth about that day in 1982.'

The lawyer asked for a break in order to speak to Valerio alone. Balistreri took the opportunity for a cigarette in his office.

'He's guilty,' said Corvu.

'I'm not sure,' said Piccolo.

'He's certainly guilty, but I don't know what of, and that's the point,' Balistreri muttered.

When they went back into the room, he saw Valerio Bona's expression straight away: a look of resignation, but also of relief, almost resolute. He was gripping the crucifix tightly.

'My client will make a voluntary statement about the events of the afternoon of July the 11th 1982,' said his lawyer, 'and he will respond to all your questions on the matter. He will not reply to any questions about more recent events with which he declares he had absolutely and totally no connection.'

'All right,' accepted Balistreri. 'Now, Signor Bona, let's hear what you have to say and then we'll decide.'

Valerio was now resolved, like a child who's been persuaded to take some very bitter medicine and wants to do so quickly, so he can get it over with.

'I couldn't settle down in Villa Pamphili's park. I was sure that Elisa had someone else and I wanted her to tell me to my face. A little after five I went to Via della Camilluccia to speak to her. I parked the moped around the corner and saw you, Dottor Balistreri, with Count Tommaso, who had just arrived. It must have been about a quarter to six, more or less. You and the Count spoke for less than a minute, then he went off to Block A and you went round the long way to the Cardinal's.'

Balistreri nodded. He remembered every instant well.

He wanted to go up to see her.

Valerio took a breath and went on. 'I was hiding round the corner. I saw Paul coming in a hurry – you'd probably spoken to him. He got into his Volkswagen with Gina Giansanti who was going to Mass, and they went off together.'

While I was looking up at that window and couldn't make up my mind.

'The door to Block B was open. I went in. The lift was occupied – it was you going up, Dottor Balistreri. I waited a little – I couldn't decide. Then I made up my mind and went up to the second floor on foot.'

Valerio Bona stopped. His face reflected the horror of the memory.

'I knew that Elisa wouldn't have let me in, but the door to the offices was only pulled to, not locked. I went into the lobby and was immediately struck by the absolute silence. I thought she might have gone out to buy some cigarettes and then left the door like that. I paused outside her office.'

Valerio broke off to take a breath. And in that moment, before he could speak, before he could open that door that had remained closed for twenty-four years, Balistreri knew that the mistake he'd made that day was far worse than he had imagined all this time. Now the spectre glimpsed while he was attacking Linda Nardi took on a vague shape.

'If I hadn't gone in, my life would have been different. I'd have stayed with IBM, got married, and have children today. But I wanted to speak to her. I was desperate, so I went in. Elisa's body was on the floor next to the wall. Her blouse and bra were torn and there was blood on her breasts. She had a black eye that was swollen, a cut lip, and a bruise on her cheek. I didn't go any closer, but stayed there a few moments. Then I pulled the door behind me and bolted. A minute later I was on my moped.'

The Prosecutor looked at Balistreri in disbelief and Balistreri looked at Valerio Bona. He felt no sympathy at all for him. What he felt inside himself was fury. If only he had had eyes, ears and a heart that damned day.

He shook himself out of his pointless, gloomy thoughts. He had to save Fiorella Romani. That was the only real, urgent, fundamental thing to be done. And the road was laid out – he only had to sweep aside whoever had put themselves in the way.

'There are two possibilities, Signor Bona. The first is that you're lying and you killed Elisa Sordi outside the office between six thirty and eight. The second is that you're telling the truth. In this case you realize that if you'd said these things straight away the perpetrator would now have been in prison for many years.'

'I know, and I've tortured myself enough for that precise reason. I didn't say anything because I was so shocked, and in the following days confused as well. The body had been found in the Tiber. The concierge said that Elisa had left at eight that night. I almost came to believe I'd had a hallucination.'

Have you confessed to this? Has a priest given you absolution? How many paternosters and Hail Marys? Do you think it's enough to gain a place in paradise?

All his hatred of those who had deceived him and locked him up inside his guilty feelings all these years became focused on Valerio Bona, as if by destroying him he could wipe out all the past.

'I hope you're lying, Signor Bona. I hope so for your sake, because if what you're now saying is true, then your silence has caused the death of four young women, a young Senegalese man and four policemen, as well as the suicides of Manfredi's mother and Elisa's mother.'

Valerio looked at him petrified, his hands with their chewed fingernails searching desperately for the crucifix, his eyes wandering off into space.

The lawyer spoke. 'The most my client could be accused of is making a false statement in the Elisa Sordi case. He has no involvement with anything else.'

There was no more caution, nor balance nor remorse, only his controlled anger and Fiorella Romani.

'Of course,' said Balistreri in an icy voice, 'that's the legal position. But your client is a practising Catholic, someone who believes in the Last Judgement, in heaven and in hell.'

He did what he should have done without a second thought twenty-four years before, and had not done until Giovanna Sordi leaped from her balcony while Italy again exploded into rapture.

He looked scornfully at Valerio Bona huddled on his seat. 'You thought you could bury your guilt simply by renouncing your IBM salary and making the computers work for the orphans. Is that it, Signor Bona? Would you like to see photographs of the corpses of these young women, all killed because of your cowardice?'

He caught Piccolo's disapproving look, the lawyer's contempt, the Prosecutor's and Corvu's embarrassment.

Marius Hagi. The grief you're dishing out is endless. And I happen to be the right instrument for your vendetta.

Valerio Bona lifted his tear-streaked face, the face of an old man. 'You're right, Dottor Balistreri, I can't wipe away my guilt. But the Lord will be my judge. I can only offer you this belated truth.'

'Well then, please tell me the whole truth. You lost control of your boat when I asked you if Elisa was one of Francesco Ajello's women.'

Valerio shut his eyes. 'He had his eyes on her in Ostia, once when Elisa came to watch one of my regattas. He begged me to introduce him to her and I said no.'

'And then?' Balistreri asked. 'There's more to it than this.'

'That afternoon, when I ran out of Elisa's office and went to get my moped, Francesco Ajello's Porsche was parked around the corner.'

A recent abortion, an unknown lover.

Balistreri spoke to the Prosecutor. There was insufficient evidence to hold Valerio Bona. They kept his passport and let him go. The Prosecutor would try to get a warrant for Ajello from the judge that very evening.

Now there was another priority. They had to reconstruct the journey Elisa's body made from her office in Via della Camilluccia to the gravel bed of the Tiber.

Over the telephone the Count's personal secretary said he was abroad, but that Manfredi was at home and had no objection to seeing him. He decided to go alone and arrived in Via della Camilluccia at supper-time. The area was deserted: all the residents were away for the weekend in their villas, on their boats or out at the open-air restaurants in the centre. The residential complex was submerged in silence; only the lights of Block A's penthouse were lit up.

The young secretary ushered him onto the terrace, where Manfredi joined him shortly after. He was silent; there were no smiles or the usual pleasantries. This time the atmosphere was very different from that of a few days earlier. Balistreri decided to pick up from their last conversation.

'Last Saturday you asked me to discover the truth about Elisa Sordi. Since then many people have asked me the same thing.'

Manfredi looked at him absent-mindedly. His eyes had Ulla's intelligence, yet you could now read his father's cold arrogance in them.

'Did you really need all those encouragements, Balistreri? Doesn't the truth interest you?'

'You were all lying in 1982. We couldn't uncover anything.'

Balistreri could feel the rage creeping into his voice and forced himself to control it.

Rage is not a shortcut to the truth.

'And so? You're the police, not us. And in 1982 you were taken up with your vices and prejudices. According to you a disfigured young man, and a nobleman to boot, was the perfect suspect.'

'All right, I'll ask you now. Did you kill Elisa Sordi?'

Manfredi assumed the scornful tone inherited from his father.

'After all that's happened you again come back to this?'

'Of course. Either we clarify this point definitively or we go nowhere. And this time you'd better be more convincing. Another young girl's life is in the balance. I've no more time or patience for any lying.'

For some ridiculous reason Manfredi gave a half smile, then nodded.

'Good. I see you're finally resolved, Balistreri. Will the truth about Elisa Sordi help to save this young woman?'

'Yes. It's the price being asked by Marius Hagi, the man we arrested.'

I could ask if you know him, but I wouldn't know if you're lying.

Manfredi absorbed the information in silence and asked for no further explanation. 'All right, I'll tell you something I won't ever again repeat to anyone under any circumstances. It will have to suffice to save this girl.'

'I'm listening.'

'I was attracted to Elisa Sordi a great deal. Just as you were, is that right?'

Balistreri was uneasy, but said nothing.

'You were attracted to her, as was everyone else around her. But all you wanted to do was take her to bed, while I was the unhappy kid who was in love with her.'

'The afternoon of the World Cup final,' Manfredi continued, 'Rome had come to a complete stop – it was a desert. Some people were at the seaside, others resting. It was as if every Italian had to play the final themselves. But Elisa came to work. I saw her arrive mid-morning, then I saw her leave for lunch and come back again, followed by Valerio Bona. They were arguing, then she left him outside the gate and went up to the office.'

'Where were your parents?'

'My father was at the Hotel Camilluccia, near here, at a conference for his party. My mother had taken something to make her sleep. The two blocks were completely deserted; the only two people awake were Elisa and myself. It was an ideal moment to have a quiet word with her. What would you have done in my place?'

Balistreri didn't reply. He was back again in that afternoon. An afternoon in which he was hot, half drunk, and excited about the coming evening in which he wanted to be free to do what he most wanted to do. He saw it all in slow motion, second by second.

I wanted to go up and see her.

Manfredi continued. 'I hoped she liked me at least a little. I knew she wasn't going out with Valerio, but I suspected she was seeing someone else. I couldn't stop myself thinking about it – it was an obsession. I kept switching from my room to the terrace. I took several showers. In the end I made up my mind.'

The truth. The truth you confessed to Cardinal Alessandrini.

'I saw Gina Giansanti come up and then leave.'

'What time was this?'

'I don't know exactly – I think it was a little after five. I went down, then crossed over through the interconnecting basements – that way I didn't have to go outside, so Gina Giansanti wouldn't see me from the lodge – and went up the stairs. The door was closed. I knocked and called out to her. Elisa recognized my voice and immediately let me in and said she was happy to see me. Indeed she asked if I could help her, as the new type of computer wasn't working well. I knew how to fix it and in five minutes it was sorted.'

Balistreri looked towards the window of Elisa Sordi's office. Behind the closed blind he saw Linda Nardi's semi-dark living room of the evening before. He could imagine what happened next.

'To thank me, Elisa gave me a kiss on the cheek. I took the kiss for an invitation and pulled her to me to kiss her on the mouth. With a smile, she politely pushed me away. I thought she was only play-acting, but at that moment I saw my face in the mirror and thought the smile was mocking me. Then I lost it.'

Whoever fights against monsters has to be careful not to become a monster himself. If you examine an abyss long enough, the abyss will start to examine you.

'I sent her into the wall with a slap. I held her wrists with one hand and tore at her blouse and bra with the other. She offered no resistance at all; she was paralysed with fear.'

Manfredi came to a stop. He didn't appear to be upset at the memory. He must have run over it thousands of times with the psychiatrist in Kenya. He was only slowing down so that Balistreri could take it in fully.

'Her lack of reaction turned me into even more of a beast. I gave her a punch in the face, which I think broke her cheekbone. She banged her head against the wall and fell down. I watched her for a while, she was breathing softly. I slowly calmed down. In order to make sure she was alive I took the pocket mirror from her bag and put it to her mouth. She was breathing.'

'So Elisa was alive?'

'Absolutely. But I didn't know what to do – I was desperate. I was trembling with fear hearing the lift going up to the floor above. Then I heard Angelo Dioguardi ring the bell and say hello to Cardinal Alessandrini. So I took Elisa's keys, which were in the door, locked the office and hurried back to my place, again going via the basements. It took me less than five minutes to get back up here.'

'And you did nothing to the girl while she was out cold?'

'You want to know if I put out several cigarettes on her and suffocated her? Absolutely not.'

Balistreri decided to press on further. He could have come back at another time to carve the letter 'O'.

'And once you were home what did you do?'

Manfredi looked at him calmly. 'What would you have done in my place?'

'I would have called my father, especially if he were a powerful man.'

'I called him immediately from the telephone on the terrace and told him everything. He ordered me to go to my room and not move from it. He would be home in a couple of minutes and would see to things. Before I went back to my room I looked out with my binoculars and saw you, Balistreri. You were smoking a cigarette near the lodge, chatting to Gina Giansanti. Then I went straight to my room.'

I looked up towards the balcony of Block A. A fleeting reflection, then nothing. Manfredi was acting shy that day.

'My father sent Ulla away and gave me a sedative. It calmed me down. He promised me that my life would change, that our relatives in Africa would help. He would talk to Elisa to apologize; he would give her a permanent job. In those few interminable moments my life was decided. For better or worse.'

I stopped to look up at the goddess's window. Again it was the only one open and this time there was a flower on the windowsill, which the girl must have put outside when the sun was no longer beating down. I still didn't know what to do, so I stayed there a couple of minutes, thinking about her, undecided. Then I went to the lift and pressed for floors two and three. I found Angelo on the Cardinal's landing.

'I gave Elisa's office keys to my father. He told me to act normally and go to the gym until the guests arrived for the match. A person he trusted would see about talking to Elisa while he went to his appointment with the Minister of the Interior.'

Balistreri remembered it clearly.

'I saw you leaving; he took the car with Ulla and you took your bike. But you didn't go to the gym.'

Manfredi told him exactly the same version of events as the Cardinal had. He was with Ulla at the Cardinal's. The Count had never known about this. He would rather have ended up in prison than tell him. And later he never had the courage to confess it to him.

'And the day after, when Elisa wasn't found and the police arrived?'

Manfredi reflected. 'My father never told me what happened. That night after the match, he ordered me to deny having met Elisa Sordi that day.'

'You didn't ask him for any explanation when they fished Elisa's body out of the Tiber?'

'I didn't have the courage. You don't know my father very well. He told me again to deny having seen Elisa Sordi that day. I asked him if he believed I'd left her alive. He told me it didn't matter. We had to hold out, then he'd send me to Kenya and I'd be happy there. Even when you were taking me away, he assured me that if I had the strength and patience, everything would be sorted out.'

'And your mother? Didn't she suggest you use her as an alibi? You could have said you and she were together with Cardinal Alessandrini.'

'She was upset. Ulla killed herself at dawn, the day following my arrest.'

'Manfredi, I must speak to your father urgently.'

'I'm afraid you won't be able to do that until tomorrow evening. He went away three days ago. He's with his brother Giuliano and my cousin Rinaldo in Uganda; they're sailing on the White Nile in an area not covered by communications satellite. But tomorrow afternoon he'll be in Nairobi and take a flight to Frankfurt, where we'll meet on Monday morning. From there I'll go back to Africa and he's coming on to Rome. You can meet him then.'

'So you maintain that you don't know what your father did that day. And you're asking me find out the truth? After twenty-four years?!' asked Balistreri in a fury.

'You don't have to believe me, but we've never spoken about Elisa Sordi again – it's as if she never existed. He never asked me if I killed her and I never asked him how she came to be killed and taken away from here. Someone killed Elisa Sordi after I attacked her. You accused me because it was the most obvious solution. Ulla killed herself because she saw no way out.'

Balistreri looked him straight in the eyes. 'Don't you feel any remorse for what you did to Elisa Sordi?'

Manfredi turned to look at Elisa's office window.

'I can look at that window today, Balistreri, better than you can. I haven't even changed my address, while I bet that all these years you've avoided passing this way. Remorse is a useless feeling. Look at me and all I've done for Africa's poor, while you can't even sleep well at night.'

Manfredi stared at him. In that stare was something far worse than hate, something deeper and more painful.

'It's time you made yourself useful, Balistreri. You look a sight. Go home and get some sleep, have a shower and a shave and a good breakfast tomorrow morning, because if your mind is in the same condition as your body, that girl doesn't have a hope.'

Balistreri got up. At the door Manfredi said goodbye without shaking his hand.

'At least try to save this girl, Balistreri, rather than your own soul.'

Evening

Balistreri returned to the office at ten, exhausted. Ajello couldn't be found. Corvu had checked his home, but his wife said he had left on a working weekend and didn't know where to find him. They had checked all the border controls, ports and airports, with no result.

Balistreri decided he needed to talk to Hagi again and tell him all that he'd done to save Fiorella Romani, if she was still alive. The Prosecutor was absolutely against sharing confidential information with Hagi, such as that learned from Valerio and Manfredi, but Floris was in agreement with Balistreri. He called Avvocato Morandi on his mobile phone and suggested an informal chat without lawyers, just Balistreri and Hagi alone in the prison courtyard. Morandi was helpful and said he would suggest it to Hagi right away. Ten minutes later Balistreri phoned Floris back to say that Hagi was agreeable.

Corvu and Piccolo went with Balistreri to Regina Coeli by car around eleven. They had to switch on the siren to get through the heavy Saturday night traffic. Trastevere's bars and restaurants were humming with sunburned crowds fresh from the beach – coated with moisturising cream and now in need of drinks, amusement and coolness.

Balistreri was shattered at the end of an interminable day that had begun at dawn with the trip to Gina Giansanti in Lecce. But saving Fiorella Romani allowed no time to pause.

Hagi was ready and waiting, handcuffed, in the prison courtyard. Balistreri was aware that in a few hours Hagi's physical state had deteriorated; his cough was heavier and continuous. His body was quickly being eaten up, but his black soul was holding on.

'I look like a dying man, don't I? And you're afraid it'll come to pass too quickly. But look at yourself – you look even worse than me. Take my handcuffs off and light me a cigarette.'

Balistreri did as he asked. The rectangular courtyard was empty but floodlit. The air was cool and you could hear the noise of traffic and the racket from Trastevere. They walked and smoked in silence.

'I have done what you asked, Signor Hagi.'

'Good. I'm listening.'

'First you must give me your word that Fiorella Romani's still alive.'

Hagi's deep black eyes stared at him in curiosity. 'You believe in my word?'

'In this matter, yes.'

'All right. I can't be sure she's alive, but she was certainly in the best of health when you arrested me and I have no reason to believe she's already dead. Now tell me who killed Elisa Sordi.'

Balistreri told him all the new information from Gina Giansanti, Alessandrini, Valerio and Manfredi. He saw Hagi nodding as he absorbed each piece. 'That's all?' he asked finally.

'I have to question the Count and Ajello; without them we're at a standstill.'

'Why is that?' asked Hagi sharply.

'Because we have to know what the Count did with those keys and who he sent over to Elisa. Was it Ajello or did he go himself? And was the girl dead or alive? Unless you know anything else that might help.'

Hagi looked at him. 'Really, this case is yours and has been for twenty-four years.'

'But everyone's been lying,' protested Balistreri.

'Precisely. Everyone has lied. And yet you Catholics have a commandment about that, if I'm not mistaken.'

'Signor Hagi, I will do anything you ask me to do, but I want Fiorella Romani back alive with her mother. We can't wait until the

Count comes back the day after tomorrow – it'll be too late.'

'That's true, it will be too late,' Hagi said. The brutal force of the phrase hung suspended between them.

Hagi looked at him in silence. Balistreri felt fatigue coming over him in waves, together with the memory of his attack on Linda Nardi and the image of Fiorella Romani tied up in a cave. His body was giving in to sleep while his brain was fighting to keep awake, grasping at the hope of saving Fiorella. Suddenly another image made its way into the fog of his mind.

'You were there on that hill the night they shot me,' he said, as if all of a sudden waking up from a dream.

'Of course I was there; I was the boss,' Hagi admitted simply.

'And it was you who finished Colajacono off and decided to spare me?'

Hagi smiled. 'We're getting off the subject, Balistreri. It's you who has to tell me who killed Elisa Sordi.'

'Who carved those letters on the girls?'

Hagi had a sudden bout of coughing. More blood, which he spat on the ground. 'The same person who carved one on Elisa Sordi,' he replied softly, when the fit of coughing died down.

Balistreri was in no doubt that he was telling the truth.

'So you already know who it is . . .'

'Balistreri, we're back at the beginning again. It's you who has to know. You've been going round in circles for years. Have you any idea how much damage you've caused with all your fucking amateurism? If it wasn't for you . . .' Hagi's cough swallowed up the end of the sentence.

If it wasn't for my lack of professionalism Alina Hagi would still be alive. But we only have the future in our hands.

'The letters point to Valerio Bona,' Balistreri said.

Hagi looked at him, laughing. 'The letters? At the same time you're forgetting the suicides of two mothers – that's another two letters.'

'Another two letters?' Balistreri repeated in a stupor.

'Do you really think the killer would go around carving his name? Where on earth do you think you are, Balistreri — in a crime novel from Victorian England? You haven't by any chance accused that poor wretch Valerio Bona of such a thing, have you?'

You know very well I have, you damned scoundrel, because it's you who led me there.

Hagi looked over at the surrounding prison wall, as if he could see through it to the crazy nightlife beyond.

'Are you seriously beginning to get worried, Balistreri? And has Cardinal Alessandrini repented for what he did? Will he think about it in the years to come as he recites his prayers together with the Pope?'

Balistreri knew he had lost. He had no more cards to play. Fiorella Romani was lost.

Corvu and Piccolo burst into the courtyard, panting.

'Valerio Bona's hanged himself from the mast of his boat,' Corvu said, all in one breath.

Hagi's eyes showed a gleam of interest. A Mephistophelian grin appeared on his sick face.

'Someone has finally begun to repent in earnest, Balistreri.'

Balistreri staggered as the news hit him.

He said that it would be the Lord who would judge him, not me.

He turned to Hagi. 'Valerio Bona didn't kill Elisa Sordi or any of the others. He only—'

'Only lied, like all of them. A very grave sin. But not everyone's paid the price that I have. Now it's their turn to pay. Only the judge is not your benevolent God, Balistreri. The judge happens to be me.'

'Signor Hagi, I'm also willing to pay, whatever the price. So long as you spare Fiorella Romani.'

Hagi leaned against the wall. 'Give me another cigarette,' he said, coughing.

Strangely, the smoking had a calming effect on the cough. Hagi spat a mouthful of blood on the ground.

'I want an answer by tomorrow noon, Balistreri. If you give me the right answer, Fiorella Romani's life will be saved. Now pay close attention, I already know something here. If you try to trick me, Fiorella dies.'

'What do I have to do?'

'There's another reason why Cardinal Alessandrini forced Gina Giansanti to lie. If you can get him to speak, make him give a full confession of his sins. Show me that you know how to act like a policeman outside the gates of paradise as well as in.'

Balistreri sent Corvu and Piccolo back to the office, arranging to meet them again at eight the following morning. He left the prison on his own a little after midnight on that infinitely long day. The Saturday night partying around the Tiber was in full swing with rows of vehicles tooting horns, crowds with beers and ice creams, open-air restaurants jam-packed.

Only twenty-four hours had passed since he'd fled from Linda Nardi's and himself. He walked on, staggering with fatigue. He'd been deceived by everyone: Gina Giansanti, Cardinal Alessandrini, Manfredi, the Count, Valerio Bona, Ajello, even by Angelo and Linda, up to the point where he now found himself in a labyrinth – and Marius Hagi was holding the thread.

He needed to sleep, to sort out the ideas that were scattered about like playing cards by the gust of his emotions. But he needed peace to find that sleep.

He hadn't dialled that number for over two years. Antonella answered at the first ring. She was at home, alone, and said she'd be waiting for him.

He found her in an old tracksuit, her eyes puffy and underlined with dark shadows. Despite everything, Pasquali had been a courteous and properly behaved boss towards her – something rare for the time. Balistreri knew, however, that those tears were partly wasted. Pasquali had gone to Casilino 900 with a gun in his hand, intending to kill Marius Hagi and put a lid on the whole business, but someone smarter and more powerful had decided otherwise and had drawn him into a deadly trap. But there was no point in saying this to Antonella.

Seeing him in such a state, she made him lie on the sofa with his head resting on her knees, and lit one of those joints that, during the years of their relationship, he had always disdainfully refused.

'What state of mind was Pasquali in during his last few days?' Balistreri asked.

'Just like yours tonight. For Pasquali a knot in his tie or a hair out of place was the equivalent of your miserable state right now.'

Antonella stretched out an arm and picked up a small book from the table.

'I tidied up Pasquali's office, Michele. This diary was in a secret drawer.'

It was a small black diary, the size of a playing card. It was for 2006. Balistreri was reminded of Nano's diary, handed over by his son, which had actually reopened the case. He leafed through Pasquali's diary while his eyes were closing. There were no names and no numbers, nor appointments, only circles around several dates.

Antonella slowly ran her finger through his hair and caressed his face. He remembered those dates very well. At last he closed his eyes and fell asleep.

Sunday, 23 July 2006

Morning

He was woken on Antonella's sofa by a mobile ringing somewhere. It was Corvu, it was already eight thirty, and they were waiting for him in the office. While he took an ice-cold shower, Antonella made him a double espresso and some toast. He smoked two cigarettes as he slowly drank his coffee.

'You're no longer off caffeine and tobacco then, Michele?' There was no reproach in her voice; instead she rather appeared to approve.

'I also chucked all the tablets down the toilet, together with certain old thoughts.'

Antonella smiled. 'Now you only have to get back to sex. Or have you already started?'

He gave her a light kiss on the lips and called a taxi.

He found that Corvu, Piccolo and Mastroianni had been in the office since six that morning in an effort to reconstruct the case from the beginning.

'In the light of the new information, I've checked all possible alibis for Elisa Sordi's death. I hope you don't mind, but I also checked out Angelo Dioguardi,' Corvu said, half excusing himself.

'You did very well, Corvu. Go ahead, I'm listening.'

'OK. We know for certain that Elisa Sordi was alive at five o'clock when she spoke to her mother on the phone, which shows up on her list of calls. Immediately after, or immediately before, the concierge comes up to her and takes the girl's completed work to Cardinal Alessandrini. Then Manfredi pays Elisa a visit, or he was already there when she received her mother's call. He stayed there about twenty minutes, while Dottor Balistreri and Dioguardi arrived at the main gate and were talking to Gina Giansanti. Manfredi was still in Elisa's office when Angelo came in and went up in the lift. He heard the Cardinal open the door in person. Manfredi left Elisa beaten unconscious, if we believe him. He locked the door, went to his block and called his father, who was at the Hotel Camilluccia, which is five minutes away – we checked. Then he went out onto the terrace and saw Dottor Balistreri through his binoculars talking to the concierge. He went to his room, where he started cutting himself with a razor blade and moaning, waking his mother. The Count arrived after a few minutes, met Dottor Balistreri, had a couple of words with him and went up to the penthouse, while Gina Giansanti was getting ready to go to Mass. As Dottor Balistreri was walking over to Block B he met Father Paul coming out, then went up in the lift to the top floor where Angelo Dioguardi and the Cardinal were waiting for him. Father Paul left the complex with Gina Giansanti. She went to Mass, he went back to San Valente.'

Corvu paused to consult his meticulous notes.

'Valerio Bona took advantage of the concierge's absence – she'd left with Father Paul – and, following Dottor Balistreri, got into Block B. He went up to see Elisa and found her dead. That is, Valerio thought she was dead. Manfredi swears he left her beaten unconscious. One of the two's lying, or simply mistaken. The six people in the Via della Camilluccia complex all went on the move together at six o'clock. Dottor Balistreri, Dioguardi and Cardinal Alessandrini came down and saw the Count and Ulla leaving in the car and Manfredi on his motorbike. From this point on we know exactly where five of these people were. Dottor Balistreri and Angelo Dioguardi went to watch the game, while the Cardinal, Ulla and Manfredi were in the Vatican. And we know the Count went to see the then Minister of the Interior. At the time, the police checked the registers and found he went in at six fifty and left at seven thirty-five.'

'Corvu, I want you to get hold of a complete copy of the Ministry's registers.'

'But Dottor Balistreri—' Corvu protested feebly.

'You know how it's done, Corvu. So just do it, that's all. Now let's come back to the present.' Balistreri pointed to the blackboard where they'd put the letters in chronological order.

O (Elisa)

? (Ulla)

A (Alina)

R (Samantha)

E (Nadia)

? (Giovanna)

V (Selina)

I (Ornella)

? (Fiorella)

'Three names have question marks,' Corvu pointed out.

'We can follow Hagi's point about his wife Alina,' Mastroianni said. 'Where there's no mutilation, we take the first letter of the Christian name.'

'Exactly,' said Corvu. 'Although I have my doubts about the last letter for Fiorella.'

It depends on what they find carved there, he thought, but avoided saying it.

'So in this order we have O U A R E G V I F. But it doesn't have to be in this sequence,' Piccolo observed.

'I've read many studies of similar cases. The order is part of the obsessive behaviour and is always important.'

Balistreri lost patience. 'These letters tell me nothing.' And yet in his mind a memory was stirring. It took shape, rose and fell, and disappeared. It was something he had seen somewhere.

They moved on to Piccolo. 'As regards Valerio Bona, there's no doubt he committed suicide. After being questioned he dashed over to Ostia – two witnesses saw him getting into a boat on his own and going out as it was getting dark. As soon as he was out of the harbour, he anchored in a quiet cove. The boat was five hundred metres from the shore. A finance police coast patrol sighted it around ten. Valerio Bona had hanged himself from the crosstree, on the mast. There's no doubt that he did it all by himself.'

Piccolo gave herself time to pause. She was hesitant. 'He left a note,' she said at length. 'It's his writing all right. Shall I read it out?'

She shot a glance at Balistreri, unsure.

'Come on, Piccolo, read it out.'

She looked down at the piece of paper and began to read.

'We should have told the truth then, but lacked the courage. I leave my punishment in God's hands.'

'Who's it addressed to?' Balistreri asked.

'There's no more in the note,' Piccolo said, 'but there is something else. There was a single outgoing call from Valerio Bona's mobile after he was questioned. We contacted the phone company, which was quick to supply the information. It was to the Vatican switchboard.'

This time Cardinal Alessandrini's personal assistant was adamant. The Cardinal was celebrating Mass, then he had to accompany the wife of a foreign head of state on a private visit to the Sistine Chapel and then he had to go over the Pope's Angelus address, which he would give at noon from Val D'Aosta where he was on holiday.

Balistreri knew he'd already overstepped the mark, but made up his mind to force the situation. A crisis between the Italian state and the Vatican meant a lot less than the life of Fiorella Romani.

He called Floris at nine that morning, went to meet him and spelled out his plan. The Chief of Police heard him out attentively, his reactions somewhere between incredulity and horror. Finally he smiled and shook Balistreri's hand.

Floris called the Minister of the Interior in person. The Minister was strongly opposed to it, but Floris pointed out that Balistreri was a loose canon and would certainly get in touch with Linda Nardi to call a press conference if things did not go his way.

The Minister called the Prime Minister's Undersecretary, a man famously close to Vatican circles. Only the explicit threat of a press conference, during the course of which Balistreri would attribute direct responsibility for Fiorella Romani's death to the Cardinal, persuaded the Undersecretary to call Alessandrini. He made his apologies, saying that Balistreri was out of control and would be replaced as soon as possible, but suggested that the Church, already under accusation for its defence of Roma rights, might like to try to avoid any further trouble. The Cardinal allowed Balistreri thirty minutes at ten sharp in the Sistine Chapel. Although he had lived in Rome for so many years, Balistreri had never been there.

Alessandrini's assistant was shocked and disgusted by Balistreri's scruffy appearance. The Cardinal arrived punctually, dressed in his vestments. Coming dressed like this further underlined the light years' distance between them, a gap that Balistreri had only a few minutes to bridge.

The greeting was extremely cold. 'I thought we had finished with our reciprocal confessions,' Alessandrini said instantly. 'Nevertheless, let's take a walk together – perhaps it will do your spirit good. I hope it's in a better state than your appearance.'

They set off walking slowly, while Balistreri tried to gather all his strength together. He was there for one reason only and could not allow himself to be distracted either by his contempt for the Cardinal or by the wonderful ceiling that people from all over the world came to admire.

'You haven't much time, Eminence, and Fiorella Romani has even less.'

'I've already told you all that I could yesterday, Dottor Balistreri.'

'Marius Hagi's told us that Fiorella Romani will die this afternoon unless you can tell me—'

Alessandrini held up a hand to stop him and came to a halt by the altar with the *Last Judgement*. Christ was its presiding figure, with his calm imperious gesture and severe gaze directed at those descending into the pit of hell; beside him the Virgin Mary sat with the resigned appearance of someone who can no longer intervene in judgement, only look sweetly at those ascending to the kingdom of heaven.

'What do you see there, Dottor Balistreri?' Alessandrini asked.

'I see a God who strikes fear and beside him a woman who looks unhappy because she can make no decisions. I see poor wretches horrified, on one side and the other. Perhaps it's justice, but I see no mercy.'

Alessandrini was deep in thought. 'At one time they would have burned her at the stake, Balistreri. Evil is a part of the divine plan as well. Christians like Gina Giansanti know this and accept it as a test, waiting for that moment, the one you see in the fresco, when God metes out justice.'

A lesson in theology. He doesn't want to help me. Or can't. It's part of the divine plan!

Balistreri took an envelope from his pocket and showed Alessandrini the photographs of Elisa, Samantha, Nadia, Selina, Ornella. Burns, bruises, letters carved into the flesh.

Alessandrini wouldn't touch them. He moved sharply away and walked towards the exit. Balistreri looked desperately at his watch

– his time was up. He saw the master of ceremonies with the wife of the head of state already waiting. The Cardinal was some distance away when he turned back towards him.

'Pass on our conversation to Marius Hagi. Tell him to listen to the Angelus address.'

He called Floris on his mobile to tell him about the conversation while he drove back once again with Corvu through the traffic in the morning heat to Regina Coeli prison.

'The Premier and the Minister of the Interior are very worried,' the Chief of Police told him.

'About relations with the Vatican, surely not about Fiorella Romani.'

'Balistreri, I'm not worried about my position. We already have too many deaths to mourn, and there's no point in useless debate. Offer Hagi anything you can.'

'The man's dying, *Signor questore*. We only have the truth to offer him.'

'What are you thinking of doing?'

'I can only trust what Cardinal Alessandrini said. I'll pass on what he said to Hagi.'

'But he didn't tell you anything!' Floris protested.

'Shall we let Hagi be the judge of that?'

The graffiti on the walls were inciting people to set fire to the travellers' camps. Several slogans were signed by pseudo-civic organizations. Political posters proposed drastic solutions.

If Fiorella Romani dies, it'll be the start of a massacre. Hagi's always known this. It's part of his plan.

They got to the prison at eleven thirty. Hagi was waiting in the interrogation room next to a television, as Balistreri had requested.

Balistreri passed on everything in detail – the alibis, Valerio's suicide note, his conversation with Cardinal Alessandrini on *The Last Judgement*.

Hagi nodded, pleased with the news of Valerio Bona's phone call to the Vatican, but it was the summary of the conversation with Alessandrini that excited his interest. He asked for it to be repeated to him twice with barely concealed satisfaction.

Then he turned to Balistreri. 'And so? What's the answer to my question?'

'I'll tell you after the Pope's Angelus address.'

'Then let me have a cigarette.' It was forbidden in there, but Balistreri decided to ignore the fact and lit one himself.

Twelve o'clock was the start of the link-up with Les Combes in Val D'Aosta, where the Pope was spending several days on holiday.

'Dear brothers and sisters!'

The Pope was smiling and in great vigour. He spoke about the Middle East, expressing solidarity with those unfortunate peoples. Then he changed the subject.

'Yesterday we celebrated the memorial of St Mary Magdalene, Our Lord's disciple, who occupies a prominent position in the Gospels.'

The Pope went on with his address on Mary Magdalene, then came to the conclusion. Balistreri saw Hagi suddenly look attentive.

'Mary Magdalene's story reminds us all of a fundamental truth: a disciple of Christ is someone who, in the experience that is human weakness, has had the humility to ask him for help, has been healed by him and has turned to follow him closely, becoming a witness of the power of his merciful love, which is stronger than sin and death.'

The Pope ended with a reminder of the Middle East situation, then he began to recite the Angelus.

'You can switch off.' Hagi was lost in his thoughts. He appeared to be following one particular thought that was far away, one of regret perhaps. Then he looked at the circular clock on the wall. It was twelve forty.

'I'd like the answer to my question, Balistreri.'

'The Cardinal lied because of his presumption in distinguishing good and evil, and now he's humiliating himself like Mary Magdalene before God, and asking for your help, Hagi. He lied for fear that we would accuse two young men, who he maintained were innocent, of a terrible crime. One was Manfredi. As for the other—'

Hagi was coughing more than ever, and the hollows under his eyes were darker and deeper. Balistreri could see the veins pulsating under his transparent temples and the bones sticking out over the ever-deeper hollows in his cheeks.

He's dying. And Fiorella Romani with him.

'And what will you do now, Balistreri?'

'I swear to you that Elisa Sordi's killer will be punished, whoever it might be . . . But I beg you to save Fiorella Romani, who's not guilty of a thing.'

'Do you think my wife was guilty of anything?'

Balistreri had by now gathered that this was what had unleashed Marius Hagi's lucid madness. He shook his head.

'No, your wife Alina was guilty of nothing. But it was her fear of you and misfortune that killed her, not a killer who tortures, strangles and carves out flesh—'

Hagi interrupted him. 'It was your wretched Catholic religion that killed her! It was Anna Rossi, Valerio Bona, Cardinal Alessandrini and that young priest with the red hair—'

'Father Paul.'

Hagi was now beside himself, coughing and spitting blood. 'Yes, Father Paul, who had lunch with Elisa that damned Sunday, the last day of her life. Alina told me, she'd seen them in a bar near the parish. And she saw Valerio Bona as well, spying on them.'

This was why Valerio had called Alessandrini in the Vatican before hanging himself. It was to remind him of the truth.

'Alina was terrified of you, Signor Hagi, and by something that you still don't want to tell us about. And yet your wife wasn't the kind to scare easily.'

'Well then, I'll spell it out clearly, Balistreri. Ulla had overheard a conversation of the Count's. She told Anna Rossi, Samantha's mother, about it. And she passed it on to Alina that I'd thrown Elisa in the river. And my wife, poor innocent young girl that she was, was terrified by the damnation of hell into which your God threatens to send even those who remain silent in order to protect their own husband.'

Balistreri was incredulous. 'All these deaths to punish someone who had turned Alina against you and in a vendetta twenty-four years later? You could have thought about it before, couldn't you?'

'I thought about it many times, but I don't know the name of the main guilty party, the one who killed Elisa Sordi, initiating all the rest. Because I threw her in the river, but when I took her out of that office she was already dead, you can be certain of that.'

'And do you know who did it now?'

'No, Balistreri. It's because of you that I still don't know. But as of last year I do know this,' and he pointed to his handkerchief spotted with blood. 'And I can wait no longer, I have no more time. You are my help in finding the guilty person.'

'What do you think you'll achieve acting like this? The name of a killer? Or the massacre of Romanians in Italy? You're turning this country into a hellish pack of racists running amok!'

Hagi looked at him mockingly. 'Like that Nano I shot between the shoulders that night—'

Enraged, Balistreri lost control and launched himself on him. He felt the blood pounding in his ears and bursting his eardrums and temples as he squeezed Hagi's neck. The prison officers rushed to stop him. Fortunately one of them was built like an ox and pulled Balistreri off Hagi as if he were a leaf.

Hagi was spitting blood on the floor and coughing as he held his throat. But he continued to flaunt his mocking gaze while the prison officers were holding on to him.

'Call a doctor,' said Corvu.

'There's no need, it's nothing serious,' said Hagi, massaging his neck. Then he turned to Balistreri. 'You see how little it takes to kill, Balistreri? But you already know that, don't you?'

'That's enough for now,' said Corvu. 'You can take this animal back to his cell.'

'No,' said Hagi. 'Now we're going to get Fiorella Romani.'

'Let me go. I've calmed down,' said Balistreri to the officers, who let go their grip but placed themselves between the two men.

'You're not going anywhere, Hagi,' Corvu said.

'Then say goodbye to Fiorella Romani and you add another death on your conscience, Balistreri. And what's it going to change anyway? One more, one less . . .'

He wants your rage. He wants to turn you into a beast like himself.

The thought calmed him down. 'I don't believe you any more, Hagi. You can't know if she's even alive.'

Hagi glanced at the clock on the wall. It was a minute to one.

'Switch your mobile on, Balistreri, right now.'

There's still one thing he wants to do and that is to destroy you. It's his price for saving Fiorella.

As soon as it was on, the phone rang. 'Hello?' said Balistreri.

The voice was a terrified whisper. 'It's Fiorella Romani. I'm begging you, come get me and bring Titti to me!'

The call ended abruptly.

Balistreri called Fiorella's mother. 'Who is Titti?'

Franca Giansanti's voice gave a start. 'It's her favourite cuddly toy, her pet Titti. Her grandmother Gina gave it to her as a present. Dottor Balistreri, what's happening?'

'Just trust me, Signora. I'll let you know before this evening.'

In order to let Hagi out of prison, even though under escort and in handcuffs, the Chief of Police had to make the decisive call to the Minister of the Interior and the Minister for Justice.

'This is sheer madness, Balistreri. But I don't care if we all sink in order to make one last attempt to save this girl,' said Floris.

'You're a decent man, *Signor questore*.'

'Thank you, Balistreri. So are you. Do be careful.'

Balistreri instinctively felt for the Beretta in his holster.

He came back into the room. 'Where do we have to go, Signor Hagi?'

'It's a beautiful sunny afternoon, they tell me. So today let's go to the seaside. I'll come in the car with you.'

'We should go in a police van,' said Corvu.

But Hagi didn't agree.

'No, let's go in a lovely ordinary car. I want to enjoy the view, seeing as it'll be the last trip I make. And if I don't see the view I can't show you the path to her salvation.'

Afternoon

They formed a line of five vehicles, the first and last two containing four armed policemen. In the middle was the car with the four of them: Corvu at the wheel, Piccolo next to him, Balistreri in the back with Hagi in cuffs. They left at two thirty in the scorching hot afternoon. The car's thermometer said it was 40 °C outside.

'Take the Via Pontina towards the coast,' Hagi ordered.

As they left the centre of Rome, Hagi was silent, looking keenly at the pavements crowded with tourists, the Tiber and the open-air restaurants. There was little traffic. In that heat everyone was at the beach or up in the hills. It took them only twenty minutes to get onto the Via Pontina, an almost motorway leading south of Rome to the coast.

'Where are we going?' Corvu asked.

'Straight on. There's still time.' Hagi seemed completely absorbed in the panorama.

Balistreri gathered this was not going to be a short trip.

'Take the cuffs off and give me a cigarette, Balistreri,' Hagi ordered.

'Not the handcuffs,' said Corvu.

'Then you can turn the car round and go back. These are the last cigarettes I'll ever smoke and I want to smoke them with my hands free, as I've always done.'

'Free his right hand and cuff the left to the seat,' Balistreri told Piccolo.

Then he gave Hagi a lit cigarette.

'Don't you have the Bella Blu lighter any more?' Hagi asked him, inhaling.

So you want to talk, damn you? All right, let's talk.

'Who's waiting for us at the seaside?' Balistreri asked.

Hagi gave a little laugh. 'Don't be impatient; you'll see when we get there. But if you have any other questions, I might answer some of them. Go on, take advantage of it; I'm happy to do it today.'

Balistreri saw Corvu's warning glance in the mirror, but he had no wish to be cautious. By now he thought he knew who had killed Elisa Sordi, but this would not help save Fiorella Romani. It was a mosaic in which several faces were still missing, one in particular.

'Very well, Signor Hagi, let's start with Samantha Rossi. Why her?'

'I've already told you. It was Anna Rossi who passed on to Alina that I'd seen to the removal of Elisa's body and then persuaded her to run away. It was as if she had killed her. I could have avenged myself on Anna right away, but I'd already learned to my cost that a greater pain is the death of someone you love. And so I chose her daughter. And please, I must insist, tell the lady that if she'd minded her own business, her daughter would still be alive today.'

He heard a deep intake of breath from Giulia Piccolo and placed a warning hand on her shoulder. Hagi wanted to provoke them, but they had to remain calm and focused on the single objective that day: saving Fiorella Romani.

'And why Nadia?'

'Oh, Christ, why all these questions I've already answered? Because she looked like Alina and Alina had also hurt me.'

Balistreri wasn't convinced, not for a moment. 'I think you're stretching it here. The more so after Camarà saw you with Nadia in Bella Blu's private lounge.'

Hagi shook his head. 'It wasn't me. I could meet up with Nadia any time I wanted. It was someone else who wanted to meet her there.'

Piccolo turned around instantly. 'Colajacono,' she exclaimed.

Hagi had a fit of coughing mixed with laughter. 'You are such a fool to be fixated on that poor man. Colajacono had been invited that evening so that he'd be more deeply involved in what was about to happen. Poor fool, he thought it was about blackmailing a politician and that Nadia was being used for that. He was an idiot, but a useful one.'

'But it was you who telephoned Vasile. You went to get the Giulia GT at the top of the hill with Adrian's bike, left the bike there, picked up Nadia, took her to Vasile and left on the bike . . .' Piccolo came to a halt, confused.

Hagi laughed. 'You're missing out something, aren't you? Who killed Nadia?'

'No,' said Corvu, correcting him. 'You went up on the bike, took the car and left the bike on the hill, then you went to pick up Nadia in the car towards six thirty. You slowed down when you mistook

Natalya for her, then you were lucky to find Nadia on her own . . .'

'I've never been lucky in my life; I've only ever had an excellent assistant,' Hagi said placidly.

Balistreri had already reconstructed that part.

'It was the man who couldn't get it up with Ramona, to give you time to make off with Nadia, the one you went with on the bike to collect the Giulia GT that would be used to pick up Nadia on Via di Torricola. Then you both came back from the hill separately, one on Adrian's bike and the other in the Giulia. At six o'clock you picked up Nadia while he kept Ramona busy. Then you handed Nadia and the car over to your assistant. It was he who took her up while you went home to where the bike was hidden and then on to Casilino 900 to take presents to the children.'

Corvu and Piccolo stared at him amazed via the rear-view mirror. Hagi clapped his hands. 'Bravo, Balistreri, you're beginning to understand something after all these years. Carry on, you'll see what comes up from the distant past . . .'

Balistreri ignored the provocation and continued.

'Your assistant waited two hours while Vasile had sex with Nadia and then dropped off asleep through the drink. Then he strangled her and carved the letter E on her. Alessandrini was right about you, Hagi – you're not the kind of man to rape, strangle and carve letters on girls.'

Hagi nodded. 'I prefer to torture the ones who remain alive, not those who're dying. That's my speciality, Balistreri.'

Making no comment, Balistreri went back to his reconstruction of events. 'You went to pick up your assistant with the bike after the celebrations at Casilino 900, while the others went to St Peter's Square. You left the car up there and came back down together on the motorbike.'

Hagi seemed genuinely pleased with Balistreri's progress, as if someone could finally understand his plan and admire its grand strategy.

'That's right, Balistreri, exactly like that. It was he who carved the letters on them all, including Elisa Sordi. It was an ugly thing, I wouldn't have been able to do it, but that's how my assistant is, you see. He enjoys these things.'

'A collaboration that came into being twenty-four years ago,' said Balistreri, carrying on regardless. 'The Count assumed Manfredi hadn't killed Elisa and wanted someone to go and talk to her, calm her down and offer a deal. The first thing he did was call Francesco Ajello.'

Hagi made a slight bow. 'Bravo, Balistreri. I see your brain is working today. Francesco was to make a deal with her in exchange for her silence. But when he went into the office, he found she was already dead. He called me to help him out. We gave the office a good clean-up, then we carried the body away in the boot of my car. Ajello went to watch the match with friends and I saw to disposing of the body in the river. That wasn't very pleasant. Before dumping her in the river, I had to see to the cuts and cigarette burns to make it seem as if she'd been tortured a long time there. But now I'm tired, Balistreri. Hand me another cigarette and leave me in peace.'

They didn't speak for a while. Hagi smoked in silence, watching the road signs go by one after another. Pratica di Mare. Pomezia. Anzio. Nettuno. It was nearly four thirty in the afternoon and Via Pontina in the sun was absolutely deserted.

Balistreri was unsettled. Something wasn't quite right. That insistence on Nadia was ridiculous. Without her and the broken headlight on the Giulia GT no suspicions would ever have been aroused.

'I want to talk about the letters of the alphabet,' said Corvu all of a sudden.

'A childhood passion of my assistant, perfected over time,' Hagi replied, as if they were talking about art or sport.

'I'd like to know if we have to use the initial of the Christian name for Ulla and Giovanna Sordi, as with your wife Alina.'

Hagi was amused by the question.

'You're quite gripped by this puzzle, aren't you, Corvu? I, on the other hand, find it childish, and also dangerous for my assistant. But he's determined to finish it. For Ulla the initial "U" is correct. But ever since her daughter's death, Elisa Sordi's mother wore a pendant on her bracelet with an engraving.'

'A golden heart with the letter "E",' Corvu remembered, thanks to his infallible memory.

'But there's already an "E" immediately before, the one carved on Nadia,' Balistreri protested.

'You're very alert today, Balistreri. It's true, there are two consecutive "E"s. My assistant is very particular, a little like Corvu. He insisted there needed to be two. As to the rest, killing Giovanna Sordi was a simple pleasure.'

'Killing her?' Piccolo echoed, turning pale.

Hagi sniggered, coughing and spitting blood into his handkerchief.

'A stroke of genius that your idiotic World Cup final made quite easy. My assistant met her that morning at Mass and told her that he would reveal the truth about her daughter's death. But in exchange she would have to join her daughter that same evening.'

'I don't believe it,' said Corvu, 'Signora Giovanna was a self-righteous woman, her life ruined by grief, but she wasn't a fool – she wouldn't have believed him.'

'Ah, but you see, it was easy for my assistant to persuade her. He told her he knew the killer's name and offered it in exchange for her jumping off the balcony. She swore on the Virgin Mary that she'd do it. And besides, what better occasion than another World Cup? Who knows, perhaps if Italy had missed the penalty, the lady might not have jumped. But in that case my assistant would have seen to matters and helped her see it through to the end.' Hagi was coughing and laughing.

Piccolo turned round, furious, and Balistreri shot her a warning look.

'And how did your assistant make her believe he knew who the killer was?' Corvu asked.

'Very simple. He revealed a detail that only someone who had witnessed the attack on Elisa would have known. And he could do that, without any doubt.'

'So,' concluded Corvu, 'the sequence is OUAREEVI plus the last letter.'

Hagi was clearly amused by this insistence. 'I see that this is an irresistible puzzle for Corvu, and so I'll give him a little help. The sequence is correct, but it's still missing the first letter.'

Corvu had to correct the skid, swearing in his native Sardinian. Piccolo turned round with her eyes ablaze, pistol in hand. Balistreri put his hand between the barrel and Hagi's face.

'Piccolo, put the gun away and put the cuffs back on.'

Balistreri tried to remain icy calm, but the restlessness he felt a little earlier was slowly becoming agitation. Something was not right. He felt it as if the shocks of a distant earthquake epicentre were approaching.

The truth is never straight. Truth is a circle. The first letter, before Elisa Sordi.

The call came on Angelo Dioguardi's mobile while he was out on Linda Nardi's terrace. It was nearly five thirty in the afternoon.

He went back into the flat. She was curled up on the sofa and dressed as if she were cold.

'That was Father Paul,' he told her. 'He wants to speak to me about something important. He said an hour from now over at San Valente.'

She nodded, sad. Perhaps the decisive moment had come. She smiled at him and caressed his hand tenderly. 'Thanks, Angelo.'

Hagi was looking at the road signs. They said the Sabaudia turn-off was one kilometre away.

'We've nearly reached our goal, Corvu. Take the turning for Sabaudia,' he said. On her mobile phone, Piccolo notified the officers in the cars in front and behind.

The five cars turned and took the long tree-lined avenue into Sabaudia's white central square with its bell tower and square-shaped Fascist-era buildings.

They went on towards the beach. The seafront was full of cars, parked among the sand dunes, and beautiful villas overlooking the sea. They proceeded at walking pace under the still blinding sunshine opposite the sea crowded with swimmers, surrounded by families dressed in swimwear and carrying ice creams and rubber dinghies. Hagi had chosen the most absurd setting: here death could slowly fill the space that life occupied in the way that a colourless and odourless – but lethal – gas could invade a beautiful lounge full of people.

'The gate to the next villa's open,' said Hagi. 'Let's pull up just before it.' He looked at Balistreri's wristwatch. 'Good, getting on for five thirty, so we're slightly ahead of time. Now I can tell you exactly what to do so as not to make this a wasted journey.'

'And what do we have to do?' asked Balistreri patiently.

'My assistant is in the villa with the girl. Since five o'clock he's been holding a pistol pointed at her temple, so if you attempt to enter, Fiorella Romani will die. You'll have to let me go in alone and convince him that you're going to find out who killed Elisa Sordi.'

'We wouldn't dream of it,' Corvu burst out.

'Then do what you like,' said Hagi calmly.

'Did your assistant know that you'd be here at this time?' Balistreri asked.

'Of course. It was fixed up some time ago. He knew he had to call your mobile at one o'clock and he did so. If I didn't arrive by five thirty he would kill her. As you see, we're very precise, we leave nothing to chance,' said Hagi, pleased with himself.

He's enjoying himself; it's his big show. But he's keeping a surprise finale for us.

A five-year-old girl knocked on the car window, smiling and shaking an ice cream cone. Hagi signalled 'ciao' to her with his hand. A man with few days to live, in handcuffs. And yet he was as happy and peaceful as a little kid on a school outing to the seaside. Balistreri was trying to keep back the troubled feeling that was building up inside him. He had left Rome believing he had the situation under control: he knew who had killed Elisa Sordi, he knew who was waiting for them in Sabaudia. But now he wasn't so sure.

'I want your word that Fiorella's still alive and you'll return her to us,' Balistreri said.

'You'll have to allow me time to explain to my assistant all the lies that were told in 1982 and convince him that you will succeed in getting to the truth. I swear on my wife's memory that Fiorella Romani will be returned alive to her family.'

'I can't take off your handcuffs,' said Balistreri, 'and I'll remain outside the villa and call out to you every so often. If you don't reply, then we're coming in.'

Hagi smiled. 'OK, but don't be concerned about my safety, Balistreri. My assistant wouldn't ever do me any harm. And now I must go or it'll be too late.'

They let him get out, a thin little man in handcuffs who staggered slightly, coughing and spitting blood onto the asphalt bubbling in the sun. Hagi paused a moment to contemplate the sea and all the everyday happiness around him. Looking at him in that moment, poised motionless between life and death, Balistreri felt certain that he, too, was suspended with Hagi in that hazy borderland.

Then Hagi went in.

If I'd had a father, I'd never have had to seek the truth. If I'd had a father, the sufferings of two tortured adolescents would never have come together. If I'd had a father, then all those women would never have been killed. The Invisible Man haunting Michele Balistreri is the poisoned fruit of too much guilt and too much remorse, including my own.

Hagi had been inside for half an hour. Balistreri was waiting ever more nervously with Corvu and Piccolo under a tree in the garden, a few yards away from the noisy bathers. The police had the villa completely surrounded. Chief of Police Floris was in direct communication by mobile. Every so often Balistreri called out to Hagi, who replied: 'Everything's fine. We're still talking.'

At five minutes past six, Hagi calmly came to the door. He addressed Balistreri.

'My assistant wants you to swear to him in person that you'll be able to nail Elisa's killer.'

'Not on your life,' said Corvu, 'Dottor Balistreri's not coming in and you're coming out of there right now.'

Hagi looked at Balistreri. 'I swore on the memory of my wife that Fiorella Romani is inside here, alive. If you'll come in, I swear to you that Fiorella will go back to Rome, alive. Otherwise . . .'

Balistreri knew that only by going into that house would the girl be saved. He looked at the beach, bubbling over with life, then at the dark door of that villa. He was ready to pay his price. Absurdly, Angelo Dioguardi's face on television and his senseless bluff came into his mind.

He was risking everything.

He turned to Corvu and Piccolo. 'All right. If I don't come out with Fiorella Romani after twenty minutes, you break the doors down and come in.'

He saw Piccolo angrily wipe away a tear of frustration and heard Corvu swear in Sardinian. There were further discussions and objections, but Balistreri calmed his deputy officers down, then followed Hagi into the villa. It was six fifteen.

At six twenty Angelo and Linda embraced on the landing.

'Are you still sure?' she said, in a last moment of doubt. This was the point of no return.

'Sure,' he said, slipping into the lift. It was as if he were gathering the pile of chips towards him in the decisive hand of the game.

The house was cool, bathed in shade, the shutters closed and the lights out. The sunlight barely entered. They went into the living room. Fiorella was blindfolded, gagged, handcuffed and tied to a chair, but she was alive.

'I'm from the police, Fiorella. In a while I'll take you home – just a few minutes more.' The girl gave a start under the emotion, Balistreri stroked her hair reassuringly.

Hagi was sitting in an armchair. The pistol in his handcuffed hands was pointing directly at him.

'Sit down, Balistreri. We still have something to say to each other before we say goodbye for ever.'

Balistreri sat down opposite Hagi. He was ready to look evil in the face.

Today your life has to end in order to save an innocent girl.

'I expect you to keep your promise, Signor Hagi,' Balistreri said, indicating Fiorella.

'I always keep my promises, Balistreri. But I always avenge the wrongs I've suffered. This is our last meeting.'

He seemed like Lucifer in person. Dark shadows under his eyes, the thick eyebrows, his eyes a feverish red.

'Light me a last cigarette, Balistreri, and put it on that little table without coming any closer.'

Holding the gun in one hand, Hagi took the lit cigarette in the other cuffed hand and stuck it in his mouth. The sunlight filtered in from outside along with the muffled sounds of the bathers. The divide between life and death was a wooden shutter discoloured by the sun and salt air.

Hagi inhaled the smoke greedily, at ease in the armchair. He was enjoying every moment of his victory. He seemed to be in no hurry at all.

'Why have you done all this, Hagi? Plotting with a maniac killer for an accomplice and also with the Secret Service, then all those deaths among your Romanian friends too.'

'They were my troops, Balistreri, and died in a war against your civilized people who are nothing more than deceiving bigots, whorish wives and corrupt police, like those who plotted with Elisa Sordi and urged Alina to turn against me. But they will all pay for their guilt.'

'I can understand the vendetta against Valerio Bona, Anna Rossi and the Cardinal. And I can understand the one against me, because I let Elisa's real killer go free. But what have the Secret Service, the Roma, ENT and Dubai got to do with it . . .?'

Hagi greedily took a few last drags on the cigarette.

'One year ago I was diagnosed with lung cancer. Incurable. I had to move quickly and a lightning war requires soldiers and allies, Balistreri.'

'You dragged the Roma into this business, Signor Hagi, in order to unleash the hatred of the Italian people on them, you and the part of the Secret Service that lets itself be used for such ends, that is.'

'The Secret Service used me and I used them, Balistreri. I wanted revenge and they wanted to subvert once and for all the political equilibrium on which this rotten country of yours has rested for the past sixty years. They counted on doing it by setting off a wave of general and uncontrollable violence against the Roma people. We gave each other a helping hand with great pleasure.'

'Nothing of that kind will ever happen, however. The Italians have many defects; perhaps they are racist, hypocritical conformists and corrupt, but they're opposed to violence. There will never be an uprising against the Roma, even less against Romanians.'

'You're mistaken, Balistreri. Mistaken once again. The next death will be a truly dreadful one. The victim will be a young Italian woman and she'll be butchered to death. The Italians will certainly rise up.' He gave a diabolical smile and a sneer. 'And you, Balistreri, will be in the front rank leading the slaughter.'

You only deliver suffering to those who survive, not to the dead. Eternal suffering.

'You coughed on purpose while they were raping Samantha and while you were speaking to Vasile on the phone. You smashed the headlight on the Giulia GT on purpose to help the investigation along. And finally, you chose Nadia just because she was connected to you, so as to lead the police to you, so you'd be captured and brought here.'

Hagi's ice-cold eyes stared at him in irony. The glow of his last drag on the cigarette lit up his face in the darkness. 'Are you afraid at last, Balistreri?'

Hagi was only one half of the evil. The other half was the Invisible Man who had killed the girls and who had spared his life that night on the hill.

Incredulous, Balistreri felt the cold knife blade of fear. He had never been afraid of death, not since that moment thirty-six years earlier when he had stopped liking himself. But this fear was worse than death – the fear of dying while still alive. A punishment demanded by the devil, not by God.

★   ★   ★

The Invisible Man was feeling euphoric and a little depressed at the same time. In a little while the debt would be settled. By that evening all his enemies would have been annihilated and his grand design achieved. He thought about what was passing through Balistreri's mind at that moment one hundred kilometres away and allowed himself to smile.

Nothing compared with what he will suffer later. And later I will no longer have a mission to accomplish.

He had left Sabaudia at a quarter to three, when his informant confirmed the departure of five police cars from Regina Coeli, one carrying Marius Hagi. Before leaving he had had time to eat sea bass baked in salt with an excellent glass of white wine in a restaurant near the villa that looked out onto the sea.

He had arrived in Rome at five o'clock, in time for his first task, which he handled with great facility. Another debt paid, another enemy eliminated.

At a quarter past six he parked below the apartment. At twenty-five past he saw the man leaving in his car. The trick had worked. For an hour she would be alone while Hagi kept Balistreri busy in the Sabaudia villa. More than enough time to really enjoy himself and leave the traces of evidence collected by Hagi in Casilino 900 to implicate the Roma.

He decided to wait ten minutes, to make sure the other man didn't come back. It was now six thirty. Another five minutes.

At six thirty Balistreri suddenly got up from his seat. Hagi did nothing to stop him, only followed him with the pistol in his hand. He had understood what was going on: Hagi wanted to keep him there as long as possible, but was not authorized to kill him. This was Hagi's pact with the Invisible Man.

He quickly crossed the hall and opened the door to the cellar. Immediately he smelled the sickening odour of death. He didn't even think of taking out his Beretta. While he went down the wooden steps he felt every step taking him closer to both evil and the truth.

He came down into a dark humid place, Hagi behind him with the pistol in his hand. Light was filtering in from a door at the end of the room. The smell of death was coming from it. He opened the door wide.

Francesco Ajello was stretched out on his back, naked, his wrists and ankles bound to the four corners of a bed, his castrated testicles and penis stuck in his mouth. His guts had been torn out from a huge gash in his abdomen and were spread over the sheet and the tiled floor.

Balistreri staggered and retched. Hagi gave him a push and made him fall among the vomit, guts and blood. Then he pointed the gun at him. 'Stay right where you are.'

In a flash of understanding, Balistreri remembered that Hagi was only trying to play for time and couldn't shoot him.

Through desperation, he forced himself to get to his feet. Hagi stepped back three paces and put the pistol in his handcuffed hands to his temple. He stared at him one last time, his demonic eyes burning with a whole lifetime of hate.

'The first letter is a "Y" and you are already dead, Balistreri!'

Then he pulled the trigger. It was six thirty-five.

At six thirty-five the Invisible Man again meticulously checked the pistol he had used a little while ago, the scalpel used for the incisions still dark with Ajello's blood and the skeleton keys to open the doors. He had forty-five minutes in which to simulate a break-in and a robbery. In a plastic bag he had hairs and fingernail fragments from two Roma in Casilino 900 that Hagi had given him.

He put on gloves and a surgeon's cap. They were almost superfluous; no one would have looked for his DNA in there. Then he set off on his last mission. The main door opened for him easily. He went up on foot. Every step on those stairs took him away from his age-old unbearable pain and brought him closer back to life.

If things had gone differently on that first occasion with her, perhaps I wouldn't have killed all the others. I often wondered about this at the beginning. After all these years I don't even know how many I killed any more and the question has changed: would I be a better person if I had killed only her in a single moment of madness?

While Corvu and the policemen made a search of the house and Piccolo saw to Fiorella Romani, Balistreri briefly informed the Chief of Police and asked him to organize a helicopter in order to save time in getting back. After a few minutes, at six forty-five, he, Corvu, Piccolo and Fiorella Romani were in the air.

Clouds were gathering in the sky and were about to deliver one of those wonderful storms he had come to love over the years. But this summer rain reminded him of another time on that grey dawn when Ulla dei Banchi di Aglieno had leaped from her penthouse.

Unsettled, Balistreri put on his headset and stretched out on his seat. From up on high he could see bathers running for shelter as the first drops of rain hit the beach.

The first letter is a Y. And the last one isn't for Fiorella Romani. So it's YOUAREEVI?

He remembered where he'd seen this written: YOU ARE EVIL.

It was where he'd felt he should look right from the beginning. Right back in 1982.

'Linda,' he cried. 'Linda.'

A living death, Balistreri. The eternal punishment.

At six forty, the Invisible Man had entered with no trouble and without making any noise. The apartment was calm and quiet.

The setting sun was shining in from the French windows leading onto the terrace. She was sitting out there, her back to the flat, looking over to St Peter's.

'Ciao, Linda,' said the Invisible Man. He had waited twenty-four years to be able to say those two words again to his first victim, Y.

She turned slowly, her face calm. 'Ciao, Manfredi.'

She had already seen his photos, the ones taken with his face remade, handsome, smiling in his surgical gown, as he was opening the hospital wing in Nairobi on Christmas morning, only a few hours after killing Nadia in Rome.

When he met her at the Charlemagne School he was the same as she was: young, intelligent, sensitive, lonely and suffering deeply from his deformity and an impossible father, as she was from never knowing her own father. He was a tortured adolescent looking for a love that would reassure him that life was worth living.

Over the years, Linda had often reflected on this.

If, on that first occasion with him, things had gone differently, if I'd only considered how intelligent and sensitive he was and hadn't rejected him because of his deformity, perhaps Manfredi wouldn't have killed all the others.

But in the last twelve months she'd understood that by now, whatever the change in Manfredi's face, nothing could change what that lonely adolescent had become: a benefactor of Africa's poorest and a killer of innocent women. The boy beast who wanted to become the handsome prince was now a handsome prince with a caged beast inside him that could never stop killing. A deliverer of pain and death to punish the world that had rejected him.

Manfredi came towards her. 'I gave you notice I'd come.'

'Yes, your card came a year ago. Then the girls started to be killed and disfigured. I knew that you'd be here sooner or later. But you've been a bit careless.'

This was true, thought the Invisible Man. That card had been a weakness, and careless of him. But the desire to terrorize her had been too strong in him. And then, after all, he was invincible.

'Good, Linda. Luckily we have a bit of time for what I have in mind. Do you like my face a little better now?'

'I've already seen many photos of you, Manfredi, taken in Africa.'

'Really? And who gave them to you?'

'Angelo Dioguardi. He went in search of you for me in Kenya ten days ago. And he discovered about all those young Kenyans killed and disfigured over these past twenty-four years.'

Manfredi laughed. 'That was my training for you, Linda. It wasn't so much fun with the natives, but I made up for it with Samantha, Nadia, Selina and Ornella.'

'If you kill me, Angelo Dioguardi will report you.'

Manfredi looked at the pistol in his hand and felt the scalpel in his pocket. This would be fun.

'You know, Linda, today I'm settling scores with my old enemies and untrustworthy accomplices. I disembowelled one before lunch, then I paid a visit to that worm, Father Paul, Elisa's confidante. Before killing him, I forced him to call Angelo and ask him to come over. I wanted to save Angelo because he was the only one in 1982 not to accuse me, and he's only a harmless fool. But right now I'm going to dedicate myself to you and then I'll wait here for him, as I'll have to sort him out as well.'

Linda's mobile rang. She looked at the display panel and then at Manfredi. 'It's Michele Balistreri.'

Any one of them could have found himself in my place that first time. And it is to these men who have lived without remorse or honour that I intend to dedicate myself. And to one in particular.

It's too soon. There must have been some hitch with Hagi, Manfredi thought, mildly unsettled. Then he decided instead that it was a magnificent occasion. Indeed, an irresistible one.

He knew he was committing a small error, another act of arrogance like the card he'd sent a year ago to Linda. Two faults in a genius plan. But they were justifiable risks. The thought of delivering terror to Linda Nardi and Michele Balistreri brought pure joy to his heart.

He took Linda's mobile and hit the reply button.

'Hello? Linda!' Balistreri's voice was a cry of desperation above the deafening roar of the helicopter blades.

'No,' said Manfredi in his calm voice.

'Is that you, Angelo?' Balistreri asked, uncertain.

'No, Balistreri. Remember that night on the hill? My name is death.'

Manfredi hung up, pointing the pistol at Linda. He was a little displeased because now he would have to hurry, while he had been hoping to spend more time with her. But that conversation paid him back for everything. Balistreri would pass the rest of his days cursing himself.

'I'm sorry, Linda, unfortunately I have to hurry. In a little while Balistreri will be here to shed tears over your corpse.'

She hesitated. She still felt a few crumbs of sympathy for him, for all the suffering that being what he was had brought him. It was her rejection of him that had pushed him into violence and to his first criminal act. A very sweet adolescent who had really loved Linda. She had rejected him only because of his deformed face, and he had wiped her out and set off on his journey of death.

It's not a vendetta for what you did to me. It's for all those murdered girls. For all the ones you'd murder still. Because you are the deliverer of evil, Manfredi.

Linda closed her eyes. 'Kill him,' she said softly.

Manfredi felt the voice at his back before even hearing it.

'I'm here, Manfredi.'

He recognized the voice and smiled. He certainly wasn't afraid of that big kid with no guts, he who had never been afraid of anyone. He turned round slowly, in no hurry, preparing to shoot.

But Angelo Dioguardi had been ready for this moment for a long time. His Beretta Combat Combo, 40 calibre, exploded five times in rapid succession.

Balistreri landed on the Ministry roof at seven. While Piccolo took Fiorella Romani to the office, he and Corvu rushed over to Linda Nardi, sirens wailing. They arrived in less than ten minutes. 'Wait for me downstairs, Corvu. Don't let anyone up.'

Corvu protested, but Balistreri was already running upstairs, pistol in hand, his heart in turmoil.

Linda's dead. And so is my life.

The apartment door was half open; he rushed in and came to a stop. Linda was on the sofa. Angelo Dioguardi was rigid next to her, his eyes swollen with tears, his hands trembling, the Beretta Combat Combo at his feet. Manfredi's body was face down on the tiled floor in a dark pool of blood.

Balistreri felt the tears stinging his eyes, his legs giving way from tension and what felt like a lifetime of fatigue. An uncontrollable trembling ran though his exhausted body as he slowly sank down on his knees before them.

He wanted to hug them both but couldn't manage to lift his arms. He wanted to share in their desperation and their joy but couldn't manage to open his mouth either.

Now he finally knew. Not only what was now clear, but also what pain had buried over time, even the most unmentionable truth. He looked at his hands, then at Angelo, then at Manfredi's corpse.

Every one of us could have found himself in his place that first time. We're all capable of killing. Me, Hagi, Manfredi, even Angelo.

Then Angelo spoke, his gaze lost in space. 'Michele, there's never been anything between Linda and me.'

The words were pathetic, misplaced, pointless, and yet indispensable. That was Angelo Dioguardi. The former likeable big kid, good humoured, a bit crazy and simple minded, who had become a poker player of international fame, and a man who would help anyone who needed it, exactly like Manfredi.

He had shared twenty-four years – nights of poker and talks till dawn in the car – with that kid and that man. And now he had sacrificed himself in his place. He had done for her what Balistreri had refused to do.

Today I'd only kill someone if I were forced to do so. But she wanted him dead, not in prison. And Angelo was the right man.

'I know, Angelo. I know now. You were protecting her from him. But you should have told me. I should have done it, not—'

'It was right this way, Michele. It was something I had to do.'

Balistreri bowed his head and gave him a caress he couldn't restrain. Then he looked at Linda, but she avoided looking at him. She would never look at him again. She was holding Angelo's hand as if he were a small child who had to be protected.

Instead of calling the police, Balistreri told Corvu to come up, and together Linda and Angelo told them everything.

Linda was extremely calm. Holding Angelo's hand, without ever looking at Balistreri, she told her story. 'We both went to the Charlemagne School. I was at middle school, he was in the upper school. Manfredi was an intelligent, sensitive kid. There was no one who could listen to me and understand me like he did.'

Balistreri was watching her, trying to meet her eyes. But what he was looking for was no more.

'We were two kids suffering from life. I had no father, he had a domineering one and that disfigured face.'

Linda was quiet for a while. It seemed she was searching for measured words even for that dreadful memory.

'One day, at the beginning of spring in 1982, we were taking a stroll in a distant corner of the Villa Borghese Park. Manfredi declared his love for me and tried to kiss me. I smiled to play down the rejection, but he felt I was mocking him and he gave me a slap, then he started lashing out at me.'

She paused again, without ever looking at Balistreri.

'He couldn't manage to rape me; he was impotent. And he lost his head. He was screaming that he'd been reduced to this state because of his face and us – all the girls who kept teasing him. He went crazy. He took a razor from his pocket and carved a little Y between my breasts.'

With an involuntary gesture she brought a hand up to her breasts, to the breasts that had suffered the offence. While Balistreri was attacking her, she had held her arms over her breasts, not her pubis. 'In the end he left me there and I managed to get to a first aid station. I told the police I'd been attacked by a group of drug addicts and only told the truth to my mother.'

'Why didn't you report him?'

'I was a mixed-up kid, always stoned on marijuana, and I had no problem going off with other boys. The only one I rejected was him, the most sensitive of them, the only one who really loved me. And you know why? Because of his face.'

'You had every right to, Linda. It was up to you to choose.'

Finally, she turned to look at him. 'Oh, sure, it was up to me to choose. But I gave him no choice, neither then nor today.'

'Didn't you think he could have done the same to other girls?'

'In the beginning, no. It was this too that stopped me from reporting him. Then, when the TV said he'd been arrested for Elisa Sordi's murder, I wanted to report him. But his mother committed suicide and they said it'd all been a mistake. I didn't want to be the one to make him suffer any more.'

'And he never contacted you again in person?'

'No. Manfredi went to Africa and I started to live again, and with a lot of help from my mother I tried to forget. For years I thought of Manfredi not as a monster but as a victim. My victim.'

By now he knew Linda Nardi. She had accepted the evil that Manfredi had done her with the tolerance of St Agnes.

'Then he came back,' said Balistreri.

Linda nodded. 'A year ago, the day after Samantha Rossi's death, I found a card in the letterbox. It said: *I'm back.*'

The Invisible Man's one true mistake. It had been stronger than him, stronger than the danger he knew he was running sending that card. He, the invincible, had to terrorize Linda Nardi, his first failure. It was the start of his accursed path.

'But why didn't you report him even then?' Balistreri protested.

'In the beginning I wasn't even sure that it was him. You didn't want to tell me if there had been any letter carved on Samantha. I had a private investigator make some inquiries, but Manfredi didn't seem to have been present in Italy at the times of the deaths of Samantha and Nadia.'

'Then I told you that Ramona's client was impotent and you managed to persuade yourself,' Balistreri remembered.

'Yes. And you told me about Alina Hagi's death at that time. So then I also began to think of Elisa Sordi. After Giovanna Sordi's suicide I knew he had to be stopped. In a permanent way.'

Because your tolerance is equal to your decisiveness. I would have arrested him and you wanted him dead.

She read his mind once again. 'Thanks to his father they would have judged him to be mentally unstable and put him in the psychiatric ward instead of prison. Then he would have escaped to Africa and killed other women.'

Balistreri looked at Angelo Dioguardi. 'And you persuaded Angelo to help you.'

'I couldn't do it on my own. I explained the situation to Angelo, telling him everything. The idea was mine and mine alone; he bears no responsibility.'

Angelo made a feeble protest, but she continued.

'He accepted and we made ready. Angelo was with me always. We expected Manfredi to come forward in some way. Today, when Father Paul's call came, we knew it was him. Angelo went out to show himself to Manfredi, then he came back in via the garage before he came up and hid himself in the kitchen.'

Balistreri shut his eyes. It was premeditated murder. Even with all the extenuating circumstances the sentence would be a good many years for both of them.

But Balistreri didn't consider it for a moment. Whatever different kind of justice Manfredi deserved, God would see to it, if he existed. And whatever injustice he'd suffered in his life, including that dished out by Balistreri, Linda Nardi and Angelo Dioguardi, Manfredi had in any case lived twenty-four years too many, killing many people. Angelo Dioguardi and Linda Nardi had done what he should have done if he'd still had the stomach for it.

Balistreri and Corvu instructed them in the details of all they should and should not say to the police. Then they called Floris, and only after Balistreri and the Chief of Police had reached an agreement did they call the police in.

No one asked Balistreri and Corvu what they had spoken about for over half an hour with Angelo Dioguardi and Linda Nardi before calling the Chief. There was no record of that half hour in any report. Despite the clear conflict caused by the friendship that linked them, Floris and the Public Prosecutor happily allowed Balistreri and Corvu to take statements from Angelo Dioguardi and Linda Nardi. No one else questioned them; the Public Prosecutor confined himself to recording their replies in silence.

The story Dioguardi told was very simple. He had been a member of a shooting range for years and had even been there that Sunday morning with his lover Linda Nardi, and there were witnesses. Then he'd been to lunch at Linda's, and preferred not to leave the bag containing his ear defenders, gloves and pistol in the car, which was parked on the road.

At six twenty he'd gone down to look for a tobacconist, but as soon as he set off in the car he realized he'd left his wallet containing his driving licence in the bag in Linda's kitchen. He'd gone back in through the rear entrance in the garages. Linda was out on the terrace, so he'd gone straight into the kitchen to look for the bag.

Then he'd heard Manfredi's voice, the threats to Linda, his confession about having killed all those girls, and the phone call with Balistreri. He'd pulled his Beretta out of the bag and gone out onto the terrace. Manfredi had his back to him. He'd told him to throw down his pistol and put his hands in the air, but Manfredi had turned round quickly with the pistol in his hand and Angelo had shot him five times.

Evening

At the late evening meeting with the Chief of Police and the section head no one raised any objections about the incredible coincidences: Dioguardi's coming back via the garages, his possession of a loaded pistol and, above all, his incredible reaction time when Manfredi had turned to face him and Dioguardi had taken him out, as if – beyond having the pistol – he was already mentally prepared to shoot him dead.

Therefore, it was neither excessive use of self-defence nor premeditation.

The reconstruction of Manfredi's movements was equally simple. He'd left Via della Camilluccia on the Saturday evening after his meeting with Balistreri and had joined Ajello at his villa in Sabaudia, where the lawyer had been entrusted with guarding Fiorella Romani. On Sunday morning he'd given Ajello a sleeping pill and tied him to the bed. When he woke up, Manfredi had disembowelled him. One more inconvenient witness less, like Colajacono and Pasquali.

Then he had calmly left Sabaudia, after having lunch in a restaurant whose receipt was in his wallet. Next, as the telephone company's records showed, he'd called Father Paul on his mobile, asking to see him.

He'd arrived at San Valente parish church a little after five. Paul was alone; the children were all at the beach with the volunteer workers. Under threat, he'd forced him to call Angelo Dioguardi and asked to meet him. Then he'd taken him down to the cellars, shot him and shut his body in a storeroom, taking away the key. Finally, he had gone to Linda Nardi's. The police had found Father Paul's body that evening in the storeroom in San Valente.

Ramona recognized Manfredi in the photo sent via e-mail to Bucharest. He was the famous client who had made her waste time because he couldn't get it up. Hagi had handed Nadia over to him in the Giulia GT and had come back to pick him up with Adrian's bike at Vasile's farmhouse after Manfredi had killed Nadia. Then they'd left the bike in Hagi's garage and taken the hire car with which Manfredi had picked up Ramona.

Hagi had taken him to Rome's Urbe airport, where they handed back the hire car and where the ENT aircraft was waiting for Manfredi to take him to Zurich in time for the Nairobi flight. In this way, despite the two-hour difference in the time zone, he'd arrived in time to open the hospital. They still had to clarify why Manfredi's name didn't appear on any passenger list, but Balistreri had his answer for that.

This was all purely investigative reconstruction; there wasn't even any proof of Manfredi's presence at the crime scenes, not even in the cases of Ajello and Paul. As regards Giovanna Sordi, it was probable that he'd approached her on the Sunday morning after Mass. Manfredi was with Elisa when her mother called, therefore he knew the subject of that conversation and so had persuaded her. But this was only more investigative speculation.

The only certain thing was the attack on Linda Nardi. During that long evening meeting on the evening of 23 July, the government, the Chief of Police, the Prosecutor's Office and the police all chose to keep the matter quiet. Manfredi's tragic end was minimized and set apart from the rest. An old Charlemagne School friend who was showering his attention on Linda Nardi. An argument with her actual lover and then his tragic death. Nothing about a serial killer, nothing about scalpels, nothing at all.

The death of the young women and the desecrations were all attributed to Hagi, who had been present the whole time – the perfect scapegoat. Hagi had been killed in an exchange of fire with the police during Fiorella Romani's dramatic liberation. Francesco Ajello had been his accomplice and Hagi had killed him while he was alone in the villa. How he came to do this, given that he was handcuffed and unarmed, was never explained.

Count Manfredi dei Banchi di Aglieno was informed of the tragic accident in which his son lost his life by an apologetic Chief of Police while he was in Nairobi and embarking on the night flight to Frankfurt.

Balistreri accepted everything without making any objection. He was able to obtain the concession that the name of Linda Nardi's lover who accidentally killed Manfredi dei Banchi di Aglieno remained hidden away in the Prosecutor's Office archives. It was a feeble secret, but one that nevertheless would enable him to buy a little time.

Sunday night 23–Monday 24 July 2006

Balistreri sent everyone away and shut himself in his office for the whole night. He thought again of Marius Hagi's words: *A lightning war requires soldiers and allies, Balistreri. They used me and I used them. We gave each other a helping hand.*

At a certain point in his life Marius Hagi had met one of his allies, namely Manfredi. Was it a chance meeting? Highly improbable. Someone had brought them together. Someone who knew them both very well and knew the origins of their hatred and desire for revenge. Hagi wanted to avenge himself against the Catholic circles that had turned Alina against him. Manfredi hated the young women who had humiliated him since he was a boy.

First Linda, then Elisa: he had desecrated them, but not killed them.

So he and Hagi had chosen the first victim. A young woman, Samantha Rossi: perfect for Manfredi and even more so for Hagi, being the daughter of Anna Rossi, who had alienated Alina from him. But it wasn't enough. There were other personal enemies: Linda Nardi, the original guilty party for Manfredi. And naturally that loudmouth show-off Michele Balistreri who had provoked his mother's suicide and let Elisa's real killer go free. It was here their destinies had been joined.

Corvu had been his usual efficient self. He had mobilized the right contacts and had a photocopy of the Minister of the Interior's appointments register for Sunday, 11 July 1982.

It showed that Count Tommaso dei Banchi di Aglieno had entered the Ministry at six fifty and come out at seven thirty-five, as Balistreri knew twenty-four years ago – nothing new there.

But it was another signature in that register that Balistreri wanted to check. The signature that countersigned the times – that of a young Ministry assistant in 1982, Dottore Antonio Pasquali.

He leafed through Pasquali's diary, the one Antonella had given him containing the dates and a few cryptic notes in English.

3 January 2006	B. End
11 July 2006	B. restart
16 July 2006	damn!!
20 July 2006	my call
21 July 2006	OK 27

They were stupid notes, hiding nothing. But then Pasquali had made them only for himself, a memorandum of his contact with the voice that told him what to do. The same one that, by chance, Selina Belhrouz and Ornella Corona had the misfortune to hear.

3 January 2006	Belhrouz killed in Dubai.
11 July 2006	Balistreri opens investigations again, after having spoken to Camarà's girlfriend and Fred Cabot.
16 July 2006	Selina and Ornella killed. Personal danger! Selina's body found near his house.
20 July 2006	Pasquali calls, for the first and last time, to ask to eliminate Hagi.
21 July 2006	Pasquali receives the go-ahead to eliminate Hagi in caravan number 27. It was a trap.

It was a perfect plan, one that only Manfredi's card to Linda had rendered null and void. But for Manfredi, the terrorizing of Linda Nardi and Balistreri's eternal remorse were indispensable, worth much more than the murdered and disfigured girls.

Nonetheless, Balistreri recognized something else in that plan, something grandiose, which had to do with a philosophy of life – an authentic personal signature.

Everything had been expertly planned, brought together and carried out. Hagi's vendetta against the Catholic world that had taken Alina from him and Manfredi's against women had been ably inserted into a much wider plan to destabilize democracy in Italy. A plan that took advantage of the growing racism towards the Roma and Romanians, and of the Italians' fear of the barbarity coming from Eastern Europe. Young girls raped, tortured and killed, as always by the Roma in the travellers' camps, up to the point where the people would turn and attack them. And then the police wouldn't have been enough any longer – the army would have been needed. And, along with help from the friendly part of the Secret Service, a new strong political leader would emerge, who wasn't involved in the catastrophe and was incorruptible. A man of honour.

Everything had served this design, even the private vendettas of Hagi and Manfredi.

ENT's nightclubs and amusement arcades were used to launder money of dubious provenance; the purse of the Secret Service's rogue element that financed the whole operation, and unfortunately became caught up in it thanks to the lighter Nadia took from Bella Blu; the accomplices who became superfluous or dangerous – Belhrouz, Colajacono, Pasquali and Ajello – abused, and their guts torn out. Accusers from the beginning – like Giovanna Sordi, Valerio Bona, Father Paul – forced into suicide or silenced. And the necessary sacrificial victims – Samantha, Nadia, Selina, Ornella – slaughtered without mercy. Accidental obstacles, like Camarà, eliminated immediately.

The most atrocious part of the vendetta had been reserved for the two greatest enemies, Linda Nardi and Michele Balistreri, who had ruined Manfredi's life when he was still a teenager. And also the unscrupulous use of the Romanians, Hagi and the others, and the exploitation of the Roma and the travellers' camps; fodder that was indispensable for extending the plan beyond the limits of personal vendetta and developing it against the whole democratic political class, both government and opposition, and the Vatican too.

The effects had been seen: crimes rightly or wrongly attributed to the Roma, the travellers' camps such as Casilino 900 still remaining in the city to exasperate the already heated souls of the Italians, hostile graffiti on the walls, the growing number of public declarations from the usually politically apathetic that confused Roma with Romanians, the growing tension with the government in Bucharest, and the Vatican as the sole defender of the rights of these people who felt almost under siege.

Certainly, the intention of Pasquali's low-profile role was to support a change in Rome's city council. But above him there was someone who was aiming higher, much higher: if a famous Italian journalist had been attacked, tortured and killed in her own home near St Peter's, if it had all been arranged so that the murder could be attributed to the Roma by means of the false evidence planted by Manfredi, the situation in Italy would have exploded. With the Secret Service's help there would have been an indiscriminate witch-hunt against all gypsies, a call for 'ethnic cleansing', a severe diplomatic crisis with Romania, and increased tension with the European community that would call upon the Italian government to arrest and put on trial those Italians who attacked any Roma and Romanians.

At this point Italian democracy would be on the edge of the abyss into which somebody wanted to throw it. If Italy didn't obey, it would be expelled from Europe. If it did obey, the much-tried and well-fomented people would have gone out onto the streets to topple the government and Parliament. And the Vatican, by now marginalised, would keep silent.

In either scenario, the Head of the Special Section was certain a solution was ready: a strong man with an impeccable image who would have taken over to put things back in order.

Balistreri recognized the absolute conviction of someone's rights and the wrongs they suffered, the use of the lives of others as if they were pawns in a game, the defence of one's honour as an absolute right. Balistreri recognized the style; in the end it was his own adolescent point of departure.

There remained one last aspect of Hagi and Manfredi's vendetta: who had really killed Elisa Sordi. In their absurd and twisted logic, this person was the true culprit of all their troubles, and couldn't remain unpunished. Hagi and Manfredi had died without knowing the name that Balistreri had just barely glimpsed when he'd attacked Linda Nardi.

Now that everything was clear, now that he had all the answers, he wondered what the young Balistreri would have done.

A shot to the back of the neck. But then his accomplices would have taken revenge and I couldn't protect everyone in eternity. They would have slaughtered Angelo, Linda, me, Alberto and his family, Corvu, Piccolo, Mastroianni.

He wondered what the adult Balistreri would do.

A charge and arrest. A well organized trial, a just sentence. Same outcome as the one above. Or rather, one that was worse, because with the support the man had it would be difficult to get him condemned.

He racked his brains the whole night. The Count would have thought the same as he did, not like the Cardinal. He wouldn't wait for divine justice. But where was the happy medium between the two?

Monday, 24 July 2006

Morning

At dawn, under the pretence of identifying Manfredi and taking advantage of the fact that the Count was still travelling, Balistreri had the Count's personal secretary, domestic staff and the residential complex's concierge brought in. They were taken to the mortuary and before being allowed to enter were asked to hand in all metallic objects, including keys.

'See to it that they're kept busy with bureaucratic procedures until I get back,' Balistreri ordered Piccolo, taking a copy of the penthouse keys.

He took Corvu and Mastroianni with him. They arrived at seven thirty and entered the deserted apartment. They went immediately to Manfredi's room, where he and Teodori had questioned the boy in 1982. Nothing had changed, apart from a laptop computer he was working from, a new full-length mirror in the private bathroom and the removal of curtains from the windows.

The walls were still covered in Heavy Metal group posters. The one he remembered was in the dark corner in which Manfredi had taken shelter during the stormy exchange with him and Teodori.

A man dressed as Satan and ten small women, each one of whom was wearing a T-shirt with a letter of the alphabet from which white blood dripped. The ten letters made up the album title: YOU ARE EVIL.

He opened all the drawers, then rummaged under the jumper at the bottom of a wardrobe. It was all there: Elisa Sordi's missing earring, the blouse with the initials S. R., Nadia's little sweater worn away at the elbows, the glasses worn by the myopic bookworm Selina Belhrouz, Ornella Corona's winking watch.

They photographed it all, without touching a thing.

And lastly, folded away in a drawer below some underwear, he found a crumpled sheet of paper. It was a capable drawing, done in pencil. He recognized the view – it was the one from the terrace. There was a window and a withered flower in the picture and beneath it, written more recently in another pencil, were a couple of sentences. Balistreri recognized it as Manfredi's handwriting.

If things had gone differently with Linda on that first occasion perhaps I wouldn't have killed all the others. I often wondered about this at the beginning. After all these years I don't even know how many I killed any more and the question has changed: would I be a better person if I had killed only her in a single moment of madness?

Afternoon

Pasquali's state funeral took place in the afternoon in a church in the historic centre in the presence of the President of the Republic, the Prime Minister and many other ministers, politicians, civil servants and policemen. Hundreds of ordinary citizens gathered outside the church in the churchyard and the square beside it, together with the vans of the television crews.

After the public ceremony, the coffin was taken to Verano for the private ceremony and burial. There, inside the cemetery church, his wife had asked for a private Mass for his closest colleagues, friends, and relatives from the small Abruzzo town where Pasquali had been born and raised.

Balistreri entered last, settling himself near the entrance, enjoying the smell of incense and cool in contrast to the nearly 40 °C of humid heat outside. Standing up, he followed the Mass while Corvu, Piccolo and the others sat in the pews further down.

I confess to Almighty God and my brethren that I have greatly sinned.

The priest's incipit caught him unawares.

The ceremony went on swiftly and silently.

Mea culpa, mea culpa, mea maxima culpa.

The words he'd rebelled against in 1970. The words that had slowly caught up with him like a nemesis, paralysing the rest of his existence.

Count Tommaso dei Banchi di Aglieno materialized beside him. He was not in penitent mood, but had accepted the meeting Balistreri had asked for.

And here he was, the supreme evil, the single architect of the grand design, whose voice on the telephone terrorized Pasquali. The man who hadn't hesitated to exploit his son's private vendetta to aid his programme of destabilization, the man who had littered his path with corpses not for money but for power, out of the total and blind conviction of his own ideas.

The man who for once should have given up, faced with the impossibility of knowing who had finished Elisa Sordi off after his son had beaten and disfigured her and left her unconscious in that room.

They went outside into the open, without waiting for the Mass to end, and took a last stroll among the graves in the sunshine.

Balistreri was sweating copiously while the Count was his usual impeccable self, well groomed, and not a drop of sweat on his dark suit.

His first-class night flight from Africa hadn't tired him; the crow's feet around his eyes were only slightly deeper.

He's a father who's just lost his son. His only Achilles heel. My life insurance policy.

'I have only a few minutes, Balistreri. I must pay my respects to the widow of my very dear friend Pasquali and see the Minister of the Interior, who wants to extend his condolences to me. Then, before I return to Africa, I have to see my legal team about transferring Manfredi's body to Kenya. I don't want him to be buried in Italy. Kenya was his real country.'

Balistreri was ready to say what he had to to him, but the man standing there among the graves, without pity or fear, was something more complex than a simple enemy.

He is the supreme evil, not Hagi or Manfredi.

It was pointless giving the Count a summary of what had happened. He knew it all, and the little he didn't know he'd come to know in a few days' time. It was pointless as well to threaten him by talking about his calls to Pasquali recorded in a simple diary. There was no proof; the Count would have squashed him like a worm.

'I want to propose a pact,' said Balistreri at last.

Walking in silence and showing little interest, the Count listened to the description of the absolutely certain proof of Manfredi's guilt. He didn't appear to be surprised, let alone worried.

'I'll proceed in such a way that no one will know a thing. In everyone's memory, your son will remain a benefactor of the poor. In exchange, I want your word that you will not kill or have anyone killed any more.'

The Count fixed him with his gaze. There was no anger, no threat, but only again that same subtle contempt of 1982.

'It's a pity that you've turned out this way, Balistreri. I know your CV. As a young man I shouldn't have disliked you – you had promise, you rebelled against the forces of obscurantism and corruption. A real pity. Quite a wasted life, yours.'

'Don't you want your son to be remembered as a benefactor rather than a killer?'

The Count stopped among the graves.

'Manfredi was a murderer, Balistreri. He became one because of the preconceptions of this Western society based on bourgeois hedonism and Catholic hypocrisy. He was a kind, cultured little boy who was fearful. He was rejected by women because of his face. For the same reason you accused him of a crime he didn't commit and we still don't know who the culprit was. And then he was even manipulated by me, his father. It was I who introduced him to Marius Hagi, in order to bring their personal vendettas into my plan.'

'Manfredi didn't know that Hagi and Ajello had shifted Elisa Sordi's body, desecrated it and thrown it in the Tiber?'

'He knew nothing of it. He knew neither Hagi nor Ajello. But I knew from my brother what Manfredi was continuing to do in Africa – killings, disfigurements. I knew my son had an illness that wasn't his fault. Then, a year ago, Hagi came to tell me that he had lung cancer and before he died he would kill Anna Rossi. Manfredi was in Rome. We spoke together on the terrace, the three of us, for a whole night. And we decided that it would be more efficacious to kill Samantha Rossi. But everything has a beginning, Balistreri, and you are a fundamental part of that beginning.'

The Count stretched out his arm and pointed to three headstones side by side. Balistreri turned and froze.

In the centre was Elisa Sordi's grave, on either side those of Amedeo and Giovanna.

'Look at them, Balistreri. Under there lies buried the only thing that has always escaped me: the truth, the name of Elisa's real killer. Can you disinter it from there? Then I'll honour the pact, you have my word.'

The Count fixed him with his stare one more time, then turned his back on him and walked away.

Balistreri looked at the three graves. It was exceedingly hot, but there were fresh flowers on all three.

Monday, 31 July 2006

The order of the day, at all levels, was *to let things settle*. Central government, city council, the opposition, the Vatican, Secret Service and the police were all agreed: they had to let the dust settle on memory's antique furniture.

For a few days, that bloody July in Italy even reached other national and international media. But the press never knew the reality. It wasn't necessary, nor was it prudent. The press knew what the politicians and the Vatican had agreed on. A deranged Romanian living in Italy, Marius Hagi, together with his gang and with the help of a nightclub owner, the Italian lawyer Francesco Ajello, had killed four young women and four courageous members of the forces of law and order: Coppola, Tatò, Colajacono and Dottor Antonio Pasquali. The deaths of Father Paul and Manfredi had nothing to do with the above crimes, and there was no link between the two either. Elisa Sordi received no mention. Count Tommaso dei Banchi di Aglieno left for Kenya with the body of his son Manfredi, the victim of a crime of passion after a disagreement over a woman.

By the end of July the newspapers were already busy with the latest infighting of internal politics, the Pope's vacation and the football transfer window.

Chief of Police Andrea Floris ordered Balistreri, Corvu and Piccolo to take the whole month of August off, something they hadn't done for years. Corvu and Piccolo set off by car for Albania and the Ukraine with Rudi and Natalya as guides. Balistreri accepted his brother's invitation to spend the month in his house in the Dolomites.

Before leaving Rome, he tried many times to contact Linda Nardi. Both her landline and her mobile rang and rang, but there was never any reply.

On 31 July, his last night in Rome, he arranged for a goodbye supper with Antonella before going on holiday. They sat down together at one of the little wooden tables on one of Trastevere's many crowded pavements. Suntanned and relaxed in front of a pizza and a beer, Antonella seemed much more attractive to him. Her hair was cut to make her seem much younger, her eyes were more luminous, her skin softer.

'You look terrific tonight.'

'After Pasquali's funeral I switched off from the outside world. Five days at the beach and a beauty farm. I haven't relaxed so much in fifteen years, Michele.'

'*Brava*. You finally allowed someone else to pamper you instead of always looking after everyone else.'

'They really did pamper me. Face masks, sunbeds, relaxing massages . . .' and she shot him a wicked smile, '. . . actually not very relaxing; the basic ingredient was missing.'

Balistreri was feeling lighter in his soul, which he felt had been lost for years. He made a sudden decision. Fortunately the restaurant toilet was sufficiently large, clean and private. It was something brief, a little uncomfortable, but very satisfying for both of them.

Afterwards, tottering somewhat from the drinks, they set off on foot to Antonella's place, laughing like idiots at the idea of two adults taken up with the mad idea of having sex on top of a restaurant toilet seat.

At her place they made love for a long time, more relaxed and with less urgency. Then, stretched out on the bed, all the lights out and the windows open for the cool and the silence of the night, she lit the usual joint and began caressing his hair. He was drinking his third whisky.

They were lying beside one another, worn out but alive, in a way that each of them hadn't felt – for different reasons – for a long time. Balistreri wasn't aware she was trying to hand him the joint. The glowing end was a small point in the semi-darkness, following the movements of her hand.

He was lying on his back, staring at the old beams and panels overhead. Despite the semi-darkness he could make out the plan perfectly.

He was rejected by women on account of his face and accused for the same reason. But he was innocent.

He could make out marks on the wood inflicted by time and damp.

A kid who was impotent. A love that was impossible. A recent abortion.

There were cracks in the wood at the points where the wood-worm had been most at work.

A faded tulip on Elisa's desk. A fresh tulip on her grave.

Now seeming detached from his body, his eyes wandered towards the ceiling.

I should have fucked you like an ordinary whore. Yes, Michele, you should have. Perhaps then you'd have understood this business, at last.

While he was attacking Linda he had guessed the truth. Then, at that time, all his efforts were concentrated on Fiorella Romani and he'd put the intuition aside. But after the pact with the Count in front of those three graves, it had come back to him. His brain, however, was proving to be lazy and reluctant, incapable of getting into alignment the perpetrator, the motive and the opportunity. The marijuana and the whisky were mingling in his body, in the silence of the night, as he was lying beside a woman to whom he had just made love.

The beams on the ceiling were the features of a face, the cracks were its lines, the marks were its eyes and mouth. All of a sudden he saw it, the face that was desperate and upset: perpetrator, motive, opportunity.

Not only our reason, but also our conscience, submits to our strongest drive, the tyrant in us.

Epilogue

I arrived in the Dolomites on August the 1st and was welcomed by Alberto, his wife and their two adolescent sons. I was put into the quiet and spacious guest room with a view of the mountain peaks.

And thus my long summer began. I slept a great deal, went for bicycle rides, facing up to the steep slopes and crazy descents, played tennis with my nephews, went shopping with my sister-in-law, and chatted about everything with Alberto and their friends and neighbours.

Even the two house martins with shiny black heads that had made a nest under the portico guttering aroused my interest. One day, while they were off fluttering about, I climbed a ladder and saw the two eggs in the nest. At the end of the first week in August two chicks were born and the father disappeared. My sister-in-law told me that on the plain this happened in June, but that at a height of 1,500 metres the eggs hatched in August and from that moment it was up to the mother alone to look after the chicks for about twenty days. Sitting in the sun, I watched the mother coming back with worms in her beak, welcomed by the chicks' insistent twittering. I found myself in an emotional state counting the days leading up to the first flight for the two house martins and, for me, the first autumn rain.

I gave no thought to work, to crimes, deaths and perpetrators. Inevitably, from time to time, I thought about Linda and Angelo, losing myself in imaginary conversations with them, as if nothing had changed. Then I rapidly fled from those thoughts and retreated to nature and rest.

In the late afternoon I would sit out in the large garden, facing the green mountain slopes, looking down at the dots that were houses in the valley below. Every day I hoped for the rain that never came. I waited for sunset, feeling the days growing shorter and coolness overtaking the heat. Then, when dusk fell and the dots of the houses began to light up, I went into the house with the others.

The last Saturday in August a small house martin took flight from the nest and landed not far from me, where the lawn ended and the rock overhang began. As I was wondering how to help it, the little bird looked up at the nest where the mother was watching it together with the other fledgling. Then it took flight, singing happily, towards the valley.

That evening Alberto told me that Angelo had called. He was coming by and would stop and say hello. He came for lunch in his old beaten-up vehicle with presents for the boys and my sister-in-law. He looked different. He was surer of himself and at the same time more subdued.

We ate together out in the sunshine in the garden, talking of this and that: the vacation that was coming to an end, the school term that was about to start, and poker tournaments. After lunch, Alberto announced that he had to take his wife and the boys to an end-of-summer festival in another little village. It was his excuse to leave us alone. Before setting off, Alberto took us both by the arm.

'When Angelo comes back from Australia, let's get back to our poker with Graziano, shall we?' It gave me a tender feeling to hear my brother trying to sound convincing, more to himself than to us. Then they left for the festival.

The silence in the large garden was broken only by a desperate cry. The second house martin, much smaller than the one that had flown away, was on the ground right under the nest. Its mother was hopping around it, concerned. The little bird seemed injured in one wing; it must have fallen during its first attempt to fly.

We watched it, not sure what to do. We decided to let the mother take care of it and went to sit on the lawn facing the huge green valley with cigarettes and whisky. Many years earlier we would have started to talk of women, poker and Paolo Rossi. Now we smoked in silence, contemplating the mountains and the valley below. The twittering of the two house martins was the only sound in the whole valley.

Two old friends with their memories, many of them good and a few that were very bad.

I came out with the question more to break that absolute silence than anything else. 'Do you know where she is?'

'She phoned me in the middle of the month; she was about to leave for Africa. She's set up a project to collect money for a foundation in Manfredi's memory. She's got together a whole bunch of financiers and wants to build a new hospital along the lines of the one in Nairobi.'

I wasn't surprised, nor was I indignant. I knew by now that Linda Nardi belonged to another world.

'She believes that if she hadn't rejected Manfredi, he wouldn't have killed the other women,' Angelo explained.

'But at the same time Manfredi couldn't have made Elisa pregnant, and Linda knew that from direct experience,' I added.

Angelo nodded in confirmation, lost in a distant thought. 'Linda knows that Manfredi attacked Elisa, but she also knows that it wasn't him who killed her.'

I didn't ask him how Linda came to know with such certainty. By now I knew the answer.

'You both risked getting yourselves killed, Angelo. A moment's hesitation and Manfredi would have shot you both.'

He turned to look at me. 'There are moments when I have no hesitation, Michele. I've tried to let you know that in every way I can.'

All of a sudden, a dark cloud came out of nowhere to obscure the sun and a cold breeze swept the grass of the lawn. Angelo Dioguardi was relaxed, observing the valley from a distance that could have been a metre or infinity.

'I went by the cemetery before leaving,' I said. 'There were fresh flowers on the three graves.'

Angelo nodded. 'Elisa adored tulips. She told me that a Turkish legend has the flower's origin in the drops of blood shed by a young woman out of love.'

I had that flower before my eyes in 1982 and 2005, but didn't want to see it.

'A tulip on Elisa's windowsill. A tulip on Manfredi's chest of drawers. A tulip on Margherita's desk. All of them withered, Angelo, all but the fresh one you placed on her grave.'

Angelo Dioguardi looked at me with an apologetic smile, the same childlike smile as on that first day at Paola's as he was rolling about in the bathroom between feigned bouts of retching. It seemed another lifetime, but the man was the same. The same man who always apologized for his highly successful bluffs in poker. Now he was excusing himself to me for the bluff with which he had risked everything to play with life itself, winning and losing everything at the same time.

'Margherita's a bit like her,' Angelo went on, 'she's full of life, trusting, naive. The evening we met she told me she adored tulips. For a while, I deluded myself into thinking I could go back to living again. Then I thought of Elisa's mother throwing herself off the balcony and it reminded me who I really am.'

Who are you, Angelo Dioguardi? You crossed the line only once in your life and it was over that young goddess. And out of the blue you found out about a pregnancy. Michele Balistreri would have resolved everything with a brutal 'Goodbye, my dear'. You, on the other hand, took it all upon yourself, lying to your girlfriend and uncle, the Cardinal, the abortion, the tears and remorse of Elisa who was about to confide everything to Father Paul. And for a moment, one single moment out of your whole lifetime, crushed by all those weights, you gave in to desperation and rage.

It was getting cool. The sky was filling with dark clouds and the rumble of thunder was approaching. There were flashes of lightning in the distance.

Angelo Dioguardi had reacted by facing up to life, trying to act kindly to others and performing good deeds for many. But it wasn't enough for him. When Linda Nardi asked him for help with Manfredi, he had told her the whole truth and had accepted killing Manfredi as a last act of expiation for his enormous sin.

Angelo wanted to explain to me what I already knew and had never wanted to hear.

'When I went up to Alessandrini, he was furious. He knew that Paul had had lunch with Elisa and he ordered me to fire her. I was terrified, afraid that Elisa would tell Paul about the abortion, as they were talking to each other a lot in those days. Then Alessandrini and I called you from the terrace and while you were coming over I told the Cardinal I had to go to the bathroom.'

I should have gone up to Alessandrini with you, but I was blinded, my eyes tearful with lack of sleep, smoking, drink, the blinding sunshine that afternoon, the mad idea of going to see Elisa . . .

'I know, Angelo. I called the Cardinal yesterday. He didn't know the reason for the question, but he still remembered that you went to the bathroom.'

Angelo went on with his pointless explanation.

'I didn't go to the bathroom, I went down to see Elisa. I wanted to talk to her, calm her down, comfort her. Thirty seconds later I was on the second floor. The office door was locked, which was odd. Now we know it was Manfredi who locked it. I opened the door with my set of keys. Elisa was flat out on the floor, not moving, with her eyes and cheek swollen, half naked and bleeding from a cut on a breast. On the table, I saw a letter she was writing to Father Paul, telling him about her affair with me and the abortion. I put it in my pocket and then lost my head.'

To Valerio she appeared to be dead. Manfredi swore he'd left her no more than injured. One of the two was lying, or they were both mistaken.

So Corvu had pronounced at the end of his detailed analysis of the alibis. But rather they had both spoken the truth. Manfredi had left her alive and a few minutes later Valerio had found her dead.

'You were coming up, Michele. I had half a minute, a chance that wouldn't come again.'

I should have understood straight away, when I saw you trembling on that landing and I saw you desperate and upset for the whole of that incredible night. I should have understood when I saw that faded flower on Margherita's desk. You did everything you could to tell me, in your own way.

Angelo gave a last apologetic smile.

'There was a cushion she used to sit on. I used that. Thirty seconds later I was up on the floor above, waiting for you.'

You can throw the whole of your life away in a moment of madness. A cushion pressed against the face of a girl who was almost dead already. A boat in the middle of the African sea and a boy wearing a wetsuit.

I knew he had thought about Elisa every day for all those years and that the suffering of those two parents had tortured him every night and that, unlike me, he had tried to make up at least in part for it by performing goods deeds for everyone, as much as possible. But I also knew they had been his hands holding that cushion.

The first drops of rain began to fall. I glanced at the mother that was jumping and twittering around the injured bird. The thunder exploded very near, almost shaking the mountainside, and the twittering suddenly stopped. The little house martin was lifeless by now. The mother looked at me uncertainly.

Any one of you could have found yourself in my place.

Manfredi dei Banchi di Aglieno had written those words – the evil man we had all been pursuing and then caught in a trap and, in the end, crushed. It had started like this, in a moment of madness.

It started to pour down. We remained there in silence, while the pale light of day was growing faint. The rain bathed our heads, faces, and bodies and soaked into our shoes. Then, one by one, the dots at the bottom of the valley began to twinkle in the dusk.

The mother looked one last time at the little lifeless bird. Then it hovered in the air and soared away alone, not happy, but it was singing.

ACKNOWLEDGEMENTS

Thanks to the publishing team at Marsilio, firstly to Marco Di Marco and Jacopo De Michelis, not only for the great professionalism they put into their work, but also for their exceptional passion. Also to Filiberto Zovico and Chiara De Stefani for guiding me safely along roads not well known to me.

And then to my very first and only three readers during the course of the work, who were patient and full of good advice that has influenced the book: my wife Milena and my two great friends Valeria and Fabrizio.

COMING SOON

THE ROOT OF ALL EVIL

Roberto Costantini

One man alone killed them all. And it all began in Tripoli.

I had to go back to the real starting point:
Nadia Al Bakri, 3 August 1969.

If I could find out Nadia's killer, then I find out who killed
all the others. I had to go back to the very point that I
tried in every way to forget.

To the roots of evil.

BOOK TWO OF THE MICHELE BALISTRERI TRILOGY
PUBLISHED AUGUST 2014

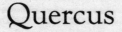

www.quercusbooks.co.uk

On 11 July 1982,
Elisa Sordi was beautiful.
Commissario Michele Balistreri was fearless.
Italy was victorious.
A killer was waiting…

On 9 July 2006,
With Sordi's case twenty-four years cold
And Balistreri haunted by guilt and regret
Italian victory returned.
And so did Sordi's killer…

But this time Michele Balistreri would be ready.
This time he would fear no evil.

'One of the most fully realized protagonists in modern crime fiction' BARRY FORS... *INDEPENDENT*

'Utterly compelling...

WWW.ROBERTOCOSTANTINI.COM

www.quercusbooks.co.uk

ISBN 978-0-85738-932-9   UK £7.99

9 780857 389329

e book available

Quercus Fiction/Crime

Cover design & photography: www.henrysteadman.com

For Lorenzo
For the People of Libya

First published in the Italian language as *Tu sei il male*
by Marsilio Editori in Venice in 2011

First published in Great Britain in 2013
This paperback edition published in 2014 by

Quercus Editions Ltd
55 Baker Street
7th Floor, South Block
London
W1U 8EW

A CIP catalogue record for this book is available
from the British Library

ISBN 978 0 85738 932 9 (PB)
ISBN 978 0 85738 931 2 (EBOOK)

10 9 8 7 6 5 4 3 2

Typeset by Ellipsis Digital Limited, Glasgow

Printed and bound in Great Britain by Clays Ltd, St Ives plc

THE
DELIVERANCE
OF EVIL

ROBERTO
COSTANTINI

Translated from the Italian by N S Thompson

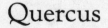

Roberto Costantini was born in Tripoli in 1952. He is an engineer, a corporate consultant, and the director of Luiss Guido Carli in Rome, where he teaches the MBA program. *The Deliverance of Evil* is the internationally acclaimed first novel in his crime trilogy featuring Commissario Michele Balistreri.

N S Thompson's translations include Leonardo Sciascia's *Sicilian Uncles* and Massimo Ciancimino and Francesco La Licata's *Don Vito: The Secret Life of the Mayor of the Corleonesi.*